The ReVered and the Pariah

FAE OF ALASTRÍONA

J. E. REED

THE REVERED AND THE PARIAH

Cover design by Story Wrappers

Interior formatting by Painted Wings Publishing Services

ISBN: 979-8-9873410-5-6

Visit the author at jereedbooks.com

Also available in ebook, hardcover, and audio.

To Rowan —
Because holding you in my arms was the greatest gift I've ever received.

Pronunciation Guide

Characters:
Alec - AL-uhk
Arianna - ahr-ee-AH-nah
Avalon - AV-uh-lon
Eimear – ee-mer
Eithne – EN-ya
Ellie - EL-ee
Eoghan - O-wen
Evelyn – EV-uh-lin
Gavin – GAV-in
Irial - IR-i-al
Kaylee – KAY-lee
Kirian - KEY-rey-an
Lillian - LIL-ee-uh-n
Máili - MAH-lee
Myrna - MUR-nuh
Raevina – ra-vi-na
Rion - REE-on
Saoirse - SUR-sha
Talon - TA-lon
Whelan - WEE-lin
Zylah - z-IH-l-ah

Places:
Alastríona - al-as-TREE-na
Ashling - ASH-leen
Brónach - BRO-nah
Fiadh - FEE-ah
Levea - le-V-ah
Móirín - MUY-rin
Nàdair - nay-DEER
Pádraigín - PAH-druh-geen
Púróg - pure-AH-g
Ruadhán – ROO-awn

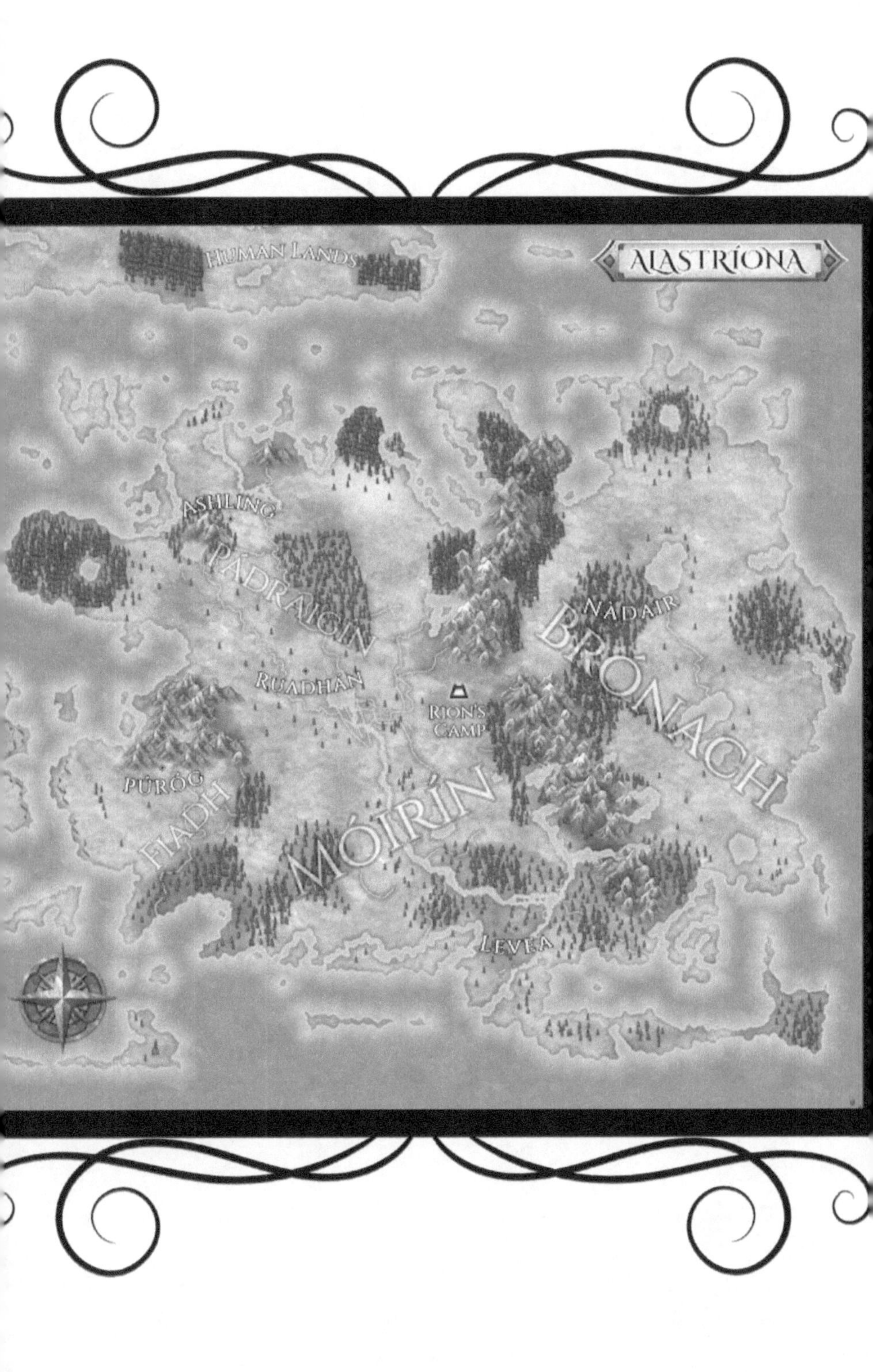

ALASTRÍONA
HUMAN LANDS
ASHLING
PÁDRAIGÍN
RUADHÁN
NÁDAIR
BRÓNACH
RION'S CAMP
PÚRÓG
FIADH
MÓIRÍN
LEVEA

THE ReVeReD AND THE PARIAH

J. E. REED

CHAPTER ONE

RAEVINA

Raevina raced down the cavernous hall, her black boots echoing off the stone walls where her people's home had been carved inside the grand mountain ages ago. Her dark braids bounced with every stride, hitting the backs of her elbows, and the knives in her belt clinked with her quick pace, drawing the gazes of those she passed. She bared her teeth at them without slowing, and they quickly turned away.

Sweat rolled down her golden brown skin and Raevina flexed her shoulders in an attempt to work the morning's training tension from her muscles.

Her attention returned to the elaborate halls and their magnificent carvings. Legends of their home's creation were numerous. Some in Fiadh claimed shadow weavers were responsible for melting the stone smooth, while others said their ancestors had chiseled the massive dwelling by hand.

Then there were the fanatics. Those who swore the nations had once been united beneath a single monarch. A time before High Lords and Ladies existed. Those devoted to the ancient texts—a version of them anyway—sang lullabies to their children about the nations working alongside one another. They even told stories about how magic wasn't separated back then as it was now.

She snorted. She'd believe the four countries could work together as soon as peace formed between humans and Fae.

Raevina glanced up, allowing herself a rare moment to appreciate the smooth stone and glittering jewels within the grand chamber. It reflected the dozens of braziers' firelight like a black sheet of glass, and eight columns of solid stone as thick as Nàdiar's redwoods rose toward the ceiling to hold it all in place.

The ceiling arched at the top and the doorways mimicked the architecture. Harsh and cold and empty, some called it, but to her and everyone else in Púróg it was a glistening gem city full of iridescent lights that promised stability and protection. Something they desperately needed with the dark creatures prowling the mountains of late.

She kept moving, trying not to think about her father's negligence as her muscular legs carried her across the main hall. Whispered voices drifted up from the rows of tables crowded with both Fae and their slaves. Typical for the afternoon hour.

She wrinkled her nose when a human limped past and wondered how long it'd been since the creature had bathed. Or eaten. Its frail body was hunched from the weight it carried and the clothes hanging from its body were tattered and far too loose. She noted the bones jutting out from its shoulders and shook her head. She'd tried to mention lightening the humans' load to her father once, but he'd threatened to label her a sympathizer.

Raevina clicked her tongue. She'd never sympathize with a human. They deserved their fate after what they'd done, but dead slaves couldn't work and purchasing new ones was an unnecessary expense. It'd be far more efficient to care for them properly and extend their lives another decade than to keep replacing them.

Raevina turned her attention away from the slaves. Four exits led out of the grand room, at least on floor level, but only one led to her father. He wasn't a male one kept waiting.

She followed the enclosed hall, the space built large enough that she could swing a sword without hindrance if need be, and turned right before pausing at the throne room.

A guard bowed before her and rushed inside to announce her arrival.

Raevina knew her father's summons had something to do with the rumors floating around.

The Divine.

Those within Brónach and Móirín claimed to have found a female with the ability to heal. A magic only the queen of their continent was prophesied to possess.

Their queen.

Raevina couldn't imagine the four countries uniting. Who did they have to fight except for themselves? The humans to the north posed no threat. The continent to the south had yet to be explored and it was believed no other land stretched around their world. None that could pose a threat anyway.

She sincerely doubted that.

Raevina had felt a calling once. A need to set sail and see what else might lie beyond the land they dwelt upon. But she'd been young and foolish then.

The guard hurried back. "He waits for you."

Raevina brushed past him and heard another voice echoing from within.

"Lady Raevina, Your Grace." The male bowed at the waist, his head low, and didn't rise until she'd passed him.

Fire surrounded the inside of the throne room, warming the space enough that sweat was already beading on her brow. Intricately carved chests sat open on the tables, all full of glittering jewels. A show of power and a taunt for any who craved it.

She hated this room. Torches and braziers lined the walls and corners in unnecessary numbers. They made the shadows tug and pull in a menacing dance.

Her father sat in the large, stone chair carved from the rock itself at the back of the room, with more chests and jewels on either side of his throne. A glass of wine rested in one hand while a plate of food sat on the opposite arm of the chair.

Raevina knelt. She didn't lift her eyes to look at his face but she knew that hideous crown still sat upon his head as it always did when he was in here. Five jagged spikes rose from the top of the wretched thing with large jewels inlaid between each. Other stones decorated the rest of it, all of them finely crafted and without flaws.

She swore she'd melt the blasted thing as soon as she took her place as High Lady.

"You summoned me, My Lord."

Never "Father." Not in here.

She waited, counting the seconds as her father ripped off another piece of the chicken leg then sipped his wine. He'd never been one to hurry and she knew better than to grow impatient.

As a child, her knees often hurt from kneeling on the floor for hours. He claimed the lesson was to teach her patience and obedience.

She'd learned it well. And had used the time to contemplate all the ways she might kill him.

"Your brother's scheme failed."

She clenched her jaw but managed to keep the distaste from her voice. "I see."

Raevina heard someone pour more wine into his glass. "I've convinced Brónach and Móirín that Fiadh had nothing to do with it and that my traitorous son acted of his own accord." She heard the hateful smile in his voice. "They believe he was attempting to start a revolt against me to claim the throne for himself. As such, he's been banished from the city."

The words didn't surprise her. Nor did her father's lack of empathy for one of his children. Either you were strong enough to survive, or you weren't.

She'd never been close to her siblings, and her younger brother was the only one she'd seen in the last few decades. The others were leading warriors or gathering intel on their enemies. Which seemed to be everyone these days.

She'd managed to listen in on her brother's schemes in recent years. His words were enough to convince Raevina of her youngest sibling's insanity. Still, she'd kept an eye on him.

And despite his questionable mind, her brother had forced Brónach and Móirín into a decade-long war. She knew the lady of Móirín had perished at The Demon's hands, but Raevina wasn't sure what her brother's role had been in it all.

She was certain of one thing though: If her brother had gotten anywhere near that creature, The Demon would have ripped him in half.

Raevina refocused on the present. "Is there a task you'd like me to complete in his place?" Perhaps now was the time she could rise in rank. Prove herself, get close enough to her father so she could end him and his neglectful rule.

He took another long sip from his glass. "You've heard the rumors."

It wasn't a question, but she answered anyway, her head still bowed. "Yes, My Lord."

"I need someone to investigate. Pádraigín is making their move to claim the female and I want a close eye kept on the situation."

"You don't trust their word?"

He hissed and she bit the inside of her cheek. "Have I not taught you better? We trust no one and nothing but ourselves. I will not get dragged into a religious mess over some false claim to a throne that doesn't exist." He sat back, but she remained still.

"You'll go and put an end to it." He swirled his glass. "And once you've done that, maybe you'll finally earn your place in my council."

Raevina tried to keep her heart steady. A place on his council. She'd get everything she wanted. Access to his whereabouts, his secrets, the plans he kept hidden from everyone else. She'd finally get the opportunity she'd sought for decades. A chance to put an end to the tyrant ruling Fiadh.

"You'll also take account of those who are summoned to the royal city. I want names and descriptions along with the location of the city. The High Lord never saw fit to trust me with such information."

She resisted the retort on her tongue. *Because he knows what you'd do with it.*

"Yes, My Lord."

She watched the shadow of his hand wave her off. "You're dismissed."

Raevina rose with her head still bowed. She risked a quick glance at her father, a large male who hadn't let his physique wane in the slightest in the centuries he'd ruled. His skin was dark, his jaw squared. He'd always kept his head shaved, with a dark, short, braided beard that carried beads within the twisted knots.

She averted her gaze, stepped back, then pivoted on her heel, her heart still hammering in her chest.

A chance. She finally had a chance, and all she had to do was kill a female the world claimed as their queen.

CHAPTER TWO

TALON

alon twirled the bloody knife around his fingers as he leaned against the cold, damp wall of the dungeons beneath Levea. The short blade swung back and forth while frustration coursed through his veins.

Mate.

The word tasted like bitter poison on his tongue and left his heart aching.

He should be more grateful. He *was* grateful. Without that male, Arianna and their entire company of warriors would have died before help arrived.

But that knowledge didn't ease the pain.

When he'd left, Talon knew Avalon intended to execute The Demon, but he'd also anticipated Arianna's intervention. He just hadn't counted on the creature staying or him returning to find—Talon slammed his fist against the wall, bruising his already injured hand. She'd run into *his* arms, not The Demon's. Talon had thought if he found the male responsible for her mother's death . . .

Talon shook his head. But he hadn't. He'd just found another lead that was proving to be a dead end.

Talon and his second, Aiden, had been trying to break the male for a week, and the shadow weaver had given them absolutely nothing.

Talon glanced up to watch Aiden land another blow across the male's jaw. Blood and spittle flew from the male's mouth, along with a tooth that clattered across the stone.

Talon had never been one for prisoners. They were messy and took time, but his predecessors had always told Talon he'd learn their value eventually. Right now, the only thing he'd learned was their annoyance.

Aiden landed another blow and Talon finally pushed off from the wall. "That's enough." His second stepped back and shook out his fist. After the vile comment their prisoner had made about Aiden's mother, he couldn't blame the male's brutality. Part of him welcomed it, especially when their captive was protecting a murderer.

Lillian had been such a gentle creature. Innocent. Likely the only one among them who could be called such. He wished he'd been old enough to protect her back then. Perhaps he could have scented The Demon's presence before the creature whisked her away. He knew The Demon hadn't delivered the killing blow, but that didn't mean he wasn't at fault.

After that fateful night, Avalon had more than doubled the security around his daughters, and their High Lord had remained vigilant ever since.

Talon had never quite understood how Lillian and Avalon had worked out. They'd been polar opposites, but mates were mates.

Talon's jaw ticked as Arianna's face flashed through his mind. He bit the inside of his cheek. He knew full well what that bond meant. No one else mattered anymore, not in the way he *wanted* to matter. Any thoughts or desires he carried for his childhood friend—Talon shook his head and prowled into the cell.

He flipped the knife in his hand. "This would go over a lot easier if you just gave us a location."

The male spit at Talon's boots, splattering them with saliva and blood. "As I told your friend, I don't know anything."

The lie burnt the inside of Talon's nostrils. They'd been close. He knew it now. If he'd led his warriors just a little further into those caverns, Talon knew he would have found the male responsible for Lillian's death.

"Your lies piss me off."

The male scoffed. "As if I care."

Talon slammed his fist into the male's jaw. "You will. One way or another, you will break."

The male slid his tongue across his split lip. "Why don't you take these shackles off and we'll see who breaks?"

Talon stared at him. Maybe it was stupid, but he was too pissed off to care. These people had attacked his city, killed his comrades, stolen his High Lady, and erased her from the world.

Talon jerked his head toward Aiden. "Remove his cuffs."

His second looked ready to protest, but stopped as Talon shot him a look. He shrugged and grabbed the keys.

Aiden had been patient with him. Patient as Talon prowled around training until his body ached and paced the compound all hours of the night. Avalon had been all over him since his return. He'd commanded Talon to remove The Demon from the city, kill him if he was able. Talon had refused. He'd screamed at him to get their forces organized, account for how they'd been infiltrated. Talon hadn't succeeded. And his High Lord had demanded what use a prisoner could possibly be, to which Talon still didn't have an answer.

A failure at every turn.

One latch fell to the floor followed by the other. Aiden took a step back, eyeing the prisoner.

"You're going to re—" Talon's boot collided with the male's face, sending him sprawling across the damp floor. Talon grabbed a handful of the male's hair and covered his arm in a sheet of ice when shadows crawled across the male's skin.

Talon slammed the male's head into the side wall. Again, and again, and again, spluttering those shadows each time his head collided with the stone. The male raised an arm to shield his face and pulled his legs beneath him. He drew his fist back and landed a blow to Talon's gut, but the raging snarl that ripped from Talon's throat had the male's face paling.

Talon's magic burst from his body, coating the floor in a thick layer of hoarfrost. It crawled up the male's leg and steam rose from the male's body as he desperately tried to fight against the bitter cold.

Fear shown in the male's gaze and Talon threw him to the ground, disappointment flooding through him at the male's weakness. Aiden moved to clamp the shackles around his wrists and tightened the chains.

"I'll give you an hour to reconsider. When I come back, we're moving on to different methods."

The male didn't look at him or bite back. He simply lay on the floor, the other side of his lip busted, and shivered from the cold surrounding his shirtless form.

Aiden followed Talon out of the cell and locked the door behind them. "Do you want to talk about it?" his second asked, not for the first time that week.

Talon ignored the question. "Have the troops arrived?"

"The last of them were set to file in early this morning. They tell us there's been more attacks close to home and they're ready to march again at your command."

"Tell them to stand by."

More attacks. More to defend. Rumors were spreading about Arianna being The Divine and not everyone was happy about it.

Talon stomped up the stairs, passing cell after cell. Most cowered away, but there were an arrogant few who strayed too close, some even leaning against the bars, hoping Talon might carelessly stumble within their reach. He knew they'd snap his neck without a second thought.

The brisk morning air met his sweat covered face and Talon took a deep breath, letting the soft breeze chase away the dampness in his lungs. He spent too much time beneath the ground. He wanted to soar through the air, feel the wind beneath his wings, but he couldn't stop until he had answers.

Talon marched straight for the warriors' barracks, washed his hands and face, changed his clothes, then headed for the manor.

Ellie was waiting for him.

Again.

She'd sat in the same place all week, asking the same question whenever he emerged from the dungeons.

"He hasn't talked."

She bristled, anger rising from her. Talon knew she wanted vengeance just as much as he did. "Maybe you should let me in there with him."

"Absolutely not. Your father would have my head."

"Yeah, well, he doesn't have to know, does he?" She eyed him as he came to stand beside her, gazing out at the falls. "You're both so edgy lately."

Talon didn't respond; instead, he glanced toward her wounds, noting her missing bandages. "You've healed nicely." He remembered her extensive injuries and the worry that had plagued them all as they wondered whether she'd make it.

"Arianna healed the rest of them yesterday. She'd heal your wounds, too, if you went and saw her."

She would, but seeing her meant also seeing—Talon felt anger rise in him like a white hot flame. What was wrong with him? It wasn't as though he had a right to Arianna. She wasn't his. She didn't belong to anyone. Yet some stupid instinctual part of him thought that maybe if he'd finished that Demon off on the battlefield . . .

Ellie cleared her throat. "You know, you don't have to hide it from me. I've known how you felt about her since we were kids." She leaned against the rail beside him. "I know you go down to that cell every morning to blow off steam."

Was it jealousy? Is that what fueled his rage?

Ellie tapped her finger and tried again. "I saw more warriors arrive this morning. Is that the last of them?"

Talon finally nodded. "Their stay home might not be as long as they'd like. Many are celebrating The Divine, but it seems just as many are raging about her being a fake."

"A simply flick of her wrist will prove them wrong."

"Even if we wanted, we couldn't take her out into the open. Not with the reports I've heard. They've killed females just for looking like her."

"Don't tell Arianna that." She sighed. "How do we quell the hostility?"

Talon shrugged. "I don't know yet."

"Well, she can't just hide in Levea."

No, she couldn't and if their High Lord had a say in the matter, it seemed she'd be leaving a lot sooner than any of them planned. "I've overhead Avalon mention those in the royal city are coming for her."

"Soon?"

"I don't know."

Ellie scoffed. "I'm sure she'll love that."

"She's the queen. She has responsibilities now."

Ellie side eyed him and he knew she wanted to retort, but held it in. Instead, she clasped her hands. "Are you going with her?"

"Of course I am."

"And how will you handle her mate?"

He bristled and that damned anger rose in him again. "I've been around him before, I can handle it again."

"Can you?" she asked. "Because from where I'm standing, you look like a bomb ready to explode."

Talon ran a frustrated hand through his hair. "I don't mean to be. There's just so much going on. Diplomacy with Brónach hasn't exactly been easy. The slaves we rescued are having a hard time adjusting while those from Brónach claim we stole their property. Avalon is riding me about The Demon in his city and Arianna—"

"Is happy," Ellie said. Talon's blood ran cold, his anger abated. "She's happy, Talon. Safe. You don't have to search for her anymore. She's home."

His hands fell. "I know." But she'd never felt so far away.

CHAPTER THREE

ARIANNA

Arianna violently scrubbed her palm for the third time, letting the blistering hot water wash away the soap from her callused skin.

She didn't know how many she'd healed today, only that it would never be enough to fill the chasm of grief in her heart. She'd killed for Rion and her sister and her own survival, but the reasoning didn't matter. Only that she'd tainted her soul and there was no going back.

The morning after her father attempted to execute Rion, she'd left the safety of their summer cabin with Rion in tow to search for her sister. Ellie had been trying to get out of bed despite her remaining injuries and Arianna had promptly healed her, telling Ellie the same thing she told everyone: She wasn't a miracle worker, some healing the body had to do itself.

Rion had watched just inside the doorway, holding one hand over his side, nursing wounds of his own. His body was still cold and sluggish, but he didn't complain.

Because Ellie wasn't the only one who'd suffered.

Arianna had wanted to run straight to the barracks and heal until her body crumpled, but she couldn't do that with Rion at her side, let alone an injured Rion. And there was no way in the seven hells she was leaving him behind. He might have saved a few lives during Fiadh's attack, but the scars he'd inflicted throughout the decades ran deeper than she could reach.

She'd almost cried in frustration, desperately wanting to protect her mate and aid her country.

Then Myrna, the servant who'd been with them since they were children, suggested the estate's infirmary wing. Myrna had even offered to have those who were critical brought in, to which Arianna was eternally grateful.

Anger flooded through her whenever someone glared at her mate, and Arianna could feel the same anger mirrored down the bond whenever males so much as glanced her way.

Arianna knew they should be alone, letting the bond solidify. They should be laughing at one another's stories, going on dates throughout the city, eating food until they were ready to burst.

But that wasn't a life she'd get to live. Not with Rion. And not as The Divine.

She didn't get to just idly sit by. And maybe she'd never get to rest again. She had responsibilities and she'd shied away from them for too long.

Arianna rinsed her hands and tears pricked the corners of her eyes as she grabbed the soap again, desperate to remove the invisible stain. Rion was there moments later, his palms gently resting atop her trembling shoulders.

His fingers glided down her arms and Arianna let him turn her hands over in the scalding water, then he shifted her body, ignoring the droplets hitting the tiled floors.

Rion wrapped a towel around her fingers then he caught her tears and Arianna finally glanced up at him. Her heart ached at the anguished look covering his face.

She buried her head in his chest. "It's never going away, is it?" He knew what she meant. She'd woken up screaming almost every night, her nightmares carrying her back to a time of chains and carnage.

"It'll ease with time."

Had it eased for him? For her father? Talon? Had they all grown numb to the years on the battlefield, killing their way toward victory?

Arianna let out a long breath and pulled back. "I'm sorry." She shouldn't be crying. She'd chosen her own path and he carried far more regret. She was sure they all did.

Rion gently hooked a finger beneath her chin and lifted her face. She gazed into those deep, emerald eyes so alight with flame. "Don't ever apologize for the way you feel."

"It just seems wrong."

His gaze softened and he rubbed his thumb back and forth along her jaw before leaning close. Arianna's breath hitched when Rion's lips brushed against her own. "Does this feel wrong?" She hummed against his mouth. Rion trailed his nose down her cheek and she tilted her head, letting him place another kiss to her throat. "This?"

"No." She could hardly breathe.

He pulled back slightly. "Then let your other feelings be just as valid. Let—"

A female cleared her throat and Arianna's gaze shot toward the older woman standing in the doorway with graying, shoulder length hair. Her wrinkled face was tight with concern. "I'm sorry to disturb you, but we could really use your help. It's urgent."

Arianna bolted after the woman, following her down the hall to find a male sprawled across a table, two Fae desperately trying to stop the bright red blood pouring from his thigh.

Their eyes lifted upon scenting her and one of the females tending to him stepped aside, loosing a breath of relief at her presence. Arianna began pouring her magic into the wound. She found the artery first.

"It was a training exercise," his friend said, watching her from the end of the table. "I didn't think—"

"He'll be all right," she assured.

Arianna felt Rion's presence behind her and the territorial aggression down their bond as he gazed upon the two males. One was injured on the table before her and the other was standing far too close. She felt his rage and restraint warring against one another, then the male standing at her side snarled, pulling his lips back to reveal razor sharp teeth.

But it wasn't Rion who lunged for him, crashing into his full frame. Before she knew what she'd done, Arianna had the male pinned beneath her body, her hand at his throat, and her fangs bared.

His eyes flew open wide and his hands released their grip on her arms, pulling back to open his palms in surrender.

She couldn't stop the growl in her voice. "Threaten him again and it will be the last threat you make."

The room fell silent and the male only nodded, his gaze darting toward others in the room as if they'd intervene. But no one moved.

Arianna regained her composure and pulled herself upright, shame already creeping through her body. She quickly finished healing the male's leg, knitting the skin and muscle tissue back together before she stepped away, her hands once again covered in blood.

"I'm sorry," she whispered and ducked from the room.

RION FOLLOWED his mate. Guilt and shame shot down their newly formed bond and Arianna's magic flared with her emotions, water and snow circling her body in a mild storm. Her abilities were stronger in Levea, no doubt fed from the abundant supply of waterways throughout their massive city.

He hurried after her, ignoring the way everyone stared at the pair racing through the halls.

They loved their queen already, their awestruck gazes told him as much. It was him they had an issue with. He was a blight. A sickness cast upon her they hoped to remove.

But he wasn't going anywhere. He'd already made a promise. At least unless she gave him the order.

Arianna wound her way through the corridors, past the main hall to her usual sanctuary: a pool of water closed off from the rest of the estate with a small bridge overhead.

She'd jumped straight into the clear pool and hidden herself beneath the shadow of that bridge.

Rion's heart pulled at his mate's distress. He'd allowed her solitude the first time, thinking his company unwelcome, but she'd tugged at their bond so hard it had sent him into a frenzy. She wanted solitude, just not from him.

Rion waded into the crisp water, sucking in a breath as the bitter chill lanced through his core. He wasn't sure what the council's magic had done to him, but he'd never quite recovered, even with Arianna's healing abilities. It still felt as though a sliver of ice was trapped somewhere in his body and it left him shivering most nights.

Not that he'd told Arianna about it.

Arianna's shoulders shook and she'd drawn her knees up, hiding her face in her arms. Steam rose around her body and he knew she'd warmed the water there for his sake.

Rion sat beside her, wrapped one arm around her shoulders, and pulled her close. "It's only instinct." He hated seeing her this way. She felt a sense of obligation to everyone else, but she was the one who needed rest.

"I don't see you raging at people." Oh, if only she knew. The sheer restraint he had most days surprised even himself. He wanted to roar and tear through everyone who so much as looked at her.

"Because no one has threatened you. And though I loathe having them around, it's difficult to be angry when they treat you like the queen you are." Her people revered her, worshiped her, and some still didn't even know who she was yet.

Arianna sighed and wiped the tears from her face. "Maybe I'm in over my head."

He waited for her to say more. When she didn't, Rion pulled her closer. "My offer still stands." She tilted her head slightly and he glanced into her red-rimmed eyes, the blue of the irises so bright even in the shadow of the bridge. His heart pulled at the pain reflected there and he wanted nothing more than to ease her burden. Rion tried a faint smile. "I offered to take you away from all this. You declined."

She huffed out a laugh and turned back to gaze at the crystalline pool before them. It was shallow, only about waist deep, and he didn't miss the ripples as the Fairy Folk played among the foliage at the bank. "They'd hunt us down."

That wasn't a no. Rion swallowed, leaned closer, and whispered, "I'm very good at disappearing." It's what he'd done half his life. "I promise it would take them a very long time to find us." He could take her north into the mountains. The Fae there were darker, more dangerous, but he'd already established dominance over them. They'd steer clear of the harpy's territory, but the rest—

Rion's breath hitched when she pushed him back, submerging his upper torso in the water while his head rested on the bank. His heart thundered, fear pulsing at the thought of being pinned. Trapped. But Arianna's body straddling his own had his blood racing for other reasons. Rion placed his hands on her hips, his mind going from a plan of escape to his mate in a single breath.

She leaned down, her mouth inches from his and Rion zeroed in on the movement. On the way her breath quickened. The way her eyes grew heavy. He'd never get enough of her wanting him. The desire that flowed down their bond matching his own. He still couldn't fathom how she seemed to need him as much as he needed her.

"Ellie would find us." She ran her nose down his throat and his heart beat even faster. He no longer cared that his body was submerged, leaving him vulnerable to every Fae in Móirín. Didn't care because Arianna's legs were around him, her scent stealing every rational thought from his mind. She was his center now.

"Arianna," a female voice called.

He sighed at the disturbance and Arianna pressed her forehead to his. "See?" She was right about one thing. Even if they ran to the edges of the world, Ellie would find them long before he planned. The solitude would never be long enough.

"Arianna," the voice called again, closer and with a bit more force.

"Do you think she'd catch us if we ran?" he asked, hoping to bring a smile to her face.

Arianna gave him a knowing look. "You're soaked to the bone. She'd have you pinned before you even left the water."

CHAPTER FOUR

SAOIRSE

Night had fallen, bringing with it those who frequented the old tavern. Some filed in, greeting the barkeep like an old friend. Others stumbled through the doorway, sinking into the nearest table before raising their hand for a drink. She'd happened upon it that evening, hoping to drown away the week in a tankard of ale. To prop her feet up, perhaps chat with a female or two.

Then Saoirse had stopped in her tracks. A female buzzed behind the counter, listening to another who gave her instructions. She took the glasses and placed them on a tray, but before Saoirse could escape, the female's hazel gaze locked with hers.

Màili.

The same female who had declared them only friends after the happiest six months of Saoirse's life.

Màili waved, a wide smile breaking across her face that reminded Saoirse of summer nights spent beneath the redwood canopy. A knot formed in Saoirse's gut, but she forced herself to smile and wave back.

Then she found a seat in the rear corner. It was too late to run now, not without it being obvious why.

Thankfully, Màili wasn't the one who glided toward her table when Saoirse signaled for a drink. It was another female, beautiful and elegant in her own right, with streaming dark hair and a pair of legs she might have loved to appreciate any other time, but Saoirse couldn't tear her gaze away from the one behind the bar.

Even after three tankards of ale and two shots of whisky, the female still pulled Saoirse's gaze. She'd look up every now and then and Saoirse would glance away, pretending to chat up the waitress, but after a while her gaze would drift back, hoping beyond hope that maybe one day Màili would give her another chance. Maybe Saoirse could compact her work schedule a little more, give the female more of her time.

She shook her head. Saoirse honestly hadn't known Màili would volunteer to come, but Màili had always been one for adventure. When they'd called for a supply wagon to aid Levea in the wake of the attack, Màili had likely been one of the first in line.

Friends.

Gods, she'd messed up and she couldn't just blame it on a busy schedule. Saoirse had missed not one, not two, but three dates they'd planned and the last one had been important to Màili, a showcasing of her latest paintings in a small square with about a dozen other artists. It wasn't a huge event, but it was the first time Màili had shown her work to the public.

She'd sold out within an hour.

And Saoirse had missed it.

A loud thud at her table startled Saoirse enough that she spilled her drink. She cursed, ready to explode on the arrogant Fae who thought they could waltz over to join her. A male more than likely, but when Saoirse looked up, her world froze anew.

Not a male. Not a male at all. The female before her straddled the stool and settled herself across from Saoirse with a wide grin plastered across her face. Ocher eyes that were warm and gentle, yet also haunted in a way she couldn't grasp, sparkled with mischievous amusement. Shoulder-length chestnut hair that carried all the hues of a majestic sunset hung loose around her angular face.

Saoirse swore she'd been struck by a dream.

"If you're going to gawk, you could at least say hi."

"Hi," she breathed, waiting for the exquisite mirage before her to vanish.

The female giggled and it was the most beautiful sound she'd ever heard.

But Saoirse realized she'd misunderstood when the female pointed a long, tan finger toward the bar. "You've been staring at her since you sat down."

She'd been caught, but Saoirse didn't bother looking at Màili again. She cleared her throat, hoping to sound relaxed and flirtatious. "And I suppose you've been watching me?" Gods, her heart was hammering in her chest.

The female shrugged. "Perhaps. Perhaps not." She reached for her drink and it was an effort not to stare at the way her throat curved. At the pulse, the delicate skin, the scars . . .

Saoirse took a breath to steady herself then made a show of swirling her drink. She glanced at Màili once, then back.

"Well?" the female prodded.

"Friends," Saoirse said. The female's smile faltered and Saoirse inclined her head toward the bar. "She declared us friends."

The female took another drink and brushed her hair away from her face. Her cheeks were tinged pink and her eyes carried a gentle haze to them. Saoirse wondered if the female had been watching her, drinking her own liquid courage before she'd approached. Or perhaps she'd simply seen her and stopped. Maybe it was pity.

The female raised her hand to call for more drinks. "If we're going to talk past lovers, we need the proper material."

Saoirse couldn't stop the smile that pulled from the corner of her mouth. She'd talk about anything if it kept this female at her table. "You're quite a forward one."

The female paused for a moment, then batted her eyes. "Oh I'm sorry, do you prefer dainty and meek?"

Saoirse laughed. "Not in the slightest." *I prefer you.* "It's just not something I'm accustomed to."

"Well," the female said, pausing to take two drinks from the waitress, "perhaps that's where your love life has gone wrong." She handed Saoirse one then took a long drink from her own, grimacing while she swallowed. "Gods, this is nasty."

Saoirse laughed again, loud and full. "Then why in the blazes are you drinking it?"

The female glanced around. "I assume for the same reason everyone else is."

Saoirse signaled the waitress. "There are better things." Then she held her hand across the table. "Saoirse."

The female took her outstretched palm with a firm grip. "Zylah."

Saoirse's gaze locked onto the scars around her wrist. "You're one of the half-breed refugees." Her scent was off though. A mix between two nations. Pádraigín perhaps?

"And you're a pureblood from Brónach."

"And yet you still came over."

Zylah shrugged. "Maybe there was something inviting about you." The female didn't hide the way her eyes roamed over Saoirse's body. "And I've been alive long enough to know not everyone from Brónach agreed with the way the High Lord ran things. I've seen the worst in purebloods, but I know the best is still out there."

Lived long enough. Saoirse noted the words. Perhaps this female had inherited long life from her Fae parentage. From her appearance, Saoirse had thought she was no older than twenty, but if she possessed a longer life span, there was no telling her age.

Something else caught her attention then, her mind addled by the alcohol coursing through her system. The High Lord. She said it so casually like she—*shit.* Zylah didn't know who Saoirse was and why would she? As a slave she'd never seen the inside of the royal estate. Being in the war camp, she'd likely never set foot in Nàdiar at all.

Zylah bobbed her head to the music and raised her hands up to cheer with the rest of them, but Saoirse was still reeling. Sure, she'd never abused the slaves in her care, but she'd still kept them like property. A choice this female might find unforgivable.

"Were you in Rion's camp?"

Zylah's head whipped toward Saoirse and Saoirse's heart skipped a beat. "Yes." Zylah studied her face. "Most just refer to him as The Demon, yet you say his name."

Saoirse didn't know how to respond, but before she could open her mouth Zylah wrinkled her nose. "Were you lovers?"

Saoirse snorted. "By the Gods, no."

A smile returned to Zylah's face. "It's not really my business anyway."

Tell her, something in Saoirse begged. Yet another part didn't want to. A selfish part wanted to keep this female at her side, talk to her just a while more. Maybe if they got to know one another first—no, that would only make things worse, she was sure of it.

Saoirse cleared her throat, but when Zylah gave her an expectant look, all truth slipped away. "Females are more my preference. I've bedded a few males, but most aren't to my liking."

"Males are disgusting." Both females laughed.

Saoirse called for another round of drinks and ordered something sweeter for Zylah. "Tell me something about your life before, well, before the scars."

Zylah's gaze roamed toward those dancing. Saoirse watched the shadows enter her eyes, a darkness she hadn't anticipated. "Those memories were a lifetime ago."

"How long?"

"Fifteen years that feel like a hundred."

Saoirse glanced down at her drink and lowered her voice. "Most of your life then."

Zylah didn't respond at first. "I knew happiness once. But it was stripped away. Those are years I'll never get back, but I have to focus on what's ahead."

Right, because even if she were a hundred years old, she might only have a hundred more years to go. Or she could live a thousand.

Or two thousand. But even with that length of time, it still didn't compare to a Fae who could remain on the earth for eternity.

"What about you?" Zylah asked. "What's your story?"

Tell her the truth.

Saoirse swallowed hard. "Did you inherit the Fae ability to detect lies?"

Zylah smirked. "Why, is your past so bad that you need to lie about it?"

"Yes."

Zylah's smile faltered. "Let me guess, there's someone waiting on you back in Brónach."

"I wish." That would have made things simpler. Zylah inclined her head for Saoirse to continue. Here goes. So much for her planned weekend. "I have two brothers," Saoirse began. "One you already know and it's the reason I use his given name." Zylah stopped sipping her drink. "The other is in Nàdiar likely pacing his floor and muttering about how the discovery of The Divine is going to be as much of a headache as the war."

"Your brother is the High Lord?" Saoirse hated the way Zylah's voice had lost all of its earlier bravado. Saoirse only nodded.

Zylah placed her mug on the table and splayed her fingers across the old wood. "You're the Saoirse said to rule at his side? His diplomat?"

"The very same." Zylah's jaw clenched. "But that doesn't mean we have to stop—"

The words lodged in her throat when Zylah's sharp gaze shot up. Anger flared in the female. Not anger. Rage. Then fear and rage again.

"You had a choice," she said through gritted teeth. Saoirse's lips parted. "You had a choice and did nothing."

Saoirse glanced at her drink, shame filling the pit of her stomach in a way it never had before. "Would it ease your mind if I told you I'm coming to understand just how wrong that was?" Watching the humans and half-breeds in Móirín had jarred her at first. She'd never seen them roaming free on their own and the absolute normalcy of it had her questioning everything.

"I was a slave for fifteen years because people in power, people like you, did nothing to help us." Zylah stood.

"Don't go."

But Zylah scrunched her nose up and for a moment Saoirse thought the female might actually spit on her. Then she pivoted on her heel and was zigzagging through the tables and bodies, headed toward the door.

Saoirse stood as well, leaving a pile of coins on the table that probably added up to double what their drinks cost. She didn't care. She knew she shouldn't chase after Zylah. She knew she had no right to, but something in her didn't want to let the female go like this. She wanted to explain herself, explain that she planned to take more of a stand against the laws in her country.

But it was too late to make those changes. Half-breeds like Zylah had already suffered. Half-breeds like Zylah had been killed because she'd sat around and taken the easy path, letting laws already in place dictate her life and the way she lived it.

Saoirse should have acted sooner. She should have marched to Rion's war camp and others like it to demand better treatment. She should have delivered supplies. Something. Anything.

But they were slaves. Little more than cattle as far as those within Brónach were concerned. Cattle with a bloody history that the Fae still held them accountable for.

Saoirse stepped into the light drizzle that had started outside and scanned the dark street. She barely saw Zylah's silhouette against the dim lanterns, but her scent was still strong enough to follow.

She pushed a male out of her way and ignored the way he hollered after her. Saoirse sprinted down the street and those she passed stared after the female in their territory. An enemy. She didn't miss their looks of disgust.

Gods, she should have worked her way around the truth, given it a day or two. Maybe then the female would have paused to listen.

"Wait," Saoirse called. The rain picked up, already soaking the top of her shoulders. "Please."

Zylah spun around. "Please?" she spat. "Do you know how many times I've heard that word?" Saoirse didn't answer. "Did you know the slaves constantly begged for scraps? Water? Hell, a warm pair of clothes, and you have the audacity to say 'please'?"

"I'm sorry," Saoirse started, but Zylah cut her off again.

"I don't care."

"You said there was good in us that you hadn't seen yet."

"In warriors," she seethed. "In those who were forced to follow orders lest they risk treason. Not for the High Lord's sister who could have done literally anything." Zylah took a deep breath and lowered her voice. "Can you honestly say you've never owned a slave?"

Saoirse's mouth went dry as she imagined the female tending to her room back in Brónach. A female who had asked Saoirse for things only to be denied them. A female she owned.

"I've never mistreated her."

Zylah scoffed and the sound stung something in Saoirse's soul. "Do you know what it's like to wear chains? To fear a whip and those who wield it?" Saoirse shook her head. "And you never will because you are a Lady." Zylah stepped forward. "I spent fifteen years of my life in suffocating fear and I won't ever let it happen again. And I'd rather die than be caught associating with someone like you."

"It was wrong, I know that now. I—" Desperation flooded through her when Zylah turned away and Saoirse reached for the female's arm, her fingertips lightly grazing Zylah's skin before wind tore from the night air and collided with Saoirse's chest.

Saoirse shielded her face as she flew back a few feet and landed on her backside. Water soaked through her pants, but she didn't try to stand as Zylah closed the distance between them and bared her teeth.

"Do not assume I'm weak just because I'm a half-breed."

Then she was gone, leaving Saoirse in shocked silence as she sat in the middle of that dark street utterly alone.

CHAPTER FIVE

ARIANNA

Arianna released her trembling grip on the bloody dagger and let it clatter to the cold stone floor. She stumbled away from the bodies littering the ground, their lifeless faces upturned in silent horror. Her breathing came fast, faster as she peered into their eyes, all wide in shock as if they hadn't expected what fate dealt them. But she couldn't have—

Our queen, some whispered in reverence.

Murderer, others added, the two voices echoing over and over and over.

A sob tore from her chest and she stepped back again only to leap away when her foot collided with a stiff hand. They surrounded her. Still and lifeless and cold.

She startled when Rion stepped through the shadows, prowling toward her as if he couldn't see the carnage. Or didn't care. The whispers turned frenzied and for a moment fear seized her heart at what the voices might do to him.

Rion paid them no mind. Arianna opened her mouth to warn him about the bodies but they were suddenly gone. Vanished on a midnight wind with no trace left behind.

She could have sworn there were more . . .

Rion halted mere inches away and lifted her bloody hand. He pressed a kiss to the back of her knuckles, seeming unfazed by the red liquid that now stained his lips.

Fear griped her anew "What's going on?" Rion only smiled and handed her another dagger before he turned her to face the waiting crowd. She could sense them. Smell them. But all she saw were more shadows.

A civilian stood before her, shackled with his head bowed, as if he'd already accepted his fate.

The shadows chanted at her in a language she didn't understand, but somehow she knew what they wanted.

And she couldn't. Not again. She—

"Arianna." She turned to his voice, but the Rion she remembered had vanished. The male before her wore that wicked smirk she'd glimpsed when he slayed his enemies. He was looking at her now like—

"Arianna."

The image shattered and Arianna bolted upright, her heart slamming against her ribcage. She sucked down air, her gaze shooting around the dark room, then she focused on the disheveled sheets, the drawn curtains, and the light layer of frost covering everything.

"Breathe," his gentle voice coaxed, nothing at all like the slick nightmarish one she'd heard seconds ago. And his face, it didn't carry that horrid smirk. His eyes were calm. Concerned. "You're safe."

She did as he commanded and her breath clouded between them. Rion's body shivered then she saw the ice. Not like the dusting of frost coating the dresser and floor. This had thickened around his hand and arm, covering it enough that the skin held a bluish hue.

Her heart jolted again and she lunged, quickly heating the cold limb.

"It's fine." She ignored the words and plunged her magic through his body, searching for anything amiss. That cold remained, his temperature still lower than it'd been before her father's ritual.

And Gods, she'd just—

Rion tilted her chin up, forcing her to look at him. "I'm fine," he repeated.

Arianna breathed in his scent and the truth in his words. She couldn't count how many times they'd both woken from nightmares in the last two weeks. Too many times. And though their magic flared and raged, neither had harmed the other.

She fell into his arms and Rion pulled her back down into the thick blankets, holding her close.

Arianna had hoped returning home would lessen her fear. She'd hoped for some freedom, and yet it'd made everything worse. Instead of feeling calm, all her emotions were rushing to the surface, clawing against her restraint like a rabid beast. She cried, lashed out, and loved more fiercely than she'd ever done in her entire life.

Ellie had told her those thing were normal, that it was simply her mind finally processing everything it'd been through, but she wished it would process it differently.

Arianna's gaze traveled toward the morning light filtering through their window. She'd hoped to sleep a little later today and let her body rest but even after a night tangled in her mate's arms, her nightmares wouldn't subside.

She tilted her head and scooted closer, nuzzling his throat before nipping at the tender skin.

His grip tightened. "Never satisfied, are you?"

She ran her fingers over his muscled chest. "I think we could lie here for centuries and I'd still want to be here centuries more." His heart sped as it always did whenever she touched him, but it wasn't from fear anymore. Not fear of her, anyway.

Rion captured her lips in a greedy kiss, his body pressing against her own, then he stiffened. All desire vanished as panic took its place. His magic rose from the small piles he'd deposited around the room, and the hairs on the back of her neck stood on end when he emitted a low growl.

Arianna's magic responded to his and she craned her neck to listen for the intruder. She'd learned just how keen his senses were. Far more delicate than her own.

Then she scented the female. Ellie. Arianna sighed in relief. Ellie didn't normally bother them here, but maybe there was an emergency.

Arianna swung her legs from the bed and pulled on a thick robe before padding toward the door. Rion followed close behind and Arianna pulled the door open before her sister even had a chance to knock.

She could feel Rion's anxiety radiating down the bond, especially with Eoghan's scent so close. The male kept far enough away from the door, but he never left.

Ellie stood a few feet from the threshold as she always did when she visited the cabin. Arianna took the gesture with gratitude. She could handle females while they walked the halls and within the infirmary, but something about this place had her instincts screaming. It had become their sanctuary.

Her little sister clasped her hands behind her back. "I'm just here to make sure you don't forget about our plans." Plans. The blank look on Arianna's face must have been answer enough. "We're supposed to go to Elview Falls today."

"Why?" But Arianna stopped herself as memories began flooding back. It had been a pact between her, Ellie, and Talon made years ago. They were to return home for the event no matter where life took them. A promise between friends to reconnect no matter how busy their lives became.

And she'd missed the last one. An ache flew through her chest. Another blistering wound she was sure would never heal.

Ellie's smile faded and the shadows of her nightmare returned.

Rion was behind his mate before she realized he'd moved. He wrapped one arm around her middle and drew her close, placing a gentle kiss on the nape of her neck.

Ellie cocked her head in a playful smile. "You have to share."

Rion held her closer and Arianna felt her instincts rise as the two stared at one another. The Fae world had always questioned whether males or females were more territorial. She'd like to believe she had more self-control than most, but after yesterday's incident—

"It's just going to be Talon and me. I promise."

Talon. Her heart tugged again. Ellie had told her about the male he'd been trying to get information from and she knew Talon was busy with other tasks, but he hadn't been to visit her since his return. Not once. She glanced at her mate. She knew they'd fought beside one another, but would they get along now?

"I want to, but—"

"I know, I know. Growl and carry on all you want, but you're coming."

"This afternoon?"

Ellie's face lit up. "Yep. I'll clear the area and swing by to pick you up. Got to make sure you don't skip out on me." She winked, then pivoted on her heel and marched back down the path, past the pillars of ice Arianna kept up as a barrier around the guest house.

Arianna closed the door and leaned against it. Rion was there then, his lips devouring hers and hands tracing her body until their robes hit the floor and they found themselves in the safety of their blankets once again.

His essence consumed her. She relished in the gentle caress of his touch and the way the sensations brought her body to life. He chased away her worries and erased her fears with a single touch.

And Arianna would have it no other way.

RION KISSED her forehead and tightened his grip, cradling her body against his chest. She'd curled up on her side, idly playing with the sheet that covered them.

"What's your favorite color?" he asked.

Arianna paused, trying to process the simple question. She propped herself up on one elbow and looked at his face to find him wholly serious. "What do you mean?" She couldn't hide the smile in her voice.

Rion played with a lock of her hair. "I want to know your favorite color."

She tilted her head, studying the firelight dancing in his emerald gaze. "Green."

Rion chuckled. "I'm serious."

"So am I." She relaxed back into him, relishing his warmth. "It's the color of nature. The trees, the grass, and sometimes the ocean when the currents shift. It represents life." He was silent for so long that Arianna tilted her head to look at him again. "What's yours?"

"You'll laugh."

"I won't."

"I'd rather just focus on you."

She pushed him down into the pillows. "You can't just ask questions and not expect me to ask them back. I want to know as much about you as you do me." She folded her hands on his chest and rested her chin there. "Now tell me."

"Black."

Arianna furrowed her brow. "Why black?"

His gaze swam with the emptiness she wanted to avoid. "It's the color of shadows." She stared. "I've always been more comfortable hidden away from the world."

"Do you still feel that way?"

"Honestly, yes. I love our relationship. I love you." He pulled her close again. "But this has all felt like a dream and I keep waiting to wake up." He swallowed hard and her heart clenched. "With our relationship public I'm afraid of what you'll learn and how others are going to influence your thoughts. I'm afraid of losing this. Of losing you."

"You're not going to lose me," she said. "And no one is going to influence you away from me. I won't let them."

Rion gave her a weak smile. "It's not a matter of manipulation. They'll all be justified in their actions and words. I'm afraid you'll finally hear something that crosses a line you can't bear. I'm afraid you'll be disgusted by it and never want to see me again."

Arianna silenced him with a kiss. "I'm not disgusted by you."

"Maybe you should be."

"You're as much a victim to the world, you know."

"It doesn't excuse what I've done. Plenty of others have had their share of difficult lives without resorting to killing."

Arianna lowered her voice. "Let me love you. Let me in despite your demons, and let me face them myself when the time comes."

ARIANNA STOOD before the door dressed in a dark tunic and pants, her heart pounding as she thought about seeing Talon. Ellie and Eoghan had delivered their breakfast as they usually did, leaving it just outside the door. They were the only ones she could trust to not poison her mate, though she doubted anyone would risk poisoning her in the process.

Food. A bed. Clean clothes. Everything felt so strange, as if they'd been thrown into an alternate world and were left grasping at the straws of their old life.

Arianna grabbed the knob and a jolt of panic swept down her spine. Irrational. The fear was irrational. They'd been out all week, but they weren't going to the infirmary this time. And she'd finally see Talon.

She'd strapped a long knife to her thigh, as she did every morning and two smaller blades slid easily into her boots. She'd never carried blades in Levea before, but somehow with everything that had happened in the last year and a half, she needed them.

Arianna tugged at the energy in her body, pulling a fine mist from the air just to remind herself that she had another weapon in her arsenal as well.

Plus, there was Rion. She wouldn't be put in chains again.

Her mate pressed a feather-light kiss to the side of her neck. "We don't have to go."

Arianna sighed, wishing she could just run back to their furs and blankets. "Ellie would have a fit."

He chuckled and his hot breath on the back of her neck sent a pleasant shiver down her spine. "She's had a few. We survived."

Right, but refusing to go shopping or participate in social events was a lot different than ignoring a promise.

She braced herself and turned the knob, letting the brisk spring air wash over and through her. This was home. This was Ellie and Talon and Eoghan. Fae she could trust, even around her mate.

Rion followed Arianna as she passed the thick ice that jutted up from the swirling streams of water carved into the platform. She touched one and solidified it. The magic was constantly melting with the warm air, but the maze of swirling walls did something to bring her comfort.

Ellie and Eoghan sat at the end of the walkway, speaking to one another about something that had Ellie waving her arms with excitement. The falls, no doubt. Rion's magic rose around her and she felt a sharp spike of irritation. Eoghan.

Her magic responded, though it wasn't to soothe her mate, rather herself as she gazed out into the open world. They weren't just rushing across the path to the estate today.

"You'll let me know if this gets to be too much, right?" she asked.

He squeezed her hand. "Only if you do the same." Right. One step at a time. That's all either of them had to take.

She took a breath, then started toward her sister with Rion at her side. Ellie's gaze shot toward them and her sister beamed, placing her hands on her hips. "It's about time, I thought I was going to have to drag you out of there."

"Most mated couples get a few months of solitude." She hadn't meant for the words to have such a bite to them, but her sister responded as if she didn't notice.

"I could list a million reasons why you're not most couples. Least of all are the sheer number of people we keep away on a daily basis. And their questions." She threw her hands in the air. "Half of them wonder if you're still a captive." Her sister winced and shot an apologetic look toward Rion. "Sorry, I didn't mean it to sound like that."

But Rion only shook his head. "No need for apologies, captivity is exactly how it started. I won't hide the truth."

Ellie lowered her voice. "Perhaps you should." Her gaze darted between the pair. "I don't think I need to tell you tension is high right now. It'd be best to avoid doing anything that might aggravate the masses. Arianna was already loved as the daughter of the High Lord, but now that she's The Divine, there are those who seek to protect her and don't quite believe the whole mate thing." She sniffed and wrinkled her nose. "Though, let them get close enough and they'll change their minds."

Heat rose to Arianna's cheeks. "We'll be discrete with the details," she promised and squeezed her mate's hand.

Ellie inclined her head. "I've had to keep your sister away, too," she said to Rion. "She wants to see you before she returns to Brónach."

Something about his sister made Rion wince. "I'll make time."

Eoghan had remained perfectly still throughout the exchange, a statue rooted to the path he stood upon. He'd followed the pair through the estate all week, but it'd been at a distance. This was the closest he'd been to her since he'd delivered the key to release Rion of his shackles.

Rion's gaze ran up and down the male's form, taking in the weapons sheathed at his side and the way he stood. She could feel the sheer dominance radiating from her mate, but when Eoghan bowed his head, something in Rion relaxed, if only by a fraction.

"Thank you," Rion said, much to her surprise. "For before."

Eoghan simply nodded. "I live to serve, My Queen."

Ellie clapped her hands together, causing them all to startle. "Enough with the serious stuff, are we going?"

Despite the anxiety rushing through Arriana's veins, a smile tugged itself free. "Lead the way."

THEY WALKED along the neat cobblestone path in easy silence, Ellie and Eoghan to their front. The swirling channels of water were ever present, gently flowing toward the stairs that would lead them into the city.

But they weren't going into the city and when Ellie veered from the main path, leaping over the freshly budding bushes that lined it, Arianna knew their route.

And Ellie had cleared the way, just as she'd promised.

No sentinels walked the area nor stood guard. No servants raced toward the estate. No children played nearby.

It was almost eerie, but it made the journey easier.

Or she thought it would make it easier. Arianna had leapt over the garden beds that lined the walkway only to be tugged back by Rion. He gave her a questioning look, his eyes swimming with memories from his past.

She squeezed his hand again in reassurance and pulled him along. There weren't assassins waiting for them in the trees here, nor ambushes set up by those who had promised to be their ally. She knew he'd suffered both and likely a lot more, but her mate had nothing to fear from her little sister. She hoped he'd learn to trust her one day.

The roar of Elview Falls wiped her worries away as they drew closer. Arianna's adrenaline spiked when the trees thinned and she ran ahead, dragging Rion with her. Her legs pounded against the forest floor until she hit rock, then stopped at the very edge of the cliff that dropped two-hundred feet.

Mist collected on her clothes and she lifted her face toward the sky, relishing in the gushing water that flowed past. It came straight from the mountains, its icy temperature a constant that kept most Fae from daring to dive into its depths.

But aside from the view of the Falls, spread out before them was the entire city of Levea in all its wondrous glory.

Arianna spotted the main waterfront that stretched from one side of the city to the other, then the five smaller waterways that jutted out from the main, each turning and twisting their way between buildings. She knew from history class that the paths had been carved that way on purpose, to allow enough water throughout the city in the event of attacks.

Then there were the small channels that surrounded everything, carved like an intricate piece upon the land that left it looking like an artist's hand had delivered the final touch.

Fae ran to and fro, though most were too small to make out. The rooftops glistened black, a special liquid applied to the structures to ensure water didn't cause unnecessary damage.

She breathed in the scent and turned to find her mate smiling slightly. Did he know how much this place meant to her? Could he feel it down the bond?

Despite reuniting with her sister and Talon, this was the first time she'd truly felt at home.

Ellie walked closer and stood by Arianna's side. "I should have brought you here when you first came home."

Arianna didn't let her smile fade. "I'm glad you didn't." She knew she wouldn't have appreciated it as much then. Because now she felt whole, like nothing in the world could bring her down.

Arianna turned to her mate again and Rion's entire body went rigid. Her smile faded and a deep growl rumbled from his chest. She turned at the same time he did and her lips parted when she spotted Talon standing just outside the tree line.

The wind ruffled his long honey-brown hair and he no longer wore fighting leathers. Talon stood before them in a neat blue tunic, his pants a shade darker. No weapons hung at his side, but something about his face seemed pained as he took in the four that stood beside the cliff.

Well, three. Eoghan remained about three yards away from the sheer drop.

Rion pulled his lips back, revealing those razor sharp fangs, and the male she'd slept beside these past two weeks vanished. A cold warrior stood beside her now, his lethal gaze trained on her best friend.

A bad idea. This had been a stupid and ridiculously bad idea. Arianna's worried gaze traveled toward Ellie. Her sister's brow had knotted.

Then Talon stepped forward.

One step and the world exploded.

CHAPTER SIX

ARIANNA

One minute, her mate's hand was in hers. The next it was gone.

Rion and Talon's snarls sliced through the air raising the hairs at the back of her neck. Then their bodies and magic collided exploding in a hurricane of swirling debris, snow, and ice.

The force of the impact shook the earth and Arianna's stomach dropped, dread sweeping through her when the two males clashed again and again and again.

No.

No, no, no, no, no, no . . .

Their bodies danced around one another in a whirlwind of flying fists and pounding magic, both grappling for dominance over the other.

A twist, then Rion's fist slammed into Talon's jaw. He dodged, pivoted, then an icy shard skimmed Rion's cheek. She saw the flash of anger in his gaze. The rage as his magic rose in answer, slamming down on her friend only for Talon to skid to the side, barely avoiding the deadly blow.

The scent of their blood wafted toward her, sending Arianna's panic over the edge. She sprang forward, ready to intervene, but Ellie grabbed her arms, pulling her back.

"Let go," she demanded, the dread turned to nausea when Rion wrenched Talon's arm behind his back. Talon flipped out of the movement, ice spreading in his wake. He drew a knife from his boot and threw it only for Rion to catch it and send it sailing right back.

Talon dodged and the blade buried itself in the ground, left forgotten as he surged forward again.

"There's nothing you can do," Ellie said, gritting her teeth as she, too, watched the pair. The females backed away as icy shrapnel flew too close, landing mere inches from their forms.

"We have to do something." Arianna couldn't bear to watch them tear one another apart. Not over her. Her heart jolted again. No, this wasn't just about her. These two had been fighting on the front lines far longer. Talon had spent his teen years learning everything about The Demon. The way he fought, his magic, his patterns.

Sand whipped up like a viper from the ground and locked around Talon's leg, wrenching him to his knees. It swirled in a familiar spiraled pattern and her mind flashed back to Lan and his comrades. Their severed limbs. The blood.

Talon screamed in fury, blood dripping from the corner of his mouth, and the sand burst away from Talon's leg in frozen shards.

Talon launched from the ground and clamped his hand around Rion's wrist. Ice ran up Rion's arm and terror shot through her as she remembered the arm she'd turned into nothing more than a shriveled husk on the battlefield. Talon had that kind of power. One touch and—the ice exploded away and Rion's elbow slammed into the side of Talon's face.

Her friend fell, then righted himself and the pair crashed into one another again.

Arianna pulled against her sister's iron grip, but then Eoghan was there, pulling them both back. "We need to move," he said, but she wouldn't leave them. She couldn't.

A pulse shot through her body as she screamed their names, pleading with Rion down the bond, but her words hit a wall, as if he'd shut her out entirely.

It didn't matter what she said. What anyone said. These were two warriors on the battlefield again, locked in a fight to the death. One lethal storm pitted against another.

Water rose from the river to their right and earth ripped from the ground at the same moment, both magics monstrous before they flew toward one another at unnatural speeds.

Eoghan summoned thick wooden trucks from the ground and wound them around the trio to shield them from the debris that flew in all directions.

They were going to kill one another. Nothing could stop this. Not even Arianna.

Then warriors emerged from the tree line, their weapons drawn and magic ready. Her heart thundered as the warriors watched, their deep-seated hatred trained on her mate as they gauged the best way to assist their commander.

Snarls and growls echoed through the air and water rose, but Talon roared, stopping everyone in their tracks. He spared them an icy glare that relayed his message loud and clear.

He's mine.

Blood coated their mouths, but their swift movements didn't pause.

A pulse shuddered through Arianna again. Ellie spoke, but she couldn't hear the words. Couldn't hear anything over the deafening roar suddenly filling her head.

She didn't know when it had started, only that something in her veins crackled like thick ice over a river, the sound thunderous and deep.

Ellie and Eoghan released her arms and Arianna thought she heard her sister curse.

She stepped toward the chaos, the sheer force of the males' powers causing a whirlwind to rise up that whipped her hair around her face.

Something in her core pulsed. An ancient, brutal thing crawling beneath her skin, waking from a long slumber.

She should have feared approaching, should be shielding her face from the magic flying as the males closed in on one another. Her arms raised, but it didn't feel like her own movement.

It pulsed again, coursing through her like a heartbeat.

The warriors watching shifted their attention from the two males. Some backed away, others called out warnings she couldn't hear.

Arianna stepped into the whirlwind. Her arms fell and the drumming pulse burst from her body, racing toward the males.

Ice coated the ground in a split second, shooting from her feet in a wave that collided with their bodies.

Their gazes whipped toward her, but not before ice covered their forms, forcing both males to curl in on themselves as they struggled to shield from it.

It strummed through her body again, pulsing out over and over and it felt . . . familiar. Safe. Cold, yet welcoming.

The males tried to call forth their magic, but the creature within her stirred and pulsed harder and faster, time and time again.

They were on their knees before her, their hands raised to cover their faces.

Arianna.

It whispered, caressing her soul in a sweet symphony of power.

Those at the tree line recoiled as a wave swept over them.

Arianna.

It whispered again, but the voice had changed.

One male rose to his feet and her eyes locked with his emerald green gaze. She studied it, as if she should know the one who dared to rise. As if he—

Rion.

The voice murmured a third time. No, not a voice, a tug. A plea.

He took another stepped forward, ice crunching beneath his frozen boot. His skin held a bluish hue, his lips, too.

That power strummed through her, begging for release, but she clamped it down as the hazy picture before her cleared.

Talon was on his knees, staring up at her, struggling to rise. Those at the tree line huddled together, hiding behind the large trunks. And Ellie, she turned just in time to see her sister directly behind her.

The ancient magic pulsed through her again, ready to intervene, but Arianna pulled back, gritting against the sheer force of will it took to restrain the magic.

"Arianna." Someone grabbed her wrist and the pulse within her vanished, stripped away so suddenly she crumpled to the ground, sucking in air as if the wind had been knocked from her body.

Rion knelt with her. Not knelt, collapsed, his body shivering violently.

Blood coated his teeth when he asked, "Are you okay?"

He was hurt. Gods, what had she done? Arianna only stared a moment before reaching for him. He flinched away, catching her hand, and the movement sent a pang of confusion through her. "Are you okay?" he repeated.

"I—" What just happened? "I think so."

Her mouth gaped as she took in the scene before her. A thick layer of glassy white covered everything reaching all the way to the tree line where the warriors hiding behind the trees stepped around icicles as long as their arms.

She'd felt the strum of power, but she hadn't—

The river cracked behind them and giant sheets of ice broke from the bank, carried by the rapid current toward the waterfall. It'd even created a slippery overhand with icicles that stretched beyond her line of sight.

Arianna loosened a breath and it clouded in the chilled air.

"What the hell was that?" Ellie shouted.

Talon struggled to rise, but fell again, cursing to himself. Arianna's head whipped toward him then. She studied her friend then turned to access Rion. He held his ribs tight, blood dripped from his lip, and his eye had already swelled.

Horrified, Arianna clamped one hand around his wrist and rested the other on his chest, melting the ice not only on his skin, but in his blood. Gods, she'd just done the same thing as her father. She'd almost—

A sob choked her, but Arianna shook it off, forcing her body and magic to concentrate. Ellie was already at Talon's side, warming him as he also warmed himself.

She sifted through Rion's internal wounds and an audible crack echoed as his rib slid back into place. She patched a large gash in his side and his breath came easier.

Talon moaned and Arianna turned to find him attempting to stand.

"Sit still for a minute," Ellie chided. Talon ignored her and Arianna was sure if Ellie had been anyone else, he would have shoved her aside.

Arianna gave her mate a warning look to stay put then ran to Talon's side.

"Don't," Talon growled, stumbling as he tried to step around her.

Her anger and pain and fear bubbled over and she grabbed his arm, forcing the male to look at her. "You're going to sit," her voice shook, "and I'm going to fix you and if you have a problem with that, I'll make sure you can't move for the next week."

He eyed her then relented, though his gaze looked in every direction except hers.

She placed her hands on his chest and he winced. Four ribs broken, but— "Some of these are old." He didn't respond. Had he been hurt all this time? Why hadn't he come to her? They cracked back in place and he gasped from the pain. "You should have come to me sooner."

"Right, because that would have turned out well." The bite in his tone had her shrinking back, then he clicked his tongue and stood, stumbling before he turned his back on her.

"I'm not done," she said, but Talon kept walking.

Ellie grabbed her hand. "Let him go, I'll watch over him."

Those at the tree line stepped forward and one of the warrior reached for Talon's arm, but he shoved the male away. Others clutched their weapons and stepped toward her and Rion—

"Leave it," Talon shouted, his tone clipped and harsh.

Arianna could see their indecision, especially as she looked back toward her mate still sitting on the ground. Catching his breath, she realized, but he was watching the warriors, too, knowing he might have to fight despite his injuries.

Arianna crossed the distance to stand in front of him, shielding his body from their line of sight. Some regarded her with awe, others with fear and uncertainty. Then they turned and disappeared into the trees, following their commander.

Ellie gave her a grimaced smile then chased after Talon, leaving the three of them at the edge of the falls.

Arianna studied the brutalized landscape. The ice and deep scars in the earth. A battlefield. One of so, so many.

She turned back to her mate and found him studying her. He didn't pull at their bond, didn't move.

"What happened?" she asked.

Rion opened his mouth to answer and closed it again. His body shuddered and she rushed to his side, kneeling beside him to pour her magic into his frigid body. He was always so cold after the incident with her father and she'd done nothing to help.

"I'm sorry," he said, avoiding her gaze.

"It's done now. Does anything else hurt?" He didn't answer. "Rion, are you hurt anywhere else?" She followed his gaze and placed her hand on his thigh, healing another gash.

Then Arianna slumped down beside him, letting the roaring falls fill the uncomfortable silence.

"What happened?" she repeated.

"The shift." Arianna jumped at Eoghan's voice and Rion's head snapped toward him. His nostrils flared, but Arianna grabbed the torn sleeve of his tunic.

"Enough." She looked at Eoghan, his face pale as he scanned the vicinity. "What do you mean?"

"You're of that age now. Seeing those two fight," he tilted his head toward Rion, "probably pulled at it."

"Sometimes the magic sparks," Rion said, his voice hushed. "But I've never seen anyone's do that." They scanned the frozen field.

"She's The Divine," Eoghan said simply. "I'm sure she's going to show us a lot of things we've never seen."

Arianna's body shook. She felt as though she'd run for miles on end without food or water. Like she was a slave again, starved and expected to work grueling hours in the sun.

The shift. Gaining her animal form would certainly be a cause for celebration, but if this was the result . . . she didn't want to hurt anyone in the process and she'd half frozen her mate and Talon.

Her gaze traveled to the tree line. He hadn't even let her heal him completely. How long would this go on? Would he avoid her forever because she'd chosen to be with Rion?

"I can't control it," Arianna said. For a few moments she hadn't even recognized Talon or Rion. Had she even been herself?

"You will, eventually," Eoghan assured. "Everything takes practice. Shifting means you finally unlock your power's potential and sometimes it takes a bit to learn how to control the change."

Silence filled the space again as she looked over the frozen landscape. It was a miracle her father hadn't shown up. What would he think about Talon and Rion's fight? He'd probably scold Talon for not finishing it.

"Thank you, Eoghan." She glanced at her mate. "I think I'd like to be alone with him. If you don't mind."

He bowed at the waist. "Absolutely. I'll be around the cabin if you need me."

She nodded and watched him walk across the icy terrain leaving her and Rion in the frozen stillness.

Rion struggled to his feet, but he still didn't meet her gaze. A trickle of shame floated down the bond. Not due to the fight, she thought, but at how it'd made her feel. The panic and despair it had caused.

Her shift. Being The Divine, she wondered if she'd get one at all. That maybe she'd be like Rion and left without one.

"Were you ever able to shift into a half-breed?" They looked human, but the Fae scent didn't disappear entirely, thus, most Fae assumed those with a combined human and Fae scent were half-breeds.

He furrowed his brow at the question. "No, I'm not permitted a shift." Right, she knew that, she'd just thought that maybe he had that part and never showed it.

Arianna closed the distance between them and cupped his cheek, gently turning his gaze to hers. His eyes softened and she poured her magic through his jaw, healing the bruises and scrapes and cuts. Her fingers traced up to his eyes and he closed them, letting her fingertips graze over his eyelids to heal the blackness forming there.

"It's okay if—" she pressed a finger to his lips and he hesitantly rubbed a hand along her arm. The last thing she wanted was a confrontation with him. She knew what had happened; there was no reason to explain it or wallow in guilt over the situation.

"Do you trust me?"

The way he looked at her almost made her heart break. "Always." *You and only you* the bond seemed to say.

Arianna threaded her fingers through his, then turned her attention to the waterfall. She pulled Rion toward the edge and closed her eyes, breathing in the fresh scent of her childhood.

Memories flooded back of hot summer days when the grass beneath their bare feet was lush and soft. Of cold winter mornings when she and Talon couldn't say no to Ellie because her sister couldn't use magic yet. Of camping at the edge, a fire roaring and her parents sitting beside one another whispering sweet nothings their children balked at.

She smiled, the sun and memories warming the chill in her bones.

Ellie's light hearted giggle as they jumped from the falls. Talon's roaring laugh when they leapt over the edge, racing toward the bottom, carefree and young.

She teetered on the edge. "I won't drop you," she promised. Rion glanced at her, then the cliff.

"You intend to—"

She cut him off with a swift kiss that turned deep, then tilted to the side and let their bodies fall.

His grip tightened but a smile spread across her face and she tilted her head back letting the rush of the wind steal her breath and worries. Rion clutched her hand and she held his in return. She knew how many seconds it took to reach the bottom like she knew how to walk the estate in the black pitch of night.

Arianna pulled droplets from the air, letting them surround their bodies and slow their descent. He didn't resist and the pair pointed their feet, pressed their hands into their sides, then their bodies broke the surface of the deep, glittering pool.

Breath left her at the sheer frigid temperature, and the pounding of the falls pushed them deeper, a strong current rolling the pair along.

A sudden spike down the bond had Arianna diving for her mate. She propelled them away from the current and both gasped when they broke the surface.

Then Rion was laughing, really laughing, the sound full and loud and Arianna couldn't help but laugh along with him.

A fight. That's all it had been. No one was hurt. Not really, and compared to what they'd faced before and all the losses they'd suffered, it was a blessing.

Arianna splashed water on his face. "I thought you were panicking."

Those alluring emerald green eyes lit up in such a rare way. Then he pulled her close and kissed her. She melted into his touch and let her magic spread to warm the water surrounding them.

"I'm sorry," he said again, brushing the wet hair from her face as they treaded water.

She shook her head. "We knew it was too soon." Steam rose in the air around them. "How many times have you two done that?"

"A few," he admitted. "Though we were interrupted a lot for one reason or another. The only other time we fought unhindered—well, that's the night a beautiful female chose to save my life rather than end it."

She ran her hand down his torso. "I'm glad I did."

Rion pressed his forehead to hers. "Me, too."

"Do you think it was instinct?"

His mouth brushed hers and her heart leapt, need instantly demanding she pull him closer. "I don't know." They kissed, long and slow and her need turned more fierce and demanding.

The pair swam closer to shore and as soon as Rion's feet touched the bottom, Arianna wrapped her legs around his waist, feeling a desire that matched her own.

His tongue dove into her mouth and everything that was Rion became her. They had eternity to work together, learn, and grow as a mated pair. And once that bond solidified, she'd feel things from him she'd never feel from another.

His pleasure. His pain.

And she wanted nothing more.

AFTER LETTING his presence consume her, the pair laid in the grass at the edge of the shore, watching the falls and the sky as it shifted to orange and purples above them. She'd dried their clothes and Rion had one hand behind his head and the other wrapped around her shoulders.

"Who taught you how to swim?" she asked.

"My mother. There's a lake not far from Nàdiar. She liked to visit, so my father built her a house next to the water."

"That was kind of him." She bit her tongue, remembering exactly what his father had done, but Rion just shrugged.

"He was a different male when my mother was around."

"Do you think your life would have been different if—" Arianna couldn't finish her sentence. What was she supposed to say? If his mother hadn't vanished? Died?

"You don't have to tiptoe around the subject." He glanced skyward. "I like to think my mother would have protected me as Saoirse did, but I'll never really know."

It was so difficult to imagine him as a child. To envision a young Rion with joy in his heart and fear absent from his life. If his mother had remained, Arianna might have met Rion under different circumstances. Perhaps during a meeting between their nations. He would have proudly worn the colors of his country, standing at his siblings', no, his father's side as a representative of Brónach.

Once they were alone, she might have snuck out onto a balcony. Arianna would have been too shy to approach, but Rion may have introduced himself, offered her a walk through the gardens. She'd have asked him about his magic and how it worked, watched his demonstration of it as one might watch an artist.

Once signs of the bond appeared, he would have courted her, taking her on late afternoon strolls and to dinners and perhaps stealing a kiss or two beneath the stars.

But that was another life. Another universe.

One she couldn't let herself dwell on because what she had now was as close to perfect happiness as she'd ever experienced. And she'd never take it for granted.

CHAPTER SEVEN

ARIANNA

ays later, horns blared in the distance and Arianna shot up from the blankets, magic curling around their bodies while her heart threatened to beat out of her chest.

They sounded again, the low bellow unfamiliar and eerie. Rion sat up at her side, gripping the sheets with one hand, his magic dancing around their forms as he studied her reaction.

This wasn't Brónach. He wouldn't know what one alarm meant over another, but one look at her pensive gaze had him pulling his clothes on.

"What is that?" he asked.

Arianna swung her legs off the bed and shoved yesterday's shirt over her head before reaching for her pants. "I'm not sure."

She opened the front door and the horns sounded again, still distant yet clear. She craned her neck. They were at the northern gate. Good, better than the western side considering the gates and bridge were still in ruins. She clenched her fists, hating that Levea was vulnerable at all. They had temporary measures in place, of course, and the bulk of their military forces were finally home, too. But still—

When the pair emerged from the spiraling wall of ice surrounding the summer house, Arianna looked at Eoghan with a hopeful expression, but he only shook his head, confusion covering his face as well. No Talon or Ellie.

Rion didn't bother growling at the male, not where there was another potential threat to eliminate.

"Is it another attack?" Eoghan asked. Arianna couldn't imagine an enemy announcing themselves, but then again, it would incite fear and cause many to scramble.

"It's not Fiadh," Rion stated, his gaze locked on the path to the stairs as if someone could emerge any second.

Arianna scented the air. No smoke. That was a plus, but could Levea stand another invasion so soon? Were they about to fight for their lives again after they'd barely survived the last encounter? There were still so many that roamed the estate halls in their black mourning clothes. Would they get no time to honor their dead?

Arianna darted toward the main path with Rion and Eoghan on her heels. The servants were gone, but she could see the sentinels up ahead, their hands on their weapons. Dread swept through her anew, but a male's voice called before she could reach them.

"Arianna."

Relief and fear flooded through her at his voice. She hadn't seen Talon since his fight with Rion. She gripped Rion's hand tight, but her mate didn't growl or snarl or so much as bare his fangs. Right, another threat; maybe if they were always in danger Talon and Rion could tolerate one another.

"What's going on?" She took in his fighting stance and pensive gaze, but there was also uncertainty there that had her wishing for more weapons.

Talon blew out a sigh and stared out over the horizon refusing to meet her gaze. "Avalon just told me an escort from the royal city is here."

"What?"

"The officials in Ruadhán have been requesting your presence."

She bristled, already knowing the answer to her next question. "And?"

"And since they didn't get the answer they wanted, they've come to get you."

AN ICY storm billowed just beneath the surface of her skin as Arianna marched through her family's estate with Rion and Talon trailing her. Eoghan had opted to stay with the cabin, just to be sure no one tampered with it in their absence.

The royal city, Ruadhán. It was a mysterious place rumored to float high above the land. A civilization where all four nations worked together to create a haven for The Divine to enact her will.

Yet, if they represented such serenity, where had they been during the war? Why hadn't they intervened or helped those displaced and left to rot?

If they were so noble, why hadn't they put a stop to every war before this one?

Servants and warriors both paused to watch the trio pass. Some smiled at her, but upon seeing her mate they all ducked their heads and either grimaced or outright fled.

Arianna couldn't stop the way her magic spun around her body with warriors so near to her mate. This wasn't the infirmary wing. This was where the council members dwelled. Where their High Lord ran the country of Móirín. Every warrior in these walls would give their life for her father. And Rion was enemy number one.

She didn't want to see any of them. Her father, the council, those more than willing to take Rion's life.

It was difficult to remember exactly who'd been present at Rion's execution, but Arianna remembered a few.

And she loathed them with every fiber of her being.

A growl rumbled through her chest and she didn't miss the way the nearby warriors stepped back. Good, they should know their places where her mate was concerned.

They continued down the outside corridor that ran parallel to a massive waterfall. The droplets collected against her skin as they passed several pavilions and the giant fountain that depicted a phoenix and dragon.

These falls had cooled her face weeks ago when she'd first entered Levea with nothing but sadness in her heart. But she wasn't sad now and they did nothing to quell the anger threatening to burst free.

Arianna wished she had more time to sort through her feelings about her father. She'd wanted to wait until the bond settled when her emotions wouldn't be so high, but it didn't appear as though Ruadhán was giving her a choice.

She could always tell them to leave.

Arianna inwardly sighed. Did she have a right to be angry with her father? At the time of Rion's execution, Avalon had thought Rion responsible for his mate's death. Ellie had informed him otherwise, though Arianna hadn't bothered to listen to the details. She should have. She should be doing more for her people, for the entire city as The Divine. Yet, some healing was all she'd managed. She'd been selfish, the instinct to protect her mate overriding everything else—

Her father's scent wafted toward her and Arianna's anger soared, ripping a snarl from her that had everyone in the vicinity running.

"Calm down," Talon urged, but the anger burned through her veins like wildfire.

Calm, right, she needed to be calm to actually speak to her father so she wouldn't just march in and rip his godsforsaken head off. She needed to discover what he'd told the royal city and figure out her role.

"What do you know?" she asked Talon, hoping to distract herself as they crossed the last hall before entering the building. Only two doors stood between her and the High Lord.

"Just that the royal city has summoned you. Avalon said you'd come to him when the time was right."

She growled again. Which meant he let them come. Or maybe those in Ruadhán were just as impatient as her father and didn't care what she had to say. Would they try to drag her against her will? One look at Rion told her that wouldn't happen, though she seriously doubted Talon would let anyone touch her against her will either.

Her mind returned to her father. One issue at a time. Her father hadn't summoned her or sought her out in the time she'd been with Rion, either because he understood the mating bond or she'd humiliated him so much that he didn't want to see her. Maybe this was as much of a strain for him as it was for her.

But . . . would her father hate her forever? He was the only parent she had left and the thought sobered her just a bit. What if Rion was a problem they'd never be able to work past?

"I've read a lot of books on the royal city," Talon said. "From what I've gathered about their past, I'd err on the side of diplomacy where they're concerned."

"Because they were so diplomatic by letting a war rage on for a decade."

Talon sighed. "I know." He'd been there to witness it just as much as she had. Rion, too. They'd all glimpsed different parts of the darkness war brought on, and it had changed them all. Arianna had just recently begun to wonder how much.

They entered a large foyer and Arianna paused to stare at the door that led to her father's study. Two sentinels stood on either side, as they always did when he wasn't preoccupied with meetings.

She took a deep breath, tapped her foot, then glanced toward her mate. She didn't want her father anywhere near him, but she also didn't want to be separated from him either.

"It's probably not a good idea for you to come in there with me," Arianna said, unable to tear her gaze away from the guards. An emotion flew down the bond, but Arianna couldn't discern whether it was anger, fear, hatred, or a combination of all three.

"For you or Avalon?" Talon asked.

"Both."

She sighed and gritted her teeth. Why did she have to see her father? Ruadhán had sent an escort, so what? Would they try to convince her to come with them? Sure. Could they force the issue?

Not a chance. Unless of course her father exiled her from the city, but even then, she had other options. She could just as easily travel to Brónach or the little cabin nestled in the trees of the mountains. No one would follow them there. Except maybe Eoghan.

Arianna pivoted away from the foyer. "They can wait."

"Come again?" Talon asked.

"The royal city. They can wait."

Talon looked her over, likely seeing the same stubbornness in her that Ellie displayed on a daily basis. He cleared his throat. "There's been concern over your safety."

Rion bristled at the comment. "What about it?"

Talon shifted beneath her gaze. Not Rion's. Hers.

"What happened?"

"Word is spreading. People have gathered outside the gates. Most just want a chance to see you, but—"

"But what?"

"There have been . . . issues," Talon said and Arianna thought she might burst at the seams.

"Stop trying to coddle me and tell me what's going on."

"What Talon doesn't want to say," Ellie rounded the corner. "Is that there have been attacks on the outskirts of Levea. They've had a few fatalities, but the guards are trying to keep everyone in order."

Talon glared at Ellie, but Arianna's heart jolted. "Fatalities?" People had died over her and she hadn't even known it? "What do they want?" If she could prevent—

"You. Dead, if their chanting is anything to go by," Talon finished.

She gaped at them. "Why?"

"Why does anyone want anything? You represent change; not everyone likes change."

"But I haven't done anything."

Ellie's face turned serious. "Your name unified two nations that have been at war for a decade. It freed the slaves positioned at a major war camp and it's forcing all three of those groups to work together. Quite successfully, I might add."

"For now," Talon said and Arianna wondered if there was more he wasn't telling her.

"Why didn't I know?" she asked him, hurt rising in her chest. Gods, she wanted to end death and torment, not bring it to her home city.

"You have enough going on."

"I don't care," she exclaimed. "If there are people dying on my account, then I want to know about it. Gods," she paced the balcony, fear and worry coursing through her anew.

What was she supposed to do now? She couldn't stay in Levea if people were dying outside the city gates just for wanting to see her. And Levea was still recovering. What if the mass of followers attracted another attack? They'd be left completely defenseless outside the walls.

She startled when Rion took her hand. He pressed a kiss to her knuckles then clenched his jaw. "You should speak with your father."

She didn't very well have a choice now, did she? "I don't want to be away from you."

Rion took a half step closer. "I know, but I've seen what rogue factions can do. So has Talon." He didn't need to say the rest. She understood. They'd rage war and even if the factions weren't strong enough to penetrate Levea's walls, those outside of them would suffer.

Ellie's chipper voice broke the tension. "I can stay with him."

Arianna eyed her younger sister, then Rion. Would the guards respect Ellie enough to not attack Rion? She couldn't be sure what kind of orders her father had given them. Was her mate in danger even as they stood inside the estate? Could there be—

Rion pulled her gaze back to his with the feather-light touch of his finger on her chin. "I can defend myself, you know."

"The bond letting you read my mind now?"

"No, the worry is written all over your face. Trust me, you'll be the first to know if anything goes wrong."

Ellie closed the distance, far too excited for Arianna's comfort. Her little sister only got that excited when she had a plan in mind. And Ellie's plans weren't always the safest.

Ellie shooed her. "Go see what our father wants and give me a few minutes to get to know my future brother-in-law."

Talon coughed and heat crawled up Arianna's neck, warming her ears then her cheeks. She turned before Rion could see her reaction.

They were mates, after all; she'd want to marry him eventually, right? Settle down, start a family?

Arianna couldn't steady her voice. "Just don't go too far, okay?"

Ellie beamed. "You got it."

Arianna turned back toward the door that led into the foyer and sighed. "Let's go see what kind of mess my father has gotten me into."

CHAPTER EIGHT

RION

ion watched his mate walk through the thin sliding door with Talon at her side and every part of his body ignited, begging him to follow.

His mate. And yet another male was escorting her to see her father. He hated how close they stood and loathed the way Talon's gaze lingered on her slender form when she wasn't looking. A low growl rumbled in his chest and Rion's eyes locked onto Talon's hands, daring him to touch her. If he so much as—

"Rion?" His jaw clenched. Arianna was the center that rooted him to the continent and he'd do anything for her. Kill anyone for her. *Be* anyone for her.

But right now she needed him to leave. Well, not leave exactly, but he knew whatever Ellie had planned wouldn't involve waiting on the balcony.

Slowly, he turned to face Ellie. This female who was so similar to her elder sister, yet different in a magnitude of ways. Both females resembled their mother in appearance and Arianna's scent carried the same sweet allure as the late Lady Lillian. But Ellie's scent was harsher, forged from the basins of the earth like her father's, though she probably resented being anything like the High Lord of Móirín.

"Come on." She skipped down the hall away from Arianna, and Rion followed, tugging against his instincts like a wild animal desperate to escape the leash. Even when she'd gone to the infirmary, he'd never been far behind. He couldn't stand the distance. Couldn't stand it now and there were only two doors between them.

So how in the seven hells was he going to handle the royal city taking her away? If Levea didn't welcome him, those sworn to protect The Divine certainly wouldn't open their doors.

"Where are we going?" he asked, his soul rending with every step.

"You'll see." She spun and walked backward, holding up one finger. "I do have to make a quick stop though, is that all right?"

She likely meant in the city, around civilians who would be less than welcoming to his presence.

"Sure." As if he had much of a choice.

They exited the main part of the estate, entering the bright sunlight of late morning. Intricate gardens lined everything it seemed, hiding the manor beneath floral bushes and trees of all sizes and varieties. He wondered which was Arianna's favorite. Perhaps something as wild as the wisteria that grew no matter the obstacle in its path. Or perhaps she liked something a bit more contained. Roses, foxglove, or hydrangeas.

Maybe she didn't like flowers at all.

Gods, what was wrong with him? He should be paying attention to his surroundings and the female leading him from the estate. He should be counting every footstep, searching every shadow.

But he couldn't get Arianna out of his head. Not for a second and she was with another male and—

Talon. She was with Talon, he reminded himself. He was a respectable male from the way Arianna spoke of him, and Rion had seen Talon's tenacity during the war. The male fought for his comrades with a fierceness that so few possessed. He was the type to lay down his life for those in his unit and, in Rion's experience, that kind of loyalty was akin to a rare gem.

But he'd also been the male who—

Rion clamped an iron door around the thought. Arianna was his. No, he was Arianna's. She'd chosen him.

Ellie hummed as they ambled down the cobblestone path toward the stairs where a pair of sentinels stood. Weapons and armor glistened in the sun and Rion braced himself. One movement. One flick of their wrist and a dagger could be in his back. There was no room for error or distraction.

"Good morning," Ellie chirped, but their bodies were so stiff Rion wasn't sure the pair were breathing. A male to his left. A female to his right.

They both carried swords at their sides and knives were already clutched in their palms. He watched their gazes drift from Ellie and snap back to him, likely wondering if they should risk her wrath and end The Demon if they could. They wouldn't.

It was then that Rion noticed it. Ellie often acted childish, but in that moment, Rion saw the way her body shifted. He scented her magic rise, the droplets forming so close to her skin, an untrained eye would never see it. And he watched the way her gaze scanned over the pair, as if she could see through to every movement of their bodies.

The guards didn't move and Rion waited until they were halfway down the stairs before speaking.

"What was that?"

"What was what?" She kept her back to him, taking the stairs two at a time.

"Back there."

She cocked her head back to look at him in the playful sort of way she always did to others. As if he wasn't different. As if he wasn't a monster. "I don't know what you're talking about."

He opened his mouth and closed it again. Well, how was he supposed to respond to that? He'd seen Arianna on the battlefield. Relished in her flawless movements that only came from years of training. Yet Arianna claimed her younger sister had always bested her.

But Arianna hadn't been the one lying unconscious, barely clinging to life during Fiadh's siege. Thank the gods.

The trees thinned as they neared the base of the stairs and the area opened into a large courtyard full of fountains, budding trees, newly turned over soil, and those same circling waterways that wove their way through the city.

Fae, half-breeds, and humans roamed the streets dressed for the cool weather. They conversed and laughed with one another in a way he'd rarely seen. No fear drifted through the air and the only sound of chains came from those wearing jewelry around their neck and wrists.

So different from Brónach. So peaceful. He'd advocated to release the slaves once and his brother had thought the idea absurd. Yet if those from Brónach saw what he saw now, perhaps they'd change their minds.

But he was no stranger to how ghosts from the past could haunt the minds of the living. They were taught to hate humans just as much as they were taught to fear those born with his type of magic.

"You think too much," Ellie said, leading him past another set of guards. Her shoulders shifted again and her magic reappeared telling him she knew exactly what she was doing. "Arianna does the same thing." Talon had said something similar once. "Care to share your thoughts?"

He supposed leaving her in silence would make for a very awkward time together. "I was just observing how different Móirín is from Brónach." He let his gaze follow a Fae and half-breed with their fingers interlocked, smiling at one another as if nothing could dampen their spirits. "We don't have humans and the half-breeds aren't free to . . . wander."

Ellie slowed her steps and followed his gaze. "Do you have anything against them?"

Rion recalled Kirian. A brave male who'd stood guard over Ellie's body. A male willing to die to protect the one he loved. "No."

"Good." They passed the final set of guards at the main gate and Rion's magic crawled beneath his skin, begging for release as those in the vicinity realized who walked beside their future High Lady.

Women and children ducked from the streets and males pulled their families from harm's reach, ushering them along.

Ellie didn't react, though he could tell from the way her gaze darted around that she was watching.

He followed her down the cobblestone street, passing a collection of shops marked with colorful storefronts before pausing at a door. A bell sounded when she opened it, but before Rion stepped onto the threshold, fear hit him hard, the scent burning like harsh smoke. He took one look at the frightened female inside and stepped back.

"I'll wait out here."

Ellie gave him a sorrowful look. "Just promise you won't go anywhere." He nodded and she ducked inside, returning less than a minute later with a bag in hand. "All done. Let's get out of here."

Happily. They were drawing too much attention for his comfort. Not for himself—he could handle a few civilians—but Ellie could get injured and he didn't want his first time out with Arianna's little sister to result in bloodshed.

The pair walked back toward the estate then past it, the same guards watching his every move. The bustling street thinned until the shops turned into homes and homes turned to land and rock and water. It wasn't until Ellie veered from the main road that Rion paused.

"Where are we going?"

"Somewhere we can talk." The hair raised on the back of his neck and she seemed to note his discomfort. What would he do if Arianna's younger sister attacked him? There weren't any witnesses out here. It would be their future High Lady's word against his. He'd been so preoccupied with others gunning for him that he hadn't paused to consider this might be a trap as well.

Shit. He needed to avoid going any further with her, get back out into the open at the very least.

Not that the citizens would take his side. Hell, no one would. Separating from Arianna had been a fool's hope.

"I can see that brain of yours churning," Ellie said. "So let me settle something right now. Coming after you in any way would only hurt my sister and after watching her wallow in grief for a month, I'd rather not witness it again."

A month. Pain hit him hard. He'd done that to her.

"Why in there?" he nodded toward the trees.

"Because I don't want certain entities to overhear what I have planned. Arianna is going to Ruadhán whether we like it or not and unless you want to be left behind, I suggest you follow."

Rion loosed a breath and searched their surroundings, letting small grains of his magic wash over the area. She was right about one thing. They weren't alone but who was to say the spies wouldn't follow them into the trees?

He almost laughed to himself. He knew the females were close but relying on the strength of their relationship felt like fate mocking him. Like it paralleled exactly what he'd always wanted from his own family.

"Okay." He followed and she grinned, spinning around to jump from the path and into the trees.

The sounds of the city faded, replaced by the scents of the forest. Rion caught the Fairy Folk peering at them from around the branches and stumps and he watched Ellie's expression brighten in their presence. Maybe she felt it was a good omen. He certainly hoped so.

A male scent drifted toward him and Rion stopped in his tracks, his magic rearing up to wrap around his body.

"Relax," she said. "It's just Kirian."

"Why is he here?"

"Because I want him here." They rounded a tree to find a tiny clearing and Kirian sat on a blanket with an assortment of food spread out before him.

The male stood awkwardly and though he smiled at Ellie, Rion noted the trace of fear in his scent. Ellie hugged him and planted a chaste kiss on his cheek before the two sat beside one another.

"Kirian, I'm sure you remember Rion. And Rion, this is Kirian."

The male bowed his head slightly. "It's nice to meet you. Officially." Right, because the last time he'd seen the male, he'd been fussing over Ellie's unconscious form. Well, he'd seen him in the infirmary wing too, but the male had paid no attention to Rion. His focus had been entirely on Ellie.

Ellie handed Kirian the bag and grabbed a wrapped sandwich. "What'd you bring us?"

"Your favorite, of course." He glanced at Rion. "I wasn't sure what you liked, but I made you one as well."

Ellie patted the blanket. "Come here, sit."

His lips parted as he stared at the pair. He doubted the sandwich was poisoned, but there was no telling who else might have overheard her plan, who might have watched them enter the trees and who might lay waiting just outside.

He turned, feeling a pulse of aggression down the bond and stared toward the estate.

"Don't worry about her," Ellie said. "I'm sure our father will piss her off, but he won't hurt her and neither will Talon."

Rion clenched his fists. "Why am I here?"

Ellie stopped filling her plate. "I told you."

"So get to the point."

She sighed. "I was looking forward to eating first, but I guess hoping you'd relax was a just wishful thinking." She wiped her hands on her pants. "I overhead my father talking to a representative of Ruadhán last night. He arrived before the others and they plan to leave with Arianna first thing in the morning."

"Let me guess, I'm not invited."

She made a mocking voice. "The Demon is not to come near the city." She ground her teeth. "I'm sure you can guess the rest." He could. He was no stranger to assassinations.

"Yeah."

She clenched her fists. "They don't even know you, they're just going off some stupid prophecy."

"Neither do you."

A smile tugged at the corner of her mouth. "I'm starting to learn you might not like sandwiches."

"I don't make a habit of eating food from—" He stopped himself, remembering this was Arianna's sister.

"Strangers?" she finished. "I get it. I mean, I've never had people try to kill me so I wouldn't really know, but," she met his gaze, "I can promise you one thing: I would never hurt my sister and as I said before, if anything were to happen to you, it would hurt her far more than anything anyone has ever done to her physically."

His heart swelled with the knowledge. To have someone care for him so deeply was a concept he'd never grow accustomed to. To think he was worth something to someone . . .

"You mentioned a plan."

"Right," she stood, "since they already know your scent and your magic, you can pretty much guarantee they'll have an entire unit dedicated to keeping you out of the city walls. But what if they can't scent you?"

Rion furrowed his brow. "What do you have in mind?"

"Covering it with my magic. Making you smell like Móirín."

"How?" Gods he hoped she didn't mean—

Ellie stepped closer and he watched her magic slowly rise. His answered in kind but Ellie observed it with child-like fascination. Not an ounce of fear. "Arianna mentioned you didn't like physical touch, but what about magical?"

"I'm not fond of either."

She studied the grains floating in the air. "You could create a barrier beneath it. You'll be fully robed, no one would notice."

"What's your plan exactly?"

"To cover your skin in a thin layer of water just long enough for you to get into the city. After that, they'd have to demand something of their queen, which, as you can imagine, won't go over well."

Her magic would be so close. The thought of just having a small layer separating himself from someone as powerful as Ellie made his skin crawl, but what other choice did he have? He could try to fight his way in, but they all knew it would end in a disaster.

Rion's magic collected around his body and he swallowed down years of dread. "Do it."

CHAPTER NINE

ARIANNA

Arianna stood on the threshold of the familiar office and stared at her father. His lips were pressed into a thin line and sunlight filtered in through the window to their left, giving his short dark hair a brownish hue. His eyes were cautious, darting between her, Talon, and the door as if waiting for someone else to join them.

Thank the gods Rion wasn't with her. Arianna's nostrils flared at her father's scent and molten anger coursed through her body, wild and unrestrained.

He had hurt her mate and the horrid magic they'd used was still hurting him. She hadn't been able to pinpoint the source of the icy current flowing through Rion's body. And it drove her mad.

Avalon's eyes narrowed. Eyes that had judged her since her mother's death. He'd deemed her worthless and had stripped her of the title as his heir.

She'd been fourteen and her sister only twelve. Ellie had never forgiven him. Likely never would, and though Arianna had grown up as the submissive daughter, she thought now, in this moment, that perhaps she'd never forgive him either.

The guards outside hadn't moved and Arianna wondered if they'd been commanded to restrain her in the event she lost her temper.

"What's going on?" she demanded, unable to keep the growl from her tone.

Avalon clenched his jaw and gestured to the cushioned chairs at the table. "Have a seat."

She debated refusing or turning and leaving, ignoring him altogether, but Talon stepped forward and pulled a chair out for her.

Calm, she reminded herself. Just remain calm and get it over with.

Arianna sat and Talon slid into the chair beside her, watching father and daughter as if he weren't sure what to do with himself.

Avalon carefully folded his hands and the sunlight caught his wedding band, pulling at an old wound in her chest. It wasn't just anger that flowed through her; before now, she'd struggled to name the emotions tied to it. Grief. Loss.

Because if her mother were around, Arianna would still be the heir. She wouldn't have deemed her daughter worthless. If her mother were around, she would have given Rion a chance to explain and prove himself. If her mother were around—

Arianna's lips quivered, but she bit the inside of her cheek. She refused to cry in front of her father. He didn't deserve to see her break down and she wouldn't give him another reason to call her weak.

"I'd like to talk to you first." She clenched her fists on the table, but he continued as if he hadn't noticed. "I want to apologize."

"For lying about my mother or attacking my mate?"

His shoulders stiffened for a heartbeat, then relaxed. She wasn't the only one struggling to stay calm. "I didn't know he was your mate."

"You knew I loved him. You saw what it did to me to not have him around."

"You were his captive. I'd hardly call whatever feelings might have emerged love." She growled and her father laid his hands flat on the table. "You're my daughter. You were held against your will. Did you expect me to feel anything other than anger toward the ones who caused you pain?"

"You know nothing about my pain."

"I know what it is to lose a mate. The anger you feel now is the same anger I've harbored for years. Anger I thought I could abate by ending the creature who stole my mate." His gaze softened when he looked her over. "Can you blame me for wanting to avenge your mother? It's instinct to defend our mates. It's a drive we can't control. But when they're gone . . . well, let's just say it's a wonder I didn't go mad." He pressed a hand to his head. "Though who can be sure I haven't?"

She'd never seen her father vulnerable. Not even in the weeks after her mother's death. But . . . he'd been absent in those weeks. No. Months. Their father had abandoned them. Left the girls to wallow in their grief with only Talon and Myrna to comfort them.

"I won't ask you to forgive me," he said. "I know that's beyond you, but I still offer my apologies and hope we can move past it in the near future."

"Are you going to hurt him again?"

"No."

"Have you commanded anyone to hurt him?" Her father didn't reply. "If you want to move past it, then you can start there. I want him safe while we're inside these walls."

Her father sat back. "He caused quite the disturbance yesterday." His gaze flickered to Talon. "I received several detailed reports." His eyes shifted back to hers. "They told me other things as well."

"Did you also receive a report about me putting a male on his back in the infirmary wing, or are your reports only skewed toward those you wish to damn?"

He chuckled. "No, I received that report, too. Your mother did the same once, but she didn't stop and it took three seasoned warriors to pull her off the male who had threatened me."

Arianna's lips parted. Her father never talked about her mother. Never. What had changed? She studied him and his movements. His racing heart. The sweat on his brow.

Her father was . . . uncomfortable. Grieving. Had Rion's innocence brought all this on? Did knowing he'd been angry and hunting the wrong male bring other feelings to the surface?

"Promise me," she urged. "Mother would have."

Her father sat straighter at that, seeming to think before he finally caved. "Yes, she would have." He folded his hands again. "As long as he doesn't pose a threat to you or any civilians, I will command my warriors to stand down. They won't quarrel with him unless they're provoked."

Arianna nodded. "Good."

He studied her, really studied her, and Arianna resisted the urge to shrink beneath his penetrative gaze. "You're not the same female who was taken two years ago."

"No." She wasn't. She'd changed so much and she still didn't understand it. Perhaps she didn't even know herself anymore. She'd grown. Loved. Hated. Fought.

Her father's gaze drifted to the open window and he was silent for so long that Arianna wondered if he would speak again. "You look like her," he began, voice whisper quiet. "You look so much like your mother that I wanted to protect you from . . . everything. I know it's selfish. I know it doesn't make sense, but when I saw Ellie standing over you, I knew you weren't strong enough." His gaze slid to her hands. "Or thought you weren't strong enough." He shook his head. "I thought if I kept you out of the fray, out of politics and the war, that I could protect you when I couldn't protect her. And now here I am, about to send you into the wolf's den and you have no training at all."

Her mouth had gone dry. Protect her. He'd acted out to protect her, yet the way he'd made her feel, the words he'd said. They were all projected anger at his own failings, but they'd left a permanent scar on her heart.

Her father cleared his throat. "Despite what you may believe, I tried to hold them off, but those in the royal city are insistent, thus their arrival." Avalon pulled an envelope from inside his tunic. The black paper had been crinkled, as if he'd clutched it in anger. Gold lined the outside, creating an interwoven border along the edges. He slid it across the table.

"They know nothing of your mate. They know The De—" he stopped himself, closed his eyes for a moment, then spoke again. "They know Rion is here, but they don't understand why or the delay. I tried using your recent situation as leverage, but—" He gestured toward the gates.

Arianna eyed the envelope but refused to touch it. No one knew. Her father had kept it a secret. Would that make things easier or harder and what did it mean to have a mate to begin with? Her mate was supposed to come from another country altogether. How had things gotten so turned around?

"The son of Pádraigín's High Lord is acting regent of Ruadhán. I expect you'll be met with confrontation where Rion is concerned. As such, I'm sending you with a few of my handpicked warriors." He nodded toward Talon. "Which Talon is among."

"Yes, sir."

Arianna's head whirled toward him and the surprise on her face caused hurt to flash across his. She hadn't been sure if he'd come with her after what had happened with Rion. They hadn't spoken since. Hadn't seen one another.

"They want to leave tomorrow morning."

"Tomorrow?!"

"I know it's soon."

She stood. "Don't they know what just happened with Fiadh? I can't leave when there's still so much to do." Not that she'd helped with the relief effort.

"Your presence in the city has been noted. As has your absence. Your people worry for you and some have started to question why you haven't addressed them as their queen." His eyes sparkled with something like pride on the word. "I'd venture to say those in the estate know Rion is your mate, but others don't and wonder if you're a captive within the walls of your own home."

"So I just abandon them?" She'd been so occupied, so distracted with her mate and healing those in the infirmary. No, not distracted.

They were an excuse. An escape. She was running all over again. Arianna clenched her jaw.

Avalon stood. "You make a grand exit worthy of your country. You dress and act the part. You reassure your people and leave with a smile on your face, promising to change the continent for the better."

Promises. But did she have the strength to fulfill them?

"Even if you hate me," he continued. "You are still my daughter. And if you need aid, need anything, you have but to call. I won't leave you to their selfish agendas." She'd frozen in place. "Which is why I'm also sending Ellie with you." He chuckled when her eyes widened. "Not that she would have stayed even if I'd ordered it. Your sister may not seem like it, but she's attended enough classes to help you negotiate. She'll also function as an adviser in my stead until you acclimate to your new home."

Home. "I'm not coming back." It wasn't a question. Of course she wasn't coming back.

Her father gave her a sad smile. "Ruadhán is meant for The Divine. They've, no, *we've* waited on you for centuries." That pride returned to his face. "I only wish your mother was here to see you now."

"Me, too." Arianna pushed up from the table and Talon did the same. She wasn't sure what to do with herself, but her father spoke again before she could leave.

"There's something else." He grimaced and gestured to the letter. "They stated The Demon wasn't to come anywhere near the city, else there'd be consequences."

CHAPTER TEN

ARIANNA

he didn't leave the following morning. Nor the morning after that or the one after. In fact, she'd refused to leave the family estate at all, just going to the infirmary and back with Rion at her side.

He'd told her all about Ellie's plan. It was reckless, stupidly dangerous, and it just might be their only choice.

She'd said three words to her father before she'd stormed from his office.

I'm not going.

The finality in her tone must have been enough because he hadn't summoned her again. Talon hadn't stopped by either.

Despite the promised dangers, Rion didn't push the issue, even if she could see him watching the shadows a bit more closely than before.

Was staying wrong? They could travel to Brónach, but she knew the masses would follow and the violence along with it.

Maybe her entire life would turn into her hiding all over again, running from one place to another with Rion at her side. No. She couldn't hide anymore. She had responsibilities, people who were relying on her. She just needed to figure out how to navigate Rion's existence into the mix.

A knock at their door had Arianna sighing. Rion was already on his feet, the book he'd been reading forgotten on the wooden stand in the living area. She pushed the eggs she'd been cooking onto a plate and brushed her hands over her apron.

Arianna scented the air. Ellie. Of course it was Ellie.

Arianna's annoyance rose. Ellie had begged her at least half a dozen times to reconsider traveling to Ruadhán. She'd declined.

Arianna prepared herself for an argument, but when she opened the door, her sister's haggard expression had Arianna biting her tongue. "What's wrong?" Rion was behind his mate a second later.

Ellie's red-rimmed eyes shone with unshed tears. Her voice shook. "Talon didn't want me to come, but I think there's something you need to see."

Arianna exchanged a quick look with her mate, then pulled on her boots and slid a few knives onto her person.

Arianna's heart thundered as she and Rion followed Ellie from their cabin refuge toward the stairs.

The city. Ellie was taking them into the city.

Arianna paused. "I'm not sure—"

"You need to come." Was Ellie's only response and the cold sad tone had Arianna's feet moving. Arianna's magic churned in agitated swirls when they passed the sentinels standing guard, but the pair stepped back, giving all three a wide berth. Those stationed at the base of the stairs did the same.

Arianna couldn't remember the last time she'd come down from the family's estate, but the way Ellie's heart raced prevented Arianna from appreciating the sights.

They marched through the city, winding between buildings before crossing a bridge over the central river. Ellie stepped onto the main path and quickened her pace.

The smell of blood hit Arianna first, thick and nauseating. Grim memories surfaced, stealing the warmth from her bones. She thought of iron chains, of empty painful stomachs, of the way freezing rain had made her body shiver so violently she was sure she wouldn't see another sunrise.

She always had.

Arianna didn't know when she'd started running, only that Rion and Ellie followed close behind.

She pushed through a small crowd, heart thundering in her chest but instead of helpless humans or half-breeds, Arianna found a dozen purebloods on their knees. Their hands were bound and Móirín warriors stood over them with weapons and magic out.

She glimpsed a split lip, a few black eyes, and splattered blood across their clothes. Arianna stared into their eyes and her lips parted.

They were … Angry. Afraid.

She ventured closer and one spit at her feet. Rion's magic hit him hard and the male's back collided with a nearby structure that groaned from the impact. He fell limp then screams filled her head. Arianna thought it was more ghosts from her memories at first, then turned toward the gate. Her stomach dropped. Not memories. This was real. Very, very real.

Arianna took off again. The thick scent of blood wasn't from the dozen Fae they'd captured. It was coming from outside the northern gate.

She ran through it and came face to face with a scene that looked exactly like the war camps she'd spent sixteen months surviving in. Tents lined the area and their occupants were wrapped in thick blankets, all huddled around fires to stave off the morning chill. Warriors and civilians alike rushed past carrying bandages while others stirred what she could only assume would be their breakfast.

Her body was shaking now.

Nightmare. This had to be another nightmare.

Arianna spun at the sound of a whip and her hair rose on her arms, but it was only the crackle from a fire. A chain rattled—no, not a chain. Her head whipped around when the wind shifted gain and the revolting tang of blood drew her into the unfolding chaos.

Arianna could see them now. The injured. Those moaning in agony.

A dozen. Two dozen. Gods, what had happened here?

Bodies were being carried on gurneys, the healers from Móirín doing their best as they bandaged wounds and administered medications for those screaming in pain. A child sobbed to her right. A female to her left.

Arianna's mind had gone silent. Fatalities. Factions. Danger. They'd warned her and yet . . .

Later. She could think later. Arianna darted to the child first and sank to her knees. The female youngling clutched her arm close and her wide frightened eyes begged to be taken from this hellish place.

Arianna's hands glowed. She didn't have time to coax the child into trusting her, not with everyone hurt. Dying. Screaming.

The child's eyes widened, she cried out, but the bone in her wrist shifted back into place and Arianna held her tight, reattaching the muscles and ligaments that had snapped off from the bones.

Someone to her right gasped and Arianna pointed to the child. "Take care of her." Then she was running to the next body. This one a male, his leg pouring blood. They had a tourniquet around the limb, bloody hands pulling it tight as healers tried to shove medicine down the male's throat.

Arianna's hands were on him then, right over the blood and she let her magic work, finding the artery to stitch it back together. Then the muscles. Then she was moving onto the next, not bothering with their questions.

She healed another child. Then a female with fractured ribs that had penetrated her lung.

Arianna absorbed the scene with every person she healed. Black soot, broken pieces of wood, and still burning bits of tent lining a small circular area. Those in the immediate vicinity had suffered the worst of the explosion while those outside it were hit with shrapnel.

Some hadn't made it at all.

The Divine, they whispered.

Arianna didn't meet their gazes. She was still scanning the area, looking for more, but when she reached down for a male, he smacked her hand away and pulled a knife from within the folds of his tunic.

Her adrenaline spiked and Arianna's magic materialized from thin air, deflecting the sharpened blade, but it slid across her cheek anyway.

A blood-chilling roar cleaved the world in two and shadows poured from every corner of the earth, rising to block out the sun.

No, not shadows. The earth itself.

Arianna's ears rang from the collective screams echoing across the area. They scrambled back, desperate to separate themselves from The Demon and his monstrous magic.

Sand whipped out and snatched the male by the throat, crushing his windpipe in an instant. Arianna turned to look at her mate and the others who'd stood, drawing weapons against him. Eyes flickered toward her, some filled with so much unfathomable hatred. She'd never met these people. She'd never—

A female roared and charged Rion, but Arianna sprang to her feet, water ripping from the air as she sprinted forward and leapt over a tendril of Rion's earth. He followed her movements, his magic aiding her charge as she snarled and blocked the female's magic in a clash of raining icy.

Arianna thought the female would stand down. That maybe they'd only attacked Rion because of his reputation. But the female's low growl sent a jolting spike of fear through Arianna's body.

And this female wasn't the only one baring her fangs. Seven stood around them, their magic taking form. Water from Móirín. Vines from Brónach. Fire from Fiadh. Sweat trickled down Arianna's face and she steeled herself, sinking back into the persona of the female she'd been months ago.

An icy current pulsed through her veins and instinct screamed for her to protect her mate. She'd tear them apart, rip them from the world before they even got close. Her magic rose as high as Rion's and spun just as furiously.

Ice cracked and raced across the ground followed by a wave of water, both coming from unknown sources. Two snarling figures joined the frenzy, placing themselves between the seven and Arianna.

Ellie stood in front of Rion, a rapier clutched in her hand as she crouched in a low stance. Talon stood before Arianna, his frost spreading along the ground and down the blade in his grasp.

Then others joined, ready to defend their queen, but they weren't all from Móirín. Warriors and civilians surrounded the seven nameless assailants from all sides, weapons and magic poised.

The world slowed.

A female glanced toward the male to her right and she gave him the slightest of nods. Arianna understood the gesture when the female's hateful gaze turned back.

They didn't intend to live. They had one goal. One mission.

Destroy the would-be queen.

The seven lunged as a unit and the world exploded in a kaleidoscope of color and pain.

A spear of ice flew from Talon's palm and hit a female with so much force it blasted her off her feet. A stranger summoned brush from the ground that ensnared a male's legs, sharp thorns digging into flesh and twisting to lock his movements in place.

Frost crawled up another's lower body, spreading like fingers across the male's body until it immobilized him entirely. Chunks of earth split into tiny particles, then wrapped around two bodies and squeezed. Their bones ground, then snapped. Two gasps. Two silent hearts.

Arianna stood before the carnage, both distraught by it and equally thankful for those who'd intervened.

The female was the only opponent left. Arianna knew she should have summoned her magic when the female charged, her battle cry echoing in her wake as she pointed her sword, intending to drive it straight through Arianna's torso.

Arianna knew she wouldn't make it. The female knew it, too, but she was still willing to die. To throw her life away for the mission.

But why? What aspect of life did they fear her changing so much that they were willing to die to protect it?

Talon's fist slammed into the side of the female's face and she slumped to the ground in an unconscious heap.

He huffed out a breath then turned to her. "Are you all right?"

Arianna only nodded, her gaze lingering on the bodies spread across the area. Her heart cracked, bleeding from a wound in her chest that wouldn't heal. Reality swept through her like an icy current.

This wasn't a nightmare and she wasn't waking up.

ARIANNA HEALED those injured from the explosion, trying to rein in the raw emotion forming in her throat. Those in charge speculated the event had been a ploy to lure her from the safety of the estate walls. It wasn't the faction's first attack and nobody thought it would be their last.

Arianna clenched her fists. This was her fault. No matter how she spun it, their deaths were on her hands. She should have left days ago, then maybe those who'd died could have returned home to their families.

Arianna hadn't bothered to wipe the blood from her face or hands as she healed body after body. Rion stood directly behind her, his sand circling in a protective embrace. Most hesitated before approaching, their eyes darting between the queen they longed to see and the creature they all feared.

Talon had forced the masses to form a line and the warriors under his command searched the people for weapons.

They'd all tried to usher her back to safety, but she'd refused to turn her back on the sick and wounded.

Many had traveled from nearby towns after hearing rumors from Brónach's traveling forces. They'd thought the warriors crazed or delusional, but those who believed had traveled to glimpse the impossibility for themselves.

Her stomach knotted.

Dusk came swiftly, but the injured were thinning. Thanks to Ellie and the healers, the ones with severe ailments had been some of the first in line. The rest simply wanted the chance to witness her power first hand. To have their faith proved true.

She wanted to keep healing them, to keep pushing, but her eyes were so heavy. Rion gently took her arm, his movements causing those around the area to step back. "We should get you inside. You need to rest."

Arianna didn't deserve rest. She'd been selfish, wanting to remain in the little cabin for the rest of their lives. For days, years, centuries. Anything to delay what she was about to face.

The royal city.

Her new home.

Her new prison.

CHAPTER ELEVEN

ARIANNA

She shouldn't have been surprised to see all the dresses, but when Ellie led her into a room with an assortment of fancy gowns, shoes, and no shortage of elaborate jewelry, her mouth gaped.

"You've been planning this for weeks," Arianna accused.

Ellie beamed, running her hands down a beautiful flowing gown that sparkled with hues of silver and blue. But there was another in the back that drew Arianna's gaze.

This dress was darkest obsidian with black glittering gems inset in the bodice. A gold floral pattern wrapped around the waist and extended down the floor length skirt.

Ellie stood at her side. "Really, that's the one you want?"

"No," Arianna said, shaking her head.

Ellie cocked a grin. "Doesn't seem that way." Arianna eyed the open back of the dress and scrunched her nose. Did she like it? Absolutely. But it was bad enough having people stare at the scars around her wrists. She didn't even want to imagine how they'd react if they saw the ones across her back.

"I'm not sure I want to wear a dress at all." Not with the way those outside the gate had attacked her. She touched her cheek, fingers trailing over the cut across her skin. Rion had been furious and fussing over it. She'd assured him a million times she was fine.

But it had been too close. Had the blade sliced just a few inches lower, it would have been her throat. She could see the pain in Rion's gaze and feel his guilt every time he looked at it. Ruadhán was a three-day journey and despite the armed escort, she needed to be vigilant.

"Well, I mean, we could dress you up as a warrior if you preferred, though I'm not sure what kind of patches to put on your uniform."

"They won't be looking for patches," Rion said from the doorway. "And you don't want to wear anything that'll become a conversation piece you can't explain." Right, because she'd be under intense scrutiny.

Arianna sighed. She'd debated asking Rion to take her to the mountains to disappear for a few years, but then she'd be forsaking a promise, no, multiple promises. Not only to herself, but to all the people that had fallen. The slaves. Zylah. She clenched her jaw.

"So we go with simple, yet elegant," Ellie said. "The only question is whether you want to wear Móirín or Ruadhán colors."

"Móirín, obviously."

Ellie smiled and reached for something in the drawers before darting to another dresser.

"If we're leaving tomorrow," Ellie said in Rion's direction, not pausing to look up. "Then you should probably visit your sister."

Rion straightened. "You've seen Saoirse?"

Ellie nodded, rummaging through another drawer. She scowled. "We've had lunch a time or two. She's staying on the outskirts on the eastern side." Her face fell. "She's a little upset that you haven't been to see her, but she's good at hiding it."

Rion's jaw clenched.

Of course she'd be upset.

A lump formed in Arianna's throat. What had he said to her? Had she tried to fight for him? Had she even known about the execution? Arianna couldn't imagine the pain she'd feel if Ellie—

"Go see her," Arianna said. Rion's face fell and she felt the sting of hurt mirror her own down the bond. This is what their lives would be like now, constantly having to leave one another to tend to various tasks and meetings. Alone. Separate.

Arianna tried to smile. "Go see your sister. I assure you, you don't want to see mine piece me together."

He glanced at Ellie and the items she held in her hand. Arianna knew the emotions that warred within him without feeling for the bond. It was instinct to constantly question their mate's safety.

"I won't be gone long," he assured her.

"Take Talon with you?" The words left her lips before she could think better of them. Rion bristled, but Arianna heard footsteps across the floor moments later. Fear coiled in her gut when Talon peered at them from behind the wall. She braced herself for another fight, though she doubted the small room could handle the impact. All the dresses, the jewelry, the things Ellie had spent her time planning out would be ruined. And her sister would be furious.

The males were so close they could touch, but neither so much as acknowledged the other's existence. Arianna swallowed, praying she wasn't making a huge mistake. "Just so the citizens don't give you trouble." Both males seemed to note the shakiness in her tone.

Her father had made her a promise, but Arianna didn't trust him to keep his word. And having Rion stroll down the streets of Levea unaccompanied was equivalent to asking the civilians to take matters into their own hands, which wouldn't end well for anyone.

Both males looked at her reluctantly, but who else could she ask? The guards didn't know Eoghan, anyone under her father's command was out of the question, and Ellie wasn't about to let Arianna dress herself. She enjoyed the task too much.

"Please."

Talon sighed and Rion nodded. Her mate closed the distance between them and placed a longing kiss on her lips that had Arianna's heart aching already. He met her gaze and gently swept his thumb across her jaw before following Talon out the door.

The room fell silent. Arianna counted their retreating steps. She listened for Rion's heartbeat, straining to hear the comforting rhythm until it faded with distance.

"Do you think they'll ever be friends?" Ellie asked, holding up a royal blue tailcoat.

Arianna eyed the fabric and the intricate swirling patterns that ran down the front and over the shoulders and sleeves.

"I don't know." She was just glad they weren't tearing one another's throats out. She prayed the incident from the other day would be their last. Arianna wasn't sure she could handle another.

"I feel like I've wronged Talon."

Ellie stopped shifting through the pants. "You found your mate."

She sighed. "A mate that was his enemy. Talon blames himself for what happened to me. I can see it written all over his face. And now . . . I think he's angry."

"Oh, he's angry all right, but not with you." Arianna gave her sister a questioning look. "I'd say he's pissed at the gods. Fate. Whatever you want to call the thing that runs the universe around us." Ellie gave her a gentle smile. "It's Talon. Just talk to him."

"I don't know what to say. Part of me feels like I should apologize, but I can't apologize for finding my mate. I'm not sad to be with Rion, I'm just upset it hurt Talon in the process."

"You were gone for almost two years." Arianna didn't miss the sadness in Ellie's tone. "People grow. We change. And we can't help who we fall in love with. Take me, for example. Kirian isn't my mate, but that doesn't mean I don't love him. If my mate showed up," she shrugged. "I suppose he'd just have to deal with me being taken."

"You wouldn't be curious?"

Ellie glared at her. "You know I'd be curious, but I love Kirian. I believe if you truly love someone, you can't fall in love with someone else." She eyed her sister, holding up two pieces of fabric. "If you'd loved Talon, truly loved him, then you wouldn't have fallen for Rion the way you did. The truth is, you and Talon didn't have the time to form that kind of bond. You were friends, you love him as your friend, and that sort of love is just as deep but different than a romantic sort." She huffed and stuffed something back in the drawers. "Besides, it might not have worked out between you and Talon even if you'd stayed. Which would have made things super awkward."

"Cause they're not awkward now."

Ellie chuckled. "You two will figure it out once we settle in at Ruadhán."

"Are you nervous?" Arianna asked, feeling the same butterflies soar through her that she'd experienced earlier.

"Hell no, I was born for this. What's to miss?"

A lot, Arianna wanted to say. The familiar sights and smells of home. A comfortable bed where one could fall asleep knowing they're safe. Familiar faces that smiled in greeting with no ulterior motive. Loved ones willing to protect their own.

"Is Kirian coming?"

A wide smile spread across Ellie's face. "He sure is. His mom is worried, but she's also excited. It's not like the royal city has its doors open to come and go as you please."

"Or pictures."

Ellie giggled. "I'm telling everyone everything there is to know about the place as soon as I get back."

Arianna laughed, knowing the secrets of Ruadhán were about to be made public.

"Okay, let's try this on," Ellie said. "And please tell me you two are staying in your room tonight instead of that dusty guest house."

"It's not dusty," Arianna argued.

"Yeah well, the tub sucks and you deserve a long, hot bath before we parade you in front of the world."

CHAPTER TWELVE

RION

The two males marched through the compound in silence with Rion trailing just behind Talon. Rion could sense the male's reluctance, though Talon didn't express the animosity Rion expected at being asked to escort him. He seemed to be taking the request quite seriously.

And as much as he loathed to be in the male's company, Arianna was right in requesting it. The eyes that had followed him when he'd walked through the city with Ellie were the same gazes that stared him down now. All with a deep-seated hatred he'd more than earned.

Rion carefully watched each sentinel they passed. Avalon had made his daughter a promise, but Rion wasn't one to rely on such things. He knew better. Words were empty. They accomplished nothing. At least, that's what he'd always believed before Arianna.

Gods, how had their paths crossed so perfectly? She was the light in the darkness. A sweet summer rain after a long drought. Perfect and resilient and full of hope. He deserved none of it, yet he drank it up greedily, like a man starved for bread. To feel her soft skin against his was a drug. To know every sweet caress came from a place of love was his addiction.

He'd craved it for so long. Feared it even longer.

Curious gazes drew his attention. Confused, but not resentful. He'd saved more than a handful during their battle with Fiadh and he'd fought beside one of their commanders rather than against him. The same male he followed now.

Pain lanced through Rion's core from the memories. Ellie's body, Arianna's desperation, and the look of relief on her face when he'd showed up at just the right time. A lump formed in his throat. He'd almost been too late. He'd almost lost her and—

A tug on the bond. Rion sucked in a sharp breath and Talon turned, regarding him oddly before he resumed walking.

Rion brushed the memories aside for another day. Right now needed to keep his feelings in check for Arianna's sake, especially if he didn't want her running from the estate to find him. Not that he'd mind.

Rion tried sending feelings of reassurance down the bond, but he couldn't be sure if they made it. The entire concept wasn't just new, it was entirely impossible. He was The Demon. He was an affront to nature. And the gods had still somehow seen fit to bless him in the most beautiful of ways. He'd gladly walk the path of heartache again if it meant winding up in Arianna's arms.

Rion tried to focus on the male walking before him. His posture was steady, his footsteps smooth and sure. Talon wasn't a timid male, but nor was he arrogant. He understood his strengths and weaknesses and Rion knew the male would lay down his life for Arianna. It was one of the many reasons Rion found himself glad to have Talon accompanying them to Ruadhán.

Rion briefly wondered what Talon thought of him now. Did the male still view him as nothing more than The Demon? An enemy? Had earning Arianna's affections caused more hatred or less?

Another light tug on the bond and he paused, turning to stare toward the estate looming in the distance.

Talon turned with him, concern twisting his features. "Everything all right?"

Rion brought one hand to his chest. "The bond is . . . strange." Like she lived in a fragment of his soul.

Talon resumed walking. "You can feel emotions down the bond, right?" His voice was clipped. Uncomfortable, but at least he was attempting conversation. Rion supposed he could do the same.

"Somewhat. I think they become stronger as the bond solidifies." It was strong, like a braided rope holding them together. But rope could be severed and he'd do nothing to risk such a thing.

"Don't do anything that might upset her." Talon said. "If she thinks there's something wrong, she'll come running." He already knew that, but Rion found himself wondering about the things he didn't know. Arianna had lived an intricate life before she'd been stolen away. There was so much to learn about her and Rion had a myriad of questions.

They continued through the city quickly and crossed the bridge at Levea's eastern gate. The two veered right, then a rather large house entered their view. It was nestled between several trees, giving the illusion of solitude despite being so close to the main city.

A wraparound porch greeted them first, complete with several swings hanging from the roof and tables decorated with floral arrangements. Gardens lined the edges, but a dirt path was the only thing leading up to the stairs.

A stream flowed nearby and several fountains with trickling water stood every few feet. Everything in Móirín had water around it in one form or another.

His sister burst from the swinging door before they even made it near the porch. She stood at the edge of the steps, her feet bare, dressed in a simple pair of loose blue pants and matching shirt. Her shoulder-length blonde hair hung loose around her shoulders.

Her appearance surprised him. He'd expected to find her armed in the presence of their enemy, but then, Móirín had only been an enemy for a decade. She'd had many friends here before the war.

Guilt flew through him. A war he'd caused.

Her gaze darted between the two, then she placed her hands on her hips. "It's about time, what took you so long?"

Rion gave her a grimaced smile. "I've been a bit preoccupied."

Saoirse waved a hand in disgust. "Spare me the details. There's a lot I'd like to know about my little brother, but what he does behind closed doors isn't one of them."

Rion closed the distance and Saoirse wrinkled her nose at Talon. "Are you required to have an escort?"

"Arianna requested it. She didn't want me running into trouble."

Saoirse's gaze softened. She knew what kind of life he'd lived in Nàdiar.

In an air of politeness that didn't quite reach her eyes, Saoirse gestured to Talon. "Do you want to come in?"

Talon shook his head and his sister seemed to sag with relief. "I'll occupy myself elsewhere while you talk. I'd head back, but if I go without him," Talon inclined his head. "I'm afraid Arianna would venture outside the city gates on her own."

"All right then. Well, if you need anything, you know the staff better than I do. Help yourself."

Talon nodded, then Saoirse opened the door and Rion ventured inside.

His sister wasted no time and headed straight for the kitchen, putting on a kettle to boil water. She stared at it, her expression changing as her mind wandered. He'd seen that look a hundred times.

Rion turned from her to study the cabin. It seemed comfortable, complete with a three cushioned gray sofa on one side, beige blankets draped over the back and dark end tables at its sides. A bowl of chocolates even sat on one, and judging from the empty wrappers, Saoirse was enjoying them.

A bookshelf stood against the opposite wall and Rion wandered toward it, running his fingers over the titles.

"You seem calmer now." Saoirse held a glass in her hand, but Rion knew it wasn't tea. She leaned against the counter, studying him with a careful eye.

He let his hand fall from the books. "I guess I am."

Saoirse tapped her fingers on the counter. "Have you spoken with Avalon?"

"Arianna didn't feel it was a good idea."

"I see." Silence.

"I should have visited sooner."

"You really should have." Her voice cracked, but she turned away before Rion could see whatever emotion covered her face. His heart filled with aching guilt. The last time he'd seen her, he'd told Saoirse he'd had enough. That he couldn't handle this life without Arianna.

"I—" He stopped himself, searching for the right words. He'd spent a month with his sister. They'd rekindled their relationship, but the years that'd separated them felt like a wide chasm capable of swallowing that newfound relationship whole.

Saoirse shook her head. "There's no need to explain it to me. I understand how the mating bond works. You probably couldn't have left even if you'd wanted to."

He smirked at that. "I still didn't want to, but something came up."

"I heard about the attack at the gate. Has she decided to go to Ruadhán?"

He nodded. "She doesn't want anyone else to get hurt."

"Good luck preventing that," Saoirse murmured. "What about you, where are you going?"

"With her."

She raised a brow. "And they're okay with that?"

"No."

It was Saoirse's turn to smirk. "Of course, how silly of me to think my little brother would start caring about the rules now."

"Ellie has a plan."

Saoirse scoffed. "A plan from a sixteen-year-old. That should go over well."

"You shouldn't underestimate her."

"I don't. I just worry she's in over her head." Saoirse cared, he realized. About Arianna's little sister. Ellie had mentioned them having lunch together. Initially, he'd wondered if those meetings had annoyed Saoirse, but now he realized it was quite the opposite.

He changed the subject. "Are you heading back to Nàdiar?"

The kettle whistled and Saoirse poured them each a cup, placing a bag of tea inside. "For now." She joined him on the sofa and set the cups down to steep. "I'll be back when Ruadhán calls for us to pledge our allegiance."

"Arianna wants to meet you."

"Everyone speaks highly of her. Most were surprised to hear she'd survived." She studied him. "The warriors didn't think her strong enough."

His fists clenched. "Those who opposed her thought that, too." She was a fierce warrior too many had underestimated.

Saoirse regarded him for a moment then removed the tea bags and handed him his cup. Rion took it and watched Saoirse curl up with her own, drawing her legs up on the sofa.

"I poured them from the same kettle," she tried.

Rion sighed. "I know." He eyed the liquid. He hadn't forgotten his last bout with poison. He'd sworn he'd been condemned to hell. Perhaps he would be someday, but for now he belonged to Arianna.

"I want you to promise me something." Rion met her gaze. "Don't go giving up again just because you two have a disagreement. Fights are expected between couples. Mates are no exception."

"Dying would mean hurting her. I won't do that." Not now. Not when the bond tied them together and she'd suffer every agonizing second of it being torn away.

Saoirse gave him a sad smile. "When are you going to start valuing yourself?"

Himself? Probably never.

CHAPTER THIRTEEN

ARIANNA

arkness cascaded over Arianna as she walked the dirt path that led to the base of Elview Falls. Moonlight trickled between the bare branches overhead and Rion clutched her hand tightly in his.

She breathed in, relishing the cool air and the memories it conjured. Night was a time for whispered secrets and hidden prayers.

When she was a young teen, it had allowed her to wallow in her failures until Talon had come to offer reassurance and quell her fears.

It was her turn to quell his. Maybe. If fear was something he felt. Perhaps anger was a better description, but that anger stemmed from something.

Arianna swallowed hard. It had started with her. She'd caused that anger—or at least her decisions had—but she couldn't regret those decisions. She wouldn't regret loving Rion.

Arianna tightened her hand around her mate's. She'd voiced her plans earlier that evening knowing exactly how much he'd despise them.

Rion had ground his teeth and turned away to stare at the fire before reluctantly nodding. Now he walked with her, following Talon's scent down the path until they were staring at the large waterfalls in the distance. Talon sat alone and Arianna's heart pulled at the sight.

She squeezed Rion's hand once. "I won't be long."

He kissed her brow. "I'll be nearby."

Arianna nodded again, forever grateful for his understanding even if she knew it killed him. But they were getting ready to head to the royal city, to Ruadhán, and this was a conversation she needed to have before they left.

Arianna walked across the grass on silent feet. At one time in her life, she might have jumped at every sound and crack in the night, but she'd experienced a different sort of danger while in captivity. A darkness that made the natural night beautiful by comparison.

Talon turned at her approach but didn't smile. He stood and placed a glass down on the stone before glancing behind her form. His eyes scanned the tree line.

"He's not coming," she said simply.

His brow furrowed in confusion then he took her in, eyes traveling over her casual top and pants. She didn't know what he searched for exactly. "What are you doing out here?"

She moved past him and Talon followed her with a heavy gaze. He grimaced when she picked up a bottle and examined the amber liquid inside.

Arianna raised a brow at him. "You drink now?"

Talon didn't snatch the bottle away. He didn't even reach for it. He just sat back down on the large flat boulder and stared out across the water. "Not really."

Silence stretched between them, then she sat at his side and placed the bottle within his reach.

He'd seemed so relaxed from a distance, but now her friend carried a new sort of tension in his shoulders. His breathing was strained and his heart beat faster than it should.

"I wanted to thank you," Arianna said, staring at her hands. "For coming with me to see my father and for escorting Rion through the city." Talon stiffened and more memories of all the things he'd done for her drifted through her mind.

Him standing with her as they fought for Levea. Him showing up just in time to save her mate. The fact that he was still searching for her mother's murderer even after all these years.

She shook her head. "You've done so much for me." And he'd asked for nothing in return.

"You're welcome." Silence. Arianna swallowed the lump forming in her throat. This could be goodbye. If they couldn't reconcile, if Talon didn't want to stand by her anymore because of Rion. She swallowed again. She wouldn't force him.

"Are you coming to Ruadhán with us?"

"My High Lord has commanded me to."

A stone settled in her stomach. Commanded. She studied the rock they sat on and lowered her voice. "And if I commanded you otherwise?"

She saw his head turn but didn't possess the courage to meet his gaze. "Is that what you want?" Pain lanced his voice so deep it splintered her heart.

"No," she said too quickly. She'd wanted to appear calm about it so he wouldn't feel any sort of guilt, but her voice betrayed her. Gods, she hated this. "I want you with me, but if you don't want to come—"

"You think I'd just let you walk into unknown territory without protection?"

"I'll have Father's elite with me. I have Ellie and Rion." Talon clenched his jaw. "I want you with us, I just don't want you to feel obligated."

Silence stretched between them again. The water fell, its relentless weight crashing into the pool at its base. The moon cast its light upon the land, bathing everything with an ethereal glow. And Arianna's heart ached at the sight of it all.

Because this used to be the easy part. Beneath the stars she'd found solstice and sanctuary, stealing moments with friends and family. It was the one place they could escape the heavy expectations put on them by those of higher rank.

But now. She swallowed the lump in her throat. She wanted to run, but there was nowhere left to turn. No other refuge to which she could retreat.

"I think about that night all the time." He reached for the bottle and the glass he'd deposited earlier. Arianna inclined her head to listen. "I've run it through my head a thousand times over. All the things I could have done differently, that I *should* have done differently." He didn't look at her. "If I'd simply gone with you …" He shook his head.

Arianna opened her mouth and closed it again. "None of it was your fault. I don't blame you for anything that happened to me."

Talon tightened his grip on the glass and for a moment Arianna thought it might shatter. Then he poured from the bottle and knocked back the liquid. His face pinched together.

"Does it still taste as bad as I remember?"

"Worse," he said. "Though I think you stole a cheap bottle when we were kids."

She was fifteen and feeling rebellious. She'd hated the foul liquid on her tongue and Talon had visibly shuddered from a single drink. She'd felt so guilty afterward that she'd returned the bottle and no one had ever found out.

"Do the stars still keep our secrets?" he asked, his voice so low she barely heard it.

Arianna's chest tightened. Talon remembered this moment and this place. How they'd shared their dreams beneath the dimly lit sky and how, sometimes, they'd stayed until dawn, hoping to escape the responsibilities to come. Talon probably knew her better than anyone else in the world.

"Yes, always," she whispered. She tried to keep from fidgeting and failed.

Talon laid back and draped an arm over his eyes. She heard his heart pounding and he inhaled deeply before saying, "I'm in love with a queen I can't have."

Arianna froze, her breath hitched, and the world around her shifted to ice. One wrong move and it would shatter into a million pieces.

"I've loved her since we were children. I don't even remember when it started but I knew, at one point, that I wanted to spend the rest of my life with her." He didn't move and she wasn't sure she was breathing. Her heart ached, breaking for things she couldn't fix or control.

"But I was a coward. I was too afraid of ruining our friendship and decided to bottle my feelings up instead of sharing them." Silence stretched in the darkness and Arianna's heart wouldn't stop racing. She didn't know how to respond. What could she say that wouldn't hurt him further?

Arianna opened her mouth to explain, but Talon beat her to it. "Don't," he said simply, keeping his arm over his face. "It's for the stars."

Right. When they were younger, they'd whispered their secrets to the stars. Wishes and dreams that could never be. Some were impossible, others insignificant, but this—this was so much more.

"Are you sure you want it to stay there?"

His racing heart was the only indication Talon hadn't fallen asleep.

"Yes," he whispered, "though I'll probably regret telling even them in the morning."

"But right now?"

He sat up slowly and met her gaze. So many emotions swam across his face. "Now I need that queen to give me time. I'm with her, through everything." He offered her a half-hearted smile. "But I—"

He cut himself short, unable to finish his sentence, but Arianna didn't need him to. She understood, and time was something she could give.

"All right."

He chuckled. "I wish Ellie complied that easily."

Arianna gave a bitter laugh, then Talon pressed the glass into her hand. She raised a brow at him, eying the half empty bottle. "You've had a lot, haven't you?"

"I'm not going to answer that." He poured her a small bit and she sniffed it before taking a sip, only to cough from the burning in her throat.

Arianna's body shuddered and she pushed the glass back to him. "That is foul."

Talon chuckled, the sound fuller than she'd heard in weeks. "It tastes better the more you drink."

"I'll take your word for it." She eyed the bottle again. "You realize you're going to have a monster of a headache tomorrow."

Talon raised the bottle. "If it's the price I must pay, then so be it." Comfortable silence enveloped them only a moment before he said, "Obligated, really? You know me better than that."

"You've been so distant, I didn't know what else to think."

"I've been distant because you have a moody partner who tried to rip my head off."

"He's not—" she stopped herself when she saw him smiling. This was Talon. This was her friend and he was coming with her. He'd stand at her side, and they'd face whatever the royal city had to throw at them together.

CHAPTER FOURTEEN

ARIANNA

Arianna smoothed the fabric of her royal blue tailcoat, running her fingers over the metal buttons that lined the front. She absent-mindedly traced the swirling patterns of silver trailing over the bodice and down the sleeves. The dark pants Ellie had chosen fit snugly against her skin. Tight, yet comfortable. She loosed a shaky breath, silently thankful the coat provided enough room to hide several knives at her waist. They were fashionable, of course, per Ellie's request, with smooth gems of various colors lining the handles.

Black boots with shining silver buckles rose halfway up her calves and Myrna had gifted her a long necklace with a pendant to represent the waterfalls of Móirín. A token of home while she was away.

Ellie had pulled her hair back in a braid decorated with fresh flowers but left a few tendrils loose to frame her face. She looked just as Ellie had promised. Simple, yet elegant.

Arianna carefully scratched the corner of her eye, hoping to avoid smearing the kohl her sister had lined them with an hour ago.

She fidgeted with the gloves, lacing then unlacing her fingers. Sweat rolled down the back of her neck. Her foot tapped. A clock ticked, her throat went dry, then Arianna tore the gloves off and threw them to the ground. They'd only hinder her if she needed to defend herself anyway.

The room swayed and she swallowed hard, her breath ragged. She was leaving home. Again. In just a few moments she was expected to parade before the citizens of Levea as a happy queen who was ready to sacrifice her freedom for the continent.

Only she wasn't. Arianna wasn't the ruler they needed. She wasn't some great war hero full of brave tales that bards could spin into legends. She was just an eighteen-year-old female who wanted to read her books, sip hot cocoa, and curl up in a quiet part of the world with the male she loved.

Arianna tried and failed to draw in a breath. She pulled at the collar of her coat and the world spun in a sudden rush of colors.

Pure white gloves to hide the calluses and scars. Neatly pressed clothes to display her unearned status. Perfectly clean blades that concealed the secrets of her stained hands.

Her body shook and suddenly the scent of rotting flesh and unwashed bodies consumed her, throwing her back into irons and torn ragged clothes. She sloshed through mud instead of pacing clean plush rugs and tasted moldy cheese in place of the chocolates she'd consumed earlier.

Arianna's throat tightened. Bodies lined the floor and their blood spilled down the walls. Were the souls she'd claimed chanting her name or was that the wind whispering a harsh reminder?

She gripped the sides of her head, willing the images to disappear, but they kept spinning in relentless torrents. Her magic pulsed, the ancient thing calling and cooling her skin.

A hand touched her shoulder and she whirled, that magic spreading at her feet. Her heart pounded in her ears but strong arms pulled her close, cradling her against a solid frame.

She breathed, the jagged thing in her chest loosening a fraction. They weren't at war. But weren't they? Isn't that why she was here? Why she was traveling to Ruadhán? Because the world was at war with itself and the nations divided by hate and prejudice?

"You're safe," Rion said, his voice almost a whisper. "I'm here." She buried her face in his chest, inhaling his earthen scent. She clutched the fabric of his new tunic, wrinkling the material. Her breathing returned to normal. The sounds and memories faded and Arianna finally pulled away, taking a shaky breath.

"If this is too much, you can tell Ruadhán to wait. They're here to serve you, not the other way around."

Arianna shook her head. "I have to go." Especially after what had happened at the city gate.

A knock, then Talon entered, his nostrils flaring as he scented her fear floating in the air. "You okay?" There was genuine concern in his voice.

"Yeah. I think so." Talon's gaze drifted to the thin layer of frost covering the rug at her feet and Arianna grimaced. "How soon does the shift happen?"

"Depends," Talon said. "Could be today, could be in another year, but that," he nodded to the frost. "Is only going to get worse."

Rion glared at him. "She has enough to worry about."

"She just needs to work it off. Preferably in the sparing ring. Her magic is craving an outlet and she isn't giving it one."

"I would be happy to volunteer as first in the ring," her sister said, popping her head around Talon's shoulder. She carried a tray of refreshments, dressed in a pair of trousers and decorated jacket herself. "Drink this." Arianna took the steaming mug and almost moaned at the sweet taste of warm chocolate. "I brought you one, too," she said to Rion, "but if you don't want to drink it, don't worry, she will."

"Is everything ready?" Talon asked.

Ellie waved him off. "Yes, yes, Rion and I have it under control." She shrugged. "And if the worst happens, we'll just fight our way in, then Arianna can come to our rescue." Talon rolled his eyes. Ellie winked then turned to Rion. "Our only hiccup could be you losing control. If your magic sneaks out, they'll scent you before we get inside."

Arianna rubbed her temples. "Remind me again why he's not just walking in with me?"

"Because the council will want to argue and it'll be months before they agree on anything." She picked Arianna's gloves off the floor and handed them to her sister. "Finish your chocolate and let's get this over with. I hate processions."

Arianna chuckled, downed her mug, and took the gloves "Okay. Let's go."

COOL SPRING air cleared the tension from her shoulders as Rion led her toward the throng of people. Her father had tried to request Talon escort her down the walkway, but she'd refused. She wouldn't let Rion be cast aside. If they wanted to accept her, then they'd have to accept him as well.

She gaped at the scene before them. Her father had spared no expense. Drum beats echoed through her chest and warriors led a procession of horses, their freshly brushed coats shining in the morning light. Many pulled intricately decorated wagons filled with trinkets to serve as an offering for the royal council. More than one warrior carried Levea's banner, the image reflecting the necklace Myrna had gifted her.

Arianna held Rion's arm, but she didn't feel the need to cling to him as she'd thought she might. And as soon as the masses spotted her and Rion, they erupted into applause so loud Arianna had to fight the urge to cover her ears. A blush crept to her cheeks as they chanted her name, some bouncing in excitement and many falling to one knee as they passed.

Arianna kept her chin high, waving back and smiling. Really smiling at the citizens she'd known all her life.

All the bakers. The shopkeepers. Those who'd stood guard over her family without complaint. The librarians. The cooks. Kirian's mom. Myrna.

Arianna wished the human female was joining them, but such a journey was too difficult for someone Myrna's age. And Arianna would never ask the female to leave her grandchildren behind. Not when every year was so precious to a human's short life. So Arianna waved, tears pricking the corners of her eyes, and bid the female farewell.

Home. This was her home. No matter where she ended up or where life took her, Levea would always be her place of refuge. A safe haven if life got too rough.

The walk lasted forever and not long enough. She turned to find her mate smiling down at her, proud in a way she was certain only mates could be.

She approached the open door of a large carriage. One of seven. Once she stepped inside, she'd be headed to a new world. A new home. But the people who mattered were with her. Her friends. Her family. They could face anything as long as they were together.

"Ready?" Rion asked.

She bit the inside of her cheek, loosed an excited breath, then took his outstretched hand.

As long as she had them, she could conquer the world.

CHAPTER FIFTEEN

RAEVINA

Sweat rolled down her the sides of her face, dripping to the stone floor beside her brown leather boots. Raevina slowed her breathing, the racing of her pulse, then spun into another series of pivots and thrusts.

She'd woken early, unable to sleep from her newfound excitement. Plans were in motion. In less than a year, she could be crowned High Lady of Fiadh with her father left as nothing more than a cold corpse in the ground. If she buried him at all. The crows had to eat, too.

Raevina rolled her shoulders then joined her second, Cahira, in hand-to-hand combat. The females were an almost perfect match as they clashed with one another in a test of strength and will. But Raevina had always been a touch faster, able to feign just enough to get around Cahira's defenses.

Cahira cursed and fell on her backside. Raevina smiled in triumph but only for a moment before extending her hand. She wasn't her father. She wouldn't degrade those she trusted with her life. And she trusted Cahira with so much more.

The two clasped arms, a promise between sisters. Not born of blood but forged with steel. Their day to rule was coming. All they needed was a little patience. Raevina would fulfill her father's wishes and kill the false Divine, then return and sit at his table. She'd learn his plans and earn the favor of his warriors.

Then she'd put a knife in his throat. Or his back. He'd never been one for honorable fighting methods so she wasn't about to let pride get in her way of destroying him.

Raevina shook her braids from her shoulders and took a long drink from her water canteen. Ridding Fiadh of her father was only the beginning. Once she battled his secrets and weeded out the disloyal, Raevina needed to deal with the monsters that had bred out of control. If she—

A piercing scream echoed from the cavern's top floor and Raevina's head shot toward the sound far above. Those surrounding her froze. Waiting.

The scream echoed again, bouncing off the rock walls and Raevina's shifted with a quick flash of light. Her body shrank and she sprouted blue-gray wings that catapulted her through the air. The wind glided down her spotted brown chest and she tilted her tail, weaving between others already airborne.

Raevina pumped her wings hard and let a shrill cry fill the massive cavern telling whoever needed to know that she was on her way.

At the top, she spotted five adults and two younglings. Raevina shifted back to her Fae form and landed before them, searching their grave faces for clues.

"What's going on?"

Raevina recognized the youngling that stepped forward. Ty. A male who had just celebrated his ninth birthday. Her gaze ran over the adults' faces, two civilians, three warriors. "T-The Chimera." Her blood chilled. "They took Axel." His voice broke and tears streamed down his young face.

Raevina marched toward the small crack in the wall that led outside. The younglings weren't supposed to play up here. They knew that. They'd been warned countless times that the Chimera were growing bolder. There might have been a time when the creatures wouldn't have dared to cross a Fae's path, but those days were long gone.

Apprehension pricked her scalp as Raevina inched her way through the crevice and found a large lion-like body digging at something on the other side of the platform. The air whipped at its thick mane and taloned claws gripped the rocky surface to maintain its balance. Icy wind howled between the mountain peaks and she shivered against it.

The creature growled in frustration. Its bat-like wings flared and the barbed tail swished back and forth with impatience.

Another landed at its side and the creature snapped its massive jaws, a warning to its companion that whatever it hunted belonged to it and it alone.

Axel's scream rang through the air and Raevina tightened the hold on her weapon. The Chimera pulled Axel from his hiding place and she grimaced at the sight of a long claw embedded in the boy's leg. He screamed again, begging for someone to save him, knowing it was forbidden for the citizens of Fiadh to interact with the creatures.

Screw that.

Raevina launched from her hiding place in the wall and Cahira appeared behind her a second later. She threw Raevina her longsword, a better weapon than the small dagger she'd palmed moments ago.

Fire erupted down her arms and shadows gathered from beneath her skin, speeding across the ground toward the beasts. The one holding Axel roared, baring its fangs. The other beat its massive wings and charged, raising a paw to swipe at the nuisances daring to interrupt their meal.

Raevina detested these monstrosities. They'd killed too many warriors of late and now they had a youngling. Enough was enough.

She ducked around its claws and hit the ground, skidding beneath the beast's underbelly before thrusting her sword straight up through the creature's gut. It howled in pain and Ravina rolled to her right, scarcely avoiding its writhing body as it bucked and clawed at the pain lancing through its core.

The other Chimera left Axel forgotten on the bloody stone. It bared its teeth and that barbed tail curled up over its head, flicking in agitation as it reassessed the threat.

One glance from Raevina told Cahira to get the youngling to safety.

Raevina stood before the massive creatures. The two predators pinning one another in place. Their shadow loomed over her, those wings fanning wide in an aggressive display that might have frightened others.

But Raevina had buried her fear long ago.

She shifted into her falcon form and shot forward. The Chimera jolted, stepping back to separate itself from the now tiny predator barreling toward him. Raevina shifted again, yanked a knife from her belt, and plunged it into the beast's shoulder. She shifted again, veering around the claw aiming for her and the beast roared in frustration as she appeared at its other side and plunged another blade into its side.

Cahira pulled Axel through the crevice in the mountain and peered back to study Raevina, gauging whether she'd need her second's assistance.

The Chimera's tail whipped out a venomous barb and aimed for her torso, but Raevina shifted again and spun, her speed carrying her to the creature's front where she shifted back and planted another blade in the beast's throat.

It slammed its massive head into her and Raevina's back collided with hard rock. Breath left her. A wet strangled sound told her the Chimera wasn't long for this world, but that didn't stop the creature from lashing out one final time as if determined to take her with it. She rolled, but the edge of its venomous barb caught her abdomen, tearing through her leather and grazing her skin before the beast collapsed.

Its wings beat frantically as if it might fly one last time, then the Chimera fell still, its body lying mere feet from its companion.

She gulped down air, adrenaline pumping through her veins. Cahira grabbed her arm and pulled Raevina to a seated position. Her second moved the bits of shredded armor to observe the wound and hissed.

"You're—"

Raevina clamped a hand over Cahira's mouth and shook her head. Cahira glanced back at the faces poking through the fissure then unfastened her cloak and draped it over Raevina's shoulders. Raevina held it tight to hide the wound and let Cahira assist her to her feet.

Raevina tried not to limp but couldn't stop the wince that escaped as they scurried back through the crevice before any other Chimeras arrived to avenge their fallen comrades. She had yet to determine their level of intelligence. Maybe they wouldn't even notice two of their kind gone.

Someone had already taken Axel to the infirmary. The warriors were staring, likely wondering if Raevina would receive punishment for disobeying her father's orders.

She wouldn't accept it and the citizens shouldn't either. Raevina straightened and addressed the three warriors. "Seal it off." She didn't care what her father said anymore. They had to take action. They couldn't afford to lose a single youngling. She wasn't surprised when they nodded in agreement. She was of royal blood after all. Disobeying her orders meant disobeying the crown.

Cahira led her down a flight of stairs and Raevina kept outward appearances up until they were in Cahira's room.

They closed the door and Raevina let the cloak fall to the floor. She hissed when Cahira helped remove her leathers and shirt, leaving Raevina in nothing but the wrap around her breasts.

Raevina carefully sat on the bed and Cahira retrieved a bowl of water and a towel. She seated herself beside Raevina to clean the wound and clicked her tongue. "You shouldn't travel with this."

Raevina cursed at the contact. The venom felt like fire as it pulsed within the wound. "I don't have a choice."

"Moving will slow the healing process." Cahira pulled a long clean cloth from a drawer and began wrapping the area.

Raevina knew that. It would be both slow and agonizing. None of their antidotes seemed to counteract the poison. The most they managed to do was slow the spread until it faded or the Fae died.

Gods, it couldn't have happened at a more inopportune time. "Can we cover the scent of it?" She didn't need those loyal to her father knowing she was injured. That'd only make her a target.

Cahira studied the gash, prodding at the already reddened skin around the area. "I can get some herbs that will help, but if anyone gets too close . . ."

"We'll make sure they don't." Raevina was taking her own warriors to Ruadhán, too. A unit she trusted with her life. They'd sooner die than betray her. The rest . . . well, they'd stop at nothing to impress her father, and killing the High Lord's daughter was a quick way to display strength. He disgusted her.

Sarcasm flooded her tone. "Maybe if the female really is The Divine, she can just heal me."

Cahira paused. "You shouldn't doubt so much."

Raevina lifted a brow. "I didn't realize you were a believer."

"I think it's been a long time since we had any hope."

"For good reason." Hope was dangerous. A crutch for those unable to carve their own path.

"Two countries putting their trust in something is a lot to discard as a mere rumor. Have a little faith."

"I have faith in myself, my companions, and the things I can see with my own eyes."

"And if she turns out to be legitimate?"

Raevina furrowed her brow but didn't answer. The Divine. Fiadh's sole purpose had been to protect the previous one and they'd failed. Residing in the mountains was often thought to be their punishment.

"Then maybe I'll get the chance to restore my family's honor."

But that chance was little more than a shimmering dream and Raevina had stopped believing in dreams a long, long time ago.

Chapter Sixteen

Saoirse

aoirse collapsed onto the plush sofa and plopped her boots on the wooden table, knocking back another glass of amber liquid. She winced and smacked her lips, feeling the burn glide down her throat.

Zylah. The name tasted like warm honey on her tongue and Saoirse cursed herself for ever owning a slave a day in her life. She should have taken a stand with Rion; maybe the two of them could have changed things for those in Brónach. Then maybe, just maybe, that female would have given her a chance.

She shook her head, sat forward, and poured another glass. Saoirse studied the liquid and her reflection in it. How many times had she turned away from a half-breed's plight, deeming them nothing better than the rug she walked upon? How many times had she seen the foul way they were treated and ignored it despite how she treated her own?

She could have put rules in place, implemented policies for the longevity of their care.

And she'd done absolutely nothing.

Her mind summoned the memory of Zylah's disgusted face. The way the female had stared at her reminded Saoirse of the way everyone glared at her younger brother. A hatred so deep it would take an absolute miracle to cure.

Even Arianna was rumored to have scars around her wrists, which meant their world was about to change. Slavery would become a thing of the past. History books would be written by souls like Zylah and they'd pen the Fae of old as cruel, wicked beings.

And maybe they deserved to be labeled as such.

She drank the glass and let her head fall back on the pillows.

Could she redeem herself in the eyes of that female? A rueful smile crossed her face and Saoirse closed her eyes, succumbing to the buzzing in her head.

Probably not, but perhaps it was worth it to try. For the female who reminded her of sunrises and the fresh windswept plains of the southlands, she would try.

CHAPTER SEVENTEEN

ARIANNA

She never wanted to see the inside of a carriage again. Her legs and backside were cramped, every bump jostled her nauseated stomach, and if she had one more guard tell her the inside of a tiny box was safer than walking alongside it, she thought she might scream.

Three long days had passed and she'd counted the swirling lines on the carriage's lacquered interior at least a hundred times. She knew the back left wheel was looser than the others, its constant squeak driving her to the brink of insanity. Then there were the hooded priests and priestesses who whispered words of reverence whenever she passed. Arianna didn't understand why those in Ruadhán had sent them along. Maybe to pray to the gods for their safe passage. Maybe to appease her with some sort of religious acknowledgement.

Arianna shivered. Every one of them made her skin crawl. And she wasn't the only one trying to avoid them. Móirín's warriors barely sat beside them at mealtimes and made a point of staying far away during their morning and evening prayers.

Maybe it was the way they covered their hair and faces, save for their eyes, that brought her unease. Or the fact that they so rarely left the temples.

She shook her head. But today Arianna didn't care who she encountered when she opened the small side door and jumped to the ground. She hadn't bothered commanding them to slow down. It would just waste more time and she wanted this journey over.

Móirín and Ruadhán guards swarmed toward her, concern knitting their brows but she waved them off with a silent gesture.

"My Lady," one said, his head bowed.

But she interrupted him. "I just need to stretch my legs." He nodded and gave a signal to those from Ruadhán. The guards switched their formation and her face heated from the attention.

Talon joined her, a hand resting lightly on the pommel of his sword. "I don't think I've ever seen a group of seasoned warriors so jumpy. One would think them inexperienced."

Two shot Talon a glare and she elbowed him in the ribs. "Say it a little louder why don't you?"

He smirked and Arianna had the distinct impression Talon was enjoying their discomfort. At least one of them was having fun.

Arianna eyed the carriage. Her sister sat within, head back and eyes closed. To an onlooker, she simply appeared road worn and weary, but Arianna knew the truth.

Arianna's gaze roamed across the faces of her entourage. Her mate was somewhere among them, concealed with Ellie's magic.

Just yesterday, Rion had been at her side. He'd stood watch while she bathed in the nearby river, much to her guard's dismay. She wouldn't enter Ruadhán smelling of old sweat and gods only knew what else.

She'd undressed beneath the protection of Rion's magic and her body had ignited with the way his heated gaze scorched her skin.

It had been three days since she'd had him in her arms. Three days since his hands caressed her skin and his lips pulled moans of ecstasy from her throat.

Three days and she was ready to combust.

But that was yesterday. Today she was ready to explode for entirely different reasons.

She'd watched Ellie lead Rion away early that morning. The bond had pulled tight, their worry mirroring one another's. The plan was in motion and she had to remind herself that he'd be back at her side within a matter of hours. So long as everything went smoothly.

Arianna chewed her bottom lip. She didn't miss the way the warriors had relaxed with Rion's absence. Though they remained vigilant, their hands no longer hovered above their weapons. Their moods had lightened and she even caught a few laughing.

Sadness washed through her. She wondered how long it would take others to grow accustomed to her mate. Would they ever laugh with him? Smile instead of grimace in his presence?

After an hour of walking and at least three guards begging, Arianna finally relented and crawled back inside the carriage. Talon remained outside and Ellie helped her change back into the blue tailcoat. She spent the rest of the trip seated on the floor with Ellie working to tame her hair with pins from her bag and wildflowers an attendant had picked that morning.

"Where is he?" she asked her sister.

Arianna could feel Ellie's smug smile even if she couldn't see it. "He's here, don't worry."

Arianna tried not to pout. "I really don't see the harm in telling me."

Ellie stood and pulled Arianna up to sit across from her, then pinned stray strands away from her face. "Because if I do, you'll look at him every five seconds and blow our cover."

She wanted to argue, but Ellie wasn't wrong. She would look at him. Then she'd look at those beside him and wonder if they were too close. She'd want to know whether he was okay and—Arianna bit the inside of her cheek and breathed.

"There you go," her sister said. "Relax. I think we're almost there."

Her heart threatened to beat from her chest, but she could do this. She was ready. Rion was close by, he just couldn't use his magic right now. Ellie and Talon were with her, too.

But her stomach churned with nervous tension.

Ellie finally finished with her hair and Arianna settled back as the carriage continued down a well-worn dirt path. She shifted the soft curtain to glance out the window and her heart jolted at the sight of the village ahead.

Smoke curled from stone chimneys, rising up to blend with the late afternoon sky. Figures chased chickens and other livestock away from their intended destination and silhouettes were already gathering at the edge to greet them.

Her palms turned sweaty. She'd opted to leave the gloves this time and had stuffed them in Ellie's bag. Arianna counted the seconds. The minutes. The seemingly infinite lifetime before the carriage finally slowed to a halt. A fury of movement outside told her the warriors were assembling.

Ellie squeezed her hand in reassurance. "You'll do fine. Just remember to maintain eye contact and pretend you're in charge."

Right, that wasn't hard at all. Why couldn't Ellie have been born The Divine? Her little sister was already eating this up and they weren't even at the gates.

Eye contact. Smile. Pretend. It wouldn't take long. She'd blink, then Rion would be at her side and they'd be hidden in a room together. The tension would fall from her shoulders and she could pretend they were back in the little cabin safely nestled in the woods.

A light tap on the door. Talon. Ellie opened it and bright sunlight flooded in, reflecting off Ellie's silver buttons. Her sister gave her a final reassuring look before taking Talon's hand and stepping outside.

Arianna was alone now and could already feel the excited energy buzzing beyond the door. A hushed silence fell over the crowd that told her Ellie had taken her place. They were waiting.

Smile. Make eye contact. Look for Rion.

No. Don't look for Rion. He was nearby, the bond told her as much. She tugged on it slightly and felt a gentle caress on the other end.

It's all right, he seemed to say. *I'm here, you're safe.*

Arianna inhaled and closed her eyes. She imagined her mother in this moment and how she might have felt the day she was crowned High Lady of Móirín.

One more steadying breath and Arianna stood, reaching for Talon. His fingers wrapped around her own, passing his strength onto her as she stepped down the tiny stairs and onto the dirt path.

Talon released her, closed the carriage door, then stepped back.

Alone. She was utterly alone before these people.

A myriad of faces gaped at her. Some old, some young, others indistinguishable due to eternity freezing the hands of time. But they all held a reverence in their gazes that told her they expected far more from their queen than she felt ready to give.

Arianna let her hands fall to her sides and lifted her chin. She braced herself, then stepped forward.

She wouldn't trip. She wouldn't bow. She wouldn't hesitate.

But her heart beat faster than a hummingbird's fluttering wings. Sweat rolled down the scars on her back, reminding her just how weak she'd once been, and the fabric of her undershirt clung uncomfortably to her skin. She stepped again, half expecting someone to dart from the crowd and offer her escort.

No one did.

Arianna kept walking, putting one foot in front of the other as she made her way down the path, passing face after face after face. They bowed as she went, some lowering their heads and whispering prayers to the gods while others fell to their knees and sobbed.

Arianna stepped over a crack in the road and around a loosened stone. She kept moving. Maybe they intended for her to walk through the village and greet everyone present. Maybe she'd walk too far and look like a fool.

A shift on the path, then Talon was following with Ellie close behind. The guards trailed after them, but she resisted the urge to glance back.

A light breeze lifted the hair on her shoulders, shifting the loose tendrils as if it too greeted her. Despite her nerves, Arianna refused to lower her head or fidget as she passed civilians she had no idea how to lead.

The air shimmered and she blinked, trying to focus on the moving image. It shifted in a way she couldn't quite describe, then four Fae stood on the path as if they'd materialized from thin air.

They waited in a near perfect line dressed in robes of deep cobalt with swirling gold patterns embroidered down the center. It reminded her of the gold and black dress she'd first eyed in Levea.

Her eyes scanned them. Two females, two males, though their ages were impossible to identify.

Old, she told herself. They were very old. It was something in the way the air crackled around them, like their magic couldn't be contained. Or maybe it was the way their bodies stood so still one might have mistaken them for statues.

The council, she realized.

Arianna sensed a shiver down the bond, but she couldn't discern its meaning. A warning perhaps, but Rion needed to wait until they were within the city walls. Arianna glanced past the Fae. Unless . . . this was the city.

As a unit, the four bowed low, their heads parallel to the ground. Arianna watched them closely, eyeing the weapons jutting out from the thick fabric. Not robes, she realized as the wind brushed past. Cloaks. Rich velvet cloaks.

She hardly thought the weather warranted such an extreme, but they were spectacular to look at.

The four didn't rise.

Arianna chewed her lip and almost turned to Ellie for answers when she felt another tug on the bond. Right. She needed to command them.

"Rise." Her voice was too soft, but the four obeyed, once again moving as a unit. Their gazes scrutinized her and it took every ounce of self-control not to step back or outright flee. Maybe she should have hidden in the mountains with Rion after all. A few decades wouldn't have hurt.

A male in the center stepped forward and spread his arms wide revealing the finely pressed black tunic beneath his cloak. Along with five blades strapped across his chest. His voice was deep when he said, "It is my absolute honor to welcome you to Ruadhán." She surveyed the village again. No grand cathedral. No riches beyond imagination. Just a humble village full of humble people. Maybe the rumors had gotten it wrong.

"It's an honor to be here," Arianna said, rehearsing the lines Ellie had drilled into her.

"Not many are afforded more than a glimpse of the village before you." He gestured to their right and Arianna followed with her eyes. "It's part of Pádraigín's magic to keep our city hidden and to ensure those who reside within its borders are safe."

Before the attack outside Levea, she might have called them paranoid, but if rogue factions were willing to kill just for an idea of who she might become, Arianna didn't want to imagine what they'd do to this place.

His arms raised and like steam on a hot summer day, the sky— no, reality parted, splitting at the seams.

The crowd gasped and even Talon couldn't contain himself as the underbelly of an entire city materialized in the distant sky above.

Arianna couldn't make out much beyond a circular mass and the way sunlight seemed to reflect from an unknown source. Rainbows surrounded the underside in a ring of light as water spilled from the edges, only to evaporate in the air above.

"If you step onto the platform to your right, we can begin the ascent."

Arianna followed him with Talon, Ellie, and the guards close behind.

She wondered if she hadn't noticed the platform due to magic or because it fit so perfectly into the ground.

Hexagonal mosaic tiles covered the surface in a kaleidoscope of colors. Azure of the sky, scarlet and rusty orange of the sunset, emerald and sapphire of the glittering ocean. The council caught her staring and Arianna closed her gaping mouth. Her cheeks heated, but they only smiled.

The platform was wide enough that fifty people could have easily stood with enough room to move about. Talon, Ellie, the council, her guards from Móirín, and the priests and priestesses stepped up. The others watched in longing as the platform lifted from the ground in a smooth motion. So smooth it barely jostled anyone.

Panic surged through her and the council male, who strangely hadn't introduced himself, whipped his head in her direction. "It's quite safe," he promised. "No need to worry, we'll have your feet back on the ground in a moment."

It wasn't the height that bothered her. It was the worry of whether Rion stood among them. She looked over the faces, at least those she could see. Even if Ellie had hidden his magic, it wasn't as if he could pretend to be someone else.

The bond didn't stretch and that same soothing feeling reached out to caress her mind with a gentle touch.

He was here. Despite how impossible it might seem, Rion was here. Was he hidden among the hooded priests, and if so, how did they not recognize one of their own? She'd figure out exactly how Ellie had done it later.

The city drew closer and closer, the massive structure larger than Arianna had previously imagined it. Her breath hitched when they crested the top. She saw the metal woven fence first as it expanded the perimeter of the floating city, rising six feet high with thick bars that promised to keep the citizens from stumbling to their deaths. Ivy covered the bars, bringing life to the otherwise cold metal.

A large crevice marked the space where their platform would land and smooth eggshell colored stone formed a street lined with shops and homes and bustling people.

Each residence had its own small yard complete with a garden, balconies on the first and second floors, and immaculately cared for exteriors of neutral tones offset by brightly colored flowers of all varieties. Everything glistened and shone as if it were as eternal as the Fae that lived there.

Their platform lowered and disappeared as it became one with the street before them.

"We have several of these throughout the city," the unnamed council male said. "You're welcome to use them as much as you like."

Arianna only nodded, her attention focused on the landscape as she stepped forward. Flowering trees circled the space with potted plants and trickling fountains every few feet. A floral aroma filled the air and gold lined the railings, sparkling in the sunlight. Other jewels adorned the space as well. They were placed into pottery, on the doorknobs, in the windowsills, and she even thought she saw some shining within the garden beds themselves.

A city of beauty. Of extravagance.

Of waste.

Arianna swallowed her disgust and followed the male down the polished street. Her stomach soured with each step.

They wore clothes without wrinkles, their bodies free from blemish or scars or bruising. They crowded the edge of the street with smiles on their faces. Smiles for her. She should be happy to find one small space in the world devoid of hardship.

But resentment flooded through her instead.

The male's excited voice penetrated her dark thoughts only to drown and die. He spoke of their history, but for some reason she didn't care how long it had taken to build the structures or how they maintained them to near perfection. She didn't care where or how they obtained their riches or what foreign lands traded in strange jewels.

The only thing she could think about were the citizens below and how different the wooden homes and dirt streets looked compared to the glittering city above it. Did the citizens of this city care anything for the village below them? Would they offer them sanctuary should war break out, or food if they faced starvation?

"My Lady?" The male must have addressed her more than once because when she turned, his brow had knitted with worry. "Are you not pleased?"

Pleased. No, she wasn't pleased. She was appalled by the extravagance, but—Arianna glanced around. This used to be her life, too.

She'd lived among the wealthy. She'd always gone to bed with a full stomach and fresh clothes and she'd never questioned the wellbeing of those beyond Levea's gates. What had she ever done in the sixteen years of her youth that had actually mattered?

These people lived in ignorance just as she'd once done. It wasn't that they were cruel and unkind, they were simply unaware. And maybe that's exactly why she was here. To bring awareness to the masses and change everything. Maybe that's what peace truly meant.

Arianna shook her head and did her best to smile. "I'm just a bit tired."

"Oh," the male's eyes brightened before turning apologetic. "Of course, forgive me, the council discussed giving you a tour much later and I must have gotten carried away. Please, come this way and we'll get you settled in the manor."

She followed, trying not to stare at everyone who shouted praise and threw petals at their feet. She tried to avoid Talon's look of worry as well and the way her sister's face had lost its smile.

They turned right once and Arianna gawked at the structure looming before them. Hedges surrounded the property, each bush cut to perfection. They rose above her head by a foot and domed into arches that led into the courtyard.

The courtyard. She gasped at the near pristine lawn. Twisted and balled topiaries decorated the yard with flowers surrounding the greenery in a multitude of colors. Only magic could make so much beauty bloom all at once.

The sentinels at the gate bowed low, one even dropping to his knees. Those escorting her nodded in greeting.

The sun bleached stones shifted to a dark burgundy once they stepped inside the gate. Another fountain stood in the center of the path and the burgundy stones split around the carving of a giant tree-like creature with the Fairy Folk dancing at its feet. She recognized those flaming eyes. The talon-like branched fingers.

The Dark Fae.

Did the citizens of Ruadhán realize what stood before them? Did they know stories she didn't? Surprise flew down the bond telling her Rion felt the same. She'd be sure to ask about it at some point, though she'd keep the details of their time in the mountain to herself.

The manor itself, with large open windows, gray walls, and dark brown trim, stood four stories tall with gardens wrapping around either side. The hedges seemed to call out, beckoning her to follow their mysterious paths.

She grimaced. It was too perfect and neat. A monument of wealth and abundance.

She followed the council up the large stone steps and another set of guards opened the doors. Everyone paused, almost as though they'd been frozen. Arianna and those accompanying her were forced to do the same.

The male who still hadn't introduced himself bowed low. "We didn't expect to see you, My Lord."

A voice smooth as silk answered as a male stepped from the shadows of the manor and into the light. "I wouldn't dream of keeping our queen waiting." He wore a midnight black long sleeve coat with gold buttons that ran down the front. Smoky eyes drank her in, studying her frame, her clothes, her weapons. His sandy blond hair shifted with the cool breeze and a warm smile broke across his angular face.

Territorial anger flared down the bond aimed directly at the new male. No, not anger. Rage. It bubbled and simmered and Arianna wondered if they were about to have another incident like the one between Rion and Talon back in Levea. She certainly hoped not.

Six warriors flanked the male, fanning out once he crossed the threshold. Their clothes were also pristine, not a wrinkle or speck in sight, as they stood with their shoulders squared and hands on their intricately decorated pommels. She wondered if those immaculate blades had ever seen combat.

The new male's calculating gaze ran over Talon. It was only now that she realized Talon had closed the distance between them, his hand on the sword at his belt.

The male's smile didn't fade. He floated down the stairs as if he were riding a phantom wind and the council bowed lower before backing away.

Her throat went dry when she scented the air, and realization had fear lodging itself in her throat.

The council bowing. The raw power rippling from his windswept scent.

"My Lady," he said in an easy seductive tone. She'd frozen in place. He closed the distance and gently took her hand. She should have yanked it away but something in his gaze wouldn't let her. Those eyes held her as if she were a captive all over again. "It is an absolute pleasure to meet you."

She wished she had worn the gloves. His eyes drank her in as he lifted her hand, but before his lips could make contact, a vicious snarl ripped through the air, echoing off the manor walls.

Swords and knives tore from their sheaths and the new male stepped back, his guards closing around him. Water droplets materialized, shifting to deadly spikes of ice. Vines tore from the immaculate gardens and shredded the perfect stone path. Fire sparked and crackled, dancing in the unnatural wind that whipped loose tendrils of Arianna's hair around her face.

A solid wall of muscle pressed against her back, warm and welcoming. Sand and rock surrounded her on all sides, cascading like water at their feet and towering above their heads in silent challenge. A low growl vibrated through her chest and she imagined her mate pinning the new male with his cold emerald gaze.

Arianna smiled and leaned back into his strong frame. Rion hadn't attacked. He'd come to her aid, a weapon waiting to be used.

The smoky eyes before her narrowed, studying her posture and the dominance of the male at her side. The male's hand flexed once, the only outward indication that he wanted to intervene.

The council members and warriors stationed to guard the estate all gaped and Arianna scented their rush of panic when Rion's grains of sand caressed her body.

She scented Talon's magic next, then Ellie's. The only two who were willing to stand so close, right in the path of Rion's magic.

The council member who'd spoken to her before tried to clear his throat, but his voice broke anyway. "Your father was given clear instructions." He pointed a shaking finger. "That creature defiles this sacred place and everything we stand for. He is—"

"Her mate," Ellie declared, voice ringing loud and clear. The male shrank back, stunned as if she'd slapped him. Fear twisted his features and his eyes darted between the new male and Rion. Back and forth. Back and forth. Ellie walked right through Rion's magic, standing before them as if she were their representative. "Rion," she emphasized his name. "Is her mate. As such, I'd choose your next words to your queen," she emphasized again, "very, very carefully."

The council member sputtered. "Mate?" Others began murmuring. "T-That's not possible. Her mate is—"

"That's quite enough," the male with smoky eyes finally said. His features were calm and collected. A stark contrast to everyone else's. The rest were gawking, likely wondering if they should run or if they'd be reprimanded for the cowardice act. "Put your weapons away." They obeyed even though fear still laced their scents. Then the warriors at his side returned to their previous positions.

The male offered her a wane smile. "Forgive me, I wasn't informed of a recent mating bond." His gaze flicked toward someone in the crowd and he raised his voice a fraction. "If I'd known, I would have given you more time to acclimate and I certainly wouldn't have paraded you through the city." His eyes returned to hers. "I'm sure the strain has been taxing."

The male stepped forward, but Rion snarled in response, flashing his teeth. The male cocked his head, wavy shoulder-length hair shifting with the movement. He didn't turn his wrists up in submission, nor did he challenge the tone in Rion's voice. He simply nodded as if answering some unspoken demand.

"I'll keep my hands to myself."

They remained like that for what seemed like an eternity. Arianna took it upon herself to break the tension and placed a hand on Rion's forearm.

She addressed the male. The regent of Ruadhán. "I wasn't given much of a choice about coming."

It's all right, she willed down the bond. His body shifted slightly.

The new male's brow furrowed. "You are the queen of Alastríona. You have a choice in everything." He studied Rion's slowing magic, then her face, which, despite her bath in the river, probably showed how little sleep she'd gotten the night before. "You must be exhausted." He stepped back and extended his arm, gesturing inside. "We have food and rooms prepared. Please, come in, we can speak more tomorrow." He paused. "If you feel so inclined, that is."

Rion's magic finally stopped moving and she took in the devastated landscape. Not just from him, but everyone else. "That sounds wonderful."

"If you'll follow me."

They did. She stepped over the threshold and Ellie beamed at her sister. But the tension in Talon's shoulders hadn't subsided. She doubted it would for a while.

They entered a large foyer that led into an even bigger sitting room. Lush rugs covered smooth marble floors and large paintings of floral arrangements, the Fairy Folk, and Fae she didn't recognize hung along the walls. Pottery set atop lacework lined the dark wooden tables and fresh flowers were being tended to by passing servants.

Arianna tried not to stare but found the task impossible. Her eyes betrayed her self-control and ventured toward the vaulted ceilings. Glass chandeliers illuminated the space, bathing everything in their pleasant glow.

She felt as though she'd just stepped back in time. The modern world had done away with so many designs. It was almost a crime. She would have given anything to gaze upon the lifelike artwork back home. She wanted to run to the library and study who had painted the pieces lining the walls, then inquire whether or not the artists still lived so she could thank them for their work.

Centuries. No, longer. They'd kept this place in perfect order as they waited on The Divine. On her. But did she need so much space?

Fae servants roamed the halls, but otherwise the corridors seemed lonely. No one sat upon the soft sofas or wrapped themselves in the plush throws. No one used the glass cups that begged to overhear a quiet conversation. Something about the disuse pulled at a familiar ache in her chest.

It was a beautiful, lonely cage desperate for an occupant.

Arianna shook the thoughts away. This was it. Everything in their lives was about to change. She wouldn't be returning to Móirín, not for a very long time. She wouldn't gaze upon the waterfalls she'd longed to see while clasped in irons. She wouldn't speak to the friends and servants she'd neglected and pushed away while she'd mourned for Rion.

Time slowed and a nauseating sensation filled her gut. She had a lot to learn and even more to change. Were the Fae of Ruadhán trustworthy? Could she confide in the council? The regent? Or had deceit and manipulation weaved too deep into their politics? Ellie and her father both seemed to think so.

Would Arianna become a slave once again, bound to her duties and left at the beck and call of others?

Rion tightened his grip on her arm and she turned to find those bottomless green eyes studying her, his brow pinched with concern. Rion. She had Rion and Talon and Ellie. They'd watched her back and she'd watch theirs. Despite leaving home, Arianna had the people who mattered.

One day at a time, that's all she needed to worry about.

Arianna gave her mate a gentle smile then turned when the regent stepped to the side and the guards pushed open a pair of doors covered with frosted glass.

Her mouth watered when she spotted the tables laden with food. Spiced chicken, a multitude of casseroles, steaming bread, and pastries oozing with warm chocolate.

Teardrop chandeliers sparkled above row after row of tables. Countless Fae filled the seats and paused to stare at the small group filing in. The blond male led them down the center path and Arianna smiled shyly at the many faces she made eye contact with.

They whispered, smiled, and Arianna tried not to blush when many placed a hand over their hearts and bowed their heads.

The regent paused before a table at the back of the room. The only one turned parallel to the door. It made watching everyone easier, but they were also watching her.

"Please," the regent gestured, "enjoy yourself. Everything you need will be provided and when you're finished, someone will be nearby to escort you to your rooms."

He turned, but Arianna stopped him. "You're not staying?"

He gave her a warm smile, so perfect and sincere that her heart tugged, drawn toward the kindness in his gaze. "You're very kind, but I'd like you to enjoy the festivities in the company of those you know. As someone who once traveled from their homeland, I understand the value of familiar companionship in a strange place."

Ellie whistled. "Are dinners always this extravagant?"

The male chuckled. "Only when the Queen herself is gracing us with her presence." His eyes seemed to sparkle with emotion.

"Thank you."

He bowed slightly. "It is my absolute pleasure." Then he was gone, his guards following, and Arianna felt a knot in her stomach unwind. Everyone was still watching, staring in silence and she realized the food hadn't been touched. They were waiting.

Ellie was first to find a seat. Rion took Arianna's hand and led her to the chair beside her sister. Then the music started.

SHE'D NEVER eaten so much in her life. Arianna leaned her head back against the chair feeling as though she might burst at any moment. Ellie was still grabbing cakes.

Musicians played in a corner to their left, their soft, upbeat music filling the silence. Many still stared and others hadn't taken their eyes off her, but she'd tuned them out after a few minutes. Mostly because Ellie kept her distracted.

Rion had waited before digging in, but when Ellie didn't fall over or pass out, he made a plate for himself. Arianna wasn't sure which of the three ate more.

Her mate squeezed her hand beneath the table, but before he could speak, a hushed silence fell over the hall that had them all straightening.

A female entered from a door to the right carrying a violin in one hand and a bow in the other. Those seated twisted to look at the female and for a moment, Arianna flashed back to her time in the war camps, dreading the way males leered at the defenseless females.

But this female didn't carry scars or shackles around her wrists and ankles. She wasn't malnourished or starved. She was clean. Whole. And happy, if her gentle smile was anything to go by.

She wore a cream colored dress with gold laced through the seams that contrasted perfectly with her olive skin. A simple necklace held a pendant shaped like a bird and her waist-length dark hair was braided back from her face and rested across one shoulder.

No one moved.

And when the bow grazed the strings and coaxed a long, soft note from the instrument, Arianna understood why.

The music began, slow and ethereal, reminding Arianna of the Fairy Folk when they sang to the forest. Arianna's heart rose and fell with each note, the music cascading over the room like soft moonlight streaming through a window.

The female's eyes closed, then her body swayed as if she played with the entire force of her soul.

It beckoned forgotten dreams and memories of a life Arianna had left behind and another that had been stolen. The tempo rose and her heart swelled with it.

She never wanted it to end.

The haunting part of the melody returned, then slowed, and when the bow pulled free from the strings, the last note echoed through the hall and their hearts.

No one moved.

No one breathed.

Then the room erupted in applause and Arianna was on her feet joining them. She swiped at a stray tear and smiled at Rion. Her mate smiled back, eyes bright with life and love and joy.

Arianna leaned in. "I've never heard anything so beautiful," she said over the roars of whistles and cheering.

Rion's breath caressed the shell of her ear. "Neither have I."

Ellie plopped back into her seat and sighed in contentment. "Good food, good music. I might just have to stay in Ruadhán for a century or two."

Arianna laughed. A century. A mere drop in time for them. It was five times the life she'd already lived and it was only the beginning. She glanced back at Rion and the smile on his face.

A beautiful, rich beginning.

Chapter Eighteen

Arianna

After the female's spectacular performance, the musicians returned to playing a far more upbeat tune. Arianna's feet throbbed. Her eyes were heavy with exhaustion, but when Ellie dragged her out onto the dance floor, she couldn't tell her little sister no.

Talon and Rion remained at the table, watching the pair despite being invited. She saw Talon's smile when Ellie twirled, and the girls danced and spun across the floor laughing until their stomachs ached.

Others joined, drinks feeding a frenzy of joy and excitement, but Ellie remained at Arianna's side, keeping those who wanted to draw too close at bay. When they reached for her, Ellie took their arm instead, spun with them around the dance floor, then quickly returned to her sister. The gathered crowd eventually took the hint and settled to clapping for the females instead.

She'd missed this. This carefree joy that came so easily to Ellie. Emotion swelled through Arianna even as they kept spinning. She was a stranger in a strange place and yet Ellie made it feel like home.

After a few more songs, Arianna pulled Talon out onto the floor despite his playful protests. He understood enough when she longingly gazed toward Rion. Or maybe it was the bags beneath her eyes. She craved a soft bed and quiet after the long journey.

Talon took Ellie's arm and they danced and danced and danced, weaving through the crowd of strangers without missing a step.

Arianna laced her fingers through Rion's hand and her mate smiled at her, though she couldn't discern his emotions even with the bond. They were jumbled, an explosion of colors all at once that were impossible to pick apart.

She glanced around the room once and just as the regent had promised, a servant swiftly crossed the room.

He bowed and gestured toward a door rather than raising his voice above the music.

Arianna watched her sister spin into Kirian's arms, a wide smile covering her face. Talon grinned too before bowing to a petite female and taking her hand. Arianna followed the servant with Rion at her side.

The nimble male opened a side door and as soon as it closed, the sounds of music and laughter faded to a distant hum.

The halls were quiet and dark, lit only by a few lanterns hanging on the walls and the moonlight filtering through the tall floor-to-ceiling windows. They were open, allowing the cool night breeze to billow the sheer cream colored curtains.

The trio walked in silence, Rion's hand clutching hers as she observed the artwork in the dark. She kept to the hall's center to avoid accidentally knocking over the fine vases perched on the edges of tables.

The male turned and gestured them up a carpeted staircase. His footsteps were near silent as he ascended. The wooden railings were smooth and intricately carved and she watched Rion's fingertips graze over the patterns as if he could memorize them in the dark.

Her throat went dry and his head whirled toward her when her scent changed. A dark gleam in his gaze told her she wasn't sleeping tonight no matter how much she needed it.

The male's footsteps, to his credit, didn't falter, though he seemed to move at a faster pace now.

They turned down another long hall, but this one only had two doors, one to her right and the other further down to her left. A double set of glass doors also stood at the end of the hall and likely led to a balcony. The servant faced the one on the right, bowed his head, and held out a key.

"I hope you find it to your liking. Someone will be here tomorrow to escort you to breakfast."

"Thank you," Arianna said, taking the key from his gloved hand.

The male bowed again and scurried away. Arianna thought she'd glimpsed a blush on his cheeks.

She inserted the key into the lock, but a gentle tug from Rion had her stepping back. He opened the door first, his magic spilling from inside his blue jacket. He'd discarded the priest's robes at dinner.

Arianna counted the seconds then Rion's shoulders relaxed and they stepped inside.

She flicked on the light switch and had to stifle a gasp.

This wasn't a bedroom. It was an entire living area.

A massive four-poster bed leaned against the left wall covered in delicate silk sheets with far too many pillows propped against the carved headboard. Heavy midnight curtains hung around the frame, held back with golden ropes. A chest stood against the foot of the bed with several more blankets neatly folded on top.

A gaping fireplace covered half of the back wall and a pair of cushioned chairs were positioned before it. A mirror hung over the mantel, with gold roses wrapped around the corners and vines trailing across each long side.

The room was already decorated in colorful floral arrangements, candlesticks, and ornate trinkets.

A mahogany vanity to her right. Plush rugs at their feet. Three chandeliers overhead.

Finery. Extravagance.

Two doors lined the far wall on either side of the fireplace. She crossed the room and pushed open the left one revealing another massive room covered in gray and white marbled tile. A double sink on the left. A hexagonal shower toward the back and a tub large enough for five to the right. Fluffy bath towels were neatly stacked on shelves and two robes hung from golden hooks on the side wall.

She backed away and proceeded toward the second door. Rion was quiet the entire time as she explored their new living space.

She gaped at the closet that rivaled the size of her old room. It was already packed with clothes. So many clothes and hats, canes, jewelry, and shoes, shoes, shoes. Heels, flats, boots.

Her stomach churned.

"What's wrong?" Rion's soothing voice cut through her nervous tension and his tender caress up her arm calmed her throbbing pulse. She leaned into him, burying her face in his tunic. Arianna idly traced a silver button and briefly wondered where Ellie had gotten the outfit.

"It's all—" Gods, how could she explain? She should be grateful for everything. Others would kill to be where she was now, but—

Rion pulled her close and rested his head atop hers. "Tell me," he whispered. Words she'd once spoken to him. A gentle pull.

"How am I supposed to live up to this? What if I mess everything up?"

"You have centuries and Ellie," he joked. Rion shifted. His head lowered and his warm breath caressed her ear. Arianna tilted her head back, allowing him access to her throat. His lips grazed the sensitive area and pleasant shivers ran down her spine. "And if you ever decide you want to leave," he said, voice husky, "I'll gladly take you away."

She laughed and he met her gaze again. "That'd give them something to talk about. The new queen kidnapped by The Demon and whisked away from her throne."

He smirked. "Only if the queen wishes it."

Arianna studied the seriousness in his expression. "It's tempting," she admitted. "I rather liked that little cabin."

He leaned close and his heated gaze promised everything she'd been imagining for days. "Just say the word."

His teeth grazed her throat and Arianna tightened her grip on his shirt, ready to tear the fabric in half. His lips trailed kisses to the base of her jaw and Rion pulled her flush against his body.

Arianna's knees threatened to buckle, but he slid strong fingers up her back until they threaded through her hair.

Gods she needed him, ached for his touch.

Rion removed the clips from her hair one at a time and she swore he moved slowly on purpose. A quick glance at his wicked grin confirmed her theory.

But she was done waiting.

Arianna's mouth crashed into his and she shoved him against to the nearest wall where they became a flurry of movement. Their hands desperately pulled at buttons and tucked clothes until it all lay in piles at their feet.

Rion pulled her closer, his tongue diving deep, and she savored the feel of it and the way his hands gripped her body like he couldn't get enough.

He pulled away to whisper in her ear again. "What do you want?"

She thought that was obvious from the way she gripped his shoulders, but he always gave her a choice. Every single time. Arianna smiled and said, "A bath." Rion paused. "And you in it."

CHAPTER NINETEEN

ARIANNA

*P*ounding metal jolted Arianna from sleep, her mind suddenly back inside a cabin with a male she needed to protect from a world hell-bent on his destruction. Water pulled from the air forming into tiny droplets that were ready to shift at a moment's notice. Earth rose seconds later, the grains dancing with the liquid in a union of deadly promises.

Pounding again. No. Knocking, then her vision cleared and she was back in a fluffy bed with her mate's arms tightening around her, coaxing her fear into submission.

His lips brushed over her upper arm and she settled back into the silken sheets, breathing deeply.

They weren't in the cabin. They weren't trapped in the middle of a war. Not a physical one, anyway.

Arianna pressed her forehead against his shoulder and he stroked her long hair as if he could pull the worries from her haunted mind. Would the nightmares ever end?

Whoever stood outside the door knocked a third time, though it was softer now and Arianna wondered if their escort had sensed her distress. She hoped not; she didn't need rumors flying through the manor.

Arianna fought her tired body and crawled from the comforts of the bed with her mate right behind her. Both pulled on their robes and Rion flicked on the light with his magic. She blinked against the offending brightness, then turned the handle.

A female with short brown hair stood on the other side with an apologetic smile. Surprisingly she wore a pale blue gown. After yesterday Arianna wasn't sure anyone wore colors other than gold and black.

The female's eyes widened and she seemed to remember herself by curtsying. "My Lady, I'm Victoria. I'll be helping you adjust to your stay. I'm here to escort you to breakfast. The Lord thought to let you sleep longer after your travels, but he didn't want you to miss your first day exploring the manor."

Right. She couldn't just hide in the room. Or maybe she could. Arianna peered around, glancing down the hall for any sign of the male. "Does he plan to escort us himself?" He was the acting Regent. The one said to be their future king. Even if she had no intention of a union, Arianna knew she'd be working with this male to ultimately change Alastríona for the better.

"Of course, but he wanted you to dine in peace before your schedule began." Courteous, but was it genuine or a show to earn her favor?

"We'll be out in a few minutes."

The female nodded, bowed low, then stepped toward a bench down the hall. Arianna hadn't noticed it last night, though she'd been more than a little worn out. Not that either of them had slept much. Her cheeks heated.

She stepped back inside and Rion emerged from the closet, buckling a new belt over a pair of pressed black slacks. The muscles in his chest flexed with the movement. Her heart began a steady rhythm as images from last night clouded her judgment. His powerful body behind her own, pinning her against the wall. His fingers pulling a rush of ecstasy from her even after she was sure she couldn't feel any more. The way her name fell from his lips, over and over worshipping her as if she were a goddess.

His heated gaze slowly lifted from the buckle. She watched his chest rise and fall and his pulse quickened.

Her mate swallowed hard and his nostrils flared. "Come here." And she was across the room, pushing him against the wall all over again, their movements feral and desperate. His hands wrapped beneath her thighs and Rion picked her up with ease, tore the robe from her body, and lowered them back into the silk sheets.

ARIANNA THANKED the gods that servants had already delivered her things to their room. She ripped through the chest and tugged on a pair of dark pants and a simple lavender colored shirt before running to the vanity. Five brushes sat before her. Arianna grabbed one at random and yanked it through her hair.

Rion wrapped her up from behind and kissed the side of her neck. She smiled at the contact even as she shooed him away. "We can't make her wait any longer."

Rion didn't hide his amusement. "It wasn't my idea to make her wait at all." She huffed and her cheeks burned. It wasn't her fault he looked as though he'd been carved by the gods. "And," Rion continued. "Last I checked, *you* were the queen. They wait on you."

"It doesn't make for a very good first impression."

Rion hummed in response and pulled on a long sleeved shirt, buttoning up the front with nimble fingers that had just previously—

"If you keep gawking like that, I'm not going to be held accountable for my actions."

Arianna bit the inside of her cheek hard, then took him in as a whole. Fresh clothes, no weapons, hair combed, though parts seemed to stick up in defiance.

"You look so—"

"Normal?" he teased.

"Calm."

His gaze softened and he closed the distance, pulling her into an embrace. He smelled the top of her hair and breathed a sigh of relief. "You make me feel that way. Calm somehow. Like the anger that plagued me has finally abated."

It was her turn to hum. Arianna glanced at herself in the mirror again. She didn't look like a queen. She looked like a normal female with her normal lover and they were in a normal house ready to tackle normal duties.

She loosed a breath, then crossed the room and opened the door to their not-so-normal world.

Arianna had hoped the female might have taken a stroll, but she sat on the little bench at the end of the hall with her legs crossed and hands folded neatly in her lap. The female jumped to her feet when the door clicked shut.

Heat flooded Arianna's cheeks and she wrung her hands together. "Sorry to keep you waiting."

The female, Victoria, bowed and gave Arianna a sweet smile. "Not at all. We're here to serve you, My Lady. Please, follow me."

They walked down the decorated halls and Arianna found herself gazing out the tall windows.

All manner of Fae walked the grounds. Some weaved through the gardens, disappearing and reappearing around the thick hedges. They wore beautiful pastel colored silks, exposing much of their skin to the sunshine as if they could shake away the remnants of winter's chill.

Inside, she continued observing the art spread across tables and hanging from the walls. She wondered if she'd ever be able to take it all in.

So many plants and colors and life. Arianna found herself envying those in Brónach. She knew the residents crafted their homes from the trees and lived among the landscape as if they were part of it.

"Does Brónach look like this?" she asked.

Rion was studying the area too, though she doubted he was taking in the lace beneath the vases or the pictures hanging along the walls. She imagined him counting dark corners and planning a number of escape routes.

"The finery is a bit extreme, but if you're referring to the nature aspect, then yes."

"It must be beautiful."

"It is," he admitted and she thought it was the nicest thing he'd ever said about Brónach. "Though Levea's waterfalls are a sight to behold as well."

"I wonder if the other cities are just as grand."

"Fiadh's cavernous halls are."

Her brows rose. "You've been there?"

Rion chuckled. "I'm over ninety years old, I've visited a fair number of places." His brow furrowed. "Though Ashling has always been as mysterious as Ruadhán." Ashling. Pádraigín's capital city. Arianna tilted her head. "They don't allow outsiders in."

Right, she'd forgotten. Although clearly its residents could leave. She'd scented a number from Pádraigín yesterday. "I wonder why?"

Rion shrugged and they continued down the hall, taking the same staircase from yesterday that led them to the first floor. "They claim it's for their safety. They're a small country with little in the way of resources aside from their trading port."

"You don't sound like you believe them."

"I take very few people at their word." She gave him a wan smile, remembering everything he'd told her after she'd saved him from her father. All the pain and haunting memories.

The female led them through a pair of familiar doors, but the sight was quite different from last night. In the early afternoon hours, the long tables sat empty and no one played music in the corners. The hall seemed too large a place for just her and Rion to dine.

"Please, have a seat. Your breakfast will be brought out shortly."

Arianna searched the walls for a clock but didn't find one. She was certain they'd missed breakfast by a few hours. "Don't you mean lunch?" She had meant it to sound lighthearted, perhaps elicit a laugh from Victoria.

But the female's face paled. "O-Of course, I can have them bring whatever you wish."

Arianna waved her hands frantically. "No, I was only—"

"Whatever you have prepared will be acceptable," Rion cut in. Victoria's concerned gaze darted between Arianna and Rion a moment, then Arianna nodded and the female disappeared through a side door.

Arianna sighed. "Thanks for that. I didn't realize everyone would be so serious."

Rion scooted out the same chair she'd sat in the night before. "You're the queen. It'll take a while for them to feel you out, but I doubt anyone will ever throw caution to the wind."

"Any tips?"

"You're asking me?" A playful smile.

Right. "Well, what would your sister do?"

Rion laughed, his voice echoing through the hall. "Trust me when I say Saoirse is the last person you'd want to take advice from. She'd have the servants shining her shoes and ironing every garment in her closet."

"I didn't realize she was so intense." Dread swept through her. She'd eventually have to meet his sister. She *wanted* to meet his sister and yet—

"She can be if the situation calls for it, but she has a softer side, too. I think the power would go to her head through. It's why, despite his overly serious demeanor, I'm sure the citizens of Brónach are glad to have Alec as the older sibling."

A shadow flickered to her right and Arianna's head snapped toward the door that led into the hall. She squinted, trying to find the individual she was certain had just walked through it. She scented the air but found nothing.

"Something wrong?" he asked following her gaze.

"No." She really needed sleep. "The light must be playing tricks on me." She glanced back only once before studying the space where the musicians had sat last night. Perhaps she would have gotten to hear them again if they'd been on time for breakfast.

The first servant emerged, carrying a large tray laden with cheeses, bagels, fruits, and steaming chocolate pastries. Arianna sat straighter, ready to dig in, but another servant followed a second later, his tray full of eggs, bacon, sausage, and dishes she couldn't identify.

Each wore long sleeves, their dark tunics clean and tight against their frames.

Another emerged with a tray of steaming breads and silverware. The female hesitated at first and decided to lean across the table to set the plates before them. Arianna wondered if it was because of Rion's reputation or due to their new mating bond.

Arianna thanked them, but before she reached for anything, another servant emerged. Then another and Arianna's mouth gaped as they placed tray after tray before the pair.

She turned to Rion when the servants were finished and kept her voice low. "Surely they don't expect us to eat all this."

He eyed the food, but his gaze didn't swim with uncertainty. He seemed excited and Arianna wondered how often he'd gotten to enjoy extravagant food in his life. "I'd venture to say the cooks are trying to make a good impression."

A moment later, Victoria appeared, her expression nervous as she clasped her hands together. "Is everything to your liking?"

Arianna tried to choose her words carefully, afraid to upset the female again. "It all looks delightful." She almost chewed her lip, then stopped herself. "Do you know if my sister has eaten?"

Victoria nodded. "They were all here this morning." The female clenched her hands tighter when Arianna's face fell. "But," she continued. "It's almost the lunch hour. I could send for them if you wish for their company?"

"That would be wonderful."

Victoria beamed, bowed, then pivoted on her heels and all but fled from the hall. Arianna eyed the food. "Please tell me you're going to help me eat this."

Her mate stabbed a pancake and the simple motion almost had her laughing. "Considering you're the queen, I seriously doubt anyone is going to make an attempt at poisoning you. At least not yet, so yes."

He poured her a cup of orange juice from the glass pitcher before filling his own. "I think I will."

Rion froze and Arianna sucked in a breath, her gaze darting around the room to locate the source of his distress. She didn't think she'd heard anyone enter but— "What is it?" she whispered.

"I didn't ask if you liked it."

She blinked, struggling to discern his meaning, then couldn't hide her laugh. "I thought something bad was about to happen and you're just afraid I don't like orange juice?"

He gave her an amused look that quickly faded. "I want to know everything about you."

She stabbed her own pancake. "No need to get dramatic over breakfast."

Rion took her hand and pressed a kiss to the back of it. The motion sent heat coursing straight through her. "No detail is too small." They locked eyes and Arianna seriously considered skipping breakfast altogether, or having the servants deliver it to their rooms. Maybe they'd hide for the rest of the week wrapped in one another's arms.

"Ugh, I'm invited to breakfast and you two are already ogling each other like you've been apart for weeks. Honestly, how is a girl supposed to eat?"

Arianna grinned. "Good morning, Ellie."

"More like afternoon, but I suppose the queen gets her meals anytime she wants." Kirian followed close behind with a book in his hand that made Arianna curious. She knew Ruadhán had a library and judging from the extravagance she'd already witnessed, Arianna was willing to bet it would be the grandest thing she'd ever seen.

"It's nice to see you, Lady Arianna," Kirian said, bowing his head.

Ellie chuckled. "You don't have to do that." She grabbed a plate, plopped down in the seat next to Rion's, and began filling it. Arianna gaped at her little sister, but it wasn't until Ellie took her first bite that she noticed.

"What?"

Arianna shook her head, the ghost of a smile creeping to her face. "Nothing." Ellie had helped sneak Rion into the royal city, but Arianna didn't know when her sister had gotten so comfortable around her mate. Even Rion looked surprised. Ellie ate and passed food to Kirian. She either pretended not to notice the grains of sand floating around the table or didn't care.

Talon's scent drifted in when he burst through the door with one hand on the weapon at his side. He surveyed the scene, took in the food, his friends seated at the table, then straightened.

"When you summoned me, I assumed the worst."

"Serves you right for assuming," Ellie said, raising her glass.

Talon studied the table again. "Was there something you needed?"

Arianna waved her hand toward the steaming trays. "Help eating. Apparently they think I need a feast."

Talon's shoulders loosened, but she didn't miss the dark circles beneath his eyes. She wondered if he'd gotten any sleep at all.

Ellie reached for seconds. "If she gets a meal like this every day, I'm joining."

Talon hesitated when Rion's sharp eyes pinned him in place, but Arianna tapped his leg and her mate settled. Talon chose the seat beside Kirian.

Arianna reached for her drink. "I'm going to talk to them today. I'm only one person. I can't stand seeing all this go to waste." Ellie and Talon exchanged glances, but Arianna tried to ignore it. She didn't want to dwell on the dark thoughts crossing their minds. She knew she was thinner than before. It was a task to put on lost weight when the body was accustomed to living off so little.

"As I understand it," Talon said. "The leftovers are packed up and delivered to the citizens in the town below. They've taken in a fair amount of refugees and Ruadhán helps care for them."

Arianna's eyes brightened. "Really?"

Ellie added. "They're struggling from what I've heard. There's too many refugees, and not enough homes to go around."

Talon tore a biscuit in half. "They claim they're working on it."

Her sister downed a glass of water. "Clearly not fast enough."

So Ruadhán was doing something. Perhaps Ellie was right, maybe it wasn't enough, but a small effort could be expanded upon. It would give her a foothold.

Rion's jaw ticked. Arianna knew the refugees weighed on him, especially with his part in the war, but the blame couldn't be placed on one person alone.

The High Lords, generals, captains, and warriors had all made decisions with lasting consequences. And she was no exception.

ARIANNA SAT back, full and content until a strange scent drifted toward her as if carried in on a phantom breeze. Rion stiffened, Talon sat straighter, and Ellie's eyes darted toward the doorway where the smoky eyed male from yesterday stood. The Regent.

He still wore black, a color she'd always associated with mourning. She wondered if she could convince the council to change Ruadhán's banners to something a little brighter.

The male's gaze lingered on the food then rose until their eyes locked. Arianna didn't move, afraid even swallowing would result in his judgement. She could have sworn something shimmered in her mind, gliding along some invisible barrier like the cool caress of a finger.

Every muscle in Rion's body coiled in on itself and he stood, drawing everyone's attention. His magic rose and Arianna reached for his hand, locking her fingers with his. A low growl rumbled through her mate's chest.

The Regent's eyes narrowed a moment, then that easy smile spread across his face and he ambled toward them as if Rion wasn't preparing to tear him apart. "I hope the food was to your liking."

Arianna eyed the leftovers. "It was delicious, though a bit over the top," she admitted.

"I'll be sure to pass your compliments along. The cooks were eager to please and I'm afraid talking them out of a single dish proved impossible."

He pivoted and gestured toward the main doors. "Do you feel up for a tour?"

Arianna folded her napkin and rose, pulling Rion along. She didn't release her mate's hand, afraid the simple movement would have Rion lunging.

Arianna eyed the Regent's wavy blond hair and the neat clothes that clung to his form, revealing a warrior's body underneath. Just like yesterday, an ancient air drifted toward her and she couldn't help but wonder how long he'd held his position in Ruadhán.

"I never caught your name," Arianna said.

His eyes widened. "My sincerest apologies, My Lady. I'm Niall, son to the High Lord of Pádraigín and acting Regent of Ruadhán."

She'd thought as much. Arianna glanced at Rion, wondering what Niall made of their mating bond. This was the male prophesied to be her mate. The future king of Alastríona.

"It's a pleasure to meet you. I'm Arianna." He already knew her name. Everyone probably did, still it felt rude not to introduce herself. "And this is Rion."

Niall's intense gaze surveyed Rion, locking on the sand still dancing at his feet. Like a predator assessing another in its territory.

"I've heard a great many stories about you. You're rumored to be quite a formidable force." He studied their hands. "Yet, instead of the hell storm I anticipated, I see a protective newly mated male like any other."

"Stories can be exaggerated," was Rion's only reply.

Niall laughed bitterly. "That they can be. Shall we begin?"

Arianna glanced back to look at Talon, Ellie, and Kirian. "I'll see you later?" she asked them as a group.

Ellie nodded, her face far more serious than it usually was as she glared at Niall. "We'll be here." Something about the male must have made Ellie uneasy, or perhaps she'd heard something unpleasant. Arianna would be sure to ask her sister at dinner.

They followed Niall down the hall in strange silence. She wasn't sure what to say, and speaking to Rion without including the male seemed awkward. Within minutes they exited the manor and Arianna found herself face to face with the entrance to a hedge maze. The stone path only appeared large enough for a couple to walk down hand in hand.

She breathed a sigh of relief when Niall guided them down the wider path that circled the manor.

"The hall leading into your room has a balcony that oversees the gardens. I know you likely haven't had a chance to see it yet, but I hope it pleases you. It's the best view in the manor." His steps slowed to a crawl. "Is the room to your liking?"

"It's quite . . . large." Too much. Far too much when the resources could be spent elsewhere.

Niall laughed, the sound full of light and mirth and Arianna swore the breeze laughed with him, ruffling the flowers and carrying a few petals in the wind. "I'm sure a great many things seem," he paused, searching for the word, "extravagant. I hope you'll forgive us for it. Many of us have waited a very long time to see you. Most have been preparing their entire lives and here you stand. A young, modest queen."

She felt her insignificance at the word young. To him and the council she was likely nothing more than a child.

"It's just—" She wanted to tell him it was horrible. She wanted to scream that she couldn't stand the plush pillows, the silken sheets, the warm fireplace, and all the gold and glittering jewels.

Niall's face faltered. "You seem displeased."

Arianna composed herself. "I'm just not accustomed to such finery."

Niall offered her a warm smile, one full of strange promises, and her gut knotted. "I hope you're able to acclimate to it. The High Lords will want to shower you with gifts beyond measure. They would take offense if you refused." Surely she could pass certain treasures along and help those in need.

Arianna studied him. There were so many things to plan, but Arianna wanted to feel Niall out first. See if he offered his ideals before she shared her own.

Walled hedges grew to their left with green and floral topiaries cut into windowed slots that gave the scene life. Flowering vines grew up the side of the manor on trellises. Everything was in bloom and the sweet fragrance pulled at her senses, begging Arianna to take a moment and appreciate its beauty.

She'd spent so long surrounded by death, drowning in a misery she was sure would never end.

And now. And now. . .

Arianna extended her hand toward a wisteria bloom on the edge of a trellis. She let her fingers trace the soft petals and leaned closer to smell the delicate blossoms.

"Is it a favorite?" Niall asked.

Arianna withdrew her hand, suddenly self-conscious. Both males had paused to stare at her. She recalled what Rion had said at breakfast about nothing being too miniscule and suddenly she didn't want Niall part of this moment. She wished it were just Rion and her walking the gardens, discovering everything there was to know about the magical estate prepared just for her.

"Yes," she backed away from the flower and Niall furrowed his brow. "But I favor a lot. It's difficult to choose when they're all so beautiful."

"Gorgeous," he agreed, stepping forward as if he might close the short distance separating them. Rion flashed his teeth and Niall stopped himself, unfazed by her mate's aggression. "Of course, how could I forget? It's simply years of ingrained court pleasantries. I meant nothing by it."

Arianna eyed her mate, studying the chaos of emotions that radiated down their bond. The feelings were muddled, like a veil stood between them. His agitation was the only thing she sensed loud and clear.

"Right. The tour. Inside, you'll find a vast library where you'll be completing most of your studies. It's the only thing that competes with the garden's beauty. I'll look forward to hearing which you prefer. Everyone seems to have a favorite."

Arianna already knew which she'd prefer. Books had always held a special place in her heart. But before her mind could wander too far she asked, "Studies?"

Niall angled himself to look at her while they walked. "You might know Móirín's history, but you have three other countries to learn about now. Some records we've lost to the ages, but a vast majority of our ancient knowledge resides in old tombs carefully preserved in our library."

"And I'll be expected to memorize it all?"

Niall laughed. "Gods, no. There's not a final exam." His eyes sparkled. "There's even a few texts written in a language we can't translate."

"No one knows it?"

He shook his head. "Decoding it hasn't proven successful. Some scholars will even claim the books change, shifting letters and symbols."

She raised a brow and Niall continued. "They say the books are cursed thus most refuse to touch them. Others believe they're written in the language of the gods and our minds aren't able to process the knowledge." He shrugged. "Maybe one day they'll share their secrets."

"That's sad," she said. To know there were histories they couldn't access, that some piece of their everlasting lives could just be gone. They were Fae, history wasn't supposed to fade into nothing. But how many Fae did she know who'd lived a thousand years? Her father wasn't even much older than that. War and jealousy and sickness befell them just as much as humans.

"You carry weapons here," he said, his voice soft.

Arianna had thought she'd done a decent job at hiding those on her waist, but the knife in her boot was easy enough to see.

Arianna looked him over, cursing herself for not identifying whether he carried any. She was sure Rion had, but—

"Do you not?" she asked.

He shook his head. "Only the guards do. I understand you went through quite the ordeal, but—"

"You understand nothing," Rion said between clenched teeth. It was the first time he'd spoken since they'd left the manor and his tone made the hair rise on her arms. "And if you think for one second that Arianna is going to walk this place unarmed . . ." He didn't need to finish his sentence.

Niall raised his hands in defense. "I only meant to say that it might make a some uncomfortable. The citizens may believe you don't trust them."

"Because we don't," Arianna said. And why would they? They were strangers. Complete strangers, no matter what they promised.

To her surprise, hurt flashed across Niall's face and his gaze traveled toward her wrists. They were covered by the long sleeves of her shirt, but she couldn't resist tugging them down.

"I suppose not," he said simply. "But I hope, given time, I'll be able to earn your trust and that of your companions."

"Me, too." Two years ago, she might have trusted this male already. She might have spilled her secrets at his easy smile. Done anything he and the council asked of her.

But those days were long gone. The world had shown its cruel ugly face in the years since her kidnapping and she'd sworn the people she cared for would never suffer the same fate.

Another easy smile and they rounded the manor, walking along the back side. "This is the only place on Alastríona where the four nations work together. Those from Fiadh keep the fires burning in our hearths and stoves. Aside from your room, of course, as a safety precaution. Those from Móirín keep our waters clean and flowing. They feed the plant life grown from the Fae of Brónach, thus both keep us fed. As a bonus, we're able to enjoy sights such as the ones before you."

"And Pádraigín?" she asked.

He smiled. "We keep this place hidden from the world and remind those of home when they need it."

"I've never met an illusionist," she admitted. Not even in the time she'd been kept as a slave, though she was sure none would have done her any favors.

His smile widened. "I have the ability myself, though we prefer the term glamour, as it's not quite an illusion."

"Oh, I'm sorry. I didn't know."

"Don't apologize, My Lady, most don't. It's our own fault for keeping ourselves secret from the outside world. The gift has followed my bloodline since before my father can recall." He seemed to note her curiosity. "Would you like to see it?"

Arianna bit her lip. "Do you have to touch me?" Because if he reached for her again, Rion might very well implode.

Niall's gaze drifted toward Rion, her mate even more pensive than he was moments ago, if that were possible.

But Niall only chuckled. "Unlike Móirín's extreme gift, we only need to be in the remote vicinity."

"Gift?" She interrupted. "I'd hardly call it a gift." She shuddered at the memories of the shriveled bodies she'd left on the battlefield. Their husk-like forms were one of the many terrors that haunted her nightmares.

His brows rose again. He seemed surprised by everything. Or was acting like it. "I wasn't aware you had the ability." She hadn't given it much thought really, she'd just . . . done it and regretted it but didn't regret it at the same time. Because in battle, it was her or them, and she'd chosen to live.

"Sometimes I wish I didn't."

"You've never seen it work to benefit life." Niall studied the garden as if looking for something. He pointed to a wilting flower. "Instead of taking the particles, try giving them back." She stared at him and he stepped back, expectant. Could she do that?

Arianna reached toward the purple flower, its petals barely clinging to the stem, and searched for the tiny current every living thing possessed. Instead of taking, Arianna studied the trickling current and carefully poured magic into its almost dry path. Like a creek suddenly flooded with water.

The flower perked and rose, spreading its petals toward the sun in silent greeting.

She supposed she'd once done something similar with Rion. When he'd been poisoned, she'd pulled the particles from his body and replaced them with water. She just hadn't realized—

"Gift," he said again and smiled at her. Arianna couldn't help but smile back. "Now," he led them back outside the hedge. "While I don't need to touch you, I will ask your permission before entering your mind."

"Will you be able to read it?"

He laughed again. "No, nothing like that. I'll simply be projecting images."

She nodded and Niall gestured toward a bench. "In case you get dizzy," he clarified.

Arianna could feel Rion's instincts raging against the idea, but she'd never encountered their magic before and if someone could project false images, then she needed to understand what she was up against in the event their promises ever proved false.

Arianna sat and Rion stood at her side, his intense gaze focused on Niall.

"Ready?" Niall asked and she nodded again.

Moments later, a breeze rustled through the garden and a chilling mist seeped through her head ever so carefully. She shivered. Gentle. Giving. Subtle. Another moment passed and Arianna wondered if anything had changed. Then she saw a single white butterfly floating in the breeze. It drifted toward her, then past. Three more appeared from around the hedge, then an entire flock covered the garden, their translucent wings beating as they soared around her, Niall, and her mate.

Rion didn't seem to notice them at all.

One landed on her finger and Arianna studied it closely. Dark veins shown through its velvet wings and its tiny feet walked across the back of her hand. It felt so real she would never have known it was a glamour unless he'd told her.

"This is incredible," she said.

Niall seemed more than satisfied. "Would you like to see more?"

"Please." Rion's magic circled her faster now and she felt his desperation down the bond. *It's okay*, she willed to him, but it didn't seem to make a difference.

The ground shifted beneath her feet, shimmering like the far off distance on a hot summer day, then she heard Niall's voice whispering in her head as if he too, were somewhere distant. "If you wish to stop, you have but to say the word."

Arianna gasped when the vision jolted, then she was standing in a great hall covered from floor to ceiling in white marble. Columns reached toward the ceiling and Arianna noticed familiar intricate carvings inlaid into the marble with gold. Vines and plants that seemed to tell their own complicated story.

"This is Brónach?" she asked.

Arianna thought she heard a hint of surprise in Niall's voice. "You've seen the palace of Nàdiar?"

"No, I—" Arianna paused. She didn't want to tell anyone about Rion's cabin, not when the place was so personal to him. It was a sanctuary he'd only shown her and a place they could run should they ever need to. "I've read a lot."

The answer seemed to satisfy his curiosity. "What you're seeing is a memory, so I'm afraid some parts won't be as clear as others."

The vision moved forward as if they were walking and they stepped through a pair of doors at the end of the hall. The vision blinked as if they'd lost a moment in time, then the doors to the throne room swung open.

Most of the figures darting past were nothing but shadows, remnants within the memory, but the image of the woman standing beside the High Lord of Brónach was as crystal clear as if Niall had studied every strand of her long auburn hair. It flowed to her waist in beautiful waves. A braid wrapped around her head, holding a thin silver crown in place.

Arianna couldn't see the male as clearly, though he carried Rion's strong jaw. Something in the shape of his eyes told Arianna this was his father, not his elder brother.

A memory. A memory of Rion's parents. Of his mother.

Arianna's head turned toward the blurry image of a child running down the aisle all the way into his mother's arms. His face came into focus for a moment and Arianna's heart pulled hard at the emerald green eyes and the same colored hair. The smile on his face spoke of a childhood full of love and admiration.

And the way the Lady of Nàdiar looked at her son. Arianna's heart swelled.

"She's beautiful," Arianna said a bit breathless. "Rion," she squeezed his hand. "Your mother is beautiful." Something hit her chest hard, some long buried pain that had Arianna clutching the area. The vision vanished suddenly and left her gripping the sides of the bench for balance.

"Are you all right, My Lady?" Niall made to reach for her again, but one glance at Rion had him stopping. But Rion wasn't watching Niall. His gaze was locked on her, full of anguish and longing.

"I'm fine," she promised. "Nothing to worry about." She took a slow breath and Rion averted his gaze. She thought she saw his throat bob and the swell that shot down the bond had tears pricking the corners of her eyes.

"Are you sure?"

She blinked them away quickly and gave Niall a pleasant smile. "That was incredible." She wished she could be alone with her mate right now, give him some space. She hadn't realized voicing it would hit him so hard. Instead, Arianna tried to divert Niall's attention.

"Can everyone with the ability to glamour do that?"

"Gods, no. Showing a memory only comes with decades of training. The mind is an easily distracted thing. It takes an incredible amount of focus. Most would only be able to shift the environment around you into something of less or equal value." He thought for a moment. "They could change someone's face or clothing for instance. Or whether a weapon is present."

She glanced over his clothing. "And how do I know you aren't casting a glamour right now?"

He smiled again. "I guess you wouldn't, though one can usually feel some sort of twist in reality. Some describe it as a brush or even a light breeze that seems to float past their mental barriers." She'd felt something like that when he'd showed her the vision, but she'd also felt it upon entering Ruadhán. The veil that kept them hidden from the world, she realized.

"Shall we continue the tour?"

Arianna nodded and Rion helped her stand. She cast a quick glance at her mate and he seemed to have reeled in his emotions. He'd mentioned her not tiptoeing around the subject and had thought that meant he'd come to terms with his mother's disappearance, but it clearly still bothered him a great deal.

Niall guided them back up the path and down another that led toward a series of unmarked structures. More immaculate gardens. More statues. More extravagance.

He spoke about each in turn. She learned the locations of the royal vaults, the temple, and the training barracks.

He pointed. "And if you head down that path, you'll find the market. There are a number of shops, as I'm sure you saw when you first arrived, but if you can't find what you're looking for, we can arrange to have it brought in from outside."

"I'm surprised you have shops at all."

"Did you think we were simply a floating castle in the sky?" Her face heated. "Ruadhán is self-sustaining. It's been that way for centuries."

Centuries.

"How old are you?"

Niall cocked his head. "I've lived for seven hundred thirty-nine years, though I've spent the last five hundred here."

Arianna almost tripped. Seven hundred? Holy gods, she *was* a child.

"Don't let it bother you," he said, brow furrowed. "The fact remains if we'd found you when your powers first emerged, you would have come to us younger than you are now."

"And you'd still have let me sit on a throne?"

Niall chuckled. "We'd have had rules for you until you came of age, of course, but yes, your input would still have been seriously considered. You are the one blessed by the gods, after all."

Arianna tilted her head toward the manor. "Are we going to tour the inside?"

Niall looked thoughtful. "I thought to let you discover that part on your own. If you wish to join the council meeting tomorrow, I'll have someone ready to escort you." He paused. "Unless you prefer not to attend."

Arianna shook her head. "No, I'd like to go." She needed to learn as much as she could about this city and those who ran it.

"Fantastic." His gaze darkened and darted toward her mate. "I should mention the council is rather strict about those in attendance."

Her mood shifted as if he'd plucked the sun from the sky. "He's my mate. He goes where I go."

Niall inclined his head and gave her a sorrowful look. "I understand completely. It took quite some convincing for them to allow his presence in the city, but I'm afraid they won't budge on this matter. Many harbor deep-seated feelings toward his past actions."

Her anger bubbled over, threatening to burst free but—could she fault them for it? Her instincts wanted to rage against ill feelings directed at her mate, but was that logical? No. He'd hurt people, and their feelings were something she'd have to consider as queen. It would be a long road of healing for everyone.

"Talon will attend in my place," Rion said. She raised a brow at him.

Niall shifted on his feet. "I'm afraid the male doesn't carry the . . . appropriate social standing necessary to warrant hearing the details within that room."

Arianna flashed her teeth. "One of them goes," she stated. "Or I don't."

CHAPTER TWENTY

ARIANNA

iall had dipped his head in apology then dismissed himself, leaving her and Rion to explore the interior rooms of the manor alone.

"You lied to him," Rion said.

Arianna studied painting after painting down the first floor hall. She gave Rion a sheepish grin. "Omitting the truth is different than lying." Word manipulation was the only way a Fae *could* lie unless they were talking to a human or half-breed.

"Why omit anything?" Rion asked.

She fidgeted with the hem of her shirt. "I just didn't want him knowing something you don't is all."

Rion pulled her to a stop and brushed the hair away from her face. His fingers lingered and he studied her eyes as if he could memorize every hue of blue within the iris. "What is it? Your favorite flower."

Arianna pulled away with a mischievous look. "Perhaps I won't tell you." She glanced over her shoulder with her arms clasped behind her back and a teasing smile on her face.

Then Rion spun her, his hand behind her head to prevent it from hitting the wall as he pressed her against it. She gasped when his hungry lips moved against her own, reminding her exactly what his mouth and tongue could do.

She was at his mercy and trembled beneath his touch. Sudden need had her grasping his shirt. Rion moved his mouth with aching slowness, drinking her in, owning her, claiming her.

He pulled back slightly, leaving her breathless and reeling. "Will you tell me now?"

"That's not fair."

He smirked. "I never promised to play fair."

His gaze flicked to her lips then back to her eyes and Arianna thought she might implode from the feelings barreling through her. "Irises," she swallowed. "Purple irises."

Rion didn't pull away. Instead, his fingers caressed a tendril of loose hair hanging along the side of her face. His knuckles brushed down the length of her throat then over her collarbone. Lower. "It suits you."

Arianna couldn't breathe.

Someone cleared their throat and she jolted. They were in the middle of the hall where anyone could see them. Suddenly Rion was too close, his roaming hands too public, but her mate was slow to move. Reluctant to pull away.

His gaze locked onto the male standing across the hall. Perfect eyebrows, strong jawline, and eyes as pitch-black as his hair. Fear pulsed from him. He bowed. "My deepest apologies for interrupting." His straight hair hung over round eyes as he tried to look everywhere else but at the couple.

Arianna noted the familiar Pádraigín scent as she took in his green tunic and dark brown pants. The male even wore a braided leather bracelet on his left wrist with small jade stones threaded throughout.

"The Regent sent me to find you in case you required assistance."

Rion straightened and stepped away from her. "You mean he sent you to spy on us."

The male had enough sense to step back, his head bowing as low as it could while maintaining eye contact. He looked like he wanted to run. "Yes," the male stammered. "Though he didn't want you to know that part." His words were rushed, clipped. "I-I wouldn't dare intervene, though."

"Why?" Rion demanded.

The male lifted his head slightly, his gaze darting to her then back to Rion. "Because she's The Divine and it isn't my place to question the queen."

She regained her senses then placed a gentle hand on Rion's chest. Her mate regarded her with eyes full of unspoken promises. "I'd love to see the library, if you have the time."

The male's eyes lit up, but he maintained an air of caution. "O-Of course, please follow me."

Rion's magic didn't stop moving around them and the male kept a healthy distance away. "I'm Gavin, by the way." His gaze flicked toward Rion, trying to gauge his reactions. Submissive, almost . . . childish.

"How old are you?"

"Seventeen."

Rion's magic relaxed at that. "The Regent sent a child to spy on us?"

"I resent that," he said, then quickly stepped back as if he'd forgotten the threat that stood before him.

"Rion isn't going to hurt you."

"Unless you hurt her," Rion added.

"Hurt her? She's the queen," he said, as if that was reason enough. "To even be talking to you," his face turned red, "gods, I didn't even bow properly, I'm sorry, I—"

"Don't," Arianna said when he made to drop to one knee. She glanced around, glad to find the hall empty. "Please, I'm not really used to the whole queen thing yet."

The male smiled and for some reason she knew she could trust him. She couldn't explain it. Maybe it was the childlike mirth in his eyes or the fact that they were basically the same age.

"How long have you been here?" she asked, taking a few steps down the hall.

Gavin jumped forward to lead the way. "A year. I mostly function as Lord Niall's assistant. I keep track of the paperwork and take notes at the meetings."

"The council meetings?"

"Yes, I'll be the one leading you there in the morning. As long as you want to go; Niall made sure to stress that you're free to decide if you're not ready. I mean, of course you're ready, I just mean to say he doesn't want you to feel—"

Arianna held up her hand and he quieted. "I'll be there and I appreciate your help." Silence settled over them as they continued, but the way the male kept wringing his hands together told Arianna he was brimming with questions and no shortage of curiosity.

"What do you do when you're not working?" she asked to break the silence.

"I read. The library is my second home, but I guess it'll be yours too, with all the studying you have to do." He grimaced. "Sorry, I just overheard the council talking. I didn't mean to insinuate—"

"It's okay. It's actually refreshing to have someone talk to me like I'm a real person instead of," she paused.

"A queen."

"Yeah."

He loosed a sigh of relief. "Well, just make sure to tell me if I do anything to offend." His gaze darted to Rion. "Preferably before you resort to violence. I swear if I do something, I don't mean it." He scratched the back of his head. "What's your name?"

Rion's brow rose and her mate actually looked a bit taken back by Gavin's question.

"Rion."

The male slapped his forehead. "Right, of Brónach. I knew that." He grimaced again. "They keep threatening to send me back to Pádraigín if I don't get my facts memorized."

"Why is someone so young the Regent's assistant?"

"We're related. They're all about family bloodlines in Pádraigín and I'm the only remaining living nephew." He grimaced at her sympathetic expression. "Don't worry, I never knew my older siblings. They passed long before I was born." He cleared his throat. "Lord Niall actually wanted my sister, but she was blessed with a little one recently and refused to leave the child. He wasn't happy when I first arrived, but I think I'm growing on him."

They turned a corner and Gavin ran ahead, wrapping his hand around the brass handles attached to a set of thick wooden double doors. "My Queen," he said proudly. "May I present to you the most fantastic room in the entire city of Ruadhán." He made an exaggerated bow and pulled one door open. "Welcome to the grand library of the elders."

Arianna thought she had prepared herself. She thought it would be somewhat similar to the one back in Levea. But when Gavin opened the door, Arianna forgot how to breathe.

She wandered inside, utterly captivated, and her gaze swept from top to bottom of the four story library. Three times the size. It had to be at least three times the size of the one in Levea.

A glass roof let in slightly dimmed natural sunlight that shone on a small garden in the center of the room. Water flowed down five stone leaves, each growing smaller until emptying in a crystalline pool. Gold and black koi swam beneath the water's clear surface, seemingly unaware of the queen who stood at the edge of their world.

Along every wall and spreading across the floor on all levels were shelves upon shelves of books. Vines wrapped around thick wooden bookcases and the heads of various snarling creatures were carved into the aisles. Their eyes watched those within as if they knew every secret and every soul who'd ever walked the polished floors.

Magic buzzed heavily in the air and Arianna spotted those responsible. Some manipulated the vines, guiding them to better sunlight or away from precious tomes. Others pulled water from the air, keeping the humidity in the space low to preserve their ancient texts. Móirín scribes watered the plants and Arianna thought she even scented someone manning a fire on the second level.

"What do you think?" Gavin asked, his excitement obvious from the way he bounced on his toes.

"It's marvelous," she said, taking another step forward and spinning to observe the space. She met Rion's gaze and found him watching her with a crooked smile.

Gavin bowed. "I have some other things to attend to. I'll let you enjoy the sights." She nodded, though knew he only left to give her time to explore. There was so much to look at, so many pages to explore.

"You like books."

"I *love* books," she corrected. Rion had already seen her room, but perhaps he hadn't realized how much she adored them. "I can't remember the last time I've read one."

Rion took her hand and she relished in the feel of his callused palm. "We'll have to fix that. What do you prefer?"

Arianna's face flushed. She'd hoped back in her room that he hadn't looked too closely at the titles. "Nothing you'd read, I'm sure."

"Try me."

She lowered her eyes to study one of the spindly green plants in the pond and the fish that nibbled at its roots. "I like romances. Fairy tales."

Rion snorted. "Of course you do."

He led her toward the giant carpeted staircase where at least four people could walk shoulder to shoulder comfortably. "What about you?" she asked.

"Nothing of the fiction variety." Rion scanned the shelves as they walked up and up, seeming to know exactly where he was going. She couldn't stop gawking at the aisles, the decor, the plants thriving beside delicate volumes that looked as though they needed protection from the foliage.

"Maybe I should take notes from your books," she said, her eyes still roaming. Arianna imagined Rion reading titles that taught strategy and tracking, and all manner of war related topics that would give him an advantage over his opponents.

They stopped on the third floor and Rion pulled her to the left. "You won't like them, but they're irrelevant until you satisfy your craving for a happy ending and true love." He tilted his head back and gave her a teasing smile that had a blush rising to her cheeks.

"I shouldn't have told you."

"I already had an idea from the books in your room, I just wasn't sure if you still liked them after . . . well, since you're older." She was thankful he didn't linger on the subject of her captivity, even if it had brought them together.

They walked down the main part of the aisle, then Rion slowed as he scanned the categories listed at the end of each shelf. She let him lead her between two of the ancient structures where he paused, gesturing to the spines.

Arianna stepped forward and hesitated. "I really shouldn't. Aren't there other things I should be doing?"

Rion reached over her shoulder and his scent engulfed her, dragging her anxieties to a full halt before he handed her a small book bound in leather.

"You, of all people, deserve a break. There's nothing wrong with a book."

Arianna ran her fingertips down the spine, tracing the gold letters pressed into it. Rion guided her further down the aisle where the next row of shelves split wider. Tables lined the area, at least two between each shelf, and her mate pulled a chair out for her to sit.

She lifted her brows. "Wait, right now?"

He smiled, and it reminded Arianna of the child she'd seen in Niall's memory. She wished the image had been clearer, that Arianna could have watched the boy play at his mother's feet if only for a few moments more.

"We have at least an hour before dinner."

Arianna stared at the book again. "What are you going to do?"

Rion pulled the chair out next to her and sat down, tugging Arianna into her own. "I'll be right here."

Arianna scoffed. "I am not reading while you sit here bored out of your mind."

Her mate gave her another childish smile. "I hoped you might read it to me."

Her face flushed again and she glanced down the aisle. She hadn't noticed anyone at the nearby tables. The last thing she wanted to do was disturb anyone's studies.

Out of excuses, Arianna adjusted her seat and opened to the first page. She glanced at Rion again, suddenly feeling shy. She'd read to Ellie countless times. Even Talon had joined them before the fireplace while she read tales of heroes who rescued their lovers. "You're sure?"

Rion leaned forward, propping his chin up on a closed fist. "Read me a story, Arianna."

CHAPTER TWENTY-ONE

ARIANNA

Arianna read well into dinner. She lost herself in the pages of the story like she hadn't done in an age, living through the first part of the character's trials like they were her own. It was magical, freeing, and Rion clung to every word.

He tensed when others crept near, but no one came into view, as if they somehow knew the pair needed the time to themselves.

Arianna didn't mind. In fact, she barely noticed anything until her stomach growled. Rion had gently closed the book, making her promise to finish it soon.

She would. When he looked at her like that, Arianna would have happily given him anything.

Dinner was lively again with Talon and Ellie detailing their busy first days. All parties had a lot to learn and it appeared they'd be passing one another in the library frequently.

Talon said he needed acclimate himself with the layout and Ruadhán's guards. He needed to learn their rotations then include Móirín's elite so his warriors could become better acquainted with their new allies. And watch their movements. When they weren't guarding the city, Móirín's elite would guard her—from a distance, Talon assured.

Ellie had busied herself meeting the council members, hunting each of them down to introduce herself. She'd called them old snobs a little too loudly for Arianna's comfort, but no one in the dining hall seemed to notice. Arianna was thankful for the musicians.

It wasn't until they were up the stairs and almost to their room that Arianna let out a deep sigh, the muscles in her chest unraveling.

Rion was immediately attentive, running his hands up and down her arm. "Do you need anything?"

She needed a lot of things. Him in a bath with her. To sleep for an entire year undisturbed. To stuff so many chocolates in her mouth she'd be sick. She'd processed so much information and seen so many sights that it all felt like a dream. She wasn't even sure their meeting with Niall that morning had actually happened.

Arianna was thankful Rion had made her settle down with the book, but she still felt drained, like she hadn't had a moment to herself in months.

Arianna looked longingly at the double doors at the end of the hall. "Do you think we could sneak out for some fresh air?"

"Say the word and you're back in Móirín." He wasn't kidding.

Arianna interlaced their fingers. "I think I'll settle for the balcony view Niall promised us."

Arianna didn't miss the way Rion stiffened at the male's name, but he didn't comment on it, either.

When they reached the doors, she pushed them open, letting the crisp night air wash through her.

A loveseat and a set of chairs stood upon the balcony with two tables that held vases of fresh flowers. Vines crawled up from the first floor, their stems so woody she was sure she could have climbed down without the fear of falling.

Everything they'd walked through earlier lay before her. The maze of hedges stretching toward the far gate, the bench she'd sat upon, and the arches that now had large white moonflowers reaching up to greet the crescent moon overhead.

Arianna wasn't sure she'd ever grow used to the beauty. She rubbed the scars on her wrists. She couldn't. Not until everyone experienced the same life. Until everyone had a choice.

"Better?" Rion asked.

She rested her hands on the edge of the balcony and leaned her head against his shoulder. "Much." Her mate made a satisfied sound and she traced her finger over a leaf. "What about you?" she asked. "How are you handling all this?" She knew he'd struggled around Niall. Everyone knew the ancient texts and who the male was prophesied to become. Not to mention the new area and dangers Ruadhán brought. Rion had followed her to this place, but . . . had she stopped to ask if he even wanted to come?

Guilt washed through her. Had she forced him here?

"I'm happy as long as you're happy."

Arianna tilted her face to look at him. "If you don't want to be here, you can tell me. Gods, Rion," she shook her head, "I've been so focused on everything else that I didn't stop to consid—"

Rion pulled her close and pressed an achingly gentle kiss to her lips, but before she could deepen it, he leaned back. "I want to be wherever you are. No matter where that takes us."

Arianna smiled softly. "I know, but you should get a say in where that place is."

His gaze turned serious. "I will never hinder you. If you feel you're needed here, then I'm here. If you want to run back to Móirín, I'd make it happen." He swallowed. "And if you ever decide you want to leave this continent altogether, I'll make sure we're never found."

Arianna tapped his nose. "I think this mating bond has gone to your head."

He took her hand and pressed a lingering kiss to the inside of her wrist before putting it against his face. A movement he wouldn't have done with anyone months ago. She trailed her palm down his neck and stopped over his heart.

"You don't understand." His voice was thick with emotion. "I never thought I'd have something like this. I never thought I'd get the chance to feel this way about anyone or have them feel anything for me in return. I'd walk through fire and sell my soul to keep it even if it were only for a few seconds more."

Hot tears pricked the corners of her eyes. She recalled the horrid memories he'd shared the night the bond had presented itself. A father and teacher who tried to murder him. A lover—she growled, unable to stop the reaction, and Rion's magic flew up to surround them.

"What's wrong?"

She shook her head. "I was just thinking."

"About what?"

"The ones who hurt you." She clenched her fists. "I hate them so much."

He closed his eyes and pressed his forehead to hers. His fingers trailed along her spine, tracing the scars through the fabric of her shirt. "I know."

A comfortable silence filled the space and they stood in one another's arms for a long while. She studied the shadows among the hedges, swearing some moved of their own accord, but whenever she tried to look closer, they returned to their normal state.

Guards patrolled below, some looking up to glance at the pair before turning away. Animals tried to blend in with the natural surroundings, but Arianna knew the prowling creatures were more than they appeared.

Rion caressed her hair then grief barreled down the bond so heavy it had her gasping. Arianna tilted her head to look at him again.

"What's wrong?"

His fingers flexed. "I wish I could have seen her," he said, his voice whisper quiet.

"Who—" she started then stopped herself. His mother. A female who'd disappeared from their lives without rhyme or reason. A female they'd presumed dead.

Arianna had lost her mother too, but she couldn't fathom the pain of never knowing. To wonder every day if she were in trouble, if she'd abandoned them, or if her body lay in an unmarked grave.

"Was there ever a hint about what might have happened to her?" Arianna studied his emotions down the bond carefully. She didn't want to upset him too much, but if he wanted to talk she was ready to listen.

Rion shook his head. "None. Despite what my father did, I know he loved my mother. I understand the bond now, so I can honestly say he exhausted every possible avenue to find her."

And he'd failed.

"I'm sorry," she said. "I didn't know what Niall would show me."

A slight smile crossed his face. "You apologize too much for things out of your control."

She rested her head against his shoulder again, feeling the ache in his heart within her own. Why had Niall chosen that particular memory? He could have shown her anything and yet he'd chosen something that would strike out against her mate. Arianna knew it wasn't a coincidence.

Niall seemed genuine, but that one moment revealed more about his character than he probably realized. He was just another person on a long list who wanted Rion out of her life.

Arianna clenched her teeth. If he tried to provoke her mate again, she'd address it with him directly.

She tightened her hand around Rion's and wondered how his father had coped with the pain. To feel that bond, alive and thriving, and be unable to reach the one you cherished above all others. Perhaps he'd declared his mate dead for the sake of his children. Maybe he'd continued the search in secret.

Arianna sighed and tried to shift her thoughts to tomorrow. She'd be alone with the council, a group of people she didn't know. Rion couldn't come with her, at least not yet. It was another thing she'd address with the council, but the more she thought about everything, the more she wondered if she even wanted to be here.

"Are you really okay with Talon escorting me tomorrow?"

He played with a strand of her hair. "No, but given no alternative, I'd choose him to protect you a thousand times over."

He might hate Talon, but at least Rion trusted her friend enough to protect her.

"Will you be okay while I'm gone?"

He huffed out a laugh. "Honestly?" She nodded. "Tomorrow is going to completely wreck me. I detest the thought of you under another's protection. I hate everything about it and it makes me want to roar at the stars for the hand fate dealt me." He paused, collecting himself. "I trust you, please don't mistake that. It's not you that—"

She pressed a finger to his lips. "I'm going tomorrow." He nodded. "But only tomorrow. I'll tell them if they want another meeting with me, then my mate will be there or I won't. I will not let them shove me around."

"Good." Rion tilted her head and trailed kisses down her throat. His magic danced across her skin, caressing her with a featherlight touch.

"I love that," she breathed.

Rion's mouth didn't stop moving. "Love what?"

"Your magic. The feel of it."

He pulled back just enough to stare into her eyes. "I thought I might have been annoying you with it."

She raised up on her toes and Rion tilted his head to the side, granting her access to his neck. A gesture he'd do for no other. "How far can you reach with it?"

"Far." His hands were already under her shirt, fingers playing at the edge of her pants.

"Far enough to keep it with me tomorrow?"

"You'd want that?"

"Yes."

His lips met hers again. "Then you'll have it. Even if I have to sit right outside the door."

She giggled. "And if I asked for the moon?"

He tilted his head up toward the half crescent in the starry sky. "Then I'll spend the rest of my life reaching for it."

CHAPTER TWENTY-TWO

ARIANNA

Arianna stood inside their closet wearing a light green silk gown with thin straps at the shoulders. They'd just gotten out of a warm bath where she'd taken full advantage of the soaps, shampoos, and lotions.

But now she was faced with an impossible decision. The dresses hanging before her were all delicate flowing masterpieces fit for a queen. She loved them and knew someone had poured their heart and soul into the fabrics. But no matter how long she stared, Arianna couldn't convince herself to put one on.

She'd woken early from another nightmare and Rion had kissed away the remnants of her darkest days. But the haunting feelings continued to plague her, making Arianna feel vulnerable in a way she couldn't stand.

Arianna ran her hands over the fabrics again and sighed. She'd worn a dress for her father, but that was when she'd been numb to the world. When she'd missed Rion so much it felt as though her heart was bleeding. And she hadn't even discovered they were mates yet.

Rion stood on the threshold, fully dressed in midnight black. The short sleeves wrapped around his muscled arms in a way that had her thoughts diverting from her decision.

Arianna cleared her throat. "They want to see a queen," she said as if that was enough explanation for how long she was taking. But she didn't feel like a queen.

"Who do you want to see?" he asked.

She chewed her lip. "You're an artist, what would you dress me in?"

Rion raised a brow. "You want me to choose?"

"I just—" Gods, why was this so hard?

Rion pushed off from the wall and gently guided her toward the rear of the closet. "I'd start with something you're comfortable in, and clearly that isn't a dress."

"But they have expectations."

"You think *I* care about others' expectations?"

She grinned, unable to hold it back. It reminded her of a time when she'd been concerned about his reputation. "No, I guess you wouldn't."

"Then you shouldn't either."

Right, like that was possible. She was only meeting the most influential group of Fae on the entire continent.

Arianna eventually pulled a pair of black slacks from a shelf. The material unfolded like liquid in her hands, the fabric light and flowing. She studied the shirts and reached for a long sleeved, light blue top with cream colored buttons.

Simple and something she could move in.

Safe. Safe. Safe, she chanted to herself. She wouldn't need to fight. Still, it didn't stop Arianna from grabbing a few knives.

She found a matching belt and eyed the jewelry before settling on a pair of silver teardrop earrings and the necklace Myrna had gifted her.

The items felt out of place in her hands. So new and such a waste when there were children outside with barely enough food to fill their stomachs.

But that's exactly why she was here. To make a difference. It's why she cared about the council's opinion of her at all. Because if she wanted to change the world on a grand scale, then she needed to impress the people with enough power to do it.

THEY MISSED breakfast again and Arianna was beginning to believe it was females who lacked any sort of self-control where their mates were concerned.

To her growling stomach's relief, Victoria met them in the hall and had the cooks warm a quick meal. Not long after, Gavin appeared in the doorway along with Talon, who surveyed the young male with a questioning gaze.

Arianna took a breath, wiped her hands on a napkin, then walked toward her friend with Rion in tow.

The males exchanged glances and Rion's jaw ticked, but Arianna leaned up on her toes to kiss him.

Rion addressed Talon. "You'll watch her?"

"With my life."

Arianna huffed. "I'm not helpless, you know." The males smiled a bit, breaking the tension. Gavin didn't move.

"I'll see you after?" Rion asked.

She nodded, pressed her forehead to his again, then stepped away. Her heart tugged hard as he walked down the hall, but grains around her wrist told Arianna he wouldn't be far. And he could sense her emotions down the bond. He'd come if anything happened.

"Morning," Gavin offered.

"Good morning," Arianna replied.

Talon continued his scrutiny. "Who's this?"

Gavin extended his hand. "Gavin of Pádraigín. I'm Lord Niall's assistant and here to escort Lady Arianna to the council meeting."

"I have it covered," Talon said.

Gavin pouted. "Can you at least pretend I'm leading you there then?"

Talon raised a brow but Arianna said, "If it puts you in your uncle's good graces, lead the way."

He beamed and Talon looked between them. "You know him?"

"We met yesterday when he escorted me to the library."

"What did you think of it? Best room in the city, right?"

"She hasn't seen the whole city."

Gavin slowed to walk at her other side. "Trust me, it's the best, though there's also a chocolate shop in the city square that's to die for." He lowered his voice. "Just don't tell Fiona I said that."

"Who's Fiona?" she asked.

"The self-proclaimed best dessert chef in Ruadhán. She and Sorcha have a contest at every party to see whose desserts are eaten faster."

Arianna didn't ask who Sorcha was, assuming she was the other pastry chef.

"I'll be sure to try both."

The trio paraded down the hall, their boots echoing off the marble floors. Servants and court ladies flitted past and Arianna caught many giggling when they glimpsed Talon.

"What's that about?"

"I don't want to talk about it."

A smile crawled to her lips and Talon turned away with a hint of pink on his cheeks. "Oh, now I have to know."

"It was nothing," he insisted.

Gavin laughed and Talon shot him a glare.

"What?" she pressed.

"Your friend was training outside yesterday morning."

Arianna waited for an explanation, but Talon turned away. "So?"

"At least half the court females were watching him from the windows. They've been gossiping ever since. They're beside themselves."

A smiled curled her lips. "Okay, but surely they've seen someone train before. What's so special?"

"He was soaked and wasn't wearing a shirt. By the time he realized they were there—"

"If you want to keep your teeth, you'll stop talking."

Gavin snapped his mouth shut but Arianna burst out laughing. She gripped her sides and doubled over.

"Haha," Talon mocked, but she glimpsed a smile.

The trio rounded a corner and they collected themselves in preparation for meeting the council. She'd seen them on her first day but hadn't been properly introduced.

They arrived at the door moments later and a guard bowed to her before twisting the golden handle.

Conversation in the room halted.

Two males and two females stood in a tight group, their hands paused mid movement.

Gavin scurried in and headed for the far corner. No one looked at him. They were all focused on her. Arianna swallowed hard and walked in, reminding herself that they'd invited her and she wasn't intruding.

Arianna was suddenly glad for the weapons she'd brought. The council studied Talon and for a moment, she feared they might order him to leave. Would she walk out with him, or demand he be allowed to stay?

Their gazes shifted then, turning . . . softer. Kinder. Welcoming.

The male who'd first escorted her through the city inclined his head. "Please, join us." He gestured to a pair of chairs across the round table.

They sat when she did. Talon took up a position at her left, standing close with his hands clasped behind his back.

The door opened again and Arianna twisted in her seat to find Niall pausing on the threshold. He glanced at the large clock hanging on the rear wall and sighed in relief. "For a second I thought myself late."

"My Lord." A female with straight black hair and a thin frame rose, but Niall gestured for her to remain seated. "Since we're all present, should we begin early?"

They nodded and shuffled the papers before them. Niall crossed the room and pulled out the only remaining chair at her side but thankfully slid it an entire foot away before sitting down.

She exhaled in relief. Close, but not too close. She wasn't sure if he'd care about the promise he'd made to Rion without her mate present. She hoped Rion hadn't felt too much of her anxiety. The last thing she wanted was for him to come barreling through the doors before introductions had even been made.

The guard stationed at the door closed it and everyone in the room fell silent. They were staring at her, waiting, and for a moment Arianna wondered if they expected her to speak first. She was their queen, but Ellie was the one who'd always been present during her father's council meetings.

"Forgive us," Niall said, startling her. "We're a bit excited to be in your presence." He gestured to the other four in the room, seeming to ignore Gavin in the far corner. "Some of us have waited a very long time to meet you and we often wondered if we'd fade from existence before we were given the chance." He leaned forward and clasped his hands on the table. "But now you're here." Niall gave a nervous laugh. "And probably more than a bit overwhelmed yourself."

Arianna let her shoulders relax. "A bit," she admitted.

"Let's start with introductions then, shall we?" Niall gestured to the first male, the one who'd escorted her to the manor. His deep set eyes were kind, and now that she wasn't overwhelmed by the sounds and smells of the city streets, Arianna could focus on him.

"This is Declan. He oversees Ruadhán's main affairs, works with the other council members when shifting supplies and finances, and is also head of decisions when I'm not available."

"It's a pleasure to officially be introduced, My Lady." The male stood and bowed at the waist. Shaggy brown hair hung to his chin and when he looked at her again, she noted his deep brown eyes. Arianna scented the air. Fiadh. The male was definitely from Fiadh.

Niall pointed to the female on Declan's right. The same one who'd stood to greet him. "Meegan oversees the guards stationed throughout the city and keeps careful tabs on any skirmishes that arise between nations. Should we ever find ourselves faced with the possibility of a confrontation, she'll be the one we turn to." Brónach.

Meegan bowed and sat back down. The female might have been small, but something in her steely onyx gaze told Arianna she wasn't to be trifled with.

The next male stood without Niall's prompting. Short cropped light blond hair, bright blue eyes, and definitely from Móirín. "I'm Felic, overseer of the city's finances. Should you ever need to enter the vault, please don't hesitate to ask." Arianna watched his fingers wrap around something beneath his tunic. A key? The male bowed, then sat again.

"And finally we have our dear Fina who has studied the ancient texts for centuries and has memorized every line written therein."

The female stood, but the seriousness behind her hazel gaze made Arianna want to run in the other direction. Her skin was so pale it seemed to be crafted of marble and her waist length black hair did nothing to add warmth to her cheeks. Courtesy of too much time spent within a temple.

Small beads were woven through her hair and she wore gold bracelets and a necklace carrying a pendant that depicted a crescent moon with a star in the center.

The chosen symbol of those who worshiped The Divine.

She rapped long fingernails on the table. "The mistreatment of our fellow priest will not be overlooked. We expect an apology and an offering to be made at the cathedral."

"Fina," Niall's tone was a warning and the way they glared at one another told Arianna they'd had this conversation already.

But she slammed her hand on the table. "We will not be ridiculed. What they did to our brother was of the highest disrespect and we demand retribution."

"I'm sorry," Arianna said carefully. "I'm afraid I don't know what you mean."

Arianna swore the female's temple pulsed. "That creature you let accompany you stripped one of our brothers of his robes and stuffed him into a wagon as if he were nothing more than a trunk of luggage." Arianna groaned, knowing full well her sister was to blame.

"Later," Niall hissed, his tone far sharper than before. This time the female straightened. She still wore an irritated expression, but Fina sat back in her seat and crossed her arms. Pádraigín. Arianna might have asked the female about their mysterious city if she didn't look so ready to murder someone.

Niall sighed. "Forgive that . . . outburst, if you can."

Fina visibly pouted. How was Arianna supposed to make it up to them? And what kind of offering did they want? Hopefully nothing of the living variety.

"I've been told you've already met my assistant, Gavin."

He gave a little wave and Arianna waved back. "I did, he was very helpful yesterday."

Fina sat straighter. "Helpful how?"

"He escorted me to the library."

"She has an amazing reading voice." Gavin's face reddened before he admitted, "I might have stuck around."

Arianna returned his smile. "That's okay. I knew I had a small audience."

Instead of looking annoyed, as Gavin had claimed he often did, Niall seemed pleased. "It's good to see you already making friends. Do you enjoy reading?"

Arianna nodded, feeling a bit self-conscious. "I know I have other duties to attend to, though."

Niall chuckled. "You just arrived after a long journey. And, as I understand it, you suffered quite an ordeal prior." His gaze traveled to her covered wrists and Arianna had to resist the urge to hide them beneath the table. "Rest assured, you have nothing you're obligated to attend to so soon."

That took her by surprise. "You don't need me?"

Meegan spoke, her voice far softer than Arianna thought it would be. "My dear, you're our queen, of course we need you. What Lord Niall is trying to convey is that there's no need to stress. You're entitled to a book, a stroll, an entire decade to acclimate if you wish it."

Niall nodded. "She's right. It's just as important for you to have a clear head."

A decade? Did they just expect her to prop her feet up while the world suffered? What about peace? What about the humans and half-breeds who died of neglect every day?

Niall continued, oblivious to her inner turmoil. "This room is where we've met every week for the last few centuries. As the Regent, I've overseen a few major developments, but we've kept everything minimal and in working order in preparation for your arrival. You're welcome to attend these meetings anytime you wish, and your input will be valued above all else." Niall looked at her with something like reverence in his gaze. "I anticipate great changes in our future."

She swallowed. "No pressure."

His eyes widened. "None at all, My Lady. I simply mean things have been stagnant in recent years and it will be nice to finally have something more to discuss than just numbers and parties." His gaze darkened and something in the pit of her stomach clenched. "As such, I think it's time we discuss a very important detail."

Her stomach flipped. She'd been hoping to speak with him privately, not in front of a group that would judge her as she rejected the one prophesied to be her mate. Arianna braced herself.

"We need to arrange the welcome ball."

Her jaw fell slack as Declan nodded his agreement. "The citizens are tearing apart the hedges hoping to catch a glimpse of their queen. I'd like to stop ordering them fixed every five minutes."

"Not to mention the security issues it's bringing about," Meegan added. "It's difficult to want to punish those who simply wish to pay tribute." Her eyes met Arianna's. "I can't say I blame them."

"What about the coronation," Felic asked. "There should be a ball for that as well."

"Yes, and afterward, we'll travel from nation to nation with a—"

"Have you not seen the riots already forming?" Meegan interrupted. "We can't risk taking her out in public."

"She needs to be seen by the people."

"I will not risk our queen's life just so they can see her."

Felic raised his hand. "Are we paying for both through the royal coffers or by other means?"

They argued back and forth, making decisions for her without so much as glancing her way. One spoke of safety, another of presentation. It wasn't until they mentioned who would meet her at the end of the coronation's procession that their tones turned hushed.

Niall cleared his throat. "The plan was not to overwhelm our new queen today." The council members snapped their mouths closed and a few ducked their heads in a sheepish manner. "Forgive them; again, this is all a bit exciting for us. How about we just focus on the welcome ball?"

"Will the High Lords attend?" Arianna asked, wondering if she'd have to face her father again so soon.

Niall shook his head. "They'll send their representatives."

"Wouldn't it—" she paused when every eye snapped toward her. Arianna tried to sound more confident than she felt. "Wouldn't it be better to simply have one ball?"

Fina chuckled but Niall answered with a slight glimmer of amusement in his gaze. "While we appreciate your frugal nature and humility, those of us who are older are always searching for a reason to celebrate. It keeps eternity interesting. And what better reason could we have than the arrival of our queen?"

"If she's even legitimate," Fina added with a touch of malice.

"Legitimate?"

Niall glared at the female, his gaze so icy she actually shrank away. Niall grimaced. "There are . . . rumors. We have a long history of false hope. After a few demonstrations, I'm sure you'll win everyone over."

Arianna looked at each of the council members in turn and noted the way Fina kept glaring. "But some of *you* doubt me?" Declan turned away.

Niall kept his voice soft. "We want to believe, it's just that The Divine is a miracle and miracles come around so seldom for our kind."

Arianna stood and the council watched her carefully. She pulled a knife from her belt. Meegan straightened. "I'd cut my own hand, but I'm unable to heal myself." She motioned to Talon. "I'd ask him to do it, but I don't think that would help the rumors since he's close to me. So," she stared into their expectant faces, "who wants to volunteer?"

Niall huffed out another laugh, but she could tell he was just as curious. Eager even. "I don't think we need—"

"I will." Gavin's voice was breathless, chest heaving as he stood, notepad forgotten. No one berated him or offered themselves in his place. Arianna crossed the room. He met her half way and rolled up his sleeve.

Arianna pressed the knife against his skin and hesitated. Maybe they sh—

"Don't worry," he assured. "I can take it."

Arianna would have liked to just cut his finger, but she knew it wouldn't erase the doubt from their minds, and if she wanted them to listen to her, then all doubt had to be eliminated.

With a swift apology, Arianna dug the blade in deep and quickly drew it across his forearm. Gavin flinched and gasped as his blood welled up before rolling down his arm and dripping onto the marble floor. She turned to the council to ensure they were watching. No one blinked.

The blood tugged at her darkest memories and the lives she'd claimed. She prayed no one would ever find out. If they did, they might not think so highly of their new queen.

Arianna rested her palm over the wound and her magic spurred to life. The grains around her arm stopped moving, as if they, too, were watching. Her palms illuminated and she let that light pour into the deep cut. The skin knit itself back together with an invisible thread until all that was left was the blood staining his skin. When she looked up, the male's dark eyes glistened with unshed tears.

Then he slowly sank to his knees, keeping her hand in his. His voice shook. "I pledge myself to your service," he said. "You have my undying loyalty from now until the day I'm no longer part of this world."

Her lips parted at his sincerity. She nodded, unsure how to reply, then turned to find awestruck faces around the room, Niall's included.

Arianna cleared her throat and pulled Gavin to his feet. "Does that clear things up?"

Niall opened his mouth to speak, stopped, then tried again. "Yes, yes, that was brilliant."

Gavin bowed and stepped back a few paces.

"Perhaps," Niall said again, his voice still unsteady. "That is enough for one day." The others nodded and began collecting their things. While they'd appeared graceful before, now they fumbled. Fina swiped at her eyes, her anger no longer present.

Arianna wasn't sure what to do with herself until Niall drew her attention. Talon stepped forward at the same moment Niall did. "My Lady," Niall said with reverence in his tone. "I wondered if I might have a word with you?" She glanced at Talon and Niall's gaze followed. "Your companion is welcome to join us."

"Sure," she said, still studying those in the room. The pair followed Niall into the wide hall, rounded one corner, then into the gardens.

Warm spring air greeted her as they continued toward a circular platform with a stone handrail. It stood on the edge of the gardens, floral patterns lining the stones beneath their feet.

Talon leaned against the outside wall of the manor, his gaze focusing on something in the distance.

"That was quite a performance."

She blushed. Maybe it had been a little too bold. "I just didn't want anyone to think they were wasting their time."

He didn't look at her; his attention was on a lilac and the tiny yellow and black creature crawling from bloom to bloom. "So you acted to prove yourself for their sake?"

"Yes," she said a bit uncertainly.

His laugh was gruff and more to himself than anything. "So truly humble. Such a rare and refreshing trait among the Fae." He turned to face her. "Perhaps you'll bring peace after all."

It was her turn to look away. "That's what everyone keeps saying."

He cocked his head. "And yet it weighs on you."

She chewed her lip. "It's not exactly an easy thing to ask of someone."

A breathless laugh. "It most certainly isn't, but given time, opportunity, and patience, I believe you just might be able to accomplish it."

"You don't know me; what makes you think so?"

"I haven't seen Meegan with that look on her face since her last grandchildren were born, and they're a century old." Niall let the small creature crawl onto his finger. "She's been through many hardships that have hardened her heart. Yet in that room, in a single moment, you gave her the one thing we all desperately crave."

"What's that?"

"Hope."

Hope. She was a child compared to them. Her body was struggling with her animal shift and yet Niall claimed she could bring them hope.

Niall. She risked another glance at him and her cheeks heated when he caught her staring.

"You're still troubled."

"I just," she steadied herself. She might not get another opportunity like this. "You're the son of the High Lord of Pádraigín."

"Yes?"

"That means we're meant to be—" She couldn't finish her sentence, but Niall only chuckled. Arianna looked into his eyes. Deep. Ancient. With varying hues of grey. Now that she was closer, Arianna could see the touches of blue within the iris.

"I wasn't going to broach that topic."

She lifted her brows. "Why not?" She hadn't stopped thinking about it.

"Because there's no rush. You're young and you have much to adjust to. Why would I put another burden on your shoulders?"

Arianna lowered her voice. "Because I already have a mate."

His jaw ticked, but she didn't scent any anger. Weren't males supposed to be more territorial than this, or was it because a bond hadn't presented itself? Could a Fae have two mates, and if so, how would Rion handle such a complex situation?

He leaned against the stone railing. "The council has been in an uproar about that."

"But you don't seem bothered."

He offered her a half-hearted smile. "I'll admit, it was disappointing to find you already with a male, but I'm not angry."

She quirked a brow. "You discover your prophesied mate belongs to another and you aren't angry?"

"I'm not certain you'll like hearing the truth."

She straightened, her nerves suddenly on edge. "I want to hear it anyway." She needed to know if the council was a threat to Rion. And if so, then they needed to leave. What if they were plotting something against him? If the council removed Rion from the picture then—

"I have multiple lovers, so the knowledge that another male is warming your bed doesn't bother me in the slightest." Arianna didn't move. "As far as the bond goes, the council and I have discussed it at length and believe you're experiencing a rare phenomenon we call a pseudo bond." Her heart pounded harder and a sharp pain lanced through her core at the mere thought.

"It's only been recorded a few times in our history. The bond forms under great stress and serves as a means to protect against unknown threats." His gaze darted to her wrists. She hated the pity in his stare. "And I imagine you went through a great deal of stress if rumors are to be believed."

She clenched her fists, anger rising. "It is not a pseudo bond."

Niall hung his head. "I don't want us to be enemies, My Lady. You asked for honesty and I gave it."

Her jaw ticked and Arianna tried to rein in her anger. She turned to face the gardens and studied a droplet that had settled at the base of a leaf. Arianna took a deep breath. "What do you want from me then?"

"Before you arrived, I had plans to court you, woo you, if you will, and had hoped to one day make you my wife."

She cringed at the thought. "And now?"

"Now, I'd simply ask to be allies. Perhaps even friends."

"And that's enough to satisfy you?"

"For now." Arianna studied him. "I'm not a young male by any means. I've come to understand that eternity requires patience, and I'm quite capable of being patient for the things I desire."

"What if those things never desire you in return?"

"Then so be it. It doesn't stop our need to aid Alastríona. If the queen doesn't wish for a relationship on an intimate level, then I won't push the issue."

She wasn't convinced. "And how will the rest of the world see us?"

"Just as they need to. As a united front."

"You mean as a couple."

"It harms no one to let them believe what they want to believe. Nothing needs to be formally announced."

Arianna didn't know how to respond to that. How would Rion feel about others viewing her as belonging to another male, and would it matter in the long run? How would she feel about holding Niall's hand before the masses, lying to them as she claimed to change their world for the better? Or was the detail so miniscule that it shouldn't matter?

"All I ask is for you to consider it."

"And Rion?"

"I can work with the council to convince them he isn't a threat. He's done nothing since his arrival that leads me to believe otherwise. He's proven quite protective of you and with how powerful he's rumored to be, that protection is invaluable at the moment."

She scented the air for a lie, but to her surprise, Niall seemed to be telling the truth. "That . . . makes me happy."

Niall beamed and reached for her, but a growl ripped from the doorway and echoed across the stones. Talon jumped to his feet, suddenly before Arianna, but Niall barely reacted.

Rion's sharp gaze swept over her, his magic billowing forward. It ignored Talon and moved until it was close enough to dance across her skin before wrapping her in its protective embrace.

"I didn't touch her, just as I promised," Niall said, his eyes locked with Rion's. Rion stalked forward, his fangs bared. Niall watched as the particles crawled across her skin, his brows knit together. Regardless of what he claimed, Niall clearly didn't like Rion touching her any more than the council did.

Arianna crossed the remaining space separating her from her mate and leaned into him. She wrapped her arms around Rion's torso and a satisfied sound reverberated through his chest.

"I've seen males with better reputations turn into savage animals with another male so close to their mate. Especially with a new bond. You have unbelievable restraint."

Rion ground his teeth. "It's not without difficulty."

Niall smiled at her. "Thank you for speaking with me. This is where I take my leave. I hope you'll consider everything I've said, but know there's no rush to make any decisions." He bowed. "Enjoy the rest of your day."

Talon glanced between the two as if debating whether he should leave. She nodded to her friend and he gave her a simple wave before following in Niall's wake.

Rion kissed her, threading one hand through her hair until he cradled her head. His tongue dove deep into her mouth and she pulled him close, gripping his perfectly fitting shirt in one hand.

Rion pulled back just enough to press his forehead to hers. "You have no idea how many times I wanted to bust down that door."

She hummed. "I'm glad you didn't, though I can't say I would have minded either."

He pulled back further. "Did you learn anything?"

"Names. The fact that a lot of people seem to doubt me and that we're going to be subjected to a ball."

Rion winced. "Wonderful."

She tilted her head. "Do you know how to dance?"

"I'm afraid I was already an outcast before that sort of training began." Right.

"I guess we better find my sister, then. We have a lot of work to do."

CHAPTER TWENTY-THREE

TALON

Movement drew his attention and Talon halted at the edge of the gardens. He studied the entrance to the hedge maze, swearing he'd seen someone or something enter, then disappear.

Talon crossed the space and angled himself on the other side. Nothing.

Either he was losing his mind or someone had just been standing there. He might have chalked it up to his eyes playing tricks on him, but it had happened too often now to be mere coincidence.

On their first night in the manor, he'd seen a shadow pass down the hall from his room, but when he'd followed it to investigate, he'd found nothing. Not even a lingering scent.

The second time, he'd been taking a stroll to the library. The doors had opened of their own accord. No one had gone in or come out, but he could have sworn he heard feet hitting the marble floor as someone ran in the opposite direction.

He didn't believe in ghosts and even Ellie had noticed similar oddities. The knowledge raised the hairs on the backs of his arms.

Talon marched out of the maze and further down the stone path but instead of a shadow or explanation, Talon found Niall lingering at the edge of the gardens.

His hand fell away from a wisteria blossom as he turned to acknowledge Talon's presence. "May we speak?" Talon's jaw clenched but he nodded.

The son of the High Lord of Pádraigín. Talon hadn't cared for the male from the first moment he saw him. Something about his aura whispered of false pretenses and secrets. If a Fae could lie, Talon was certain this male had found a way to do it.

"As you wish," Talon said, bowing his head slightly. He couldn't show even the slightest hint of dislike or mistrust. Because this male was the future King of Alastríona. He was the one Talon would serve beneath for the rest of his life. That was, if Arianna chose to marry him. Talon was certain Rion's presence threw an unexpected hitch in his plans.

"You and our queen are very close," Niall stated. Talon remained still, even as Niall's gray eyes scanned his body. "I'd even venture to say you love her." Talon inwardly cursed but kept his expression neutral. "It's all right, you know. It's quite normal to fall for our childhood friends. They're the first ones we love outside of our family. It's an easy love. Comfortable, even."

Talon wasn't sure how to respond so he kept quiet. Better to let this male talk than risk his fury. Niall paced the garden. "Did she ever return your affections?"

Talon thought back to that day so long ago. About how her soft lips had felt against his and the way his hands had shook. Niall might as well have shoved a knife through his heart. "It was a long time ago and she's found her mate."

"That remains to be seen."

Talon hadn't meant to overhear their conversation, but it wasn't as though he was far enough away to avoid it. A pseudo bond, Niall had called it. "You truly believe the bond isn't legitimate?"

"There's a bond. One doesn't experience that much trauma without forming one. But I don't believe it's the bond our young queen hopes it is." Niall studied the garden for a moment. "I fear for her. Tell me honestly, do you trust the male?"

Trust was a strong word, but he'd seen the way Rion treated her with utmost care. He'd also witnessed how much she'd suffered without him. "I trust him not to hurt her."

"I don't," Niall said. "I think she's coaxed a tiger into a pretty cage, fed him delicious food, made him a comfortable bed, and thinks her kindness means he won't turn on her. But eventually the tiger always grows bored. He'll begin pacing that pretty cage before he finally rips it open." Niall turned to face Talon. "I don't want her caught in the middle when that happens."

"Mates can't hurt one another."

"And if he isn't her mate?"

"Are you asking me something?" Talon clenched his fists before remembering himself. He wouldn't hurt Arianna, and Rion's absence would do just that.

"I want us to be allies." Niall closed the space between them and rested a light hand on Talon's shoulder. It felt as though wind ripped from Niall's fingertips, and one small movement would have it diving into Talon's body to tear him apart from the inside out. "I want someone watching them. And I want to know if he starts pacing the cage."

Talon only nodded. He was already watching. Every second they spent with one another, he watched. Part of it killed him, but Talon had seen The Demon out of control before. He'd witnessed the blood lust, fought against the rage in his eyes.

And if that rage ever turned on his best friend, Talon would put an end to the creature himself.

CHAPTER TWENTY-FOUR

ARIANNA

Her little sister was missing. Well, not missing exactly. It seemed everyone had seen her at one point or another, but tracking her down was equivalent to locating a ghost.

"Can you have her meet me in the library?" Arianna finally asked one of the servants.

"Of course, My Lady." The female had bowed and run off, hopefully to find someone who could find Ellie.

"She's the ambassador of Móirín," Rion pointed out.

"If she's just doing her job," which would be a first for Ellie, "then why can't anyone find her? She should be with *someone*." Arianna wrung her hands together. "She's not exactly the workaholic type."

Ellie and Kirian had given her father enough grief to last a lifetime. They were always skipping classes together and sneaking into places they shouldn't.

"Maybe this is different," Rion offered. Or maybe her little sister had grown up far more than Arianna wanted to admit. Arianna had been gone for almost two years. What if Ellie wasn't the same young female who snuck out of her history lessons? What if she and Kirian no longer met beneath the stars to steal a kiss and share their secrets?

Arianna tried not to let worry plague her. "I just hope she's not getting herself into trouble."

"Avalon wouldn't have sent her if he doubted her abilities." Rion had a point. Her father was strict and expected great things from his daughters. But the knowledge only made Arianna wonder if she truly knew her little sister at all.

THE PAIR entered the library and proceeded to the third floor. A stack of books sat atop the table they'd occupied yesterday. She almost chose a different place to sit, but the folded piece of parchment resting on top of the stack drew her attention.

Her name was written across the center in elegant script. Curious, she unfolded the sheet and read:

The table is yours by order of the head librarian; therefore, I left you a few books to help with your studies. They're some of my favorites and easier to understand than the ones Lord Niall will try to offer you.

P.S. Don't let him read this.

Gavin

Arianna glanced at the first title and sighed. History. "This is going to be torture."

Rion chuckled, took the second book and flipped through a few pages. "I thought you enjoyed books."

She made a disgusted sound. "Not boring ones."

He turned the book over, examining the back. "Turn it into a story," Rion offered. "Don't think about the names and dates. Pick a general and learn about their life, then connect it to others that lived in the same time period." He set the book down. "It'll read more interesting that way."

"Is that what you did?"

He shrugged. "More or less. The more you know about someone, the more you understand the reasons behind their actions. I focused on their strategy—or lack thereof—then what ultimately led to their downfall so I wouldn't repeat their mistakes."

"As I said, torture."

He chucked again and Arianna lifted the third book from the pile. She opened it to a detailed map of Alastríona and lingered there.

There were so many places she had yet to see. So much to learn and do. Her fingers glided over the page starting at the human lands in the north, then traveled down to the islands off the coast of Móirín's southern borders.

This was a world she had yet to see but would one day know like the back of her hand. She'd learn everything she needed to know about Ruadhán first. She would earn the council's favor, make a few changes, then begin a slow journey across the vast land.

They would visit the capitol cities, where she'd spend time with the High Lords and Ladies. Afterward, she'd venture to other major towns and make a name for herself. And maybe she'd finally figure out what peace meant along the way.

"Do you th—" Arianna paused when she found Rion at the end of the aisle staring at something on a shelf. Grateful for the excuse, Arianna set the book down and wandered over to find him studying a glass chess set.

He carefully lifted it with both hands before asking, "Do you know how to play?"

Arianna let a wide smile spread across her face. "Not in the slightest, but I'm willing to learn."

A game. Her mate liked a game.

He crossed the room and placed the board on the table, moving his seat across from hers. "It's a game of strategy with the singular goal of trapping the opponent's king."

She shrugged. "How hard can it be?"

HARD. So impossibly hard. Rion explained the pieces and their movements and after a few practice games she understood a majority of the rules. But for the life of her, she couldn't predict anything Rion did. She'd move one piece, thinking herself clever, then he'd claim another. Or outright win because she left her king vulnerable.

"It's not about taking your opponent's pieces as much as it is forcing the king to surrender."

She huffed and propped her head up with one hand. "Don't you do that by eliminating players?"

"You do that," he clarified, "by making as few moves as possible to accomplish your goal."

Arianna furrowed her brow and studied the board again. She didn't know how long they'd sat there, but her bottom hurt from the wooden chair and her stomach rumbled, reminding her they'd missed lunch.

Arianna looked up through the glass ceiling, trying to read the way the sun sat in the sky before giving up and searching the area in their immediate vicinity.

"Why don't they have a clock in here?"

Rion tilted his head to one side. "They do, it's just down the hall."

The doors downstairs flew open, as they'd done at least a dozen times since the two had seated themselves in the corner, but when Arianna scented Ellie, she was on her feet.

Ellie huffed upon seeing her, threw up her hands, and spoke in an angry whisper. "I've had a least a dozen people stop me in the last ten minutes with the demand that I come here."

"Where have you been?" Arianna asked.

"I was busy. What do you need?"

It had taken the servants hours to find her. Hours. She knew those in the manor would do anything to please her and if it'd taken them that long to locate Ellie—Arianna shook her head. She didn't want to imagine what the word "busy" meant to her sister.

Without inquiring further, Arianna said, "We need dance lessons."

CHAPTER TWENTY-FIVE

ARIANNA

"Two weeks is not nearly enough time to get you ready," Ellie said, exasperated. Dark bags hung beneath her sister's eyes as they rushed through the dimly lit halls in the early morning light. Niall, or rather, his assistant, had informed Ellie about the ball.

"Did you get any sleep?" Arianna asked her little sister.

"Sleep is for the weak. I have too much to do."

"Like what?" She still hadn't asked what had kept her so busy yesterday. Whatever it was seemed to be keeping her up at night, too. Were they working her too hard? Did the council have unrealistic expectations of a sixteen-year-old?

Ellie shooed her away. "Don't worry about it, there's enough for you to focus on without adding my problems to the mix."

"Problems?"

Ellie sighed. "You know what I mean. It's too early for all your questions. I haven't even had coffee."

"You drink coffee?"

Ellie gave her a playful smile. "Only if it's full of chocolate and comes with a croissant." Fine. She'd let her sister divert the conversation, but Arianna wasn't letting it go. She'd have a talk with Niall later and inquire about her sister's duties.

They entered a room full of body length mirrors that stretched the length of the wall. Stacked crates lined the right side of the room, but otherwise the space was wide open. The wooden floor looked polished and new as if no one ever walked across it. A shame.

A thrill of delight ran through her. Arianna loved to dance. It was the only thing her father ever complimented her on. That and her cooking. She'd never felt nervous to stand before the other students, not like she did during sparring sessions where every gaze burned through her like a hot iron. Dancing was just . . . freeing somehow. She couldn't explain the rush.

"So how are your skills?" Ellie asked Rion.

Rion was studying his mate and took too long to answer. "I don't have any."

"You've never had a single lesson?" Ellie ran her hands through her hair. "Gods, my father started us at five."

"We mostly played," Arianna reminded her.

Ellie ignored her sister. "You've never danced a single time in your life?"

Rion shrugged. "Can't say I had many willing volunteers."

"Right." Her sister made a face. "The opening dance will be the most important. Everyone will be watching, so I think it's best if we focus on that one. Two weeks should give us plenty of time for one. If we have time, we'll touch on the basics of another." She glanced around the room. "I think it's safe to say you won't have to dance with anyone else, but," she held up a finger, "you should know that a great deal of males and females will be dancing with Arianna."

Rion clenched his jaw and suddenly Arianna was questioning the entire event. Of course they'd wanted to dance with her. She bit her lip. She hadn't thought this through. There would be males putting their hands all over her, and she'd seen how Rion had reacted to Niall touching her. How did she expect him to handle an entire room of eager Fae?

"Maybe this is too soon," Arianna said. They'd promised she could have a decade if she asked for it. "I'll tell Niall we need to wait and let the bond settle for a while before—"

Ellie shook her head. "You're doing this. The invites were sent this morning."

Her face paled. "So soon?"

"The council seems to think everyone will be scrambling to attend. You literally have citizens climbing the fence to get to you. The ball will give them a chance to settle down."

"Oh gods."

"And I heard about their little theory." Ellie rolled her eyes. "They don't want to believe you two are mates, so they're likely going to use this ball to try and expose Rion as the monster they believe he is."

Arianna furrowed her brow. "What do you mean?" Either her sister had gone snooping or the council had already openly discussed it with her. Arianna guessed the former.

"Think about the impact it would create if Rion acted the way he did with Talon and Niall. No offense," Ellie added quickly. "The nation's most trusted advisors will be in attendance. It's a test and Niall hopes to gain the upper hand." Rion cursed and Arianna paced the room, wondering, not for the first time, if they should just leave altogether.

"But," her sister said. "We aren't going to let that happen because you," she pointed at Rion, "are going to learn to control yourself for a few hours and I," she gestured at herself, "am going to make sure no one provokes you."

Arianna gave her sister an exasperated look. "And how do you plan to accomplish that?"

"I have a secret weapon." Ellie raised her voice. "You can come in now." Talon stepped into the room but leaned against the threshold with his arms folded. The expression on his face told Arianna he didn't like Ellie's idea any more than she would.

"I'm failing to see how this helps the situation," Arianna said.

Ellie looked straight at Rion without faltering. "Would you rather have a stranger's hands on Arianna or someone you know who will respect her boundaries?"

His gaze darted toward Talon and back. "I'd rather not have either."

"Well, that's not an option. You held yourself together with Niall, but Talon seems to set you off by simply being in the same room, so we're going to practice and you're going to get all your growling and snarling out here." Arianna opened her mouth to speak, but Ellie interrupted. "And if any of you touch your magic and destroy this beautiful room, you'll be stepping into the sparring ring with me."

Rion surveyed Ellie and Arianna blanched as he seemed to size her up. No way she was letting those two into the ring together. Rion wouldn't hurt her sister, she knew that, but Ellie didn't always understand boundaries.

"Furthermore," Ellie continued. "I'm going to have a dance with you," she gestured to Rion, "to prove to the other ambassadors that it's not just Arianna who trusts you." Arianna bristled at that, her own instincts taking over despite it being her sister who suggested it. Ellie pointed a finger at her. "And you're going to control yourself, too."

Arianna's face fell. If she felt like this with her sister, how was Rion going to manage with complete strangers? "What if we can't?" she asked.

Ellie shrugged. "Then the whole thing blows up, rumors start, and we'll have a kickass story to tell when all the heat dies down." No one mirrored her humor. "Lighten up, that's why we're here. To practice." She turned toward Talon. "Now get over here and let's get started."

Talon hesitated, his gaze darting from Arianna to Rion and back to Ellie. "This isn't a good idea."

Arianna agreed, but Ellie only shrugged. "We won't know until we try." She looked at Rion, whose knuckles were already white. "And Talon is the least of your worries. Arianna will be expected to have at least one dance with Niall." Rion actually did growl at that. "See?" her sister said. "Better to get it all out here."

Arianna wasn't sure she remembered how to take a steady breath. They were erratic, coming in short bursts as she tried to process how the upcoming event might unfold.

Ellie started a music player and turned the sound low. She clapped her hands together, startling Arianna. "All right." Her gaze turned expectantly to Talon. He sighed and finally pushed off the wall. Rion didn't move. He was too busy studying Talon, roaming over every inch of the male as if assessing a threat.

But Talon wasn't a threat. He never had been.

Her friend stopped a few feet away, still looking like he thought this was as much of a bad idea as she did.

Rion's chest rose and fell, his shoulders pensive and muscles tight. She could cancel the ball. She could ask them to wait, but how much time would be enough? Arianna owed her life to those who'd died before her. To the many she hadn't been able to save. It was time to stop waiting.

Arianna exhaled, trying to let the tension fall from her shoulders, then she rested a hand on Rion's arm. "She's right. We need to practice."

Arianna sensed his reluctance warring with his need to please her. And though it felt like it took every ounce of his restraint, Rion stepped back. He squeezed her hand once before releasing her, then stood beside Ellie.

Arianna struggled to pull her eyes away from her mate, then she turned to face Talon with a half-smile.

"Just like old times?" she asked.

He smirked and offered his hand. The other circled her back and she stiffened, afraid her friend might feel her scars through the thin fabric.

"You're just as tense as he is," Talon said, pulling her through movements so familiar they were second nature.

"Watch their feet," Ellie instructed Rion.

"Sorry," Arianna said, willing her body to relax. She didn't scent any anger from Talon. Good. He didn't need to know. No one did.

"All right," Ellie said, stepping forward to interrupt them. "Now, let's get Rion in on this." Ellie stood beside Arianna, then raised her arms and looked at Rion as if she expected—holy gods above.

Rion eyed the trio, his gaze still locked on Talon before he crept toward Ellie.

"Technically your hand can go anywhere between the woman's hip and her shoulder blade. Whatever feels comfortable for you. Your other hand will take my free one." Rion looked at Ellie then, suddenly seeming to realize what she expected of him.

He stepped toward her and grains of sand eased out from beneath his tunic. Talon stiffened as the magic crawled down Rion's arms and covered his hands to create a barrier between himself and Ellie.

Ellie didn't react to it at all. Didn't so much as flinch as she took Rion's hand in her own.

Arianna wouldn't call what shot down the bond fear. More like uncertainty as he watched both Ellie and Talon for various reasons.

"The male leads," Ellie said, "but if you forget, just let Arianna guide you." Ellie lightly kicked his foot. "Think of dancing as its own fighting form. It's a push and pull between two bodies, just like a battle." Ellie stepped and Rion moved with her. "Good. Again."

The morning wore on one agonizing step at a time. Her mate didn't grow frustrated or seek reassurance. He simply moved and absorbed the information so fast, Arianna couldn't help feeling a touch jealous.

He asked a question here and there and they reset back to the beginning a lot, but he was learning. Day one and Rion was actually learning the first part of the dance.

They only had two weeks to prepare, but grim thoughts took root as she remembered she'd be expected to dance with ambassadors to the other nations.

And suddenly Arianna wondered if her mother's murderer would be attending the ball.

Chapter Twenty-Six

Arianna

"Absolutely not," Niall said as they strolled through the manor two days later. "We confirmed with Fiadh's High Lord that his son was the only one responsible for what happened in Móirín. It was his plan that resulted in Lady Lillian's death. The High Lord claims he hasn't had contact with that son since the war began."

"Claims," Rion said. "Which means you didn't speak with him directly."

Niall gave Rion a sidelong glance and Arianna thought she saw malice glint through his gray eyes, but she blinked and it was gone. "We've been preoccupied with other matters. I can't oversee every meeting while also acting as the regent to Ruadhán."

"You don't think the High Lord of Fiadh had any part in the war?" Arianna asked.

Niall's gaze softened. "I don't. Lady Lillian," Niall stopped himself and shook his head. "It's too early to speak of tragedy. I think it's better if we focus on your studies instead."

Arianna wanted to argue it was too early for that too, but she didn't want to risk sounding like a whining child.

They'd finished dance lessons before breakfast, stuffed themselves on cream pastries and breakfast meats, then she'd found herself face to face with Niall. She'd been informed her studies were to begin this week.

Niall pushed open the library doors. "You've learned a great deal about Móirín, and I'm certain with your social standing that you know a bit about the other countries as well."

"Probably not as much as I should," she admitted.

Niall laughed and led them to the top floor. "The books up here generally don't leave this area. Many are delicate from age and it's important we preserve them."

"Are there any books unavailable to the public?"

"Forbidden, you mean?" He chuckled. "I'm afraid you might have read a few too many fictional tales." Her face heated. "As I said before, we have some texts that are written in a language we can't decipher, but aside from those, no, nothing in this library is forbidden."

The trio turned down an aisle to find a librarian balancing on top of a ladder as he placed a heavy tome between two others. His shaved head and muscular build made the male look more like a general than someone who spent time around books.

The male's eyes lit up when he saw her. "My Queen." He clambered down the ladder. "It's such an honor to have you grace our halls."

She nodded in return. "It's good to be here. The library is beautiful."

He looked around as if seeing it for the first time. "We put a lot of time and hard work into preserving this small paradise." He clasped his hands together. "How can I be of service?"

"Our queen will begin her studies soon and I thought your suggestions would be a good place to start. We have the welcome ball coming up and I want her to be prepared for those in attendance."

"Oh, of course, right over here." The male gestured them down a side aisle, prattling on about the collections he'd gathered over the decades, but a shadow caught Arianna's eye and she paused to study a bookcase in the corner. She squinted at it and a pair of eyes encased in darkness widened upon meeting her stare. She blinked and they were gone.

Arianna couldn't explain why, but she sprinted toward the shelf as if she might prevent the person or thing from running. But when she rounded the corner, the space was empty. Arianna looked between the aisles and Rion watched, likely trying to piece together why she'd suddenly taken off.

"What is it?" Rion asked, keeping his voice low.

"I just saw someone," Arianna answered. She was sure of it. She didn't know how or why, but she was certain a person had been standing there just a second ago.

Niall called after them. "Find something interesting?"

Arianna shook her head and rubbed her eyes. "I must be seeing things." She tried to smile through the lie. Arianna knew they could smell it, but Niall's smile only widened.

Warning bells were echoing through her head as she continued following Niall and the librarian, not bothering to listen to their conversation on balls and those who might attend.

Something was off; she could tell from the way her hair stood on end. Had Niall or another with the power to glamour used their magic to veil a person from her sight? And if so, why?

She hadn't scented magic or felt the thickness of it in the room, but she was certain of one thing: Niall had locked eyes with the librarian. A quick movement she wasn't meant to see. Niall was most definitely hiding something from her. She just had to find out what.

DINNER WAS more than fulfilling and Arianna couldn't help but giggle at her sister's enthusiasm. Honestly, Ellie acted as though she'd never had a decent meal in her life.

The ethereal violinist made another surprise appearance that had the entire dinner hall erupting into applause. Arianna wanted to meet her and ask the performer about her life and how long she'd practiced to sound so otherworldly breathtaking.

But even with those distractions, Arianna couldn't shake the feeling that something was amiss.

Rion walked hand in hand with her to their bedroom. "Something's bothering you," he said.

Arianna looked around as if she might glimpse another pair of eyes watching her from the shadows. "Have you noticed anything weird?"

"Define weird."

"Earlier in the library, I saw someone around the corner, but it was like they were . . . cloaked in shadow or something. Then they just vanished."

Rion led them up the stairs. "I didn't smell anyone."

She hadn't scented anyone either. Arianna sighed and rubbed her temple. "I might be losing my mind."

"You most certainly already have." He tried to stifle a grin. "No one in their right mind would have brought me here." Arianna gave him a playful shove, but Rion pulled her close. "Don't doubt yourself. If you saw something, then chances are it was real, we just have to figure out what it means. Pádraigín's talents could be responsible."

But why? What were they hiding and was it worth waiting to find out? If they were laying a trap for her—or worse, her mate—then she needed to intervene. Then again, maybe Niall didn't know about it, either.

Arianna thought about all the things she'd been sure of months ago and the way many of those things had changed in such a drastic way.

She'd believed Rion was a monster. That the Dark Fae in the mountains were mindless creatures that murdered any who ventured into their territory. Both had proven to be false. Then there was the bond that wasn't supposed to exist, yet lay before her so clearly. Maybe she needed to get her hands on a copy of the ancient texts and read them herself.

"I'm starting to feel like everything I know is a lie."

Rion led them past the bedroom and out onto the balcony where she could see the last rays of the sun dipping below the horizon. "Maybe it is," he said too quietly.

"That's reassuring."

Rion didn't reply at first, so Arianna tugged him close, waiting for him to collect his thoughts. "Before you came into my life, I'd stopped believing in anything. Hope was a thing for fools. There was only power and obedience." He shook his head.

"Then you told me I wasn't a monster. You told me you loved me." His voice grew thick. "Then the bond appeared. None of that was supposed to happen. I'm not supposed to have the ability to create anything aside from destruction."

"And yet here you are."

He nodded. "The texts are adamant about what and who I am. But they're just as adamant about what and who you are."

"So how did they get one of us so wrong?"

He shrugged. "It makes one wonder if we should be listening to them at all."

"Well, maybe we can try to read and decipher it together."

He raised a brow. "You want to solve the great mystery of the ancient texts?"

She grimaced. "Maybe during down time. I just don't know where to start. All this," she gestured with her hand toward nothing in particular, "is just as confusing as your stupid game of chess."

Rion took her hand and angled her body to face him. "One," he held up a finger. "Chess is not stupid." She huffed out a laugh. "And two, this world you're part of now is exactly like that game. They want the upper hand. They want to stay three steps ahead of you at all times."

"So what do I do?"

He smirked. "You're the queen. The queen can do anything she wants. You've been compliant and played their beginning round. I'd say it's time to make a few plays of your own."

Arianna couldn't help but admire him. She'd come here to change lives, and now she had a real opportunity to do it.

Arianna nodded. "I'm going to bring it up at the next meeting and you're—" A female yelled off to their right and Arianna startled. Rion's magic flew up to surround them but upon realizing no one was attacking, Arianna leaned over the railing to get a better look.

She couldn't make out their faces in the dimming light, but three sentries stood around a lone figure with their weapons raised.

"Who are you," she overheard one guard demand. "And how did you sneak into the garden?"

A female voice answered. "I already told you. I'm here to see Arianna. I came with those from Móirín—"

"Half-breeds are not permitted here at this hour. You will return to your quarters and await instructions."

"I—" A guard grabbed her wrist from behind. One moment, they were standing, the next, they were off their feet, flying back as if they'd been struck in the chest by an invisible force.

Arianna leapt from the balcony, using her magic to slow her fall. Rion followed close behind. Her heart thundered in her chest, beating with an ache of impossibility. She recognized that scent and voice.

The sentries jumped to their feet, ready to strike, but they pivoted upon hearing Arianna's approach. "Stay back," a male commanded. "We don't know—"

"Zylah?"

The female whipped her head toward Arianna and the guards hesitated. Their gazes darted to their commander, waiting for instructions.

But the only one Arianna was watching was the female before her. A female who'd been her friend and had accepted her as she was. A companion she had thought she'd lost in the blast against Rion's camp.

Zylah placed her hands on her hips. She was free. No chains. No shackles. "Do you have any idea how hard it's been to see you?"

Zylah. Arianna's lips quivered. Zylah. She ran, unsure if she was saying the name in her head or out loud. Arianna threw her arms around the female and Zylah gasped, hesitating before returning the embrace. "I guess no one brought you my letters, either."

Arianna clutched the female a moment longer before pulling back, swiping at the tears rolling down her cheeks. Zylah smiled. "You're a queen, you're not supposed to break down and cry."

"I don't care," Arianna said, her voice cracking. "I thought you were—I thought everyone had—"

"I'm more resourceful than that," Zylah said, but her gaze softened. "I got Irial and a few others out, too. The warriors from Móirín took us to Levea, then set us free."

Freedom. They'd done it, at least for a few.

"You have magic," Arianna said, gaping at her. "I had no idea."

"We all have our secrets."

"My Queen," the commanding guard said in a careful tone. Arianna turned to watch his gaze flicker toward Rion before returning to her. "The half-breed snuck in without authorization. We have strict rules and safety protocols that—"

"My name is not 'half-breed,'" Zylah sneered.

The male stiffened and anger blotted his face, but Arianna interrupted before he could speak again. "It's okay, she's with me."

"With all due respect—"

"I've always hated anything that came after those words," Zylah said. "They're never wise or beneficial."

The male's face pulled taut, but Zylah ignored him. "They have slaves here."

Arianna's stomach dropped. "In Ruadhán?"

Zylah nodded. "And you're not going to like what you see."

CHAPTER TWENTY-SEVEN

ARIANNA

ear drifted from the guards and Arianna realized she wasn't supposed to know about the slaves. But who were the guards afraid of? The council? Niall? The entire lot of them?

Arianna and Rion followed her friend with the guards trailing after. They wound through the hedge maze, exited the rear gate, and crossed the immaculate yard.

Arianna could feel the anger radiating from Zylah. Were there really slaves in Ruadhán? The royal city, of all places? This was a sacred city with the sole purpose of allowing her a space to bring about peace. What sort of peace could they hope to gain on the backs of the oppressed?

Their small group walked through another metal gate. Vegetation grew wild here along a gravel path, the area clearly not as maintained as the manor's yard.

Lights faded, leaving them surrounded by darkness, and Arianna didn't notice the buildings ahead until they were almost upon them.

"Who's there?" Another guard, but the commander trailing strode ahead, making his presence known. Zylah didn't stop as the commander informed the guard of the situation in hushed tones.

The buildings were the complete opposite of everything she'd seen in and around the city. Instead of fancy gardens and stone paths, Arianna's boots crunched across plain gravel. The buildings, three in total, were sturdy and well-kept, but they were painfully plain.

Windows were spread along the sides with curtains already drawn. Zylah grabbed a door without knocking and pulled it open.

Light spilled from within along with dozens upon dozens of scents.

Half-breeds.

Arianna's brows shot up as she followed Zylah inside. It was clean, thank the gods, but at least thirty bunk beds lined the left wall separated by small oak dressers with a single drawer and pocket underneath.

Across from them, tables lined one part of the wall while a kitchenette filled up the rest. Dishes were clean and stacked. Glass pitchers of water sat half empty and a single, large bathroom stood to her immediate right. Arianna glimpsed shower spouts lining the rear wall inside.

Half-breeds who were housed together and forced to eat and bathe together as well. She'd wondered if they were allowed in the city at all and now Arianna had her answer.

So long as they wore iron.

She clenched her jaw. All this time she'd thought Ruadhán functioned like Móirín with paid servants. But she'd been wrong. So painfully wrong.

All the shadows and flickers of movements that had caught her eye were slaves going about their daily routines. They'd placed a glamour over her. Niall and the council had violated her by tricking her mind into seeing what they wanted her to see.

And she'd been naïve enough to believe those from Pádraigín wouldn't use their talents without her permission. Niall had played his part well.

A slave stood and fear washed through the area as silence settled over the room. Their heads turned toward her one by one and iron gleamed in the overhead light.

Another rose to their feet, then backed toward the rear of the room. Still another glanced toward their bunkmate as if questioning what they were supposed to do in her presence.

Some pulled on clothes, their hair still dripping from a recent bath. All gaped, pushing family and friends behind their bodies as if . . . as if she were a threat.

Arianna wasn't sure her heart could handle much more.

She stepped forward and the five closest to her stepped three paces back.

Her lungs seized and she held up her hands. "I'm not here to hurt you."

The two closest, both males, eyed one another and bowed their heads low. "Is there something we can assist you with?"

"You're slaves." They nodded slowly. "You're slaves in the royal city."

"I'm afraid we don't understand, Your Grace."

Arianna clenched her fists, hating the fear that leaked from their bodies. "Who did this to you?"

"Don't bother." Arianna spun to find Ellie standing in the doorway. The bags beneath her eyes had grown and her clothes were wrinkled as if she'd rushed to throw them on. Her sister looked more haggard than Arianna had ever seen her. "They're bound to secrecy and far too scared to speak."

Fear. Survival. Pain. Arianna knew those feelings too well. The memories were too recent and floated near the surface. "This is unacceptable." It was far more than, that but she couldn't find the proper words.

Her breath clouded the air, that ancient thing in her blood writhing beneath her skin. She twisted back to face the slaves. "Are you the only ones?"

They exchanged glances again as if speaking a language only they understood. She knew that language. It was a myriad of brief gestures they prayed would remain unnoticed by their captors. If it didn't—she cringed, remembering the sound of the whip as its bite hit her skin.

Rion's deep voice broke the silence. "Your queen asked you a question."

Arianna whirled on him, her anger seeping out as ice cracked along the concrete floor in his direction. Rion visibly flinched back and immediate guilt flooded through her at the sight. Arianna tried to rein herself in but her voice still shook. "Don't—"

She'd meant to say don't intimidate them. Don't frighten them or force them into anything they didn't wish to do. But words failed her.

Rion bowed his head and stepped back. She hated his submission almost as much as she hated the iron around their wrists.

One of the male slaves swallowed before saying, "There are a few more buildings like this one down the path." He pointed, still unsure. "And another set on the other side of the city." His voice lowered. "But some of us sleep in our masters' quarters for their convenience."

Convenience. Arianna bristled at the word, remembering things she'd rather have forgotten.

She searched the sea of faces. Their clothing might not have holes, but their wrists still carried deep scars. Their bodies might be freshly washed, but none were granted the privacy they all deserved. They might be fed, but they didn't choose their meals. And they might have the ability to roam the most beautiful city in Alastríona, but none were free to make their own choices.

Arianna pivoted toward the commander. She didn't bother to soften her tone. "I want every single slave, owner, council member, and anyone else who matters brought to the main dining hall in ten minutes."

He glanced at those standing behind her as if they might try to intervene. They didn't. "Most have retired for the evening."

Arianna squared her shoulders, anger bubbling to the surface. "Then wake them. That's an order."

Chapter Twenty-Eight

Arianna

The slaves readied themselves and Arianna instructed the guards to lead Ellie to the other buildings and anywhere else slaves might be kept against their will.

Ellie's wrath matched her own. Arianna knew her little sister would ensure the slaves weren't treated cruelly. She'd be the first to intervene if they were.

Some slaves tried to put on their formal attire, but Arianna told them it wasn't necessary. As gently as she could, Arianna asked them to dress casually and wear whatever was comfortable. Most were uneasy and their whispered worries reminded Arianna exactly why she'd agreed to come in the first place.

She wanted to destroy all this. Form a new world. She knew Móirín was the only nation that had outlawed slavery, but before coming, she'd been certain Ruadhán shared similar ideals. So much for peace.

"What's your plan?" Rion asked, his tone far gentler than it usually was. She hadn't meant to snap at him, especially not in front of others. She just didn't want the slaves scared, not when they already feared so much.

"I'm giving them an ultimatum." Arianna watched groups file from the warehouse-like building they claimed as home. "I won't spend another night in this city if there are slaves."

Her mate nodded in agreement. "Good."

Arianna knew she was outnumbered in her beliefs and that making demands would likely only result in more enemies that wanted her dead, but she had vowed to make a difference. How was she supposed to look Zylah in the eye if she didn't honor those vows?

Arianna and Rion followed the last of the slaves from the building, bringing up the rear. Zylah had gone ahead with Ellie.

Zylah. She still couldn't believe the female was alive. But who had kept her away and why had they deemed it appropriate to toss her letters aside? Was it because the female was a half-breed, or had the letters contained information others didn't want her to see?

Arianna's heart tugged and broke, bleeding and patching itself together again. Their reunion should have been different. The females should have run straight to the kitchens and stayed up all night talking about their time spent apart while they stuffed themselves sick with chocolates and pastries.

But Zylah's eyes had barely left the slaves. Arianna's, too. Zylah had suffered in captivity far longer than Arianna, surviving in a world hell-bent on breaking her.

It hadn't succeeded.

They reached the dining hall and Fae were already filing in, but Arianna paid them little attention. Her focus was upon Ellie as she entered the room, jaw tight as two females trailed after her, clutching tiny bundles in their arms. Chains dangled from the female's wrists.

Icy rage rumbled beneath the surface of her skin.

Mothers. Mothers of newborn infants and they had chains around their bodies.

Niall strolled in next and the Fae crowded him for answers. He spoke in reassuring tones, promising an explanation soon. Niall shook their hands, greeted them with a smile, then walked right past the females cradling their infants as if they were nothing.

The slaves bowed their heads low when he passed, confirming what she already knew. It was *him*. Niall had given the order to keep slaves hidden from her. He was the Regent, the one who watched over Ruadhán in The Divine's place.

Arianna stormed to the front of the hall, the very place where her table usually stood. Ellie, Rion, Talon, and Zylah flanked her and a hushed silence fell over the space.

Niall, still circled by several court Fae, gently pushed them aside to address her. His brow furrowed and he gestured around the room. "Can I ask why we are here at this hour?" She hated the calmness in his tone. The way he outright ignored the slaves as if they were nothing above furniture.

Ice had started to form, crawling from beneath her black boots. It had already spread a few inches out, coating the marble floor in a thick jagged layer. Niall eyed it, then shifted his uneasy gaze back to her face.

"You hid them from me," she seethed, unable to control her temper. "You knew how I'd feel about it and you hid them anyway."

He didn't look surprised. A first for him, though maybe everything before this point had been a show to win her over. "Things are done differently in Móirín. I simply didn't wish to upset or overwhelm you with—"

"I will *not* stand for slaves."

"I assure you, they're well cared for," he gestured with one hand. "Look around. They receive clean clothes and adequate food daily. I—"

Arianna growled, baring her teeth and Niall stopped talking. She stepped toward him, ice crunching beneath her boots, and pointed a shaking finger at the slaves gathered along the benches to her right. "Cared for?" She growled again. "I see a mother, no, two mothers with chains around their wrists." Arianna stepped again. "I see fear whenever one of you," she gestured to the court Fae, "walks by." Arianna shoved her sleeves up and held her wrists high for all to see.

Audible gasps flew through the crowd, but her eyes never left Niall's. "And I see the same scars that I carry."

A multitude of emotions flashed across Niall's face before his eyes softened with the one she hated the most. Pity. "I'm sorry for the pain you endured. It's a—" An infant began wailing. The mother, truly horrified, stood to soothe the child. She rocked her back and forth in a gentle motion but the chains still clinked together, unraveling the last shreds of Arianna's self-control.

Niall cleared his throat, but Arianna wasn't looking at him anymore. She'd focused her attention on the male crossing the room, his jaw tense with annoyance.

"Quiet the child," he hissed, working to keep his voice down. But Arianna heard him, as did every other Fae in the hall.

The female whimpered. "I'm trying."

He looked down on her with so much disgust that Arianna's stomach twisted with loathing.

He clicked his tongue when the child's wailing increased. "I knew I should have just done away with it. When we get back—" He reached for her, but his hand froze in place, held there by a branch of Arianna's magic. Arianna didn't know when it had happened, only that the creature in her slumbered no more.

"You'll what?" Arianna was already across the room.

The male with short brown hair, narrow dark eyes, and more jewelry than it should have been legal to own, looked down his angular nose at the female who was supposed to be his queen.

He sneered at her. "The half-breed chose to lay with another. The babe is a result of her disobedience." He scoffed as if remembering something unpleasant. "She wailed so much after its birth I decided to let her keep it." He looked at the slave and wrinkled his nose in distaste. "But clearly, that was a mistake."

Let her. He'd *let her* keep it. The way he said it—oh gods, how long had they been separating children from their mothers? And what did they do with them after? She was going to be sick.

The female clutched her infant tighter and tears poured down her cheeks. The male clicked his tongue again.

"Ellie," Arianna called, unable to keep the rage from her tone. The male looked at her, noted the challenge in her gaze, and smirked as if she were as powerless as the slaves.

But she was far from powerless.

Boots thundered as Ellie crossed the silent hall. Too silent. As if they were all holding their breaths in anticipation. "Take this female to my room, remove those chains, and give her anything she needs."

The male laughed and looked toward the gathered Fae as if his next words were law. "That female is my property. You won't be taking her anywhere."

"Not anymore."

All mockery left his face. "I will not be undermined by a naïve child." He reached out and right as his fingertips brushed her skin, Arianna exploded.

Ellie stood guard over the slaves, shielding them with her own magic as Arianna glowered at the male. A layer of ice covered everything. The floor, the tables, the chairs, and the male's body. He stood frozen mid movement, eyes whirling in frantic circles.

"Do not," Arianna said through gritted teeth, "touch me." She felt a trickle of pride down the bond even as Rion's magic joined her own, circling, ready to protect.

Arianna slowly turned to meet several stunned gazes, Niall's among them. "I'm not here because I want to be. Your city, grand as it is, means nothing to me. I was brought here because of a prophecy. I was brought here to bring about peace." Her voice lowered. "And already I see how little peace means to you.

"You want a queen you can control, one that will act as your puppet and grant you power over the masses. I am not her.

"Peace," she continued, "can't be found when we have chains around the innocent." She locked eyes with Niall. "I will not be paraded around, I will not be manipulated to your will, and I most certainly won't stand for slavery, whether they're Fae, half-breeds, or humans."

Silence. Deafening silence.

Arianna steadied herself. "Every slave in this city is now free to make their own choices. If they wish to leave, I'll arrange an escort to Levea first thing tomorrow morning. If they wish to stay, they'll be paid a fair wage for their services." The slaves began whispering to one another. "And if anyone takes issue with either of those things, then every slave in this city will accompany me back to Levea where I'll stay for good."

"You would leave Ruadhán?" Niall asked. "For them?"

"And I won't think twice about it." The Fae murmured amongst themselves but they watched her and Niall with bated breaths.

"You'd cleave this continent in two."

"Then maybe that's what it needs."

Seconds ticked by, agonizing and uncertain. They watched the Queen of Alastríona and the Regent of Ruadhán. Two who were supposed to be one, yet a pair that stood with so much separating them.

Then Niall did the last thing she expected.

He started laughing.

The near hysteria in his tone had her stepping backward. Rion crossed the room in an instant, separating her from the male Arianna was certain had just lost his mind.

Niall waved his arms, trying to collect himself. "They said you'd bring peace, I didn't imagine you'd bring a backbone with you." After a few more breaths he calmed and raised his voice to address everyone in the room. "The Queen has given us her first command. It's time we see to the arrangements."

"But My Lord," a Fae male started, then stopped himself.

"Things are going to start changing and change is never easy," Niall said. "But we've prepared for this our entire lives and we must be willing to make sacrifices." Niall glared at the male still suspended by her magic. "And I'll personally see to it that those in defiance of our queen's rule are swiftly dealt with."

The male's eyes bulged and he moved his chattering lips enough to say, "You filthy traitorous—" A current of wind seemed to rip from every corner of the room at once. It rushed past and hit the male in the chest hard enough to steal his breath and render him unconscious.

Niall glared, then his anger turned into a smile that had Arianna reeling, unsure how to respond. He only said, "Don't worry, I only knocked him unconscious."

Then Niall turned to face the slaves. He ran a hand through his shoulder-length hair, the only indication he gave that this wasn't going to be as easy of a change as he was trying to present. "Do you have someone you'd like to appoint over the project or should I see to it?"

Arianna opened her mouth then closed it again. She'd been prepared for a fight. She had thought of all the ways the situation could end badly. She had wondered if she'd acted in haste and should have planned an escape route first. She never expected—

"Zylah," Arianna called, though her tone was far less demanding now. Her friend gave Rion a wide berth before standing at her side. "Would you like to oversee them?"

Zylah looked over the sea of faces as if she might memorize every single one. "I'd be happy to."

"I want the shackles removed immediately," Arianna said. "And I want every child who has ever been stolen returned to their parents."

Niall frowned a bit. "The question will be asked, so forgive me if it sounds insensitive. Will those who paid for the children be compensated for their lost revenue?"

She could have crammed his teeth down his throat. If he'd just done something, anything, they wouldn't be in this situation. But he didn't care. Not really. He was only trying to please her.

"If anyone," Arianna clenched her jaw, "makes their money by enslaving children, then they deserve to have their livelihoods stripped away." She turned to face the Fae who were looking at her and Niall as if the pair had lost their minds.

But the slaves. They'd raised their heads. Some were scared. Others were excited. But it was the glint of hope in their eyes that made Arianna's heart swell.

THEY WORKED for hours on preparations for those who would travel to Móirín and the slaves who would remain, which were a lot more than Arianna had anticipated.

They'd spent their whole lives in this city. They claimed to know their place in the world and that leaving it behind would be the same as living without a purpose.

Arianna respected their wishes even if they worried her. Fear still permeated the air like a thick cloud as whispers of uncertainty flew through the dining hall.

Most had turned in for the night and she was about to do the same, but Arianna had one more task to complete before she did.

Arianna braced herself and approached Eoghan. He'd been standing on the sidelines the entire time they had been in Ruadhán. There wasn't a need to follow her around. Not with Rion, Talon, and Móirín's elite keeping a close eye on her.

So she had assigned him the important task of guiding the slaves back to Levea where they'd be safe. Arianna was happy to hear the two mothers would be joining him on the journey.

"Hi," Arianna said by way of greeting.

Eoghan bowed low. "My Lady. Grace," he corrected himself.

She scrunched her nose. "You don't have to be so formal."

"It sets a good example for the others." She smiled at him and he returned it. Both shifted their gazes to watch the former slaves flit about the room.

Iron shackles littered one corner where they'd cast the barbaric things aside. She'd demanded they be melted down and stored far, far away.

Eoghan opened his mouth and stopped himself, but not before Arianna noticed.

"What is it?" she asked.

He lowered his head. "I don't feel worthy to ask anything of you."

"Eoghan." He looked up when she said his name. "Please, tell me what you need." He'd never asked her for anything. Not once.

He averted his gaze. "I have a family back home," he began, but cut himself off.

Rion cut in. "You're overdue for your leave."

Guilt flooded through her. She'd never asked about his family or his life. She'd never had the opportunity. Until recently, it always felt like they were surviving from one moment to the next mostly on borrowed time.

"Go home," Arianna said, even as her heart ached with the command. "Go be with your family."

Eoghan bowed his head low. "It has been an absolute honor to serve you, My Queen." Her heart swelled. He'd been the first to know her secret, aside from Rion. He'd protected her and stood by her side. But it was time for him to move on. At least for now.

"My wife is expecting our third child. She said she'd like to meet you someday."

Arianna fought the rising emotion. "It's a promise. I'll visit and you can show me all around Nàdiar." He bowed again, but Arianna threw her arms around Eoghan's neck. He stilled, unsure, then patted her shoulder.

"Thank you for everything," she whispered and pulled back.

"Of course, and I swear to keep them safe."

"Send word when you arrive in Levea."

He nodded and Arianna watched him walk away and sit with a group of warriors she'd assigned to join him. She'd trust no one but her father's best.

Arianna turned to her mate who had gone stiff. She took his hand and he pulled her close. They stood there for several moments, watching Zylah write things down while others did her bidding.

"You've already changed their lives."

"I hope I can change a lot more." Then Arianna smiled despite the long night. Because this was why she had come. This was the difference she wanted to make. This was worth everything.

Chapter Twenty-Nine

Arianna

Arianna and Rion arrived at breakfast the next morning to find Eoghan and the slaves already gone. She wasn't surprised. He'd informed her they'd be leaving before sunrise to avoid confrontation, but her heart still ached. She'd only known Eoghan a short while, yet it felt like a lifetime. It would be strange to not have him watching over her.

Arianna glanced at her sister who had been strangely quiet all morning. Ellie nudged the food on her plate, her mind clearly elsewhere.

"How did you know about the slaves?" Arianna asked. Last night, her sister had appeared out of nowhere. Arianna hadn't questioned it at the time, but now she wondered how long Ellie had known. And if it was the reason she always looked so exhausted.

Ellie pushed over a piece of fruit, watching it roll through the syrup. "I just found proof last night."

"What do you mean, you *found* proof?" Arianna pressed.

Ellie side-eyed her, then glanced around the crowded room as if someone might overhear. Arianna almost preferred a late breakfast if only for the privacy it afforded. "You know how."

"Ellie," Arianna hissed. "You can't just go around doing that here. You don't know what these people might do."

Ellie straightened in her chair. "They were hiding slaves and I think they're hiding a lot more. Last night just proves you don't know who you can trust, and that leaves us at a disadvantage. We need to learn more about them by whatever means necessary."

Rion spoke up, his voice cautious. "There could be consequences if you're caught." His tone didn't exactly sound disapproving.

"And there could be consequences if I stop." She waved her arms. "They've had centuries to put their plans in place and I'm not just going to sit around and let them use my sister."

"What else did you find?" Talon asked. Arianna threw her crumpled napkin at him, but found herself leaning forward to listen. Arianna knew her sister wouldn't stop no matter how much she complained, so listening was her only option.

Ellie returned to rolling the fruit around on her plate. "I haven't gotten into their main offices yet; we're still learning the rotations."

"We?" Arianna lifted a brow. Ellie gestured to Kirian and Arianna pinched the bridge of her nose. "Gods, she dragged you into this?"

"He's quite crafty for a half-breed," Ellie joked, but her smile quickly vanished. "There's something big going on. I don't know what they mean yet, but I found ledgers detailing recent large shipments. They're all written in code."

Talon sat back in his seat. "Well, that's obvious. It's just supplies for the coronation. It'll be the biggest event on the continent since," he shrugged, "well, since forever."

Ellie shook her head. "The dates were from over a year ago. No one knew about Arianna then."

"It could be anything," Rion said, but Arianna could see the doubt in his gaze.

"It could be," Ellie agreed. "But you don't go through the trouble of hiding something in a secret compartment *and* writing it in code if it's not important."

"Ellie," Arianna said, her tone serious. "I want you to be careful." Ellie rolled her eyes. "I'm serious. We don't know what these people are capable of."

"They don't know what we're capable of, either. Speaking of which," her eyes brightened and a feral grin spread across her face. "You've been way too sedentary. I think it's time we start up a little training routine, don't you think, Talon?" Arianna paled.

"I couldn't agree more."

HER MUSCLES already hurt and they weren't even to the training yard yet. She had looked to Rion to save her, but to her dismay, he had also agreed, claiming he needed to do the same. She supposed sculpted muscles didn't maintain themselves.

Arianna would have preferred to return to the library to study, or visit the slave quarters to see how things were progressing, but her sister claimed there would be time to do those things later. She wasn't getting out of it.

The trio ambled down a long path filled with gardens, fountains, and strolling Fae before descending a flight of stairs carved into the side of a small hill. At the base, five massive circular platforms made from thick stone slabs stood close together in a ring.

As they neared, Arianna glimpsed the differing colors in the stone, telling her it had been broken and replaced more times than she could probably count. The outer bricks looked original, at least.

Ellie threw the bag she'd run back to her room to collect against one of the stone benches and extended her arms toward the sky. Talon joined her, stretching his joints even though Arianna was pretty sure he had already run before breakfast. She'd eventually need to join them. Maybe after dance lessons were over.

Arianna sighed. "I'm not getting out of this am I?"

Rion chuckled. "It'll be good for both of us."

"Gods, please don't let my sister hear you say that."

"Too late," Ellie called. She'd seated herself on the ground and was pulling at her legs. "Now get stretched out; some of us have important things to do later."

Right. Important and illegal and dangerous things.

Arianna sat beside her sister. With last night's excitement, they'd skipped their dance lesson. It didn't feel right after recent events. Neither did training, but Arianna knew her sister was right. She needed to start moving again.

Arianna reached for the ground and wrapped her hands behind her ankles, letting gravity pull her forward. When she felt loose, Arianna sank into a stance and glided through several forms. She summoned her magic, keeping it light and easy as she lost herself in the flow of familiar patterns. She only paused upon noticing Rion's stare.

She blushed, suddenly shy in his presence. She'd never done well with an audience. Not after her father had publicly humiliated her in front of his council and stripped her of her title as heir. It had been a horribly humiliating day that she would never forget.

"What's first?" Arianna asked no one in particular.

She assumed Talon would lead as he usually did, but a mischievous smile spread over Ellie's face. "How about we spar and test that new magic of yours?"

Arianna blanched. "It's not new magic. It's the shift. It's just making things crazy right now."

"Yes, but the shift also unlocks the rest of your abilities," Ellie said as if reciting from a textbook. "Your magic isn't fully matured until then." She grinned. "Maybe all you need is a little push and," she clapped her hands, "perhaps you'll grow wings or a tail, or itty-bitty feet."

"Wings would be nice." Arianna had always wanted to fly, ever since she'd seen Talon take off and soar through the clear sky. She glanced toward Rion, then those who were gathering at the top of the stairs. She grimaced. "We don't need to spar."

"Of course we do. How else are we going to know what you need to focus on?"

"Your sister," Talon interrupted, "acts as though you were in a hole the entire time you were . . . gone." A painful expression crossed his face. "But last I checked, it wasn't Arianna who almost died. Perhaps her abilities aren't the ones we should be worried about."

Ellie huffed. "I was excessively outnumbered and I doubt even you could have fought your way out of all that."

"I don't know," Rion cut it, closing the distance separating them. "I've seen him fight his way out of a lot." Silence fell over the group. Had Rion just . . . complimented Talon? She knew her friend had almost killed Rion once and, in turn, had almost died. They were two males on almost equal grounds, both on the same side, willing to fight for the same things, yet not quite allies.

Ellie scoffed, ignored them, then stepped back a few paces before sinking into a stance. Rion stiffened. His magic crawled from the edges of the ring, rolling across the stone before rising to circle around her.

Ellie rolled her eyes. "You don't seriously think I'm going to hurt my sister, do you?"

Arianna sighed, lifted her hands, and shifted her feet. "He doesn't, but our instincts don't care."

Ellie rolled her eyes again. "Stupid Fae instincts."

"I'm using that one later," Kirian called out. Arianna eyed the book in the half-breed's hands, wondering at the little journal he had been writing in since he arrived.

Ellie snapped her fingers. "Focus." Arianna did. She looked at her sister. The younger who should have been the elder. The daughter who might have made a better queen if fate had only willed it.

Ellie dashed forward and Arianna moved with her. Ellie kept her movements easy, slowed a fraction as the females parried and struck, falling into a familiar rhythm. They used to meet one another three times a day. Once beneath her father's unforgiving gaze. Once with Talon correcting their forms. And once beneath the stars where they could practice without judgment.

The pair had always been close.

Ellie pushed a little harder and sweat beaded across Arianna's forehead. Her forearms stung as she blocked Ellie's strikes, and she winced when her sister grazed the side of her cheek.

Rion was as still as the stone beneath her feet. She could feel his instincts warring, wanting to protect her yet reminding himself she wasn't in any real danger.

Arianna glanced at him. A mistake. Ellie twisted her arm, but to avoid injuring her sister, Ellie pivoted to catch her instead and both lost their balance. Rion softened their fall with his magic.

Ellie stood and brushed the dirt from her clothes with a scowl on her face. "You shouldn't look away. You know better."

She did know better. All those lessons and one would have thought she would have learned by now. But Arianna had never been capable of focusing when so many eyes judged her every move.

But Rion wouldn't judge her and neither would Talon. They were her allies. Her friends. And both had stood with her in the face of death.

Arianna stood, brushed off her clothes, and faced her sister again.

TWENTY MINUTES later, both were panting, coated in sweat, and Arianna was fairly certain her forearms would be covered in bruises by morning. Rion had relaxed enough to busy himself with his own exercises, which had distracted her more than once, earning her a sharp rebuke from Ellie.

Talon was at the opposite end of the platform pulling water from the air. Arianna looked between the two males and part of her wondered if they would ever be more than, well, she wasn't sure what to call them exactly.

Ellie swung again, her movements faster and more focused. Arianna ducked and shifted to the side. Had they been using magic, she might have struck out at her sister, but they'd save that sort of training for another day. She hoped.

Someone coughed and Arianna risked a glance toward the stairs. Gods, when had so many people shown up?

"Eyes on me," Ellie commanded, her voice breathless.

Arianna tried but faltered when Ellie struck her again. Her sister winced when her fist collided with Arianna's ribs then Ellie drew back entirely.

Her father's words began echoing through her. Weak. Useless. *She's two years younger than you and you can't even best her?*

"My Lady?" Niall's concerned voice echoed from the top of the staircase and every head whipped in his direction. His brows furrowed. "What are you doing?" He wore a tan tunic today with black pants and boots to match. His hair wasn't unruly and no bags hung beneath his eyes, making Arianna wonder if last night had affected him at all.

"She's training," Ellie said, irritation practically radiating from her tone. "What's it look like she's doing?" Ellie wasn't one to forgive easily, and after seeing those mothers clinging to their children, Arianna wasn't sure she wanted to forgive Niall either. She still wasn't even sure she'd stay. As queen, could she command his removal? Was it even worth trying?

He glided down the stairs all grace and elegance. She couldn't forgive his outright violation of her person. He'd altered her mind without her permission. He'd made her look like a fool.

Niall stopped just outside the training ring. "Why?" he asked.

Ellie let out an exasperated sigh. "For the same reasons anyone trains."

"But we have people in place to protect you."

"A lot of good that did her when she was in chains."

Niall shot Ellie a hard look. He was usually so irritatingly composed, but Ellie's tone seemed to irk him. At least one of them could get under his skin. "If she'd been in Ruadhán, where she belongs, none of that would have happened."

Ellie growled. "If—"

"Ellie," Arianna warned. Her sister snapped her mouth shut, but she didn't turn away. Arianna wondered if the slaves had reminded

Ellie of the kind of hardships Arianna had faced at the hands of the slavers. She'd told her sister a few stories.

Arianna rolled her shoulders and felt her scars stretch. Her sister didn't even know half of it, and Arianna didn't possess the heart to tell her. She didn't want to see the pity or anger that would follow. She hadn't told Talon for the same reasons.

"I like to train," Arianna offered. "It gives me something physical to do." Niall's eyes glinted in a way Arianna wasn't sure she liked.

"We have the best instructors around. I could fetch one for you."

"She's fine with us," Ellie said, her tone still hostile.

"And yet, she was kidnapped and held hostage for a very long time." He glanced at Rion and Arianna could have sworn her mate flinched before anger trickled down the bond.

Niall stepped back. "But you seem confident in her abilities so," he gestured, "why not give us a demonstration?"

All color drained from Arianna's face as she stared at Niall's expectant expression. She lifted her gaze to the stairs where the council had also gathered.

This wasn't happening. If they saw her fight and determined her abilities less than adequate, it would be like facing her father all over again. They'd view her as nothing more than a weak, defenseless female. A female that needed their protection and coddling.

"Arianna," Ellie called, but her sister wasn't smiling and she most certainly wouldn't be holding back. But it wasn't arrogance that sparked through Ellie's eyes. No, her sister honestly believed in her. Arianna just wished she possessed the same level of confidence to believe in herself.

Arianna shifted into a stance, but her legs had gone heavy, as if they were one with the stones beneath her feet.

Her arms suddenly felt ridiculous by her face, as if she were holding them all wrong. Her breathing was off, too fast and shallow. Were they already laughing?

Ellie sped forward, her feet light and virtually silent against the stone. But Arianna missed the first block. Ellie pulled back at the last second, her hand barely grazing Arianna's stomach. Arianna blocked the next strike, but missed the one after and felt Ellie's knuckles graze her cheek.

Ellie slowed, pulled back, and scrunched her face. Arianna's heart fell. Disappointment. Disappointment would come next and Ellie would be another person—her sister turned toward Rion and raised her voice. "I need you to do me a favor." He raised a brow. "Block."

Ellie's magic ripped from the air, the particles moving so fast they crashed into one another and solidified before shooting toward Arianna's mate in deadly jagged spikes. Arianna's heart leapt into her throat. Rion blocked them easily enough.

But Ellie continued throwing her magic again and again and again.

The crowd murmured. Rion stepped back and confusion knitted his brow.

"Stop it," Arianna said, but her sister ignored her. The icy mixture struck out again, peppering Rion's barrier. He retreated another step and Arianna sensed his fear when Ellie's magic shot at him from his left.

"I said stop it," Arianna demanded with a bit more force. Again, Ellie didn't respond and when Ellie's magic drew too close, Arianna snapped.

The ancient power spilled through her blood, coating every cell with raw energy. She felt like a storm, like a bolt of lightning ready to lash out from the building pressure.

Ellie's magic barreled toward Rion again, but this time Arianna screamed and ice cracked the stone they stood upon. It shot between her mate and sister like an asp, so fast she didn't register what had happened until it was already over.

Frost coated Arianna's feet, rooting her to the stones, and a sheet of ice thicker than her body separated the two people she cared for. It towered over their heads, three times the size of the hedges that wrapped around the gardens.

Arianna's breathing came too fast and she struggled to rein herself in. Panic gripped her in a steel vice threatening to suffocate all rational thought.

She just—she had barely moved. Hardly thought about what she had wanted. But her magic had responded.

Kirian still sat on the stone bench, a quill in his hand. Talon stood on the sideline with his lips parted. Rion was already crossing the slick stones and Ellie—Ellie was smiling. Smiling so wide that it infuriated her.

"What's so funny?" Arianna growled at her sister.

Ellie shook her head but her gaze drifted toward the council members. They'd visibly paled and shrank back looking as though they'd seen a ghost. Or the destruction of their perfectly crafted plans.

"I think that ought to cover it for one day," Ellie said. She marched around the ice wall, ignoring Arianna's glaring expression. Rion paused, wary as Ellie motioned for Kirian to follow her. Then the pair ascended the stairs, right past those still gaping at the massive wall Arianna had formed in the middle of the training yard.

Chapter Thirty

Arianna

"Chocolate or vanilla?"

Arianna pinned Rion with a stare. "You should already know the answer to that one."

He smirked. "Just confirming in case you have a secret favorite."

"What about you?" Rion moved his knight and Arianna made a face. She had no hope of beating him. None whatsoever.

"Vanilla, if I had to choose between the two, but I prefer strawberry over anything."

"It's heresy to prefer anything over chocolate."

Rion placed a hand over his heart. "Then consider me a heretic."

Arianna laughed and moved a pawn. After a quick shower, they had escaped to the library where Rion had bombarded her with a sea of questions.

And they'd talked for what seemed like hours. He knew what her favorite games had been as a child, what books she preferred, the season she loved most, and her favorite meals.

He'd had to answer all the same questions, of course. Unsurprisingly, he'd been playing chess since he was old enough to comprehend the pieces. His mother had taught all her children. He enjoyed fall when the trees and ground were littered with color. And roasted chicken was his absolute favorite if prepared correctly. Arianna tucked the information away, determined to have the cooks make something soon. Or perhaps she could sneak into the kitchens herself.

Their light conversation cooled Arianna's temper and though she still wanted to scream at her sister, she also understood.

Ellie had attacked Rion to show Niall and the council that Arianna wasn't to be trifled with. She'd done her a favor, really, but that didn't mean Arianna was ready to forgive her. Maybe tomorrow. By breakfast she'd see her sister's smiling face and have no choice but to smile back.

Arianna huffed, studying the board. "Music," she said, moving another piece. "Tell me about your favorite music."

Rion started to respond but the entrance doors opened a second later. Arianna groaned. She just wanted one evening. One evening with her mate where she could pretend no one else existed. Especially a certain blond male who had pushed Ellie into action.

But despite hoping he had another reason for entering the library, Niall's footsteps paused on the third floor and headed right for them.

Rion eyed her and something in his gaze told Arianna he'd intervene if she wanted him to. She just slowly shook her head. The only reason she was even still in the city was the sliver of hope that Niall might actually help her free the slaves across the continent.

She massaged her temple. Though this was also the same male who had walked by a new mother in chains without sparing her a second glance.

Niall prowled down the aisle at a snail's pace, pretending to study the books as if he hadn't spent five hundred years memorizing the shelves. Rion studied Arianna's face, awaiting the command.

Niall finally stopped before them but she refused to look up. In fact, she didn't even acknowledge his presence. Childish? Maybe, but she didn't care. He leaned against the thick bookshelf and studied the game board.

Several tense seconds passed.

No one moved.

"Do you play?" he asked with a strained tone.

Arianna finally moved a piece, knowing full well that Rion would take it. "Not well," she admitted.

Niall grimaced when Rion stole the piece she'd moved. "Perhaps your mate should take it easy on you." Mate. It was the first time anyone here had called him that. They were all still clinging to the pseudo bond theory.

"If I do, she'll never learn." Arianna studied Rion. He sat straighter now, weight forward on his legs as if he expected to spring up any moment. His arms lightly rested on the table, fingers flexing slightly. Arianna felt his magic stir around her legs, but his eyes remained on the board.

Niall sighed in the awkward silence that begged him to leave. "I feel we've gotten off to a bad start."

"Lying tends to do that," Arianna said, moving another piece without really looking at it. She just needed something to do with her hands.

Niall didn't respond at first. "I could have handled it differently," he admitted. "I could have told you the truth up front and been better prepared. I—" He stopped himself. "I apologize. There's no excuse for my actions. With the centuries I've lived, I'm afraid I've learned to rely on deception far too often. It's a crutch of immortality." He tried to smile, but it didn't reach his eyes. "I hope it's not too late to start over. I'd like us to be friends."

"Just friends?" Arianna wasn't sidestepping the discussion. If she was going to stay, then she would lay out all the rules right now.

Niall eyed her mate. "I think we've already had this discussion, but to solidify my intentions, I'll reiterate: I have plenty of males and females to satisfy my physical desires." He clasped his hands. "Males and females who are plenty willing and free of chains unless they wish for them." She knew the comment was meant to shake the tension, but Arianna kept her face blank. "I won't ask you to join me in my bed unless you wish to." Rion growled, but Arianna could have sworn she saw something in Niall's gaze spark. "Of course, your mate is welcome to join when he's able to share."

Arianna gaped at the audacity. "What?"

"It's only the newly mated and young who feel so territorial over their coupling. As centuries pass, many couples, mated or not, grow bored physically and find alternate forms of entertainment, often with other couples." He gave her a knowing smile.

Arianna cleared her throat and returned to staring at the glass pieces. Her queen was surrounded. She couldn't let Niall distract her with his nonsense.

He seemed to sense her switch in demeanor and tried again. "Can we not be allies, you and I?"

"I won't marry you," she stated and Rion froze. She hadn't told her mate all the details of Niall's previous conversation. "Even as a political front. I'm not comfortable with it and if it's something that will be demanded of me, I'll remove myself from the city."

Niall's gaze softened. "You're so willing to leave."

"I've been given no reason to stay."

"Do you find living here so abhorrent?"

"I find it foreign and wasteful. I see strangers down the halls looking to me for answers and a council that's loyal to someone else. I see a future that's already been decided without my consultation and quite frankly, if I have to threaten to leave at every turn, then I'd rather keep some of my dignity and go now before I'm viewed as a child throwing a tantrum."

"We don't view you that way at all."

"Rion is my mate," she continued. "The council will have to deal with that. He will be present at all future meetings and will stand at my side as I fulfill my role to the people of Alastríona." Arianna met Niall's hesitant gaze. "I know what the texts say and I don't mind ruling with you, but I will not do it under false pretenses. We can be allies, but it will be on my terms and no one else's."

Arianna felt Rion's pride swell down the bond. Pride for her. For his mate rising to stand up for her values and beliefs. She waited, her attention going back to the board as if Niall's answer meant nothing.

"Not much for tradition, are you?" Arianna didn't respond. Niall seemed to be contemplating. If he didn't agree then she'd have to search for a new home. She couldn't return to Levea, not with the growing rebel factions. "I agree."

"To what?"

"Everything." Her lips parted. "Many of our rules were put in place long ago. Too long ago, it seems. I will discuss all this with the council and sort through the details before our next meeting." He paused. "We want you with us, Lady Arianna." She locked eyes with him. "We want you as our queen to guide us toward a better world."

CHAPTER THIRTY-ONE

ARIANNA

The week flew by in a whirlwind of activity. Every morning before breakfast, they joined Ellie for dance lessons. It was still excruciating, especially when she could feel every territorial thought radiating from Rion down the bond, but they were managing. If Rion could handle Talon dancing with her, then he could handle anyone. She hoped.

After breakfast, they proceeded to the training yard where Ellie detailed her adventures sneaking into office spaces. She still hadn't found much. Just more ledgers and some old notes that mentioned an affair between two married couples. It left Ellie frustrated and Arianna fearful. She just prayed her sister wouldn't get caught.

Every day it seemed the crowd watching them train grew. She hated it. Arianna was certain rumors of her abilities were circulating through the manor, but as long as no one provoked her again, they wouldn't glimpse those sort of powers.

The ancient magic baffled Ellie and Talon. Both tried to help her summon it to no avail. Ellie threatened to attack Rion again just to see if it would surface, but Arianna had promptly growled at her sister and Ellie had relented. For now.

Arianna stretched a sore muscle in her side and tried to focus on Ellie instead of the gathering crowd. She was successful for the most part. That was until Rion removed his shirt.

She could have died right there. Sweat rolled off his frame and he tossed the soaked fabric onto an empty bench before shifting back into a stance.

Her mouth went dry and her lips parted. She'd never seen him train like this. Not so openly and without restraint. The way he moved, gliding from one position to another with his magic trailing him. His muscles flexed and he pulled at the earth beneath his feet, taking it up and up and up before it all crashed back down. But it didn't hit the ground. It dispersed instead, circling his body once again.

"Gods above, one would think you've never seen him naked," Ellie said. Arianna jerked her gaze away, cheeks heating. "Hey Rion," Ellie raised her voice and Rion turned, chest rapidly rising and falling. "Care to cover yourself up? Your Queen can't focus."

Rion smirked and Arianna wanted to die. "Be quiet," she hissed, mortified. She couldn't stomach looking at the audience seated on the stairs now.

Her sister smiled. "Then focus."

Arianna refused to look at him again for the rest of the session. It wasn't until Ellie declared them done for the day that Arianna finally glanced toward her mate. He was breathing hard, a sword in hand, and moved in a way that reminded her of the warriors from Brónach.

The earth moved with him, like it was breathing.

He must have sensed her stare because when he turned, they locked eyes and a look of hunger filled his gaze.

Arianna all but dragged him back to their room.

Once showered and sated, Arianna headed to the slave quarters. Though they'd been freed of their duties, many were skeptical anything would change. Some wondered if they should have traveled to Levea or whether the few that had were suffering a worse fate.

Arianna tried to assure them their friends were fine and she promised to relay any messages once they received word.

Zylah was constantly on the move, organizing and preparing.

By nightfall, Arianna found herself in the library, studying by the light of the lanterns lining the wall. She thew her pen down, letting it clatter against her notepad. It wasn't right. She should be helping Zylah.

Arianna rubbed her eyes and Rion slid the book from her hands. "You're working too hard."

"I'm not working hard enough."

Rion offered her a gentle smile. "There will always be things to do, but they don't need to be done this week or the next. You can take your time."

"You just want me to yourself," she teased.

"I want you to be free," he said. "I want you to relax."

Arianna looked away. "I'm not sure I'm afforded that luxury anymore." At least not for a while. "But a walk might be nice."

Rion pulled her to her feet and Arianna followed him down the stairs, through the halls, and out the garden doors. Night had fallen and the manor was largely empty aside from the souls who wandered the moonlit gardens.

They walked hand in hand and Arianna breathed in the crisp air. Winter was still trying to cling to the edges of spring, reluctant to be forgotten so soon.

Former slaves ambled about, no longer bound by curfew. Her heart warmed to watch their newfound freedom, knowing how relieving something so simple could be.

She'd eventually ensure they received proper education, too. Then they could pursue whatever path they wished to walk in life. It would never replace the time they'd lost, but at least they might fulfill some of their dreams. Make their mark on the world if they wished to.

The pair rounded a corner and found Zylah seated on a bench, scribbling furiously in a little book. The female's hair fell around her face and Arianna wondered if she'd found purpose in her new task. Their reunion had been so brief. She hadn't found time to ask the female how she'd been or how those in Levea were being treated. Whether her friend was happy.

Zylah glanced up and closed her book. She smiled at Arianna, opened her mouth, then closed it again upon spotting Rion at her side. Zylah glanced at their clasped hands and her brow furrowed.

"Hi," Arianna said a bit awkwardly. "How are things going?"

Zylah's nostrils flared and her gaze shifted to Rion again before she replied. "We're making progress. Pádraigín's Lord has been helpful, though I expect his efforts are only to impress you." She sighed and glanced down at her notebook. "The Fae are already complaining there aren't enough workers now that the slaves have been freed." She twisted the pen in her hand.

"I have a meeting with the council in the morning. I'll sort out the details and ensure everyone is treated fairly." Zylah didn't respond and the way she looked at Rion again had the hairs on the back of Arianna's neck standing on end.

"I spoke to former slaves in Levea," Zylah said, but Arianna knew she wasn't talking to her anymore. "They told me what you did. Many of them regard you as their savior."

Rion shifted on his feet, clearly uncomfortable. "I am no such thing." Arianna clutched his hand tighter.

Zylah lowered her gaze to her book again. "You liberated hundreds of slaves over the decades. You reunited families and pulled them from a life of torment." She paused and Arianna's heart clenched, knowing exactly what the female was going to ask next. "So why didn't you help those in your war camp?"

The world stilled. Arianna's instincts made her want to lash out and defend her mate, but memories gnawed at a festering wound she wasn't sure would ever heal. A male who had cared for his fellow slaves, dead in an instant. The young who had resisted, gone without a sound. The many slaves who had been beaten, chained, and left to die.

Rion met Zylah's eyes without flinching. "I could offer you a million reasons, but they'd all amount to little more than excuses."

Rion's gaze drifted toward her and Arianna felt guilt trickle down the bond. "The truth is, I stopped caring."

Zylah stopped spinning the pen in her hand. "Yet, you still ran slaves to the border. I don't understand." And she'd sit here until she got an answer, Arianna realized. She wanted to know what had been different, why she'd never been given the same chance as those who'd obtained their freedom.

Rion looked off into the garden, studying the shadows. His voice was soft when he spoke again. "Some days I cared more than others. There were times when I ripped warriors from their tents and tore their bodies apart for what they were doing. Other days," he sighed. "Other days I kept walking, convinced nothing I did would change the atrocities around me. There were times I passed a slave that had been beaten and I killed the one responsible. Other times, I turned away." Rion scrunched his brow. "I was tired. Tired of trying and failing."

"You are a Lord of Brónach."

Rion chuckled, but his face looked pained, full of shameful memories. "I am The Demon first and foremost. I have no more claim to the throne than the slaves working the fields."

Zylah grimaced. "I don't know whether to hate you or be grateful for what you did."

"Hate me," Rion said without hesitation. Arianna's heart clenched. "The little good I might have done doesn't compare to the atrocities I've committed and those I ignored."

Zylah inclined her head toward Arianna. "She doesn't hate you."

Rion looked at his mate and something in Arianna cracked as she realized the words he wanted to voice but didn't.

She should.

CHAPTER THIRTY-TWO

ARIANNA

Arianna wore dark colors. A tunic and pants that breathed easily and allowed her to move unhindered. She slid knives into her boots and buckled leather straps around her waist to hold a few more. She wasn't walking into that room to bring peace today.

Rion skimmed over her attire and she found a glimmer of approval in his gaze. He knew her plans. This was her ultimatum. She would lay everything out and if they disagreed, then she'd move on, start somewhere new, and form her own council.

It'd be a slow process if she had to go that route. She wouldn't have any allies or any sort of leverage and if the council stood in her way . . . well, she'd face that possibility when she got there.

Arianna held her head high as she marched down the halls. She'd skipped breakfast, her stomach too knotted to hold anything down. She'd already canceled their dance lesson. She needed all the rest she could get. She needed her mind clear and focused.

Rion marched at her side. Death incarnate. Tight clothes showed off his warriors body and the way he walked, with a predator's gait, had more than a few darting behind closed doors.

The sight of them drew the concerned gazes of everyone they passed. Talon waited beside the council doors and acknowledged their approach. He joined the procession into the council room. Everyone was already there, waiting just as she'd planned.

Niall stood from his chair, eyes surveying her face, then her clothes and weapons. The council wasn't armed and neither was Niall, but she didn't care. Not today. Let them be uncomfortable. Let them bristle against her aggression. These were Fae willing to imprison children and she was about to tear their comfortable world apart brick by brick.

Niall's voice was steady when he spoke. "Should I call for chairs for your companions?"

"We'll stand," Rion said, moving toward one of the back walls. Talon joined him. Both males stood with their feet wide, but Arianna could scent their magic in the air around her. They were ready to intervene should things go awry. The changes she sought would dramatically unroot their entire future. She expected resistance and was prepared for it.

Everyone's hearts beat just a little too fast.

Niall nodded. "Then let's begin." He pulled a chair out for her and Arianna sat before the council. "First," Niall began. "I want to assure you that we've been working hard to meet your demands." Niall straightened the papers in his hands. "I've sent word to the High Lords that every child under the age of sixteen is to be freed from slavery effective immediately."

That stopped her. "Across the continent?" Her voice was barely audible.

Niall nodded. "I didn't see any reason to wait until this meeting as I was certain it would be something you wanted. I had hoped the action might show how serious we are about meeting your demands." He separated a few pages from the stack before him and slid them toward her. "This details that children are an exception to slavery. It also states that mothers are to be freed for five years after giving birth in order to raise their children, and infants aren't to be taken from their mothers for any reason."

"Now," Declan said, "know that this means some are going to be homeless. Not everyone will care for a slave out of the kindness of their hearts."

Niall nodded again. "So we've also outlined safehouses where refugees can gather for now. Lady Evelyn offered a few sanctuaries across Móirín and we've also made plans to expand the town below. We anticipate hostility, but with any luck we'll at least begin to make changes."

Words were foreign things lost on her tongue. Her mouth gaped. She tried to speak, failed, and swallowed once before trying again. "This is . . ."

"You're pleased?" Niall appeared hopeful.

She glanced around the room at the faces studying her, waiting for her approval. "This is so much more than I'd hoped for." This was it. It was starting. Today, there would be children freed from their shackles. Today, mothers would rock their babies without chains. Today was a day for new beginnings.

Niall beamed. "We've been speaking at length with your advisor Zylah and Lady Evelyn, and we have a list of things that need your approval for the former slaves throughout the city. You've given them freedom, but some don't wish to leave, as I'm sure you've been told." Arianna nodded.

"As of today, slavery within Ruadhán is forbidden, and those who attempt the act will be exiled and severely punished. We're giving them a one-week grace period to ensure the information is received. Those who don't wish to comply will be escorted back to their homelands, but their former slaves will remain here, just as you wished."

Niall only paused a moment before continuing. "We've implemented a system similar to the one in Levea where each slave will be offered a sum for their past service. Beyond that, they'll be allowed to choose their profession and will receive a fair wage for their work."

Arianna scanned the document. She'd have to read through it later, just to ensure everything was detailed the way she wanted. "And their hours will be restricted to a reasonable level?" There wasn't much use in wages if they never got time to spend it.

Niall hesitated. "Not yet, but we can add it in," he said quickly. "We'll make amendments as you see fit, but don't feel rushed. I'm already having notices posted around the city and surrounding towns."

Arianna lowered the papers, her heart beating fast. This had to be a dream. "Zylah mentioned there's been a shortage of staff due to the slaves who left."

Niall exchanged a glance with the council members. "Yes," he huffed out a breath. "It's an issue we're trying to resolve."

"What about those in the town below? Surely some would volunteer."

"It poses a security risk," Meegan said.

"But we need to consider it," Felic offered.

Arianna furrowed her brow. "A security risk to me, you mean?"

Meegan nodded. "We've kept threats at bay by limiting those permitted to enter."

"I'm quite capable of protecting myself and if not," Arianna gestured toward Rion and Talon, "I have others to help." Not to mention those in her father's guard. She rarely saw them, but could scent their presence everywhere she went.

Niall nodded. "Then we'll begin scanning potentials, both Fae and half-breeds."

Felic cleared his throat and opened a heavy book. "Can we discuss the extreme expenses associated with the slave's freedom and how they'll be compensated?" He looked at Arianna. "Would you be willing to pull from your personal funds?"

Arianna blanched. She looked at Niall, then back to Felic "I—" Gods, where was she supposed to find money? "I can ask my father perhaps," Arianna trailed off at Niall's wide grin and the way he tried to hide his laugher.

"I guess I didn't do a good enough job explaining the royal coffers, did I?"

"I—the what?"

The council looked at him and Niall shook his head, that smile still covering his face. "Forgive me. I thought I made it clear on your initial tour of the grounds." He thought back. "I suppose that explains why you weren't more excited when I mentioned it." She stared at him blankly. "You are probably the richest Fae who has ever walked the continent."

She swallowed hard. "So when you said royal coffers . . ."

"I meant your coffers. Your money. Money that has been collected over a very, very long time. Centuries. Longer. The contents were gifted by the four countries as payment for their queen to come so she could implement her will without hindrance."

"I—I didn't know." Arianna shook her head, trying to regain her composure. "Of course the money can come from there."

Felic scribbled something in his book.

Arianna straightened and watched for a moment as they exchanged bits of information, shuffling through papers to line everything up the way she wanted.

They had freed children, but it wasn't enough. Not by a long shot. She squared her shoulders and prepared herself for the next onslaught of questions. For the flat-out refusals or for them to laugh in her face.

"I want to abolish slavery completely."

Everyone stopped. The council. Niall. The world. Her heart.

They gaped at her as if she'd just made the most outrageous suggestion on the planet.

Declan glanced toward Niall then wetted his lips. "It is one thing to deem it illegal within the confines of a single city, but to do so across the entire continent . . ." His words trailed off. Arianna knew this wouldn't be taken lightly. She knew it would take work, but she had made a promise and she intended to keep it.

Fina, who had remained silent until now, finally spoke, though her words were careful. "This is the way we've lived for centuries. Humans serve us as punishment for their past."

"A past they don't remember," Arianna said. "A past those living had no part in." She clasped her hands on the table before her. "I know the history and I understand the anger, but when is enough

enough? Why do we punish half-breeds for their split heritage when our blood courses through their veins as well? When did we decide that being half Fae meant you weren't Fae at all?" Arianna met their uncertain stares. "Enough with the anger. Enough with the heartbreak. On both sides."

The council members kept silent, but their uneasy gazes told her they weren't convinced. She rolled up her sleeves to reveal the thick marks around her wrists.

Arianna's voice was quiet. "Do you have any idea how much pain slaves suffer through day in and day out? Do any of you know what it's like to be clapped in iron and separated from your magic? To be vulnerable?"

"No," came Niall's soft voice.

"None of you do." Arianna rolled her sleeves back down. "Slavery is a horrendous act and if you want peace, then it has to stop. It's time we move on from our hatred."

They were silent for so long, Arianna wasn't sure they would speak again. Maybe they would need to wait until next week to answer, but then Niall said, "It will take time. Even Móirín took eight years to phase it out completely and there are still illegal trading rings to this day." His face fell. "As I'm sure you're aware." She was. She'd been kidnapped in her home country. A place where slavery had been outlawed for decades.

"Merchants rely on the labor to trade and transport goods," Niall continued. "Many who care for our well-being rely on the same. There are slaves, I'm sure, who will want to set out on their own instead of accepting a wage. The loss of labor could throw an entire economy out of balance. If you want to abolish slavery successfully, it will be a slow process."

Time. Time wasn't something humans had. Most half-breeds didn't have it, either. Arianna hated the idea. Eight years was such a long time for them to suffer, but she couldn't risk economic collapse.

Niall seemed to notice the sorrow on her face. "However, there are laws we can implement that will make their lives more comfortable." Niall looked toward Gavin and the young male jumped to his feet, eager to be part of the conversation. He'd been so silent, Arianna had forgotten he was there. Gavin set his pen and tablet on the table.

Niall thought for a moment. "We can make it illegal for them to live in harsh conditions. We can demand proper meals three times a day, outlaw severe beatings, and place a limit on how many hours they work."

Arianna nodded. It was something, at least. "I want the elderly cared for too. Their bodies grow weak as they age. Hard labor is too difficult for most."

Niall nodded. "We'll ensure their comfort." Gavin kept writing, then stepped back. Niall reached for her hand, then stopped himself. He glanced at Rion and met a watchful gaze. "I hope all this pleases you."

Arianna swallowed the lump in her throat. "Very much."

"Enough that you'll stay? Enough that you could call Ruadhán your home?"

Arianna met the council members' faces one at a time and saw the hope in their eyes as they waited for her answer. They had taken her threat to leave seriously. They had met her demands instead of writing them off. And they were willing to do more than she ever imagined.

"When I woke up this morning, I was ready to pack my bags and leave this city behind."

Niall sat straighter. "And now?"

"Now I'm ready to see this continent changed for the better."

Niall loosed a breath. "I can't tell you how glad we are to hear that." He stared at her for a moment with something like admiration in his gaze, then clapped his hands together, startling everyone in the room. "Right, now that that's out of the way, on to discussions about the ball." She paled. "Which only involves you, I'm afraid."

"What?"

"The vendors and shop owners are in the next hall over. They'll be here any minute and want your input on, well, on everything."

Arianna twisted in her seat when Niall waved his hand and a guard opened the door. She looked toward Rion and Talon, suddenly wishing she'd worn something a bit more inviting.

Niall and the council stood. "Prepare yourself. They're a little excited."

CHAPTER THIRTY-THREE

SAOIRSE

Alec pinched the bridge of his nose. His dark brown hair hung over even darker eyes as he scanned the page, reading over its contents for the third time. The black envelope and gold phoenix seal told Saoirse exactly where it had come from.

She tried to be patient. "What does it say?"

Alec sighed and slid the paper across the table. "This new queen is going to start changing things faster than I anticipated."

Saoirse read over the words. A single paragraph that demanded an end to child slavery. Not a request. Not something they planned to work toward. A law that carried harsh consequences if not implemented.

"I'm sure this is going over well in Fiadh."

Alec scoffed. "Pádraigín is the one who procures the slaves. I'm willing to bet their council is in an uproar."

Saoirse popped a grape into her mouth. "Maybe, but the Lord of Pádraigín is the one who signed it." Saoirse wondered how that was being received by Fiadh too. Perhaps the council in Ruadhán felt no one would take the new queen seriously before her coronation.

"Besides," Saoirse tossed the paper and envelope back onto the table. "It's about time. Trading in children is barbaric."

Alec eyed her. "Some might label you a human sympathizer."

She shrugged. "They can label me whatever they wish. Don't you think the whole slave thing is a bit outdated anyway? I mean, Móirín did away with it ages ago and it's worked out well for them."

Alec didn't reply. The grief of their past weighed heavy on all of them. No amount of time would ever heal a wound so deep.

Alec cleared his throat and changed the subject. "Were you able to meet her?"

Saoirse ran fingers through her damp hair and reached for her steaming cup of tea. "No." Alec frowned. "She was a bit preoccupied."

He scowled. "With what? You're a representative of Brónach, the least she could do is give you—"

"She found her mate," Saoirse interrupted.

Her brother froze, knowing full well what a mating bond meant. They'd witnessed its depth between their parents. They'd watched their father fall apart, torn at the seams as he lost a piece of himself month after month until he was so cold Saoirse had hardly recognized him.

Alec sat back. "So it's true then. The Lord of Pádraigín will become the King of Alastríona." He chuckled to himself. "I guess I best start groveling now for all the petty disagreements we've had through the years." Alec picked at a piece of lint on his sleeve. "How did *he* take it?"

Saoirse blinked at her brother, confused until she remembered Ruadhán had come to collect their queen. Alec must have assumed the Lord of Pádraigín was among them.

But that wasn't the case at all.

Saoirse wrapped both hands around her mug and settled deeper into her cushioned chair, preparing for the anger about to spill from her older sibling. "The Lord of Pádraigín never came to Levea."

Alec furrowed his brow. "But you said the queen found her mate."

"I did."

Alec waited a moment, but she could see the information processing. He knew, but still asked, "Then who is it?"

"Rion," she said simply.

"That's not possible."

She shrugged. "I met with him before I left. It seemed real enough."

Alec clenched his fists. "If he hurts her—"

Saoirse laughed. "Rion would tear himself apart before he ever laid a hand on that female."

Her brother wasn't convinced. "You believe he's changed so much?"

She nodded, not wanting to argue that Rion had always been Rion. She hadn't mentioned the rest. The fact that Rion had almost died at the hands of Avalon or that her little brother had given up altogether when faced with the prospect of losing Arianna. It felt too personal of a thing to share, especially since Alec still hadn't forgiven him even though he knew the truth about their father's death and who was really responsible.

Alec crossed the room and stopped before an old bookshelf full of maps, tomes, and Alastríona's history. "The ancient texts tell us one thing. Something we've believed all our lives and it turns out to be true. Yet another part of it is false. How are we to make sense of that?"

"Maybe the scholars didn't know what they were doing after all."

He ran a hand down a book's spine. "Maybe." He looked ready to say more but stopped himself. "I want you to meet her, make your own assumptions, and report back."

"I already planned on it. You think I've been dress shopping for fun?"

He pinned her with a look. She yawned and stretched her legs. "I'm headed for bed then. I have a lot to do tomorrow."

Alec nodded and Saoirse paused in the doorway, noting the way Alec kept staring at that book. She'd never been very religious and had made a point to avoid the temples in her adult life. But one thing was becoming clear. Something somewhere in their history wasn't right, and when they uncovered the truth, it might very well fracture the foundation of their world.

SAOIRSE DIDN'T head into the office the following day. Her brother didn't expect her anyway. She had schedules to make and she needed to determine who would be accompanying her to Ruadhán. She would have loved to take Eoghan. The male was a well of knowledge. But he'd just returned and needed time with his family. She smiled. His wife might have Saoirse's head otherwise.

Her warriors moved swiftly, gathering their things and making final preparations. They were ecstatic for the opportunity to see Ruadhán up close. It was a once in a lifetime opportunity, even for an immortal.

She tried to focus on the task at hand, but the longer she worked, the more Saoirse couldn't get a certain half-breed out of her mind. The female haunted her every step. Saoirse saw her among the slaves that walked the halls. And in those she commanded when they lowered their gazes and bowed their heads.

A pang of regret flew through her. A sense of wrongness.

That evening, Saoirse studied the female slave who had served her for five years. She'd found her when she was seventeen. Half-starved and beaten, standing on the auctioneers podium with her head lowered. Saoirse had collected her and two others that now served in the kitchens. No one had dared to bid against her. They knew better.

Eithne was faithful, but what might she have become if she'd been born in Móirín instead?

Saoirse set a stack of papers down and twisted to face the female. "What would you do if you were granted freedom?"

Eithne froze and Saoirse heard her breath hitch. The female's heart quickened and she struggled to keep her voice steady. "It's not a slave's place to think about such things."

"It might be," Saoirse said. The queen would command the slaves' freedom eventually. Saoirse had heard the rumors about the scars she was said to carry around her wrists. She had once been a slave in Rion's camp after all.

Though she hated to admit it, Zylah had been right about one thing. Saoirse had never truly stopped to consider what freedom might mean to a slave. She'd always seen them as property and now she felt sick to her stomach at the idea.

"Have you ever been told why the Fae hate humans so much?" Eithne shook her head. "Millenia ago, Fae lived alongside humans on the continent to the north. Some coexisted, but most couldn't get along. Humans were ever-changing while the Fae, with their long lives, liked to keep things traditional. It started many wars and eventually the Fae lost."

Eithne's head shot up, disbelief covering her face. Saoirse continued. "They learned our one weakness. Our families. Younglings." Eithne's face paled. "They clamped iron around us and took our abilities with a knife to our children's throats. As I'm sure you are aware, we treasure our children above all else. The blessing is so rare." Saoirse shook her head.

"We complied with all their demands and they killed our children anyway. Slaughtered them right in front of their parents. It broke most, but those still willing to fight escaped and fled here. A land full of dangerous unknown creatures.

"It's a long brutal story. One that encompasses the usage of Dark Fae to do our bidding. They protected us, believe it or not, and the humans stopped hunting us down. We freed those we could, but I'd wager there are Fae still trapped in the north even now."

"That's . . . awful."

Saoirse gave a strained laugh. "Yes. Awful, yet we've done the same to humans and half-breeds, blaming those alive now for the sins of their forefathers." Saoirse looked at her slave again. "It's time for a change, and I want to know what you'd do with your freedom."

Eithne chewed her lip. "I don't know." She gestured to the clothes she'd been folding. "This is all I've ever known." She caught herself then. "I'm grateful, though; you've been very kind and I'll happily serve you for the rest of my life."

Saoirse tasted her fear, then pulled a key from her pocket. Eithne went very still. Saoirse approached her carefully and took the female's callused hands in her own. She put the key in the tiny hole, twisted, and the first shackle fell.

"You're free to do as you will, but stay by my side." The second shackle hit the ground. "Allow me to pay you to continue the work you've always done, and I'll give you whatever future you want." Tears fell from Eithne's eyes. "I can never return the years you've lost, but I want to teach you how to live on your own and when you're ready, you can set out and find the life you should have had all along."

CHAPTER THIRTY-FOUR

ARIANNA

Excited was the understatement of the century. Arianna had spent hours listening to a dozen people talk over one another about color schemes, themes, fabrics, ribbons, dresses, and more.

She had wanted to run and let the designers handle things, but Arianna had forced herself to offer her opinions and feign interest. She wasn't sure how they expected her to be excited about such things when so many suffered across the continent. She had documents to review that were far more important than the color of ribbon. Or what flower arrangements should decorate the tables.

But Arianna had to remind herself that the people of Ruadhán had never known hardship. They'd lived in finery from birth. An easy life full of color and soft fabrics.

Rion and Talon had both stood behind her, watching every move of those who'd gathered. Many had shied away from the grains of sand at first, but they grew more comfortable as the minutes ticked by until they didn't seem to notice Rion's magic at all.

That was four days ago.

Now she sat in the library with Rion beside her, reading through the documents Niall had prepared. Arianna rubbed her tired eyes. Niall had been thorough, editing each country's laws one by one and changing them accordingly with a no tolerance or negotiation message stamped in big letters at the bottom of each page. She knew the demands were bold, especially when she hadn't been in her position long, but change needed to start and it needed to start now.

Arianna looked at her mate who seemed to be studying the grains of wood on the table. "If there's somewhere else you'd rather be . . ."

Rion laughed and finally stood. He grabbed one of her romance books. "I'm quite content where I am." Arianna grinned when Rion opened to the first page. Fairy tales with happy endings might do him some good.

She was glad to have him here, even if they weren't talking. His presence steadied her.

But even with him near, Arianna couldn't shake her feelings of inadequacy. Eight years. She wished she could end it sooner. Maybe she would write a letter to her father and ask exactly how he'd implemented an end to slavery across Móirín. And what he did with those who refused to comply.

Arianna signed her name for what felt like the hundredth time, suddenly thankful for all those lessons on calligraphy.

When she finished, Arianna stood and stretched her stiff and aching body. She left the library, Rion in tow, and found the nearest servant. They pointed her toward the garden and Arianna found Niall seated on a bench, gazing into the afternoon sky.

"I finished them."

He blinked at her in surprise. "Already?" Arianna nodded. "I didn't expect—" He shook his head. "Is everything to your liking?"

"I think so." She'd asked Rion to clarify a few passages, just to be sure she understood them.

"Good, very good." Niall took the papers and waved over a female Arianna had never seen before. She bowed low, careful not to meet Arianna's gaze. "Be sure these get where they need to go."

"Yes, My Lord." The female snatched the papers and ran off. Arianna watched her, curious.

"She was never a slave," Niall said, breaking the silence. "She's been an assistant of mine for many years. She's quiet but does her job so well I could never hope to replace her."

Arianna glanced at the door where the female had disappeared.

Niall continued. "She comes from a line without magic. Many think it's a consequence to breeding with humans, though her family claims their lineage is pure. She's an outcast, so I brought her here." Niall's gaze softened. "I want to apologize. It was never our intention to place such a heavy burden on your shoulders. We wanted to give you time to adjust to your new home, but I must admit, I am glad to see you taking such a serious interest in the welfare of your country."

"I made promises," she said. "I intend to keep them."

He studied the sky again. "It's rare to find a Fae so pure in her intentions and words. So many like to weave their own agendas into the mix."

"Do you?" Arianna asked.

"Of course. How else do you think I've maintained order? One must not always tell whole truths when speaking to the Fae if one wants to accomplish their goals. I hope you never have to learn that."

She tilted her head, feeling bolder with him by the day. "Do you do that with me?"

"You're quite forward." She waited and he finally said, "I will strive to tell you the truth in anything you ask of me."

Well, that was about as Fae of an answer as she'd ever get. "Okay."

They stood in silence for a time and Arianna was just about to wander back to her room when Niall said, "I've been meaning to ask you a question involving a potentially sensitive subject. Would now be an appropriate time?" Unsure what to do with herself, Arianna only nodded.

"Your father appointed Lady Evelyn as his heir. Why is that?"

"Has she heard you call her that?"

Niall smirked. "She demanded I address her by her full name, as only her friends are permitted to call her Ellie." Of course she had.

Niall waited and Arianna summoned her courage. Ellie had made her look strong in front of the council and Arianna had made a stand against them where the slaves were concerned. But her stripped title as heir was still a wound that refused to heal.

"My father thought I was too weak to handle it."

"Physically or mentally?"

"Both?"

"You're unsure?"

She sighed. "I think—I'm relearning myself. Sometimes I think the person I used to be might have died in those chains." She glanced at her wrists. "That my years spent in iron changed me."

"Tragedy changes most. Some for better, others for worse."

"How do you know which is which?"

He paused to think. "You have several who care for you. I'd say that speaks volumes. You are brilliant and have such a fire in your soul to correct the unjust things of our world. It could be for that very reason that the gods blessed you as The Divine."

"You think the gods guide me?"

He nodded. "Many do."

One could only hope.

It was her turn to ask a difficult question. "Why didn't Ruadhán intervene during the war?"

Niall didn't respond at first. "Walk with me?" She followed him down the garden path and Rion remained close. He never spoke much around Niall, but she supposed if someone desired her mate, she wouldn't be inclined to speak to them either.

"The war between Brónach and Móirín was unfortunate, but it ultimately boiled down to a personal grudge between the High Lords. Ruadhán has always strived to let them handle their own disputes as we didn't want to project our power. You see, with no official monarch in place, we were afraid to overstep and risk the destruction of this beautiful city. However," he continued. "Now that our queen is here, we can make strides to help those as you see fit."

They entered a building Niall had pointed out during her initial tour. The vault. It was extravagant in the way that everything in Ruadhán seemed extravagant, with flowers, fountains, and decorations made of marble and stone. Some even sparkled with gold that had been melted into the cracks and crevices.

Light filtered in from a space at the top of the walls and tall windows coated with colored panes of glass depicted various scenes from the Fae's long history.

A scene of Fae gaining their freedom, iron cuffs at their feet and an unexplored land stretching before them. A scene of a child being cradled by its mother, the first sign of hope for their people after years of endless sorrow. Another with a group of Fae before a female, all bowing at her feet, reaching their arms toward her as if they might just touch the hem of her robes.

Arianna looked away and followed Niall through another set of doors. They veered right, then descended a flight of stairs. "I hope, in spite of it all, you won't think ill of us. Our priority all these centuries has been to establish a place for The Divine. For you. Nothing else mattered."

"It seems a bit excessive."

He offered her a grimaced smile. "Yes, I understand." She wasn't so sure he did.

Niall pulled a gold key from his pocket and unlocked the door at the end of the hall. She gaped when it swung open to reveal a massive vault door. The gold structure stood twice as tall as Rion and had markings of vines, water, fire, and wind carved into its surface.

Niall pulled a palm sized stone from his pocket that was shaped like an octagon. He clicked a button and it spread open. Each piece was a different length with teeth along the edges that resembled a key. Niall fitted it into the matching section of the vault door and twisted. Locks clicked. He twisted it the opposite direction and more locks moved, sliding out of place. A final time, and the door sprang open.

He ventured inside, but Arianna's stomach clenched with the fear of being locked in. He seemed to note her discomfort. "Not to worry." Niall held up the key. "It works from the inside, too. Just in case."

Lights flickered to life and Arianna gasped. Stretching from the entrance to the rear wall, and almost as long as the main dining hall, were mountains of glittering jewels and gold. So much gold. Shelves lined each wall with an assortment of crowns, raw chunks of precious jewels, and heavy necklaces, bangles, and rings of all sizes.

Niall marveled with her. "This is all your personal collection, but don't fret. It has been collected over a very, very long time and the taxes aren't enough to rile the High Lords. In fact, they hardly seem to notice the donation." His voice lowered when she turned to him at a loss for words. "We've all done our part while we waited for you. We wanted to do whatever we could to give you the resources necessary to set things in motion."

Tears threatened. They had mentioned funds, but this—this was enough to feed everyone. House everyone. She could build until the end of time, hire people to care for the sick and hungry while she made her way across the continent to heal each and every being who needed her. This could bring about real change. Change the continent desperately needed.

"I want to help them," she said, her voice hoarse. "I want to help the world rebuild and give those in need a place to rest."

Niall nodded. "Then I will seek out the best place to start."

"Thank you. Truly, thank you, Niall."

He bowed at the waist, but his eyes never left hers. "It is my absolute pleasure."

Chapter Thirty-Five

Arianna

Someone screamed.

The hairs rose on the back of Arianna's neck and her magic crackled through the air, lifting to circle her form. Rion's did the same.

Everything fell silent, the tense moment before the world turned upside down. Then Fae were running and Arianna followed, instinct and fear driving her toward those in need.

Ruadhán. This was Ruadhán. Nothing bad could happen here. No one would attack the royal city. No one—painful reminders tugged at her heart. Those injured outside of Levea. Those injured within.

The crisp tang of blood assaulted her senses and Arianna's stomach dropped. She'd sprinted through the manor hall and skidded past a few guards without stopping.

Ahead, a crowd had gathered. Panic covered their faces and one female cried, her hands covering her mouth in distress.

"Murderer," someone shouted.

"Half-breed filth." Others joined in a chorus of angry voices that rose until they blocked out all other sounds.

Arianna pushed her way through with Rion on her heels. Those in the crowd quieted upon seeing their queen and pulled their brethren back, pointing her out. Most bowed and backed away, giving her a clear view of the area ahead.

Arianna noticed the flames first, spiraling around a male's body. He didn't wear the fine clothes so many others wore and the scars around his wrists told her he'd been a slave only a few days prior.

Another half-breed with magic.

His nearly black hair had come loose from its tie and curls hung around his tanned face. A face full of loathing and contempt.

Guards were pouring from the manor, the barracks, and the surrounding grounds. Their weapons were drawn, magic out as they shouted orders for the crowd to back away and make room.

Rion stepped when she did, a constant shadow to her movements.

A charred body lay on the walkway. Blood stained the pristine stones. No one needed to check for a heartbeat to know the male was dead.

Arianna's gaze roamed across the scene and whispers floated through the air.

To her right, a female cowered on the ground, her hands covering her face. Blood dripped between her fingers from a wound Arianna couldn't see. Another female whispered to her, arms wrapped around the injured one's shoulders. The half-breed with the flames stood before them both as if he were their protector. His angry gaze hadn't left the charred remains once.

Arianna stepped beyond the crowd and a hushed silence fell over the area.

"My Lady," a male's soft voice. She didn't know him. He bowed, eyed Rion, then glanced back at the scene. "Please, let's get you back to the manor. You don't need to see this." His arm reached out as if to guide her, but Rion's resounding growl had him backpedaling, clutching the weapon at his side.

"What happened?" Arianna asked.

The male still looked uncertain and his heart beat too fast. "We can handle—"

"What happened?" she asked with a bit more force.

The male straightened. "The half-breed killed a close member of the court." He gave her a skeptical look as if it should have been obvious, but Arianna ignored him and instead studied the accused half-breed. He still hadn't looked away from the body on the ground. As if locked in a trance. His fists were clenched so tight his knuckles had gone white.

"Why?"

The male shrugged. "I imagine he feels wronged for being enslaved. I knew something like this would happen if—"

"I wasn't asking you," Arianna snapped. The male didn't utter another word. She stepped forward and he stepped back, fear rippling through him as Rion's sand crawled across the ground, forming a protective perimeter around his mate.

Arianna crept closer to the half-breed. Flames still circled his body, sparking and shooting out as if he couldn't maintain control. She finally stepped into his line of sight, breaking his trance. He focused on her face, but he wasn't afraid.

"Why?" Arianna repeated, her voice softer.

His body shook. "You promised to protect us." He swallowed hard and glanced toward the female in hysterics. Blood still dripped between her fingers. "He didn't care," the male said, voice so low Arianna strained to hear it. His head shot up and he shouted at the crowd. "None of them care."

Arianna glanced between the female still clutching her face and the male lying dead on the ground. "He did that to her?"

The dark-haired male didn't answer at first. "She refused to go to his bed last night. He claimed that if she didn't want to lay with him, then he'd ensure no one would ever want to look at her again." The male gritted his teeth. "Then he beat her and—" his voice trailed off. The male didn't bother swiping at the angry tears rolling down his face.

Arianna's heart crumbled. She knew this pain. Knew the desperate look in his eyes.

"It's okay now." His jaw went slack and Arianna turned from him, shifting her attention to the female clutching her face. Arianna carefully approached and knelt before her.

Another female tried to console the injured one. Her sister, or perhaps even a cousin, if their similar features were anything to go by.

The uninjured female bowed her head, but she didn't release the injured female's shoulders. "My Queen."

The one still crying didn't look up. She didn't appear to notice anything beyond her pain. Her thin body shook with both shock and sobs. Arianna gently pried her hands away and surprisingly the female didn't resist. She didn't look at Arianna at all. Her body just shook and shook and shook.

A deep gash ran from the top of her forehead, across the bridge of her nose, and down the left side of her face. Another mark almost crossed it, coming up the side of her cheek. Arianna swallowed back the bile rising in her throat at the way loose skin hung from the wound. Thankfully, he'd missed her eyes.

Arianna held the female's bloody hand in her own. "May I?" A collective breath went through the crowd, then the female's eyes came into focus. Tears spilled down her face, mixing with the blood and she stared at Arianna, stared until recognition filled her. The female tried to bow her head, but Arianna drew her gaze back. "It might hurt a bit, but I should be able to fix the worst of it."

Arianna wasn't sure whether the female understood, but she nodded and Arianna placed her hand right over the female's wound.

The female winced as the skin knit itself together. The wound was deep, as if her attacker had been determined to cut her straight to the bone. Or kill her.

Those standing nearest gasped and the male with the flames stepped closer, the fire around him vanishing entirely. Rion growled at the crowd when they tried to do the same.

Arianna closed her eyes and focused on the deepest part of the wound first. She worked the muscles, feeling one in the jaw reattach with a suddenness that had the female gasping.

"I'm sorry, it'll leave a scar." She'd learned from the infirmary in Levea that she could heal most things, but sometimes the superficial skin wouldn't mend completely. None cared of course, not with the pain gone, but Arianna wondered if it was a limit to her power or a skill she still needed to learn? Maybe she couldn't heal wounds entirely at all. It'd certainly seemed that way with severe ones.

The female's hand slowly rose to her face and traced the faint scar from her eyebrow to her mouth. Her eyes widened in shock and she stared at Arianna for a time before pressing her face to the ground. The female broke out in violent sobs as she whispered, "Thank you," over and over and over again.

Arianna stood and the crowd parted as guards pushed their way through. Niall emerged from their center, wind whipping around his body in agitated fury.

"What happened?" he demanded.

Arianna answered before the guards could tell the wrong story. "The male was beating a former slave." Arianna gestured to the injured female, then to the male still standing. "And this one defended her."

Niall looked at the body and anger pulsed from him. "By killing him."

"Yes," the male said, his gaze daring as he locked eyes with Niall. "It's nothing short of what he deserved."

Niall's jaw clenched and Arianna saw a flash of rage there she'd never seen before. "The crime you've committed is murder and murder is paid with the life of the accused."

The female's head shot up and her quiet plea was enough to tell Arianna what the two meant to one another.

No one moved despite Niall's command. It was as if they waited for another's opinion. The hesitation didn't go unnoticed.

"You said they had a one-week grace period," Arianna positioned herself closer to the male.

Niall nodded. "I did, as such—"

"Does it not apply to the slaves?"

Niall clenched his jaw again, looking annoyed with her for the first time since she'd arrived. "My Lady, while I can appreciate your efforts toward wanting to ensure they live suitable lives, I cannot, in good standing, condone them for the act of murder."

"But the male was aware of the new law. The half-breed," Arianna gestured toward the one behind her, "heard her scream and yet no one else did?" She eyed the guards skeptically. "None of you heard her?" They looked away and her anger surfaced anew. "They stood aside as a member of *your* court," she spat at Niall, "tried to take what he wanted. I will not have him executed when he fought because no one else would."

Niall eyed her then eyed the crowd, both half-breed and Fae. "A crime this severe cannot go unpunished."

Arianna glared at the charred body with disgust. "What would his punishment have been for harming a former slave?"

Niall's hand flexed. They had an audience. He couldn't be anything but truthful here. "He'd be exiled."

Arianna nodded. "Then that shall be the punishment served."

CHAPTER THIRTY-SIX

ARIANNA

Arianna sat on the roof, nervous anticipation rolling through her as they watched the matte black carriage pulled by two midnight horses make its way down the cobblestone street. Dark red trim lined the wheels and windows giving the whole thing a menacing appearance.

Talon had informed Arianna that the ambassador of Fiadh would be arriving that evening. She hadn't expected the anxious butterflies that had formed in her gut. She knew the ambassador was female, but that was as far as her knowledge went.

Arianna didn't know if she was older, like Niall, or younger like herself. She chewed her lip, watching the wheels roll across the stone in silence. Arianna imagined it had a red carpet inside with thick cushions and smooth panels that glittered with the precious stones Fiadh prided themselves on.

She wondered if she'd ever get to see the grand city carved into the belly of a mountain.

Arianna crossed her legs and gripped her mate's hand. Rion didn't seem nearly as pensive. He watched with an easy calculated gaze, as if he were sizing up an opponent. Was this female her enemy, or was the High Lord from Fiadh telling the truth about his estranged son? Had the attack on Levea really been an isolated event? Rion didn't seem to think so. It did feel a little too convenient, especially since that son had gone missing.

The carriage pulled to a stop before the gates. Four more carriages followed, all black.

The door opened and Arianna held her breath as the image she'd been forming in her mind shattered into a million tiny shards.

She'd been expecting the female to be dressed in a long gown, for her hands to have white, elbow-length gloves that would reach out for someone to assist her down the carriage step. Arianna had imagined the female's hair long and flowing, pinned back in elaborate braids, with jewelry adorning her wrists and neck.

Instead, an elegant warrior emerged clad in black leathers with more knives strapped across her torso than Arianna cared to count. Long braids were tied back from her dark face and Arianna felt Rion's magic spring to life, circling his mate as if she needed protection from the warrior even at this distance.

The female jumped from the carriage with fluid grace, the sword strapped across her back barely moving.

Beautiful. Deadly. Arianna swallowed.

Those in the carriages behind hers exited as well, eyes darting everywhere as they took in the manor and gardens. One female stood just behind the ambassador and rested a hand on her weapon. Her personal guard, Arianna realized.

Servants poured from the manor, rushing to make themselves useful, then the wind tugged at Arianna's loose hair. Slowly the ambassador of Fiadh lifted her eyes up and up and up until they locked with Arianna's.

Arianna scarcely risked a breath beneath her gaze. But it wasn't Arianna the female lingered on. It was the male at her side.

A possessive instinct coursed through her body and Arianna bared her teeth. "Have you ever met her?"

Rion pulled Arianna closer. "No. And I'm certainly not interested in a female who looks ready to slaughter her way through the city."

Arianna remembered dressing to make herself look intimidating. She'd hoped it might encourage the council to listen to her. But she knew, somehow, that this female didn't dress for show. She was just as deadly as the knives strapped across her chest.

When the female broke eye contact and disappeared through the main doors, Arianna loosed a breath of relief. Rion tilted her head back and captured her lips in a greedy kiss that sent shivers through her body. His tongue grazed her bottom lip and he moved to whisper in her ear. "I've never let anyone touch me like this and I never will. I belong to you, body and soul."

Arianna smiled. "You think the bond ever wears off?"

He feathered kisses down her throat. "I can't say I want it to."

"I'd like to not feel the need to strangle every female who looks at you."

Rion hummed against her open mouth. "I like it." She scoffed, but Rion drew her closer, his hands wandering over her body, leaving trails of fire in their wake. "To know someone wants to fight for me. Kill for me. It's . . . not a feeling I have words for."

He didn't need words, not when she could feel it too. A veil still separated them, like reaching through a murky pond, but she felt enough, especially when they were so close.

"Your sister will be here tomorrow," Arianna said. They'd received the reports that morning. "Do you plan on greeting her?"

"If it gets us out of morning dance lessons? Yes."

Arianna laughed. "I thought you enjoyed those."

Rion arched a brow. "I detest having a male touch you day in and day out."

Arianna didn't partially like Ellie touching him either, but she'd adjusted to it and hardly took notice anymore. Arianna eyed the carriage and those loosening the straps on the horses. "Will you be all right at the ball?"

Rion clenched his jaw. "I won't lie and say I'll enjoy it, but I'll control myself. That much I promise." He glanced away. "I won't behave like I did when we first arrived."

"You think that bothered me?"

"Didn't it?"

Arianna nuzzled his neck and nipped the tender skin at the base of his throat. A soft moan escaped his lips. "Maybe you aren't the only one who enjoys their mate's possessiveness."

Chapter Thirty-Seven

Arianna

Arianna chased Rion down the hall. Her stomach had been tossing all morning.

Saoirse. His sister. The one person who hadn't deemed Rion a monster simply from the magic he possessed. She'd saved him and hidden him from the world until he was old enough to care for himself.

But she'd also let him live in exile with the world believing he'd murdered their father. She understood why. Sort of. Arianna knew it sounded logical, but she couldn't help the spike of anger at how one could let a family member suffer so much. But maybe the truth wouldn't have made a difference either way.

"My Lady." A former slave bowed in passing. Many were still shaken from the bloody event a few days ago, but they were adjusting. The male had been escorted to Levea, along with the two females he'd protected. Arianna hoped they'd find peace there.

Arianna politely inclined her head. She glanced out the window, watching those previously shackled wander the gardens as they saw fit. They were free from burden and she'd seen some of the light return to their eyes.

Many had opted to switch professions and most refused to work beneath their former masters. Arianna didn't ask why. It would only breed anger, and Zylah had once told her that a slave's suffering was their own burden to bear. Arianna wouldn't violate them by prying.

"I want a hot bath drawn," a loud female voice echoed down the hall. "And breakfast brought to my room. Don't forget the wine," she added quickly. Wine? The sun had barely risen.

They rounded the corner and a tall, beautiful female with wavy dark blonde hair spun to greet them. Emerald green eyes locked with her own. Rion's eyes. Her scent was similar too, though hers carried a floral undertone Rion's lacked.

The female placed her gloves on a nearby tray held by a servant, then kicked off her dirty boots. That's when Arianna noticed the dry blood caking her sleeves and torso. Concern flew through her, but the female didn't appear hurt. Arianna wasn't sure she wanted to know where the blood had come from.

But seeing a warrior armed from head to toe in a pair of white socks was enough to elicit a smile from Arianna.

"I didn't want to drag in the mud," Saoirse explained. "Or blood. It's too nice in here to dirty up the floors, even if there are servants to clean it."

Servants. Not slaves. The change in reference wasn't lost on Arianna. She knew Brónach kept slaves.

A female about Arianna's age stood behind Saoirse even now, but she didn't have iron around her wrists.

Saoirse's gaze locked with Arianna's. Arianna wasn't sure what the female saw there, but she smiled in greeting.

Then Rion's magic flared to life.

Saoirse laughed. "Relax, little brother, I'm not going to steal your mate." Arianna cocked her head in confusion. "Rion knows I prefer females." She waved a hand. "As such, his instincts demand he keep you away from me. But," she said, lowering her voice. "He'll just have to get over that because I fully intend to steal a dance."

Rion bristled, then settled himself. He glanced at the blood on her clothes and frowned. "Did you run into trouble?"

She waved her hand again. "Nothing I couldn't handle, but I had to stay up for the rest of the trip and now I'm starving, filthy, and plan to sleep the afternoon away. However," Saoirse approached and Arianna wasn't sure whether she should back away or remain where she was. His sister took her hand and kissed the back of it, eliciting a soft growl from her brother that she ignored. "I wasn't going to do any of those things without officially meeting you." Arianna was at a loss for words. Something sparked in the female's gaze as she turned to her brother. "I hope my little brother hasn't told too many lies about me."

"N—No, not at all."

Saoirse's smile widened. "Relax, I'm only teasing. No need to be so serious."

The confident female before her opened her mouth to speak again, but every muscle in Saoirse's body froze. Her smile faded, earlier bravado completely forgotten as she twisted toward a doorway in the hall. Arianna followed her gaze. Zylah stood there, clipboard in one hand and a tray of food and drink in the other.

Both females stared, but neither moved.

Zylah assessed Saoirse in a way that told Arianna they'd met before. Then Zylah noticed the female at Saoirse's side. Her nose crinkled, anger poured from her body, then she spun on her heel and stormed away.

Saoirse's countenance fell, but she quickly recovered and cleared her throat. "I'm sure you have a lot to do before tomorrow, so no need to stand on formalities. There will be enough of that to last a lifetime."

Saoirse turned to those waiting to guide her to her rooms then she was gone, chatting with the servant until they were down the hall. The last thing Arianna heard was Saoirse's call for an entire bottle of wine instead of just a glass.

CHAPTER THIRTY-EIGHT

RION

Rion didn't recognize the male staring at him through the reflection of the floor length mirror. He didn't recognize the smooth black suite clinging to his body. Or the silk shirt underneath. The gold cufflinks at his wrists. The polished black boots.

The male standing there was someone else entirely. A male who might have been worthy to walk beside The Divine. Her mate in another life who wasn't burdened with scars from his past. One who was refined and could speak to others in a way that would reel them in. A male who might have been able to help her rule.

He was none of those things. His entire persona inspired fear. His past cast a cloud over his mate's good intentions. He'd seen the way everyone stared, questioning her judgment, and Rion hated himself for it.

Rion tilted his head, examining the hair that now fell perfectly around his pointed ears. Ellie had pulled him away from Arianna, claiming she had something for him to wear, and once they were in the hall, she'd declared herself his personal barber.

He'd despised every second of the experience and Ellie had swatted—actually swatted—at his magic more than once, then had threatened to shave his head entirely if he didn't give her a little room to work. She'd said if she wanted to kill him, she certainly wouldn't use a pair of scissors because it wouldn't make for a very interesting story.

He'd rolled his eyes but smiled. He wasn't sure he would ever trust Ellie entirely, but something about Arianna's little sister was growing on him. He imagined she'd gotten the dimensions for his clothes from Arianna.

Rion looked himself over again. Gods, how long had it been since he'd attended a formal engagement? Probably since his early twenties, and he'd ruined the affair by throwing someone across the room after they'd tried to put a knife in his back.

Kirian sat in a corner of the room, offering suggestions whenever Ellie asked. She held up another piece of clothing, ignoring the way Rion's sand rose to wrap around her arms when she approached. Rion didn't miss the way the half-breed's heart rate spiked, nor the way he leaned forward as if he might protect Ellie.

Rion studied the female. She never jumped away, never so much as flinched from him the way so many others did. She'd heard the stories. She knew his past.

"Why doesn't it bother you?" Rion asked.

Ellie turned to study two other vests hanging on the wall. He prayed she wouldn't make him change again. "Why doesn't what bother me?"

"My magic."

She turned to look at him. Her eyes were so much like Arianna's. A lighter color, but the sincerity in them was the same. Ellie just shrugged. "Why should it? And before you give me the whole *I've done terrible things* speech, I've already heard it." She sighed. "I had to study you for an entire semester at school when we were learning about Brónach."

"And that makes me question it even more."

She finally brought the fabric closer and held it against to his chest. Rion stiffened, fighting the urge to harden his magic around her body. She was so close to his throat. One strike and he'd be gone. He'd seen how fast she could move.

Ellie's movements slowed, but she did nothing else to indicate she noticed. "Maybe I like to draw my own conclusions. I hate being told how I'm supposed to feel." Rion eyed Kirian, wondering if the half-breed had something to do with the comment. Then again, maybe everything she did centered on defying her father, too.

"Let me ask you something," Ellie said, stepping back to look him over as if he were a piece of art. "Why do you push everyone away?"

"What do you mean?" He loosened his magic, glad for the distance she'd put between them.

"You keep reminding us of your sins as if you expect us to change our minds or something."

Rion raised a brow. "Because I do."

"Why?"

"I—" Because he didn't think they understood the depth of the atrocities he'd committed. Rion lowered his voice. "Because she deserves someone better."

He averted his gaze and Ellie cocked her head. "Someone like Niall?"

A low growl escaped before Rion could stop it, but Ellie didn't flinch. She smiled instead and moved to lean against a desk. Kirian watched. Frozen.

"You can't have it both ways, you know. You can't keep pushing her away, then get angry if someone else comes along."

"I don't trust that male."

She thought for a moment. "Okay, then what about Talon?"

His lips parted. Talon was an honorable male. Loyal. Rion knew he and Arianna shared a small history. He turned away from Ellie unable to stomach the images creeping into his mind.

Ellie sighed. "You make her sad." Rion lifted his head at that. "I don't know if you see it or feel it or whatever, but every time you speak as if you're unworthy, I can see how much it hurts her." He did too, but— "She loves you," Ellie said and walked closer, examining his clothes again. "She's never been like this around another male. Never. Talon included, and even Talon can see that. It's why he doesn't challenge you."

Ellie smiled at him. "So here's what you're going to do tonight. When Niall or anyone else takes her hand, you're going to remind yourself that Arianna loves you. That she chose you and no one else could possibly win her heart the way you have."

His own heart swelled as she continued. "You're going to watch her dance and have the time of her life and you're going to learn about the Arianna before a life of slavery. You're going to see her with new eyes and know, in your heart, that you can trust her. Because Arianna is yours and there is nothing in this world strong enough to tear you two apart."

CHAPTER THIRTY-NINE

SAOIRSE

he entire place was a mixture of anticipation, sweat, silk dresses, and alcohol. Saoirse downed her glass of champagne and wished for something stronger.

She'd already met the queen, though she hoped to have a more in-depth conversation with her once fancy obligations were out of the way.

She smirked, remembering her brother's pensive stance, but something about him also seemed calmer. Happier. It made her chest swell. To know that this young female could bring any sort of joy to her brother's otherwise miserable life was nothing short of a miracle.

Gods ordained indeed.

But something else caught her attention tonight. Despite the twirling females and handsome males that glanced her way, Saoirse couldn't stop staring at one female who lingered in the back. She twisted her gloved hands and looked so unsure of herself. Such a difference from the female who had knocked Saoirse on her ass.

Zylah. A half-breed with magic and, judging from the way she'd chosen her words, in possession of at least a bit of a Fae's immortality.

Saoirse watched her for another heartbeat. Zylah stepped forward, as if ready to join the crowd, then sidestepped and marched straight for the balcony before disappearing behind the sheer turquoise curtains.

Well, that wouldn't do at all.

Saoirse set her glass on a nearby table and marched through the crowd. She sidestepped dancers and those caught in conversation.

One male tried to coax her to dance, but she brushed past, holding up a finger. She wouldn't miss this opportunity. Not when it seemed like the female had been trying her best to avoid Saoirse at every turn.

Saoirse stepped past the billowing curtains and found Zylah standing at the edge of the balcony. Her gloved hands gently rested on the thick railing lined with ornate vines and flowers in full bloom despite the time of year.

Zylah wore a pale green dress that hung to her ankles, yet the fabric was freeing enough that it moved with the wind.

Saoirse stepped forward. "A beautiful female should be inside dancing, not standing alone on a balcony."

Zylah's head turned slowly and her eyes drank Saoirse in. From the slit that ran up her thigh to the gold earrings dangling to her shoulders. Her mouth opened once and Saoirse's heart fluttered when she heard the female's sharp intake of breath.

Saoirse's red silk dress left little to the imagination, hugging every curve of her body in an alluring way. She'd caught several staring. Several she might have tried to lure into her bed that night had she not seen Zylah standing in the corner.

Now, Saoirse could care less about the others.

Zylah scrunched her nose and turned away. "I thought I made it clear last time that I didn't want anything to do with you."

Right. That. "If it earns me a conversation, I'm making strides to better the lives of the oppressed where I'm able."

Zylah scoffed. "And yet you arrived with a slave carrying your bags."

Saoirse crossed the space and leaned her back against the balcony, facing the ball inside. She watched a male spin a female through a complicated dance step and imagined what it might be like to do the same with Zylah. "She's not a slave anymore." That earned her a sideward glance. "I gave the female her freedom and offered to teach her about the world. She chose to stay by my side to learn."

"Is that to be her payment?"

Saoirse frowned. "No. I've given her a fair wage and more to account for the time she's spent in my service. She's quite wealthy now."

"And I suppose money makes up for everything she's endured."

"No," Saoirse said carefully. "But I'm not able to give her those years back. It's the best I can offer."

Saoirse sensed Zylah's rising anger. "It's not enough." Zylah pushed off from the balcony, ready to leave.

"What is enough?" Saoirse asked and Zylah stopped. She seemed to stare at the same couple gliding across the floor. "You were angry that I did nothing. Now you're angry that I've tried something. What is it you wish me to do?"

Zylah spun and if Saoirse could have taken a step back, she might have. "One," Zylah held up a finger. "You can stop following me around and take 'no' for an answer. Two," she held up another finger. "There is absolutely nothing you can do to make up for their pain."

"So I'm condemned no matter what I do? That's it? I'm just the evil ambassador who did nothing for those less fortunate?"

Zylah squared her shoulders. "More or less."

Saoirse eyed her. "And yet you're still talking to me."

"Because you're insufferably distracting."

Saoirse quirked a smile at that. "Am I now?" She stepped forward and corralled Zylah until her back pressed against the balcony. Saoirse knew the female had magic now, which meant if she wanted to escape, she could. The extraordinary female before her wasn't frightened or submissive or weak.

Zylah gripped the railing. "Yes, now leave me alone. Surely you have better things to do than follow me around."

Saoirse closed the distance slowly, watching Zylah's body language with each step. She placed her hands on either side of the female, their chests so close they were almost touching. Saoirse could smell the jasmine soap Zylah had used that morning and the fresh mint on her breath.

Her heart answered Zylah's beat for beat, blood racing. Saoirse leaned close, her breath creating prickles along Zylah's neck. "You tell me to leave, yet you linger, allow yourself to be pushed into a corner . . ." She trailed those breaths down her throat, hovering just out of reach. "I think you want more than you're willing to allow yourself to admit." After all, it was Zylah who'd sought her out at the tavern and Zylah who had started their conversation. Saoirse's lips dipped closer. "If you want me to stop, you have but to say the word."

"Stop."

Stop. The word froze Saoirse in place. She hadn't expected the female to actually say it. Not when her body screamed for the exact opposite. Zylah's breath was ragged, but Saoirse did as she commanded. She met Zylah's gaze and watched the rapid rise and fall of her chest. Her heart beat wildly, but Saoirse inclined her head and let her arms fall away. Zylah looked at her for another heartbeat, then she was gone, leaving Saoirse reeling on the balcony with nothing but a cold breeze for company.

CHAPTER FORTY

ARIANNA

Arianna peeked through the crack in the door and felt heat rise to her cheeks when she glimpsed the crowd waiting below the stairs. She'd never visited the ballroom and hadn't realized how massive it would be or how many people waited to greet her.

Her heart thundered and she wrung her gloved hands together. Talon stood beside her, leaning against the wall with a faint smile on his lips.

"What?"

He shook his head. "I didn't think you'd be so nervous about a ball."

"And I didn't think there'd be so many people."

Gods, it looked like they'd invited the entire city, which seemed plausible considering she was to be their queen. But she thought they'd wait for the coronation ceremony. She thought she had more time to prepare.

"You'll do fine." She shot him a glare, then studied his figure.

He wore Móirín's colors. A dark blue overcoat, matching slacks, and a silver button-up shirt. He'd pulled his hair back in a loose tie that left her friend looking equal parts wild and refined.

It suited him, but also pulled at the haunting memories from the last time they'd dressed up for a celebration. A festival. An event quickly put together to honor a set of warriors for their bravery.

She'd walked with Talon hand in hand, her heart skipping with every step they took away from the dancing Fae.

She remembered how the stars seemed to greet them, their twinkling lights magical and bright. She recalled his tentative kiss and the way he'd run his fingers down her neck before chaos ripped them apart.

What if it all went wrong again? What if someone hurt him in here? What if they hurt Ellie or Rion or—

"You are the most exquisite thing I've ever seen." Arianna spun at the sound of Rion's rich voice and her throat went dry. His unruly auburn hair was shorter, the strands hanging around his ears and above his eyes in a way that drew attention to his chiseled face.

He wore a black silk shirt with matte black buttons and a midnight coat embroidered with gold. His boots were new, clothes without wrinkle or blemish, and gods he looked like a dream.

Rion's gaze roamed up and over her body, lingering on the way her dress dipped at the front. She struggled to keep her arms still. Ellie had picked it out and matched them both. Arianna didn't know how her sister had carved out enough time for herself, but she had insisted she be the one to dress them. Arianna just thanked the gods she'd managed to slip into the corset before Ellie could see her scars. Ellie had chided her, claiming it must have been a nightmare, but she'd shooed her off.

Her dress was the same midnight black as Rion's coat with gold embroidery trailing down the sheer sleeves in elegant circular patterns. She was secretly glad it covered her wrists, if only to avoid the stares from the crowd. They would be whispering enough as it was.

Arianna refocused, trying to tear her eyes away from Rion's body. She wasn't successful. "Where have you been?" she hissed, closing the space between them. Her heels clicked against the smooth floor.

"Getting a pep talk from your sister."

Arianna tilted her head. "Is she the one who cut your hair?"

He grimaced. "Only after threatening to shave it all off."

Arianna giggled. Ellie had cut his hair. He'd allowed someone close with something that could easily be wielded as a weapon. She wanted Rion to trust others, those worthy anyway. He still had too many enemies, but Arianna knew her sister wasn't one of them. Neither was Kirian.

Talon cleared his throat and bowed. "I'll meet you down there." Then he was gone, disappearing down the hall toward a side entrance. The only people who would be walking through the doors in front of her were Rion and herself.

"What did she say to you?"

Rion shrugged. "She told me to watch."

Arianna tilted her head. "Watch what?"

Rion stepped closer and cupped her cheek with his warm palm. A blush rose to her cheeks at his proximity and the way he looked into her eyes as if he could memorize the rings of color within. Emotion swam in his gaze and her breath hitched when he leaned down and whispered. "You."

Her chest tightened when he tenderly kissed her, then pulled back and ran his thumb over her bottom lip. She thought she might catch fire right there in the hall. She couldn't wrap her mind around his meaning, nor steady herself enough to remember whatever else she'd been about to ask him.

"I thought you'd be a wreck," she finally said. Arianna wrapped her arms around his waist.

"Like I said, your sister gave me a pep talk."

Arianna opened her mouth again, but promptly shut it when music began playing inside the ballroom. Her mouth went dry at the sound. She knew what that meant. The doors were about to open.

Rion looped her arm in his. "Relax," he said, voice low. "I've got you." Feelings of admiration floated down the bond and Arianna stood a little straighter. She pushed her fears aside. She wouldn't let herself be afraid. Not of the people behind this door. They were here to see her, not the other way around.

She was their queen.

The doors opened and a myriad of scents washed over and through her. Rion stiffened a bit, but his smile didn't falter and seeing him so relaxed, so at odds with what she'd grown accustomed to, brought a genuine smile to her lips.

"Shall we?"

Arianna stepped forward onto the flat platform and heard the collective gasps of awe. Whispers soared through the crowd before falling silent. She knew they hadn't expected Rion to join her, nor for him to look so, well, refined. The complete opposite of the violent creature they'd been told so many stories about.

Arianna caught Talon's eye in the crowd, then she spotted Ellie. She'd been worried her sister might arrive late, but there she stood, wearing a floor length dress of blue and shimmering silver. It gently hugged her slender frame and the neckline rose to wrap around her throat. Her hair was pulled back with waterfall curls spilling from the crowned braid around her head.

She always appeared so much older than she really was. It made Arianna envy her confidence.

Arianna drew in a slow breath and stepped down, her heel clicking against the marble stairs. Rion moved at her side with an ease that continually surprised her. His movements were always so deliberate. He didn't stumble or sway. He was rooted in perfect balance, and it gave her a sense of steadiness she hadn't realized she'd needed.

The crowd parted. Some had covered their mouths with one hand, tears springing to their eyes. Others still looked between her and Rion, likely wondering why it wasn't Niall who escorted her to the dance floor. The male had offered, but she'd declined.

This was a moment no one would ever forget—the biggest before her coronation—and it was a moment she wanted to share with her mate and no one else.

Rion led her toward the open space ahead. The crowd quieted and Arianna's heart beat so fast she was sure everyone could hear it.

But Rion held steady. He didn't shy away from their stares, nor appear nervous. Instead, he turned toward her, just like they'd practiced, took her hand, and pulled her close.

Arianna met his emerald green gaze, both breathtaking and beautiful. The music changed and when Rion stepped, her body moved with his. Time slowed. The crowd disappeared and Arianna let him guide her through the movements, gliding across the floor like water over stones.

His hand left her back, spinning her, and she returned to his arms, elation flooding through her entire body. She smiled, wide and unrestrained and Rion returned it.

After everything they'd suffered, she had wondered if their future held nothing but turmoil and shadows and fear. But this. This was magic. This was a child's dream that knew no bounds. This was a moment she wanted to bottle so she could treasure it for the rest of eternity.

Rion spun her again and his magic glided out from beneath his sleeves and circled her body, following her movements like a ribbon in the wind. Her own joined it, the two intertwining in a dance all their own.

And then she laughed. So carefree that she thought her heart might shatter from the sheer joy filling her chest. Rion held her close and they danced and danced and danced. Arianna wished the song would go on forever, just so she would never have to leave this moment.

Perfect. Beautiful.

But their movements slowed, their magic receded, and she paused to stare into his eyes, her chest rising and falling with every breath. The last note faded, then the gathered crowd erupted in applause, pulling both from their reverie.

The Fae surged forward and for a moment, Arianna feared Rion might lash out, but he surprised her again. In fact, he offered smiles of his own, acknowledging forced greetings with a nod. Most kept their distance, eyeing the magic that crawled back inside his jacket sleeves.

Rion never released her hand, not once as she greeted complete strangers who looked at her as if she were a fabled being come to life.

They kept shaking her hand, some hesitating as if they weren't sure they should, but when Niall approached, the crowd separated to allow him through.

"That was an elegant performance." He took her hand and kissed the back of it. Her gaze shot quickly to Rion. Irritation flew down the bond, but he remained calm, almost . . . nonchalant. "May I be honored with the second dance?" Arianna's eyes narrowed at Niall. She knew his game—Ellie had guessed it—but seeing him do the exact same gesture that had set Rion off just a few weeks ago confirmed her suspicions. He wanted Rion to react. All of them did.

"Be my guest." Rion allowed Niall to pull her away. She furrowed her brow in concern, studying her mate, but he only offered a reassuring smile. Arianna searched the bond, prodding him, and though it was a little forced, Arianna could feel his sincerity.

He was genuinely happy, and that happiness cracked her heart with a kind of joy she hadn't allowed herself to bask in for such a long time.

Then Niall led her out onto the dance floor.

CHAPTER FORTY-ONE

RION

ion separated himself from the crowd and leaned against a pillar off to one side of the ballroom. Ellie joined him and nudged Rion with her elbow. "I'm impressed," she said. "You didn't tear his head off."

"Trust me. I want to." But he needed to appear indifferent. Keep his temper in check, both for Arianna's sake and because every eye in this room was waiting for The Demon to make an appearance.

"Well, the mask is good." Ellie watched Arianna with something that resembled pride. Rion did the same. "Have you learned anything?" Rion only nodded. In the moments since they'd walked down those stairs, he'd learned more about his mate than he had in the weeks since his attempted execution.

He'd seen her laugh finally, the sound full of a kind of joy he'd never heard before. They'd spent so much time in darkness, surrounded by war and fear that had almost suffocated that part of her. The part flourishing as she danced. She wasn't comfortable with Niall, that much was certain, but she was at home here. Among the people who offered smiles and words of greeting and encouragement.

"She's happy," he finally said, realizing Ellie was waiting for an answer. "I never realized how much she worried about my reactions."

"She worries because she cares."

"She has enough to worry about without adding my feelings to the mix."

Ellie sighed. "There you go again. You know, asking her not to care about your feelings is like asking you not to care about hers. Would you ever do that?"

"Of course not."

"Then stop acting like everything should be one sided. She knows all this is difficult for you and she just wants to make sure you're not pushed beyond your limits."

They watched her and Niall dance a little longer. Rion never looked away from the male's hands. He didn't think the male would push things when he was trying to earn Arianna's favor, but he wasn't about to leave her alone with him, either.

"Talon is watching, too." Rion's gaze followed Ellie's across the room to find the male standing with a drink in his hand. "He doesn't trust Niall either."

"Do you?"

Ellie shrugged. "After the stunt with the slaves, I'm fairly disgusted, but we're not in Móirín, so I'm trying to be understanding about it. I feel like he has intentions toward Arianna, but I can't tell if it's for his own interests or for the continent, like he claims."

Ellie tilted her head toward Kirian. The male was well dressed with his copper hair combed back. He was watching them closely. "We'll know soon enough."

Rion looked at her then. "You found something?"

"Maybe." Her brow furrowed. "But I wonder if I'm trying too hard and seeing things that aren't really there."

"What do your instincts tell you?"

"That those ledgers weren't just for supplies. At least of the normal sort." Rion waited. "I got into Declan's office."

"And?" For the first time since he'd known her, Ellie didn't appear sure of herself.

"Pádraigín is using the strait that separates this continent from the west to send boats to Fiadh."

"They've always used that strait. It's faster than traveling by land."

Ellie watched the dancers and waited until a couple was out of earshot before continuing. She lowered her voice. "They're transporting iron cages and judging from the dimensions, I'd wager there aren't slaves inside."

"Why would the Fae want anything to do with iron?"

Ellie had gone a shade paler than usual. "I think they're transporting The Dark Fae. Some of the names they used line up with them, anyway." She shuddered. "I hope I'm wrong. It could just be code."

The Dark Fae. Why would Pádraigín or Fiadh have any interest in the creatures and what did they plan to do with them?

"So the two have an alliance then?" he asked.

"Oh, most definitely. I should find out more in a few days. Fina's office is across the hall."

Rion studied Niall again, then Arianna. "Don't get caught."

She grinned. "Never."

CHAPTER FORTY-TWO

TALON

Talon watched Rion's reaction when Niall claimed another dance. The male still stood with Ellie, both speaking in hushed tones. Ellie was safe. Arianna was safe. And his warriors from Móirín were keeping a careful eye on them all. Talon loosed a breath and turned to watch the female that had stolen his attention as soon as he'd laid eyes on her.

He swallowed hard and pulled at his jacket. Sweat had formed along his back, causing the silken material to stick to his body, but he rolled his shoulders and tried to ignore it.

Raevina. The ambassador of Fiadh. He knew they were supposed to be enemies. There was tension between their countries after the invasion, but Talon couldn't ignore the flawless dark skin of her bare leg or the white dress slitted all the way to her mid-thigh. It hugged her flawless form, revealing a sleek, muscular body likely honed from centuries of training.

Talon knew she wasn't young. He'd had to learn about the royal families and their children, and the Lord of Fiadh hadn't sired any children in well over two centuries. Not since he'd dispatched his last partner. Talon silently hoped it hadn't been the female's mother.

The silk of Raevina's dress rose to hug her throat before dipping to cover her torso. It left her arms bare and she wore thick golden bangles on her left upper arm. Bracelets dangled around her wrists and golden earrings hung low from her ears, thin and elegant. She'd painted her lips a shade darker than her skin.

He'd watched her arrival to Ruadhán, eager to examine who they might be contending with, but when the warrior dressed in fighting leathers had emerged from her extravagant carriage, his mouth had gone dry. She'd passed him in the hall and he hadn't been able to speak at all. Thankfully, she'd only looked at him once, and had likely dismissed him as another guard.

The female radiated an air of ruthless authority that told Talon approaching her was as stupid as it was brave.

He didn't care. He needed to speak with her. Meet her. Touch her, if she'd allow it.

Talon glanced at Arianna again, then set his drink on the nearest table. Raevina was surrounded by what Talon could only assume was a group of close comrades. Or friends. But they all quieted at his approach and their smiles faded.

Her eyes locked with his, pinning him in place, daring him to take another step. A warning for lesser males to keep their distance.

But Talon wasn't a lesser male, and he wouldn't bow to her intimidation. If she wanted him on his knees, there were other, more agreeable ways to convince him.

Her brow rose and somehow, despite his racing heart, Talon kept his voice calm. He placed one hand behind his back and held the other out. "Could I have the extraordinary honor of a dance?" He didn't presume she'd say yes, and he wouldn't disrespect a female by reaching for her.

Raevina cocked her head at him and swirled her drink. Her gaze swept up and down his form, but miraculously, Talon remained still under her scrutiny. "*Can* you dance?" she challenged. "I'm not at all interested in the pathetic sway some of these lot are doing."

A half grin. "I assure you, I can dance just as well as any lord's son."

She tilted her head. "I've danced with many a lord's son." He didn't take the bait. Finally, she set her glass on the high table beside her. Those with Raevina raised their brows in surprise. "I'll be the judge of that."

Talon ignored the jab and his heart soared when she slid her bare hand into his. She allowed him to lead her out onto the dance floor. Allowed, because he could tell from the way she kept her balance that this female could put him on his ass in an instant if she wished it.

Raevina spun around, almost as though she hoped to catch him by surprise, but Talon gracefully stepped into the movement. The two spun, falling into step with those already occupying the dance floor.

His fingers grazed her waist, and it set his blood on fire. Her hand was over his shoulder and when she twisted into a spin, Talon pulled her back, dipping her. The movement allowed him a brief touch of the bare skin of her back. Then they were moving again.

He kept time easily, even with the beautiful distraction in his arms. She didn't shy away, didn't balk, and even offered him a coy smile that suggested she knew exactly how she affected him. She was likely accustomed to having a similar effect on most males who crossed her path.

He clenched his jaw then slammed a lid over his territorial Fae nature. He wouldn't let it intrude upon this moment. Not when he was stealing small touches where she allowed. He didn't push nor did he let his fingers wander, no matter how much he wanted it. Gods, he wanted to do so many things with her. He wanted to please her in every way, all night. To hear his name on her lips just once.

The song ended and she pulled away too soon, her palm on his chest. He knew she could feel his racing heart. A spark lit up behind her gaze and she smiled like a feral creature, wide and unyielding.

"Well, I do believe you *can* dance just as well as a lord's son." Talon beamed, his chest swelling with pride. The music slowed then and those around them drew closer, pressing their bodies against one another. He held out his hand again but Raevina shook her head.

"I told you, I don't do the sway thing." She winked at him, but something in her gaze suddenly seemed strained. Pain? She recovered quickly then twisted on her heel and walked away, joining her friends with a smile on her face.

Talon just watched, reveling for a moment in the fact that he'd gotten to touch the most beautiful creature he'd ever laid eyes on.

CHAPTER FORTY-THREE

ARIANNA

"You look absolutely stunning tonight," Niall said.

Arianna struggled not to pull away from his grip. She hated the feel of another male's hands against her body, but if she pulled away, she would create a scene, and that was the last thing she wanted.

"Thank you, you look nice as well."

Niall's smile widened. "It's my job to look nice, otherwise I'd be the laughing stock of Ruadhán."

"You've been here a long time." She already knew that, but Arianna wasn't sure how else to fill the silence. They'd already spoken about the decor and food and he'd listed off the names of every noble. Names she quickly forgot.

He nodded. "I also came here on and off as a child, so I already knew most of the council members before moving here."

"It doesn't sound like you got to stay home much."

He shook his head. "I didn't, and I resented my father for a long time because of it, but he showed me the continent and I've come to appreciate the experience as an adult." His voice lowered to a whisper. "But now that you're here, I have little desire for travel."

She looked away, trying to ignore the subtle meaning in his tone. "I don't understand how everyone can just accept who I am. No one even knows me."

"They trust the gods and their decisions. They don't need to know you."

"But what do they expect me to do? What does bringing peace actually mean?"

"I believe," he said, "that's something only you can figure out, otherwise we would have done it centuries ago." He offered her another smile. "But we're at a party, why dwell on such things?"

"Because it's stressful."

"We don't expect a miracle." He grinned, seeming amused by her frazzled state. "Fae live very, very long lives. We have plenty of time."

She loosed a breath. She often forgot that part, especially when she'd spent every day of the last two years fighting for her life. "Then what do they expect from me first?" She didn't want to disappoint them, and the way they all kept looking at her told Arianna they expected great things.

"How about I just tell you to live?"

"Live?"

He grinned again. "You're so young. Live your life. Experience that life through the eyes of others. Convince those in doubt that you are good at heart and simply wish for their happiness."

Talon cleared his throat and Arianna almost jumped out of her skin. "Save a dance for me?" Arianna breathed a sigh of relief. Niall clenched his jaw, clearly unhappy with the interruption, but offered Talon a slight nod of his head before excusing himself.

Talon pulled her across the floor. "You looked like you needed saving," Talon said.

Arianna ensured Niall was out of hearing range. "Thanks for that, he can be a bit . . ."

"Intense?" Talon offered. She nodded. "I hear nothing but good things about him from the guards." He shook his head. "It almost seems like they worship him."

"That makes sense though, right? I mean, he's been here for five hundred years and he's supposed to be the king one day."

Talon was silent for a moment and a revelation seemed to wash through him. She watched his face pale and brows furrow. His heart rate spiked, then he seemed to collect himself again. But the action was strained and the smile that he tried to muster didn't quite reach his eyes.

"What is it?" she asked.

Talon shook his head and tried to take a calming breath. "The one you choose to marry will be the king. Your mate." Arianna's lips parted. "Niall doesn't automatically get the title because of the prophecy. The decision is yours."

"What are you saying?"

"Niall's position is threatened, and I think he'll do anything to ensure he gets the title he's worked centuries to obtain."

Arianna swallowed hard. She hadn't really thought it through and it seemed so stupid now. Niall had proposed a fake marriage to unify the country, but if she ultimately decided she didn't want to rule with him at her side. If she married Rion—

Gods, she'd already told Niall she didn't want to marry him. She had outright refused, which meant Rion was an obstacle in his path. Maybe all his kind words had only been to placate and win her over. What if he tried—she spun suddenly, searching the crowd for those familiar green eyes, but Rion was nowhere to be found.

Chapter Forty-Four

Rion

Rion loosed a sigh of relief when Talon cut in for a dance. He wished he could have done it himself and he cursed all the years he'd neglected to learn the art of dancing. He swore that by Arianna's coronation, he'd know every one. Even if he had to deal with Talon's hands on her for a while longer.

Rion couldn't wait for the night to end. He fully intended to whisk Arianna back to their rooms and submerge them in a hot bath with all the soaps she liked. Anything to wash away the scent of males from her skin. He planned to do other things to her as well that would make her forget everyone's name but his own.

Rion swallowed hard and struggled to focus. Niall had drifted off with a small group Rion didn't recognize, and Ellie had snuck away to dance with Kirian, the soft spoken half-breed she loved so fiercely.

His heart grew heavy as he imagined them separated one day. No one knew how long a half-breed might live. Not until adulthood. Either they displayed signs of Fae strength and longevity or they didn't. He prayed Kirian would.

Rion sensed a pair of eyes watching him and turned toward the main door to find a brown haired female approaching from the side of the dance floor. Rion looked over his shoulder, hoping to find another meeting her gaze, but no one stood anywhere near him.

She drew closer, inching her way through those who drank and conversed on the sidelines. The female stopped more than once, as if fighting some internal war with herself.

Ellie was confident no one would ask him to dance. Surely this female didn't plan to. Even if by some miracle she did, he'd politely decline. Perhaps he'd make small talk about the weather or the party. Maybe the female wasn't interested in him at all and just wanted to inquire about Arianna.

She wore a long dress, but it wasn't as elegant as some of the others and moments later he understood why. A half-breed. He relaxed a fraction and offered her a nod in greeting.

"I've been sent to take you to your rooms," the female said. Her voice, no, her entire body shook and she refused to meet his gaze.

Rion studied her, his brow furrowed. Had someone dared her to approach? Was she confused? Drunk perhaps? He scented the air around her body but didn't smell any alcohol. Tentatively, Rion said. "I know where my rooms are."

She wrung her hands together. Nervous. Uncertain. "No, I mean *your* room, My Lord."

Rion just wanted her to leave, but he didn't know how to tell her that without sounding harsh so instead he said. "I don't need to go to my room right now." Or ever for that matter. He hadn't even known he had a separate room. There wasn't a reason for it.

"There is a gift waiting for you inside." At that, Rion went rigid. His gaze swept across the room as understanding seeped through his core. Wisely, no one met his gaze and the female was smart enough to keep her head down.

"Who sent it?" His voice was firmer now and she retreated a step. Fear radiated from her, turning a few nearby heads. The female trembled harder as she shook her head, unable to find her voice.

Rion studied the crowd again. Someone had laid a trap for him, but why had they made it so obvious? Only an idiot would listen to the female's nonsense and—Rion stilled when his eyes landed upon Arianna.

Someone had set a trap for him in another room. If he refused to go, would they target Arianna's room next? Did the world know she couldn't use her abilities on herself? And if they didn't, would they risk injuring her just to eliminate him?

His gaze darted between her and Talon. Talon had given his word to protect her. The male had even made eye contact with him before asking the ambassador of Fiadh for a dance, something Rion hoped to hear about later.

Rion eyed the personal guard her father had sent, counting them as they blended in throughout the room. Six had eyes on her while the others meandered about, mixing with the crowd.

He shouldn't go. But if they came after Arianna . . .

The female didn't speak again, she simply waited, still wringing her hands. She jumped at his reluctant voice. "Lead the way."

Her lips parted as if in shock then she was moving, weaving her way in and out of the crowd with Rion close behind.

Rion stopped beside one of the guards from Móirín and the male stood straighter at his proximity. "Keep an eye on her. I won't be long."

He nodded, refusing to make eye contact.

The female didn't exit through a main door. Instead, she led Rion through a servant's door and into the main hall. A place others might not notice him leaving.

She was under threat, of that much Rion was certain. Which meant someone still had leverage over their slaves. Freedom was just a front. But he'd have to sort through that later.

He wasn't surprised to find Fae lining the hall with drinks in their hands, though the female certainly seemed to be. She'd probably never done anything like this and Rion hoped he could get to the bottom of it all so she'd never have to do it again.

She uttered apologies as they passed, but Rion met the questioning stares of each and every one, wondering if they were the cause for the female's predicament.

Most turned away.

They walked up the central staircase all the way to the fourth floor and Rion's magic stirred when he saw the shadows on the walls. They were an easy weapon for the Shadow Weavers of Fiadh and the too few lamps down the hall created the perfect atmosphere for an ambush.

He expected the female to run. For assassins to leap from the corners and fight him in the hall. Maybe their blades would be poisoned. Maybe they'd hope to subdue him, then eliminate the threat to the throne.

But she pulled a key from her pocket instead and stopped before a door on their left.

Rion didn't move. "What's inside?"

"I-I don't know." She was shaking again. "I was only told to bring you here."

He grimaced and took the key. "Tell your master you've completed your task." Her heart thundered in her chest. "And know that your queen will protect you should you ever need her help."

She clenched her fists and lingered a moment too long. He saw the indecision. The want to fight whatever held her captive. Then her shoulders slumped in defeat. "There's nothing she can do." Then she was gone, bounding down the stairs before Rion could say otherwise.

Rion stared at the door then the crevice underneath. Light flickered inside. Candlelight. He paused to listen, refusing to step closer.

No movement.

Using his magic, Rion inserted the key into the lock and twisted. It clicked and he waited again, straining to listen in the tense silence.

Nothing.

He slid his magic beneath the door this time and knelt, using the particles to feel around the floor of the room. No one screamed, no increased heart rates or heavy breathing.

His sand wrapped around the doorknob and twisted.

Vanilla and jasmine leaked from the room, masking any scent within. He pushed the door open fully. Dozens of candles sat atop tables and the mantle, casting an eerie glow across the floor.

Rion eyed the fireplace that sat directly across from the door. Embers flickered within.

Not a footstep or breath.

Rion palmed a dagger he'd hidden at his waist, reined in his magic, and stepped just over the threshold. He studied the shadows. One door stood closed to the right of the fireplace. Likely a closet, but could someone be hiding inside? Surely they wouldn't be so obvious.

He scented the air again. A female. There was definitely a female in the room.

Rion quickly scanned the space from top to bottom. A few well-placed chairs, a plush rug, and a bed with dark silken—her scent hit him first and Rion's stomach twisted with revulsion.

She stood slowly, letting the sheets drift to the floor. She should have balked at his presence, but she did nothing to conceal her naked body.

The female tilted her head and leaned against the bedpost with a seductive smile.

"Do come in."

"You're in the wrong room," Rion said, keeping his gaze firmly locked on her face. He would have turned away were he not worried about her shoving a knife in his back. Naked female assassin was a first, but he wasn't taking any chances.

"I'm not," she corrected. "I'm your gift."

Nausea rolled through him again. He'd expected a trap, for the room to explode, or an assassin to leap out with weapons poised. But this—

"I don't need your . . . services."

Her hand roamed over her exposed breast and down her stomach. He refused to let his eyes follow. "I've not been touched before. I'm told that's what you like."

Rion growled and the female had enough sense to step back. Her eyes widened a fraction. Gods above the people in this city knew no bounds. They were certifiably insane. He knew what this was. The game they were hoping to catch him on. He just—

"Rion?"

Too late. He'd realized too late. His heart could have stopped and it would have hurt less. He wished it would. Maybe it would leave him on the floor a broken mess. Anything. Anything but this—

Slowly, ever so slowly, Rion turned to face Arianna. She stood in the doorway, one hand lightly on the frame. Talon flanked her, breathing heavily as if he'd been running.

Rion couldn't form words, could hardly breathe or think as Arianna took in the naked female's body then turned back to stare at him with wide eyes. How could he explain?

Arianna scented the air and that one moment bred more fear than every horrible thing he'd ever experienced.

If she believed any of this—

Arianna's gaze snapped back to the female and the most devastatingly beautiful sound escaped Arianna's lips. The female, to her credit, fell to her knees and pressed her forehead against the thick rug. Arianna hardly seemed to notice. She stalked forward, magic crackling through the air in response to her anger.

Relief spread through him. Relief that Arianna knew their game and relief that she hadn't doubted him for even a second.

He recognized possessiveness. It spilled from the other end of their bond and he gently wrapped his fingers around Arianna's elbow.

She allowed him to pull her away, but that cold feral gaze didn't budge. The female was shaking now but Rion wasn't certain he cared, not as Arianna shifted her eyes to meet his.

The deep cerulean wasn't of this world. It couldn't be. Not with the way they made his knees want to buckle.

Arianna's fingers flexed. Rion knew that emotion, too. Rage. The need to rend everything that stood in your path.

He kissed her instead.

Her response was slow, as if she were emerging from a daze. He knew she wanted to tear that female in half, but he also knew she'd regret it later.

Slowly, one small step at a time, Rion guided Arianna back into the hallway. Móirín's guards lined the far wall, their weapons drawn. He ignored them and didn't bother to acknowledge Talon either. Not right now.

The pair stepped further away from the door, Rion still walking her backward with his lips coaxing her to obey.

Yours, he tried to convey with every touch of his hands. *I'm yours.*

Arianna stopped and pulled back slightly to meet his gaze. She loosed an uneasy breath, but when she tried to look behind him, Rion took her chin between his fingers and held her steady.

She studied him, that feral possessiveness refusing to fade.

It was absolutely intoxicating.

Arianna grabbed his hand and pulled him through the hall. He didn't fight or ask questions as they ran down the stairs, twisted into another hallway, then slammed open the door to their room.

Rion promptly shut the door with his magic and twisted the lock right as she dove for him.

Her kisses were deep, desperate, as if she'd never tasted him before and may never get to again. Her hands were in his hair, running down his neck, tugging at the fabric of the shirt separating their bodies.

Rion ripped the damned thing off and buttons flew across the room.

Then she was pressed against him, her body flush with his, stealing the very air from his lungs. He wanted to tear her dress off too, but knew it would likely land him in a heap of trouble come morning.

He pulled the first layer down, then his fingers ran over the strings of her corset. He found the knot, pulled it, and began unlacing.

Her lips found his neck, tongue gliding over sensitive points that had Rion whispering her name as if he were praying to the gods. He never wanted this moment to end.

Her skin against his. Her hands holding him steady and unraveling everything he'd become all at the same time.

She nipped his throat and he moaned against the contact of her teeth. Only her. He'd only ever let himself be vulnerable like this for her.

His hands gripped her hips then they were moving toward the bed. He was done with the wall. Done with clothes, too, as he cast the last bit of offending fabric aside.

They fell into silk sheets and plush pillows and then he was gone, lost to sensations and touch and pleasure beyond his wildest dreams.

Rion drank her in, drowning in the moment in a way he'd never allowed himself before. They had loved, but this . . . this was primal and when a moan escaped her lips and her nails bit into his skin, Rion swore he'd never get enough.

Her ankle locked around his leg and before he could think, Arianna flipped him onto his back. His hands never stopped roaming, memorizing every inch of her bare skin. He was drunk on the feel of her and never wanted to sober.

Gods. Gods this wasn't real.

Her teeth nipped at his throat harder, more demanding, and his heart threatened to burst. She trailed those kisses down his chest and back up before clamping her teeth at the base of his throat. Hard.

So close. She was so close to breaking skin but then she froze, her entire body going rigid.

A surge of emotions then Rion was running his hands up and down her arms, his breathing unsteady.

"You can if you want," he whispered, stomach clenching at the thought. Her breath was ragged, heart racing, and he sensed her want. Her need. An intense, overwhelming thing. He'd let her mark him if she wished to. It was an old practice. A custom many had done away with, but that didn't stop the animalistic desire from arising. And if she wanted to, gods, he'd beg for it.

She pulled away ever so slowly to look him in the eye. Flushed. Breathless. Beautiful. Surprise and shame flickered down the bond, but Rion rose up and pressed his body to hers, capturing her in another kiss.

"No," he said, voice thick. "Don't stop."

Her body shook. "I don't want to hurt you."

Rion pressed a kiss beneath her ear. "Does it feel like you're hurting me?" Arianna didn't respond, but she tilted her head back and he kissed her neck, pausing at her racing pulse. "I'm yours," Rion said. "Any way you want me, I'm yours."

CHAPTER FORTY-FIVE

ARIANNA

rianna woke in Rion's arms, their bare bodies pressed close beneath the blankets. Time was an irrelevant concept and she refused to care that they'd slept in.

Last night . . .

Last night was an experience she wouldn't soon forget. Their bodies entwined in a sea of skin and nails and teeth, the world a forgotten whisper. A smile graced her lips and she stretched, reaching her arms overhead.

Rion's grip tightened and he pulled her into his side. She ran a hand through his newly shortened hair and he finally cracked one eye open.

"Hi," she managed. Arianna hadn't let him sleep much. Her body had been on fire and she blushed at the memory and at what she'd almost done.

"Hi," he returned. She nuzzled his neck and kissed the base of his throat. "You missed your party."

She shrugged. "There'll be others." Rion raised a brow. "It wasn't really . . . pleasant after our dance." All she had wanted to do was join him on the sidelines. Niall hadn't let her dance with anyone other than Talon. So much for meeting the ambassadors and those among the court.

And after the dance—she clenched her teeth. She didn't want to think about anything that had happened between her leaving the ball and closing the door to their room.

"I didn't know she was there," her mate said quietly.

"I know." She wasn't stupid. Rion barely let Ellie near him, let alone a stranger. And with their mating bond, she was fairly certain she'd never have to worry about him running off with another female anyway. Still, she wondered why he'd left at all. "Why were you there?"

He propped his head up and leaned on one elbow. His hand still rested on her hip, thumb rubbing lazy circles over her skin. "Someone told me a gift was waiting in my room."

Arianna furrowed her brow, trying to understand. "And you went?"

He studied the edge of the pillowcase. "I thought I knew what I was walking into." He sighed and ran a hand through his shortened hair. "I thought if I ignored it, then whoever had orchestrated the event would try a different tactic. One that might catch you in the crossfire."

If she hadn't just experienced the best night of her life, she might have throttled him. "You should have talked to me first. We could have sent someone in to check it out." He didn't respond. Arianna caught his eye and gave him a stern look. "You're not alone anymore. You can't put yourself at risk like that."

He pressed an aching kiss to her brow. "Exactly. I'm not alone and I can't bear the thought of someone hurting you because of me."

"Don't you think I feel the same?" Again, silence. "When I realized what my father was trying to do, when I felt the bond tearing apart—" She lowered her voice. "The pain was unreal, and I don't want to ever feel that again." Rion swallowed hard. "Promise me," she pushed. "Promise me you won't do something like that again."

He stroked her arm and she knew a hundred thoughts flew through his mind. Assassination attempts, poisonings, impossible missions he wasn't supposed to return from. "I promise to try."

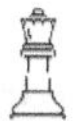

BY SOME miracle, Arianna hadn't missed the council meeting. She wasn't even sure why they were still having one. Surely the council had partied well into the night and were hung-over from all the wine.

Then again, maybe she'd ruined the whole occasion by leaving early. She was the guest of honor. They were bound to have noticed her missing. Had they gone in search of her, or had her Móirín guards informed Niall and the others that she'd retired early?

Arianna marched into the meeting room, her anger pulsing with that ancient power stirring just beneath the surface. One of them was responsible for what had happened last night, of that much she was certain. She just needed to figure out which one.

Their sleepy gazes snapped to attention when Rion followed, his magic on display for all to see. Arianna yanked her chair out, the wood scraping across the floor, and sat with her legs crossed.

Declan opened his mouth to speak, but she beat him to it. "Someone pulled a stunt last night that wasn't appreciated." Even if it had led to a rather enjoyable night.

She wanted to demand answers or hang the council over the edge of the city one by one until they gave up whoever had done such a thing.

Niall was the first to respond, his posture pensive. "What do you mean?" He looked her over, eyes roaming her body. "Were you injured?" She had hated the way his lips had grazed the back of her hand, even with the gloves. She knew he'd only done it to rile Rion. Arianna still couldn't believe her mate had remained so calm.

"No, I wasn't injured and I don't want to discuss it. Those responsible know what they did and should I find them," she met their gazes one by one, "there will be consequences."

Niall eyed the council and she wondered if there were any of the four he mistrusted or if it was all a show to throw the blame on someone else.

Niall cleared his throat. "We can persue—"

Arianna growled, her temper getting the better of her, and Niall snapped his mouth shut. "I cannot," she emphasized, "discuss the details here if you wish for me to maintain my composure."

He clasped and unclasped his hands. "Is it why you didn't return to the ball last night?"

"Yes."

"There were many who missed your company," Felic said, trailing off when she pinned him with a glare.

"Maybe next time someone won't target my mate while I'm otherwise occupied." Arianna flashed her teeth. "Then I'll be able to stay longer."

The council was silent, eyes turning to Niall for assistance on how to best handle the situation. Maybe she should have just stayed in bed. The bond was chafing at her patience.

"Whatever happened," Niall said. "You have my sincerest apologies. I'm certain none of us wanted you to miss the ball." He looked her up and down again. "You're certain you weren't hurt?"

Arianna studied him, the way he sat in the chair, back relaxed and hands gently splayed upon the table. If he'd had any part in it, he certainly hid it well.

"I'm fine," Arianna said again and some of the anger fell from her shoulders. Not one of them had reacted. No sideways glances, no shift in their posture. Maybe they hadn't been the ones to orchestrate it. But if not them, then who?

She loosed a breath. "I'm sorry, I shouldn't accuse you."

Niall offered her a weak smile. "My Lady, you are in a strange place full of strange Fae. I'd venture to say a little mistrust is healthy."

Arianna studied their worn expressions and the hazy look in their eyes. She was certain more than one had probably stumbled through the door. "Is there a reason this wasn't rescheduled?"

Niall shrugged. "We meet every week, regardless of events."

Arianna made a face. "Well, maybe that's something else that needs to change." For the first time, the council looked like they unanimously agreed with her.

Niall smiled again. "I'll make the arrangements."

They sat in silence for a time and Arianna wondered if they would dismiss early. The council didn't appear as if they wanted to be here anyway.

"If no one has anything else to report, I'd like to propose an idea," Niall said. He waited before continuing and turned in his chair to face her fully. "I've come to understand the slaves mean a great deal to you, so I'm certain at this point that the war refugees mean just as much." Arianna nodded. "It might help some of them regain their sense of hope if they were to see you in person."

Rion responded first. "I thought it was too dangerous to leave the royal city."

Niall made a point of thinking. "It is, but I think in light of all the skirmishes, it would be good for her to be seen. Perhaps it might even quell some of the fighting. The simple truth of the matter is that many can't afford to travel long distances, and many more are still recovering from the war. Therefore, they won't be able to attend your coronation.

"With any luck, we'll start some positive rumors to counteract all the negative ones." So many stood against her. Fae she'd likely never meet. They'd made assumptions about her character and it'd take something drastic to change their minds.

"We've been working with a few of the smaller neighboring villages," Niall continued. "We've provided supplies for shelters and given them food. I've even formed a rather constructive relationship with one of the village heads, and she's eager to meet with you."

Arianna's lips parted. The people. The masses. This is exactly what she wanted. To mingle and provide aid and come to know those she would eventually rule. "I thought Ruadhán didn't interfere with the war."

"In the war, no, but that doesn't mean we're heartless. There were many in need of homes and we provided them as best we could."

Arianna nodded. Perhaps they could have done more, but at least they'd done something. She would see how far their generosity stretched when she laid eyes on the villages herself. "I'd like to help in any way I can."

Niall beamed. "I know last night was . . . challenging," he offered with a slight grimace. "But I'm scheduled to arrive at one of the villages tomorrow afternoon. Would you care to join me?"

Overwhelming excitement washed through her. "Yes, yes of course."

Niall's gaze darkened and her heart plummeted when his eyes slid to Rion. "I'm afraid your companion won't make for a welcome sight."

Arianna opened her mouth to argue, ready to tell them Rion went wherever she went and she was tired of hearing otherwise, but she snapped her mouth shut.

Refugees. They were refugees from the war. Would they know her mate if they saw him? Scented him? She turned to look at Rion, but her mate had averted his gaze. Guilt swam down the murky bond. He knew.

"Talon will come with us," she declared, and to her surprise, Niall didn't object. Maybe he was finally getting the hint that one of them would always be with her no matter what he wanted.

Niall motioned Gavin over. The male was strangely pale and refused to meet her gaze. Perhaps he'd had too much to drink as well and just needed a chance to recover. Considering his age, she was willing to bet older Fae had pressured him into drinking more than his body could tolerate.

Gavin unrolled a large map that covered the area surrounding Ruadhán, then placed a weight at each end to prevent it from curling back in on itself.

Arianna stood with Niall, leaning over the page to get a better look. She'd always been fascinated with maps and the landmarks on their pages. Someone long ago had traveled the entire area, marking each river and mountain with utmost precision. Even today, map makers scouted for ways to improve upon the designs and mark the ever-changing villages that popped up and vanished overnight.

Niall pointed to a black dot just to the northeast and glanced over her shoulder to ensure Rion was watching. "We won't be far." He met her stare. "I wanted to be sure your mate knew where you'd be. Just in case."

Arianna nodded and looked at the map again. "Thank you." They wouldn't be far at all. It was difficult to comprehend just how far the war had spread. It'd affected so many lives. Changed them too.

Niall bowed. "Until tomorrow, then."

"Until tomorrow," she echoed.

Arianna left the room with a smile on her face, but Rion wasn't smiling and why would he be? She was leaving Ruadhán and he wasn't coming along. She would ensure Ellie remained close by, just to prevent anyone from trying to set him up again.

Of course, if he wanted, Rion could always accompany her to the outskirts of the village and wait for her there. Her face scrunched. No, she couldn't ask him to do that. He'd be bored out of his mind. If he didn't lose it entirely.

Before she realized where they were going, Arianna found herself at the entrance to the hedge maze. Rion still hadn't looked at her and her stomach plummeted. She knew he wouldn't want her to go for a plethora of reasons, but had she overstepped? Was traveling with Niall and Talon going too far?

He walked onto the path and she followed, trying to decipher his emotions. They were more veiled than usual, which tended to happen when one of them was overly anxious or overwhelmed.

He wouldn't even look at her.

Arianna bit her lip. Rion had promised not to hinder her, but— She could always just help with the village below the city. They housed refugees there, too.

"Rion?" He didn't respond and she touched his arm, jolting her mate from whatever dark thoughts had begun plaguing his mind. After last night—

"I don't have to go."

He shook his head. "You want to."

"I just want to help, but if it bothers you that much, I'll just find some other way. Maybe I—"

"No," he said. "It was going to come to this eventually."

Her brow furrowed. "Come to what?"

Rion finally faced her. She studied the emotions swimming in his gaze, the way his jaw had tensed. He took her hand and kissed her fingers. "I know the village he's taking you to."

Oh. She waited for more and bit the inside of her cheek. "Is it dangerous?" But she already knew the answer, even as he shook his head.

"I did terrible things there." His gaze wasn't on her, nor was it on the hedges he stared at. "Such terrible things."

Arianna pulled him close and drew his eyes back to hers. She tried offering him a reassuring smile. "It'll be fine. They're rebuilding. They have help."

Rion only shook his head. "Just send someone to tell me if you don't want me in your room when you return."

Chapter Forty-Six

Arianna

Arianna met Niall and the rest of their traveling companions just as the sun crested the horizon, bathing the sky in vibrant pinks and deep purples.

She still wasn't certain about going. She wanted to help. Gods, she wanted to help more than anything, but the way Rion had cradled her against his chest and held her tighter than he'd ever done made her question everything.

The way his kiss had been so desperate and needful. The way his hands had lingered as if he wouldn't be permitted to touch her again.

Arianna had seen the consequences of war. She knew firsthand the horrors many suffered. But something about this place rattled Rion to his core. She felt his shame and guilt as if it were her own. Her chest ached with raw emotion, but Rion wouldn't let her change her mind. He had said she needed to go, needed to see the people she was supposed to rule.

Then he'd turned away and she had walked from the room with a heart so heavy she wondered how she managed to move at all.

She wanted Rion at her side. But he couldn't be at her side for this.

Rion had confessed his sins already. They'd walked that path. He'd told her he was responsible for countless deaths. But this would be the first time she'd lay witness to those things. And it terrified her mate beyond reason.

Talon met her at the edge of the platform, glancing past those who'd gathered to finish strapping supplies to the wagons. "Is he not seeing you off?"

Arianna chewed her lip and clutched her chest as if she could ease the ache there. "He wants to give me space, I think." She hated this. Every second. Maybe it could all wait. There wasn't a reason to rush. Niall had everything under control and—

"Come on, before you change your mind."

She grimaced. "That obvious?"

"You might as well have a sign plastered to your head." Silence, then Talon shifted a long pack from his shoulder and handed it to her.

She raised a brow. "Dumping your bags on me now?"

He chuckled. "Open it." Arianna eyed him, then shifted the rolled leather bag. She pulled at the strings and slowly unrolled it, determined not to drop whatever lay inside.

"I've missed a few birthdays and Yule celebrations, and you never really had a mating ceremony, so I suppose I can lump them in with that as well."

"This is—"

"I wasn't sure when to give them to you, but since we're traveling, today seemed as good as any."

Arianna tentatively ran a hand over the silver scabbard encrusted with fine white and blue gems that lined the whirling patterns etched into the metal.

A twin pair of perfectly crafted long knives.

"You've always been faster with the shorter blades."

She opened her mouth to speak but words wouldn't form. Arianna set the leather pack on the ground and slid one of the knives from its sheath.

It glided effortlessly and without sound. She wrapped her hand around the hilt and marveled at how well it fit. At the lightness of the blade.

"I don't know what to say."

Talon grinned broadly and cocked his head. "'Thank you' would be a good start. They cost a fortune."

"You didn't have to—"

"Yes, I did, though your sister is probably going to skin me alive for giving you my present first. You can just pretend you like hers better, but we'll both know the truth." He winked, but Arianna's throat was thick with unshed tears. "And no crying. Niall already dislikes me and I don't need Rion thinking I'm over here bullying you."

She gave a strangled laugh, wiped at her tears, and clutched the blades to her chest.

"You mean you don't have a present to placate those two?"

Talon grimaced. "I'm pretty sure Niall owns at least half the city and gets anything he wants. As to Rion, I'm not sure we're at the gift giving stage yet."

"Too awkward?"

"Just a bit."

She choked on a laugh and eyed the knives again. "Thank you, Talon. Truly, they mean a lot."

"Yeah, yeah, now let's get moving before you try to change your mind again, and we'll pray you never have to use them."

NIALL HADN'T dressed down despite their destination. In fact, the pommels of his weapons were crested with jewels that sparkled in the rising sun. His boots were freshly polished, and his hair finely combed.

"Are you ready, My Lady?"

Arianna furrowed her brow at the carriage stationed in the center of the platform before her. "As long as I don't have to ride in that."

He stared at it, seeming confused by the remark. But he didn't know how much she'd loathed the three day journey to Ruadhán. "Would you rather ride on horseback?"

"I would, actually." She eyed the horses and their extravagant saddles. She couldn't remember the last time she'd ridden. Well before her capture. She hoped she didn't make a fool out of herself trying.

Niall quickly made the arrangements and a guard led a brown mare toward her moments later. The creature was strong and beautiful and gladly dipped her head for Arianna to stroke her muzzle.

They brought Talon one too, the horse as beautiful and black as the midnight sky. Talon offered Arianna a foothold so she could mount before he gracefully jumped onto his own.

Then the platform was moving, carrying them all into the clouds and down toward the ground in a steady fluid motion.

Arianna glanced up and noticed a figure that stood at the edge of the metal fence, the wind whipping at his red hair. Her heart lurched, hating the growing space between them. She gave a tentative wave and he returned it before clouds and mist hid him from view.

It's just for today. They could handle that. Talon would watch over her, and Ellie would watch over Rion.

Niall led his horse to Arianna's side and brushed a hand down the creature's neck. "Your mate trusts your friend a great deal. Talon, wasn't it?"

Arianna nodded, though she didn't believe for one minute that Niall didn't remember Talon's name. He seemed to remember everything. "I trust him and that's good enough."

His gaze floated toward the horizon and Niall was silent for so long Arianna wasn't sure he would speak again. She thought he might tell her about the village or give her some insight as to what they'd be walking into. Instead, his next words took her by surprise.

"Will there ever be a day you trust me like that?" She blanched. Trust him? She barely knew him. In fact, she was fairly certain he was at least somewhat responsible for what had happened the other night. Not to mention the way he kept antagonizing her mate. She was about to open her mouth to respond when he shook his head. "Forgive me, that was out of line."

Arianna closed her mouth. She eyed Niall over her shoulder. "Trust is built over time." His jaw feathered and she lowered her voice. "But maybe one day."

When he didn't offer anything more, Arianna said, "Tell me about the village."

Niall ran a hand through his hair as if he were trying to collect himself. "They've suffered a great deal, but its residents are strong, so they're recovering quickly.

"Before the war, the village was a central trading post. It was an obvious choice given the nearby river. Supplies were easily moved, merchants stopped by to rest and trade their wares, and their small community was flourishing into something more.

"Sadly though, Brónach and Móirín fought to dominate the territory, but Brónach's forces were harsher and did irreversible damage. The merchants stopped coming and the villagers eventually refused Móirín's aid for fear of the repercussions."

"And Rion was part of those repercussions?"

He nodded, his face grave. "I hope you'll forgive their animosity. They'll likely smell him on you."

She nodded, hoping she could contain herself, but Arianna wasn't sure how she would handle it at all.

They followed a dirt path at an easy pace until the sun beat down on them from directly overhead.

The wind caressed her hair, pulling tendrils loose from her braid and Arianna tilted her head back, soaking in the warmth of the sun's rays.

She was traveling to a village to help. She'd freed a group of slaves, was already making strides toward freeing many more, and now she was assisting the refugees.

Maybe the gods were finally smiling down on her. Perhaps all the hardships she had faced until now were the direct result of refusing her title. Perhaps the gods weren't patient and her refusal to accept her role had angered them.

Then again, maybe it was all luck and the gods didn't intervene at all.

Smoke rose in the distance, then homes dotted the horizon one by one. She swallowed, suddenly nervous. How should she act around them and what were their expectations?

She would heal the sick and injured, that was a given, but would she be allowed to help unload supplies or build alongside those crafting additional living quarters?

Did she need to worry about the rebel factions attacking her again or had Niall already weeded them out?

They drew closer and closer and Arianna spotted Fae working in the fields. They paused upon seeing the wagons, then many were bounding for the village, likely to spread news of their impending arrival.

By the time they rode into the village, it seemed as though every able bodied Fae lined the dirt street, watching with excited eyes. But they weren't looking at her. They studied the wagons, their hands seeming to itch to unpack the contents.

Many were thin, too thin, and their clothes were filthy and riddled with holes. Some of the homes that stood had fresh posts and strong roofs, but others were on the verge of collapse. And Fae still stood in the doorways as if claiming the space for themselves.

How long had Niall been helping? Not too long, from the looks of it.

Arianna watched as guards jumped from their horses and greeted those with whom they were familiar. Many of the villagers ran up to Niall and bowed deeply before bombarding him with a sea of questions.

Arianna counted the houses and stopped counting heads when she realized there wasn't enough shelter for the crowd by half.

Sleeping and nighttime arrangements were likely a very crowded and uncomfortable experience.

Niall's smile was infectious. He met a female with open arms and she offered a warm smile in return. Then she patted Niall's shoulder as if he weren't over seven hundred years old. "Our dear Niall." She stepped back and bowed. "Never one to be late, are you?" She eyed the wagons and raised a brow. "Did the council finally approve our request for additional supplies?"

"Actually, you can thank our young queen for her generous donation." He held out an open palm to gesture to Arianna.

The female's lips parted and she openly stared, those dark, haunted eyes soaking in every detail. Her hair was a sea of gold in the afternoon sun, spilling over her shoulders in gentle waves.

"You brought the queen," the female said, a bit breathless. Arianna swung her leg over the saddle and slid down the horse's side.

The female, still gaping, stepped forward, scented the air, then hissed and recoiled back. Talon drew his sword and placed himself in front of Arianna. Three Móirín guards did the same, flanking her friend. Six other guards summoned their magic and awaited instructions.

The woman growled, the hatred in her tone deep and unforgiving. "You're with that creature?" Arianna stiffened and the female clenched her hands, eyes wide and wild. "You—you—"

Niall placed a gentle hand on the female's shoulder, but she shook him off. He frowned. "If I could, I'd like to speak with you for a moment. In private."

Though they'd embraced just a moment ago, the female looked more ready to tear him apart than talk. She hesitated, clearly undecided before finally leading Niall away.

Arianna didn't dare to move. Not out of fear, but because she didn't want them to fear her, not any more than they already did.

She hated the smell and the way it glided through the air. Arianna was glad Rion hadn't come. Those staring at her would have either attacked him in a sad attempt to protect their homes or they would have outright fled.

The minutes ticking by were painful.

Talon and her guards remained exactly where they were until Niall and the female returned. She was still visibly upset, but at least she'd heard him out. Arianna only wished she knew what he'd said.

Talon didn't move.

"Niall has kindly explained the pseudo bond. I didn't realize you'd faced such turmoil. Strange how we attach ourselves to our captors, is it not?" Okay, maybe she could have done without knowing after all.

Arianna glared at Niall. "It is not a pseudo bond."

The female offered her a sad smile. "Of course not."

Arianna swallowed the urge to argue. Every cell in her body wanted to defend her mate, but before she could speak, the female said, "Come, walk with me, child."

Child. Not queen. Not lady. Arianna bit the inside of her cheek. Talon put his sword away and the others relaxed, though they seemed to keep their sharp gazes locked on the villagers.

Arianna took a steadying breath. She needed to remain calm. These people had only recently been freed from the ravages of war. They'd likely experienced things beyond her imagination and she couldn't fault them for their anger or caution.

She fell into step beside the female and Talon followed close behind.

"I'm Cadhla, the village head."

"Arianna."

The female smirked. "I always imagined The Divine as someone much older than myself, but I suppose none of us are born with the wisdom of centuries. We must grow and learn from our mistakes just like everyone else."

Arianna knew what *mistake* the female was referencing but she refused to acknowledge it.

"Five years into the war," Cadhla began. "We were still a peaceful village, kept out of the conflict sweeping across the land. We thought we were far enough away from the chaos that we wouldn't attract attention. Thus, we invited those who didn't have a home to reside here." She met Arianna's gaze. "You see, The Demon took whatever he wanted. Land, homes, supplies, and even our lives where it suited him. And he took it with no regard to how we might survive otherwise."

Her voice lowered. "We were supposed to be sending aid to their camps and we weren't. He took it as an act of defiance."

A dark look crossed her fair features. "The Demon showed up at our gates with a legion of warriors. Some tried to resist, and he tore them apart. He forced many of us to watch so we would learn the cost of disobedience. His men took all our food and—" her voice cracked as she continued. "I tried to tell my son to stand down, but he was young. Maybe even about your age." Cadhla paused, seeming to relive the horrid memory. Arianna had stopped breathing.

"My son charged The Demon head on and that monster wrapped his foul magic around him so tight that it crushed him in an instant." Her hands were shaking now. "Just like that, gone. And that horrid creature smiled." Tears were spilling down Cadhla's face now, her cheeks and nose flushed.

"No matter what you might think or how you might feel, you have to know who he is at his core. I mean truly know. You could talk to anyone in this village and they'd have a similar story. Is that the kind of male you wish to give your heart to?"

Arianna struggled for words and failed to find any suitable so she just said, "He's not like that anymore," But her voice was small and the words felt hollow in the face of this female's pain.

The female shook her head. "Males like him don't change. It's not in their nature. They don't happen upon a pretty face one day and vow to cast their bloodlust aside the next. He's a monster and a murderer and he will show you that soon enough. I just hope you're ready when he does."

The female excused herself after that, leaving Arianna reeling in the dark memory. She felt hollow, her heart aching for the people and everything they'd lost. Not just their homes, but their family members. And she suddenly realized her life had been so easy compared to theirs.

Her hard days had been spent with hope. She'd known where her family and friends were. She'd been able to sleep with the knowledge that Ellie was safe in her bed while these Fae had mourned and buried their dead.

Arianna had come to help them but barely twenty minutes in and she already wanted to go home. She couldn't. So, with a heavy heart, Arianna healed those who were injured while the villagers shared their heartbreaking stories.

Each one felt worse than the next. They spoke of a very different male from the one who had kissed her farewell that morning. Her soul felt raw and bare, like they'd ripped her heart from her chest and bruised it with their heartache.

Niall sauntered over after she healed a young male with a broken wrist. The male told her a story about losing his parents and about the nightmares where flashing green eyes haunted the darkness.

"It helps them to have someone listen to their plights," Niall said as if trying to console her.

But it wasn't helping her. Not in the slightest, and she knew Rion could feel her swell of emotions. His were silent and Arianna wondered if he'd pulled himself back on purpose, hoping to give her space, or if the distance between the village and Ruadhán had something to do with it.

I am the monster they claim me to be.

He'd said those words to her once, but they hadn't possessed much merit until now.

He'd been a story she was told as a child. Writing in a textbook while she'd attended school. A warning from Talon and her father.

Rion had been afraid to let her come here because he'd known exactly what she would see.

Rion had changed their lives forever and there was nothing anyone could ever do to make amends.

With an aching heart, Arianna spent the day healing the rest who were injured. She filled a new well and helped spread water across the fields. They even let her assist with building the skeletal foundations for a new structure. But despite the labor, it was the emotions that left her exhausted when the sun began its descent in the sky.

Arianna joined the others as they approached their horses, but Cadhla stopped her again. "I hope you'll consider everything you saw today." She offered a gentle smile. "Please come visit us again. You're welcome anytime."

Arianna maintained her smile even though all she wanted to do was run the entire way back to Ruadhán. "Absolutely. I was happy to help." Her heart was heavy. So very heavy.

Arianna swung up into her saddle and was the first down the path with Talon following and the guards scrambling to keep up. She couldn't meet Talon's gaze, nor those of the other guards. They had already known. Everyone knew the depth of Rion's actions except her.

She'd only ever seen him kill those who had attacked him first and she'd convinced herself Rion was simply defending himself. Had he really stalked villages and burned them to the ground? Had he killed innocents simply for disobeying?

"My Lady," Niall's call from behind had Arianna pulling on the reins of her mare. He pushed his horse into an easy trot then stopped before her, eyes pinched with concern. "You're leaving?"

Arianna glanced toward the sun. "I wanted to be back before nightfall."

"I see." He looked to the village and back. "I have a few more things to take care of here, but we'll join you soon. I'll send a few of my warriors to escort you." She nodded and turned away, desperate to escape his scrutiny.

"Do our efforts not please you?"

"No," she answered quietly. "They do."

Niall pushed his horse closer and lowered his voice. "I'm sorry if what I said today upset you." Arianna didn't answer. "I had to tell them something."

"But you believe it too, right?"

"That your bond isn't real? Absolutely, but it's not my place to intervene. You'll discover it on your own with time."

She clenched the reins. "Is that really what today was about? Did you bring me here hoping to speed things along?" Her temper rose. "Did you think showing me how bad he really was would change something in the bond?"

Niall's eyes filled with sorrow. "I won't lie and tell you no, but my main motive was to show you the effort we've put forth toward healing those who were displaced. I can't help that he was part of almost every effort in tearing their lives apart." She didn't respond and Niall dipped his head. "I am sorry for the pain this caused you." He lingered a moment longer, but when she kept her head down, Niall turned his horse back to the village and trotted away.

Arianna bit the inside of her cheek hard. She wouldn't cry. Not here.

Right now, all she wanted was a hot bath and to think about something else entirely. But Arianna knew she wouldn't. The pain from that one village would haunt her for weeks. They were a broken people and she couldn't right the wrongs that had been inflicted. All she could do was listen. Listen and drown in the grief they suffered day in and day out, all the while knowing it was her mate who had put it there.

CHAPTER FORTY-SEVEN

ARIANNA

The horses kept a brisk pace, seeming just as eager to return home as she was. They moved faster without the wagons, but the light was fading quickly. Rion would be a pacing, worried mess by the time they entered the city.

Arianna sighed and noted the way Talon seemed to be watching her every move. He'd witnessed Rion's merciless wrath first hand and she hadn't considered the full weight of that until now. Her friend's struggles suddenly made more sense. Did the villager's opinions reflect his own? Did he believe Rion could change, or was he also waiting for The Demon to reappear just as Niall and the council seemed to be?

Dusk fell, then light faded from the land, leaving them to walk the last few miles shrouded in darkness.

Arianna hated every second of it. She studied the sides of the road, searching for any unnatural lumps in the grass. And when they passed a small hill, her heart had nearly beat out of her chest as she craned her neck to watch for any possible assailants.

Something howled in the distance, causing the hairs on the back of her neck to rise, but it was too far away to cause them worry.

Arianna chewed her lip when she spotted the copse of trees ahead.

In the dark, the trees were woven together as one, individual trunks almost indiscernible even with her Fae eyes. Her heart quickened and even Talon palmed a knife, ready to strike any who dared attempt an ambush.

She prayed she wouldn't have to draw the twin blades strapped to her back.

They kept moving, all eyes watching the tree line as the horses trotted past. She held her breath, listening. Waiting.

Almost. Just a few more feet and the trees would fade behind them and she'd laugh about her fear in the morning. Just a few—

A twig snapped, her mare's ears swiveled, and Arianna cursed beneath her breath. Then an arrow buried itself in the shoulder of the male riding just ahead of her.

He cried out and the horse next to his bucked, sending its rider to the ground with a hard thud. The female quickly righted herself and drew her weapons.

Talon leapt from his horse and grabbed Arianna's arm, ripping her from the saddle. He pressed her against the creature's side, shielding her body as more arrows flew from the darkness. Talon knocked two away with his magic, but the sudden outburst had the horses rearing before they took off into the night. She'd never grown accustomed to the squealing noise horses made when they were injured.

Arianna yanked her magic from the air, surrounding herself and Talon in icy crystals. Even if she couldn't see the arrows clearly, the shards might throw a few off their target.

Her heart thundered and she struggled to hear beyond the racing pulse in her ears.

The guards from both Ruadhán and Móirín formed a tight circle around her, caging her from the chaos and acting as living shields. She might have balked against the action if it weren't for their magic. Even the one with an arrow protruding from his shoulder stood close, his weapon raised. But Arianna could see the way his hands trembled from the pain.

Silence engulfed the area. None moved. They waited an entire agonizing minute, then more bow strings snapped.

Magic erupted from her guards in a whirlwind of frenzied activity. Fire spun out from the arms of those furthest away, illuminating the field. They lit the nearest trees and flames raced up the tall trunks, eliciting screams of pain from the individuals hiding within.

Wind tore from the air, redirecting the raining arrows back to their owners. Shrieks of pain told Arianna more than one had found its mark.

Plant life of all forms tore from the ground, splitting the earth as they reached with spindly fingers for whoever was unlucky enough to stand in their path. Water and ice surrounded her in a protective circle, acting as a last line of defense should anyone break through the others' offensive strikes.

Arianna watched the magic work together in perfect sync, those from different countries fighting for the same cause.

Fighting together.

In unison.

Those in Ruadhán constantly talked about the peace she'd bring as if she could heal the land single handedly. But maybe it wasn't a single action that would bring that peace about. Maybe it was this, the four nations working together to achieve a common goal.

They'd been separated for so long and for reasons their history never clearly explained.

Warriors leapt from the shadows, clashing with her guards head on. But those fighting for their queen drove the assailants back.

The warriors surrounding her joined the fray at Talon's command, leaving her friend and the injured warrior to stand by her side. Almost over. Just a few more minutes and their enemy would be subdued.

The scent of the wounded warrior's blood drew her attention as it soaked though his sleeve. Sweat rolled down his neck and he gritted his teeth against the pain, struggling, once again, to raise his blade.

She swallowed hard and moved to his side. The arrow had gone straight through, thank the gods. It would make extracting the offending object easier. She studied the dwindling battles and once satisfied that none would be coming after them, Arianna grabbed the shaft of the arrow and snapped it in half. The male cried out, hissing between his teeth. She muttered an apology before yanking the shaft from his shoulder.

Arianna covered the wound with her hand and the male winced when her palms illuminated and the magic began its work. She watched the battle, her heart slowing. Three more. There were only three more fighting. Once they gave up, the rest of them could get out of here.

Only two of her guards appeared hurt, their crouched silhouettes illuminated by the fire rising high in the trees.

"Thank you," the male whispered and Arianna stepped back, his blood covering her hands. Fire spun from his body and the trio watched another of their enemies fall. Then another.

Bandits. They'd just been bandits likely hoping to collect easy coin from passing travelers.

She breathed a sigh of relief.

Talon cried out from her left. Her head whipped around to see his chin painfully collide with the earth. She ran for him, heart pounding, teeth clenched and fear tearing through her body as he continued screaming in agony.

What—then she saw them. Two tendrils of darkest black against the already shadowed earth. It wrapped around his legs and crawled up both his calves, burning through the fabric of his boots and pants as it traveled.

She didn't think, Arianna just moved, launching freezing crystals into the darkness ahead.

The tendrils didn't let go.

Talon blindly hurled his own magic into the darkness before forming a wall of ice that severed the tendrils of shadow. He scrambled away, attempted to rise to his feet, and cried out against the pain.

The guard with them stood to Talon's front and Arianna slid to her knees beside her friend, already working on the scorching wound of his left leg.

Her hands shook and every muscle in her body had tightened all over again. There were more. So many more judging from the scents and sounds. Feet sliding through the grass, ragged breathing that told her they were ready for a fight, rapid heartbeats picking up speed the closer they drew to their targets.

The ambush had simply been to feel them out, test their strength. And they'd isolated Talon as the biggest threat. They knew, she realized. Somehow they knew she was out here and they'd come for her.

Arianna worked on Talon's other leg, but she hadn't finished before fire illuminated those closing the distance. A dozen. Two. Three.

Gods. Oh gods, how many were there?

Those who'd been fighting by the tree line closed in around her, their weapons already drawn. Talon stood, ignoring the blistering skin on his right leg. He shoved her body behind his own and Arianna stared into the angry faces coming for her.

How did they know? Did someone from the village tip them off? Had there been members of the rebel factions present after all?

Arianna drew the two long knives from her back with trembling hands. There weren't enough of them, not nearly enough to fight off so many, even with their magic.

Those stalking toward her broke into a run. Magic flew from both sides, colliding in a thunderous stream of blades and battle cries. She didn't move, watching in horror as blades pierced flesh and her comrades went down one after the other. Her heart beat faster, faster, faster.

Talon spun and danced through their enemies, swinging his sword in a high arch to behead one of the Shadow Weavers. He was targeting those from Fiadh first. Two guards stood at her side, ready to intervene should anyone get too close.

Talon ducked, then those shadows reached out and slammed into his chest. Smoke coiled from his leather armor, but her friend barely seemed to notice as he launched ice across the ground. His opponent tripped, distracting him long enough for Talon to sink his blade into the male's chest.

Then Rion desperately pulled on the bond, yearning for some confirmation that she was okay. She couldn't respond, couldn't convince her body to move, even with the twin blades in her grasp.

There was so much blood and magic and her comrades were falling and the males were bathing in their triumph with each kill and the smells and flickering lights and her pounding heart and she couldn't breathe, couldn't breathe, couldn't breathe—

"Such a prize traveling out in the open." The voice came from her right and the two guards at her side pivoted to place their bodies between the male and their queen. Not just a male, but five others, all with fire and shadows and—Arianna swallowed hard. Chains. Those were chains in his hands.

He glanced toward Talon and frowned. "You know, I'd really hate to kill you all." Ice coated her veins. Not bandits. Slavers. But . . . but they weren't half-breeds or humans. They were Fae and—and this male didn't care. They'd enslave the queen and show the continent that even she could be subdued. That slavery wouldn't end no matter who stood in their way.

Her mouth was suddenly dry and her body rooted in place with gruesome memories. Cold iron grating against her raw wrists. Long winter months with little more than rags to keep her warm. Fellow slaves starving to death. Blood caked to her back from the lashings she had received. The way they'd stung as she was forced to work through the pain.

Somewhere in a distant part of her mind, someone tried to yank her free of those memories. They told her they were coming. To hold on. To fight.

Talon's voice rang through her, but he seemed so far away. So far . . .

Her breath came faster and faster and Arianna thought she might have a lead weight on her chest, suffocating her, gripping her lungs so tight it might as well have been an iron shackle.

The male prowled forward, those chains clanking together. Someone moved from her left then her right, but the shadows swallowed them whole along with their screams.

Someone was still beating against her mind, over and over as if trying to break through a wall. But she couldn't find him, couldn't reach no matter how much she wanted to.

The five stepped forward, closing in, then three icy shards shot from her left and buried themselves deep in the male's chest. She barely drew a breath, watching as they fell to their knees and the remaining two snarled.

No. No, please not again. She couldn't do this again. She didn't want to watch the people she loved suffer as she'd suffered. She couldn't— she couldn't—

Please, please, please, please.

Arianna curled into herself.

Someone, please.

A crack.

Another.

Then she looked up. Blood dripped from the male she'd healed, his arm wounded again from the blade he'd caught. Not dead. Not engulfed by shadow.

Crack.

He fought. He was a warrior. A guard. And he fought.

Eoghan had fought.

Talon was still fighting.

She needed—

The clashing came louder.

She needed—

Her vision cleared to find the male with the chains drawing closer.

She needed—

He wore a wicked smile on his face, like he'd already won. That smile she'd seen so many times when the slavers had taken a whip to their backs or kicked them while they were down.

She needed—

Arianna didn't need anything.

The ringing in her ears faded. Her lungs relaxed, pulling in air that tasted like crackling magic. Arianna lifted her head and it felt as though the world slowed around her.

Crack.

Crack.

Crack.

She wasn't trapped. Arianna flexed her fingers around the handles of her blades and fresh blood flowed through her joints.

She wasn't hiding. She stood and met Talon's gaze. The world and everything around her moved slowly, as if she had all the time in the world.

Arianna pinned the male before her with a look of disgust. She took stock of the chains in his hand and those hanging from his waist. As if he expected to enslave them all. Her. Talon. The guards. Arianna clenched her fists.

She wasn't powerless.

You're weak, her father's voice echoed from a distant memory.

The male closed the distance and she watched as he grabbed her wrist.

No. I'm not.

A final crack and the dam broke. Power surged through her and Arianna angled the knife in her right hand and swung it down in a wide arc, severing the male's arm from the rest of his body.

His scream pieced the night air and those remaining at his side hissed, their deadly magic rising, ready to engulf her, too.

A sweet voice whispered to her then, telling Arianna she was just as deadly as any of them. More so. Because she'd survived. She had come out victorious from every battle she'd ever fought and it wasn't because of luck or the gods or some coincidence or fate.

It was because she was powerful and unstoppable and fierce.

Ice burst from her feet and exploded in a wave of cold that sent the male before her sprawling to the ground, frost already crawling across his skin. She silenced his comrade's magic, snuffing out their shadows as if they were nothing more than flames on a candle.

They came at her with weapons instead. Arianna ducked beneath the first swing and brought her blade up. The sharp knife cut right through his leather armor and slid across the delicate skin of his stomach, spilling the contents on the ground at his feet. He doubled over, but Arianna left him, focusing on her next target.

She swung and missed. The male grinned, sure he had won, but she blinded him with a burst of ice. He fell back and she leapt on the male before he could right himself. Arianna buried her blade in his throat, then turned toward the rest.

Talon was still fighting, but his eyes were on her now, studying every movement she made.

She was not weak.

Arianna ran and became a series of vicious, quick movements. She wouldn't feel guilt or offer them a shred of mercy or forgiveness.

Her knives flew from her waist faster than she'd ever thrown them and they found their marks every single time. Her guards regrouped, fighting in her wake. Fighting with her. Then Talon was at her side, moving in sync with her strikes as if they were partners in a dance.

Their enemies fell, paused, then backed away. Arianna didn't let them run. She let her magic cover the ground and caught those attempting to flee. They tripped, sliding, and the ice crawled along their bodies, rising up and up until it covered every inch of their skin, forever trapping them inside a frozen prison.

Her breath clouded in the air and Arianna only half registered that Talon stood by her side, his magic still circling.

He stepped, crunching hoarfrost beneath his feet. "We probably shouldn't kill them all." Right, because they needed answers. Like who had tipped them off, where the rebel factions were gathering, and how many others they might have in captivity.

Though many were wounded and limping, the warriors followed Talon's instruction to bind those still alive with iron.

They'd been outnumbered and had emerged victorious. So many plights and challenges and she'd come out on top every single time.

Arianna made a promise to herself. She wouldn't be that weak little female plagued by darkness and memories any more. She'd place that female in a box full of plush blankets and books and chocolates and protect her from the outside world. She'd give that female love and comfort and nothing, absolutely nothing, would ever hurt her again.

The magic still roared within her veins, crawling and writhing like a creature who wanted to fight. She looked at her hands and the thin layer of frost that coated her fingers, crawling and spreading before melting again.

Kill them, it still seemed to beg. Arianna furrowed her brow.

No.

Kill them, it pushed, more demanding. *Kill them now.*

No.

The power flickered as if angry, then vanished entirely. It yanked from her body so suddenly Arianna gasped and hit her knees.

Talon crossed the field in a matter of seconds and caught her shoulders before she fell. He held her close as she gasped for breath. Her head spun and spots lined her vision, then she felt the desperate pounding again.

A wild, hysterical fear filled her head and it took Arianna a moment to realize they weren't her feelings at all.

They were Rion's.

Rion who felt like he was unraveling at the seams.

Rion who was begging for some kind of answer.

Arianna tugged back, trying to console him, but she was flooded with so many emotions she couldn't sort through them all. Not at this distance and not with his fear so palpable it felt like her own.

"Are you all right?" Talon asked.

Arianna lifted her head, the sudden silence of the night pressing in on her from all sides. She looked him over, noting the cuts on his arms and torso and the burns across his legs.

"You're hurt."

"So are you." Arianna looked at herself then. First at the large gash in her right forearm. Then at the thin line across her upper thigh. She hadn't noticed either during the fight.

Arianna ignored her wounds and reached for Talon. Her magic was sluggish and heavy, but she pushed it, determined to close the worse of his wounds and heal the burns. The ones on his legs would scar, but there was nothing she could do aside from make a salve that he likely wouldn't use.

Arianna let her body collapse and ran a hand over her face, still trying to catch her breath.

Then someone cried out. They screamed a name. Arianna moved without thinking. She ran to the warrior's side and began healing his wound. Then she moved onto the next. And the next.

Those in captivity were chained together and corralled into a small space beside the trees. None tried to speak, but they visibly shrank away when she passed by. Arianna supposed being caught and almost suffocated by ice would be enough to quiet even the brashest of warriors.

The male from Fiadh who'd taken an arrow lit a fire and guided her over to it. He draped his cloak around her body and Arianna thanked him. Cole. Cole was his name, and when they got back to Ruadhán she was appointing him as part of her personal guard. He'd stepped up to defend her against impossible odds, stepped up to defend his commanding officer, too.

Arianna's breathing slowly returned to normal, but her body still trembled.

Talon sank down at her side. "You hesitated." It wasn't exactly a reprimand. More like an offer if she wanted to talk.

Arianna replied, "You didn't." Because Talon would fight for her until the end of time and if he hadn't been here—Arianna shook her head. He'd never let her fall into chains again.

The guards built more fires at Talon's command and they pulled bandages from their packs to nurse superficial wounds. Niall would meet up with them soon enough and they'd travel the rest of the way with his group. For now, they'd stay put and rest.

Hopefully the smell of blood would keep anyone else far, far away.

Her eyes had just started to drift shut when rapid footsteps made every warrior jump to their feet. Talon had warned his warriors to stand aside when Rion arrived and stay far away from the male.

Arianna could feel Rion's apprehension and scent his fear as he took in the blood and bodies.

Arianna stood and shouted a single command. "Step aside." None wanted to, she could see it written across their faces, but they obeyed. Rion's snarl tore through the air as a warning.

Her mate's nostrils flared and his wild green eyes darted around the camp searching, searching, searching until—that intense gaze locked with hers, then his eyes drifted to the shallow cut across her forearm and the one across her thigh.

Something in him snapped.

He twisted toward their prisoners and Arianna's stomach sank. All clambered to their feet and desperately fought against their bonds. His magic rose, crawling across the ground, pulsing with his hurried steps.

A monster, that female had called him. *He'll show his true colors soon enough.*

But the only thing Arianna saw was a territorial male reacting to those who'd injured his mate.

Arianna left her cloak by the fire. She barely had the energy to pull at the water particles but forced herself to do it anyway. They mingled with his raging magic. He paused when she tugged on the bond, but Rion didn't turn to face her.

Arianna laid her hand on his shoulder and he met her gaze. Icy hatred filled his beautiful eyes as he studied her face, breath coming in rapid gasps.

"They're not worth it," she tried.

"They're not worth the air you breathe," he seethed, his voice a low dark tone she hadn't heard in a while.

"Maybe not," she eyed them. "But everyone deserves a chance at redemption."

His body shook with barely contained fury, but his magic fell away slowly, settling on the ground in piles at their feet. Rion locked eyes with one who dared to look up and he bolted toward the male, slamming his fist into the male's face so hard Arianna heard something crack.

The male howled in pain and Rion stood over him for several seconds, panting. She wondered if Rion might kill the male anyway.

Her mate turned away from the prisoners. She didn't have time to ask questions before his arms were around her, squeezing so tight she was sure she'd break. He breathed in her scent, kissed her brow, then buried his head in her neck and just held her.

Arianna wrapped her arms around his back and the knot in her chest unraveled with his presence. She breathed easier now, despite Rion's iron grip, and let her head rest on his shoulder.

Rion didn't move until Arianna shivered and even then, he didn't release the hold on her shoulders. They marched toward the nearest fire and Rion growled at those gathered. They dispersed quickly.

She sat on the ground and Rion sat behind her, pulling her flush against his body. He wrapped his arms over her shoulders and held her again, close, as if she might disappear.

His heat seeped through her clothes and exhaustion swept through her body. Arianna leaned her head against his and breathed in his scent.

Not a monster, she wanted to tell that female. Maybe once, but not anymore.

"I'm sorry," he said after a time. She merely tilted her head. "I wanted to give you space, but—"

"I don't want space." Rion's rage trickled away, but he was still a hurricane of emotions.

He'd known. Gods, he'd known how she would feel after seeing the village. He had known exactly what she would come across. The atrocities she would witness.

"Why did you let me go?" He hadn't tried to warn her or make any excuses for himself, just like he'd done with Zylah.

"Because I don't want to hide anything from you. You deserve to know."

"I already knew." But she hadn't. Not really. It was difficult to imagine that the male currently clutching her to his chest was the same monster everyone talked about. He was different now. So different, Arianna could hardly visualize his old self. But Rion could. She was sure he relived every cruel thing he'd ever done day in and day out. She wondered if he still fought against that part of himself or if it had vanished entirely.

"You still doubt my feelings." He didn't answer. How could she show him once and for all?

"Maybe they aren't real." His voice cracked and her heart shattered with it.

"You think it's a pseudo bond, too?"

He didn't release her. Didn't pull back in the slightest. His heart beat so fast she could feel it in her own chest. "It doesn't feel fake," he said. "But it would explain things."

"Why do you keep trying to push me away?"

"I just—I want you to be happy. I want people to adore you the way The Divine is supposed to be adored. I don't want the weight of my sins on your shoulders." She had seen just how heavy that weight could be today. And she'd only visited one village.

Arianna was silent for a time, watching the fire flicker and spark. "You told me our immortal lives weren't worth wasting." Arianna pressed her cheek against his. "I don't want any of this if it means I don't have you."

Rion's breath shuddered and he pressed his lips against her hair. She was certain she would fall asleep in his arms before he spoke again. "You asked once if I wanted to be forgiven." Arianna waited. "I've thought about it for a while, just to make sure it was something I wanted for myself."

"And?"

"I want to earn my place in this world. I want to show people I've changed through my actions, not just my words."

Arianna smiled. "I sense you have a plan in mind."

He nodded but pressed his head to hers again. He hadn't loosened his grip on her once. "Tomorrow." Because tonight he just needed her, to know she was safe and his and all was right in the world. Arianna felt Rion's emotions clear then, like a fog had lifted. Love. Unbridled and passionate. There weren't the emotions of a monster. And despite what everyone kept telling her, Arianna knew their bond was the realest thing to ever exist.

CHAPTER FORTY-EIGHT

RION

Niall had met them before dawn. He was beside himself and demanded explanations before he escorted their injured party back inside the confines of the royal city. Rion didn't much care what happened to the prisoners. Niall could execute them for all he cared. Arianna didn't seem to care, either.

Rion had run her a hot bath and tended to her wounds, which were thankfully shallower than he'd first thought. Then they'd spent the entire next day in the library, playing chess and reading books.

He didn't tell Arianna his plans for three days, mostly because he wanted more time with her before setting off on his own. He would have rather waited another month, but Arianna's excitement had gotten the better of her and she had run to Ellie. Everything had fallen into place after that.

Arianna supported him completely.

Now he stood outside the manor waiting for Ellie's return. Rion wished he didn't have to rely on others, but he needed materials and he knew no one on the council would be willing to give him anything. They'd likely laugh in his face anyway.

But he didn't need their approval. He didn't need anyone's approval. He just wanted to begin making amends, no matter how small.

The bond tugged, instincts begging him to remain close to his mate after what recently happened. When he'd felt her initial rush of frozen panic, Rion had darted from the library so fast he'd knocked over a table. And he was fairly certain he'd given two half-breeds heart attacks in the process.

But he needed to do this. If he wanted to stand beside the queen of Alastríona, then Rion needed to prove himself worthy. Or at least begin proving himself. He had a long road to walk on the path to redemption.

Ellie finally exited and sighed in frustration, shaking her head in a way that had his heart sinking.

"They declined?"

"No, they accepted, but the nonsense was exhausting." Rion fell into step beside her. "Apparently, you need a babysitter." Ellie scoffed.

"And you volunteered?"

Ellie waved her hand through the air. "As if I had a choice. If anyone else goes, they'll likely try to assassinate you, then we'll have a whole other mess on our hands."

"Don't you have other responsibilities?"

"None that I don't put on myself."

"What about Kirian?"

"He'll stay here. He's researching some stuff for me and after what happened with Arianna, I don't want him outside the city walls."

Rion eyed her bag. "You're ready to go?"

She smirked. "I thought you didn't want to waste time."

Rion smiled to himself and followed her toward the platforms.

THEY'D EACH taken a horse, a light pack, and nothing more. Ellie said the council would have their supplies ready by tomorrow, but Rion had his magic in the meantime.

Yesterday, Ellie had helped him scout for a suitable area on the map and now she was helping him survey the landscape. He wanted to build a village. The first of many, to replace all those he'd destroyed.

Rion knew it wasn't much—anyone could build—but the occupation of it was something he enjoyed.

Ellie stopped in the middle of a field and he followed her eyes. "This ought to be as good a place to start as any."

The land was mostly flat save for one hill that rose to their left. He might be able to keep it and use it for farming.

The trees were sparse, yet large enough that he would be able to use their timber for construction.

Rion leapt from his horse and patted its strong neck. He pulled the reins from around its head, then unsaddled the creature, allowing it to roam free and graze on the tall grass. Ellie did the same.

"You realize this is going to take forever by yourself, right?"

Rion eyed her. "It won't be as hard as you think."

She shrugged, then pulled a blanket from her pack, unfolded it, and spread it across the tall grass. "Here, I brought you some lunch."

Rion stared at the long wrapped sandwich before taking it. She plopped down to unwrap her own. "Kirian made them himself. He doesn't want to risk anyone poisoning me, either."

She took a bite, closed her eyes, and chewed slowly, savoring it in a way that almost made Rion laugh. Rion was fairly certain Ellie would choose food over gold if she were ever given the option.

He sat across from her and eyed his sandwich. He should trust her. He wanted to trust her, but he had wanted to trust so many others, too. She had been meeting nonstop with the council since their arrival. She functioned as Móirín's ambassador. If she had finally decided he wasn't worth keeping around—

"Really?" she said, seeming to follow his train of thought. Ellie sighed and swiped his sandwich before he could reply and took a large bite. Her face contorted and she shuddered before swallowing it quickly and handing it back. Rion just stared at her.

"I don't like tomatoes. Arianna said you do, so of course your stupid sandwich has to be loaded with them."

At that, Rion laughed. Arianna's little sister had to be the most authentic Fae he'd ever met. She voiced exactly what she was thinking and faced the world without fear, demanding it bend to her will.

Ellie looked out over the area. "So what's our first move?"

Rion finally bit into the sandwich and followed her gaze. He swallowed before saying, "I'll clear the trees and level the ground."

She scoffed. "Oh sure, no big deal. We'll just rearrange the landscape as if it's furniture in the sitting room."

He laughed. "I guess there are some advantages to this magic."

"I'd say so." She glanced around again. "Just don't drop a tree on me."

ONCE THEY finished lunch, Rion quickly uprooted the trees and piled them off to one side. Ellie located a spring and he shifted the dirt, packed it, and placed rocks inside to create a sturdy well. He tilled one section, preparing it for crops, then marked a space where he'd build a pen for animals.

"You really plan to build an entire village by yourself," Ellie said.

Rion used his magic to work on the first tree, blasting away the bark before carefully splitting it down the middle.

"A few villages. As many as it takes."

She shook her head and watched as the two pieces lowered to the ground. He split them in half again. "Well, I'll make time to come help whenever I'm free."

"I appreciate that."

She spread her arms. "We'll get the whole gang out here. It'll be nice to change things up a bit and get some fresh air."

"I thought you enjoyed the royal life."

"I like the food," Ellie admitted. "But they're all a bunch of old bastards who whine when one little mishap inconveniences their day. They're downright irritating. Although," She added before he could respond. "I'm having quite a nice time snooping through their things." She crinkled her nose. "Mostly."

"Mostly?"

Disgust crossed her features. "I found a book I would have rather not set eyes on. I mean, who details their," she paused, searching for the word, "encounters and sets a numeric value about—you know what? Never mind, it's too gross to even talk about."

"You read a lot of it?"

Rion thought her face might have turned a shade green. "I thought it was coded or something. I didn't seriously think anyone would—" She shook her head again. "Can we change the subject, please?"

He chuckled. "Sure." But silence stretched between them as he placed the first posts in the ground, setting what would be the framework for the first cabin. Rion planned for it to have a living area and a bedroom with a small kitchen against one wall. Four windows, for which he'd need to request supplies, and a sturdy fireplace that would keep its occupants warm come winter.

Ellie tested his posts, checking they were straight. "I've been meaning to bring something up with you and Arianna, but there never seems to be a good time." He raised a brow so she continued. "You're Arianna's mate."

"Yes," he said a bit uncertainly.

Ellie gave him a knowing look. "You're The Divine's mate."

Rion lifted another post and set it beside the others. "What are you getting at?"

She released an exasperated sigh. "Why is no one willing to talk about this? The Divine's mate is supposed to be the king of Alastríona."

Rion tightened his grip on the wood, fingers splintering the smooth post. "You can't say things like that."

"Why not? It's true. The texts are very specific. That's why they're all convinced it's a pseudo bond, because if it's not, then you are the rightful king."

"What kind of king," Rion tasted the word, "kills his own people?"

"Look, I know you've done some horrible things, but that doesn't change the fact—"

"It changes everything," he interrupted. "You see the way everyone stares at her. They're baffled by her choice in me, and some of them are angry, questioning her judgement. That wouldn't be happening if it weren't for me. Even if fate claims I'm to rule at her side, there isn't a soul on this continent who would claim me as their sovereign."

"I would."

Rion's lips parted and he stared at the young defiant female. She had made every effort to show him she wasn't afraid and just like his mate, Ellie was willing to accept him as he was, sins and all.

"That . . . means a great deal to me."

"Talon would too, you know."

He scoffed. "Talon can't stand the sight of me."

"He doesn't hate you. He just wants Arianna to be happy and his feelings are complicated right now. Give him time and you'll see."

Rion lifted another post into position and sank it into the ground. "Even so, three people aren't going to make a difference."

"Four," Ellie corrected. "Kirian counts, not to mention the former slaves residing in Levea."

Rion remembered Zylah's words. *Many of them regard you as their savior.* He shook his head. "It's not enough."

"It's a start, and more than you had a few months ago. Probably more than you've ever had," she ventured. "You're earning people's trust. Even if the progress is slow, I bet you'll be surprised before the end at how many would pledge themselves to you."

A dream, he reasoned. A dream that was so far-fetched, it might as well have been a fairytale. But then, he had believed in one of those before, too.

CHAPTER FORTY-NINE

ARIANNA

Arianna slammed the book shut and moved onto the next. She thumbed through the pages, searching chapter headings and images. Nothing. Nothing at all about the previous Divine aside from vague descriptions and passages that recited the ancient text.

It was maddening. How could a figure so important to their history not have endless books detailing her life, her accomplishments, her name? Arianna had only stumbled across one passage and her heart had plummeted.

She failed to bring peace when the world needed it most and wrought destruction in its place.

Failed. But what did failure mean exactly? And destruction? What had she done?

Had the previous Divine forsaken her duties and gone on to live a normal life? Had she died at too young an age? Had she disagreed with the council's methods and taken matters into her own hands?

Arianna placed the book on a table and moved on. She'd littered half the library with forgotten books, but they always managed to find their way back to the shelves.

A feeling of triumph trickled down the bond and she paused to check on it. Rion left every morning after breakfast with a swift kiss and a promise to return before nightfall. The task of building something brought life to her mate in a way she hadn't seen in a while. Maybe the productivity gave Rion a renewed sense of purpose.

She couldn't wait to see his progress.

Rion had been a general in Brónach's military for a large portion of his life. He'd had missions, subordinates, schedules, and had maintained it all with a firm hand. But upon leaving his camp behind, Rion had lost his purpose. Even if he tried to claim *she* was his purpose now.

Arianna rolled her eyes, sighed, and ran her hands along a leather spine. Another history book. At least Rion's task felt important. All she did day in and day out was read and search for answers that didn't seem to exist. She looked up through the library's glass ceiling and noted the sun's position. She'd missed lunch. Again.

"Distracted?" Talon asked.

She headed toward him and studied the book in his hand. Talon was here for other reasons. To keep an eye on her in Rion's place and to do some research of his own. Talon needed a fool proof exit strategy should things ever go awry. He'd been bent over maps and blueprints for days. Maybe she'd ask him to sneak her out right now. She wondered how long it would take before Niall noticed her missing.

"Bored," she admitted. Talon grunted and returned to his book. Apparently boredom wasn't a good enough reason to disappear from the city.

"Has Niall ever mentioned if there are levels below the manor?"

"Like a basement?" she clarified. Talon nodded and she shrugged. "I never asked."

"Ask when you get a chance."

She furrowed her brow. "Why not just ask him yourself?"

Talon didn't speak for a long moment. "I'd like to avoid speaking with him alone if I can."

She raised her brow, interest piqued. "Why?"

Talon ran a hand through his hair, about to say something, then changed his mind. He closed his book, using his finger to mark the page. "I just don't like some of his questions, is all." He nodded toward the book in her hand. "Any luck with your research?"

Arianna tossed the book on the table with a loud thud. "Just more of the same."

"Anything I can help you with, My Lady?" The smooth glide of Niall's voice seemed to creep from the shadows like he was a relic among the ancient items. She hadn't heard him enter and the way Talon had crossed the short distance told her he hadn't, either. Arianna hoped Niall hadn't overheard Talon's comment.

She took a calming breath. Maybe this was good. He had been here a few centuries. Maybe she had just been searching in the wrong place. "Do they have a section dedicated to the previous Divine or something? I can't find anything about her."

Niall's face faltered. "I'm afraid there isn't much written."

Arianna just eyed the library and raised a brow. "She was The Divine. What do you mean there wasn't a lot written?"

"I misspoke. There might have been records at one time in our history, but that was before the great library was burned to the ground."

Arianna blanched. "Then how do we know anything?"

"Word of mouth. Rumors. I, for example, am very old. I've spoken to many across the continent and even more in the continent to the north. There are stories that have too many similarities to be labeled a mere coincidence."

"Is that part of the reason they claim she failed?"

Niall grimaced again. "Would you care to join me for a stroll? There's something I'd like to show you."

"Sure." She needed to get outside for a while anyway, clear her head of all the words tumbling around like pieces of a puzzle that refused to fit together.

"The story of the previous Divine is a tale of great tragedy. Legends claim she was as beautiful as a setting sun and brought life and abundance wherever she went. The Divine traveled the land, healed the sick and injured, and put a stop to wars and civil disputes with her presence alone." He shook his head. "But it wasn't enough. Despite everything she did, there were still those who stood against her, determined to prevent the world from changing. In a cataclysmic turn of events, she lost her mate."

Sudden pain filled Arianna's chest and she gripped the area, unable to hide her horror. "That's awful."

Niall nodded, his face grim. "It was, but what followed was even worse."

"What do you mean?"

"You have to understand, she lived in a very different time and not everything was recorded as it is now. We've pieced together some documents over the years and heard even more stories. History claims she was in love with another before she found her mate. She'd promised herself to him and broke those promises. Some say he lost his mind and was consumed by jealousy."

"That male killed him?"

Niall shrugged. "That's what the stories say."

They exited the manor and Arianna followed Niall down the garden path, past the vaults and storehouses until they stood before the quiet cathedral. She'd never visited before, afraid to run into Fina. Arianna was certain the female still didn't like her.

Niall held the door open for her and Talon and they filed inside.

Seven statues depicting the gods and goddesses stood around the room, their eyes watching all who entered with stern expressions that raised the hairs on the back of her neck. Incense burned at their feet, giving the air a hazy glow. Light filtered in through large rectangular slats in the ceiling. Candles and a few massive braziers were lit all around the area. But it was the central statue standing on a pedestal against the back wall that drew Arianna's attention.

The statue was massive, at least three times the size of the others, and depicted a female who was equal parts beautiful and ethereal. Powerful and calm. Her face was both serene and anguished in a way Arianna had never seen and it pulled at something deep in her heart, forming an ache so vast she felt Rion's concern from the other end of their bond.

She briefly sent waves of calm to let him know she was all right.

Dozens upon dozens of fresh floral bouquets were laid out at the female's feet, piled high and around as if worshipers delivered them every day. Arianna wondered if the gods were jealous of the female.

The Divine.

Niall's voice was soft when he spoke again. "You might see her as a failure and perhaps others have labeled her the same, but there are a great many who still worship her despite her faults."

Arianna studied the statue and the water droplets across the female's skin. They rose around the female's body in a wave. "What do you think of her?"

"I think she suffered a great loss. I think the world put unfair expectations on a young female and her heart was split in two for most of her life. And those are the exact things I'd like to prevent from happening again."

Arianna glanced at Niall, but he wasn't looking at her. She recalled all the times he'd mentioned Arianna taking her time and how he didn't want to burden her with too much too soon. It suddenly made sense now. Niall didn't want to see history repeat itself.

Niall continued. "She made enough of an impression that someone built this structure in her likeness. So I won't fault her, even if she did cause irreversible damage in the end."

"What do you mean?"

He tilted his head and sun-kissed strands of hair hung over his pained expression. "Her history was burned because she, herself, set fire to it." He turned back to the statue. "She waged war across the continent, searching for the one responsible for her mate's death. She was grieving and wasn't in her right mind. Countless paid the price for it and that grief is what killed her in the end."

The ache rose in Arianna's chest, bitter and binding. Arianna studied the female's face again. She'd lost her mate. Her tie to happiness in a world that expected too much.

A sense of obligation settled through her. Arianna could do it. She had her mate. She had her family and friends. She could bring about peace and set the previous Divine's heart to rest.

But Arianna would do it one day at a time. She'd take up the mantle and do what the previous Divine hadn't been able. And she'd do it with her mate at her side.

CHAPTER FIFTY

RION

ion returned to the village for the seventh day in a row and studied everything he had accomplished.

He'd completed one building and had the framework set for three others. Each had four walls, a roof, and sturdy floors. He'd finished a chimney yesterday and planned to build another today.

Ellie had dug a second well, just in case the first dried up, and he had discovered a pond not too far south, but it was so murky and foul smelling that he'd steered clear and would advise others to do the same.

It felt too much like the Harpy's lands, ancient and menacing in a way that made his skin crawl. Rion hoped to never know what lurked in the shallow depths.

Rion jumped from his horse but paused at the unknown scents floating through the air. Footprints littered the ground as if they'd examined each structure before settling on one.

He immediately thought of bandits and slavers, neither of which he'd tolerate living in the place he'd built for those displaced.

Rion's magic rose, humming in an angry swarm as he marched up the two stone stairs and slammed the door open.

He froze.

At least two dozen people sat inside, all on the floor curled up with their blankets and packs. They leapt to their feet and backed away. The children ran to their mothers, fear covering their faces, and more than one drew their weapons. Old, rusted blades Rion was fairly certain wouldn't hold up in a real fight.

The world fell silent. Their breaths turned shallow, then one heart rate spiked followed by another as they noticed the magic and realized who stood before them. One stepped back, tripping over his pack.

Not bandits. Not even slavers. There were wanderers without a home. Fae who had nothing to their names. Their clothes were tattered, their bags dirt-covered and worn. He noted the food they'd spread across the floor, a meager meal that wouldn't even come close to feeding half.

A young male stepped forward, a pure-blood, and though the adults shot pleading looks at the youngling, they didn't appear to possess the courage to command him to back down. To keep his mouth shut and bow his head so maybe, just maybe, The Demon would let them live.

Rion swallowed the lump in his throat. Why had anger risen in him every time he entered a village? Why had he looked at everyone with so much hatred in his heart?

Because none would have hesitated to kill him. Even now he saw it in their eyes. The abomination. The creature that would wreak havoc upon the world. A festering wound that needed to be cleaned before the infection spread to the rest of the body.

That was him.

Rion cleared his throat and eyed the young male. He couldn't have been older than eight. No magic, which meant the youth likely hadn't grown into it yet.

Rion slowly set his pack on the floor. Their wide eyes watched his every move. He didn't have much, some fresh water and Ellie's packed lunch, but it would be enough for the children at least.

Rion backed toward the door. "I'll be outside working. There's food in the bag if you need it."

The young male clenched his fists. "You're not mad?"

"About what?"

"Us being in your home."

"It's not mine."

His young eyes widened. "Whose is it?"

"Yours, if you want it to be, as is anything else I build here." Those in the room looked between one another, but he exited before they could ask him any more questions.

Rion wasn't sure what he expected, but when the boy finally left the house, others joined him, watching Rion as he used his magic to build the chimney of the cabin next door to theirs.

Rion's heart beat just a little faster. He'd given someone in need shelter. Even if they decided not to stay, they were safe for a time. He'd shown a stranger he wasn't going to hurt them and they hadn't fled at the first given chance.

Maybe Ellie was right. Maybe things could change for the better.

The afternoon wore on and Rion continued working, pulling down trees before splitting them apart. He left a few that were thick and sturdy to provide shade during the warmer months.

The youngling never stopped watching him. Not once.

He had short, dark blond hair that seemed to carry every shade of the earth and golden amber eyes that contrasted against his tawny skin. His pants were torn at both knees and stitched together across the top of one thigh. The shirt was at least three sizes too large even with the tie he'd used to tighten it at one end.

A glimmer of something caught his eye then, but Rion couldn't identify the object until the male drew closer.

Iron. The boy wore an iron bracelet. It wasn't a shackle, and the thin material looked as though it would slide off his slender wrist easily enough. But he wasn't a half-breed. Even if he possessed magic, it shouldn't overwhelm him. Such a phenomenon was rare. Fae were made to possess magic, it was part of them.

The youngling stepped closer and Rion angled his body so it appeared he wasn't watching. He didn't know what the male needed, but he could sense his fear, along with those watching from the doorway. It looked like they wanted to intervene, but once again they didn't. None were the young male's parents, then.

Rion finally turned to face him and the male startled. "Do you need something?"

The youngling balled his fists then loosened them. He moved his feet in the dirt, then finally steeled himself and marched right up to Rion. "You come from somewhere, right? If this isn't your home." Rion nodded. The male's lip trembled slightly, but he bit the inside of his cheek. "Can you get medicine?"

Rion sniffed the air around the youngling, then looked him over for any injuries. None. "I can. What's wrong?"

"My friend. She hasn't been feeling good. The adults won't tell me anything, but I think it's bad."

"Take me to her." The youngling stared at him for a beat then pivoted on his heel and ran back toward the cabin. Those surrounding the entrance stepped aside, though one braved standing on the threshold as if he might stop Rion from entering.

"I won't hurt them," Rion promised. He kept his magic in check, even as he eyed those clutching one another as if this moment might be their last. The male's chest heaved, then he relented and moved inside.

Rion followed. On a small pile of blankets, a female sat beside a young half-breed and stroked the little girl's hair, whispering words of comfort. Her head shot up when she scented him and the female froze, her hand still resting on the child's head.

Rion kept his voice soft. "What's wrong with her?" The female's lips trembled. She didn't speak. Instead, she lifted a corner of the blanket to reveal the child's foot. It was swollen and severely discolored. Infection. Rion studied the half-breed's breathing, then marched for the door. Those outside retreated upon his swift exit, but their expressions were hopeful.

"I'll be back," he said and swung up onto his horse before kicking it into a gallop.

Rion chided himself. He should have gone back the minute he found these people hiding out. He had no way of knowing how long they'd gone without food or water or clean clothes. They needed supplies and help, and that little girl needed a lot more.

THE SUN had almost set by the time Rion arrived back in Ruadhán. Arianna was waiting for him, as she usually did. He grimaced upon seeing the worry in her eyes. He must have unknowingly sent his feelings of desperation down the bond.

"We need to pack a few things, then I need you to come with me." Arianna nodded. She didn't question him or even hesitate as they ran to the kitchens together.

Rion quickly explained the situation as they gathered everything they could get their hands on. The cooks weren't pleased, but when Arianna had asked for a basket, they'd jumped into action, packing a feast for their queen. He hoped it would be enough.

Rion snagged two large waterskins, stole several thick blankets, and loaded down three horses with more than they should probably carry.

The guards had rotated their shifts by the time they returned to the back platform.

"Going somewhere, My Lady?"

"Only for a little while. I'll be back before morning."

The three guards exchanged nervous glances as they eyed her and Rion. "I'm sorry, you want to leave in the middle of the night?"

"It's urgent," she insisted. "Someone is hurt."

He shifted, clearly uncomfortable. "I'm not sure it's wise. Please consider taking a few warriors with you at the very least." Rion knew news had probably spread about the attack, but they couldn't waste any more time.

Arianna shook her head. "I'll be fine. But please, keep this between us. There's no reason to cause alarm." The guard glanced between them again, fear and uncertainty rolling from his shoulders. "Please," Arianna pleaded. "I'd rather not jump with this many supplies and I think the horses might die of fright."

At that the guard blanched, then commanded the four standing with him to get into position.

They were on the ground in minutes.

"My Lady," the guard called, still looking torn with himself.

Arianna gave him a thankful smile. "I'll be fine, I promise." Then they were gone, pushing the horses as fast as they could go while she and Rion trotted alongside.

Rion knew the guard would inform his higher ups. He was obligated to. And once Niall discovered the guard had failed to stop Arianna from leaving, he'd lose his position and likely never serve in the guard again. Rion would be sure to tell Arianna later, just to ensure that didn't happen. She needed all the allies she could get.

They rode in silence, letting darkness encase them with its cool embrace. The chill in the air bit against his warm skin, but after a week of hard labor, he found it refreshing. His body was starting to warm again. Whatever damage had been done from Avalon's magic was finally starting to mend.

Flickering lights came into view within thirty minutes and they slowed to a trot. Two males exited the cabin, those rusty swords drawn as they studied the pair in the darkness. They scented the air and lowered their blades.

Arianna's gaze swept over the clearing. She studied the little silhouettes of the homes he'd built and raised her brow. Rion shook his head. She could ask questions later. After she'd tended to the child.

"I brought someone to help," Rion said by way of greeting. But unlike before, Rion couldn't restrain his magic. It circled his mate and kept close. He wanted to help these people, but he wouldn't risk his mate's safety in the process. They could still be part of the rebel factions against her rule, willing to do anything to tear her down. If that proved to be the case, Rion wasn't sure what he would do.

Arianna entered and he followed, pausing on the threshold as she studied their desperate faces. "There's food outside," Arianna said, "and fresh water. And I packed a few blankets as well." No one moved. She turned to glance at him before clearing her throat again. "I was told someone was sick?"

The male youngling from earlier stood and pointed to his friend. Rion remained where his was, but his magic trailed Arianna's every step. Many watched the grains floating around the strange female before them, seeming to marvel that she wasn't screaming in terror.

They stepped back, pushing themselves into the wooden walls as if they could blend in with them.

Arianna crouched before the girl and pulled back the blanket to examine the wound, then she placed her hands on the girl's ankle. The child groaned, but the adult female held her still, desperate eyes watching Arianna's every move.

When her hands began glowing, every Fae watching in the cabin sucked in a collective breath. More than one hit their knees, sending whispered prayers to the gods above.

None moved, caught in a trance as they watched the queen in their midst. Arianna pulled foul smelling liquid from a small wound and the swelling visibly decreased. The redness leached back and skin that had once been purplish and ashen returned to its normal color.

Tears ran down the adult female's face and she bowed her head in thanks even as sobs raked her thin body.

"I'd heard the rumors," a male whispered from the opposite corner. "But I didn't believe—" he took a tentative step forward. "The Divine is among us. The prophecy is true."

"She shouldn't be," another woman said, her voice low. Arianna glanced at her and the female bowed her head. "It's too dangerous out here, your Grace. If you knew what some were saying . . ."

But she did know. From the attack in Levea and the one just recently. But Arianna didn't share those stories. She just looked at him with those bright gorgeous eyes and smiled. "I'm in good hands." Their gazes followed hers and studied Rion, taking in the male they'd been told was a monster. A male who had acted as one for most of his life.

Arianna stood. "I'll make sure to have more supplies delivered first thing tomorrow. There's also medicine in the bag that should help bring down her fever."

"Will you return to the royal city tonight?" another male asked.

Arianna studied the cabin. "I think I'll stay here, if that's all right."

Six jumped to their feet and Rion's magic responded. They regarded him carefully, but somehow with Arianna near, they didn't appear as afraid as before. "We don't have much, but—"

Arianna held up a hand and shook her head. "I don't require anything from you. Really, it'll be nice to be outside of the manor for a while."

They stared at her, their mouths gaping as she exited the crowded cabin. Rion followed and watched as she stopped in the center of what he'd built. She examined the space, taking in all the posts that marked where more cabins would go. Where they would build fences for animals and where he hoped to plant a few more trees. Her gaze lifted to the stars.

Rion wrapped his arms around her from behind and Arianna leaned her head against him.

"Thank you," he said.

Rion thought he felt her smile. "You seem happy."

"I am." He squeezed her tighter, his heart pounding just from a small touch. That he was allowed to touch her at all. "And even happier now that you're here."

"It's so quiet."

He listened to her easy breathing and looked at the sky with her. "I could build you a home here." She tilted her head. "If you wanted a place to escape every now and then."

Arianna smiled again and his heart swelled. "Only if we keep it a secret. Otherwise, it won't be quiet for long."

Rion looked at those watching them from the doorway. "I doubt they'd say anything."

"Then it's a deal."

CHAPTER FIFTY-ONE

ARIANNA

They spent the night in one of Rion's unfinished cabins. It didn't have windows and the chimney wasn't quite done, but knowing she was in a structure he'd built brought her joy.

And the people. There were people here. She'd sensed how much concern her mate carried for the girl's wellbeing and it had made her heart soar.

They were important to him, so Arianna would make their welfare a priority. She'd visit every week as long as the villagers promised to keep those visits a secret.

She smiled to herself. A home. Rion was going to build them a home right here in this little piece of heaven. Maybe he'd design the interior the way he'd done at his old cabin in the woods.

They exited the cabin in the early hours of dawn to find the villagers outside. Two stood over a fire, heating up some of the food she and Rion had delivered last night. And the little girl was awake, standing before the flames with bright round eyes.

Arianna clenched Rion's hand and he watched the girl dance on the tips of her toes. She'd be okay. More than okay.

Rion's magic still floated around Arianna, as it always did, but those watching didn't seem to mind as they bid the two good morning. Perhaps they knew he was protecting her and it gave them a sense of comfort.

Is this what she could look forward to every morning? A community breakfast they prepared together? Rion assisting those who worked in the field while she tended to the animals and made cheese and bread?

It wasn't a life of riches and gold, but it provided things of far greater value. Community, trust, family, and friends. Here, there wasn't court life to dance around or the half-truths that came with it.

Here, they simply lived, and she could spend eternity doing just that.

Arianna shouldered an empty pack. "I'll be back shortly with more supplies, and Rion will keep building until there's enough homes for everyone."

"We'd like to help," a male said. He shot a tentative gaze at Rion. "I mean, if we're going to live here, we should earn our keep. And we'll get more done that way. I-If that's all right."

Rion nodded, but before he could reply a thunderous sound filled the air and Arianna spun to find a dozen horses, all with riders clad in black, shining armor barreling toward them.

The villagers stepped back and the children ran back into the cabin. Arianna positioned herself at the village's center with Rion at her side, his magic whipping out and springing to life.

Not again. This couldn't happen a second time. She'd only told one guard where she was going. And they'd left under the cover of darkness. Surely no one could have figured out her location that fast.

But as the dozen horses drew closer, Arianna recognized Niall at the front. He wore metal armor of black and gold and his face was drawn into a strained grimace.

She tried to resist rolling her eyes as they neared. Every one of the warriors drew their weapons and the villagers standing behind her stumbled back.

Arianna waited patiently until Niall was close enough to dismount. He looked her over from head to toe then examined the village and those within. He wouldn't even look at Rion.

"What's going on?" he demanded. "Are you hurt?"

She sighed. Arianna had told the guard she'd be back before morning. She supposed she should have kept that promise.

Arianna shook her head. "Someone needed my help. I was just on my way back."

"Someone—" he faltered. "The guard said you'd left in a hurry last night and hadn't returned. I thought—" Niall let out a shaky breath and ran his hand through his blond locks. She'd never seen him so disheveled.

"I'm fine," Arianna assured.

"You can't just leave like that, you need an armed guard at all times. We need to know—"

"I have Rion," she said.

Niall pinned her with a sharp look. "It's not enough. Not after last week. If anything happens to you, if the world were to discover their queen—" he cut himself off again. "What were you thinking?"

Arianna furrowed her brow. "I was thinking I'm free to come and go as I please. I didn't realize I was a prisoner."

"You're not. You—" he loosed another breath and took a few moments to collect himself. "You're okay then?"

She nodded and Niall finally surveyed those standing behind her. "These people. They need further assistance." It wasn't a question, but Arianna nodded anyway. Niall looked them over again, then studied the cabins. One finished and three under construction.

"This is your doing?" he asked Rion.

Rion nodded and Niall finally let the stress fall from his shoulders. "Put your weapons away," he commanded his guards. He looked ready to say more, perhaps reprimand her further, but stopped himself.

"When do you wish to return, My Lady?" His face was pulled taunt, like he loathed the idea of her spending another moment in this place.

"I was just heading back. They need more food and supplies and—"

"I'll have a team put everything together right away, along with additional building supplies and seed so they can begin planting. We'll also gather a few animals that are well maintained. They'll be here before the afternoon."

Arianna's brows shot up. "So soon?"

Niall nodded and a shadow of a smile graced his lips. "I keep telling you, all you need to do is ask and it shall be done for you. We are here to serve, My Queen."

AT ARIANNA'S request, they stayed until the supplies were delivered.

Rion was glad to see the villagers' smiling faces, glad they could eat without worry and have new clothes and fresh water.

But something in Rion ached at the sight of Niall's easy interactions with those around him. They'd all bowed to the male, curious about the Regent of Ruadhán. None cowered or backed away.

And none so much as passed Rion another glance.

They were just excited, he told himself, and after an extended period of time living with nothing, it made sense to crave everything.

And thank the one who delivered it.

Rion clenched his jaw, wrestling with feelings he refused to acknowledge. He'd grown accustomed to the shadows, lived there for decades, so it shouldn't bother him to dwell in the darkness now.

But in the shadow of this male, Rion wanted to rage. He'd seen Niall's sideward glances, the tiny smirks. He was enjoying this and it wasn't for the reasons Arianna thought. Niall wanted to show Arianna the kind of power he possessed and everything he could give her if only she asked.

And gods, he hated it.

Once they returned to Ruadhán, Rion spent two much needed days with his mate. They had walked the gardens, talked about everything he had planned for the village and played chess until Arianna was ready to throw the board. Then those two days were gone and he was back at it.

Rion adjusted the heavy pack on his shoulder. Arianna had given him more herbs, just in case others arrived injured, and she'd made him promise to come get her should another situation unfold like the one before. She didn't care what Niall thought, nor about his request. She'd go where she pleased.

The knowledge shouldn't have made him smirk the way it did.

His horse kept an easy pace down the familiar path. He would finally finish the second cabin today and was planning to install windows by the end of the week. The villagers had already built two more by themselves.

And they were growing more accustomed to him day by day.

Smoke rose in the distance and Rion studied it with his brow furrowed. He supposed they could be burning the collected brush or their old clothes.

But then the wind carried a familiar smell that stung his delicate senses.

No.

Heart thundering, Rion leapt from his horse and let the pack fall from his shoulder. His feet hit the ground hard and he flew over the hilly terrain.

The smoke didn't bother him. He could rebuild if something had caught fire. But the other scent. The one as familiar to him as Arianna's, sent a jolt of fear through his body so profound, Rion wasn't sure how he convinced himself to keep moving.

A cruel mixture of blood and fear swirled through the air and only grew thicker as he closed in.

He cursed. Why hadn't he requested Arianna to station an armed guard here, at least until the villagers got established? Their weapons were mediocre at best and even if they'd been supplied with better steel, there hadn't been nearly enough people to wield it.

Rion skidded to a stop, chest heaving as he surveyed the empty field. Blood dotted the grass and bare ground and heavy boot prints told him a group was responsible for the assault. But where were—

Rion froze when he noticed a female kneeling beside the tree line. He bolted toward her, craning his neck to view the bundle of clothes laying in the grass at her feet. Rion slowed and swallowed the lump in his throat. He bent to kneel at her side, desperate to help in any way he could. Arianna could be here—

Too late. He noticed the blade too late as she pivoted and shoved the knife deep into his abdomen. She twisted hard and Rion gasped, ground his teeth, then leapt back. Rion pressed a hand to the wound and felt blood already soaking his tunic.

The female stood, fury making her hands tremble as she pointed the bloody knife at his face. "Is this all a game to you?" Her eyes were wide and red-rimmed. "Do our lives mean nothing?"

Rion had a hand raised between them, as if it might stop her from lashing out at him again. "What are you talking about?"

Her laugh wasn't kind. It was the kind of sound one made when everything had been stolen away and others thought they could steal more.

"We knew it was a trick. We knew and still—" Her lips trembled. "You are nothing but a monster."

The words hit like a blow to the gut, then a brief memory surfaced of a female from his past. Her kind smiles and gentle touches. And the words that were far, far too similar before she, too, had buried a knife in his body.

Rion opened his mouth to tell her he'd only just arrived when Fae warriors crawled from the trees. He paused, blood racing. He hadn't heard them or scented their presence.

Rion stepped back and surveyed the warriors as they prowled forward. Was he losing his mind? Was this really happening or was it all in his head? A nightmare.

The female's fury turned to grief as she beheld the familiar black and gold armor. Rion studied the faces again. He recognized a few.

They'd been part of Niall's escort when he'd delivered supplies to the villagers.

"What happened?" a male's gruff voice asked. Had Niall sent warriors to look after these people after all? But if so, where had they been hiding and why hadn't Rion been able to scent them upon his arrival?

Rion's stomach sank. The male's eyes glinted as if he didn't need to wait for the female's answer.

Rion scented the air again and beyond the blood and fear, he pinpointed their magic. Pádraigín's magic. They'd been here the whole time, waiting.

They'd—Rion clenched his fists and the warrior drew his weapon. Wind whispered through the trees, but it wasn't the natural sort.

Not a nightmare.

Rion stepped back again and winced from the pain in his stomach.

"What happened?" the male asked again, but Rion knew it was all for show. They'd done this. This bastard and the warriors following him were the ones responsible.

The female pointed and it seemed she didn't need words. Because what were words when he already carried a brutal reputation?

More warriors emerged from behind as if they'd been cloaked by a veil. Was Niall behind all this or had the council helped? Whoever was responsible had taken great care to map everything out. They'd even left a few witnesses.

His word wouldn't matter to anyone except Arianna. She'd seen him off and knew he hadn't been here long. There was no possible way for him to—

A sudden rush of bodies had Rion cursing. He jumped to the side, trying to avoid anyone who might strike out, but—blood splattered across his clothes. Rion gagged from the stench and tried to dodge more flying his way.

Their blood. The villager's blood, among other things. Bile rose in his throat. Whoever had planned this out was definitely determined to get rid of him. They were taking every measure to ensure he looked as guilty as possible.

His heart beat wildly now. He had to make it back to Arianna before they did. He needed to explain the situation. Tell her exactly what had happened before they filled her head with lies.

But they wouldn't smell like lies and that made everything so much worse.

Rion honestly wasn't sure what she'd believe. It all looked so convincing and he had a dark history and so many had been telling her that he'd snap eventually.

Rion's heart had never beat so fast in his life. He couldn't breathe. Didn't know which direction any of this would go.

This was hell. He'd stumbled into hell and he needed to crawl back out before the dark, fiery chasm consumed him entirely.

He couldn't lose Arianna. He could lose his sanity, his freedom, his body, but he couldn't lose her.

Rion pivoted on his heel and ran. For the first time since he was a child, he ran as fast as his legs could carry him. Fled from a fight as if he wasn't certain he'd win.

His lungs cried out as though razor blades were piecing through the tender organs. Pain shot from his stomach with every long stride and the wound bled even more. But still, he ran. And prayed to the gods that he'd make to Arianna first.

CHAPTER FIFTY-TWO

ARIANNA

*A*rianna sat at her desk twirling a pen between her fingers. Talon had left just a few moments ago, promising a swift return, but she'd told him to take as long as he needed. She seriously doubted anyone was going to attack her in the library.

Arianna sighed and rested her head on the book she'd been reading. She'd been trying to take Rion's advice and study individual generals, but it wasn't proving easy. History books were written in a way that cataloged battles and dates, the number of warriors beneath their command, and how many of those warriors survived their confrontations.

If they mentioned wives or children, it was little more than an afterthought. Maybe she needed to create her own stories. Perhaps even write them down for future generations.

Many had taken multiple lovers throughout their lives and the conflicts from that alone echoed through the generations. Their children—

An alarm blared through the library and Arianna shot to her feet and covered her ears, bracing against the sudden shrill sound.

Those browsing began scrambling toward their peers. The double doors slammed opened and the head librarian whispered to a colleague before he began shouting orders for everyone to take cover.

Arianna followed the panicked crowd down the stairs, trying to push past their frenzy. She grabbed the head librarian by his sleeve, wishing she could remember his name. "What's going on?"

"There's been an attack."

Her blood turned to ice. "On the city?"

The male shook his head. "On a village nearby. The injured are arriving now, but the one responsible hasn't been apprehended." Recognition flashed across his face and the male promptly bowed his head. "My Lady, I'm so sorry."

She furrowed her brow. "About what?"

He licked his lips, unsure at first, then lowered his voice to a near whisper. "I'm told The Demon is responsible."

The room went cold and she staggered back a step. "The Demon?"

The male nodded, his expression grim. "Please, let us take you somewhere safe. The guards are afraid—My Lady!"

Arianna hadn't waited for him to finish speaking before she was sprinting through the hall, dodging those filing toward the safest rooms in the manor. Rooms that would be heavily guarded.

They'd mentioned protocol at one point, but Arianna hadn't absorbed the information. She wasn't certain if she was supposed to join the civilians or if they had a special place where they hid The Divine. Not that she'd allow herself to be separated.

Arianna desperately searched the silent bond. Why hadn't she felt anything? Why couldn't she find him even now, when the alarms were echoing through the city and their world had been plunged into chaos?

Rion, where are you?

Arianna tried to ignore the whispers as she passed, her feet pounding against the polished floors.

I thought he'd changed.

I can't believe he'd betray the crown.

Did you see the victims?

Monster.

Demon.

Traitor.

The crowds by the front door were too thick so she stopped at a window and threw it open. The scent of blood hit her then, thick and repulsive.

She backed away, her breathing coming faster and faster.

Rion didn't do this. He wouldn't.

"My Queen." A guard stopped before her and dropped to one knee. "Please, come inside, let us—"

But she was running again. He called her name, but Arianna ignored the guard and raced up the stairs. She darted down a hall they never frequented, her legs carried by some unseen force.

Then she felt him. Finally. His desperation. His pain. The plea as he tugged on their bond in a frantic rhythm, almost as if he'd been doing it for hours.

But before she could sort through the reasons, a hand shot out from behind a door and dragged her inside.

Arianna didn't attack or resist and twisted to find her mate staring at her with unguarded fear. It wasn't often she saw him vulnerable and she'd never seen him so utterly undone. Like the world had collided in on him all at once.

"I didn't do it," he said, his voice a broken plea. She looked him over and tried not to recoil at the scent of blood covering his body. Arianna reached for the wound in his abdomen and his hand reflexively covered her wrist. His fingers squeezed lightly and he groaned when her magic stitched the deep wound back together. He was too pale. He needed rest.

"What's going on?"

His eyes were wide and wild, so unlike the calm general who won every battle he'd ever faced. "I didn't do it," he repeated. His hands were shaking, his entire body trembling and his eyes wouldn't stop scanning the room. "Please, you have to believe me, they—"

"Rion."

"Set me up. They came out—"

"Rion." She shook him.

"Of nowhere and they—"

Arianna grabbed his face and forced him to look at her. Rion stilled, but his breathing was still raw and ragged.

"Calm down," she urged, her voice gentle. She'd never seen him like this. Like he—gods, was he having a panic attack?

"Breathe," she coaxed and made a show of inhaling. Rion drew in a breath and slowed the rise and fall of his chest to match hers. His wild eyes calmed slightly, but his heart still pounded.

"It wasn't me," he said again.

Feet beat against the floor down the hall and she knew the guards would find her any minute.

"Are you okay?" she asked. "Are you hurt anywhere else?"

"No."

"Good. Then stay out of sight and find me later. I need to help those injured and figure out what's going on."

He gripped her shoulders tight, almost painfully. "They're going to tell you it was me."

Arianna pressed a gentle kiss to his lips and Rion loosened his grip, seeming to melt into her touch. "It's okay. I'll sort through it, I promise. Just lay low. Can you do that?" He nodded. "I'll call for you soon."

With a final look, Arianna darted from the room and gently closed the door. She rushed down the hall, glanced back once, then took the stairs two at a time.

A guard stopped her on the second floor. "My Lady, Lord Niall is looking for you. He wants you in the central hall with the others."

"No," Arianna shook her head. "You'll take me to the wounded where I can help."

He bowed low. "Please, your Grace, we don't know where the threat is and our top priority is your safety."

He was right about one thing: They didn't know where the threat was, but if they were trying to pin it on Rion, then it wasn't the kind of threat that would jeopardize her safety.

Anger pulsed through her. They wanted Rion gone so badly that they were willing to kill innocents to accomplish the task. Maybe she had made a mistake in staying here. Maybe she should have returned to Levea and made her demands from afar.

But she would have to deal with that later. Right now there were people who needed her help.

"You can either lead me to the wounded, or I'll find them myself, which I'd wager will put me more at risk than is necessary. What's it going to be?"

His eyes widened, but the male bowed again. "Please, follow me."

Arianna tried to brace herself for what she was about to face. Again. The blood, the cries, the chaos. It seemed like no matter where she went, death followed and Arianna wasn't sure how to escape it..

CHAPTER FIFTY-THREE

RION

Arianna had gone silent down the bond as she cared for the wounded. Thank the gods there *were* wounded. He'd peered over the edge of the roof just once before darting away. Most of the children had made it out and he'd recognized a few of the adults as well. But the rest—

Rion had felt his mate's initial spike of panic and the ache in her heart, but he hadn't sensed the sting of anger he'd expected from her. At least, no anger directed his way. He knew what the villagers were telling her and he knew none of it would smell like a lie. Because someone from Pádraigín had made it look like he was guilty.

Rion let her work. He wouldn't risk distracting her, especially in the event she was trying to save someone's life. Had that little girl made it out? The boy with the iron on his wrist? Rion had never gotten the chance to question him about it.

Gods. He threaded his fingers through his hair and tugged on the strands. How had everything gone so horribly wrong? He knew why, the why was easy. They wanted him gone. Eliminated so they could follow through with their initial plans of putting Niall on the throne.

But to resort to this.

Rion had seated himself on the roof in the shadow of a chimney that jutted out at an awkward angle. It was the only place he could think of to go with the amount of guards patrolling the area. They wouldn't search up here, he hoped, and the smoke would drown out his scent. If they found him and he had to flee—Rion shook his head. He'd face the possibility if it came to that.

She believed him. Rion still couldn't quite wrap his mind around the idea. He was so sure she would doubt him, that those around her, especially the victims, would be able to convince her of his guilt, but Arianna never doubted him for a second.

He marveled at it. Marveled at her.

Someone was trying to get rid of him. He'd known it since the ball. Hell, he'd known it from the first time Niall had shown Arianna a memory of his mother, likely hoping to anger Rion into action.

No one wanted him here. No one aside from Arianna. And maybe Ellie. He wondered what Ellie was making of the chaos.

Rion stretched his legs out. He needed a hot shower. He needed to change his clothes and rid himself of the stench of the villagers' blood.

Someone clambered onto the roof, slipping once, before righting themselves. Rion's heart jolted and he shot to his feet, but kept his magic restrained. If they rounded the corner and saw him, perhaps he could render them unconscious. Great, now he was considering taking prisoners.

Rion peered around the corner and a male's face paled when he glimpsed Rion in the shadows. Rion moved, launching forward, determined to knock the male out.

"Wait," the male pleaded, raising his hands to shield himself. Rion paused, suddenly wondering if Arianna had sent him. He hadn't felt her down the bond in a while. The male's voice shook. "They have her." Rion went very, very still. "They captured the queen and we don't know what's going on. We can't find her." His chest was heaving. "I heard her scream, but—"

Rion was moving before the male finished his sentence. His magic sprang to life and Rion no longer cared about secrecy. Not if Arianna was in danger.

What the hell was going on? What if whoever had attacked didn't just want him gone, but wanted Arianna subdued as well? What if the rebel factions had broken in during the chaos? What if they'd been in the city the whole time and had finally found the perfect opportunity to act?

Rion hit the ground hard, barely registering those who scrambled away from him in terror. They didn't matter. Only Arianna mattered. That male had heard her scream . . .

Everything in his body recoiled at the thought, begging him to hurry, hurry, hurry.

He raced through the door and down the hall, following her scent. Rion desperately searched the bond. Was she hurt? Calling for him?

He furrowed his brow. She felt distressed, sure, but it was the same sort of stress she'd been experiencing. Unless the bond was having some kind of lapse. Maybe that's why she hadn't responded to him earlier. He gritted his teeth. How long had she been in danger?

Rion sprinted toward the grand ballroom glad to find the hallways mostly devoid of life. The citizens had been corralled by the guards toward areas of safety. He'd read all about the plans put in place in the event of an emergency. They had three areas to usher residents toward, but the ballroom wasn't part of those plans. Maybe they had just moved the injured there until they could prepare rooms.

It was too open and left everyone vulnerable. The guards could easily be pinned inside. Was Arianna a hostage? Was she the only one? Where the hell was Niall?

A thousand questions flew through his mind at once but when Rion shoved open the heavy golden doors, he stilled.

The ballroom was well lit with sunlight filtering in through a few well-placed windows. The balcony doors were open, letting in a fresh breeze and standing in the middle was a single male who spun around at Rion's sudden entrance.

A sadistic smile pulled at the corner of his lips.

Rion didn't recognize the male's face, but there was no mistaking the velvet black uniform embroidered with gold. One of Ruadhán's elite.

"It took you long enough."

Rion surveyed the balcony, the corners, then counted the weapons slung across the male's torso. He stepped closer, ready to demand answers when Arianna's scent slammed into him.

Rion's body went unnaturally still. The male smiled wider, drinking in the emotions playing across Rion's face. He couldn't shake his fear, nor stop the images of her injured body from flashing through his mind.

This male had Arianna's scent all over him. He smelled so much like her that—

No. He didn't register saying the word out loud but the male cocked his head in a knowing way.

Rion clenched his fists and his nails bit into flesh, drawing blood. "You *touched* her?"

He kissed his fingers in a dramatic fashion. "And truly divine she was."

White hot rage blasted through Rion's body. His earth ripped through the solid marble floor, sending large chunks of it flying in all directions. They slammed into the walls, knocking large holes through the wood and plaster before thudding against the ground. The floor splintered and cracked, moving in a wave that mirrored his fury.

The male blanched and had enough sense to step back.

"Where is she?" Rion's voice was low. His anger visible through the billowing cloud rising behind and around him. He would annihilate this male, rip the skin from his flesh until the male answered every single question. Rion would repeat every atrocious act he'd ever committed if that's what it took to get her back.

The male stepped back again. "I don't—"

Rion's magic snapped forward quick as an adder and wrapped around the male's left arm. In one motion, it wrenched his forearm back at a ninety degree angle and snapped the bone in half.

The male howled in pain, but Rion closed the distance and gripped the male's throat next. Rion stared into his dark eyes, feeling an old sort of anger course through his body that exhilarated the darkest parts of him.

He'd get Arianna back or they would discover exactly what kind of monster he could be.

"I will ask you one more time." Tears were streaming down the male's face now. *Pathetic.* Rion glanced at the male's broken arm. The bone jutted from the middle of the forearm at a nasty angle and blood dripped onto the destroyed floor. He'd remove it next. "Where is she?"

The male whimpered and reached up to grasp his wrist with his uninjured arm. "Please—" Rion growled, shook the arm off, then sank his fangs into the male's throat.

He'd tear him apart right here, make an example out of him. He'd—blood filled Rion's mouth and he violently recoiled, stumbling back as if something hard had slammed into his body. No, not something.

Rion blinked, trying to clear his vision. Everything shimmered and spun and he studied the figure slumped against the broken marble floor as if seeing her for the first time.

Tear-filled cerulean eyes stared back. He fell back a step, registering her pain and anguish and betrayal. So much betrayal.

The bond frayed. What once had been a solid rope spun apart until it was nothing more than a bunch of single threads.

Then those threads broke, snapping so hard Rion gripped his chest as if he could hold everything in place. Another snapped. Again and again and again as if they were being pulled apart by the pressure of emotions flying between himself and Arianna.

It sent him reeling.

His lips couldn't form words. His body couldn't move. He just stood there frozen, watching, trying to convince himself this moment wasn't real.

Arianna wasn't kneeling in a puddle of her own blood. She wasn't gripping the side of her neck where his fangs had just been. Her body wasn't trembling with fear and pain. Her arm wasn't—gods. Her *arm*.

Her blood coated his teeth. Bile rose in Rion's throat and his stomach clenched so hard, he was sure it would empty its contents right there.

Another thread snapped, leaving the remaining few pulled so taunt, Rion was certain they'd break in the next few seconds.

Then a roar filled the room. A male rushed from a side door with long brown hair. His magic ripped from the air and slammed into Rion's body.

Rion couldn't catch himself. He did absolutely nothing as his body was thrown across the space, putting ten feet between him and his mate.

But Talon didn't run to him first. He ran to Arianna's side and knelt to examine her injuries before rounding on him again. That look. That was one he recognized. Those were the eyes Talon had given him on the battlefield, except the anger ran deeper now.

Rion didn't known why Talon hadn't killed him already. He didn't know why the male wasn't moving from beside Arianna. Rion's gaze drifted back to his mate.

He couldn't move. He was frozen, trapped in a capsule of his own perfect hell.

She had been afraid once before. In the beginning. Before their relationship had soared to heights he'd never allowed himself to imagine. But this—this was different. This fear, no, terror, was a bottomless cavern and ingrained in a way he'd never be able to fix.

Rion had just attacked his mate. She was the one person who might have stood by his side until the end of time. The only one who'd ever helped him. Healed him. Made him feel worthy.

Now. Now there was nothing.

Arianna looked at him, for the first time, as if he really was a monster.

And he was. Gods he was the worst creature to ever walk the land. He was an abomination that should have been eradicated long ago. He was foul and horrid and—

"Run."

The word was hardly a whisper. He thought he'd misheard her, but Talon's sharp eyes shifted to her, a question there.

Ellie entered the room next followed by several guards. She surveyed the scene in what felt like both a second and forever.

Rion hadn't looked away from Arianna. Her brow had furrowed and tears still fell as she clutched her injured arm, trying to hold it still.

Everyone was shouting. More had stormed in from behind. He could hear their voices, but not their words, as if the world had somehow been turned off to everything around him.

Another thread snapped and Rion clutched his chest, his own eyes glistening with unshed tears.

"Arianna . . ." His voice was frail. Weak as if he hadn't used it in months. His heart was heavy. His stomach tight.

"Seize him," Niall's voice thundered through the room, echoing off the walls as if projected by some form of magic.

He smelled it as the guards' magic sprung to life. It was angry. Vengeful.

And Rion did nothing to stop it. He just kept staring at Arianna, his heart so broken he wasn't even sure how to pick up the splintered pieces. Their bond was breaking. His soul with it.

"Run," she whispered again and Rion felt the desperate pull in his heart. But he still couldn't move, even as hands rushed toward him.

He was stone welded into the floor, his limbs and body useless to obey her commands.

Fear flew through her and into him, coating his tongue with its acrid taste. Then the ballroom exploded in translucent walls of blue and white.

Rion blinked, trying to process the scene. Everything was too slow and fast all at once.

Ice had spread from Arianna's feet and he followed it with his eyes.

It stretched between her body and the doorway behind him with no one else in its path. The tall, jagged walls reached all the way to the ceiling and his breath clouded in the now frigid air.

Guards were already pounding against the glass, their blurry figures full of rage.

He locked eyes with Arianna again and somehow, through the pain, she'd steeled herself.

"I command you to run."

Rion didn't know how he did it. He wasn't sure where the strength in his legs came from or how his lungs figured out how to draw in air again. As if in slow motion, he rose from the floor, took one last look at his mate's beautiful, tormented face, and ran as fast as his body could carry him.

CHAPTER FIFTY-FOUR

ARIANNA

Tears stung her eyes and Arianna gritted her teeth as she watched Rion run for the door. But his steps were unsteady and his movements sluggish. She wasn't sure what might happen if the guards caught him and she could only buy him so much time. They'd already almost broken through her ice.

Pain radiated through her arm forcing Arianna to release her hold on the magic. Now more than ever she needed the strange ancient magic that had been making itself known to come forth, but the ancient creature buried in her bones was silent.

Arianna couldn't get the words out of her head.

Rion's frantic voice from just hours ago claiming his innocence. The low growl when he had demanded to know her location.

He hadn't been looking at her. It wasn't her arm he'd broken. It wasn't her throat he'd tried to rip out, but even knowing those things, Arianna couldn't stop the overwhelming fear that coursed through her now.

Her heart pounded. She had never feared him, but maybe it was just the adrenaline. They could talk later, fix everything, find whoever had orchestrated this entire mess.

She'd never considered executing someone before, but right now, the idea didn't sound unpleasant.

Arianna gripped her chest as if she could grasp the last three threads binding them together. Her body trembled so hard she wasn't sure she could move. But maybe that was from the blood loss too.

Arianna tried not to look at her arm and the horrible angle of it.

A fresh wave of tears fell. Why was someone doing this to them? Why did it matter who she chose to love?

She wished she had never come here. She wanted to be back in Levea. She wanted to go home, where they might be safe.

But they wouldn't be safe. Rion wasn't safe anywhere. Everyone had always wanted him dead. From the first moment his magic had appeared, he'd been on the run. And Arianna didn't want that life. Not if this was the kind of pain she'd be forced to face.

The ice shattered and Arianna's head snapped up. She hadn't realized someone had been talking to her. Several people were calling her name, trying to snap her out of whatever state she'd fallen into. Shock? Was this shock?

The pain hit her anew and Arianna hissed, doubling over as it ricocheted down her arm in violent waves.

Guards were running out the door now. And Rion wasn't himself. He hadn't even summoned his magic. If they caught him— Her breaths came quicker. If they caught him—

"Talon." She couldn't get enough air and spots flew across her vision. She couldn't look up, couldn't see past anything except the bloody, broken floor beneath her knees.

"I'm here," he said, his voice close. Concern laced every word.

"Don't let them catch him." He didn't answer, so Arianna forced herself to turn her head and look straight into those honey brown eyes. His brows were pinched, but unsaid words were on his lips. He clamped his mouth closed at her expression. "Please. Find him. Hide him." Arianna doubled over in pain again, sucking in breath, then she cried out in agony, screaming against the fire in her arm.

Talon wrapped one hand around her good arm and leaned in to whisper. "I will." She felt him leave and a small sense of relief washed through her. Talon would do it for her, even if he didn't understand. He would prevent anyone from hurting Rion until she could get to the bottom of things.

Ellie's body hovered over her next and she heard her little sister growl. Arianna didn't possess the strength to look up. She couldn't move anymore, not with the pain and heartache and agony ripping through her body.

"You'll stay away from her." Her little sister left no room for argument.

"We only want to help." Niall. His voice was gentle but strained somehow.

"Then get a healer," Ellie barked, her hands still around her sister's body.

"Can't she heal herself?" another asked, but Arianna didn't know his voice, or maybe she did, but the pain was blinding her, dulling her senses.

"No, she can't," her sister hissed. Arianna scented Ellie's magic then, wrapping around them both. Another stood close, but she couldn't . . .

She couldn't . . .

The world went black.

CHAPTER FIFTY-FIVE

RION

command you to run.

The words were like ice in his heart, but she'd given him an order and Rion had obeyed.

He'd fled from the manor, then the city, then the village below. The world around him blending into a kaleidoscope of colors, sounds, smells, and feelings. He'd become incapable of discerning one from the other. He couldn't identify his surroundings. He couldn't name the things he passed or the objects before him.

Rion's body and mind only knew one thing.

Run.

Images flew through his head. Arianna's fearful expression as she gaped at him, the trust they'd formed shattered in a single moment. The gaping hole in her neck where he'd sunk his fangs into her flesh. The bone protruding from her arm—bile rose in his throat and Rion vomited, the remnants of his small breakfast hitting the forest floor.

He wiped his mouth and kept running.

Gods, what had he done? His heart beat so hard in his chest Rion thought it might explode. He gripped his shirt, trying to quell the pain there, to calm down, but it did little good.

His head spun. He fell, then righted himself, ignoring the stinging pain in his hands. It was nothing. Nothing. Nothing. Nothing.

He was a monster. A demon. A creature from the darkest depths of hell. An abomination no longer afforded a care in this world. He had injured his mate. His *mate*. She was the one person he wasn't supposed to be able to harm. It was impossible. Impossible. Impossible.

Voices closed in on him, blending with everything else. Voices echoing from his past, screaming at the top of their lungs. Telling him he should die and be done with it. They said he had no purpose in this world. That he was beneath the filth that ran through the city streets.

No. No, no, no, no, no . . .

There were voices nearby. Far away and close. Real and imagined. Rion scented magic and twisted, but he couldn't make sense of the world around him. Didn't know if the light he saw was the sun or the moon or fire.

Fire—Rion blocked his face, his magic barely coming up in time. His hands singed and he fell back, hitting the ground hard. More voices, but Rion scrambled to his feet, desperate to obey that single command.

Run.

Wind tore at his clothes and Rion hit the ground again, his chin slamming against the hard earth. He gasped, but the pain was nothing compared to what still coursed through him, tainting his blood, coating his mouth.

Something was pulling the air from his lungs and he grabbed his throat, gasping for breath. He clawed at the earth, his body still begging him to run, run, run.

Why? Tears fell freely down his face now, even as he fought against the unseen enemy. *Why was this happening?*

Because you deserve it, a voice seemed to answer.

Fight left him, his vision darkened, and Rion knew nothing more.

Two weeks …

Four weeks …

Six weeks …

Eight weeks …

CHAPTER FIFTY-SIX

RION

He screamed into darkness that wouldn't hear him and fought against the shadows depicting his worst nightmares.

And no one bothered to save him.

Chapter Fifty-Seven

Talon

She was a ghost, barely moving, hardly functional from day to day as she lay in her room, tears staining her cheeks. She wouldn't eat, couldn't sleep, and only did either when her body absolutely demanded it.

Talon clenched his fists. Niall had resumed command of Ruadhán and had agreed to give Arianna space to grieve and heal, but even he was growing impatient. He was a constant face in the hall where Ellie had erected a barricade to shield Arianna from the inquiring masses.

No one made it within a dozen yards of Arianna's door. No one aside from him, Ellie, and a servant named Victoria.

Arianna rarely spoke, and they'd learned after the first week not to mention Rion's name in her presence. If they did, she broke down all over again and withdrew so far into herself that Talon worried she might never emerge.

He sighed and continued down the hall, leaving dust and ash in his wake. He hadn't stopped searching. Arianna had asked something of him and he was determined to fulfill her request. He'd been out every night, sometimes for nights on end, following tracks and scents just as he'd once done to find his friend. Ellie called him the best tracker Móirín had ever seen.

He scoffed. Best tracker indeed. He hadn't been able to locate Arianna in a year and a half and he was proving no better where The Demon was concerned.

Rion. He corrected himself. He'd accidentally called him The Demon in front of Arianna and she'd given him the most heartbreaking look he'd ever seen.

Talon had searched and searched, but now he was out of leads. He'd traced every location. Followed every discernable trail.

And nothing.

Talon didn't know what to do. He didn't want to return to Arianna empty handed, but he didn't have the heart to break the news to her, either.

Rion was alive. Of that much everyone was certain, but no one could find him. Not Saoirse with her warriors from Brónach. Not Niall with Ruadhán's elite. And certainly not him, no matter how many experienced Móirín warriors he took with him.

It was like the male had just disappeared and, according to Ellie, he'd been completely silent down the bond. Or what was left of it. He'd overheard the sisters talking.

Talon shook his head. They were in a mess. The council wanted a coronation. The world wanted their queen. He needed his friend. But all Arianna desired was her mate returned to her, safe and sound.

"This is ridiculous," a familiar voice echoed from the hall. Talon broke into a sprint and rounded the corner to find four guards with pensive gazes, a very angry Ellie standing before Arianna's open door, and Raevina staring them all down with her arms splayed outward. "She's been in there for two months. The ambassadors aren't here to pledge themselves to the city's regent."

"She's indisposed," Ellie said, but Talon could hear the warning growl in her voice.

Raevina clicked her tongue. "He's not even her mate, and the sooner she accepts that and gets out of that room, the better off she'll be. You think our enemies are just going to sit by forever? Have you heard what's happening out there?"

"I know well enough what's happening."

"Then why isn't she—"

"What's going on?" Talon demanded, and he could have sworn the guards sighed in relief at his presence.

Raevina turned on him and something in Talon's heart pulled toward the female. He hadn't had a chance to speak with her since the ball. They'd both been busy with their own tasks, but her beauty hit him just as hard now as it had then. Long braids around her perfectly shaped face. That flawless skin that seemed to call to something in his blood.

Talon shook his head, trying to clear it.

Raevina said, "She needs to come out of that room."

"Why?" He stepped closer to Ellie, trying to peer inside. Shit. Arianna was awake, but for the first time in a while, she was focused on something. On Raevina, but Arianna didn't appear to be absorbing her words. She was just staring at the female.

"Why?" Raevina looked stunned. "What do you mean, why? She's the queen. There are things that need to be done."

Talon noted the sweat beading on Raevina's forehead. Her slightly labored breath. "Are you feeling all right?" he asked.

Raevina waved one hand. "Don't change the subject. It's been two months. If The Demon hasn't returned by now, then he isn't coming back, and it's time for you two to stop coddling her and demand she fulfills her role."

"If people like you don't leave her alone," Ellie seethed, "I'm taking her back home to Levea."

"And how do you plan to do that? There are factions everywhere, both for and against her, demanding she make an appearance. Civil war is breaking out over her demands with the slaves and she's done nothing to sort it out."

"I'll take care of it," Ellie said between clenched teeth.

"Talon?" Arianna's small voice had him in the room in seconds, Ellie on his heels. Raevina remained in the doorway, watching, her arms crossed as she leaned against the threshold. Arianna gave him a hopeful look and Talon's stomach plummeted when that hope died in her eyes. Like it did every time he returned.

He hated it. Hated himself for being the one to cause it.

"When are you—" A sharp hiss and intake of breath had Talon's head swiveling toward Raevina. She'd collapsed against the door frame, holding her side. Talon stood, ready to assist her, but she righted herself. Her color had paled a shade and bags appeared beneath her eyes. Talon thought she might be sick, but Raevina straightened and stepped back. "You're the queen," Raevina said. "Start acting like it."

Then she was gone, her boots echoing off the smooth floor. Talon thought he smelled something acrid in the air. He turned toward Arianna who still watched the doorway as if Raevina might reappear. As if someone else might appear too.

CHAPTER FIFTY-EIGHT

SAOIRSE

aoirse sat on one of the many stone benches in the garden, head between her hands as she stared at the dirt path, watching the beginnings of rain gently pepper the ground.

Saoirse knew she should move. She should go inside, sort through the plans and details, but despair had grabbed hold of her that morning and left her plummeting into a deep chasm.

Her brother was gone. Disappeared. Vanished without a trace. Just like her mother.

Only this time, no one really wanted to find him. Aside from Arianna, of course, but even she'd been huddled in her room, both recovering and mourning for her mate.

Saoirse knew firsthand how much grief could tear someone down. She'd seen it in her father when he'd raged through the estate and everyone had feared to so much as speak to him.

He'd become a different male then, someone unapproachable rather than the loving parent she'd always known. And he'd remained that way until his untimely death.

She'd never understood why her father had stopped searching. She certainly never had. Saoirse hadn't cared what others claimed, but when her father had demanded resources be spent elsewhere, she'd flat-out disobeyed and used her own funds to continue the hunt.

Saoirse still had maps dotting the walls of her room. Along with details of other High Lords and Ladies within the court. Saoirse had detailed every aspect of their lives until she knew what brew of coffee or tea they preferred and whether they took sugar or milk with each. She'd stalked them to an unhealthy level, always searching for anything out of place.

She'd broken into homes and searched through records she had no business seeing and she'd stolen diaries and combed the pages for any mention of The High Lady of Brónach

All that effort wasted.

Saoirse still remembered the day she'd collapsed in the middle of her room and cried. She'd exhausted all possibilities and had come up completely empty.

Now she stared at the earth as it slowly faded from a bright color to a darker shade and wondered if the same fate would befall her little brother. Would she never see his face again? Never have a chance to right all the wrong she'd done to him?

A footstep. A scent. Saoirse closed her eyes as the female stood on the path, likely staring at her. Maybe if she didn't look up, the female would get the hint and leave her alone. No one came to the rear corner of a garden if they wanted company. And Saoirse certainly didn't want company right now. She just needed a few minutes to take in the grief and feel the heaviness of her family's absence. A few minutes, then she'd march back to her warriors and begin another search.

The footsteps receded and Saoirse breathed a sigh of relief.

They were in the royal city, which meant her list of suspects was short but complex. These were the council members, Fae who were hundreds of years older than she was, and probably far better at playing a long-term manipulative game.

But she needed to play smarter. She couldn't let her brother just vanish. Saoirse wasn't sure she'd survive losing another member of her family. And what would happen if they decided to come after her brother Alec next? She'd just be a useless leader who couldn't protect her own family.

The footsteps sounded again and Saoirse gritted her teeth. "I'm not in the mood today." She didn't think she could banter with the female without also biting at her.

But the footsteps drew closer and Saoirse reluctantly lifted her head to find Zylah standing with a steeping cup of tea between her hands. Zylah didn't look away, wasn't embarrassed or shy or anything Saoirse might have expected from bringing tea.

Zylah stepped close enough to place it on the bench then stepped away. Light rain hit the hot liquid, but Saoirse glanced back at the female who seemed to be observing her.

"You looked like you needed it."

Saoirse laughed, but the sound was hollow. "Is it poisoned?"

Zylah tilted her head as if she might be considering the idea. "No, I've thought about a lot of ways I could kill you, and poison is the furthest down the list."

Saoirse took the cup in one hand. "Glad to know you've been thinking about me." But her gaze turned back to the dark liquid that reflected her worn face.

"They'll find him," Zylah said after a beat of silence.

Saoirse's heart seized but she wouldn't let Zylah see it. Though if she'd brought her tea, Saoirse ventured to guess her feelings were already fairly obvious. "Careful," Saoirse warned. "Someone might start thinking you care."

Zylah didn't respond at first so Saoirse looked up to see her face tilted toward the heavens. The misty rain clung to individual strands of her hair.

"I had a little brother once," she said, her voice full of bittersweet memories. "I wouldn't wish the pain of losing a sibling on anyone."

Saoirse felt a lump in her throat, then tore her gaze away and studied the tea again. She sipped the steaming beverage and let the bitter taste drown her threatening tears. "Thank you."

CHAPTER FIFTY-NINE

RAEVINA

Raevina hissed against the pain in her stomach as Cahira unbound her wound. She cursed the creature that had given it to her, vowing to slaughter every single one of them when she returned to Púróg. To hell with her father's demands and rules. Maybe she'd just confront him right then and there and be done with the whole mess.

She cursed when she peered down at the red skin lining what was once a superficial scratch. The wound had festered and deepened, and Cahira cleaned pus from it every morning and every night. She'd developed a fever too. Just another reason for Raevina to annihilate those blasted Chimera. She'd always hated the Dark Fae as much as anyone else, but now things were personal.

"If you'd just lay down and rest for a week, it would heal," Cahira chided, grimacing at the wound.

"I already tried that."

Cahira dipped a rag into the warm bowl of water at her side, wrung out the excess, and dabbed it against her stomach. Ravina hissed and bit the inside of her cheek so hard she tasted blood. If not for the venom eating away at her skin, the damn thing wouldn't hurt so much.

"Two days is not a week."

"And those two days made no difference. I don't have time to sit around. I need to know what these people are planning and I need to make myself a part of it."

Cahira prodded the skin around the cut and Raevina hissed again. "I'm out of herbs," her second said. "We need some of the weed at the base of the mountain."

"We don't have time to make the journey." Nor did she have time to keep waiting. "If I could just get this Arianna to leave her room for a few minutes, I could end all this and we'd be back in Fiadh before the next full moon."

Cahira pulled out some fresh gauze. "If you don't plan it out carefully, they'll know, and your father will exile you like he did your brother."

"I will not end up like that loud-mouthed—" Raevina stopped talking when the door opened. Cahira jumped to her feet, weapon out and shadows filling the space that separated them from the doorway.

Then everything fell silent.

There she was. Alone and completely unguarded. A ghost of her former, cheery self. The Queen, dressed in nothing more than a white nightgown that gave her far too ghostly of an appearance. Raevina didn't move and Cahira's shadows withdrew. They exchanged an odd look and the Queen stepped inside.

Her bare footsteps were silent against the cool marble floor, and Raevina offered the young queen a strained half smile. "Any chance you could pass some of that healing magic my way?" She didn't believe. Hadn't from the moment she'd spotted this female on the rooftop with the male lesser warriors had labeled The Demon. Then again, maybe he'd given himself the title just to inspire fear.

Arianna didn't respond and Raevina almost felt sorry for her. This was the moment she'd been waiting for. Raevina could push the would-be queen back into the hall with a single thrust of her hand, then slit her throat. It would be easy and painless. Then Cahira and

Raevina would disappear to another floor and mingle with various parties until the body was discovered. No one would ever suspect them.

Another week, and she'd be on her way back to Fiadh and the world would return to normal.

Raevina eyed the blade resting on her dresser. An armlength, that's all that separated her from her goal. It was perfect and yet—and yet she couldn't convince her body to move, as if it had a will of its own.

Was she curious?

A few more minutes wouldn't hurt. She could see what the female planned to do. Maybe she honestly believed herself to be a healer.

The Queen stood before her now. Her cheeks were hollow, her face gaunt and shoulders far too slim.

Cahira stepped aside, her head bowed, and Raevina rolled her eyes. Her second had always been the more religious of the two, believing in all the old fairy tales written within the ancient texts. Her second had even gone so far as to steal one of the heavy tomes from the temple. Raevina was pretty sure that was sacrilegious in itself.

She inwardly smirked. Those texts were nothing more than children's stories told to keep people in line so they would follow the laws of the land.

The Queen knelt and Raevina quirked a brow. She'd had a few females on their knees before her, but this was certainly a first. Arianna's hands lifted and Raevina winced when she pressed them over her wound with no regard to the foul smelling liquid seeping out.

Well, the Queen certainly wasn't squeamish.

Raevina eyed the blade again. Right here, she could do it right here, but then a glowing light formed beneath the Queen's touch and warmth spread through Raevina's abdomen.

She froze, then her breath hitched when her abdomen lit on fire. Raevina clenched the edge of the mattress even as she watched the greenish liquid pour from the cut and drip onto the floor. The skin around her wound shifted back to a normal color and closed, leaving nothing more than a thin line in its place.

Raevina breathed easy for the first time in months. Her lips parted as she met Arianna's gaze. Impossible. It had to be impossible, but her blood was racing, telling her otherwise.

She hadn't performed any fancy rituals or long chants. She hadn't even bowed her head to pray to the gods first. This Arianna, their queen, had just placed her hands on Raevina and healed her as easily as Raevina could light a candle.

Arianna stood, but before she could turn away, Raevina grabbed her wrist. She winced when frost shot down her arm and fragments of ice seemed to bury themselves straight into her bones.

Arianna turned back and Raevina saw it then. Saw the cold, calculated look of an individual capable of ruling this country. Of changing everything they'd ever known.

"I don't like to be touched." Her voice wasn't of this world. It echoed to some long forgotten part of Raevina's soul, calling her home.

Raevina slid to her knees. The Queen didn't react. She simply pulled away, leaving Raevina to question every legend and story she'd ever been told.

The Queen. The Queen of Alastríona had healed her and she was walking away and she'd—Raevina clenched her teeth. She had almost killed her. That was her whole mission, to kill the imposter. But she'd never imagined, not once, that this female might be the real thing.

Raevina tilted her head to find Cahira with her forehead plastered against the floor. Maybe that's what she should have done too, but Raevina's body refused to move. As if she were rooted to the spot.

Her hand thawed and though she could have sat there stunned for the rest of the night, Raevina grabbed her tunic and weapons, then followed Arianna into the hall.

She'd been sent on a mission. Her father had commanded her to kill The Queen. He planned to reward her. But when had her father ever kept his promises? She swallowed hard. To hell with her father. She served a new monarch now. And she'd regain Fiadh's lost honor, no matter how long it took.

CHAPTER SIXTY

ARIANNA

aevina's words had shaken her awake from the darkness clouding her mind.

She couldn't leave. They wouldn't let her join the endless hunt for Rion.

She couldn't remain in her room. Too many were beginning to worry about her health.

And she couldn't face the masses. Because she might break down as soon as they asked a question Arianna wasn't ready to answer.

All she could do now was wait and hope and pray. But was that right? Shouldn't she be doing more?

Arianna felt for the three threads that still tethered her and Rion together. She tugged on them lightly every single day, running the fingers of her mind across the taunt strands, trying to coax something from the other side.

But her mate was silent. So utterly silent.

Arianna didn't know what that meant. Could she no longer feel him because of how weak the bond had become? Was he too far away for that part of the bond to work? Was it even real to begin with?

Tears sprang to her eyes at the last thought. She'd never doubted the legitimacy of the bond before, and part of her wondered why she doubted it now. But it was a small whisper, a horrible voice, telling her a true bond wouldn't unravel so easily. That a mate couldn't hurt the other.

Arianna stared at the heavy double doors looming before her. She didn't remember the walk through the halls. Not really. She didn't look at the people or the intricate carvings or appreciate the floral designs as she'd once done. She was too tired to even lift her eyes as she trudged up the stairs, feeling like the weight of the world held her back.

Arianna stood before the shelves of the second floor. She knew what she sought, yet didn't possess the energy to find the tomes. Because if she found anything that pointed her toward an answer she didn't like, Arianna honestly wasn't sure she'd survive.

"Can I help you, My Lady?" Arianna slowly turned to Niall's worried expression. His blond hair was dripping wet and he looked like he'd barely had time to throw on his clothes. Two buttons were still undone at the bottom of his shirt. His shoes weren't tied, rather the laces were stuffed into his boots and he was breathing hard enough to tell Arianna he'd run all the way here.

Right. The servants had likely been in an uproar upon seeing her. Talon was out searching again and she'd woken to find Ellie asleep in the armchair. Her sister never left.

Arianna opened her mouth to speak, but words refused to form. The tears surfaced again and Arianna reached for Rion, begging him to answer. He'd looked so heartbroken when she had commanded him to run and now all she wanted was to command him to return. Whatever it took.

Arianna tried clearing her throat, but her voice was soft and raspy. "I want to read about pseudo bonds."

Niall didn't respond at first. He merely stood there as if debating whether he should assist her. If he didn't, she supposed she'd simply wander until her body gave out. Curl up in a corner maybe. Was this all she'd amounted to? A worthless being without her mate at her side? If he was indeed her mate.

"It hurts me to see you like this," Niall said.

She clenched her fists. "Then don't look," she snapped. But as soon as the words left, so did the anger and her energy with it.

Arianna sank to the floor and drew her knees in. She didn't care who saw.

Niall knelt at her side and tried again. "I only meant that I want to help." When she didn't respond Niall clasped his hands together. "I'm afraid there isn't a lot of literature on the matter. We have a few stories that detail bonds being formed from those who were traumatized or so obsessed with their lovers that they claimed a bond had formed." Arianna listened but didn't move. "I can find those volumes for you, but I have a condition." Arianna raised her head slightly. "I'd like you to join me for lunch."

"I'm not hungry."

"Please?" he tried, but she just stared at the floor, studying the swirling designs in the rug that lined the walking areas. Arianna searched for specks of dirt in the fibers, but they seemed unnaturally clean. Everything always seemed so damn clean and perfect. Where were the flaws that made things irregular and beautiful?

Where were the flowers with missing petals? The statues with cracks down the sides? Where was the dust that coated books worn with time, or the yellowing pages of tomes that were older than her father?

"I understand you want to find him," Niall said and Arianna's stomach clenched, grief flowing through her anew. "But if you continue like this, you won't be able to help him when you do."

Arianna stopped studying the fibers and pushed through her waning energy to stare into Niall's gray eyes. Such beautiful gray eyes. They drew her in, made her think of the sky right before summer rain. His wet hair hung down in his face and she studied the locks, transfixed for a moment by all the colors that made up hair she'd only ever thought of as blond. It was so much more, like a sunset had been woven into the strands.

"Arianna."

"Fine. I'll eat."

His eyes widened. "Great. I'll have the cooks prepare something in the—"

"No." Niall fell silent. "Right here. And you'll find me the books."

His face turned grave again, but he nodded. "As you wish, My Lady."

It took Niall less than five minutes to find the volumes she needed, and a steaming bowl of potato soup appeared moments after that. Arianna's mouth watered at the smell of it and the considerably large chunk of bread on the side.

She took the book first and began flipping through the pages, but the words were blurring and her head pounded as if someone had bested her in a sparring match.

"Please, eat something," Niall said gently, then sat down beside her. She imagined what they must look like. A Lord of Pádraigín and the Queen of Alastríona both seated on the floor of the library with a small pile of books and a bowl of soup.

Arianna took the warm bowl in her hands and raised it to her lips. One sip and heat flowed through her, welcome and filling. She couldn't remember the last time she'd eaten. Ellie had all but forced things down her throat, but Arianna had not tasted them, not really. They were pale and cold and dull. This was full of color and promise.

Strength. She needed strength if she wanted to find Rion. She needed to read about pseudo bonds and real bonds and find out exactly what it all meant. She knew a bond had to solidify, but did that mean it could also fall apart as hers and Rion's was doing?

Before Arianna knew it, the bowl was empty. Her stomach twisted and she closed her eyes, fighting to keep the contents down.

"Good?" Niall asked.

"I think I ate too fast."

He chuckled a bit. "Yes, well, have some bread and see if that helps your stomach."

She obeyed, refusing to look at him. What did he think of her like this? What did any of them think? This was worse than the time Rion had outright left her. At least then she'd known where he was. Now, she didn't know if he was suffering, hiding, or still running despite her wanting him to return.

"Thank you," Arianna said once her stomach had calmed down.

Niall held a book in his hand. She hadn't realized how closely he sat to her until now, nor had she considered that she was dressed in nothing more than a night dress. It covered her body, but it was far from the garb a queen might wear in the presence of her subjects. And Niall hadn't bothered to berate her about it.

"You were a slave." He already knew that, but Arianna found his eyes on the scars of her wrist. She didn't bother hiding them.

"Yes."

"To him?"

Her heart jolted with a fresh wave of pain and Arianna set the bread down. It had turned to ash in her mouth. "For a while."

Niall seemed to straighten slightly. His jaw worked, but he kept his expression neutral. "Did he ever . . . hurt you?"

He had. His magic had grazed her skin. Cut her hand. Held her still within its clutches. But she couldn't voice those things now and certainly not to Niall. Instead, Arianna said, "He ignored me most of the time."

Niall seemed to wait for more before saying. "I'd love to listen to your story, if you ever feel inclined to share it."

Niall picked up another book and for some reason, Arianna added, "Talon almost killed him once." Niall froze. "I saved him."

He ran one hand across gold lettering. "Is that what started the bond?"

Arianna shook her head. "My father tried to execute him and I—" She gripped her shirt, right over her aching heart. "I felt it. I could feel him being torn away from me and I knew what he was."

Silence filled the space again. "I'm sorry for the pain you're enduring."

Seconds later the library door burst open and Ellie stormed through. Her gaze roamed the aisles until they landed on Arianna. She outright glared at Niall, but he didn't return it.

"I'll take this as my leave. If you need anything else, please don't hesitate to ask."

"Thank you."

CHAPTER SIXTY-ONE

TALON

nother night. Another failure. But at least Arianna was up and about. Talon had decided to leave the search to his warriors after today. He'd done all he could. Arianna needed him now.

He sighed. He had retraced his steps one final time, but the results were the same. He'd wound up in a barren wasteland covered in ash. It felt like the world ended there somehow. Like the fires that had swept across the earth were unnatural.

But there weren't footprints in the ash, nor much in the way of animal life. He'd still sent four warriors to scout the perimeter. Just in case.

Talon walked through the manor, watching the moonlight filter through the tall glass windows. He kept his footsteps light, determined not to disturb any who had already retired for the evening.

Then a door opened and Talon paused to stare at the beautiful female who emerged. Her scent drifted toward him, full of flames and shadows and secrets. He didn't mean to stare, but Talon couldn't look away from her disheveled state.

The belt around her pants hung loose and the top three buttons of her blouse were undone, revealing far more skin than he'd seen at the dance. Then a voice called her back and Raevina turned with a wide smile toward the person inside.

A male emerged and Raevina closed the distance and pulled him in for a deep kiss. She nipped his lower lip and Talon's stomach twisted in knots. His breath turned ragged at the sight. She kissed him again, her tongue sliding between his lips, pulling a satisfied moan from the male. A whisper of words, then the door closed. She turned to find him staring like she'd known he was there all along.

Talon couldn't move and Raevina did nothing to cover herself. Her feet were bare against the marble floor and her pants were rolled part way up her calf. Well, one of them was; the other had likely fallen while she—Talon shook his head, trying not to think about what she'd been doing.

She gave him a crooked smile that ignited his blood. "Little glorified bodyguard skulking around in the shadows." She cocked her head. "One might think you're up to no good."

"Says the one leaving another's bedroom in the middle of the night." He hated the edge in his voice, but her smile only widened as if he'd said something funny.

"Jealous I'm not leaving yours?"

"If you'd been in my room, we wouldn't be done." Gods, did he just say that?

Raevina threw back her head and laughed and Talon wondered if she didn't care whether the male inside heard. "So confident in your abilities to please, are you?" She stalked forward, her hips rolling from side to side and Talon's mouth went dry as he studied the skin she left exposed. He wanted to replace that other male's scent with his own, to make her forget she'd ever been with anyone else.

Raevina stopped mere inches before him, that grin still on her face. "I'm willing to bet a month's wages you've never even had a female in your bed."

Talon was glad for the cover of darkness if only to hide the heat that rose to his face. Her hands reached up to caress the collar of his shirt and Talon swallowed hard. Then she patted his chest. "Come back to me when you have a bit of experience."

She turned, but something in him couldn't let her walk away. Not like this. He wouldn't be treated like a nobody novice even if she was right.

Talon spun Raevina around and crushed his lips to hers, backing her against the nearest wall. Talon pressed into her hard, the lines of his body melding with her sweet curves.

He would never have done such a thing with Arianna or another female who would be surprised and possibly reject the aggressive advance, but something about Raevina seemed to crave it, and judging from the way her hands moved in his hair and the way she tightened her hold to an almost painful level, this was exactly what she wanted.

Talon kissed her hard enough to bruise and reached down to grasp her thigh before pulling it level with his waist. He wanted to tear the clothes from their bodies right there in the hall, but then her hand was on his chest pushing him back.

"You're just full of surprises, aren't you?" He stepped back when she pushed him further, his hands falling to his sides even as his chest heaved. "Maybe another night." Then she walked down the hall, her boots slung over one shoulder and hips swaying with every stride.

Talon just stared after her, his breath still ragged and blood screaming that she belonged to him.

No, she doesn't, he corrected himself.

Gods, she'd be the death of him.

Chapter Sixty-Two

Arianna

Arianna took dinner in her room that night and already felt her energy returning. She stuck to soups and bread, trying to bring her stomach back to life after so long with meager meals. Niall was right: She needed her strength if she were going to find Rion. She couldn't wallow in her grief anymore and expect everyone else to do the work.

"Are you sure you're up for this?" Ellie asked the following morning. She had called for a meeting with Saoirse, Rion's elder sister. She'd still never had a formal conversation with the female, but Arianna knew she was the only other being who would be searching without reservation.

"I need to do this," Arianna reminded Ellie. She needed to get stronger too, begin training her body again. She didn't know what had come over her. It felt as though a veil had been lifted from her mind, or maybe that was the anger, fueling her movements as she thought about whoever had done this to her and her mate.

Pádraigín's magic was responsible, of that much she was certain. She'd discussed the events in detail with Ellie last night and both had agreed that Rion had been glamoured. Or she'd been glamoured. Arianna still wasn't quite sure how it all worked, but someone had thrown them into this mess and when she found out who, Arianna was going to tear them apart.

But first, she needed to find her mate. She'd wanted to storm from the city and begin the search on her own, but Arianna didn't possess any tracking abilities, and if Talon hadn't found him, then she'd fare no better. She wasn't even sure if she could follow the bond in its shattered state. And Rion still wasn't answering.

Arianna entered the small room to find Saoirse already seated with a mug of tea clutched between her hands. Someone had stripped the female of her weapons—Raevina no doubt—and left Rion's sister to sit in the comfortable room in silence.

Arianna locked eyes with the female from Fiadh. She barely remembered doing it, but Arianna had wandered to the female's bedroom and healed her. Afterward, the female had followed her down the halls until Arianna was back in her own room. There, she'd pledged her undying loyalty and confessed her motives for coming to Ruadhán in the first place.

Arianna had just stared at Raevina, and Ellie had done the same. At least, until Ellie bombarded her with questions. Raevina had answered every one in acute detail until Ellie was satisfied she wasn't a threat. Raevina only left to sleep and eat and reluctantly relinquished Arianna's safety to Ellie or her second in command, Cahira.

It was a strange alliance, especially since the battle with Fiadh was still such a raw wound, but Arianna accepted it. The female was strong and her loyalty could be the key to forming an alliance with Fiadh in the near future.

Arianna focused on those in the room. Talon stood on the left side of the loveseat while Raevina leaned against the wall at the other end. Her friend kept eyeing Raevina and it occurred to her that she hadn't explained the whole situation to Talon. Arianna swallowed. She hoped that wouldn't turn into a mess.

Arianna sensed Saoirse's gaze on her as she circled the furniture and seated herself nearest to Talon. The female's green eyes tugged at the grief still filling Arianna's heart.

Saoirse sipped her tea. "Finally reentering the land of the living?"

"Watch your tone," Talon warned. Arianna didn't reprimand him. She couldn't, because everything about the female was sending her back into that dark, spiraling abyss. Saoirse reminded her of Rion in so many ways. Saoirse carried her head high and her shoulders squared. Her magic stood at the ready, barely contained, and she watched the corners of the room, yet made herself appear relaxed and—

Ellie cleared her throat and Arianna broke her gaze. She clasped her hands together, suddenly unsure about everything she wanted to say. She'd been in her room for two months and Saoirse hadn't found him. Neither had Talon. What did Arianna think she could say that might change anything?

"Sit up straighter," Saoirse said.

Arianna jolted. "What?"

"You're slouching."

What did that have— "I-I don't—"

"Don't speak unless you're sure of your words, and put more authority in your tone."

Talon growled, but Raevina just looked amused.

Saoirse sat forward. "You are a queen. I don't care what rumors say you've been doing. I don't care what people have seen. You act like it. You make demands. You're not a servant begging for a favor."

"I—right."

"Has no one taught you proper etiquette?"

Arianna risked a glance up from her lowered head, then remembered herself and sat straighter, but it was Ellie who answered. "She's not exactly been in top form."

Saoirse's gaze slid to Ellie. "But no one needs to know that. No one needs to know anything. You're here now."

"I'm here to find Rion."

Saoirse looked away at that. "I'm afraid I don't have anything to report if that's what this meeting is about."

"What else did you think it was about?"

"The continent. Slaves. Your rule." Saoirse offered a grimaced smile. "There's a lot that hasn't been addressed."

Right. She'd never even been properly introduced to the ambassadors. And to have Raevina in this room while she was speaking with Saoirse probably wasn't the wisest choice.

"I apologize for the delay, but my first priority is finding Rion." Arianna choked on his name.

"The council disagrees."

"The council can go to hell." Arianna felt that earlier anger bubble to the surface again.

Saoirse's brows rose. "And why is that?"

"Because someone caused all this. Someone who had enough knowledge and power to plan it. I intend to find out who before I move on with anything else."

Saoirse smiled. "Now you're thinking like a queen." She clasped her hands. "But this is going to be tricky. Those in power have an infinite amount of time and resources. They've waited centuries to enact their plans and they're not about to make a mistake now. But Rion—" Saoirse chewed her lip. "I'm not sure how much time he has." Fear welled up in Arianna and her stomach clenched. "My brother is alive, right?"

Arianna nodded. "But he's been quiet. I can't sense anything from him."

"Whoever has him knows exactly how powerful he is, which, sadly for us, tells me they're not stupid."

"So how are we going to find him?"

Saoirse inclined her head toward Ellie. "I think this one has been doing a bit of digging, have you not?"

Ellie didn't hide her smile. "I might have found a lead. But I need a distraction to get to him."

Arianna whirled on her sister. "Who is it?"

"Wait," Talon said, interrupting the females in the room. "Should we be discussing this with her here?"

"*Her* has a name," Raevina replied coolly.

Arianna chewed her lip. "It's fine."

Talon looked between them. "It's fine? That's all I get?"

Arianna's face heated, knowing he was likely to reprimand her. "I—well, I kind of went to her room a few nights ago and healed her."

Talon shot Raevina a look. "You said you were fine."

"I was. Mentally."

"So you *were* hurt?" He stepped closer as if he might examine her himself, but Raevina stopped him with a glare.

"It was an old injury that's no longer a problem."

Talon was looking between them like they'd lost their minds. "I still don't understand."

Arianna took a breath. "Okay, there's a whole conversation you missed out on because you were out in the field." He crossed his arms as if to say he was here now. Her gaze flickered between Raevina and Talon. "Raevina was sent here to kill me."

Talon's mouth went slack as he observed the room, seeming to note that no one had a weapon drawn on the female. Arianna was surprised he hadn't drawn his own.

"Care to elaborate?"

Raevina pinched the bridge of her nose and sighed. "My father send me here to kill an imposter." She tilted her head. "Well, I doubt he'd care whether she was an imposter or not, but once I realized she wasn't, I decided to forsake my father and dedicate my life and my people to our queen."

Talon arched a brow. "Just like that? No loyalty to your family?"

Raevina's eyes darkened. "If you knew how things were run in Fiadh, you'd understand family means absolutely nothing. My father has killed all but a few of his children, either because he deemed them too weak or he saw them as a threat. The High Lord's seat is something constantly fought for. It is not kept with respect, only fear and strength."

"Still not seeing how that makes you trustworthy."

"I've wanted to overthrow my father for a very long time. Longer than you've been alive. Fiadh lost their honor when the last Divine died. We were meant to protect her and we failed. I wish to restore that honor."

Talon scented the air, slowly accepting the truth in her words. Arianna glanced at Saoirse, who seemed amused by the whole scene.

After a few silent moments, Saoirse cleared her throat. "While that was interesting, I'd very much like to return to our previous conversation." She nodded toward Ellie. "You were saying?"

Ellie eyed Talon, waiting for another interruption. "Right, I think Niall's assistant, Gavin, knows something."

"What do you need?" Saoirse asked.

"Thirty minutes and a silent room."

"Consider it done."

CHAPTER SIXTY-THREE

RION

Rion pulled her close, breathing in the heavenly floral scent of his mate. Summer lilies, cascading waterfalls, and just a hint of flame, as if she carried a spark of him somewhere deep in her soul. She was here, safely wrapped in his arms where the gruesome remnants of his nightmares couldn't touch her.

He leaned in and brushed Arianna's wavy dark hair aside, desperate to catch a glimpse of her sleeping face in the darkness. She was growing it out and he couldn't wait to see it waist length again. She'd told him that she and Ellie used to—his hand pulled away wet.

Rion furrowed his brow and sat up, reaching for a light he couldn't find. Didn't they have a lamp at their bedside?

He pulled for his magic, but it didn't respond, then the starts of a pounding headache pulsed behind his eyes. He winced and black specks flew across his vision.

"Arianna?" he tried, voice whisper soft. He hated disturbing her, but she'd always assured him he could wake her anytime he needed. He just wanted to hear her voice. Just once.

She didn't respond.

"Arianna," he tried again and shook her shoulder. It was cold, too cold and her body was stiff. Dread coursed through his gut and somehow a light he couldn't locate flickered on in the distant corner, or had it always been there?

Rion rolled her over then leaped from their bed, chest heaving as he stared at her ashen face contorted in pain.

He looked at his trembling hands next, heart thundering when he found them red and dripping. The tang of her blood filled the room, choking his senses. Rion stumbled back when his eyes fell upon the bite mark on her neck.

Rion licked his lips and tasted her blood.

He'd done this.

His gaze dropped to her arm next and his stomach tightened at the sight of the mangled limb. Not just bent at a horrid angle, but the flesh torn from bone, laying on the once pale sheets—he retched.

Rion backed away further, leaving her lifeless body on the mattress, splayed out as though she were some kind of sacrifice. The darkness swallowed her form as through it were an animal, then he was falling, falling, falling.

Rion jolted awake and bolted upright. He blinked several times, shielding his eyes from the warm afternoon sunlight, then Arianna was there, her hands on his chest, rubbing soothing circles through his tunic.

"You're all right, it was just a nightmare," she assured.

Alive. She was alive.

He reached for her face, cupping her cheeks between both hands and pressed his brow to hers. She offered him a soft, heartbreaking smile. He breathed in over and over again, struggling to calm his racing blood.

They sat on top of a thick blanket in the middle of a meadow surrounded by trees. He blinked against the bright sun and took in the scents and sounds. Nothing seemed amiss. He startled when she handed him a wrapped sandwich.

Her face fell. "That bad?"

Rion shook his head, trying to clear it. "It's nothing."

"We can talk if you need to."

He tried offering her a grin but knew it didn't quite reach his eyes. He couldn't remember how they'd gotten here or what the occasion was, but she was here, safe.

Rion's heart slowed and he unwrapped his sandwich only to toss it against the nearest tree. He jumped to his feet, swiping away the squiggling larvae that had fallen from the wrapper.

"Rion?" He met Arianna's gaze, but her eyes weren't the deep cerulean blue he loved. They'd turned dull and her face had shifted to a paler shade. She was thin and bony and when he blinked again, blood poured from her neck.

She didn't seem to notice the change. Arianna just tilted her head. "What's wrong?"

Then a crack echoed through the clearing and her arm bent backward. The bone protruded from her skin, and Rion's chest was heaving all over again.

He blinked and she was gone. So was the meadow.

He stood beneath barren trees, their branches reaching toward the sky with spindly fingers. A cold breeze ruffled the dead leaves and Rion turned to find a single headstone at the end of the path. He closed his eyes, unwilling to approach. He didn't want to see the name etched into the surface.

Then he was falling all over again and the visions kept coming. Them at breakfast with Ellie and Talon only for the room to explode in a mass of hysteria. Ellie begging him to stop, pleading with him over and over. She screamed that she'd trusted him and he saw the betrayal behind the tears in her eyes.

Then they were at the training grounds. He was trying to command his magic to stop, but it kept moving of its own accord, just like it had done in his youth and before he could shout a warning, Talon's lifeless body fell against the stones.

He tried to run but couldn't. Tried not to listen and failed.

Arianna's voice kept echoing through it all. Sometimes she'd smile, other times she'd beg, but her screams were the worst of hells and they shattered every last shred of his sanity.

RION'S EYES fluttered open and for a terrifying second, he thought he'd gone blind. His body felt leaden and his blood sluggish. Drugs? Dehydration? A mixture of both?

He tried to focus on his surroundings, but everything was black save for the dim flickering light beneath a door. Not blind then, but his vision still blurred. A bitter copper taste coated his mouth and his throat burned like he'd swallowed fire.

Rion flexed his wrists and grimaced. He tilted his head up to stare at the iron shackles biting into his skin and the chains that held his body upright. He didn't know how long he'd been hanging there.

The chains loosened every now and then, of that much he was certain. He had vague memories of lying on the cold stone, saliva and blood and filth pooled around his freezing body.

Rion gritted his teeth and dragged his feet beneath him, fighting for the strength to lift his aching limbs.

Blood rushed back to his hands and his fingertips tingled. Rion tilted his head to the side to stretch his neck and instantly regretted the movement.

Nothing was broken, though his fingers were certainly bruised enough to suggest otherwise.

For the first time in what felt like days, Rion's head was clear. This wasn't a nightmare, or a vision, or anything of the sort. He was awake, finally, through he had no idea how long he'd been here.

Rion rolled his wrists again and surveyed the room. It was too dark to see much, but he could tell the cell was small and no one else occupied it. No blanket, no bucket, not a single thing lay on the floor aside from a drain at his feet.

The darkness smelled of mold and water trickled down the walls. Water he would have gladly sipped from the floors if he wasn't restrained. Gods, his head was pounding.

Rion shifted a foot only to hear the rattle of more chains. They'd shackled his ankles, too.

Was he back in Móirín, or had they thrown him in some underground dungeon beneath Ruadhán?

Did Arianna—everything came rushing back to him then. The bite on her neck, her arm bent at an awkward angle, the bond snapping.

The bond.

Rion desperately reached for it and stopped himself as if hovering outside a forbidden room. Three small fraying strands were all that was left. They were so weak compared to the braided rope that had stood in their place. He didn't dare reach for them.

Did Arianna know he was here? Was—was she the one who had ordered him imprisoned?

She'd told him to run, but in that terrible moment, the warriors in that room had wanted to kill him. And rightfully so. Maybe someone she'd ordered had put him here. Hell, maybe Talon was his overseer.

Pain echoed through his heart and body as if someone was beating a drum. He ached beyond reason and his mind plagued him with images of her distraught face.

The betrayal hurt the most. She'd trusted him and he'd broken every scrap of that trust.

Rion gritted his teeth and his chest heaved, throat burning with tears he tried to swallow down. He could still hear the echo of her arm cracking and he swore he could still taste her blood on his tongue.

Rion tried to assess himself in the darkness. His chest was bare and itched terribly as if something were coating his skin. Blood, most likely. Parts of his body burned, whispering of old wounds that had yet to fully heal.

Some of the images were real, then. Like a fist flying from the shadows to collide with his jaw or a sharp object sliding just beneath his rips and left there for what felt like hours.

But Arianna wouldn't have allowed those things to happen to him. She wouldn't have wanted to save his life just so he could be tortured. He hoped.

Keys rattled from the doorway and Rion went still. He inclined his head slightly, straining to listen. The thick iron door swung open and Rion blinked against the small light of a candle.

It took several moments for his eyes to adjust. He tried to rally his magic, but a sharp current shot through his body. His legs collapsed and Rion gasped for breath. Right, he was in iron. His magic wouldn't help him here.

Iron. He'd only experienced it once before, but back then he'd surrendered to it. He hadn't wanted to escape and thus hadn't suffered the repercussions of trying.

Rion drew in another breath, attempting to steady his shaking body. Gods, how long had it been since he'd eaten? His stomach clenched and his body felt slimmer somehow.

The individual stepped forward, but the light was only a few feet off the ground. He squinted past the flame—a child.

Rion stared at her matted brown hair and the look of sheer terror in her dull blue eyes. Her clothes, a too big tunic and torn shorts, were dirty and riddled with holes.

She stood there, unmoving, studying him as she worried her lower lip. Rion wondered if she'd chew right through it, but the child finally set the candle—no, oil lamp—on the damp stone in the doorway.

Rion scented the air. She reeked, though he probably didn't smell much better. This wasn't a youngling of pure blood. She was a halfbreed. A glint of metal revealed the shackles around her wrists. A slave.

Arianna definitely wasn't responsible for his capture, which meant she was likely looking for him. Or he hoped she was looking for him.

After what he'd done, he couldn't fault her if she wasn't.

The girl retreated into the hall only to emerge balancing a tray in one hand and a stool in the other. She let the stool clatter to the ground then set the tray beside it. Rion spotted a bowl full of an unidentifiable white substance, a cup that he prayed contained water, and what appeared to be a block of moldy cheese.

She approached him slowly and placed the stool close before darting back. She was going to feed him, he realized with a start. Maybe whoever had confined him here didn't trust Rion with a utensil. Or wanted to see if he'd lash out at a child. Or maybe they didn't care either way.

She grabbed the bowl and slowly crawled onto the stool. The girl wouldn't meet his gaze and her hands trembled as she offered him a spoonful of the foul looking mush. Rion's stomach rolled and he turned away.

The girl drew back and her lower lip wobbled. "Please," she rasped, her voice frail. "He'll punish me if you don't."

Punish her. Of course they would. This was one of the many reasons Arianna wanted to outlaw slavery. Rion's anger flared and the girl almost fell off the stool in an effort to put space between them. His heart tugged for the child and he tried to calm himself.

"Water." His voice cracked.

The way she moved reminded Rion of a rodent trying to flee from a cat. She grabbed the cup and he licked his lips but couldn't wet them. Rion knew the water was likely laced with something unpleasant. Something that would send him back to that state of delirium, but he was so thirsty that he didn't care.

She pressed the cup to his lips. The water was old and stale and he tried not to shrink back from the tiny things that seemed to be wriggling against his tongue.

It spilled down his front and the little girl gasped. She scrambled away as if he might strike out.

He needed more, so much more. Rion finally cleared his throat, but it was raw. "You don't have to be afraid of me," he said when he caught his breath. Gods, why was he so tired?

"You won't tell him I spilled it?"

He barely had the energy to look at her. "I'm his prisoner too, why would I tell him anything?"

She twisted the fabric of her filthy shirt. "The others do."

Him. Others. Rion tucked the information away.

"Can you get the key?" he asked, signaling to his chains.

She shook her head and offered the mysterious mush to him again. Rion took the spoonful and struggled not to gag when the cold, chunky half-solid hit his tongue. He swallowed quickly.

"How many others are there?"

"I—I don't know."

"It's okay," he assured in a gentle tone. He couldn't push her, not yet. He'd get the information he needed. And when he found a way out, he was taking this child with him and annihilating whoever had dared to lay a finger on her.

CHAPTER SIXTY-FOUR

TALON

Arianna joined them for breakfast. She was finally getting out of her room, though he hated how much time she spent in Niall's company. Niall was a male with an agenda. He was the one who was prophesied to rule the continent at Arianna's side. Now with Rion out of the picture, he seemed inclined to spend every waking moment with their queen.

But should that bother him? The Lord of Pádraigín was said to be her mate. Could Talon blame the male for wanting to get to know her?

He supposed not, but he didn't want anyone taking advantage of his friend in her fragile state. She'd locked herself in her room for weeks. She needed time to process and plan her next moves without the influence of others.

Talon stood when she entered the room. Arianna stared at the table laden with an assortment of breakfast foods. Familiar pain flashed across her features.

Somehow Ellie was always one step ahead.

She had removed Rion's usual chair and had replaced it with her own. Kirian sat beside Ellie as he always did, and if Talon read the room correctly, he was to sit at her opposite side.

Arianna hadn't moved from the doorway.

For a moment, Talon thought she might retreat back to her room, skip breakfast altogether, which wasn't the best of ideas considering how thin she'd become. She needed to eat. She needed to train and move and have a purpose.

"I think Ellie has some news," Talon offered, hoping the way Ellie was fidgeting meant she'd gotten the information she needed from Gavin. It worked. Light stuttered to life in those blue eyes and she joined them at the table. Talon didn't wait for her to serve herself. He filled a plate with all of Arianna's favorite things and set it before her.

"You didn't have to do that," she said, but set to slowly chewing a piece of cheese.

Talon filled his own plate and seated himself at her side. "It's nothing."

Ellie was oddly quiet and stared at her empty plate. Talon suddenly noticed her tense shoulders and the way Kirian sat with his hands in his lap, strangely avoiding Ellie's gaze. Were they arguing?

Talon cleared his throat. "Did you find anything?"

It took a long moment for Ellie to register that Talon had addressed her. Ellie's face flushed and anger rolled through her body. "I don't want to talk about it."

Arianna furrowed her brow. "Did he tell you anything?"

Ellie clenched her fists. "Nothing that will help us."

"What does that mean?" Talon asked.

"It means he's a racist, arrogant ass that I never want to hear from again."

Talon reassessed Kirian's discomfort. Gavin must have said something about her relationship with the half-breed, but Talon didn't understand the anger. She'd dealt with nasty comments just fine in Levea and had put individuals who were centuries older in their place. She hadn't even backed down from her father.

Ellie withdrew a paper from her pocket and tossed it to Arianna. She grabbed it and Talon leaned over to read a single sentence.

He's watching.

"Who is this from?" Talon asked.

"The arrogant ass."

"This is it? That's all he gave you?"

Ellie relaxed her hands and took a steadying breath. "Yes, now can we move on please?"

"No," Talon said. "He was supposed to be our lead. I thought you said—"

"Talon," Ellie warned and he followed her gaze to Arianna. Her face was grave and some of the color had faded from her eyes. "I was wrong. We have to try something else."

Something else? What else was there to try? Saoirse had a team of her best warriors searching for her brother around the clock. Talon took shifts with those from Móirín and Niall claimed to have sent a few of his warriors out as well, though Talon wasn't sure if he trusted the male's claim. With Rion gone, Niall had Arianna all to himself; he didn't exactly have a lot of motivation to find her mate. Pseudo bond or no.

Rion had to be out there somewhere. It wasn't like someone could just disappear.

Arianna stood, her breakfast mostly untouched, and left without a word. His heart plummeted. She was a female without her mate. A soul in the world that had lost half of herself.

Talon had never been religious and sometimes he wondered if the gods reached down to help them at all, or if they sat on their grand thrones in the sky and laughed at the misery of their subjects.

Chapter Sixty-Five

Arianna

Arianna paused in her doorway and stared at the folded letter resting on the floor. Arianna glanced up and down the hall once and spotted Raevina regarding her cooly from the other end. The female had brought her own guards to stand beside those from Móirín. No one entered the hall or left without Raevina's permission. Had she seen the one responsible for the note?

Arianna entered her room and picked up the folded letter with trembling hands.

I'm looking. Don't give up hope.

Was this from Gavin? It certainly looked like his handwriting. *Don't give up hope.*

She was trying, but every day was harder than the last. Arianna gritted her teeth, fighting back tears, clenched the paper in her hands, then marched from her room and straight to Raevina. The female stood straighter at her approach, if such a thing were possible. "Did someone pass by my room this morning?"

"Not that I'm aware." Her gaze drifted toward those who'd been stationed to stand guard while she was at breakfast. They shook their heads, not needing Raevina to repeat the question.

Raevina gripped the hilt of her sword. "Is there someone in your room?"

Arianna quickly shook her head. "No, no, I just thought—"

"Best if I have a look, just in case. Don't write off a gut feeling."

Arianna nodded, thankful for the female's help, and followed her to the doorway. Raevina searched her closet, the bathroom, beneath the bed, and even along the walls as if someone could be hiding in the shadows. Which, in Fiadh's case, she supposed they might be.

"All clear." She scented the air again. "Though it smells a bit like Pádraigín's magic in here. Perhaps we should move you to another room, just to be safe."

Arianna shook her head. "No, I'm sure everything is fine." She clutched the note in her hand, hoping she wasn't giving herself away.

"You're hiding something."

Arianna's face heated. "It's nothing, really."

Raevina's brows pulled together. "I want to protect you, but to do that, I need to know everything that might put you in danger."

"It's not dangerous," Arianna promised.

"You're absolutely sure?"

"Yes." Raevina scanned her a final time before walking toward the door. "I really am here to help you, my lady. Please don't hesitate to ask for my assistance."

Arianna sighed, closed her door, then waited for the female's footsteps to echo back down the hall before she pulled the piece of paper from her pocket again. Gavin. He'd pledged himself to her in the council room, right in front of everyone, yet something had happened between him and Ellie.

He's watching.

I'm looking.

Who was watching and what was he looking for? Rion? Could she trust Gavin to help her? And if he didn't know Rion's exact location, did he at least know who might be responsible for taking him? Could he confirm that Rion *had* been taken?

As much as she wanted to seek Gavin out, Arianna realized he was warning her. And if she raised suspicion, she could very well be killing Rion in the process.

So now she just had to wait and hope and pray that a stranger she barely knew would give her the information she needed to find Rion before it was too late.

ARIANNA STOOD in the gardens and gazed up into the night sky, watching the stars twinkle against the black void overhead. She wondered if Rion stared at the same sky and how he was faring. He was still silent. So still and silent. She thought she'd felt a flicker of him earlier that day, but when she'd searched the bond, there had been nothing.

She needed him. Gods, she needed him and she didn't understand why she had cowered in her room for so long. She had let herself waste away. Allowed her body to fatigue and had wasted valuable time that could have been spent searching for her mate.

Arianna glanced at her arm and the scar that had formed. She could still recall the pain and the way the snap had rippled through her entire body. It still ached even now.

Looking back, Arianna recognized she could have fought against him, maybe even prevented some of the damage, but she hadn't thought to defend herself at all. Because she never imagined in a million lifetimes that Rion could hurt her.

Her heart quickened at the memory and Arianna forced it away, clearing her thoughts. She feared how she might react upon seeing him again. The mere thought of her bone breaking sent distress coursing through her anew. Would she be scared of him? Would she run into his arms or hesitate? And how was he feeling about the whole situation?

Terrible, she presumed, but she didn't really know, wouldn't know until he wakened from the other side of the bond.

"Can't sleep?" Niall's voice floated from behind and Arianna turned slightly to lock eyes with Raevina and Talon. They stood at opposite ends and often avoided conversation. She couldn't fathom why, especially when Ellie mentioned they'd danced with one another at the ball. Maybe things hadn't gone well after that.

Arianna nodded toward the pair, indicating all was well.

"I don't sleep too much anymore," she admitted.

"Raevina seems to have taken a liking to you."

Arianna followed his gaze before turning back to the sky. "That tends to happen when I heal people."

He chuckled. "Yes, I suppose it would." Silence fell between them. "Worried for your mate?"

"Pseudo mate, according to you and everyone else here."

Niall grimaced. "I'm sorry if that upsets you."

Arianna sighed and ran a hand over her face. "No, I apologize, I didn't mean to snap." She was so tired, but Niall had helped her the other day by locating the books she needed. He'd even sat with her and coaxed her into eating. He was the last person she needed to be snapping at.

"You're very kind," Niall said. "You have an intense loyalty toward your friends. Your subjects—at least those within the manor—have taken note of it." He smiled. "I'd venture to say you'd be worried if any of them disappeared. It's a good trait to possess as a queen."

"They're probably happy he's gone."

"They're not happy to see you so distressed and neither am I. Your arrival is meant to be a joyous occasion, and it seems there's been sadness thrown into the mix at every turn." She recoiled slightly when he brushed a strand of hair from her face.

Niall's voice lowered. "You should be picking out decorations for your coronation and trying on dresses. You should be tasting wine and visiting with those who run the vineyards. You should be swapping your ideas with the council, as you used to, and helping to usher this continent toward an era of peace." His brows softened. "Your absence has been noted and you are sorely missed."

"I've heard the rumors. Are they really rioting?"

He sighed and looked away. "We expected resistance. It's inevitable where change is concerned, but I'll admit, it's a bit more than I'd anticipated."

"What can we do to fix it?"

"You could make a public appearance."

"I thought that was dangerous."

"It is, but I'll be with you and we'll be ready should things go astray. In different circumstances, I'd be against it, especially with what happened last time, but I think the people need to see their queen." He smiled again, this one fuller. "They need a face to worship instead of words on a paper."

Her lip quivered. "How am I supposed to celebrate or do anything of consequence knowing he's out there, likely hurt and in need of help? What am I—" Her throat tightened and Arianna's voice cracked. "What do I do if the bond snaps completely?"

Niall caught the tear that rolled down her cheek and his hand lingered, rubbing against the side of her face. She wouldn't meet his gaze. Part of her wanted to pull away, but another part coaxed her to linger.

"Look at me." She obeyed. "You push on. You rest in the knowledge that you are doing everything you can, and others are doing the same. You do the things you originally set out to do and no matter what, you never give up." He offered a gentle smile. "And know that if you ever need someone to talk to, I'll be right here."

Arianna stepped out of his reach and crossed her arms over her chest. "How are you okay with any of this?"

"With your desire for another male, you mean?" She nodded. "The bond hasn't made itself known to me. I might be less inclined to be so . . . patient if it had, but I'd still try. The fact of the matter is that you don't know me well enough. You've been thrust into a new world full of strangers, and a few months isn't enough time to form any sort of bond." He leaned against the balcony and clasped his hands together. "Though I'd like it very much if we could be friends."

"I think I'd like that."

"Shall we exchange favorite colors then? Books? Music?"

"I didn't think the Regent had time for things like that."

"My Lady, I will always make time for you."

Arianna surveyed the dark garden. "I want to do more for the people, but I don't think I'm ready to tour the country yet. I need to be here in case any news shows up. But I do want to help."

"Fair enough." He seemed to think, gazing at the stars the entire time. "I know it might prove painful, but we could proceed with your coronation. That would allow the leaders to gather and news to spread through the papers. It would give the people something to look forward to."

A gentle breeze blew through the area and her head swam. Niall allowed her to stand in comfortable silence. The coronation. She had wanted Rion present for it, to see his smiling face as she marched down the aisle and was officially crowned queen.

But Rion wasn't here and she didn't know when they would find him. Soon. Gods, she prayed it was soon. But what if it wasn't? What if she went weeks, months, years searching for him? Would she make the slaves wait that long? Would Zylah forgive her if she did?

Zylah. Why had she not thought about her friend until now? Was the female doing okay with the arrangements of the former slaves? Was the transition to a paid role going smoothly, or had it all crumbled in on itself? And what about the children across the continent? Were some free and others not? Had the council appointed someone to enforce her new law or were they waiting on her, not daring to act until she gave confirmation?

"I'll do it," she finally said.

"You're certain?"

Arianna nodded. "You're right. I can't just sit around and do nothing. Everyone is searching for Rion and in the meantime, I will do my part for the people."

Niall shook his head, but a smile still graced his features. "Every day I have to remind myself of your youth, and every day you prove you're just as capable as someone ten times your age." He eyed her. "The gods chose their queen well."

Arianna flushed. "Most of the time I feel like I'm in over my head."

"Don't worry," he said. "I won't let you drown."

She smirked. "Not sure someone from Móirín could drown."

"Good point." He turned to face her again. "I have my warriors out searching for him as well."

"You do?" She searched for the lie and didn't find one.

"That surprises you?"

Arianna studied a couple strolling through the gardens. "Without him, no one stands in your way."

"Without him, you're unhappy. And your sister is still a barricade I have yet to break through."

Arianna laughed. "She just doesn't trust strangers."

"I see."

"You're not the one who took him?"

"Are you accusing me?"

Arianna stared at her clenched hands. "Without Rion, I'd be more inclined to lean on you. Trust you."

"And what would that trust amount to if you discovered such actions? After centuries of waiting, what's a few more decades if need be?"

She finally looked up. "Friends, then?"

Niall smiled again. "Friends. Though if you ever decide you want more," he kissed the back of her hand and his heated gaze twisted her stomach. "Know I'm already yours."

Chapter Sixty-Six

Rion

A female's high pitched scream echoed through the walls over and over and over again. Rion could hear her chains rattle and swore he heard a male's voice laughing. He tried to scent the male, to identify his captor, but whoever it was didn't feel the need to visit him yet. Maybe he never would. Maybe his captor's goal was to leave him here to starve to death or die of dehydration.

Rion licked his parched lips and a shiver ran down his spine when the female screamed again. He wondered how long she'd been here and what kind of horrors she was facing.

The girl who'd given him food and water hadn't visited today or yesterday. He knew it was because their captor was present. Either he'd beaten her so hard that she couldn't fulfill her duties or he'd commanded her against it.

Rion still didn't know how long he'd been here. He would ask the next time he saw the girl, maybe even inquire about the female's wellbeing. Perhaps he could get them both out if fate allowed it.

Fate. It had trapped him here against his will and Rion had no way of escape. The chains were too sturdy, his body was too weak, and the girl was too afraid of her master. He wasn't sure what options he had now. He supposed he could pray for a miracle, but the gods had never answered him before.

Rion waited by the bond with fear and trepidation. Three strands. That's all they had left. Three little pulses of life that told him his mate still sat at the other end.

She didn't stir and he still refused to touch them, afraid they'd snap with the slightest amount of pressure. He just needed to know she was there. He wouldn't survive the visions otherwise.

Time passed. Sometimes his arms were loose, hanging free at his sides; other times they were above his head and Rion swore his shoulders would be ripped from their sockets. His vision blurred and heat rose through him, flooding his body in agonizing waves. He tried to lick his dry lips to no avail and struggled against the haze forming behind his eyes.

Dying. He was dying.

He needed water, food, rest, heat. Anything. He'd gladly take anything.

The door hinges squeaked, but Rion couldn't open his eyes to see who had entered. His arms were overhead again, joints pulled tight. His head pounded. His ears rang, then a cool cup met his lips.

Rion all but lunged toward the lukewarm liquid, taking large gulps without caring what he might be drinking. He pulled at the chains, wishing for the freedom to yank the cup from the bearer's hand.

His stomach churned and Rion gasped when the last of the liquid ran down his throat. He needed more. So much more.

Then, by some miraculous blessing, the cup found him again. Rion drank it down greedily. She offered again. And again. Maybe the gods were watching after all.

Rion finally opened his eyes to find the girl staring at him, holding the cup between her small hands. The oil lamp burned in the doorway as it had last time, and it cast a wide shadow over her frail form.

Bruises lined her jaw and her left eye was swollen shut. He clenched his fists but tried to keep his anger at bay this time. He didn't want to frighten her.

"Hi," he managed in a weak voice, but the girl still jumped. She stared another moment, then reached for something on the tray and scrambled up on the stool to offer it to him. Bread.

"It'll help you hold down the water," she said. Rion took a few bites and she backed away again, still staring. "You didn't tell him."

Rion raised a brow. "Didn't tell him what?"

"That I spilled the water."

"He didn't visit me."

"Oh."

"But I wouldn't have said anything."

She twisted her bare foot in the dirt on the floor. Did he not give her shoes either? "Do you want some more water?"

"Please." The girl ran from his cell and returned a moment later. "He won't be back for a while."

"How do you know?"

"He said so. I have to ration the food when he leaves, but sometimes it still isn't enough. I don't think he cares."

Rion cleared his throat. "I heard someone screaming."

She eyed the cup. "He calls her his favorite. She's down the hall."

"How long has she been here?"

"I don't know. A lot longer than you."

"How long have I been here?"

The girl paused to think. "A few weeks, I think."

His heart stuttered. A few weeks? Weeks? His breath turned ragged. He'd thought a few days maybe, but *weeks*? Gods, what was Arianna thinking right now?

The girl backed away, but Rion couldn't calm his racing heart. "Don't go."

"I shouldn't be in here too long. I'll get in trouble."

"I won't tell," Rion promised, desperate to glean any information from her that he could. "Does he let you go outside?" She shook her head and stepped back. "Do you know where we are?" Another step. Shit, he was scaring her. Her eyes had gone wide, but before he could ask anything else, she closed the door and left Rion in the dark.

Weeks. Rion returned to the bond, examining it. His body shook. He could feel Arianna on the other end, almost as if she were breathing. He wanted to reach out, needed to know if she was okay, but—what if she rejected him? What if he touched that strand and it snapped? What if they all snapped because she wanted nothing more to do with him?

No. No, she'd told him to run. The bond was still there, even if it was weak. She wanted him.

His body trembled and his fear almost won out, but Rion carefully reached out a tentative hand and ran invisible fingers down one of the frayed strands. Just the ghost of a touch lest the strain prove too much.

Desperation flooded his body. Her desperation. A plea. A calling. Tears rolled down Rion's face when her essence flooded that little space tethering them together. Her worry engulfed him and he knew for certain then that she wasn't responsible for his capture. Of course she wasn't. She'd never condone imprisonment like this.

He wished he could feel more, but the weakened bond wouldn't allow it. He could do nothing aside from attempt to send feelings of reassurance. Her questions, however, bombarded him.

Where are you?

Why haven't you come back to me?

Are you okay?

I don't know, he wanted to say. *I wish I could and no, I'm not okay.* Not in the slightest. Because he'd hurt his mate and he wanted to fall to his knees before her and beg for her forgiveness.

But he couldn't say any of those things.

THE DOOR opened again hours later. Or what seemed like hours. The girl stood there, looking at him with a wary expression. She carried another tray and more water.

"I thought you might still be thirsty."

"I am," he said, determined to keep his emotions in check. Arianna hadn't stopped prodding him, but he didn't know what else to do aside from bask in her presence. He was powerless. Maybe the iron prevented him from sending anything her way. He wasn't sure whether it affected bonds or not.

The girl dragged the stool over. He needed to be careful. Make this child trust him before asking anything that might make her run away again. Rion decided to start with something easy. "How is the female?"

The girl lowered her eyes. "She's okay, but I couldn't get her to eat." He wondered if the female conversed with her as well. Maybe she hadn't today and that's why the child had returned so soon.

"How long have you been here?" She shrugged. "Do you know how old you are?" The girl shook her head and Rion had to rein in his anger. *Calm.* He tilted his head. "I'd say you're probably eight or nine."

"You think so?"

He shrugged as best he could. "We can pretend you are."

She offered him a rare smile. "When do you think my birthday is?"

Her excitement surprised him. "That depends. What's your name?"

"Kaylee."

Rion made a show of thinking. "Kaylee," he repeated, then examined her dark hair and eyes. "Let's say March eleventh?"

Her smile could have lit up the universe and he wondered how long it had been since she'd smiled at all.

"When is yours?" she asked.

"October twenty-fourth."

"That's a long time away, isn't it?" He nodded. "And how old are you? What's your name?"

"Ninety-three. And Rion."

Her mouth gaped. "Wow, you must have seen so much outside." He rotated his aching wrists. "Can you tell me about it?"

"You've never been outside?"

She examined the cup. "He lets me go to the surface sometimes, but he doesn't like me doing it much and I get in trouble if I try to sneak out." She wrinkled her nose. "It stinks out there."

"What does it smell like?"

"The fireplace after it's burned. It looks like it, too." Her head shot up. "I once found a book and all the trees inside were painted green." She wrinkled her nose. "The ones around here are all black."

So they were underground and whoever had trapped them had also burnt the area. Hiding their scents, he realized. Shit. That meant there wouldn't be any landmarks either.

"Where do you go when you sneak out?" he asked carefully.

"No where, I just like to look at the sky."

"Are there any towns nearby?"

She shrugged. "I don't know. He said the hounds will get me if I go too far. I saw one once. It was super scary and I didn't go outside for a long time after that."

Hounds. Great. Something else he'd have to deal with when he escaped.

She sat. "Will you tell me what it looks like? Outside?" she clarified.

"Can I have more water first?" The child jumped to her feet and raced from the room. The pounding in his head had started to subside and his senses were returning.

After he'd drank three more cups, Rion tilted his head back.

"Better?" she asked.

"Much. Are you allowed to take all the water you want?"

She nodded. "There's a well."

"I see." Her eyes were expectant. "What do you want to know?"

She thought for a few moments and Rion swore he could visualize tiny gears moving in her head. "Forests," she finally said.

His heart ached for her. She'd likely been here her entire life, confined to the dark walls of this prison. She'd never known the joy of sunshine or felt the cool breeze hit her face. Hell, she'd likely never seen a flower or played with other children. Damn her captor. Damn that male to the deepest level of hell.

Rion began recounting every detail, down to the tiny insects that lived within the barks of trees. He told her about his home country and how the residents all lived as one with nature. Her eyes lit up when he mentioned the three hundred-foot trees that surrounded the main city and she asked a million questions, constantly interrupting as if her brain couldn't absorb the knowledge fast enough. Then Rion made a promise: If he ever got out of these chains, he would ensure she escaped these bland walls and he'd show her the beautiful city of Nàdiar himself.

CHAPTER SIXTY-SEVEN

ARIANNA

Arianna sat before the council members and shifted uncomfortably in her seat. She hadn't been here since the incident with Rion and their stares were doing nothing for her nerves. All carried questions in their gazes, but none of them dared voice their concerns. She wondered if Niall had a hand in that.

He'd been more than ecstatic to have her join him, even if he seemed a bit wary that the task might prove too much. But just as she'd said before, she wanted to help. That was the entire reason she'd come to Ruadhán, to help those in need.

Ellie sat in today, mostly because her sister refused to leave her side and Talon was present as well, standing behind her chair.

Declan cleared his throat and looked between her and Niall. "What are we to discuss today, My Lord?"

"Everything," Niall said. "There's no reason to hide anything from Arianna. If she decides the information is too much, she needs not push herself." He eyed her again and offered a gentle smile.

The council glanced among themselves, but picked up their papers and began.

Two months had erupted into pure chaos. Her stomach twisted at the thought. They'd sent as many teams out as they could to help manage the situation, but while some cities had readily agreed to end slavery with children, others were capturing those who had been freed and slaughtering them, claiming they wouldn't have humans roaming their streets without a master.

Children. These were children and mothers. People who couldn't defend themselves. Arianna hadn't even demanded the freedom of adults yet and already the Fae were striking out.

Her father, the High Lord of Móirín was doing everything in his power to take in those displaced, as was Alec, the High Lord of Brónach. Fiadh's High Lord had burned those longing for freedom at the stake then had dumped their bodies along the road to send a clear message. Pádraigín seemed quiet about the situation, neither complying nor standing against it.

But while Brónach had their main cities under control, there were smaller villages and towns that had taken matters into their own hands. The situation was dire in many cases, with citizens refusing to pay taxes. One city was even attempting to separate themselves into their own nation.

All over children. Her stomach rolled and Niall glanced at her before continuing. "I'll leave to visit with the council in Pádraigín soon and set things straight. It's important we stand as a united front on this matter, even if things seem dire. We'll continue to provide aid wherever we can and use the Queen's money to fund the events." He glanced at her. "If that is still acceptable to her?"

"A-Absolutely." Maybe Niall was right. Maybe she did need to make a public appearance to sooth the masses. She could take Talon and Raevina, not to mention Niall and his seasoned warriors, to protect her. They could—breath left her when she felt Rion's silent caress, so tentative, so gentle and yielding. Arianna grabbed at the threads and pulled him as close as was possible.

Those in the room had fallen silent. Arianna hadn't realized she'd jumped to her feet.

Her hands were shaking. "He's there. He's alive. He's—" Arianna stopped herself and glanced around at the council members, then to Niall and her sister. "Rion," she said simply. "He's there."

"Is he okay?" Ellie was on her feet, their meeting forgotten.

"I don't know." She tried to study the bond. "He feels so far away. The bond's so weak." Or maybe he was.

"Can you tell where he is?" Niall asked, but something in his gaze told her he wasn't happy. Not really.

"No." Her hope faded and she tried to send a million questions down the bond. She needed to know where he was and if he needed help, but he didn't answer. He just kept holding on and caressing that single strand. Tears welled in her eyes. "I'm sorry, I have to go."

"My Lady," Declan said. "We still have—"

Niall held up a hand and the male fell silent. Niall turned to her. "Take all the time you need. We'll finish up here."

Ellie followed her into the hall with Talon's footsteps close behind. She could hear both of their heartbeats. Feel their excitement. Arianna didn't know where she was going, not until she found herself in front of her room.

"What do we do?" Ellie asked. "Can he tell you anything?"

Arianna tried to focus on the bond again. She sent him more questions, but it didn't feel as if he received them and Arianna's new found hope flickered away. She could feel her mate, but it changed nothing. Her stomach soured. They couldn't communicate. She still had no way to find him.

"Hey." Ellie rubbed her back. "It's all right, we'll figure it out. Can you feel where the bond is coming from?"

Arianna tried to focus again, but a lump formed in her throat. "No. I can't. I can't sense anything." Arianna felt her face drain of color. "He's scared, Ellie. And I think he's hurt and I can't do anything to help him."

Her hands shook but her sister took them and squeezed. "It's okay, we'll find him. He's alive and he finally answered."

Arianna's earlier panic rose though, billowing through her like smoke. "They saw him. Everyone saw what he did. How am I supposed to convince anyone that he didn't mean it?" Her throat burned with unshed tears. "Gods, Ellie, they already viewed him as a monster before. What are they going to think now? They're not even going to let him back into the city."

Ellie rubbed her shoulders. "Shh, it's okay, calm down. The first thing we need to focus on is finding him. Even if he comes back in irons and has to sit in a prison cell, at least you'll know where he is."

"He will not sit in a cell," Arianna seethed, anger rising at the horrid idea.

"I know, I know, but you can't break down again. We need you. Your tie to him might be the only thing that helps us find him."

Someone had him. Someone was hurting him and there was absolutely nothing she could do to stop it.

Anger burst through her anew. She was done waiting. Done sitting around. Arianna needed to find her mate and she needed to find him now.

"Where is Gavin?"

TWO DAYS later Gavin returned and Arianna stalked through the manor with Ellie, Talon, and Raevina trailing behind her. She didn't care that they drew the stares of almost everyone they passed. She didn't care what rumors would start or how the council and Niall felt about it. She was done being helpless and pathetic.

Somehow, it felt as though a veil had lifted from her shoulders. Like her pain and grief had faded entirely, or maybe her anger had burned it away.

It was stupid. So selfish of her to simply lie around for all those weeks when her mate was somewhere hurt and battered. She could feel it from him. The fear. The uncertainty. And his sorrow. Such deep, deep sorrow that her bones hurt down to the marrow.

Arianna scented Gavin in the gardens. Thank gods for that. She stormed through the hedges, winding down the path to find the docile, light-hearted male picking through some of the flowers. He clutched a few in one hand and turned at her approach.

Surprise lit his features and his gaze briefly flickered toward Ellie before refocusing on Arianna. He bowed at the waist. She kept marching and it wasn't until she was almost upon him that he tried to step back. Arianna grabbed him by the collar of his shirt and slammed his body against one of the stone pillars. It cracked and water spilled from one side.

Gavin's eyes went wide. "My Lady," his voice shook, hands splayed out to either side of his head and flowers forgotten as they floated to the path. Ellie stood at her side, but Talon and Ravina had taken up stances at either end of the hedges.

"Enough with the notes." Arianna growled. "Where is he?"

"I don't know what—"

She gripped his shirt tighter. "You said you were looking. What did you find?"

His voice lowered. "Shh, you don't understand. I can't tell you anything—" The ancient thing in her pulsed and ice crawled across Arianna's hand. It coated his jacket first and spread along his tunic, moving with quickening speed until it seeped through his shirt and onto his skin.

Gavin shivered, his voice forgotten until he turned to Ellie. "Are you just going to let her do this to me?"

"That depends. Are you going to tell us where Rion is?"

"I already told you, I can't," he hissed, his entire focus now on her sister. "He'll know."

Ellie watched the ice. "Then I guess this garden is about to have another statue."

He gaped, looked between them again, and kept his voice low despite the desperation in his eyes. "Fine, fine, but it has to be tonight, otherwise—"

"No," Arianna said, slamming his head against the stone again. "Now. You will tell me right now."

Gavin tried to look around. His gaze went to the balconies first, as if he could see everyone who stood upon them, but Arianna drew his attention back with a low growl. "Now," she reiterated.

"I found a map," Gavin finally said. "It's vague, but I recognized some points laid out. Just north west of here, there's a section of land that's been charred by repeated fires. Most say they spring up because the air is so dry, but it's really just a front for an underground prison. I think Rion is there, but I can't be sure, so I didn't want to say anything."

"And whose prison is it?"

Gavin looked between her and Ellie. "I thought you already knew." His gaze traveled back to the balcony and her frustration spiked again. "Niall," he whispered. "He's had you glamoured since you arrived."

CHAPTER SIXTY-EIGHT

RION

The keys jingled, the lock twisted, then Rion lifted his head. The male's scent hit him first and every hair on Rion's body stood on end. Pure hatred burned through Rion's veins like wildfire and a low growl escaped his lips.

Kaylee followed behind him, carrying an oil lantern. She set it toward the center of the room then backed away, her head low.

"Leave us," the male's voice echoed through the tiny cell and Kaylee scrambled away, her body so full of fear.

"You," Rion seethed. Anger boiled in his veins, seeking some sort of release. Had Rion been able to reach for his magic, he would have torn this male in half right then.

"Me," Niall echoed, a smile plastered across his face. The shadows danced over his angular features. "How's the iron treating you?"

Rion's only answer was a resounding snarl.

Niall clicked his tongue and picked up the oil lamp. "That's no way to greet me." He carried it to the edge of the room and lit a brazier that Rion hadn't seen before. Rion turned away from the glaring light, his eyes burning. Niall moved to light the other one, then blew out the small flame.

Then Rion saw it, the contraption above his head that held the chains in place. Several anchors were bolted into the ceiling and his chains slid between each. They stretched all the way through a hole in the wall that was just wide enough for the links to fit through. He imagined a lever and crank sat on the other side of the stone. If he could break it—

"Don't bother," Niall said. "I've had a hundred prisoners in here before you and every single one of them has tried. No one ever succeeds."

"And where are they now?"

Niall shrugged. "At the bottom of one lake or another."

Rion ground his teeth, but Niall's disturbing smirk didn't vanish as he prowled closer. If Rion had been able to lift his legs, he would have wrapped them around the male's neck and snapped it without a second thought. But the chains around his ankles weren't nearly long enough.

Niall drew back and planted a hard fist in Rion's gut. Damn him. Damn this male and all his scheming and plotting.

Rion slammed his body against the chains, pulling and screaming as hard and loud as he could. He yanked at his magic, determined to break through, but an electrical current surged through him, matching his strength.

Rion screamed again before collapsing, breathless.

Niall laughed. "Never been in irons before, have you? Oh wait, you have. Though I'm glad Avalon didn't finish the job. It would have removed the best piece on the playing board."

"Do you fight any of your battles or do you only beat those already down?"

Fast as lightning, Niall had Rion's face in a steel grip. "I fight those I need to and render the rest useless." Niall released his grip and Rion worked his jaw.

"Does Arianna know I'm here?"

Another wicked smile. "Would that cause you more pain or less?"

Rion didn't answer.

Niall stepped back and rolled up his sleeves. "She doesn't. No one aside from my closest advisors know about this place. Sorry if you expected a rescue. It won't be coming."

"Why am I here?"

"I think you mean to ask why are you still alive?" He leaned against the far wall and crossed his arms. "I don't like killing things I can play with." He smirked. "It irks my father to no end."

"She'll look for me."

Niall shrugged as if the knowledge had no effect on him. "Maybe she will, maybe she won't. She won't find you, of course, even if she does break my spell."

Rion clenched his fists. "What did you do to her?"

"Nothing of consequence. I just amplified her grief a bit, made the idea of finding you seem impossible. Emotions are quite easy to manipulate, especially when I've already been in someone's head. They hardly notice the prod."

"She'll break it." She had already reached out to him. She wanted to find him.

Again, Niall shrugged. "Doesn't matter if she does. She still won't find you. And with the distance and heartache, it's only a matter of time before the bond breaks entirely. Quite a number you did on that, by the way."

"Because of you."

Niall touched his chest as if Rion had given him a complement. "Clever, wouldn't you agree? Oh, the tragedy of turning a mated pair against one another before the bond has solidified."

"You're sick."

Niall's face hardened. "Maybe so, but the throne is mine, and someone like you isn't going to stand in my way."

"She'll never trust you."

"No?" He leaned forward. "Funny you should suggest such a thing, considering I was the only one who could pull her out of her room. She's been in there for two months and the poor thing was withering away. I couldn't have that, of course."

Rion froze. His stomach turned upside down and panic flew through his core.

Two month? Not weeks, months.

Niall turned to him. "Something I say shock you? The poor thing even confided in me the other night. After a careful talk and some well-placed feelings on my part, she even volunteered to do the coronation. She really is quite brilliant, thank the gods. I don't know if I could have dealt with being married to a child for the rest of my years."

"She will never marry you."

Niall smiled again. "Oh, she will. You see, unlike you, I've been alive for a very, very long time and in my position I've come to learn exactly how others think, especially young females. You don't think she'll grow lonely while she searches for you? You don't think she'll look for someone to lean on? And who better than the male who goes out of his way to please her at every turn? Eventually, she'll also want to please me. Of course, a little persuasion goes a long way, too."

"You keep your hands off her."

Niall stood so close now that Rion could see the sharp glint in his eyes. "Don't worry. I'll keep you up to date on everything I do with your mate," he spit the word. Rion's eyes flew wide. "Oh, were you starting to believe the pseudo bond façade, too? I'm honestly a bit disappointed."

Rion snapped his teeth and yanked at the chains overhead. Niall stepped back, eyeing the male before him as if he were a toy. "Now, let's get on to the fun part." He moved faster than the wind itself, then a blade sank deep into Rion's gut.

VISIONS SWAM through Rion's mind. Visions of his past, his future, things that were and things that had never been. But they were getting harder to discern, harder to predict, and he struggled to ground himself.

Images of Arianna happy with another male. Images of her angry, standing over his body with a weapon in her grasp. More images of his mother and her screaming that he was worthless and should have died at his father's hand.

They came again and again and again along with physical pain. So much searing pain that Rion was sure he should have died by now.

Darkness floated around and through him, then he heard the familiar drip, drip, drip of something hitting stone.

He'd lost track of days and time. Of minutes or seconds or hours. Rion didn't know up from down for a while, nor how long he'd suffered through Niall's gruesome torture. All he knew was that he needed to stay alive for Arianna's sake. He needed her. He needed—

"Gods, you're stubborn."

Rion didn't react to the voice. He didn't possess enough strength to even lift his head.

More images assaulted him. He felt the slap of her hand. The words that pierced his soul as she called him a monster. She didn't want him anymore. She couldn't rule with someone who'd committed so much destruction. The people hated him and after she discovered what he'd done a town over, she did, too.

No, that wasn't right. He could still feel her down the bond. Her caress. The way she begged for him.

It went silent, like a light had been flipped off.

Rion struggled then and blindly grasped for it in the dark. He was frantic, ungrounded, desperate as his hands fumbled for the threads of light and the small room that guarded them. He couldn't find it. He couldn't see.

His heart beat wildly even as more blows slammed through him.

Drip, drip, drip. All over the stone.

The bond. Arianna. *Please.*

Then something snapped and it went through him like a whip cracking against his spine. Rion broke through the veil of Niall's magic and gasped for air, yanking on his chains in anguished fury as he screamed against the severing of yet another thread.

Tears mixed with his blood and he wanted so desperately for this to end. He just wanted to see her again. To have her chase away all the horrible thoughts and dreams like she'd done for months.

He just needed her.

"You know, this would go over a lot easier if you would just let the bond go." Niall snapped his fingers. "Let it break and everything will go back to darkness. Sure, you'll still feel her—such is the curse on the male's side of things—but the rejection won't hurt as much."

No. He didn't want to let go. He didn't want *her* to let go. *Please. Please, please, please.* He wanted to make her understand, but everything was so hazy. Her emotions. His. He couldn't weed through them.

She doesn't want you, something in him whispered, but somehow Rion knew it wasn't true. That didn't stop the accompanying terror. He knew she deserved better, but he didn't *want* her to have better. He didn't want another male touching her.

But what if she did? Would he let her go? *Could* he let her go if she chose another? Females could release the bond at will, at least until it solidified. If this kept up, if Niall kept pushing, would she eventually let it fall?

Niall chewed on something and Rion's stomach knotted. "You realize she can feel everything you're feeling right?" That stopped him short. "You're making her suffer with you."

No, you're making her suffer, he wanted to scream, but couldn't. Because blood filled his mouth and coated his teeth. It trickled down his chest, leaked from his wounds, and kept up that incessant dripping onto the stone.

The cold, cold stone.

He was so cold.

"I'm growing bored," Niall said and threw down whatever he'd been holding. Rion thought he saw the glint of a blade, but before he could open his mouth, Niall had once again buried it in his side.

CHAPTER SIXTY-NINE

ARIANNA

Glamoured. The thought was outlandish and yet made so much sense that Arianna felt stupid for not realizing it sooner.

Gavin had explained that Niall glamoured the entire city to make it appear grander than it actually was. He'd claimed it was to spread news about Ruadhán's splendor so the four countries would continue to pay tribute.

Arianna wondered if Niall had ever believed The Divine might arrive or if he planned to eventually run the continent on his own, claiming his actions were what The Divine would want.

Now Gavin sat on a maroon sofa with his hands splayed out before him as he explained how they could break said glamour, or in her case, glamours.

Apparently Gavin had sensed Niall casting his magic multiple times around her, and the very thought sent anger flowing through her like molten rock.

Arianna had known about the time with the slaves, but she hadn't imagined he'd done it again. Of course he had. He'd likely controlled half of her decisions since arriving.

Arianna had offered to go first, but Raevina had cut in to test whether Gavin could be trusted. Talon had opened his mouth to protest, but one look from the female warrior had stopped her friend in his tracks.

Raevina was taking the glamour quite personally.

"You can't force it," Gavin said. "It's about reconnecting with your surroundings and how your senses absorb the world. Taste the air, feel the stool you're sitting on, look closely at the specks in the rug, and you'll feel the glamour warping your reality."

Raevina was silent only a moment before she said, "I feel it."

Well that certainly hadn't taken long. Even Talon lifted a brow in surprise.

"Now shatter it. Imagine something sharp carving right through the veil and break through."

More silence. Arianna wondered if it would be so easy. Gavin had gaped and almost scolded her upon learning she'd allowed Niall to enter her mind once. He claimed doing so allowed Niall to manipulate her more easily. Niall would be able to build upon the images he had already placed and she would be less perceptive to future magic.

Glamours even allowed Fae to lie if their magic was strong enough. Arianna clenched her fists. How many times had Niall lied to her, then?

The entire room sat pensive, waiting, then Raevina gasped and jumped back as if someone had splashed cold water over her. The female stared at the room, glancing from one corner to the other. She blinked several times, then cleared her throat and said, "That's quite—"

"Jarring, I know. The feeling will pass."

"Will he know she's free?" Talon asked, eying Raevina with something like concern.

Gavin shook his head. "Only if he tries to feed her something else and she doesn't respond."

Talon studied him. Ellie didn't move and neither did Saoirse, but when Arianna stepped forward, they all seemed to intervene at once.

"How do we know you're not going to cast anything on her?" Talon jerked his eyes toward Arianna. "She's the queen. Having her under your control might prove beneficial."

Gavin shook his head. "It doesn't work like that. It's not mind control. At least, mine isn't."

"What does that mean?"

"It means there are Fae out there who are stronger than Niall or myself. The gift evolves with age and experience." He waved a hand around the room. "The only things I'm capable of manipulating are this room and my scent," he added. "It's helped me escape a few close calls."

"With Niall?" Arianna inquired.

He nodded. "He's not as patient as he puts off. He's been known to kill any who cross him and make an example out of them while doing it."

Arianna's blood ran cold. "And you're afraid he's going to do the same to you?"

"If he finds out anything I've told you, yes, and he'll do it without hesitation."

"But I thought you two were family?"

Gavin shrugged. "Doesn't matter. Not in Pádraigín."

"Doesn't matter in Fiadh either," Raevina said. "I guess our countries have something in common after all."

Shit. Arianna had known Gavin was afraid of Niall, but she hadn't imagined the male quite so brutal. Not with everything he'd said and done. It explained why Gavin hadn't stopped trembling since they'd dragged him into the room.

Gavin had told them everything. He'd detailed his findings of the underground prison, a document he'd run across in Niall's office. Then he mentioned Niall's ruthless court and how he'd run this place for centuries and changed it in all the wrong ways.

He'd done so many things just to impress her and earn her favor. And threatened those who could expose him. Gavin included.

Gavin was trusted with a lot of information, but nothing like the secrets he'd stumbled across.

The documents listed over a hundred prisoners, mentioned slaves, and even gave coordinates across the continent. Perhaps there were other prisons. Arianna planned to find out soon enough.

She eyed Gavin. It all felt too easy. Too convenient for him to know so much and be willing to simply part with the information. He might be nervous in the room surrounded by warriors, but he wasn't afraid. Not really.

"Why help us at all?" Arianna asked.

"You're our queen," he said as if that should be explanation enough.

"Try again," Talon chimed in. "How do we know you haven't been cloaking your scent this entire time to lure us all into one of Niall's traps?"

Gavin opened his mouth to speak and something like fear flashed across his face. He didn't have a good answer for that.

Did they risk trusting him, then? Was Rion really in this prison or would Arianna find herself back in shackles by the end?

Gavin's gaze flickered toward Ellie and Arianna didn't miss the way her sister bristled at his stare. Arianna glanced between the two, but when Gavin started to speak, Ellie cut him off.

"You keep your damn mouth shut." Ellie's aggression caught her off guard and even Raevina stood straighter, one hand venturing toward her weapon.

"If they need a reason—"

"I will cram your teeth down your throat if you say one more word."

His lips snapped shut, but Talon was already processing. "What's going on?"

Ellie's face had reddened and her knuckles went white. "Nothing," she said. "He's just an arrogant ass who talks too much."

"I am not arrogant. I only meant that it's not proper for royalty to be with someone of diluted blood."

"And I told you to mind your own business."

"It is my business when—"

Ellie stood and was across the room before anyone could stop her. She grabbed Gavin's shirt and lifted him from the couch, leaving him to scramble for purchase. Talon was on her a second later, pulling Ellie back while Raevina stood over Gavin with a blade pointed at his chest. Gavin didn't move.

"Ellie," Arianna chided. "What is going on—" She looked between them again and her mouth fell open. Gavin's eyes tracked Ellie's every move as if he drank her in, even after the aggressive pass. He watched the rise and fall of Ellie's chest and something like hurt flashed across his face when she turned away.

"You love her," Arianna said. Her sister cursed and pivoted for the door.

"Where are you going?" Talon demanded.

"For a walk."

"We don't have time for that right now. He's infatuated with you, so what? We have more pressing matters."

Ellie whirled, a retort on her tongue, but her gaze drifted toward Arianna and she swallowed it back. Her little sister stared at the rug, took a long breath, and exhaled it from between clenched teeth. "Fine."

Fine must have meant she'd stay, because she didn't reach for the door. Gavin just studied his hands.

Suddenly a snap echoed through the inside of Arianna's chest so violently that it sent her to her knees. Arianna clutched her chest, fighting for breath, but she couldn't rise to her feet. Tears sprang to her eyes and another snap reverberated through her torso, slamming through her as though she were being physically assaulted.

Hands were on her back then and whispers sounded in her ear. Her stomach churned and Arianna vomited all over the rug before clutching her chest once more. Someone pulled her hair back. Another picked her up and moved her across the room.

Wave after wave of desperation and pain flew down the bond. She tried to catch her breath, but she couldn't move, could barely think.

She was breaking. The bond was breaking and she was breaking with it. Any minute now and the last thread would snap. She'd be separated from him, left with nothing but a cold place in her chest where Rion used to be.

She wouldn't survive. Not this time.

The emotions flooding through her were intense, earth-shattering, and desperately savage.

They were . . . Rion. These emotions were from Rion. She had thought their bond was too far gone to be able to sense him like this. Now she felt everything. Every. Single. Thing. The ache of hunger in his stomach. The burning need for water that clawed at his throat. The blinding pain that wracked his body.

But the bond. It was the worst. Like someone had taken a white hot poker from the fire and skewered her alive. She was being turned over a fire, over and over again, the bond itself the cause of the flames.

Arianna tried to touch it and jolted back as if she'd been burned.

Only one. There was only one left. Then darkness claimed her.

ARIANNA WOKE with Ellie leaning over her, pressing a cool rag to her face. Talon stood close, his arms crossed as he leaned against the arm of the sofa she rested on.

Ellie noticed her first. "Drink this," her sister said, but Arianna pushed it away, fearing it might be something to ease her pain. She couldn't afford to sleep now. "It's just water," Ellie promised.

Arianna took a tentative sip, then another set of hands were guiding her into a seated position. Talon perched at her side, a vision of worry.

Her chest was raw and aching. "The bond," she said and tears brimmed to the surface. Rion had gone silent down their single strand. She couldn't sense his earlier anguish or pain. She couldn't sense anything.

Ellie exchanged a worried glance with Talon. "Tell us."

"It's almost gone." Her voice cracked. "We have to find him." She tried to rise, but Talon pushed her back down.

"We will. Gavin told us where to look, but—"

Arianna looked up at the sudden shift in her friend. "But what?"

"We have to proceed carefully."

Arianna finally focused on the male seated across from them. He appeared uncomfortable and refused to meet her stare.

Talon continued. "He has Fae in captivity beneath this manor that have been there for years."

"Why?" her voice rasped.

"To run the city," Raevina answered, a look of disgust on her face. "His glamours—"

"We have to go. Now," Arianna said and tried to rise again.

"We will," Talon promised. "Just give yourself a minute."

"We need to plan this out," Raevina said. "According to Gavin, Niall has spies everywhere. If we aren't careful, he'll discover you're gone before we want him to. I can't imagine he has kind things planned should that happen."

"First things first then," Talon said, turning to Gavin. "When is he coming back?"

Gavin shrugged. "I don't know. Soon, I imagine. He never stays away long."

"Okay, then you two will leave tonight," Raevina said, looking between Talon and Arianna. "It should give you a head start. We'll distract him for as long as we can."

"What are we going to do?" Ellie asked.

"Prepare. Things are about to go to hell."

CHAPTER SEVENTY

RION

The female's screams echoed through the hall again, chipping away at Rion's nerves. He knew exactly what kind of hell Niall was unleashing upon her. The male liked to play with the body, but the mind seemed just as fun to him. He'd filled Rion with so many gruesome images that Rion knew he would see them in his nightmares for years to come. Maybe decades.

The halls fell silent and Rion froze, straining to listen for any sounds. None, then keys jangled before his door and Rion tried not to let dread sweep through him when Niall sauntered through. The male greeted him with a sadistic smile.

Niall cleaned fresh blood from his hands with what looked to be a filthy rag. He carried the oil lamp but didn't bother setting it down.

"I'll be gone for a while," Niall said. "The child will see to it that you don't die while I'm away."

"Why tell me?"

"To gloat, I suppose. I have a female to woo, so I can't be constantly disappearing. She and her little friends will be forming a suspect list by now and I must appear as blameless as possible. She's quite smart, your mate."

He crossed the room and wrinkled his nose as if smelling something foul. "I just wanted you to know that I'll be the one standing at her side during her coronation." He lowered his voice. "And it might take a while, but when you finally feel that spike of pleasure down the bond, you'll know who's responsible."

Rion's vision went red. He yanked at the chains so hard his wrists cracked, but Niall just stepped back, laughing. "You've done all the hard work for me. The bond is barely hanging by a thread. One more move and it will shatter, and I'll be there to comfort her through it. But don't worry," he added. "I'll show you everything when I return. My name will be the only one falling from her lips and she'll forget you ever existed."

Rion yanked on his chains again, willing those bolts to rip from the ceiling.

Niall stopped then and turned back to face him. Something in the male's scent changed and Rion froze. Niall's features twisted into a smile so gruesome, Rion wasn't sure if the male before him was Fae or monster.

"And since you'll be here for an extended stay, I figured you might wish to know the name of your noisy neighbor." He pressed a hand to his chest. "She is my absolute favorite, after all." Rion waited, his mouth going dry. He knew this male thrived on pain and fear.

For a terrifying moment, Rion thought he'd hear his sister's name or Ellie's, and his gut twisted as he remembered the female's screams. But the words that fell from Niall's lips had Rion's mind reeling and heart fracturing into a million tiny pieces.

"High Lady Eimear of Brónach." Then, with a final sneer, he slammed the iron door, leaving Rion frozen in the stillness.

His world tilted and the rage that had been burning through him shifted to cold embers.

Rion ran through his memories trying to sort and piece together how it might be possible.

It couldn't—it couldn't be her. Niall was just trying to get into his head and mess with his emotions so the rest of the bond would break under the stress.

But Rion hadn't scented a lie. Was that part of his magic, too? Rion's heart pounded faster and faster.

Niall had shown Arianna a clear image of his mother the first day he'd toured them around the garden. What if the reason Niall could recall the memory so clearly was because he'd been obsessed with her?

Rion's father had been fiercely protective of his mate, that hadn't been a secret. He'd guarded her with his life as any mate would. But somehow, she'd still slipped away. Had Niall used a glamour to do it? Had he drugged his father? The guards?

But his mother was dead. No, they'd never found a body. And people had stopped searching for her because—it had never made sense until now. Niall's magic could influence thoughts and emotions. He'd said so himself. Which meant he had influenced his father to cease looking for her. To give up and give in to grief.

Because intense emotions were easy to manipulate. What else had he manipulated? And how far did that magic reach if he could influence an entire country to stop searching for their High Lady? How many were helping him?

Rion tried to clear his throat, but it had constricted. His body trembled as the thoughts kept cascading through him.

His mother. He'd been hearing his mother's screams.

The bond pulled tight and Rion felt Arianna's gentle caress. *I'm here*, she seemed to say.

Kaylee opened the door then and Rion tried to steady his racing heart. He knew she could scent the emotions coursing through him now. He couldn't name them, not with the way they flooded his system, uncontrollable and unyielding.

"Hi." His voice shook and she remained in the doorway. The slight light from the lamp revealed the new bruises on her face. The swelling.

"He's gone," she said, though she made no movement to enter.

"The female down the hall," Rion couldn't keep his voice steady. "What does she look like?"

The child twisted the fabric at the hem of her shirt. "She has red hair like yours, but it's really long and dirty. She's nice and talks to me like you do. I like her a lot." Her lip wobbled. "But he's so mean to her."

Time stopped.

Holy gods. Holy gods above. His heart was skipping all over again, his stomach twisting into knots. His mother. His mother was here. What had Niall said? That no one would find him? That no one was coming? He'd been so confident because he'd had a prisoner that the world had searched for and never found. A prisoner for over eighty years.

Anger rose in Rion anew. Fire burned through his soul and the girl took an involuntary step back.

"Do you want to help her?" Rion asked. Kaylee nodded, though he could tell she was uncertain. Rion gripped the cold metal of the chains holding his wrists. "Can you loosen these?"

Kaylee chewed her lip. "I can try."

"Please."

She exited the room and Rion heard the distinct sound of her dragging the little stool down the hall. He listened as she climbed up.

Rion hissed when she moved the crank and the chain tightened, then it moved the other way, giving him an inch, two, three. His elbows lowered, then suddenly stopped.

Rion waited and heard her grunting before she stumbled back in with her head down. "I-I'm sorry, that's all I—" Her lip trembled. Gods, he hated Niall. He'd never hated someone so much in his life.

"It's all right." He studied the chains. "I need you to get something for me." She looked up. "I need something with a sharp edge. A sword, a knife, an ax. Anything I could swing."

"W-We don't have anything like that here."

"Please." Rion struggled to keep his voice even. "You have to find something."

"Why?" Her voice was soft. So frail and small. What kind of monster did it take to beat someone so innocent?

"Because I'm getting us out of here." The girl's face lit up with equal amounts of fear and excitement. Niall had finally made a mistake. He'd told Rion he wouldn't be back, which gave Rion time.

And time was all he needed.

Kaylee nodded and ran down the hall, taking the little oil lamp with her. Rion tested the slack with a light pull. He curled his fingers tightly around the chains.

Then Rion sent a promise down the bond. *I'm coming.* He said. *I'm coming, just hold on. Hold on for me. Hold on for us.* Because when he got back, he swore he was never letting her go.

He was done with doubt. Done with letting others rule over his life with their opinions and prophecies.

Arianna had never given up on him. Not when he'd walked into that cabin half dead, not when he'd recounted every horrible thing he'd ever done, and not even after facing the brunt of his brutality.

So when he got back, when he saw her again, he would fall to his knees and take whatever pieces she was willing to offer.

I'm coming, he promised again.

Rion tightened his hold on the chains and yanked with every ounce of strength he possessed. They didn't budge. He growled and yanked again and again and again until his hands were slick with blood, until his muscles begged for relief and the metallic ring of those chains was the only noise that echoed through the chamber.

He slammed his body weight against them again and again and again and again.

Wait for me, he begged down the bond. *Don't let go.*

CHAPTER SEVENTY-ONE

ARIANNA

rianna crouched behind the cracked stone fountain and waited. The torrential downpour made Talon's silhouette difficult to identify in the dark, but that was exactly the reason they'd decided to leave.

If she couldn't see him, neither would the guards.

She was soaked to the bone already. Water pooled in the bunched crevices of her cloak before spilling onto the ground. It pattered against her hood and Arianna shivered despite the warm weather.

She was going to find Rion. Find him, save him, then bring him home.

Thunder cracked, loud and rumbling, then lightning flashed across the sky.

Talon gave her the signal.

Arianna dashed from her hiding spot and ran as fast as her legs could carry her. Water soaked through her boots and she dodged the deeper puddles, determined to be as silent as possible.

She slid behind the next statue and paused at Talon's side.

Guards patrolled in both their animal and Fae forms, stalking the entire yard at what seemed like random intervals. But Talon had studied their rotations. He'd planned this exit strategy weeks ago. Just in case.

Lightning flashed again, and Arianna cringed when thunder boomed loud enough to rattle the ground.

The gods were truly looking down on her tonight.

Talon dashed from her side again and she watched him fly across the yard like a wraith. She would follow in just a few breaths, as soon as he lifted his hand to signal that the sentinels ahead had passed.

After their meeting with Gavin, quick plans were made, then they were off, determined not to waste time.

She and Talon would rescue Rion, or at the very least, locate him. If the underground dungeon was too heavily fortified, then they'd have to rethink their strategy. All Arianna knew was that if she found her mate, there was no way in hell she was leaving without him.

The rest of their rebel group planned to go about their day as if nothing were amiss. Ellie intended to play it off as though Arianna was sick and wished to be alone. Saoirse and Raevina were setting up an evacuation plan for the half-breeds in the event things went horribly south. Arianna wasn't sure it was necessary, as she couldn't see Niall harming them, but both females had been insistent. And Gavin claimed he'd function as their spy. Provided Niall didn't already know everything and wouldn't kill Gavin as soon as he saw him next.

With any amount of luck, Niall wouldn't even notice Arianna was missing until she was too far away for him to pursue.

They just needed a few days at most. She hoped. Arianna wasn't really sure what they'd do after they discovered the prison. Hopefully exile Niall from Ruadhán, though she questioned whether the council would take her side.

Talon lifted his arm and she positioned herself into a low crouch. Her long knives pressed against her back, the metal a gentle reminder of what she might soon face.

Shorter blades lined her boots, her thighs, and the belt strapped across her chest. She felt like a walking arsenal.

Talon gave the signal again and Arianna dashed from her hiding place. She kept her breath even and her strides long before sinking into the shadow of another statue.

A mountain cat paused and the pair held their breaths. Its ears swiveled one way, then another. The feline stepped toward them and sniffed the air. Seconds dragged out before the Fae finally moved on.

Arianna silently thanked the gods for the rain. Without it, they never would have successfully masked their scents. She was relying solely on dumb luck and prayers to make this plan work.

Thunder cracked across the sky again and Arianna ran at Talon's side as they crossed the final stretch through the lawn.

Raevina was right. Everything was about to go to hell.

Even if Arianna proved Niall had taken Rion, it might not be enough to convince the council to fault him. Many believed Rion belonged in a cell to pay for the crimes of his past. The other prisoners might not matter either if Niall offered logical explanations for their imprisonment. Which he likely had prepared.

Arianna wasn't even certain they'd fault Niall for the glamours. He could spin it in a way that made it seem as though he were trying to protect The Divine.

Which probably meant returning to Ruadhán was a bad idea all the way around. Maybe that's why Saoirse and Raevina were making plans. They'd already thought this through.

Arianna continued following Talon through the dimly lit city. No one wandered the drenched streets and the pair slipped between buildings undetected. If a citizen were to glance out their window, they would simply assume the pair had likely left a tavern and were eager to escape the rain.

It wasn't until Arianna stood at the floating city's edge that her heart skipped a beat. She peered into the never ending darkness where droplets of rain disappeared into a black abyss.

"Are you going to jump or am I forced to push you?"

Arianna gave Talon a sidelong glance. He'd pulled his hair back into a low bun and water rolled down his exposed face. She eyed the long sword strapped to his back and prayed he wouldn't have to use it.

"As I recall, you were the one who needed a push all those years ago." She recalled the memory from their youth when both had been innocent of the evil in the world. Their only worry had been whether they could conquer their fear of jumping from the largest waterfall in Móirín.

He smirked at that and peered down with her. "Don't make me catch you."

"Likewise." Then Arianna tilted and the city fell away.

THE PAIR hit the ground running. The village below was as empty as the city above, with only a few patrons daring to brave the storm for a late night drink at the local tavern. No one noticed the two shadows slipping between the residences or leaping over their small gardens.

I'm coming.

They were the words she'd been repeating since Ellie had tossed Arianna her cloak.

I'm coming and somehow it felt as though Rion repeated it back.

They kept pushing, kept running through the rain even as the terrain shifted and they entered the coverage of a forest. Talon had only glanced behind once, presumably to ensure she kept pace, but Arianna wasn't stopping and she certainly wouldn't slow him down.

Talon knew exactly where they were going; he'd seen the charred land before.

So close. He'd been so close.

They ran until her legs ached. Until her lungs screamed at her to find somewhere to rest. She wouldn't. And—Arianna paused to study the building Talon had veered toward.

If it could even be called a building. Crumbling shack was more like it.

The door had been ripped from its hinges and lay on the ground, covered by a thick layer of vines and moss. Boards were missing from the walls and half the roof looked as though it had been blown away. But Talon still ventured inside and she reluctantly followed.

"Why are we stopping?" she asked. Talon didn't respond. Instead, he shifted a felled beam, then dug at a loose floorboard with one of his knives. It creaked and popped up. He reached into the dark hole and pulled up a leather satchel.

"Did you really stash a bag all the way out here?"

"Did you really think I wouldn't be prepared to flee that perverse city?"

"I didn't know you hated it so much."

"I hate the ones who govern it." He pointed to the floor. "Sit. We have a few things to go over."

Arianna looked out into the stormy night. "Do we have time for this?"

"We're making time because it's important."

She pursed her lips but relented and sat with her legs crossed. Talon crossed the room and dug a map out of the satchel. Magic flickered through the air and droplets stopped falling from overhead as Talon held them at bay.

He lit a small oil lamp he'd also lifted out of the floor and set it in the center of the map.

"I need you to listen very carefully." The seriousness in his tone snapped her to attention. "We're not going back to Ruadhán."

Arianna furrowed her brow. She thought that might be a possibility if Niall wasn't cooperative, but—

"Okay."

"Ellie sent a letter to your father. We have a safe house stationed here." Talon pointed to a random location on the map.

"But that's within Pádraigín's borders."

"It is, but they don't patrol that far south. We presume it's either because they don't have the numbers or they don't care. Either way, once we have Rion, we're to meet your father there."

She raised a brow. "That journey will take him days."

"Which is why Ellie already reached out and another reason I dispatched half of your Móirín's guards there before we left. They'll have it ready for us."

She studied the map again, trying to memorize the area and any landmarks surrounding it.

"Raevina, Saoirse, and Ellie will meet us as soon as they're able to get out safely." She nodded again. "Arianna." She met his gaze. "A mission like this is dangerous. I need you to listen to everything I say."

"Okay."

He didn't look away. "If I tell you to do something, it's for a reason. We won't have time to debate it." Her heart started pounding and Talon swallowed. "Even if you see him, even if he's standing right in front of you, if I tell you to run, then I need you to run."

She blanched. Talon was a warrior. A commander. He knew what he was doing and if a scenario like that unfolded, she knew Talon only had their best interests at heart. Still—

"I don't know if I'll be able to do that."

"You have to. He wouldn't want you to get caught or worse. We can always reconvene with others to form a new plan, but if we're captured too, that's it."

"Not if they ki—" She couldn't say the word.

"For reasons I can't fathom, Niall hasn't done that yet, so I doubt he'd do it now. Just promise to trust me. If there's a way to get Rion out, I will not leave him behind."

"Do you promise?"

Talon placed a hand over his heart. "I swear it on my honor as a Fae."

Arianna gazed out into the pouring rain again. "How long will it take us to get there?"

He blew out the oil lamp and returned it to its hiding place. "At this pace, before sunrise."

"You said you didn't notice any guards before?"

He nodded. "No prints aside from a few animals. We scouted the entire perimeter. The fire looked fresh, so we didn't pursue much further." He replaced the floorboard. "Though if they possessed

Pádraigín's magic, I assume they could have made it look any way they wished."

"Which means there's at least one person there at all times."

"Let's hope we get lucky and that's all." Talon readjusted his knives. "Don't you think it's odd that no one in Móirín has ever mentioned their magic before? They taught us enough about the wind part of it, but nothing about manipulating our vision. Seems like an important detail to leave out."

"Maybe they didn't think enough Fae could do it, so they felt it wasn't necessary."

Talon rolled his eyes. "Then the right teachers aren't making our curriculums."

Arianna offered him a silent laugh. So many people had gotten so much wrong. Could they trust any of their written history? She tried to breathe and work the tension from her shoulders. Any moment now and they'd be running again, headed straight into what could be a bloody confrontation. She wished she had spent the last few weeks training, but Niall, it seemed, was responsible for manipulating her emotions.

"Does it still hurt?" Talon asked and Arianna followed his gaze to her arm. She hadn't realized she'd been massaging the muscles there.

"A bit," she admitted. The area carried a thick scar where the bone in her forearm had snapped in half and ripped through the skin. Arianna grimaced at the memory. "It wasn't his fault," she said. The words were awkward and uncomfortable.

Talon loosed a long sigh. "I know." His voice lowered into a growl. "But when I find the one responsible for casting that glamour—" His teeth clenched and she understood. There'd be no mercy. Even if it was Niall himself.

Talon stepped closer and reached out a hand. "May I?"

Arianna eyed him then extended her arm. His thumbs moved across her forearm gently at first, then narrowed in on the injury. She flinched and he mumbled an apology before lightening his touch.

Talon ran his fingers over the area in soothing circular motions. He stretched her wrist and bent her fingers and elbow, pulling and pushing the muscles until they released the gathered tension.

Arianna just watched in fascination. "Where did you learn that?"

"From someone on the field. She liked to keep us moving and claimed the manipulation healed our injuries faster."

"Did it?"

"I wouldn't be doing it otherwise."

She watched his hands work. "Is it—" Arianna stopped herself and chewed her bottom lip.

"What?" He slowed.

Arianna shook her head and swallowed back tears. Her voice was still thick when she said, "What if I'm afraid of him?"

Talon's fingers stopped moving. "What do you mean?"

She chewed her lip again. She hadn't even voiced her fear to Ellie. "I keep having these nightmares." She risked a glance at Talon and quickly turned away. "About that day." She knew he understood. "And whenever I see him in my dreams, I'm happy, but I'm also—" Arianna chewed her lip again, shame and doubt consuming her.

"Then I'd say you're completely normal." Arianna studied the sympathy in his gaze. "He attacked you. Even if he didn't mean to, the natural response to that is fear."

"But he'll know."

"And you'll work through it." She turned away and Talon released her arm. He scratched the back of his head. "You know, Ellie is better suited for this kind of conversation."

"Yeah, well, Ellie likes him too much."

Talon stiffened. "Do you want me to talk you out of saving him?"

"Gods no, I don't want him in pain. I love him. I'd kill for him, but the only thing I keep seeing is that—" She hesitated. "That dark look on his face. The way he—" She choked on the word. "I just want everything to be like it was."

Talon was silent for a long time and both watched the rain hit the puddles on ground. "Let him move first," he offered. "See where that takes you."

Arianna waited. "That's it?"

He chuckled. "I told you, this is a conversation you should have had with Ellie. I'm not exac—" Talon cut himself off and his gaze darted toward the ice slowly making its way along the undergrowth.

It coated the grass one blade at a time. Frost shot through the puddles, zigzagging across the surface, freezing the water in its wake. Talon's breath clouded in the air. "Is that you?" he whispered. When she shook her head, Talon's face went pale.

He backed away and she followed, watching that ice inch its way toward the base of the stairs then it began climbing up, one wooden plank at a time. Talon took her elbow and guided her toward the rear wall of the shack on silent feet. They climbed through the broken boards without disturbing them and stepped several paces away from the nearly crumbled building.

The ice continued to move.

It coated everything it touched: the ramshackle structure, the trees in its path, and even the rain as it was still falling.

Arianna tried to draw Talon's gaze, afraid to speak in the unnatural stillness that'd fallen over the forest, but he pressed a finger to his lips. She sucked in a breath at the urgency in his eyes. The fear.

She'd never seen Talon afraid. Not since the day he'd sent her up river with a promise.

The ice crawled faster, consuming everything in its path as if it were fire. Talon pulled her back further before spinning her in a silent, dizzying motion that left her unbalanced. He pressed her body into the nearest tree, then stepped close and clamped a tight hand over her mouth before pulling the collar of his shirt up to cover his own.

They stood like that, frozen as the rain shifted to solid pebbles of ice and bounced off the frost coated earth.

But why was Talon afraid? Ice meant Móirín. It meant Fae from their own nation were close. But the ice didn't explain why nothing else in the forest seemed to move. Why her hair stood on end and her instincts begged her to run.

Slight rustling sounded in the bushes nearby, so faint she almost didn't hear it. Talon only tightened his grip on her mouth and pressed closer, his large frame shielding her from view.

She wanted to ask questions—she just needed him to look at her—but before she could move, claws reached out from the darkness and sank into Talon's shoulder. It violently ripped him away and the cold air swept over her body.

His resounding roar filled her ears and he spun to sink his now drawn blade into the—what the hell was that?

The creature howled in fury and the tattered hood covering its head fell back, revealing pointed teeth and black lips. Its dark, spindly hair covered a gaunt face pale from the lack of sunlight.

Its limbs looked too thin, as if all the fat had been sucked away, leaving loose skin to hang from muscles and bone. Arianna tried not to cry out when the creature lunged for Talon again, those black eyes drinking in their target. Its teeth snapped and Talon sank his blade into the creature again.

Or she thought he did. To her horror, the blade bounced off as if it had struck rock.

Dread pooled in the pit of her stomach.

A piercing wail that had Arianna clasping her hands over her ears echoed from the darkness, and a second creature with a slightly smaller frame emerged from the shadows, causing Talon to trip backward. He righted himself, but not before the wicked thing sank her fangs into his forearm.

Talon cursed, then Arianna was moving, ripping her own blades free. She let them fly, first into the larger creature, then into the second. Both rebounded off and hit the ground.

She spun her magic down her arms next and launched it at the spindly creatures, sending both flying backward into the trees.

"What the hell are those?" she screamed, her voice high and desperate.

"Run," was his only answer. Arianna turned to obey, then heard him unsheathe his long blade. She pivoted to find him standing before the hissing pair as if . . . as if . . .

Arianna grabbed his shoulder. "Let's go."

He shook her off. "I'll buy you time. You have to get ahead of them, get away from the cold. Find the river, jump in, and heat it as hot as you can stand. They can't take the heat."

"I am *not* leaving without you."

Talon launched another bolt of water at the creatures, knocking them back again before he turned to her. "I'll be right behind you."

No, he wouldn't. In every story she'd ever read, in every recounting of events told from older warriors, the one who stayed behind rarely ever made it back. They sacrificed themselves for their allies.

Arianna drew her long knives and stood at his side. "If you stay, I stay."

"You're so damn stubborn." He cursed and Arianna summoned her magic again, knocking the creatures back a third time. The pair were furious now, clambering to their feet and wrestling against the icy restraints she tried to clamp around them.

Talon shifted tactics. She watched steam rise from the ball of liquid between his hands and she mimicked it. Hot. Right. If their magic utilized ice, then they wouldn't be able to stand anything hot. She'd give anything to have Raevina here right about now.

Talon launched his sphere at the larger thing and it let out a horrendous hiss and collapsed in a writhing heap on the ground. Arianna hit the smaller one, then Talon grabbed her hand and they were bolting through the forest.

Another high-pitched scream echoed from the shadows. Then another. There were more. Gods. Gods. She tried to look back, but Talon shoved her forward.

"Don't look, go straight for the water."

"What are they?" she panted.

"Damn it." He spun and the creature caught Talon's blade between its pointed yellow teeth. It almost seemed to smile at him with those milky white eyes. Its flattened nostrils flared and Arianna used the same tactic as before. She heated a sphere of water and blasted the creature away.

Talon grabbed her arm again and they were sprinting through the dark, ducking beneath branches and leaping over fallen logs.

"I don't know," he admitted. Well, clearly he'd encountered them before, but they could talk about that later, when they weren't running for their lives.

Dark Fae, something in her gut suggested. But they were so different from the ones on the mountain.

Arianna ducked to avoid another spindly body that leapt at her with its arms stretched wide. It growled like a feral animal and hit the ground screeching.

"How much further to the river?" she asked, surrounding herself in boiling water that spun rapidly around her body. It sizzled against the rain still pouring from the sky.

"Not far." Thank the gods. She could practically taste Talon's panic. The high pitched cry echoed through the branches again and Arianna cringed at the sound, her feet pounding against the ground harder and harder as she sprinted.

There. She could smell it, even through the downpour.

She could hear it, too. The rain had swelled the river already. It crashed against the bank, but Arianna didn't have time to consider it as she took a deep breath and leaped from the edge, plunging right into the freezing water.

The current ripped through her, tossing her body along its wild path. It tugged her down, down, down and she tumbled along, no longer able to discern up from down. Arianna wrapped her arms around her head, hoping to protect it from the rocks below.

Calm, she told herself. *It's just water.*

Arianna summoned her magic and pulled everything around her to a violent halt. A log flew by, nearly colliding with her head and Arianna adjusted the current directly in front of her and sent a stream outward to intercept anything else that might be barreling her way.

So many things flew by at such a rapid pace that Arianna couldn't focus on any one object. The water was too murky and she couldn't sense Talon within its depths.

She grew frantic, prodding the water until—there. Magic. Talon. Thank the gods. She swam toward the almost electric hum in the water, calming the swelling current one inch at a time. She needed to surface for air.

Then tiny shards of ice began to fly past. Arianna looked through her calm sphere of water and dread sank into the pit of her stomach. Frost. That was frost coating her bubble of protection.

Hurry, Talon.

The ice crawled faster and faster. Something touched her arm and Arianna spun.

Not Talon.

Milky eyes locked with hers mere inches away and those black lips stretched wide, revealing pointed, yellow teeth.

CHAPTER SEVENTY-TWO

RION

Time held no meaning. Rion just kept slamming the weight of his body against the chains over and over and over again.

He ignored the blood rolling down his arms and the sharp pain that radiated from his wrists. His body begged for a break and his bones threatened to crack with each agonizing movement.

Rion wouldn't relent. Not until he was free. And he'd shatter his entire body if that's what it took to get there.

A single thread. That's all that tethered him to the one person he cherished above all others. And he was holding onto it for dear life.

Kaylee watched him, young eyes wide with worry. She'd found him a tool. A dull one, but a tool nonetheless. An ax. She'd done her best to drag the worn weapon that was twice her size all the way down the hall. He'd find a way to make it work; otherwise he was going to be here a lot longer than he intended.

Rion slammed against the chains again and again, the rhythmic rattle echoing like a broken song. He winced when new pain bit through his shoulder and burning seared the uppermost muscles of his left arm.

Great.

Rion let his body fall limp and his chest heaved with every breath. Kaylee ran forward to offer him water as she always did whenever he took a break. He was covered in sweat and his stomach growled, but Rion only stopped long enough to consume a few bites before he was at it again.

Iron wasn't going to keep him away from his mate. Nothing was.

Rion pulled again.

Again.

Again.

A groan. His heart jolted and he pulled harder. A slight shift this time.

Rion glanced up at the brackets that held the chains to the ceiling. They didn't look like they were loosening, but—

"Step back," he ordered Kaylee. She obeyed. She always obeyed and Rion hated the amount of fear that still radiated from her small body. As if he could hurt her even shackled.

Another pull, another groan, then the ceiling cracked and Rion barely moved out of the way fast enough as a large chunk of rock came barreling toward him. It hit the ground with a resounding thud, seeming to shake the entire room from the impact. Rion shielded his face with one arm against the dust billowing throughout the cell.

He glanced up. Another room. So there *were* multiple levels to this hellhole, just like he'd thought. Rion scented books and ink and wood. He squinted into the darkness. It wasn't a cell, but the space above was too dark to discern anything else.

Rion rotated his free shoulder. His left arm still hung above his head but his right was loose at least. Rion pulled the length of the chain out from under the rock. It still stretched up in a diagonal line toward the ceiling but he had enough slack to swing a weapon.

He stared at the ax but winced when he rotated his wrist. Both were swollen and discolored. Minor injuries. He'd deal with them later.

Of course, there were his other wounds to consider as well, courtesy of Niall. They'd closed, thank the gods, but Rion could still feel the ache from where the blades had penetrated deeper. It was a miracle he hadn't bled to death.

Rion breathed deeply and steeled himself. Newfound hope coursed through him. Just a few more minutes and he'd be free, his mother would be free, and Kaylee would finally get to bask in the sunlight.

"Bring me the ax," Rion said and inclined his head to examine his left arm. Hopefully the weapon would cut through in one swing. He just needed to keep enough tension on the chain before he brought the ax down. Easy. He just wished his hands would stop shaking.

Rion raised his gaze to look at Kaylee, but she hadn't moved. Her eyes were wide, her breath just a little faster and her scent—

Gods. She hadn't expected him to succeed.

Of course she hadn't. How many others had likely tried and failed to break their chains? How many had she watched mangle themselves only to give in to their fate?

She stepped back and Rion felt a familiar tang of fear sear through his chest. He was close. So close to tasting freedom, but if she didn't help him—Rion looked at the remaining brackets in the ceiling. He didn't know if he could break the rest, nor was he certain he had the energy to try. With the relief of success, Rion's body had lost part of its earlier determination. As if it knew it could finally relax.

She took another step back. Even if he broke the brackets, there was no guarantee he could break the chains. His mother hadn't...

"Please," Rion tried, his voice full of pleading. His entire future was riding on a child who'd been beaten her entire life. Someone whose only friends had been prisoners.

"You'll leave." Her voice trembled. Her entire body trembled. "You're going to leave me and then he'll be mad."

"I won't. I already promised you I wouldn't."

She twisted her tunic so tight Rion was sure it would rip. "He'll hurt me. He'll punish me for the broken wall. He'll—" A terror filled sob escaped her lips and Rion's heart cracked. If his other arm had been free, he would have knelt to make himself appear smaller.

How was he going to convince this child to trust him?

"Someone I love needs me," Rion tried. "Niall is going to hurt her if I don't get out of here and stop him."

The girl wiped tears from her eyes. "Is she your mate?"

His brows rose, surprised the child knew the word. "Yes," he said. "She's my mate. Please," he tried again. "Help me get back to her. I can't do this without you."

The girl eyed the ax, then his outstretched palm. "Promise," she said. "Promise you won't leave me here."

"I swear it." Her lips trembled, but she lifted the handle and began dragging the weapon toward him. Rion felt his hope return when he wrapped his hand around the wooden handle and prayed it'd withstand the impact.

"Step back for me?"

Kaylee ran for the door and hid behind the wall. Rion eyed the chain, dropped his weight to pull it taut, shifted his grip on the weapon, then swung in a wide arc.

The chain snapped and he fell to the floor, his heart thundering with more hope than he'd experienced in weeks. Rion shook out his free arm, forcing blood back into his fingers before he slammed the ax down on the chains holding his legs and remaining arm.

He'd left a considerable length of chain dangling from his right wrist, just in case he needed another weapon.

Free. He was free.

Rion turned to face Kaylee. She eyed him warily and stepped back again, ready to flee. Rion didn't rise. He sat there, catching his breath and slowly reached out a bloody hand.

Neither moved for what felt like an eternity.

Kaylee had never known friendship, but she had trusted him enough to bring him a weapon. Now she needed to decide if she trusted him with her life.

Slowly, tentatively, the girl stepped toward him. She eyed the blade at his side and Rion released his grip on the handle.

She stepped again and again until her small hand settled in his. Rion gently wrapped his callused fingers around hers. "Now show me where the Lady of Brónach is and let's get out of here."

MAYBE KAYLEE knew, maybe she didn't. Part of Rion hoped she didn't. He was certain his mother wouldn't recognize him and he didn't want to overwhelm her by popping in and saying, *Guess what? The evil psycho bastard who trapped you here took your kid, too.*

After eighty years of captivity, Rion wasn't even certain what he was walking into. Was there any hope she might still be sane?

He watched Kaylee run from the door and down the hall, carrying the small oil lamp to light the way. The half-breed seemed to like his mother enough, but that hardly gave him any hope. She probably liked anyone who so much as smiled at her.

Rion eyed the dank hallway. It was as plain as any dungeon he'd seen. Just stone with unlit braziers lining the single long hall. Darkness beckoned to him from either end, and his skin prickled as he imagined who might be waiting in the shadows.

But he focused on Kaylee. She wasn't afraid, which meant there wasn't anyone else down here. She knew how to get to the surface too, which was exactly where they'd be headed next.

Kaylee pulled a ring of keys from her pocket and fumbled through them, searching for the right one. She glanced at him once, as if afraid she was taking too long, but he remained still, a mask of patience on his face.

Inside, every instinct roared at him to hurry.

Finally, her little hands fit an iron key into the lock.

Iron. Why was everything made of iron?

Rion's heart galloped in his chest when Kaylee finally swung the door open.

His throat went dry and Rion was once again a youngling who'd gotten caught stealing sweets from the kitchens. He remembered his mother's feigned anger in the presence of his father, then her laughter afterward. She'd made him promise not to get caught again and had promptly sent him to bed with a bag full of sweets. He'd shared with Saoirse, of course.

Rion followed Kaylee inside and sucked in a breath when the soft light hit his mother's face. Eighty years and there she was, hanging right in front of him.

Her face was harsher than he remembered, the lines of her cheekbones prominent as they stuck out against her pale skin. Her once beautiful hair was long yet matted beyond repair.

But it was her. Gods, it was her.

Tears welled in his eyes and Rion couldn't stop them from falling. He'd longed for his mother like no other. He had convinced himself that maybe she could have loved the monster dwelling beneath his skin. Maybe with her, his life could have been different. Normal.

Kaylee stood there, looking between them with a confused expression on her face.

He collected himself and quickly wiped his eyes. There would be time for sappy reunions later. Right now, he needed to remove her chains and escape.

Rion approached and prayed she wouldn't recognize him based on scent alone. Unless . . . maybe she already knew. Maybe Niall had told her all about his new prisoner. Or maybe he'd kept her in the dark about her children and tormented her with false images the way Niall had done to Rion.

Rion stepped again then his mother growled. A vicious noise that sounded more animal than Fae.

That familiar emerald green gaze lifted and Rion paused, stunned by the hateful gleam in her eyes. It dared him to approach.

His mother had always been calm and graceful. Powerful yet elegant. He'd forgotten she was also one of the fiercest warriors Brónach had ever seen.

Rion had read the stories that spoke of a female warrior who had torn across the battlefield, using her abilities as a seer to predict her enemy's movements while she summoned plants from within the Earth's core to eradicate them after.

It wasn't always his father who had dealt with those giving their country trouble.

Eimear, The High Lady of Brónach pinned him with that warrior's gaze now. She surveyed him from head to toe, ready to bare her fangs and fight against anything he threw at her.

Despite eighty years of torment, Niall had not broken her.

Rion bowed his head slightly then lifted his arms to display the shackles and chains that hung there. "I am not your enemy." Her growling ceased and she studied him. Eimear scented the air and Rion went stiff. Part of him hoped she wouldn't recognize him while another part prayed she would.

"I'm going to break the chains," Rion said, carefully lifting the ax. "I'm sorry I don't have the keys." She didn't nod and Rion wondered if she understood him at all. She watched him circle around to her ankle and he pulled the chain tight before slamming the ax against it just as he'd done with his own. Rion ensured there wasn't more than a few inches hanging from the shackle. No need to weigh them down or risk tripping.

Rion rose and examined her arm. Shit, why hadn't he lowered her down already? He ran for the door and pulled the cold lever; his mother fell into a heap on the floor.

Rion cursed again and ran back. He laid the ax on the floor and bent to help her up. As soon as his hand met her skin, Eimear lunged for his throat.

Rion snatched the ax before she was over him and used the handle to keep her teeth from clamping around his throat. She growled and thrashed, snapping her teeth and snarling like a wild animal.

He had just enough leverage to buck her off before rolling out of range. Eimear lunged for him again but the chains pulled taunt and Rion cringed at the way the restraints jerked her backward. She didn't seem to notice.

Rion stared at the rage in his mother's gaze. Eyes that were so much like his own. Kaylee had fled as soon as Eimear moved. He could still hear the girl's footsteps as they slapped against the stone.

Great. He'd have to navigate this dark maze to find her before they ran to the surface.

But first, he had to convince his mother he wasn't a threat.

His heart hammered in his chest as Rion stood in the doorway. Eimear hadn't backed away. She remained close with the chains pulled taunt, eyeing him as if he were the one who'd placed her here.

Rion knew the look well. She glared at him like he was a monster. He'd taken that look from so many others through the decades. He deserved that look. Earned it.

But he couldn't take it now.

Not after all the beatings. Not with starvation and weariness trying to convince his muscles to give in. And not with his fractured bond.

Rion collapsed right there on the stone. His knees hit the surface hard and he just sat there, staring at her, broken and unsure of himself. He needed to escape, but he couldn't do that without her and if she didn't trust him. . . Rion had three other chains to break and she'd likely snap his neck before he got the chance.

Rion thought of Arianna at that moment, about all the times she'd spoken to him as though he were a cornered animal. What would she do?

"I'm here to help," Rion tried.

Eimear still stared at him, like she expected him to fade and shift back and—but that's exactly what she expected.

Niall had shown him false images for months and Rion was certain that male had done the same with Eimear. Which meant she didn't know whether this was real or imagined. Did she think him Niall in disguise? Did she believe killing him would finally end her torment?

Rion looked at his bloody hands. How distorted was her reality? How many times had Niall offered her hope only to violently tear it away?

"I don't know what to say to comfort you," Rion said. "I'm not good at these sorts of things." He peered at her and noted the softness on her face. A dangerously crafted façade designed to lure him in. A muscle in her hand flexed and he knew those claws would rip out his throat if given the chance. "But I promise I'm not with that monster."

She didn't speak, only stared.

"I'm from Brónach," he continued. "I have a mate who is waiting for me. Niall wants her for himself, that's why I'm here. And if I don't get back, the bond we have will shatter."

Eimear might as well have been stone.

"Please," he begged, still on his knees. "Let me set you free."

Something in her face changed then, just a spark, but Rion saw it through the dim light. Freedom. It was likely all she thought about now, the sole thing that kept her going.

Rion lifted the ax. She might still attack him once the chains were cut. Maybe he'd get lucky and she'd run. Either way, he had to try.

Rion stood and she backed away a step. He gestured to her arm. "Set it on the ground and I'll cut you free."

Eimear eyed him, then the ax, then him again before sinking to the ground in a way that reminded Rion of a cat.

A very dangerous cat.

Her gaze never left him as Rion dared to venture closer. She was going to kill him. He'd seen murderous intent enough times to know. Still, he couldn't just leave her here.

Rion slowly lifted the ax, then let it swing to sever the chain that bound her to the floor.

His mother didn't move. She hadn't even flinched as the sound still ricocheted through the room. Rion pointed toward her ankle and she slid it forward, her gaze still trained on him. Rion cut it quickly, right against the shackle.

Eimear finally extended her left arm, the only thing still keeping her captive.

Rion took a deep breath, prayed to the gods, then cleaved the chain in two.

He knew it was coming. Knew and still he wasn't fast enough to dodge. The High Lady of Brónach slammed into him like a mountain and Rion gasped for breath when his body collided with the hard wall across the room. His head bounced off the stone and stars shot across his vision, but Rion lifted his arm, using the metal of his cuffs to block her teeth.

She grabbed his arm and twisted it hard enough that they tumbled to the ground.

Gods, she'd just tried to break it. Rion scrambled for purchase, but before he could right himself, Eimear snatched the chain attached to his wrist and pulled it up beneath his chin.

Rion barely had enough time to slide his hand between the chain and his throat as she tugged up and dug one knee into his back. He gasped, struggling for breath. He kicked his feet, searching for a wall or crack in the floor that might give him leverage, but she dragged him toward the middle of the cell, her grip firm.

He tried dropping his weight, but she'd already prepared for the movement and pulled tighter.

He fought to no avail.

She was going to kill him. His own mother was going to kill him right here in this dirty cell. He could almost hear Niall's laughter at the irony.

"Don't hurt him," a timid voice said from the shadow of the door. Eimear paused, but his vision was already blurring from the way she'd twisted the chain. "He's not like the others." The voice said again. Kaylee. The half-breed stumbled forward, wringing her hands in her shirt as she always did.

Eimear studied her for what felt like an eternity, then Kaylee added, "He wants to help us escape."

Another pause, then the chain fell and his mother leapt back, putting as much distance between herself and Rion as she could. Rion scrambled toward the opposite wall, coughing and wheezing while he rubbed his throat. He leaned his head against the stone, swallowing down lungfuls of air. Black spots flickered across his vision, then disappeared.

Rion watched his mother as she regarded first him then the little girl who stood at the doorway with her fists clenched.

"Thank you," he rasped. She nodded and Rion took an extra moment to steady himself before forcing his body to rise. They might be free from their chains, but they still had a long way to go.

"Lead the way," he said to Kaylee.

"What about the others?" Eimear asked. Her voice. He'd forgotten that musical tone. It carried an air of roughness now, but his heart still yearned to hear it. Just one more time. A hello. A goodbye.

"We can send for them once we're safe."

"And where is safe?" she asked again.

"Ruadhán," he answered.

Eimear shook her head. "I won't go anywhere near that place. Not while Niall rules it."

Did she expect them to flee all the way to Brónach? They wouldn't survive in their present condition, not that long of a trip. Not to mention the monsters that prowled the roads at night. The sooner he got his mother in the royal city, the sooner she'd be safe, at least with Arianna at her side.

So Rion said the only thing he could think of to convince her. "The Divine resides there now. She'll protect you." As would Talon and Saoirse and everyone else who'd heard the tale of his mother's disappearance. Once the council discovered what Niall had done to Brónach's High Lady, they'd be forced to act.

"The Divine," his mother whispered, tasting the words. "It's time, then." Rion didn't know what she meant. "Fine, to Ruadhán. Show us the way out, little one."

CHAPTER SEVENTY-THREE

ARIANNA

Boney fingers wrapped around Arianna's throat and the creature used its magic to catapult them deeper into the river's cold depths. Arianna's back slammed against the stones at the bottom and she gasped, only to suck in dirty water. It tasted foul and stung her lungs and Arianna thrashed against the creature's powerful grip.

It leaned closer and Arianna swore she could already feel its fangs against her throat. Something told her this thing, whatever it was, didn't need air like normal creatures, and that it was more than willing to take its time with her right there rather than share with its kin.

The calm pocket of water Arianna had carved for herself vanished and the current tore the gangly hand from around her neck and sent them both spiraling through the raging river.

Air. She needed air. Her mind and body reacted without thought and Arianna shot up, up, up until she broke the surface, gasping for breath only to have the tossing waves throw her back under. She spun again, no longer able to tell up from down. Arianna fought, frantically waving her arms before propelling herself toward what she prayed was the surface. She gasped for breath again.

With searing lungs, Arianna spun in a circle, taking quick stock of her surroundings. She checked the bank and frantically searched the endlessly twisting surface for any signs of Talon. Nothing. She knew he'd jumped in, she'd heard the splash, but where had he gone? He had to be close. He had to be.

A log came barreling down the river, tossed like nothing more than a twig by the water's roaring swell. Arianna grabbed a branch in passing and hauled herself just a little higher above the surface. Nothing. She couldn't see him anywhere in the darkness.

Two more dark figures darted from the trees, then plunged into the river without pausing.

Arianna's blood ran cold.

Heat it as much as you can stand, Talon had said. She could protect herself from the overwhelming heat, but if Talon was nearby, he'd be caught in the crossfire. He could protect himself, she knew, but only if he was conscious.

A sharp sensation pierced through her foot. Arianna barely had enough time to draw in a breath before that gnarled hand dragged her beneath the surface. She was half blind in the murky river and spun only to have another set of sharp teeth sink deep into her shoulder.

Undiluted terror shrouded her senses as images of Rion's twisted face assaulted her mind. Arianna saw the challenge in his gaze. The unrelenting anger as he commanded her to tell him—to tell him—no, this wasn't Rion. The room shifted back to liquid and she struggled against the thin body. It had its arms around her torso and its bony legs around her waist.

More teeth pierced through her foot and Arianna lost her breath again. She fought desperately, wriggling against the iron grip of its fangs and claws. For a moment, Arianna imagined she felt Rion's panic down that single thread, followed by his anger.

But their bond was too weak. She wouldn't be able to feel those things now. She—the ancient thing in her body answered her mate's call with glowing calculated anger of its own. It lifted a massive head and cracked one eye open to survey the threats lying beyond.

It didn't crawl to the surface this time. The world didn't slow. Instead, the raw magic in her veins ruptured through the veil holding it back and burst from her in a violent sea of blue and white.

She remembered her days as a slave and the cracks of the whips. The way the iron-tipped barbs had ripped into her flesh. Arianna recalled the day her wrist had snapped and the endless days after when she'd collasped to the mud, her energy spent.

But more than the pain or tears or loss, Arianna remembered that she had always risen. Always survived. Always triumphed.

Because she wasn't weak.

The bodies pinning her down sprang away and Arianna shot to the surface. She gulped down air and again looked for her friend, using magic to calm the water around her body. Everything moved so fast. Too fast. She used dozens of tendrils of magic to search through the river's stormy current. For a heartbeat, thrashing, anything that would tell her Talon lingered in the depths.

She found nothing.

Another set of claws wrapped around her ankle, but instead of fighting, Arianna breathed deep and allowed the creature to pull her down. She could sense three pairs of eyes staring at her in triumph, all suspended in her bubble of calm. Their teeth snapped, the sound muffled to near silence by the water. She felt the current ripple further away, telling her there were even more of them approaching, ready to devour her alive.

But the magic beneath her skin roared and Arianna internally screamed with it.

Heat built in her core, down her arms, through her legs, then the closest creature jerked its hand away. Another swam closer only to snap its teeth in frustration.

The temperature rose and rose.

Bubbles formed just outside a protective layer shielding her from the boiling liquid. Her frozen skin reacted to the heat, tingling as it warmed. The creatures retreated further, using their own magic to prevent the river from sweeping them away.

One turned to flee, but she wouldn't let it get far.

Arianna felt for her friend a final time and when she still didn't find him, Arianna prayed he was out of the water and unleashed hell upon them all.

She knew now with utmost certainty that whatever creatures lingered in the mountains that separated Móirín from Brónach weren't the Dark Fae. Not even close. The Dark Fae were foul things with sharp teeth and claws that only possessed enough awareness to kill and maim.

The Dark Fae were the creatures surrounding her, beasts from legends forgotten through the ages. They were the things willing to rip the skin from a living Fae's bones. And she would eradicate them from the land one at a time.

Two more fled and Arianna sent boiling tendrils of water darting after the frantic creatures. The water muffled their shrieks of pain. They thrashed, losing control of their magic as they tried and failed to cool the liquid boiling their skin. But despite their wordless pleas, Arianna held firm.

They tore at their own bubbling flesh now as if they might stand a chance of surviving without it. Still, the water grew hotter and hotter until eventually the creatures stopped moving altogether. She pushed that heat just a little more, feeling it press against the barrier she'd created for herself. Just a little more to be certain they wouldn't survive.

Arianna bolted for the surface, her lungs straining. Air. Fresh and crisp and cold. Her body, suspended in a single cool ring of water, glided toward the bank.

The river took care of the rest. It washed the boiled corpses away, along with whatever else she'd killed in the process. Part of her felt sick that innocent animals had been caught in the middle, but something would eat well tonight, at least.

Arianna crawled onto the grass, but she couldn't allow herself to rest. Not until she found Talon. He was out here somewhere. She refused to accept otherwise.

A far off howl echoed from within the dark trees. Her skin crawled. How many more of them could possibly be prowling the woods?

She studied the tree line, then surveyed herself. She didn't know how the raging water hadn't dislodged her twin knives, but the rest of her arsenal had vanished along with the pack that held their food and a map of the area.

She peered into the darkness. The silence was deafening and she strained to hear any sound that might tell her which way she needed to go.

No hissing or screaming creatures. No sound of Talon's war cry. Just the angry swell of the river as it lapped at the bank, ready to pull her back under again.

Downstream. That would be the best place to start looking. Arianna stood only to collapse again. Pain seared through her foot and she winced at the puncture marks peppering the top of her boot.

She cursed and forced herself up. Talon could survive this, she told herself. He wouldn't let a few—whatever they were—be the death of him. But her mind kept circling back to the what ifs.

A piece of debris might have collided with his head, rendering him unconscious. One of the creatures might have dragged him under before he could draw enough breath. They could have attacked him first and—

Arianna forced herself into a poor excuse of a run as she tried to keep her body weight on her heel. The rain kept pouring down, beating against her head in an endless sheet. The wind blew and she braced against it, fighting the chatter in her teeth.

She studied the darkness ahead with every labored step. Her panic rose and the magic with it, that ancient thing refusing to slumber until she found what she was looking for.

Alive. Talon was alive. He had to be.

An eagle's cry echoed ahead and Arianna could have wept from the sound. She picked up her pace, forcing her body faster.

There. Across the bank, water ripped from the river and hit two of the creatures square in the chest. The liquid sizzled against their flesh and they screamed against the pain, but it wasn't deterring them. Either they were starved, or they weren't intelligent enough to know when they'd lost a fight.

Her injured foot hit a branch and it cracked in half. Talon pivoted. His gaze widened with surprise and relief, but the distraction cost him.

One of the Dark Fae crashed into him from the left and sank its teeth deep into his thigh. Talon grabbed the sides of its face and Arianna could see his magic working, burning the creature's flesh so it would let go. But the other one was already moving and two more were darting toward him from behind. She hadn't even seen where they'd come from.

Arianna flew.

She sprinted and jumped from the bank, right back into the raging current of the river. Except she didn't sink beneath the surface this time.

It seemed as though the swells of the river came up to meet her every stride. It solidified beneath her feet as if her magic controlled the river itself. Maybe it did, she didn't pause to think on it, didn't consider anything as she leapt across that river to get to the friend who needed her.

Talon blasted the creature from his body then encased their forms in ice. It did nothing, absolutely nothing. The creatures just bent the frozen water to their will and walked through it unhindered.

She made it to Talon's side before the next one could lunge. There were six now. Six with their thin lips pulled back to reveal those razor sharp fangs. They paced before the pair, wild ravenous eyes searching for an opening.

Blood had dyed the side of Talon's tunic crimson and she noted the other wounds along his arms and legs as well. Arianna was certain she didn't look much better, but that wound to his side . . . She needed to address it. And fast.

The largest among the group hissed and Arianna eyed the river and the water at their feet.

"Stay close to me," she commanded. Talon tried to follow her gaze and did as she commanded.

Arianna rallied her strength. She didn't know if it would work. She had never tried to control this much of her new magic at once.

She focused and the river answered her call. It pulsed as if it possessed a heartbeat of its own and Talon stepped even closer. The creatures, animals that they were, paused and turned to look at the angry swell. One had enough sense to step back and scent the air.

The current in her body surged beneath her skin, pacing as if excited that Arianna was finally paying attention to it.

The river moved with a single thought. Not a section. Not the surface. The entire river.

It lifted from between the banks like a writhing worm, then hit the ground and barreled straight toward them. Talon braced himself, moving to shield her from the impact, but the giant surge of water veered off and spun in a circle around them and the six creatures.

The puddles at their feet joined the swirling dark water. It was her weapon now. The massive force completely submissive to her will. Even the droplets falling from the sky froze on command.

Then the water heated. It spun faster and faster, the temperature rising so high Arianna wasn't sure whether it was sweat or water dripping down her neck.

The chill finally left her bones.

Then everything was moving in slow motion again.

Her heart thundered and her anger resurfaced as she imagined all the innocent lives these dreadful beings had feasted upon.

"Steady," Talon whispered, his voice a bit breathless as he watched the storm encircling them. Arianna wasn't sure if it was reverence or trepidation in his voice. Likely a bit of both.

The spiraling water tightened.

"I'm in control," she assured. The water rose high overhead before crashing down on the six creatures with all the force of the raging river. Their screams of fear were lost in the sizzling liquid. It swallowed them whole. They were nothing compared to the power in her hands. Nothing but floating corpses lost to the water's dark depths.

Arianna guided that boiling current right back where it belonged. It crashed between the banks, spilling across either side then resumed its normal path.

The rain turned cold again and the ancient being within her seemed to make a contented sound before crawling back to wherever it hid inside her body.

Arianna collapsed to her knees and nausea rolled through her stomach.

Talon slid down beside her, breathing hard, then his hands were on her shoulder. She hissed and jerked away and he mumbled an apology. Talon followed her gaze to her foot.

"Are you okay?" he asked. Yes. No. Arianna just nodded. Her body trembled too much for her to speak just yet.

"Gods, Arianna, I said hot, not to boil the whole damn river."

A choked laugh. "It worked, didn't it?" She stretched her legs out in the grass and tilted her head back, welcoming the cool rain against her face. "And you didn't exactly specify."

Talon smirked. "Whatever is happening with your magic, I like it. A lot."

She huffed out another laugh. "Me, too." Because it was answering her now, and the power that radiated through her body when it did made Arianna feel like she could conquer the world. No, not conquer it: change it for the better.

After a few more breaths, Talon stood and pulled Arianna to her feet. "Come on, let's get out of here and find some shelter before anything else decides we'd make a good meal."

Chapter Seventy-Four

Rion

It was night when they emerged. The moon glowed in the sky like a silver disc and illuminated the barren landscape. The trees were burnt, their lower trunks covered in black soot just as Kaylee had mentioned. No prints. No path.

Niall covered his tracks well.

Rion tilted his head back, basking in the slight breeze that shifted the ash at their feet. For two months, he'd smelled nothing but the dank cell Niall had crammed him into. Some days it seemed as though he could taste the other prisoners' filth. Now he breathed in the fresh air, not caring that it smelled of embers.

Freedom.

He glanced at his mother. Her green eyes were locked on the moon and her pale skin almost glowed in the faint light. Her chest expanded as she scented the air, taking in … everything.

Eighty years beneath the ground with no hope of ever seeing the sky again. Eighty years of the same four walls and chains and only a few souls to keep her company.

His throat bobbed and Rion turned away, allowing his mother some privacy.

On their way to the surface, Rion had inquired about clothes and Kaylee had led them to a side room where he'd found a tunic and a pair of boots that were slightly too small. He'd thrown them on, thankful they didn't smell of Niall. Rion imagined they'd once belonged to one of the prisoners. He wondered if they were still alive.

His mother had dressed without bothering to remove the tattered clothes already covering her slight frame. She'd found a pair of boots, then had draped a different tunic over Kaylee's head and tied the loose fabric with a rope to hold it closed.

There weren't any shoes to fit Kaylee, but his mother had layered several pairs of moth-eaten socks over her small feet. It would do for now.

"This way," his mother said. She'd kept three full arm lengths away from him since leaving her cell and Kaylee clung to her side.

"How do you know?" Rion eyed the iron on her wrists. Her abilities as a seer wouldn't work with them on.

"I can smell him." Rion scented the air and she caught the movement. "You don't spend decades locked in a cage with someone and forget the foul stench they carry."

Rion nodded, a lump forming in his throat that his mother also seemed to note. She eyed him, that piercing emerald gaze surveying his form for any weaknesses she might be able to exploit. She likely saw a lot of weaknesses right now.

Every muscle in his body burned with a combination of pain and exhaustion. He wasn't certain how far he could push before it finally gave out. His mother's shoulders had slumped, too. Even in the moonlight, he could see her collarbones beneath the fabric of her thin shirt and the way they protruded from her shoulders at sharp angles. Despite the way she'd attacked him, Rion knew she was just as exhausted as he was.

Great. Here they were, two adults barely on their feet and a child who looked more petrified to leave than to stay and face her lunatic of a captor.

Rion knelt to Kaylee's level and gently took her hand. She startled and his mother spun around, eyeing him with a look that promised death should he try to hurt the child.

"It'll be all right," Rion promised. "We're going to get out of here and I'll show you that forest, just like I promised."

Kaylee nodded and something in his mother's gaze softened. His back hurt like hell from where the High Lady of Brónach had planted her knee in his spine. It would likely ache even more tomorrow, as would the rest of him. Gods, he'd give anything for a bed. But they couldn't afford to rest. They needed to move and find shelter away from this wretched place.

He eyed the blackened trunks once more, then they were off. Rion held Kaylee's small hand and Eimear followed behind, a large gap of space still separating them. He could feel his mother's gaze boring a hole through his back as she surveyed the new male in her presence. He'd tried like hell to avoid eye contact with her, if only to keep her from recognizing the color.

He'd never seen the warrior side of his mother, but now he wondered if the skills he'd developed came from her lineage instead of his father's. The pair were legendary. They'd met on the battlefield, fighting side by side against a common enemy. Two against hundreds. Or so the stories claimed. Rion wondered if they'd discovered the mating bond before or after that battle. History claimed they were married soon after and had ruled Brónach as equals.

Rion continued trudging through the ash without looking behind. They were leaving a clear trail. Hopefully they'd run into a river soon. With any luck, it would be calm enough that they could wade into its depths and hide their scents from any pursuers.

Or maybe they'd be better of marching straight for a nearby town. Everyone knew the story of how the High Lady of Brónach had vanished. Perhaps her name would invoke enough protection against Niall and earn them a ride back to Ruadhán. Of course, that also meant his mother discovering his true identity. Only they wouldn't call him a Lord of Brónach. They'd refer to him as The Demon. Perhaps she'd tried to kill him again right then and there. Assist the world in destroying another walking monster.

Rion swallowed hard.

They crept forward, their footsteps silent in the ash. The wind shifted, a branch snapped, and Rion recoiled at the foul stench in the air.

He cursed. He hadn't been paying attention. The hairs on the back of his neck stood on end and he twisted, searching for the beasts he knew would be upon them in seconds. He remembered Kaylee's mention of hounds. The paw prints in the ash ahead proved her right.

Rion frantically surveyed his options and hauled Kaylee toward the tallest tree. He hated the way the little girl flinched when he grabbed her and lifted her onto the lowest branch.

"Climb." She obeyed without question and Rion wondered if she could smell them, too. Perhaps her bloodline favored her Fae heritage. He turned to his mother. "You, too."

She bristled at the command and held her ground. "I'm more than capable of fighting off a few dogs."

"You're exhausted," he tried to reason.

"So are you."

"Please." Something in his tone made her turn. Consider. Rion inclined his head toward the girl. "One of us needs to look after her."

His mother studied Kaylee and the way her body shook. She could definitely smell the hounds. "Fine." She grabbed the lowest branch, hoisted herself up, then urged the child to climb higher.

Rion wished the tree were taller or possessed a few more sturdy branches. They were too exposed and barely nine feet off the ground.

Better than nothing.

Rion noted the long claw marks etched into the tree's burnt bark. They stretched from the height of his shoulders all the way to the ground in four marks that dug deep.

A low growl echoed from the shadows and thunder clouds answered overhead. He suppressed a shiver and turned to face the five beasts prowling toward him on all fours.

Rion let the chain unravel from his right wrist. It hit the ground, with a muffled thud.

The hounds circled him, planning the best way to strike their injured prey. He smelled too much like blood and Rion knew it drove the animals mad. He'd be an easy target for them. A good meal in their stomachs that would cost little effort. Or so they thought.

Matted fur and a host of scars decorated their bodies. Sharp fangs dripped with saliva and Rion counted their ribs, telling him they hadn't had a decent meal in a long while. He knew the feeling.

Rion tightened his grip on the chain, suddenly glad he'd left one intact. The ax had broken when he'd hacked down the door for supplies. He'd tossed the weapon aside. But chains. He could work with that.

Rion might not possess his magic, but he hadn't worked his way through Brónach's ranks with his powers alone. There were countless times his enemies had tried to take advantage of his magic's weakness by making it too heavy or impossible to move.

They'd quickly learned he was just as deadly without it.

The hounds prowled closer, their lips curling to reveal jagged canines. Rion circled too, leading them away from his mother and Kaylee. He could feel his mother's pensive gaze, but he doubted she'd intervene if his body caved. He'd just have to ensure it didn't.

A jaw snapped, Rion hissed, then the first hound lunged.

Rion sidestepped the creature and planted his boot in its ribs, sending it skidding across the ground. A cloud of ash billowed up and the rising breeze carried it off.

A careful calculation then another jumped from his right, teeth flashing. Rion ducked beneath it, then dug his elbow deep into the hound's empty belly. He used its own momentum to send it sailing over his head.

Rion spun then and let the chain in his grip fly out, striking another so hard in the face that the skin along its snout split wide open. The hellish creature howled in pain and dug at its face, backing away.

The others growled and circled, sizing up the threat they'd previously perceived as an easy kill. One against five.

They kept moving, snarling in the moonlight, searching for a sign of weakness, a limp, a twist in his body that would make for an easy take down.

Rion feigned a lunge and the hounds leapt back only to correct themselves and continue pacing. Kaylee coughed and one of the hounds twisted toward the noise.

Rion bristled. Not a single one of these creatures was getting anywhere near those females.

Rion shook the chains around his wrists, loosed a fierce growl, then yelled, "Come on!"

He sprang forward, unwilling to wait for them to make the first move. One came from his right and Rion whipped the chain up, twisting so he caught the creature's neck in a loop. He pulled hard, ducking past another, but not fast enough. Its body collided with his legs, knocking him off balance.

Rion cursed and the pack moved as one when he hit the ground.

Sharp fangs pierced his calf first and he felt the muscles begin to tear. Another locked onto his forearm and still another sank its jaws into his side, ripping the flesh when it shook its massive head.

He scented Kaylee's overwhelming fear, saw his mother lean forward slightly. Then Arianna desperately tugged on the bond and Rion screamed in pained rage.

He slammed an elbow down on the one biting into his ribcage, then used his free leg to kick the hound clamped around his calf. Rion twisted to his knees, wrapped the chain around his fist once, and punched the canine in the head. It backed away, shaking off the pain before lunging again.

Rion shoved the chain into the hound's mouth and twisted sharply, snapping the animal's neck. It collapsed instantly.

One down.

Rion rolled to his left, hoping to use the chain again, but the hound ducked around it and sank those horrid teeth into his other arm. Rion roared, grabbed the chain with his free hand, and beat the creature on the head over and over again until its blood splattered across his tunic.

Rion quickly leaned back, narrowly avoiding another open maw, then rolled to his feet, panting and bloody and full of so much primal rage he was certain he'd explode with it.

The remaining three circled him, the fourth shaking its head in an attempt to clear it. It growled again, but backed away, its head tilted at an unnatural angle.

Rion spun the chain in one hand. He crouched, waiting even as blood trickled down his arms and legs.

He no longer felt his wounds. Just that unrelenting fury that had kept him company for so many years.

Rion growled again. After decades of survival against assassins and walking off bloody battle fields, he wasn't about to be bested by a few mangy animals.

Not here and not now.

Rion darted toward the injured hound on his right. It didn't notice in time. He wrapped the chain around the beast's neck and a crunch of bones told Rion it wouldn't rise again.

He twisted toward the others, but they'd taken a step back, still growling.

Rion let a vicious snarl rip from between his bloodied teeth. The hounds tucked their tails and ran, peering over their shoulders as if he might give chase.

Rion panted, but remained upright, watching just in case they turned back around.

His breathing slowed first, then the tension fell from his shoulders. Then the pain began everywhere all at once. His body was shaking and ash clung to his skin.

Steady. Breathe.

He tried telling himself he'd been through worse, but his body didn't believe the lie.

Rion took another shaky breath and turned toward the tree where his mother and Kaylee sat.

Unsurprisingly, Kaylee watched him with pure terror on her young face. He might as well have been Niall at that moment. He hated it and hated everything he'd had to do in front of her.

His mother watched him as one watched a worthy opponent. She sized him up, taking stock of his injuries and the single long chain dangling from his wrist. He didn't miss the way she'd tightened her grip around the child.

Monster. Demon.

His throat thickened but Rion kept his voice steady when he said, "We need to move."

CHAPTER SEVENTY-FIVE

SAOIRSE

aoirse followed the thick crowd down the hall knowing full well what she was walking into. Just over twelve hours and Niall had figured it out. His guards were patrolling everywhere now, eyes of all shapes and sizes watching from the shadows and high rises as everyone from the manor filed into the main dining hall.

Raevina was already gone, another fact that Niall was sure to have noticed and likely only fueled the rage pouring off him.

She entered the enormous room and joined her warriors who'd been standing off to one side watching the crowd as she'd instructed. The lot of them breathed a sigh of relief at the sight of her. Alec had probably threatened their positions if any harm were to come to his sister. Saoirse rolled her eyes. Males and their protective instincts.

Saoirse acknowledged her second with a curt nod. Fin was a male with a level head and one who wasn't afraid to reel her back when her temper flared too hot. She'd already informed him of the situation.

He'd keep the rest of her warriors in line should things go awry. And Saoirse fully expected them to. If Niall offered any horrible news concerning her brother or Arianna, Saoirse would leave even if she had to fight her way out. She wouldn't let Rion suffer; the gods knew he'd endured enough already.

Fin was to remain in Ruadhán along with the others from Brónach and collect as much information as possible before joining her.

She pinched the bridge of her nose. Maybe she'd made too many cautionary plans. Niall could simply want to share important news he'd recently gathered from wherever he'd visited. With any luck, maybe some of the fighting had ceased.

Zylah filed in with the other half-breeds. The doors closed and Saoirse narrowed her brows at the warriors who stood before the exits with hands on their weapons.

Shit. He definitely knew something was up. But did he suspect them all, or only one?

The crowd fell silent when Niall entered. Without the glamour, he still looked like a nearly perfect male, but his eyes and hair had lost a bit of their luster.

He marched toward the front of the room with the council filing close behind.

Everyone fell silent. Niall's gray eyes studied those in the crowd, lingering on face after face as if he could root out the problem with intimidation alone. He stopped on hers and Saoirse met that unflinching stare with disinterest.

This male was the one who'd taken her little brother. And if she found Rion hurt, Saoirse would enjoy ripping Niall apart piece by piece.

Ellie stood across the room with the half-breed she loved and Móirín's elite at her side. Saoirse frowned at the guards and the way their hands rested atop their weapons. They needed to be more discreet, though perhaps others would simply perceive their pensive stances as nothing more than Móirín protecting their future High Lady. She was the only heir now.

"The Divine has left us," Niall said, his voice somehow amplified throughout the hall. Many exchanged confused glances then murmurs began flying through the crowd. Saoirse remained still, as did Ellie.

"The Divine has left," he repeated and everyone fell silent again. "And I have been betrayed." Saoirse refused to look at Gavin. The male stood close to Niall. Too close for her to intervene should Niall lash out. She was stuck. If she reacted to save Gavin, she might be giving them all away. If she did nothing—

"I have done so much for all of you." He shook his head, as if actually pained. "So much, and yet there are forces who would see me removed from the throne." Niall began pacing before the council members who all stared out at the sea of faces as if they could find the ones Niall was referring to.

Saoirse risked a glance at Gavin. He stood just to the right of the council with notepad in hand. Sweat trickled down his temple. Would Niall kill him here and now, surely—wind ripped through the room like a violent storm and Saoirse grabbed for her weapon. The warriors from Brónach and Móirín did the same, filling the room with the sound of singing steel.

The currents whipped everyone's hair and clothes around in a frenzy of colors and she gritted her teeth, ready for a fight, knowing several civilians were about to become casualties.

But instead of coming for her or Ellie or even Gavin, that current of air shot straight toward the front of the room and hit each of the four council members in the chest and shoved them against the back wall.

Saoirse's lips parted, her face horror struck as she watched the four fall to their knees, clawing at the fabric of their clothes. Their mouths opened in silent screams and blood seeped through the front of their tunics from wounds no one could see.

Two doubled over, their bodies twisting and writhing in a way that reminded her of an injured spider. One fell backward, his head colliding with the marble floor in a sickening thud. But the last one, Declan, forced himself to his feet.

He tried to run, blood dripping from where he clawed at his own throat. Niall didn't even move as another gust of air sent the male careening back into the wall.

Dead. A blink and they were all dead.

Saoirse scarcely risked a breath, her heart pounding in her chest as she gazed upon the four bodies.

Hundreds had just witnessed Niall murder the council members who'd served in Ruadhán for centuries. Centuries. Unless they'd lied about their ages somehow. But—no one said a word.

Calm, she drilled into herself. *Calm, calm, calm.* A warrior didn't have room for panic.

She wasn't leaving her warriors here. No way in hell. Niall had lost his ever-loving mind.

But he'd not targeted her or Ellie or Gavin. Which meant the council were the ones who'd had knowledge about the dungeons. And Niall still thought they were the only ones.

But that didn't mean the rest of them were safe.

Niall brushed a piece of lint from his sleeve and continued as if he'd done nothing more than crumple a sheet of paper. "Now that the proper sentence for treason had been carried out, we can move on to more important matters." He stepped forward and those closest to him stepped back. Niall either pretended not notice or the male didn't care.

"I've already sent my warriors to collect our queen. She has been manipulated and lied to and now believes me an enemy. Let me assure you, wrongs will be set right and the one accompanying her will be tried as a traitor."

Saoirse felt the color drain from her face. Her eyes drifted toward the four bodies behind Niall. She knew exactly what waited for Talon if he returned. It was a good thing they'd already made other plans, but it also meant they needed to get everyone out of this city a lot faster than they'd originally anticipated.

Raevina had taken care of the children, courtesy of a surprise revelation Saoirse still couldn't wrap her head around. But there were the other half-breeds to consider. Arianna wouldn't want them left behind.

Niall stood before them, his carefully crafted mask gone. Now she saw a male who'd grown bored of his own game. He was prepared to take what he wanted and eliminate any who stood in his way.

And he wanted Arianna.

Saoirse glanced outside, trying to judge the sun. Would Raevina have found Arianna by now, or had she run into trouble with Niall's warriors? Had they located and freed Rion? Were the three of them on their way to the safe house?

And if not . . . if things turned completely upside down and Niall captured Arianna too, what would the female be willing to sacrifice in order to save her friends? With the queen in his clutches, no one would dare stand against Niall for fear of him hurting her.

Niall's voice rose again. "If you look around at those in this room, you'll notice we're missing an ambassador." His fingers flexed. A tic of frustration. "Which tells me the council are not the only ones who have betrayed me." Niall turned to Ellie then and Saoirse's heart jolted. He offered the young female a wicked smile that sent a chill skittering down Saoirse's spine. How did he know? How many spies roamed the manor halls?

"Tell me where Raevina is and what she's plotting."

Ellie made a show of looking at those standing around her. Their weapons were still out. "You're asking me?"

"Do not play dumb with me. I want to know what that miserable wretch is planning." Niall stepped forward. "Does she hope Arianna will find The Demon? Do they plan to reconvene at a remote location? Return to force me to pay for the crimes they imagine I've committed?"

That was exactly Arianna's plan. Saoirse looked at the bodies again. Not that it would do much good now.

Niall laughed, though it was more to himself. "You think overthrowing me would go over so easily? I've been leading these Fae for centuries. They've lived in luxury because of my decisions. They've eaten well and slept in warm beds and wanted for absolutely nothing because of me."

"And yet you're not their king."

The room drew in a collective breath as the two stared one another down. If Ellie was trying to make Niall lose his composure, she might have just succeeded. One of his fists clenched and for a moment, Saoirse thought she felt that storm again. She gripped her weapon harder. Surely he wouldn't kill the ambassador of Móirín. It would incite a war that could cripple everything he'd worked for.

But even that knowledge, despite his anger, wasn't lost on him. Niall stepped back and plastered a fake smile on his face.

"I didn't want to have to resort to this." Niall raised his hand and a pair of guards grabbed a half-breed from the crowd. The male cried out and fought against the strong arms dragging him toward Niall. The crowd only watched, their eyes darting from Niall to Ellie and back.

Did Ellie know him? Her brow had furrowed, but recognition didn't flit across Ellie's face. Kirian was standing at her side. The guards forced the half-breed to his knees. He was already shaking, his eyes wide with terror.

"Here's how this is going to unfold." Niall whipped out a blade and, fast as the wind itself, sliced it across the male's throat, opening a bright red line. Saoirse didn't turn away. The half-breed reached for his neck, trying to hold the blood in. He coughed once, spraying crimson over the smooth marble, then his head hit the hard floor. Someone in the crowd screamed and hushed sounds echoed to calm the female.

A servant handed Niall a towel and he cleaned his blade before sliding it back in the sheath at his side. He'd somehow hidden the long sword beneath his clothes. Another glamour?

Niall clicked his tongue. "Such a waste, but he can always be replaced." He turned as if the male meant nothing, but Ellie was shaking, her fists balled tight. Saoirse swore she could scent Ellie's magic in the air.

"Every," Niall made a show of thinking, "let's say, thirty minutes, I'm going to kill a former slave until you," he pointed at Ellie, "tell me what I want to know."

Undiluted hatred flickered in the Ellie's eyes. But despite the gruesome show, they still needed to keep calm. Saoirse prayed Ellie knew that, too.

Ellie didn't speak. She just stared Niall down, unflinching and unafraid.

Niall raised his brows. "No loyalty for the creatures you claim to love?" Niall's gaze flickered toward Kirian and Saoirse's heart plummeted when Niall pointed. "Bring him to me."

Chaos erupted.

Ellie's magic sprang to life as soon as the guards reached for Kirian and Saoirse's stomach fell when an iron clasp clicked around Ellie's wrist a second later. One of her guards had betrayed her. The young female fought, screamed, and beat those who tried to hold her down. One guard stumbled away, holding a bloody nose while she lunged forward, grabbing Kirian's hand once before they were torn apart.

Ellie spun, wrapped the chain around the guard's throat, and yanked him back. A sharp kick forced the male to his knees. She pulled the chain tight and eyed Niall. "Let him go."

Niall laughed. "You think a hostage will sway me to release your precious half-breed?" He gestured to the crowd. "I have an entire room of hostages."

Panic covered Ellie's face. Saoirse's heart was beating faster now. What should she do? Niall would likely kill the half-breeds anyway out of spite. Did she cut her losses, grab Ellie and Kirian, and make a run for it? Would her warriors make it out alive if she did?

Kirian was on his knees now. Niall wasn't waiting. Ellie released her hold on the guard and lunged forward. A set of Niall's warriors drew their weapons and Ellie's guards met them swing for swing.

Ice and fire erupted, then Niall's sweeping magic disarmed them all and sent the Móirín warriors careening into the nearest wall. Six guards disarmed with barely the flick of his wrist.

His sentinels forced Ellie to her knees. The young female was sobbing as she watched Kirian directly across from her, knowing she was out of options.

Saoirse stepped forward, but Gavin beat her to it.

"My Lord."

Time seemed to freeze as Niall turned those hateful grey eyes onto his assistant. His nephew. Gavin's throat bobbed but he stood straight and walked a few paces before sinking to his knees. "If My

Lord would be so gracious, I would like to take this one and the half-breed to my rooms."

Niall raised a brow and looked around as if he'd missed a conversation somewhere. He chuckled a bit. "Your father warned me you could be dull at times. You take after your mother in that regard."

To his credit, Gavin didn't flinch. "Please, My Lord."

Niall studied the blade he'd drawn. "And why would I ever relinquish these two to your hold? What purpose would that serve of mine?"

"I have unfinished business with her, My Lord."

Again Niall met the eyes of his warriors as if astounded the male had the audacity to speak. "I fail to see how that pertains."

Gavin kept his voice calm. "She has defiled herself with a half-breed. She insulted my person when I confronted her and she failed to heed my demands."

Niall tapped his blade against the marble floor. "Your point, please."

"She's my mate, My Lord."

At that, Niall's brows rose. He stood there for a few seconds before throwing his head back in laughter. The sound echoed through the large room, but no one joined him. Saoirse was fairly certain he'd lost his mind.

When Niall finally collected himself, he stepped away from Kirian and Saoirse relaxed a fraction. "Well isn't this just fantastic," he said and spread his arms wide. "The ambassador of Móirín, no, the future of Móirín, will come under the rule of Pádraigín." He smiled brighter. "Gods know we need some new blood in Móirín. I fear their High Lord's mind isn't quite as sharp as it used to be." Niall looked pointedly at Ellie, who was looking at Gavin, but Saoirse couldn't yet tell if it was with anger or fear or a combination of the two.

"Just look at who he appointed as his ambassador. A sixteen-year-old female who hasn't even come into her animal form. A child. It's like he holds no respect for the royal city and all it stands for."

Niall looked at Gavin again. The male hadn't raised his head or moved from his knelt position. "Rise, nephew." He curled his lip in disgust. "Are you certain you wish to keep the half-breed as well? I could just as easily take care of him for you now."

Gavin stood, but kept his head lowered. "He will keep her obedient and I would like the eventual opportunity to do it myself."

A wicked smile crossed Niall's face. "Of course. I unfortunately understand what it's like to have your female possessed by a lesser male." He looked between them. "I highly recommend keeping them both in chains."

"Of course, My Lord."

Niall snapped his fingers and a group of guards escorted Ellie and Kirian from the hall with Gavin following close behind. Good, he'd get them out. Saoirse hoped.

But it left her wondering how Niall planned to obtain information about Raevina.

Everything in Saoirse's body went rigid when she turned to find Niall smiling at her. Then Saoirse heard the scream and saw the female they were dragging in from a side door.

Her mouth went dry.

"You didn't think the games were over yet, did you?" He hadn't looked away, even as Màili was dragged down the aisle, tears streaming down her beautiful face.

"What is this?" Saoirse demanded.

Niall glanced between her and Màili. "This is the female you were infatuated with just a few short months ago."

"What does she have to do with anything?"

Niall chuckled. "Do you want to tell her or shall I?" It took Saoirse a moment to realize he hadn't been addressing her. He was talking to Màili.

Màili's pleading eyes met Saoirse's. "It wasn't like that. It—"

"Wasn't it?" Niall interrupted. "I recall several letters detailing events in Nàdiar that were nothing short of classified." Niall tapped his chin. "In fact, I remember one such letter when you were caught in Saoirse's office. You played that part so well that the sister of the High Lord even invited you to her bed."

Saoirse clenched her fists. "So," Niall said. "Now I have to ask what a traitor's life means to the ambassador of Brónach."

"No," Màili cried again. "You don't understand. He made me, he threatened my family—"

"Was it all fake then?" Saoirse asked, her voice deadly calm. She'd shared things with Màili she'd never shared with anyone. Not information about Alec or her nation, but secrets about herself, her dreams and goals and fears.

"No, it started that way, but—"

"But you fell in love," Niall scoffed. "It's always the same story wrapped a different way. Throw feelings into the mix and suddenly you're forgiven." Niall placed his blade beneath her throat and Màili whimpered. "We'll see if those feelings hold any value momentarily." Niall directed his cold gaze to Saoirse. "Tell me what I want to know."

"You're not going to kill a pure blood."

She could have sworn something glinted in Niall's gaze. "I killed the council."

Saoirse couldn't stop herself from looking at the bodies. "You said they betrayed you."

"And what do you think you've done?"

She shrugged. "Nothing."

"Nothing," he echoed, brows raised. "You've committed treason by plotting against me. The punishment for that is death."

Saoirse narrowed her eyes at him. "Go ahead and try it."

He clicked his tongue and dug the point of his sword deeper.

"Saoirse?" Màili's frightened voice cut through her anger. She'd deal with the female's betrayal later. Right now she just needed to get Màili away from Niall.

"You'll be okay," Saoirse promised.

Niall laughed, then tilted his head. "I'm waiting, Saoirse. And despite what I've let everyone believe, I am not a patient male."

"I have nothing to say to you."

He sighed and pinched the bridge of his nose with his free hand. "I thought I'd made enough demonstrations already. I suppose it's a good thing there are two females you admire, even if your second choice makes me nauseous." The blade gleamed in the light as he tilted it. "To think not one but two ambassadors have fallen for half-breeds."

"What are you—" but before she could get the words out, Niall had spun with his weapon.

Saoirse's scream filled the cavernous hall when Màili's head left her shoulders and rolled across the marble floor. She ran for the female, hands outstretched as if she might be able to put her back together.

Saoirse's knees slammed into the floor. Her hands shook as she reached forward then recoiled, wanting to touch Màili's head yet not daring.

A look of pure terror marred the beautiful female's face. Saoirse thought she might vomit right there.

She couldn't form thought or words. Gone. She was just gone. No chance for explanations. No second chances. Nothing.

A green cloak slowly floated down to hide Màili's face and Saoirse peered up to find Fin at her side with his head bowed.

"I do hope that's enough to convince you." Niall's voice. "Now tell me where they're going."

Saoirse didn't move. Her knees throbbed and her chest felt hollow as if someone had carved her heart right out of the cavity. She'd kill him.

"Go to hell," she seethed. Màili. Beautiful, brave Màili was no longer part of this world. She was gone. In a blink she was just gone. Saoirse had done nothing to stop it. She'd thought Niall would hesitate, play a different hand. But the male was beyond playing.

"Fine, if you need more motivation, so be it. I can keep this up all day."

Niall snapped his fingers and a familiar voice filled the room.

Saoirse's head snapped up to find Niall heading straight for Zylah, his bloody blade dragging across the floor in his wake. The sound echoed through Saoirse's ears even as her blood pumped wildly, drowning out all reason.

A pair of guards had their hands on Zylah. She kicked and screamed like a feral cat in their grip. None of the former slaves reached for her, despite the things Zylah had done to help them. Profound rage burned through Saoirse's blood when one guard reached for a pair of shackles.

Zylah's magic spun in a frenzied current, whipping her clothes with its force. She blasted her captors into the crowd, then pivoted toward the door.

Zylah. Niall would kill Zylah next or torture her until Saoirse yielded the information he desired.

He'd made a show of the council members and Màili to instill fear. He had been three steps ahead from the beginning.

Ice wrapped around Zylah's wrists and color leached from the half-breed's face. She yanked against her restraints, twisting her arms so far Saoirse was certain her bones would snap.

Zylah thrashed, but when she saw the iron shackles, something in the female broke. Her screams turned to hysteria and her anger to undiluted fear.

And that fear was Saoirse's undoing.

No way. No way in hell was Niall laying a single finger on Zylah. She'd rip herself to shreds, fight until every last bone in her body broke before she let him hurt that female.

Greenery broke from the floor and shot across the hall so fast Niall didn't notice until it grabbed his arms. The thorns pierced through his flesh and yanked the male to his knees.

Saoirse was already flying, moving faster than she'd ever moved in her life. Her instincts were shouting. Demanding. *Protect, protect, protect.*

Saoirse leapt past Niall and twisted to dodge the warriors closing in around their lord. She didn't care about them or Niall, she just needed Zylah.

Saoirse's magic was a symphony of greenery rising in her wake. It covered everyone and everything and pinned them all in place.

Many screamed while others summoned their own magic to fight. Flames rose behind Zylah and Saoirse slid across the ground, dragging her blade across two ankles before rising to her feet again. Her magic wrapped another three in a sharp embrace and squeezed until their faces contorted. She didn't care if they lived or died.

A blast of air hit Saoirse from behind and she turned just in time to see Niall rising to his feet.

Saoirse didn't think, didn't fear, didn't feel, just as she'd always been taught. She only moved. Saoirse pulled her magic forth again, a rising wave of vines and branches that interlocked, then grabbed Zylah's wrist and blasted through the doors.

Zylah didn't protest. Saoirse wasn't certain if the female was in shock or thankful.

The halls were empty and Zylah kept pace as they sprinted with Saoirse's magic doing everything it could to slow Niall and his warriors.

They exited the manor and Saoirse steered them toward the side, where they sprinted through the garden. Zylah still didn't speak, didn't question as they continued, running, running, running until Saoirse could see the edge of the city.

It was only then that Zylah tried to slow, but Saoirse tightened the hold she had on the female's wrist.

"What are you doing?" Zylah yelled, her spike of fear almost palpable.

Saoirse passed her a single glance. "Trust me." She knew Zylah didn't and maybe she never would, but when presented with the choice of Niall or Saoirse, Zylah chose Saoirse. At least it seemed that way as Saoirse leapt from the floating city's edge and the pair plummeted through the sky.

CHAPTER SEVENTY-SIX

RION

Rion panted as they continued trudging across the terrain in the dark. The adrenaline had worn off and suddenly he wasn't sure how much longer he could keep pushing his body. Sweat beaded against his brow and when the rain started, Rion thanked the gods. He tilted his head back, letting the cool water wash away the sweat, grime, and crusted blood coating his entire body.

His mother did the same while Kaylee just held her hands out, trying to catch the droplets.

Then he saw the girl's smile as she turned to him and Rion's heart melted. He'd push on, if only for her.

It was the first time she'd looked at him since their run-in with the hounds.

They'd left the ash behind over an hour ago and were greeted with an open rolling landscape dotted with trees. Night still kept them hidden from the world, but there was no telling what they'd face come sunrise. Rion didn't know if Niall would send warriors to check in on his prisoners. Surely someone replenished supplies. How long did they have? He should have asked, planned everything out.

"We need to clean your wounds," his mother said, eyeing him. Rion hadn't realized how slow he'd been walking until now. He could hardly recall the last few minutes. Gods, his head was throbbing.

"Later," he said. They had to find shelter first. If Niall discovered them missing and sent a group of warriors to retrieve them, it would all be over.

Rion didn't want to imagine what Niall would do to his mother or the girl for escaping.

Eimear didn't argue, nor did she look at him again as they pressed forward. He studied a warrior's determination and realized she wouldn't go back. Even if Niall sent a hundred warriors, Eimear would die fighting, content to let her long life end rather than be imprisoned again.

Rion steeled himself, his very bones crying out as he pushed his legs to move faster.

Thunder cracked overhead and Kaylee ran to his mother's side, clutching her leg. He thought he saw a faint smile trace Eimear's lips and Rion was suddenly pulled back to a time when he was young. Eimear had given him that smile before, offered it to Saoirse, too. A smile reserved for children and her family.

Emotion swelled through him and Rion turned away, refusing to look at her again.

The trio continued through the storm, pushing their worn bodies past the brink of exhaustion. It was his mother who found the outcropping of rock and the space beneath it.

Rion sniffed the area and studied the tracks through blurring vision. Nothing large seemed to dwell within and the thick brush surrounding it would give them cover.

The trio crawled inside right as dawn began lightening the sky.

Kaylee, little as she was, walked about without issue, but Rion and his mother were forced to kneel, and eventually Rion just shifted to crawling across the dirt floor. He spotted a few pieces of dry wood in the back and sent up a prayer to the gods for their fortune.

He'd also found a rolled blanket and an empty shoulder pack. Travelers frequented the cave, which meant they weren't far from a road. Good, his mother and Kaylee could get a proper meal soon.

Rion hadn't planned to make a fire, but Kaylee's teeth were chattering and the rain had soaked them all to the bone. He handed her the blanket and the girl draped it across her shoulders.

His mother slumped against the furthest wall and Rion crept as close as he dared before working on a spark. She watched him like a predator assessing its prey, marking every movement and hesitation.

"You can sleep," Rion said. "I'll take first watch." Though he'd probably have to stand in the rain to stay awake.

Smoke. Then a flame, and Rion slowly fed the spark to life. He'd keep it low, just enough to chase the chill from their bones. The smoke curled outside the space but there was little he could do about that. Hopefully the rain would be enough to wash away their tracks and scents. Rion was relying too heavily on Niall's word that he wouldn't be back.

"Why save me?" his mother finally asked, her voice a near whisper. Kaylee was already asleep in Eimear's lap. He wondered if the child had ever had a restful night's sleep.

Rion couldn't meet her gaze. "I heard you screaming for weeks. I couldn't just leave you there."

Tell her the truth.

No, not yet. Maybe not ever. Because if she learned the truth and he saw disappointment flash across her face, Rion wasn't sure he could survive it.

She continued to study him, undeterred. "You left the others."

"Their cells weren't beside mine. I couldn't hear them. Not really." He'd thought he'd heard some echoes, but Niall had distorted his reality so many times, he couldn't be sure they were real.

"Will you really send for their aid?"

Rion nodded. "As soon as we reach Ruadhán, I'll tell Arianna about them and she'll send for their rescue."

"Arianna?"

"The Divine," he clarified.

She lifted a brow. "You're on a first name basis with the queen?" Shit. Shit, shit, shit. "Are you Brónach's ambassador?"

"No," he said, trying to choose his words carefully. "I'm . . . no one important."

Her voice was like ice. "You should try telling a better lie." His gaze snapped up at her tone and Rion prayed she wouldn't lunge at him again. He was certain Kaylee's sleeping form was the only thing keeping her rooted down.

Rion didn't have the strength for another fight. His wounds had clotted, but his body had also begun to stiffen since he'd sat down. Eimear continued. "Everyone who is allowed within the walls of Ruadhán is important." Her eyes narrowed. "I deserve to know who I'm traveling with and why he was locked up in that hellish place." Demanding. Intimidating. Determined. Just like Saoirse.

But what could he tell her? He wasn't ready to face the truth.

"I-I helped guard her. The Divine, I mean. Or I did."

"What does that mean?"

Rion shook his head and lowered his voice. "It means she might never forgive me."

Eimear was silent for so long that Rion dared to glance her way. He found something akin to sympathy in her eyes. "You love her."

Something caught in his throat at that and he rushed to blink away the tears. "More than anything."

Silence again. The rain increased, coming down in sheets now. Rion watched the water trickle past in a groove that had formed over the years.

"How old is she?"

"Eighteen."

"Niall only mentioned her appearance recently. Why didn't she go to them sooner?"

"She didn't want to be found."

"Why?"

He shrugged. "She was young and didn't know what she wanted from the world yet."

His mother digested the information for a while. He felt his eyes drift shut, but Eimear's voice jolted him awake again. "Is she Lillian's daughter?"

The name struck a chord in him. Of course his mother had known Lillian. Their countries had been allies after all, but Arianna and Ellie hadn't been born until long after his mother's disappearance.

Rion nodded. "She had two daughters. The younger is sixteen."

"Had?"

His jaw clenched. "She passed a decade ago, right before the war."

"What war?"

"The one between Brónach and Móirín."

Eimear opened her mouth to ask another question, then closed it again. "There's a lot I need to relearn about the world."

The way she studied the rain had Rion's heart aching for her. Here he was, having a conversation with his mother, a female who had suffered beyond anything he could even begin to imagine, and she didn't even know one of her children sat across from her.

But he didn't want to hurt her more or overwhelm her already distressed mind. He saw the way she clenched her fists and teeth, the quick looks as she struggled not to flee at every sound. The struggle not to flee from him.

"They're not at war anymore," Rion clarified. "They've reconciled."

She nodded at that. "Good." And just when he thought she might not speak again, his mother asked. "Who is the High Lord of Brónach now?" Right. She would have felt the bond break when his father died. Rion had to swallow the lump in his throat.

"Alec." Her gaze shot to him again and he cursed himself. "Lord Alec," Rion corrected. "Lady Saoirse serves as his advisor and is the ambassador in Ruadhán right now."

"On a first-name basis with so many important individuals, aren't you?" She eyed him. "Or are you simply disrespectful?"

Rion lowered his head. "I'm striving not to be."

His heart pounded as she studied him. He knew what she'd ask next, and part of him wished she wouldn't. That maybe she'd close her eyes and drift off to sleep. But the words left her lips and it was everything Rion could do to keep himself in check.

"And what of my youngest son, Rion? What became of him?"

The worry in her voice cracked something in his chest. He tried and failed to keep his voice steady. "He became a war general."

Eimear's heart began racing. "Is he—"

"No," Rion said quickly, unwilling to let his mother think the worst. "He's alive, he just has other duties now."

"I see." She looked down at Kaylee, then began running her hands through the girl's hair. Rion couldn't help but wonder if his mother thought of him and his siblings in that moment.

"Do you have children?"

His jolted. "No. They're not something I deserve."

Her brow furrowed. "Why?"

Because I'm a monster. "I've . . . done things."

She laughed softly but the sound sent Rion's heart soaring. She'd laughed. Decades of torment and his mother was smiling. "If everyone thought that way, no one would have them." She continued stroking Kaylee's hair. "You didn't act surprised when I called the High Lord of Brónach and his siblings my children, which means you know who I am."

Shit. Another slip. He couldn't get his brain to think right. Rion swallowed. "You're the High Lady of Brónach."

"And does the unimportant former guard of The Divine who is also from Brónach plan to introduce himself to his High Lady?"

Rion stared at the small flame between them. "I'd rather not."

"I knew it." She was looking at Kaylee again. "You really had me fooled this time. Bravo, I suppose."

"What?"

Silver lined her eyes and his stomach plummeted. "Just be done with it. I'm tired of these games."

Tired of—oh gods. Niall. His magic. She didn't think any of this was real.

How many times had Niall let her taste freedom only for the vision to ripple and fade? How many times had she tasted hope only to feel the bitter after-sting of despair?

"This is real," he said. "You're free."

"Free." She tasted the word but still hadn't looked up from the child. "I'd give anything for her to be free, but what could I possibly offer you that you haven't already taken?"

He would kill Niall. The next time he laid eyes on the male, he'd kill him for everything he'd done.

Rion took a shaky breath and searched through the memories he'd buried long ago. He had placed them inside a box and thrown away the key, determined to keep them safe from the darkness that had devoured his life. But Rion dusted off that key now and inserted it into the lock. His mother needed this. No matter how much it might kill him, his mother deserved to know she was safe.

"Mint," he started, his voice barely more than a whisper. "You used to have mint tea every morning. There was a little jar nestled on the counter with pink flowers decorating the lid." Her head lifted.

"You liked to tend to the fire yourself and you'd sit in a rocking chair with a blanket draped across your lap as the sun rose. It was your favorite time of day."

He could feel her heavy gaze but refused to look up. "You loved the second floor garden the most. It's where you always went when you and Fa—if you and The High Lord had a disagreement. It was a gift from him on one of your anniversaries. I don't remember which one. You were always rearranging it, tending to the plants and digging through the dirt despite your magic."

Rion wasn't sure what to do with his hands. "You loved chocolate but hated when anyone added nuts to it. You claimed it destroyed a perfectly good dessert." He smiled at that, remembering her red face when she'd bitten into a brownie only for it to have a crunch. She'd been polite of course and ate it anyway, but even Alec had laughed at his mother on their way home.

"You would put us to bed and whisper a prayer of protection over us every night. Though you had to say Alec's after dinner because he claimed he was too old for his mother to tuck him in." His hands were shaking now. "And you used to sing. I remember the melodies, but not the words."

His heart was beating against his ribs so hard Rion was sure they'd crack. He couldn't escape this moment, no matter how much he wanted to. He didn't want her to look at him with disappointment when she discovered he was a monster. He didn't want her to learn that he'd injured The Divine. That he'd been cursed by the gods.

"Look at me." The command in her words forced him to obey. She studied his face. The emerald green eyes that were a reflection of her own. His auburn hair, a shade darker than the long locks she possessed. The set in his broad jaw that Saoirse claimed reminded her of their father. His frame, his hands, the way he sat.

"Come here." Rion shook his head and looked away again. He didn't trust his voice to speak. His mother shifted Kaylee and placed the empty pack beneath her head. The young girl curled tighter in on herself but didn't wake. Or maybe she was only pretending to sleep while listening to the adults.

Eimear inched closer. Rion didn't move, even as his heart rate spiked. She knelt before him.

Six inches. His mother was six inches away, her gaze combing over his features again and again and again. He'd rooted himself in place, unable to shift as both hope and dread threatened to drown him.

"Look at me," she repeated. Reluctantly, he obeyed again. Silver lined her eyes. "Rion?"

Rion's throat tightened. His mother knew. Recognized him even after all the years apart. But what could he say? What—

Her thin fingers reached for his face and Rion flinched away. The anguished look that crossed her face was enough to shatter every barrier he'd ever created. Her eyes took in the shackles around his wrists and ankles and the blood caked to his face and torso. The bruises that lined his arms and body.

"I won't hurt you," she promised and Rion's breath hitched when she pulled him into an achingly gentle embrace. He heard her heart, a familiar sound that dragged a sob from his body. He gripped the back of her shirt and just like she'd done when he was a child, his mother rocked him back and forth, rubbing his back in soothing circles.

And Rion let himself split wide open.

IT COULD have hours or days or years, but he pulled back too soon and collected himself, wiping at the tears running down his face. His mother's hand met his cheek and he let her run her fingers through his hair and study him, an adult in place of the child she'd left behind.

"You always had the biggest heart out of your siblings." Rion couldn't help the strangled laugh that escaped him. The heart that she remembered had been crushed beneath the weight of the world, but he wasn't about to bring that up now, not with her looking at him in a way only a mother could. Like she'd love him despite any flaw.

She cocked her head. "A war general?" He grasped her hand gently and pressed his cheek against it, wanting to feel this forever. He wanted to confess everything he'd ever done and hide it at the same time. He wanted to flee while she still loved him. He wanted—

"Rion."

His voice cracked. "I've done so many horrible things."

She moved to sit beside him and coaxed his head to her shoulder. He felt so young beside her, even if he towered over her now. "So have all who've encountered war. Everyone's hands are stained, my own included."

He couldn't imagine his mother stained by anything.

CHAPTER SEVENTY-SEVEN

ARIANNA

The pair kept moving through the endless downpour, determined to stay ahead of anything else hunting them through the trees.

They were getting closer now. She could smell ash in the damp air. Her heart pounded furiously. Arianna wasn't sure how she'd react upon seeing Rion again. She knew how she wanted to react. She wanted to run into his arms and pull him close. She wanted to heal all his injuries and hide away from the world where he'd be safe from anyone ever trying something like this again. But reality was a far crueler beast.

Please don't be afraid of him, she begged herself as if it would help. She hated the images her nightmares conjured. They were horrid and had her waking breathless and reeling. Arianna wondered if it had been Niall who'd initially planted those images in her mind. She might not be glamoured anymore, but the effects lingered all the same. Damn that male to hell.

He had started this whole mess. She didn't doubt that he'd do everything in his power to solidify his intensions.

Let him make the first move, Talon had suggested. She didn't want to wait. She wanted to drown in the scent of her mate, the scent of their bond, and Arianna wasn't sure her body was going to let her.

The trees stopped suddenly and opened to reveal a land covered in ash. It might have once been a meadow peppered with trees, but now the black trunks jutted up from the ground like dark pillars reaching for the sky.

Arianna searched the sopping wet ground first, hoping to find tracks that might help her identify how many warriors stood between her and her mate. To her dismay, the rain had already washed everything away.

She studied the nearby trees, searching for any Fae in disguise, but there didn't appear to be any of those either. Would Niall really leave an entire prison unguarded? Perhaps he thought the burnt ground would be enough to deter most passing by. It had certainly deterred Talon.

Dawn had just started to brighten the sky when she stepped into the clearing, still limping on her injured foot. Talon grabbed her arm. "We should scout the area first."

"He could be right there," Arianna hissed.

"So could a dozen guards."

"Then we'll take them out."

"Arianna, you have to remember to think. I know—"

"I am thinking," she growled. "I'm thinking he's been held here for two months. I'm thinking about all the ways he's likely hurt and the terrible things Niall has done to him. I am not going to stand here and let him endure one more second of it."

Talon released her arm and studied the ashen landscape again. The wind shifted, then Arianna went rigid. Not because of warriors or guards or creatures, but because of the scent in the air.

Her blood thrummed through her veins like the beat of a dream and Arianna took off sprinting through the burnt area.

She ignored the pain in her body and Talon didn't stop her. He couldn't have even if he'd tried because that was Rion's blood in the air. A lot of it, along with the smell of death and decay. She searched for their bond and found that single strand intact. It wasn't him. He wasn't dead, but he was definitely hurt.

Her heart kept racing as she flew across the wide expanse. She didn't have a tree line to hide behind now and neither had he. Who had found him and what had they done? Would Arianna find her mate in a puddle of his own blood, barely alive? Had he tried to fight his way out? Was he the reason no guards stood around the area?

She skidded to a halt at the sight of the corpses ahead. Hounds. Their bodies had been mutilated by other animals. Any tracks that might have told Talon what had happened here had been washed away by the ever-present rain.

But that was definitely Rion's blood in the air.

She turned toward Talon who seemed to be studying everything, reading signs on the ground she couldn't decipher.

"It's hard to see, but he's not alone." Talon walked to a nearby tree and pulled a string of fabric from the darkened bark. He sniffed. "There's a female with him, maybe another, but the scent is too muddled to make out."

"Are they being followed?"

Talon shook his head. "Not that I can tell. At least not from this direction." He looked around and Arianna followed his stare. The burnt land stretched so far she couldn't see the end. There were others. Niall had more people trapped against their will. More who had suffered at his hand.

"We'll come back for them," Talon said, seeming to read her thoughts. "Avalon will get them out."

"You think they'll be okay until then?"

Talon shrugged. "I can't say, but we don't have the man power to deal with a bunch of Fae who've been isolated in a prison for who knows how long. Their sanity might not be . . . intact," Talon said carefully.

Arianna nodded, then her heart jolted as she heard shouting in the distance. She didn't even look at Talon before they were both running again.

I'm coming, she tried to call down the bond. *Just keep fighting. I'm coming.*

CHAPTER SEVENTY-EIGHT

SAOIRSE

Saoirse allowed Zylah to rip her arm out of her grasp when they'd finally outrun their pursuers. Zylah had been trying to get away from her since they'd jumped from the city's edge hours ago. Saoirse had hissed at the female then demanded she stay within reach.

Zylah was too headstrong and her instincts were all wrong. She'd wanted to circle back and gather the rest of the half-breeds so Niall couldn't hurt them, but Saoirse had firmly told her it wasn't a good idea and that she wouldn't allow Zylah to get herself killed. Zylah hadn't reacted well and Saoirse had even resorted to carrying the female at one point.

That had earned Saoirse the slice across her forearm. Not from the squirming female, but from their enemy. She'd been too slow to dodge the knife. It was only after fighting and narrowly escaping another round of pursuers that Zylah finally listened to her.

Saoirse rubbed her temples. She needed wine. Lots of wine and a bath and a warm bed full of lush pillows.

Saoirse slumped against the nearest tree and let her body slide to the ground. A motion she immediately regretted when the harsh bark bit into her singed skin. She rested her head against the wide oak and tried to ignore the blistering pain.

Fiadh's shadows had caught her during a skirmish. Well, they'd almost hit Zylah and Saoirse had intervened. The flames had licked across the tops of her shoulders. Not that Zylah had noticed. She'd been too busy screaming in Saoirse's face.

Saoirse couldn't have saved the half-breeds even if she'd wanted to. It was the grim reality of any confrontation. Not everyone made it out alive. But Zylah would. Even if Saoirse had to play the villain, Zylah would be free to live the life she pleased.

But Máili—

Saoirse clenched her jaw and closed her eyes. Images of Máili's lifeless corpse replayed over and over in her mind. She didn't want to imagine what Niall would do with her body. Máili deserved the most beautiful of services and Saoirse vowed she'd honor the female's death and take her remains back to Nàdiar. She deserved that much, even if she had been a traitor.

Saoirse would never know the extent of it. Never hear the explanation.

A shadow fell over her face, then a cold blade pressed hard against Saoirse's throat. She opened her tired eyes to find Zylah's cold gaze staring back. Her jaw was set, her hair disheveled, and blood had smeared over the left side of her cheek from a dagger that had flown too close. Saoirse had killed the warrior who'd thrown it.

A tired smirk. "Is this how you say thank you?"

Zylah's lips curled back from her teeth. "You left them."

"I didn't have time to weigh my options. I made a decision and—"

"The wrong decision." Zylah sneered. "You've never cared about them."

"Don't presume to know what I do and do not care about." Saoirse's icy voice froze the female. "After what I just saw. After what he did to—" Saoirse's throat went raw and she swallowed the burning tears. "I did what I had to do to ensure you survived. And I'd do it again."

Zylah put more pressure on the blade and Saoirse struggled to swallow. "What's the plan?" Saoirse asked. "Kill me, then run off to find the queen and demand she rescue those left behind?"

"I'd never make demands of her."

"But you'll make demands of me? I'm sister to The High Lord of Brónach."

"That's exactly why I make demands of you."

"Because of where I'm from?"

"Because of your position among the powerful. Because of your ability to instill change and the refusal to do so."

"I'm making changes."

Zylah raised her voice. "Freeing one slave doesn't undo a lifetime of feigned ignorance."

Saoirse leaned back. Anger. So much anger, but Saoirse saw through it to the real emotions Zylah kept burying down. Feelings that she might not be able to let herself recognize lest they consume her. It wasn't anger at all. "You blame Brónach for your brother's death."

She glared. "Among others."

"Who else?"

Zylah clenched her teeth. "My mother, my father, and," she swallowed hard. "My fiancée." Saoirse froze. "That's right, my fiancée. I was engaged, we were happy. My entire family had everything we could ever want, then your warriors," her hands shook, "walked into our town and took everything. *Everything*," she emphasized. "I watched—" her lips trembled. "I'll never forget Brónach's colors, or the looks on their faces."

Light rain started overhead. Neither female moved. "If you believe killing me will bring them back—"

Zylah growled. "I know it won't bring them back. I don't care. I swore I'd tear Brónach apart one day. I swore I'd kill the entire royal family and put an end to your wretched line."

"Would you resort to killing children, too?" Zylah didn't move. "If I told you Alec had sired a child, would you go after the infant?"

"I'm not a monster."

"No, you're not. You are one of the bravest females I've ever met and I admire you for what you've already accomplished."

"Flattery isn't going to save your life."

"I don't intend it to." Saoirse gently took Zylah's wrist and positioned the blade lower. "You'll hit the artery better here." The blade bit into Saoirse's skin.

"You're not even going to fight?"

"Is that what you want? A fight?" Zylah clenched her jaw. "Do you want to go to war, carve up the land in the name of vengeance?"

"No."

"No," Saoirse echoed. "You just want others to suffer as you have suffered. I understand."

"You're not doing a very good job of talking me out of it."

"Do you want to be talked out of it or do you just want to hear me beg for my life?"

Zylah didn't answer. Saoirse leaned forward and the knife bit deeper, drawing a line of blood. "Easy," Saoirse whispered, then her lips were at Zylah's neck, her ear, before grazing over her delicate lips.

They parted slightly. "What are you doing?" Zylah asked, her voice uneven.

"Stealing pieces of heaven before I wake up in hell."

"I thought I already told you no."

"I won't be here much longer, so what does it matter? Unless you don't plan on killing me." She kissed the corner of Zylah's mouth and Zylah shoved away, rising to her feet.

"You're unbelievable." Saoirse blinked, staring at the female and the knife in her hand. "You," Zylah's hands were shaking. "You were really just going to let me do it, weren't you?"

"If that's what it takes to make you happy."

"You don't even know me," Zylah exclaimed. "We've had a drink and a handful of conversations. Why in the gods name would—" Zylah stopped. She stared into Saoirse's gaze and whatever she found there was enough to make her eyes widen. Zylah looked her up and down and her lips slowly parted. "Holy gods." She shook her head.

"You think I'm your mate." Saoirse's heart still thundered even as Zylah swept a frustrated hand across her face.

"And here I thought you were an overly possessive female who just couldn't stand not getting something she wanted."

"That, too," Saoirse said with a small smile.

"I'm a half-breed."

"Why should that matter?"

"I'm a female."

Saoirse quirked a brow. "Again, why would that matter?"

"Isn't the whole bond supposed to represent, I don't know, the ability to procreate?"

Saoirse chuckled. "False presumptions are often made when mortal creatures try to understand the ways of the gods."

"You're not mortal."

"Do we not die as the humans do? How many Fae have you known to fade from the land? It is a gift to live so long, and one we are not often afforded."

Zylah continued pacing and Saoirse watched as if she could see the female replaying their every encounter.

"I don't feel a bond," Zylah said. "Do you?"

"It's a pull," Saoirse admitted. "A calling to protect you."

"Protect me from what?"

"Everything."

"And I get no say in the matter? I'm just expected to see you at every turn for the rest of my life?"

"Females, for the most part, are able to ignore the bond if they wish it."

Zylah spun to face her. "And what if their *mate*," she spat the word, "won't let them? What if they're insistent and show up at every turn despite being told they're not wanted?" She loosed a breath. "If the bond is just another set of shackles, then I don't want it."

Saoirse blanched. "I'd never put you in chains."

"You already have."

"Zylah."

"From the moment you decided I was yours without any consent from me, you put a collar around my neck. I've had enough of those and I'm not interested in entertaining the Fae idea of a love match. I loved once and that was enough."

If Saoirse understood anything, it was the grief that flashed across Zylah's face. She knew, not because of the warriors she'd lost, but because it was a fresh wound in her heart. One that wouldn't heal easily.

Zylah turned toward the trees and began walking. Saoirse called. "Where are you going?"

Zylah stopped and looked up into the dreary sky. "I don't know. Another continent maybe, where I can start over and forget."

Forget about her previous life. Forget she'd ever been a slave. Forget about Saoirse.

Saoirse's throat tightened. "Let me get to you safety." Zylah glanced back over her shoulder and the defeat in her expression broke off a piece of Saoirse's shattered heart. "Let me lead you to the safe house and when all this is over, if you truly never want to see my face again, I'll disappear from your life."

Zylah shook her head. "I don't believe you."

"I swear it," Saoirse said and the words tasted like poison. "If my absence is what makes you happy, then you'll never have to see me again."

Chapter Seventy-Nine

Rion

The rain still hadn't let up and thick clouds blotted out the morning sun. Rion had slept for an hour at most before jolting awake from a nightmare so vivid it had him jumping to his feet and clawing at his throat. Kaylee had screamed and his mother just looked at him with understanding. They would all suffer through nightmares for a long time to come.

Rion had muttered an apology, fed the fire the last dry log, then set about freeing his magic.

He slammed the rock down on the shackle again and again and again. He'd gotten the first one off, but it had left his ankle swollen and bruised. Rion ignored the pain. It was nothing compared to the aches pulsing through the rest of his body. He could deal with a few bruises. If he freed his magic, it would give them an advantage should Niall's warriors intercept them along the road. He'd do everything in his power to ensure Eimear stayed out of that wicked male's grasp.

Rion glanced at his mother again, still hardly believing she was there. He prayed his magic wouldn't alienate her. Rion couldn't really remember how closely she'd followed the ancient texts. He remembered visiting the temple a few times but couldn't recall if the events were isolated to holidays.

Rion hated his magic, yet they also needed its strength if they hoped to make the journey.

He sucked in a sharp breath and swore when the rock missed his shackle and cracked against the bone of his ankle. Rion wasn't even sure how his body was still functioning. He'd been pushed hard before, but this was on another level.

Rion brought the rock down again and the metal bent inward, digging into his flesh. Blood rolled into the boot, but he kept at it, pounding over and over. Kaylee watched him in horror. She'd already begged him to stop, but his mother had shushed the girl and pulled her into her arms.

She understood, too.

Now that Eimear knew Rion wasn't a threat, she'd let her façade of strength fall and his heart ached to see her so weak.

She limped on her left leg from an invisible injury and had even tottered when she'd risen to relieve herself just moments ago. They all needed food and rest. The rain provided fresh water, a luxury certainly not lost on him.

Something in the latch clicked. Rion yanked the shackle from around his bleeding ankle and launched it into the nearby brush. He laid back to relieve the ache in his muscles. Rocks bit into his skin, but Rion ignored them, instead savoring the stretch of his lower back. He took a final breath, then sat up, ready to start on his left wrist.

The hairs on his arms rose. Rion scented the air and tilted his head to listen.

His mother had gone stiff and Kaylee peered between them confused before she began shaking.

Someone had found them.

Shouting echoed far too close for his liking. Rion shot to his feet, not bothering with the fire as he grabbed Kaylee and flung her onto his back. The child gripped his shirt and they darted into the freezing rain.

His footsteps were sloppy and Rion sloshed through deep puddles that had muck clinging to his pants and boots. His mother ran at his side, watching their back as if she expected warriors to emerge at any moment.

Damn it all. They shouldn't have stopped. They should have just kept going until they'd stumbled across a town that could protect them. *If* they could protect them. Rion wasn't certain of Niall's reach or how many villages bowed to his influence. Hell, he didn't even know where they were. They could be deep in Pádraigín's territory, which left them far more vulnerable than he wanted to admit.

The voices echoed again and Rion tried to quiet his footsteps, as did his mother. They ducked into the shadows of trees. Rion was thankful for the thick brush even as it tore at their clothes and slowed them down. It'd slow their pursuers too. Confuse them if they were fortunate. He could smell the river and hear its swell, too. They wouldn't be using that as an escape route. Not unless they wanted to drown.

The trees dipped and the pair tried not to slow their pace as they slid down the steep incline. Rion used several trees to keep himself upright and Kaylee clung to his back tighter and hid her face in his shirt. She likely understood the need for quiet better than anyone.

The roar of the river swallowed up sound and they darted for it, sprinting over the small clearing. Large rocks jutted up between the gnarled roots of trees. The river had escaped the confines of its banks and had flooded the tall grass surrounding it.

Rion spotted another outcropping in the rocks and dove for it. Perfect. He pried Kaylee's white knuckled grasp from his shirt and pushed her inside. "Stay here." Rion turned to his mother. "I'll distract them and the first chance you get, run. Ask for Arianna or Talon; trust no one else."

Eimear wanted to protest, he could see it in her eyes, but she also knew this was the only way. Whoever was tracking them had caught his scent and they were too close to outrun.

He'd fight until his last breath to ensure the females escaped.

Rion backed away, watching Kaylee's silent tears, then ducked when he heard the sharp twang of a string loosen. The arrow flew past his head, narrowly missing his shoulder. Battle cries split the air and warriors dressed in black emerged from the shadows. They sprinted down the hill, weapons drawn and magic at the ready. Rion's heart plummeted. He hadn't hidden them fast enough.

He met Eimear's gaze, but instead of sorrow or fear, he found that warrior's stare pinning him in place. She wasn't going down without a fight either. Good, he needed her if he was going to win.

His mother whispered something to Kaylee and the little girl wedged herself into a small crevice between the boulders.

He prayed she would survive even if they didn't. Perhaps Niall's warriors wouldn't notice her after the battle.

They drew closer, and Rion scented magic of all varieties. A dozen. Two. He steeled himself, willing strength into his weary limbs. Just a little more, he kept telling his body. A little further, then it could rest.

"You really shouldn't have run," one of the males said, his voice muffled by the sound of the river. "It's those two who will suffer for it." He inclined his head toward Eimear. "Niall will punish the females just so you understand what's at stake should you ever try something like this again."

The male turned toward his mother. "And you, you should know better already. Did you not learn your lesson last time?" Rion didn't want to think about what that meant. A flash of anger crossed Eimear's face. Anger and grief.

A stealthy shadow closed in from his left but Rion snapped the chain dangling from his wrist like lightning. It wrapped around the male's weapon and Rion wrenched the blade from the warrior's grasp. He tossed the slender sword to his mother and she caught it in a graceful movement that reminded Rion of a dancer.

The rest lunged as one in a storm of blades and crackling magic.

Rion used that iron chain again, harnessing months of aggression in a single blow. It wrapped around a warrior's throat and Rion pulled hard.

A resounding crunch told him he'd hit home, but the growls that followed promised he'd pay for it.

Not today. He'd win or he'd die fighting. There were no other alternatives.

Rion charged. He avoided their swings and ducked around their magic. It skimmed his body, leaving small wounds he could think about later. Don't falter. Don't hesitate. Three tracked his movements, ignoring the female warrior who followed in his shadow. She sliced through their bodies with lethal efficiency.

Another four closed in. A blade swung and Rion raised the chain to block it. His mother ducked beneath his arms and plunged her sword into the warrior's abdomen before ripping it out his side. Rion caught another blade and wrenched it away from its owner, then fire collided with his left side, singeing his tunic and forearm. Rion cried out as the wind came alive and slammed him into the ground, then ice began crawling up his leg.

Eimear sliced a throat and the frost stopped momentarily.

Slow. They were moving too slow and each twist or pivot was sloppier than the last.

More warriors appeared from behind the trees on his left, but Rion couldn't focus on them, not as he watched a wall of fire rise up and barrel straight for his mother. She stood against it, weapon drawn, a warrior who wouldn't back down from anything.

Panic seized him, then the river—the river moved. He blinked, trying to clear his vision, but the raging current that promised a watery grave sprang to life. Tendrils of black water as thick as his body flew in all directions at once, colliding with anyone in their path. The puddles at his feet rose then solidified into jagged spikes before plunging deep into his enemy's bodies. Warrior after warrior fell, clutching wounds inflicted by an unknown source.

What—

Her scent hit him like an electrical current and Rion whirled. His heart skipped a beat as he watched the most beautiful creature alive dance through her opponents. Her cerulean eyes burned with icy rage and Rion felt something in his core unwind at the sight of her.

She'd come. Arianna had come for him.

His body trembled now and he watched her as if the fight weren't still happening around him. Her hostile snarl snapped Rion back to the present. Arianna sprinted toward him, a twin pair of bloody knives in her grasp. Her face didn't light up with relief, nor did she show any signs of slowing.

Rion's heart stopped as he faced the full blunt of that anger. He had so many things he needed to say but—a myriad of feelings poured through him. Maybe—maybe she hadn't come for him in the way he'd hoped. She adjusted the grip on her weapons, still sprinting and Rion let his arms fall to his sides.

The fierceness in her gaze was magical. She was the most magnificent being he'd ever laid eyes on. If her face was the last thing he saw before hellfire consumed him, then Rion would gladly welcome his end.

Arianna extended her long knife and her magic spun down the blade in a crackling current. It whizzed past his head, barely kissing his cheek with the cold and Rion turned to find a blade of ice protruding from a male's throat.

Rion didn't know what to say or do with himself. Arianna stood before him, dressed in a way he'd never seen. She was covered from head to toe in black with places for daggers all over her body. Her twin blades dripped with water and blood and the magic surrounding her emitted a pulsing current that almost seemed alive.

Arianna was no longer just a female from Móirín. She was a warrior. A queen ready to conquer and take what belonged to her.

And her eyes. They were locked with his. So close. She was so close that he could have reached out and touched her, but Rion didn't dare.

He should be fighting. They both should, but somehow time had stopped.

Rion let the blade fall from his hand first. She didn't look away. He released the chain next and still her gaze remained locked with his. He couldn't read her emotions anymore and he wouldn't risk reaching for the bond. He wasn't even sure he could.

A mixture of recognition and disbelief thawed her icy stare. She gasped.

Then Rion hit his knees.

He was at her mercy now. Whatever she wanted from him, she could have. She was his lover. His mate. His queen.

The battle behind them ebbed, leaving only the sounds of the swollen river behind. Arianna's lips parted and her body shuddered as she released an uneasy breath. Rion turned his wrists up and stared at the Queen of Alastríona.

"Rion?" His mother's voice broke the silence, but neither Arianna nor Rion turned to look at her. It was as though neither quite knew what to do from here.

He knew what he wanted. More than anything he longed to pull her into his embrace and sob into her shoulder, begging for some shred of forgiveness. But Rion wouldn't reach for her, not until she reached first. She deserved that from him.

She deserved so much more from the world.

Talon entered his view, the male placing himself between Arianna and Rion's mother who was closing in fast with a blade still in hand. Kaylee trailed her. Talon didn't attack and Rion knew exactly what the male saw. A female and a child, both bruised and shackled, as ready to fight as they were to flee.

Eimear stepped again.

"You can trust them." Rion's voice shook. His mother paused. She studied his position on the ground then the female Rion was kneeling before. Something sparked in his mother's gaze and he wondered if she were seeing an old friend in Arianna's face.

Eimear threw her sword down, then Talon sheathed his weapon.

"You're The Divine?"

Arianna broke from Rion's stare to study Eimear. She soaked in every detail, from her waist length matted hair to the tattered clothes covering her too thin body. Arianna's gaze darkened when she glimpsed the shackles on her wrists. "Yes, and you are?"

Eimear straightened as if ready to present herself even after everything she'd been through. "Eimear, High Lady of Brónach."

Arianna's lips parted and Talon's head whipped toward Rion's mother. No one moved for a long time as they processed the living ghost who'd come back from the dead.

"We need to move," was all Talon said, but Rion could see the way he watched Eimear. As if he wanted to help but didn't quite know how.

Rion knew Talon was right. They weren't safe here, but there were so many things he wanted, no, needed to say to Arianna. This wasn't the reunion he'd been hoping for. He needed time to apologize and figure out how they were going to move forward with their relationship, if she wanted to move forward at all.

But those things would have to wait. The important thing was that he and his mother were free and Arianna was as far away from Niall as she could get.

Talon picked through their enemies' weapons and replaced the knives across his chest before fetching a bag and sorting through the contents. Rion's mother just bent to console the girl.

But when Arianna looked at him again, Rion couldn't bring himself to move. It seemed as though their world froze all over again and he was locked in an endless moment of agony.

"Tell me what to do," he whispered, his heart beating so hard he was sure it would stop. "Tell me what you need."

She didn't speak at first, but when Arianna cleared her throat, her voice was soft. Hesitant. "A-are you hurt?"

"I'll be all right." It was a lie and they both knew it. He was far from all right.

Rion rose slowly, but his knee buckled and he stumbled before catching himself.

Arianna backed away—away from him. The wave of fear radiating from her almost sent Rion right back to his knees.

She was . . . afraid. Gods. Gods, no. Guilt flashed across her face and Arianna looked away. Her hands flexed, but remained where they were.

Not Arianna. Everyone else he could handle, but not her.

Rion lifted his wrists. "They're iron," he said, unsure if it would help. Unsure of anything. "I can't use my magic." She didn't indicate whether that knowledge eased her fears, but he saw the flash of anger at the sight of the shackles. If Arianna was afraid, if she needed it, he'd wear iron for the rest of his life.

"We've lingered long enough. Let's go," Talon said, interrupting the awkwardness with the voice of a commander. He walked past, offering Rion a look of sympathy.

Kaylee yelped, but Eimear caught the girl before she fell. Kaylee gripped her ankle, then Arianna was at the little girl's side.

Arianna slowed her movements when Kaylee recoiled. "I won't hurt you," she promised.

Kaylee looked her up and down. She absorbed the black clothes, the blades and the blood and didn't release her hold on his mother. "What hurts?" Arianna asked, her voice surprisingly gentle. A voice he remembered.

Let me help you.

The girl pointed to her ankle and Arianna cupped the joint with her hands. Light filtered through the gloomy darkness. The child cried out once, then settled. He understood the sudden pain followed by relief. It was something he'd felt a million times. And something he'd beg to feel just once more.

"Would you like me to carry you?" Talon asked, but the child frantically shook her head, moving to hide behind his mother again.

"Are you hurt anywhere?" Arianna asked Eimear.

His mother lowered her head in reverence. "Nothing I can't handle until we find shelter."

Arianna nodded, then stood and followed Talon. She hesitated beside Rion and her mouth opened once as if she might offer to help. Her fists clenched and unclenched. Rion stepped, determined to show her he wasn't too bad off, but he stumbled again and cursed.

Concern flashed across her face and she turned back to Talon. "We can't travel like this." Talon's expression was grim as he surveyed the area. Gods, he hated being the one to slow them down, but there was no fixing it now.

After a minor argument, Talon and Arianna left the three of them sitting within the gnarled roots of a tree while they scouted for shelter nearby. Rion didn't have the energy to argue. He sank back to the ground, defeat settling heavy over his soul.

She was afraid of him. His mate. Rion clenched his hands into fists. *Monster.*

Eimear placed a comforting hand on his shoulder. He didn't flinch away. "You left out the part about The Divine being your mate." He didn't respond. "What did you do that's so unforgivable?"

Rion's head lowered. What hadn't he done? "I hurt her."

"How?"

Should he count his losses and confess everything right now? Did he tell his mother about the despicable creature he'd become after her disappearance?

"I—Niall's magic made me think she was someone else." His voice broke again. "I thought the male had hidden her somewhere, then I—" Rion couldn't voice the words. "I hurt her," he said again.

"Then it wasn't your fault."

"It doesn't matter."

"It does."

Rion gritted his teeth. "I deserved everything I got in that cell and I deserve more for what I did to her."

"That's for her to decide." Yes, it was and he was ready to take whatever Arianna threw at him.

He wouldn't beg, nor would he try to change her mind. He wouldn't make her suffer in his presence if she didn't want him near.

But even as he told himself those things, Rion recognized them for the lies they were. Because he knew he'd grovel on his knees for just one more second in her presence.

Chapter Eighty

Arianna

They'd found a suitable shelter that was away from the river and the bodies scattered along its bank. At least far enough that she couldn't smell them. The cave would allow them to escape the rain long enough to rest and plan their next course of action. Fleeing to the safehouse.

When Rion had stood and stumbled again, she'd stepped toward him, determined to overcome her fear, but he'd held up a hand, stopping her in her tracks. Arianna hadn't known what to make of that. He'd been in captivity for two months, chained against his will and clearly tortured.

Maybe he didn't want to be touched. That part of him had never really faded. He'd welcomed the feel of her hands before, even seemed to relish her touch, but perhaps with as vulnerable as he'd become, he couldn't bear it quite yet.

So she had swallowed the lump in her throat and stepped back, her heart cracking as he limped into the small cavern.

Once inside, Talon had collected wood, stripped it of the liquid weighing it down and started a fire for the High Lady of Brónach and the child clutching her shirt.

Now, Arianna sat before the female, gently working on her wounds. She was wild, a creature who'd been locked away and one who feared returning to any cage. So Arianna moved slowly and kept her hands where they could be seen.

His mother. Gods, Niall had had Rion's mother this entire time. How old had Rion been when she went missing? Eight? Ten? That meant she'd been in captivity for more than eighty years.

Arianna wasn't certain how the female, Eimear, had maintained her sanity. Then again, Arianna hadn't exactly had a conversation with her, so maybe she hadn't.

Arianna risked a glance at Rion. He sat at the rear of the cave, slouched against the wall with his head down. A warrior defeated. He'd refused to let her tend to his wounds until she'd assessed his mother first.

He looked so much worse.

"Give me your knife." Arianna started at the request and studied the too familiar eyes demanding a weapon from Talon.

He didn't hesitate or ask what she needed it for. Talon just unsheathed one of his blades and handed it to the female. But he kept close, an ever watchful guardian over Arianna.

Eimear tilted her head, lifted the blade, and began sawing through her hair.

"What are you—"

"It's fine," Eimear said, the blade cutting through the mats. "It can't be saved anyway." She was right. Every bit of it had clumped into a mass so thick, strands didn't even hit the floor as she sawed through it.

"Enough about me," Eimear finally said. "See to him."

Arianna nodded and stood. She winced at the burning in her foot, a constant reminder of the horrid things she and Talon had killed.

The movement drew Rion's attention. His shoulders went stiff, his nostrils flared, and a sense of dread filled the pit of her stomach.

She hated to force herself upon him, hated to touch him if he didn't want her to, but he was bleeding and injured. The sooner she tended to his wounds, the sooner they could get out of here.

She tried not to limp, but the adrenaline from the fight had worn off. She'd removed her other sock and doubled it up to pad the injury. Talon had offered his as well.

Arianna shivered and approached the male her heart longed for. He watched her as an animal might watch a predator. She wanted to tell him she wouldn't hurt him, but the words didn't feel right. He'd been hurt so much.

Slowly, Arianna knelt and examined his body. His throat bobbed and he looked ready to speak, but stopped. Arianna's hands shook and she hated it, hated every single second because she knew he could smell fear all over her.

This was exactly what she'd been afraid of. That instead of running straight into his arms, some part of her would be afraid. Her fear claimed his fangs might pierce her throat again. That he'd easily snap her arm and throw her to the ground as if she were weak and nothing, nothing, nothing.

"I'm sorry," he whispered, his voice hoarse and rough. Arianna followed his gaze and found herself rubbing the scarred part of her arm again. She quickly let her fingers fall.

"Who hurt you?" he asked, eying the line of tiny punctures along her boot.

"*What* hurt me would be the better question." Silence. "I don't know what they're called. Dark Fae of one variety or another."

"Are you okay?" He was looking at her shoulder now as if he could see through the material covering it.

"You're asking me?" And he was. His face was nothing but serious despite the plethora of wounds covering his own body. She nodded once, but she wasn't okay. Not with anything.

"Can I fix those?" She tilted her head toward his ankles, the left so horribly swollen she wasn't sure how he'd managed to put weight on it.

Rion nodded and she reached for his discolored skin. A gentle touch was all it took for a hiss to escape his lips. The selfish part of her wanted to touch so much more, but the rational part told her he deserved space.

Arianna mended the swelling before moving onto the other side. "What happened?"

"I removed the shackles."

"With what, a rock?" That earned her a tiny smirk. Her heart soared.

"Well, I didn't have much else to work with." Gods, he was serious. How long had it taken him? She reached for his wrist before stopping herself.

"May I?" His brow furrowed, perplexed, and he extended the left one first. The short chain rattled and she resisted the urge to growl at the offending metal. Arianna needed to remove those. She wasn't sure if her knife was small enough to work the lock, but she certainly wasn't going to let him take a rock to them again. She healed the other wrist, then waited.

"Where else?"

Rion sat very still before glancing toward his mother and the girl. Both had fallen asleep near the fire with Talon standing guard. Her friend was trying his best to give the two a moment of privacy in the small space.

Rion sat forward, wincing with the movement, and removed his shirt. He failed to keep the chains from rattling, but the females didn't stir.

Arianna sucked in a breath at the marks covering his body. Bites, cuts, and stab wounds that could have been days or a week old. Bruises of every size and burns, too. He looked like someone had strung him up and—

Arianna reached for the bite wound over his ribs, the worst of the bunch, then hesitated. Before she could even speak, Rion said, "You don't need to ask permission to touch me."

"I just thought after—"

"I am yours," Rion said. "Do with me whatever you wish."

Hers. He was hers. She'd claimed him and he her.

Arianna went to work.

Rion sat unnaturally still as she moved from one wound to another. His skin slowly shifted back to a normal color.

Rion's heart beat wildly and his breathing came in erratic gasps that mirrored her own, but she stayed focused—or tried to stay focused.

His scent beckoned her home and Arianna dared to lean closer. He leaned in, too. Her heart skipped a beat then Rion pressed a lingering kiss to her hair.

Every muscle in Arianna's body stiffened. She jerked back, recoiling from his touch.

Recoiling from her mate.

Hurt flashed across Rion's face before he could hide it. "I'm sorry, I shouldn't have." But he craved her, just as she was craving him, and that stupid fear wouldn't let her have him. Talon had called it normal, but it wasn't normal to fear ones mate. Nothing about this entire mess was normal.

"Don't apologize," she said, feeling her voice tremble even as she fought to keep it steady.

Silence stretched between them, but he wouldn't look at her. Probably couldn't for fear of what he'd see.

Tears welled in Arianna's eyes because their bond was hanging by a single thread and there was no telling what tomorrow or the next hour might bring. What if this was it? The only moment they'd get to reconcile? Niall could find them and just as easily tear them apart again.

Her hands were shaking, but Arianna forced herself to reach out.

Talon shot to his feet, then Rion and his mother were up, too.

"We have to go. Now," Talon said. He grabbed the pack but didn't pause to extinguish the fire. Rion threw on his shirt and they all followed him into the rain.

The downpour had finally shifted to a light drizzle as they sprinted. Rion's mother carried the child on her back now, no longer limping. Neither was Rion, and he looked far more alert compared to before.

Arianna listened to their feet hitting the soggy ground, then the echo of others closing in from the rear. The climb uphill would be too slow and there wasn't a path that led around.

They'd trapped themselves. They had to fight. Fight or give in, and Arianna knew not a single one of them was about to surrender.

"Stay with them," Talon ordered, jerking his chin toward Eimear and the child.

Stay. Let me protect you. They were always protecting her.

It was *her* mate they'd kidnapped. It was *her* mate these males wanted. And it was *her* mate she'd stand beside.

"No," he turned at the sound of Arianna's voice as she walked right past him. "*You* stay with them." Talon looked ready to protest then stopped, seeming to understand as she closed the distance to stand beside Rion.

Rion eyed her, looking her up and down as if assessing a comrade, then let the chain fall from around his wrist. Rion had never tried to push her aside when it came to a fight. They'd stood beside one another before, and she'd stand beside him now. Because if they were going down, then they'd go down together.

Talon's magic formed around them first, tiny droplets of ice that hovered in the air and coated the ground at their feet. The child clung to Eimear's legs, but Eimear didn't cower, even with the iron holding her magic at bay. So much like Rion.

Their pursuers were nearly upon them now. Three dozen at least. Arianna let a slow breath fall from her lips. She hated killing as much as she had all those months ago, but the act didn't cripple her as it once had. She knew what she was fighting for. For herself. For Rion. And the freedom of the oppressed.

Instead of outright attacking, the group slowed. One male separated himself and prowled forward. Fire rose up to surround his body. It writhed as if offended by the rain.

His gaze roamed over the lot of them before settling on Arianna. "We're here under direct orders from the Regent of Ruadhán. He has commanded us to escort you home." His gaze flickered to Rion.

"You can tell Niall I will return when it suits me. I have other matters to address first." Like getting Rion out of those shackles and freeing the others left in that prison. She wanted to hear everything they had to say about Niall, then plan the best course of action for removing The Regent from the city altogether.

The male gritted his teeth and when his gaze landed on Rion's mother, Arianna knew the talk was just a show. A last try at attempting to appease her. He glared at the High Lady of Brónach as if she were a nuisance instead of a victim.

"I'd rather not resort to violence," the male tried again. "I encourage you to come peacefully—"

"Or what?" Eimear challenged. "You'll drag your queen back in chains?"

He sneered at her. "If that's what it takes."

Arianna bristled at that. "Go ahead," she said, her voice low and daring. "Try." She flashed her teeth and jerked her chin toward his belt. "Pull that iron out and see what happens."

He sighed, but before his hand could reach into his satchel, Arianna's magic flew at him. It froze every droplet in its wake, one by one, until it slammed into his arm. Frost spread across the male's limb, then down his torso, and finally around his legs. She didn't bother listening to the string of curses that fell from his mouth.

Rion eyed her momentarily, then the warriors behind their leader howled in fury. They drew their weapons and launched forward.

Arianna's magic erupted and hoarfrost shot across the ground in an angry wave. She gripped the raw energy and commanded it, just as she'd done while facing the creatures who had attacked her and Talon.

The warriors ran right through the frost, but it crawled up their legs, freezing several in place. Others broke loose and her magic answered theirs in an explosion of smoke and debris overhead. Spears of ice and boiling water launched from behind her, and when a warrior drew too close, Rion sprang into action.

There was no need for talk or strategy. They understood each other's movements and trusted their comrades to fulfill their roles.

Flames sparked too close to her mate and Arianna's heart jolted, but he rolled out of the way and shot the length of his chain outward. The iron wrapped around a warrior's blade and Rion pulled it free.

She refocused.

He didn't need her to worry. Rion was a general, she reminded herself. A strategist who'd rarely been bested on the field. He knew how to fight, whether he possessed his magic or not. And now he wasn't hurt.

A warrior with flames spiraling around their body charged next and Arianna let water crystals dance around Rion's form. They circled him as if he were the one controlling the tiny shards. The warrior didn't balk from her magic or Rion's charging form.

The male's blade swung down, but instead of dodging it, Rion raised his arm toward the weapon. She sucked in a breath, her heart nearly stopping. Metal rang through the air and Rion shoved the sword away. He ducked into his opponent and landed several blows to his torso before wrenching the weapon from his grasp.

Talon shot a spike through the male next, then Rion circled back, placing his body between Arianna and the warriors silently strategizing amongst themselves. Their expressions told Arianna they hadn't expected the small group to put up much of a fight.

Another lunged, but Rion didn't use the blade he'd acquired. Instead, he lifted his arm again and ducked around the warrior's magic. Another strike on the metal, then another. The movement looked so strange and labored.

Another strike.

Another.

Another.

Then the shackle snapped.

Rion spun around the warrior, his wrist bleeding, and buried his blade in the male's gut.

Her eyes went wide. Of course. He was breaking his shackles. Rion was setting himself free.

Just one more to go.

Arianna moved with her mate, clearing Rion's path as he glided between the warriors and their magic. Icy knives kept flying from behind, courtesy of Talon.

Ice and water and metal moved as one, pushing and pulling. A back and forth as if they'd practiced these movements a thousand times over.

Metal rang out again and blood rolled down her mate's wrist. He pivoted, stepped back, moved with his attacker, then the blade struck again. Arianna winced at the crack of bones and the way the blade sank deep into Rion's flesh.

Her mate retreated a few steps and Arianna blasted his pursuer.

Rion clawed at the metal digging into his wrist. He grabbed it with his teeth and she could have sworn he ripped away flesh when the iron bent. Rion pulled at the cuff from a different side, his movements desperate and frantic. Then it opened and finally hit the ground.

A familiar cloud rose, shaking the earth they stood upon with its deadly force. It spread out in all directions and those who'd previously looked ready to sacrifice their lives for their High Lord's orders retreated a step. They closed ranks as if they might stand a chance together.

Arianna knew they wouldn't.

The grains of sand and earth rose around Rion's body in a billowing storm as if it, too, had been held by the iron. Or maybe that was just his rage. Months of it bottled and finally set free.

A crunch of boots from behind had Arianna pivoting and scenting the air. She tugged at her magic, ready to protect Talon and the others, but a familiar face with dark skin and serious eyes sent relief washing through her.

Flames danced around Raevina's body undeterred by the rain. Even Talon sagged with relief.

One motion from her hands and the warriors accompanying Raevina fanned out, charging those gathering around Rion.

They kept their distance from the male, as if scenting the anger rolling through him.

Raevina assessed her queen, looking her over twice before letting her gaze drift toward Rion. She studied the magic snapping around his body as one might study a battlefield and Arianna wondered if Raevina didn't quite believe her mate's innocence.

Rion knew nothing of Raevina's newly pledged loyalty. She was standing too close to his mother and he was already closing in.

Rion's billowing cloud of sand and stone drew closer. He growled, a warning meant for Raevina, but it was Arianna's heart that jolted with the sound. Images of his twisted face had her gasping for breath, then his magic fell away as if someone had flipped a switch.

Arianna watched the ground, praying it wouldn't move again. Rion stood between her and Raevina. He eyed Talon, too.

"Stand down," Raevina commanded. She adjusted the grip on her sword, then gauged the distance between Rion and Arianna.

Rion bared his teeth. "I'll stand down when my queen commands it."

His queen. Not mate. Queen. The title felt so distant and formal.

Raevina scrunched her nose with distaste. She didn't lower her weapon as she addressed Arianna. "My Lady, we have your sister, and my scouts are keeping track of Niall's movements. The High Lord of Móirín is set to arrive in two days. Discreetly. He'll have further suggestions upon his arrival."

Right, because they couldn't go back to Ruadhán. Would she have to lay low for a while? Form her own court to challenge Niall's rule? Would that just incite another war and lay waste to the land?

Arianna nodded and Rion seemed to note the faint movement.

"It's okay," Arianna assured him. "She's on our side."

Raevina studied Eimear and even though recognition flashed across her face, she didn't ask questions. Raevina was a warrior on a mission. "We shouldn't linger. Niall has sent a lot of scouts to find you and your scents are all over the place."

Which explained how the second group had moved in so quickly. All the blood might as well have been a beacon in the night.

Rion didn't protest, but when Arianna looked to ensure he agreed, she noticed the way he clutched his wrist to his chest. His face was neutral, a carefully honed mask.

Arianna eyed the fresh dirt at his feet, clenched her jaw, and forced herself to walk across it.

It was ridiculous. Rion was her mate. *Her mate*, she tried telling herself. Hurting her was the last thing he would ever do.

Arianna reached for his wrist and cursed her trembling hand. Slowly, as if afraid to startle her further, he extended the discolored joint.

A flash of light and it snapped back into place.

Arianna met that familiar green gaze. His eyes were so warm, yet full of worry and anguish.

She didn't step back and Rion's fingertips brushed the underside of her arm as if asking if he could touch her at all. His lips parted, but Raevina cleared her throat.

Right, they needed to move.

CHAPTER EIGHTY-ONE

RION

Rion remembered his teachers reading old poetry. They were stories about longing and heartache and often ended in tragedy. His young mind hadn't understood them then. Even as an adult he'd never given much merit to the words penned by those fractured souls.

But Rion understood now.

As they sloshed through the freezing puddles with Raevina's warriors providing escort. As he watched his mate limping with her head down, defeat written across her weary face. As he dragged behind, feeling as though one slip up, one mistake could separate them forever. He understood them perfectly.

He was the stranger here. So many things had happened since his disappearance. Arianna and Raevina had become unlikely allies, and Talon and Raevina had some sort of complicated history.

The Fiadh warrior still watched him closely, and he wondered if she'd been there the day he had attacked Arianna. She'd likely seen the aftermath, at the very least.

They made the slow climb up the steep, rocky hillside, then walked through an open meadow for at least a mile before they were beneath the safety of the trees again. Raevina followed a seemingly invisible path, and Rion felt as though a hundred eyes watched their every step. Birds of prey, stalking cats, wolves, the bright eyes of foxes.

Were they with Niall? Were they loyal to their queen? Or were they simply animals, curious to see the Fae walking past their dens and hunting grounds?

Raevina had informed them they were indeed in Pádraigín, but that they didn't need to worry because the countryside was wild and largely untraveled. Something about creatures prowling the roads. Rion eyed Arianna's uneven gait and wondered if they were the same ones who had injured her.

The rain picked up again, a silent blessing, even if he was tired of being soaked to the bone.

Tired. Of everything. Of pain and heartache and separation and loss.

He was just tired.

He risked a glance at his mother. She hadn't reacted upon seeing his magic. No fear or shock or disgust. Had she known all along what he'd become, or was she simply too exhausted to process it all?

He sighed inwardly, unsure his heart could take much more.

A mixture of scents told Rion they were close. Most of the Fae were from Móirín or Fiadh, but there were a few others, too. Some from Brónach—likely Saoirse's warriors—and a handful from Pádraigín. Good, at least some knew where their loyalty should lie.

Saoirse. Rion glanced at his mother again as she trudged along. She looked just as tired as he felt, maybe more so. The rain had plastered what was left of her hair against her scalp, and Talon had taken to carrying Kaylee on his back.

Saoirse was going to see their mother again. Of everyone who'd searched for her, Saoirse had been the most dedicated. She'd mourned the loss of Eimear deeper than anyone else.

Rion wondered how his sister had felt about his disappearance and if she'd looked for him with just as much passion. Part of him didn't want to know.

Fae emerged from the trees one by one, cloaked in their animal forms, but Raevina didn't react so Rion remained calm, keeping his magic in check for Arianna's sake. A wolf joined to their right and a leopard to their left. They both huffed in greeting.

The Fairy Folk appeared then, popping their little heads up from the underbrush. His mother paused to watch and their entire entourage stopped with her.

One came close and peered up at Eimear, tilting its head as if in greeting. His mother smiled at the tiny creature whose little arms were nothing more than twigs with a few leaf-like hands attached at the tip. One had to look close to see how the leaf separated into five tiny fingers.

Then it scurried away, darting between the feet of everyone else until it stood before Rion.

His heart cracked even as he leaned down to greet the small creature. Those little arms reached up and he lowered one hand to scoop it into his palm. He couldn't tell whether it smiled or not, but he understood when it lightly touched his face.

Welcome back, it seemed to say.

Rion didn't realize he had an audience until he glanced up to find their group surrounded. Many stood with their mouths gaping, watching The Demon with the sacred creature.

A creature no one else had ever touched. Except Arianna, of course, but he doubted they knew that yet.

Rion placed it back down and it scurried to Arianna. She touched its tiny hand in greeting before it raced into the brush without looking back. Then the Fairy Folk were gone, blending into the forest where they dwelled and spun their mysterious magic.

No one spoke as they continued walking, but Arianna spared him a sideways glance and Rion's heart soared as he glimpsed the ghost of a smile across her face.

RION COULDN'T help but sigh in relief when a large cabin entered their view. A small clearing surrounded it on all sides and a wisp of smoke rose from the stone chimney. Rion spotted a few rocking chairs on the porch, but otherwise the exterior was bare.

He wondered if those from Pádraigín were using their magic to conceal the safe house from unwelcome eyes. Of course they were, he just wished he could sense it. But he imagined he was missing a lot with exhaustion hanging over him like a heavy cloud.

The door swung open, creaking on its hinges, and Arianna's father stepped beyond the threshold. Rion clenched his jaw, ready for Avalon's verbal assault, but Arianna's overwhelming sense of relief sent her sprinting the last few feet to her father.

His mate dove into Avalon's arms and Avalon returned the embrace, clutching his daughter tight.

Before leaving Levea, Arianna had been furious with her father, and for good reason. Maybe she still harbored some of those feelings, but right now he was simply her parent. And as any parent should, he'd come to his daughter's aid.

Rion's gaze traveled toward his mother and he found her staring right back. She still didn't look at him with anything other than a mother's love. Perhaps his life *would* have been different had she remained in Nàdiar. He'd never forgive Niall. Not for a million different reasons.

Rion's heart ached. Their reunion should have been just as emotional. It should have been filled with warm embraces and tears. Questions and no shortage of rambling as he tried to explain how they'd endlessly searched for her. Yet it had been tainted with fangs and dirt and chains.

A growl echoed from behind Avalon that had everyone straightening. "Why is that creature allowed to wander free?" The male had already drawn his weapon. Water droplets formed to his front, all solidifying into icy spears ready to fly through Rion's heart.

Rion studied the male but didn't recognize him. He felt a growl rise in his throat, though he stifled it when he noticed Arianna watching. Rion uncurled his fists. "If my queen wants me in chains, she has but to ask."

Hurt flashed across her face, but he didn't understand it. Nor could he risk searching the frayed bond for answers. She deserved his respect, had more than earned it, but the way she reacted to his words seemed strange. Like it made her sad somehow.

Arianna raised her voice. "If one more person touches him with chains, they'll find those shackles around themselves."

The male's mouth gaped but when he realized no one else was ready to fight, he dropped his magic and bowed. Avalon didn't reprimand his guard or his daughter. In fact, he looked at Arianna with reverence. Pride.

Saoirse slipped through the door next and Rion's world froze. She looked him over once, then his sister was running. Actually running before her body slammed into his. He barely braced enough to stay upright, but the motion left him in shocked silence.

"Just let me," she said, voice thick with emotion. He wasn't sure he could have pushed her off even if he'd wanted to. How many years had it been since he'd felt his sister's warm embrace? Too many. Far, far too many.

Slowly, Rion returned it, patting his sister on the shoulder. She pulled back to look him over again. "You're all right?"

"As okay as I can be."

She gave him a halfhearted smile, but Rion nodded behind her and Saoirse followed his gaze. His sister stiffened, then her lips parted. Their mother was smiling at the pair. Smiling at her children and the relationship they shared.

Saoirse stepped once, but when Eimear opened her arms, a strangled sound escaped his sister and she was sprinting with tears streaming down her face. Eimear pulled her daughter in close and the females sank to the ground, both sobbing and asking questions through their tears that no one could understand.

Something deep in Rion's heart mended then. A hole he hadn't realized he'd carried. He just watched his mother stroke Saoirse's hair as if the female were five years old again. If Saoirse cared that anyone watched, she didn't show it.

"Come on," Avalon said, a hand still resting on his daughter's shoulder. "Let's get you cleaned up."

THE CABIN had three bedrooms and two bathrooms. Saoirse entered one room with their mother and Kaylee. Four of Saoirse's guards followed with two large washbasins, a pair of scissors, new clothes, and towels in tow. Someone from Móirín entered too, likely to fill the tub. Minutes later, everyone exited, leaving Saoirse, Eimear, and the girl alone in the room. Rion imagined they wouldn't be out for a long, long while.

Most stood outside, those from Móirín shielding everyone from the rain while warriors from Pádraigín hid the cabin from outsiders, and those from Fiadh kept the fires roaring.

Avalon quickly explained that he'd used the river to decrease his travel time and that more warriors would be arriving over the next couple of days. They were moving in small units and hiding in underground bunkers during the day.

Is that how Arianna would travel if they didn't take care of Niall? Would the roads ever be safe for her while the male drew breath?

Rion didn't yet know whether Arianna planned to return to Levea or whether he'd be permitted to accompany her. He prayed he would. The thought of spending one second without her was unbearable.

"The back room has a shower and a bed," Avalon said to his daughter. "You look like you could use some rest."

Rest. He needed an entire year of it.

Rion wasn't sure what he expected, but when Arianna inclined her head for him to follow, he did so without hesitation. All eyes in the room watched, but he didn't bother meeting their gazes. The only thing Rion cared about was the female in front of him.

A private room. This was it then. They were finally going to talk, or she was about to send him on his way. He was free and his body healed. If that's all her goal had been—Rion shook the thoughts away.

She limped more heavily now and entered the cooler room, leaving the door wide open for him to follow.

No fireplace resided here and he could already feel the slight draft from the large window beside the bed. Rion was silently thankful no one stood on the other side of the glass. He didn't want an audience for whatever was about to happen.

Arianna hobbled across the space and stood at the opposite end, wringing the dark fabric of her shirt between her hands. Her fear only amplified when Rion closed the door.

She was alone with him. Alone and afraid and he hated himself for it.

Swallowing hard, Rion stepped forward to close the distance, but Arianna stepped back.

His heart split in half, then Rion hit his knees.

Rain water rolled down his body and dirt bled into the lush white rug beneath him. They were finally together, finally alone, and Rion couldn't get anywhere near her.

Her face. The way it twisted when she looked at him. He'd finally found someone who didn't see him as just a monster and he'd ruined it.

Rion just wanted her to be happy, whatever that took.

His voice cracked and his composure shattered. "I'm a selfish creature," he whispered. "I told myself I'd give you time. I said I'd stay away if that was your wish. I thought that maybe I could convince you to lock me up where I couldn't hurt you again." Rion's jaw clenched. "But I'd give anything to stay by your side. If you want me to wear iron, I'll do it. If you need me in chains, just say the word." He gripped the fabric of his pants. "I'll beg, if that's what it takes. Even if I have to keep my distance, I'll—"

"No." The word struck him to the core and he broke. Right there. Shattered into a million tiny fragments. He'd been fighting for months. He'd refused to give in to the visions or the nightmares. He'd pushed his body beyond its limits and survived despite everything the gods had thrown at him.

But that one word.

No.
No, I don't want you.
No, I don't trust you.
No, no, no, no, no.

Rion bowed his head to the rug while the word echoed through him. He wasn't enough and he couldn't make amends.

He tried to clear his throat, failed, then his next words came out in a fractured plea. "Will you allow me to lead your armies then? I have the experience. I-I'll report to Talon or whoever you choose. And I swear, gods, I swear I won't act against you. I'll—" He couldn't finish. His breath was coming too fast. His ears were ringing and he wasn't even sure he was making sense. The world was burning him from the inside out. His insides screaming.

No.

His heart pounded so hard Rion was certain he'd die. "Anything," he whispered. "Just tell me what you want."

Silence filled the space for a long while, but Rion didn't lift his head or open his eyes. He just stayed there, head bowed, wondering if he'd ever get to touch his mate again. It felt as though fate had dangled her before him only to snatch her away, just to see what he might do in her absence.

Time crawled and sped at once, but it was the silence that hurt, chipping away at him one sliver at a time.

A small step. A breath.

Maybe she'd leave him lying there on the floor while she went to her father. Maybe he'd never see her again.

He'd be alone.

Cursed and alone.

Another step. Then another. Arianna stood before him. He could feel her, but Rion refused to lift his head. He didn't want to see the rejection in her eyes. He couldn't bear it.

She knelt and his breath hitched when her fingers brushed through his hair with so much tenderness, Rion was certain he was dreaming.

"I meant," she said, her gentle voice cascading through him like water. "I don't want you to go away."

Slowly, not believing, Rion looked up. Her blue eyes glistened with unshed tears and her body was shaking. "I need you," she admitted.

Needed him. Needed him, yet—

"You're afraid."

Arianna didn't deny it, there was no point when the scent of it filled the entire room. Instead, she settled herself on the floor, knee to knee, and studied her hands. "Then I guess it's your turn to convince me."

Rion remembered those first days. The first time she'd helped him. Healed him, thus revealing who she was. He hadn't been sure what to make of it then. He'd waited for the blow, for her to try to kill him under the cover of darkness, but it had never come and when they'd gone to the cabin—

Ever so slowly, Rion inched his hand toward her and wrapped his index finger around her own. A smile crept to her face even as a silent tear slid down her cheek.

"I'll never be able to apologize enough," he said. "I can't begin to tell you how—I'm sorry." His voice broke again. "I'm so sorry. Mates are supposed to know. I should have known and—" He cut himself off again. "If you'll let me, I'll spend the rest of my life making it up to you."

"Niall deceived you."

Rion shook his head, but Arianna pulled on their bond and breath left him. A thread, so tiny and frail, wound its way up that single strand and braided together. He almost wept when another did the same. Then another.

"You came for me when you thought I was in danger. You've always come for me."

Rion glided his hand up and rested it on the back of hers. "This time," he said. "It was you who came for me. Thank you. Without you—"

Arianna's jaw clenched and Rion stopped. The wounds were too fresh and the danger still too near. Right now they had one another. Right now they were safe.

"Tell me what you want," Rion said instead. "If there's a line, I'll stay firmly behind it. Just tell me what you need."

"There's no line." She turned her hand over and interlaced his fingers with her own. "I just want you the way I had you before all this happened."

Rion offered her a weak smile. It wouldn't happen overnight; even now, her heart was racing and it wasn't for the right reasons. She was terrified.

He shouldn't ask, but Rion couldn't help himself. He just wanted to be a bit closer. "Can I kiss you?"

She released a shaky breath and a ghost of a smile tugged at her lips. "Yes."

Rion moved with aching slowness, as if the small space between them were as fragile as a piece of glass. Arianna watched him, her breathing quick and shallow. One spike of fear and he'd pull back, content to simply hold her hand for the rest of time.

But that spike never came and as Rion's lips grazed hers, another strand braided together. He could feel her again. His stomach knotted and the sensation stole the breath from his body. She drew closer, the same need driving her, and both rose up on their knees.

Rion dared to wrap one arm around her back and pulled her body flush against his own, all the while still watching for any sign that it was too much.

She gripped his shirt in a fist and he was lost.

It had been so long. So, so long since he'd felt her, and she tasted every bit as perfect as he remembered. The bond mended itself, forming between them as their lips and hands drank the other in. He couldn't wait for the day it solidified. He could hardly control himself, but he did. For Arianna, Rion would strangle every instinct his body screamed for. Demanded.

They broke apart and Rion pressed his forehead to hers, desperate for the contact. This was enough. Just to be able to touch her again was enough.

"Do you want a shower or food first?" Neither. He didn't want to move.

"Is sleep an option?" he asked.

"Only after you eat."

"Shower, then." Because once he ate he'd probably fall asleep standing. "But you go first."

She pulled back. "You're the one who's been—" but she couldn't finish the sentence. Locked away. Trapped.

"Please."

Arianna studied the plea in his gaze and relented. "Okay. Will you be all right in here for a minute?" He nodded because if he spoke, it would be a lie. He wasn't all right at all. He needed her close.

Thankfully, Arianna didn't even need to leave the room. Avalon had anticipated their needs and one of his warriors stood outside the door with fresh clothes, towels, soap, and a tray of steaming food.

Arianna offered the female her thanks before closing the door again. She set the tray on the dresser beside the bed, then deposited the rest of the supplies in the bathroom.

She paused on the threshold. "Are you sure you don't want to go first?"

"I'm sure." Rion just needed to know his mate was cared for before he took care of himself.

She flipped on the shower, gave him a final look, then closed the door.

ARIANNA LET the hot water cascade over her sore shoulders and warm her frozen core. She'd hissed when it hit her injuries, but once her wounds were clean, she didn't linger.

She used the soap and shampoo without bothering to smell them, then jumped out and dried off before searching through the pile of clothes.

They'd given her an assortment of things. A soft shirt and shorts, a sweater and pants, two outfits for her mate to choose from, a pair of toothbrushes, a comb, and salve for the cuts and scrapes along her body.

She threw on the sweater and shorts and wrapped a towel around her hair for later.

Arianna paused at the closed door. Her heart rate picked up again and she reached down the bond, searching for him.

They'd kissed and it had been just as glorious as she remembered. She would have liked to kiss him for the rest of the night, perhaps tempt herself with wandering hands, but Rion needed a shower and food and sleep.

"I'm beside the door," he said, his voice whisper soft.

Arianna rallied her determination and inched it open. He was indeed beside the door, right beside it, sitting on the floor with his back to the wall. He tilted his head up, eyes half-lidded as if he'd fallen asleep.

"Your turn," she offered. "I put your towel on the counter and there's a change of clothes, too."

Rion peered inside without standing. His throat bobbed and she followed his gaze into the steamy room. It looked normal enough to her.

"Do you mind if I leave the door open?"

It hit her then. The white walls. The cold tile. The tiny square space.

"Of course not," she said, her throat constricting. What had Niall put him through? "And I'll be right here. I won't leave this room."

He swallowed again and nodded before hauling himself to his feet. She might have healed his wounds, but Arianna could tell Rion was still in pain from the stiffness in his joints. She wasn't sure if she could do anything about that, but she'd try once he finished.

She'd left the water running and averted her eyes to give him some privacy.

Arianna heard Rion's clothes hit the floor before he stepped beneath the water. She eyed the place he'd just been sitting. Dirt stained the wood. Then she looked at the soiled rug and decided getting rid of it would be better than Rion seeing he'd ruined it. Not that she cared.

Arianna inched her magic into the bathroom and collected his dirty clothes. She threw them in the center of the rug before rolling it up and setting it near the door. Arianna dried her hair, then used the same towel to clean up the watery stain on the floor.

Two months. Two months and she was certain those pants had been the same ones he'd been wearing the day he left. Anger rolled through her. The things Niall had done to him . . . Arianna clenched her jaw, then cracked open their door to push the rolled up rug outside.

The guard eyed her but she gave her a gentle smile before saying, "Burn it." Rion didn't need the reminder of what he'd been through and neither did she.

She studied the bond and listened to her mate scrub away the filth from his body. She wouldn't disturb him; he could take as long as he needed.

Arianna pulled the brush through her hair then sat on the bed eyeing the trays. The savory smell of roast filled the small room and left her mouth watering. She just hoped Rion would be able to hold it down.

Her foot throbbed. Arianna opened the tiny tin of salve and dabbed the thick mixture over the puncture wounds, paying careful attention to the deeper one from the creature's claw. She wrapped a fresh bandage around her limb, then trailed her fingers along the marks across her shoulder.

They were raised and burned but Arianna couldn't wrap the wounds herself.

The water turned off and Arianna was glad she couldn't see through the doorway from where she sat. She heard shuffling, more water running as he brushed his teeth, then Rion peered around the corner.

His hair dripped; it had grown a bit past his ears again. He wore a fresh short sleeve shirt and a comfortable pair of pants.

Bags hung heavy beneath his eyes.

Arianna scooted herself back on the mattress and beckoned him over. Rion moved at a snail's pace, clearly determined not to frighten her.

The springs groaned beneath his weight and Rion shifted so he sat with his legs crossed directly across from her. Arianna carefully balanced the tray and set it between them.

Rion's face turned a shade paler.

"Just try to eat some," she said. "The bread isn't as hard as it looks." He had to be hungry. She had no idea how long it'd been since he last ate.

He tore off a piece of the bread, dipped it into the warm broth, then placed it in his mouth. Rion's eyes closed and he chewed as if it were the best thing he'd ever tasted.

"Yours is better," he said after a few minutes. "Not that I'm being picky."

She smiled. "I'll be sure to make you some once we're back in Levea."

Rion swallowed hard and averted his gaze. "Is that where we're going?"

Arianna looked into her own broth and swirled the vegetables within. "I don't know, honestly." Too much had happened and she hadn't allowed herself to think this far ahead. She hadn't even expected her father to get here so soon. "We should probably sleep before we make any life-changing decisions."

Rion nodded, took another bite, then she followed his gaze to her arm. "Can I see it?" She knew what he meant. Did he really want to torture himself further?

Arianna extended her arm and Rion scooted the tray to the side. She wished he would eat more, but her attention snapped to Rion's fingers as he carefully rolled up her sleeve.

She could hear his thundering heart beat and the way he sucked in a breath at the sight of the thick scar across her skin. His fingers traced it, then ever so slowly he bent and pressed a delicate kiss to her skin.

"Forgive me," he said, his voice barely audible.

She pushed him up and brushed the wet hair away from his face. "I forgive you." His lips parted and Arianna watched his heated gaze drag down to her lips, then to the other scar hidden by the sweater. He didn't ask to see that one.

His eyes fluttered. Drifted. Then his body swayed.

"Sleep," she ordered. Rion didn't bother moving the blankets aside before he laid down, pulling her hand down with him.

"Stay," he begged as exhaustion dragged him under. His eyes were already closed.

"Always."

CHAPTER EIGHTY-TWO

ARIANNA

Arianna woke to a light tapping on the door. She didn't know what time they'd fallen asleep nor how long they'd been out. It felt like minutes.

Dim light filtered through the window, but the overcast sky made it impossible for her to tell whether it was dawn or dusk. Rain still pelted the glass. She wondered if it would ever cease. She missed the sunshine.

Arianna slid her hand away from Rion's and carefully crawled from the bed.

He didn't move. A first.

She padded across the wooden floor, limping from her injury, and cracked the door open to find another guard with a tray of food. Arianna silently thanked them and they handed her a note.

She studied it, remembering the last notes she'd received. But the Móirín warrior didn't appear panicked and Arianna certainly didn't want to risk rousing Rion with her own.

She nodded and slid back into the room, setting the tray on the bedside table before unfolding the note.

We're meeting in the living room in an hour. There's a lot to discuss. See you then.

Avalon

Arianna folded the paper and inclined her head to listen. She didn't hear anyone in the sitting room and wondered if they'd vacated the house to give her and Rion some privacy.

No, not just her, his mother and Saoirse, too. She hoped the female was resting too.

Arianna stretched and scanned the room. Rion still slept soundly on top of the tan sheets and blanket. A pair of small end tables stood on either side of the bed with a dresser directly across from it. The perfect little cabin room.

Arianna crawled back into bed, but this time Rion stirred. His eyes cracked open and he blinked a few times before looking around as if struggling to remember where he was.

Then his gaze locked with hers and relief settled through him.

"It wasn't a dream."

She smiled, her heart filling with warmth at the site of his sleepy half-lidded stare. "It wasn't a dream."

Arianna's eyes ran down his neck and chest, noting how thin he'd become. She placed a tentative hand over his heart and ran her fingers over the smooth skin. Rion stilled, watching her every move.

She wanted to touch every inch of him and let him do the same. Maybe then she could convince her mind he wasn't something to be feared.

"We have a meeting in an hour."

Rion sniffed then glanced toward the tray. He wiped a hand across his face before sitting up. "I'm afraid I'm all out of formal attire."

She smirked. "Making jokes already?"

"It's either that or wallow in misery, and I've had enough of that."

Her smile faded. "Me, too." Arianna reached for the tray and set it between them. She could have sworn Rion's eyes lit up.

It was a simple breakfast. Scrambled eggs with toast, bacon, and a side of jam. He didn't even hesitate before cramming a piece of bacon into his mouth.

"I'd eat slowly," she cautioned.

He seemed to consider before taking a bite of the eggs. Rion's brows scrunched. "What happened to the rug?"

Arianna followed his gaze to the bare wooden floor. "I had it burned, along with your clothes." He raised a brow. "I'm not sure the stain would have come out anyway."

He swallowed, though if he were embarrassed, he showed no signs of it. "What's the meeting about?"

Arianna shrugged then showed him the note.

"Your father seems . . . different."

She wouldn't say different, but perhaps he was a bit more relaxed. Especially around Rion. Maybe someone had finally talked some sense into him. Or maybe he'd just had enough time to sort it all out himself.

She hadn't thought twice about running into her father's arms. Arianna honestly hadn't admitted to herself how much she'd missed having an authority figure she could trust.

"I guess we'll find out soon."

Rion rubbed his eyes and studied the rest of his breakfast. She'd eaten a few bites of her own, but the silence in the room felt too heavy to finish it.

"I, um—"

"What is it?" Rion asked, suddenly alarmed.

"I didn't want to ask last night, but my shoulder."

Rion almost shoved the tray off the bed in his haste then seemed to remember himself and slowed. "What do you need?"

She eyed the tin and bandages on the night stand beside him. "I can't really wrap it myself." And it was burning, each little puncture mark feeling as though venom had laced the creature's pointed teeth. Arianna knew it hadn't.

Rion took the tin and bandages, then waited.

She took a breath. Her mate. Rion was her mate.

Slowly, Arianna pulled her shirt over her head, leaving her in nothing but the wrap around her chest. But Rion didn't look at her half naked form. His gaze flew to the wound and assessed the damage. She'd been lucky. One shake of the creature's head could have left her incapacitated.

She held the sweater to her chest and inched closer.

Rion studied the mark. "You said a Dark Fae attacked you?" Arianna nodded and Rion unscrewed the lid before dipping his fingers in the salve.

"I don't know what they were. Talon seemed like he'd encountered them before." Her friend had claimed he'd explain later, but they'd been running nonstop since they'd leapt from the edge of Ruadhán.

Rion applied the balm with a feather-light touch. "I used to hear rumors from my warriors about strange beings, though I never encountered any myself. I often thought they were being dramatic."

She huffed a laugh. "They're very real and very scary."

"Tell me about them."

So she did. Arianna recounted every single detail while Rion wrapped her wound, then moved to rebandage her foot. He listened intently and claimed he'd never faced anything like them even during his time in the mountains.

The thought didn't sit well. Perhaps they were some sort of abomination of nature. Or maybe they'd been created by someone other than the gods.

THEY LEFT their trays on the dresser and Arianna changed into a short sleeve gray top. Blood from her wound had stained the sweater and she didn't want anyone fussing over her any more than her mate already had.

Rion didn't bother changing. His clothes were comfortable and after months of discomfort, he deserved the small luxury.

When she opened the door, Rion didn't growl at the guard stationed down the hall, nor did the guard snarl at him.

That was a nice change.

Saoirse was already in the living room, standing before the crackling fire. Her mother, Eimear, sat in the beige armchair to the left of the hearth with the little girl on the floor between her feet. Her round eyes looked up and Arianna couldn't help but smile at the crumbs covering the child's face. Someone had brought pastries.

"Morning," Saoirse said by way of greeting. Eimear looked better, but Arianna could tell from the way Saoirse stood that the female hadn't left her mother's side.

A smile ghosted Saoirse lips when she saw Arianna and Rion's joined hands.

"Morning," Arianna returned. Morning. Which meant they'd slept longer than she'd realized. A lot longer. She hadn't even dreamed. Rion waved an arm, looking like he could use a few more days' rest before he tackled the world and its problems. Let alone a meeting with her father.

Arianna plopped into the loveseat across from Eimear and angled herself toward the warm flames. Rion sat at her side. His posture wasn't rigid as she was so accustomed to seeing. It was as if all the fight had been drained out of him.

Or he was still just so exhausted that he couldn't be bothered to defend himself. Not that Arianna or Saoirse would let anyone touch him.

Eimear watched Arianna with utmost fascination. She had a bit more color to her cheeks and she'd washed all the dirt and blood from her face and body. Eimear wore a hood to cover her head, but Arianna caught a glimpse of the cleanly shaven skin beneath.

The High Lady of Brónach clutched a steaming mug between her thin hands. "You should have some." Arianna almost responded before realizing Eimear had addressed Rion.

Her mate tried to rise, but Saoirse stopped him with a gesture of her hand. The female was across the room in a second and filled two mugs with the steaming liquid. She returned, moving a bit more carefully and handed one to Arianna, then her brother.

Arianna stared into the brown liquid and took a sip. Mint tea. Rion did the same and a mysterious emotion flickered across his face.

She squeezed her mate's hand.

A strange glint had Arianna turning back to Eimear and the bracelet around her wrist. It was thin and did nothing to cover the thick scars left from her shackles, but—

"You're wearing iron?"

Eimear casually studied the metal. "I'd rather not see what happens when my powers are released after being restrained for so long." She waited a moment before adding, "With my visions, I could enter a comatose state for weeks, and I've had enough of prisons, even ones of my own making."

Right, Arianna had forgotten the female was a seer. One of the rare few. Perhaps the only one currently living. The rest, like a large portion of their history, had been forgotten. Arianna wondered if the previous Divine had burned all that knowledge, too.

Rion looked ready to speak when Talon sauntered through the door, rain water dripping off his dark blue uniform. He noticed those already gathered and studied each in turn before carefully removing his weapons. His eyes didn't leave Saoirse's who looked ready to tear the male in half.

"Easy," Rion said from beside her.

Eimear looked Saoirse over, a mother appraising the warrior her daughter had become. "Let's not forget he helped a great deal in my rescue."

Saoirse turned back to the fire and loosed a breath. She mumbled something that sounded like an apology. Arianna sympathized. Saoirse hadn't seen her mother in over eighty years and had thought the female dead. Of course she'd be more than a little protective.

Talon took a seat in the single armchair across the room. A three-piece sectional sofa sat in the middle of the space with a coffee table to its front.

A sliding glass door to Arianna's left let in some natural light while a simple chandelier above their heads illuminated the rest of the space.

They waited in silence, the only sounds the crackling fire and Eimear sipping her tea. Then Saoirse threw another log into the flames and the door opened again.

Arianna's father entered this time, tall and proud and elegant as he'd ever been. He surveyed those within the room, his gaze almost cold and calculated. She bristled when those eyes stopped on Rion. Her mate didn't move. No growling or posturing as Fae males usually did. Arianna found herself leaning closer to her mate, a movement not lost on Avalon.

He smiled and walked into the room with the same male trailing him from yesterday.

Arianna surveyed the male now. Tall and muscular with short cropped dark hair and matching eyes. His posture spoke of years of training, perhaps even decades. Her father's new personal guard. Arianna wondered if Talon recognized the male.

Avalon seated himself on the left most cushion of the sofa and his guard stood directly behind him, eyeing everyone in the room as if they might be a threat to his High Lord. Arianna was certain his promotion had come recently.

To Arianna's surprise, Zylah entered the room next, followed by a young male that Arianna thought she recognized, but couldn't place. Raevina followed behind them, but unlike the others, she didn't set her weapons by the door.

Talon eyed her but said nothing.

Ellie entered last with an injured Kirian at her side and Gavin trailing close behind.

Arianna was on her feet in an instant. "What happened?" She'd already crossed the room before they could answer. Kirian's left eye was black and swollen shut and the way he leaned to one side told Arianna enough about how his ribs were faring.

Her sister wasn't free of bruises, either. Blue lined her jaw and a dark slash stretched along her forearm from wrist to elbow.

"We escaped," Ellie said simply.

Arianna placed her hand over Kirian's eye. He flinched slightly but kept still. "Escaped what?"

Ellie eyed their father. "Niall. A lot happened after you left." Niall had hurt her? He'd beaten Kirian? Had he discovered their plan just as Gavin claimed he would? Arianna finished with Kirian and worked on her sister.

Their father's voice interrupted before Arianna could bombard her sister with a dozen questions. "Have a seat."

Ellie thanked Arianna and clutched Kirian's hand as she walked past, then plopped down on the sofa beside her father. Kirian didn't leave her side.

Gavin paused on the threshold for a moment before opting to stand in the back. He kept his distance from Ravina, who had taken up a place behind Talon. The female leaned against the wall and studied her nails.

Zylah, with the male youngling trailing her, opted to sit on the floor near Eimear. The two children ignored one another.

Fourteen were crammed into the small space. Twelve adults and two children. Arianna could already feel the tension in the air.

She gazed at each face one by one. It was strange enough to see her father seated on an old sofa, and stranger still to see him in such ordinary clothes. No finery or showing off then.

"Arianna." She startled at her name and looked into her father's eyes. He clasped his hands and sat forward. "You're the Queen of Alastríona; therefore, I think it's safe to say our future rests in your hands." Every pair of eyes studied her reaction. Arianna merely nodded.

"Your throne has been jeopardized. The male stationed to act in your stead has done things that are nothing short of treason. He attempted to bend your mind to his will, he willingly acted against your laws, he committed murder, and," Avalon's gaze flickered toward Eimear. "He has committed atrocities far beyond anything I could have imagined.

"It stands to reason that he should be removed from the royal city and put on trial."

She couldn't disagree with that but— "Whose murder?" Arianna asked. She counted the faces in the room again. Everyone she knew was here.

"Niall killed the council, thinking they were the ones who betrayed the information regarding Rion's location," Saoirse said without looking away from the fire.

"He also figured out Ellie was involved," Zylah added. "He murdered a half-breed, then tried to kill Kirian so your sister would talk."

Arianna eyed the half-breed, who kept his gaze averted. Tried. But they were here. "How did you escape?"

Ellie turned in her seat slightly to look at Gavin. She sighed. "I guess it doesn't matter since everyone else knows." She waved her hand through the air. "Gavin and I are mates." Arianna's lips parted. Mates. She'd known the male cared for Ellie, but she hadn't imagined—mates. Her sister had a mate. They were so rare and so treasured and yet both females from Móirín had found them.

Gavin inched forward. "When I told Niall about the bond, he released her to me."

"So where'd all the bruises come from?" Saoirse asked.

"From the guards," Ellie said, her fists clenched. "They thought using Kirian to taunt me was a good idea." She flashed her teeth. "I showed them otherwise."

"Which is how her arm was cut," Gavin said.

"And what?" Saoirse questioned. "You left right then?"

"We had to. I couldn't risk him coming back in the event—" Gavin stopped himself from talking and peered over at Saoirse.

"In the event of what?" Arianna pressed.

"His other source didn't pan out." The words were soft and low as they left Saoirse's lips like a deadly promise. "You knew."

Gavin's face visibly paled. "He went through with it." Not a question. Disbelief.

"What?" Arianna pressed.

"She's dead," Saoirse said, taking a step closer. "She's dead because you didn't warn us—"

"I couldn't," Gavin said. "I wanted to, trust me, but Niall already knew someone close was involved. He put us all in a room together and drilled us with questions, trying to find the source of the leak. I think the only reason he didn't kill us right then was because he wanted to make a spectacle of it."

"Why didn't he kill you?" Talon asked.

"Because I was never privy to that information. I just happened upon it when I was looking for—."

"You mean while you were snooping," Raevina said, her voice silken and lethal.

Gavin met their accusatory stares then turned desperate eyes to Ellie. "I was just trying to get your attention."

"What I'd like to know," Raevina spoke again, "is how you managed to lie to someone like Niall and come out unharmed."

Gavin blanched. "I-I already told you: I can mask my scent with a glamour." Everyone in the room froze. Gavin had mentioned it before, but Arianna didn't think anyone had imagined he could do it so directly.

Talon leaned forward in his chair. "So you're telling us you can lie to anyone about anything you want?"

Gavin looked like he wanted to run. "Yes."

"Can everyone from Pádraigín do it?" Arianna asked.

"No, it takes training, and even then most can't master it." He hesitated. "My mother was gifted with the ability. It's the first thing she taught me and, turns out, I'm gifted, too."

Rion clenched his jaw. "How do we know you haven't been lying this entire time? How do we know you aren't working as Niall's spy?"

Ellie, to Arianna's surprise, interrupted. "Trust me, he's not."

"You're certain?" Avalon asked, studying his daughter's mate, a match he was sure to approve over Kirian.

Ellie rolled her eyes. "You all claim I have a flair for dramatics," she gestured with one hand. "I assure you he's worse. He's already sworn himself loyal to me and Arianna while wrapped in iron."

The room seemed to take a collective breath.

Zylah tapped her foot. "Shall we move on to the real reason we're here? I don't think the children need to be exposed to anything that isn't necessary."

"I'm not a child," the male youngling said. "I helped."

"Yes, you did. A great deal," Saoirse added, her gaze softening. Arianna could still see the grief in Saoirse's eyes and wondered who she'd lost at Niall's hands. To think he'd murdered the council . . .

"The youngling is also a seer," Eimear said.

Arianna's mouth fell open. A seer. Two alive in the same lifespan. Two in the same room.

Arianna studied the young male who was sitting straighter, eying every adult in the room. Then she noticed the iron bracelet on his wrist. Just like Eimear's.

"He came to me claiming Niall planned to use the children against us. The half-breeds," Saoirse clarified. "He said he saw me and Raevina getting them out alive, but that if we told anyone else, Niall would find out. We chose to act. Whelan here guided us out step by step."

"You're wearing iron," Arianna said. She hated to see anyone with it around their wrists.

"It helps with the visions," Eimear said. "They can get overwhelming and sometimes distort our reality so much that it becomes difficult to tell what is real and what isn't."

"But they couldn't get everyone out and before we left, Niall was threatening to kill the rest of the half-breeds," Zylah said.

"You think he'd go through with it?" Arianna asked. The very thought sickened her but surely, at the very least, he wouldn't waste resources.

"Yes," Saoirse said. "He most certainly would." Arianna could tell there was something they weren't telling her. Niall had done something horrible. Then again, he'd done a lot of horrible things. He'd pitted her and Rion against one another. He'd held Rion against his will. He'd lied to her and used his magic to manipulate her for his own gain. He'd murdered and—Arianna glanced at Eimear.

Niall needed to be dealt with.

"But Whelan has given us other information, too," Avalon said, pulling Arianna from her grim thoughts of vengeance. "If we choose to leave Niall in Ruadhán, he will raise an army to his side."

Arianna felt her face drain of color. "To what end?"

"I imagine to get you back and rule the continent." Avalon gestured toward Eimear. "The High Lady tells us visions are often obscured, but when they take distinct visual shape, they almost always come to pass unless intervention is made. Whelan also sees many shadowed creatures behind Niall in the visions, but it's unclear what they could be."

"So what do we do?" Arianna asked.

All eyes turned to her but it was her father who continued. "That is what we're here to decide. Each person in this room is present because you've formed a relationship with them. This is the beginning of your court and the ambassadors of the four nations."

Arianna met each eye and her lips parted slightly. "You want me to decide?"

"You are the queen," Avalon said. "It is your place to decide."

"No, that's—" Gods, they were serious. "Learning to rule a continent is a far cry from whatever this is. We're talking about people's lives. Hell, if Niall raises an army, we're talking about another war."

"Which is why we're here to weigh the pros and cons," Raevina said.

"Oh sure, let's not pretend if it wasn't half-breeds that you'd even hesitate," Zylah spat.

"You know that has nothing to do with it. He didn't just target half-breeds," Raevina countered.

Talon folded his hands. "But if we wait and those shadows really are part of an army. . ."

"What army would rise against the queen?" Ellie questioned.

"A hired one," Saoirse said. "He has access to countless funds, and mercenaries will fight anything for a high enough price."

Ellie rolled her eyes. "Humans, maybe."

"Don't underestimate humans," Raevina warned. "They have iron weapons at their disposal, and let's not forget how our ancestors ended up on this continent in the first place."

Arianna had the very distinct impression the entire group had already settled a few arguments.

"Say we storm the manor," Talon said, his gaze focused on Whelan. "Are you able to see whether we'd emerge victorious?"

"Don't ask him such complex questions. A seer isn't able to see whatever they wish to see," Eimear said.

"Then how does it work?" Zylah asked.

"I cannot explain it. Call it destiny, the universe, the gods. Something out there sends the visions our way when we need them."

"Are you sure you can't see if your visions would be any more detailed?" Gavin asked.

Saoirse gave him a warning growl but Eimear's stare was icy as she said, "Unless you wish for Niall to find us from the sheer force of my abilities alone, then no, I can't."

"What do you mean?" Talon asked, though Arianna was certain it had more to do with curiosity than anything.

"My power wants out. I started to feel it crawling beneath my skin after a decade. It's angry and ready to burst from its cage in a way I don't think anyone is prepared for. Myself included."

"Is that safe?" Arianna asked. "For you, I mean?"

Eimear offered her a gentle smile. "It's one of the reasons I'm waiting until I'm stronger before setting it free."

Rion leaned forward. "You mean to tell me that you expect Arianna to choose between saving the half-breeds and leaving them to their fate?"

"It's her choice to make," Avalon said. "Either way, we'll have to retake Ruadhán eventually. We may or may not have the numbers to do so now. A lot of that rides on how many would follow their queen over Niall."

Talon unfolded his arms. "If we allow Niall to remain in his current position, he could try to rally others to his cause. But if we advance now, we can eliminate all that and place Arianna where she belongs."

"We have the numbers," Raevina said. "I estimate at least half won't fight for Niall after what he did to the council, and the other half only pretends to serve him because they're scared out of their minds. It'll be easy to rally them to our side."

"If you go in swords swinging, he'll kill the half-breeds," Zylah said. "You need to consider stealth as an option."

"It won't do any good," Gavin said, his eyes studying the patterns in the floor. "He'll know you're coming. He likely already knows you're coming."

"I told you he had a flair for the dramatics," Ellie said.

"I'm serious. He's always three steps ahead. No matter what you plan, Niall will have a second plan in place."

"So we'll have a third," Rion said, unfazed. "No one is unbeatable."

"So are we saving the former slaves?" Zylah asked.

"Of course. And Niall is going to answer for everything he's done," Arianna said.

"Niall is mine." Eimear's voice was so demanding that they all fell silent and turned toward her. "I get to end him."

No one disagreed. If anyone had earned the right to punish Niall, it was Eimear.

"Stealth will be key," Talon said. Arianna could already see the gears turning in his brain. "We'll prioritize rescuing the half-breeds, then we'll see how many are willing to stand against Niall."

"And if it turns out we're outnumbered, then we'll retreat with the hostages and regroup in Levea," Arianna said.

They all murmured their agreement, then set to making plans.

CHAPTER EIGHTY-THREE

SAOIRSE

Saoirse found Zylah behind the cabin watching the children chase one another through the small clearing and between the trees. Their laughter filled the air, sparking pleasant memories that dragged a smile to Saoirse's lips. It was a welcome sound after arguing with their queen for the last thirty minutes.

Their group had almost unanimously agreed that Arianna should go back to Levea for her own protection. Avalon had added that Ellie and Rion should accompany her and both sisters had violently protested.

Saoirse had to give them props. They certainly weren't cowards.

Zylah eyed her once before turning back to face the children. The pair stood in awkward silence and Saoirse ensured she kept her distance.

She'd been pushing too hard. The female wanted her physically but that was the extent of things. Saoirse had been a fool not to listen to her. Now, Saoirse might very well have to bid her mate farewell for good.

"You didn't tell me you got the children out," Zylah said.

One screamed in delight when another rounded a tree and tagged them before running off again. At least the rain had let up for a while.

"Not all of them," Saoirse said, knowing there were still at least a dozen more left at Niall's mercy. They'd been in another room when Whelan had found her and told her what they needed to do. Going after them would have revealed their intent to Niall in some way.

"I'm sorry about her," Zylah said. "The female Niall—the female from the tavern, I mean. I'm sorry about what happened to her." Right, because when Saoirse had first met Zylah, Zylah had caught her gawking at the female while sipping her ale.

"Me, too," Saoirse said. Silence fell between them again.

Zylah sighed. "Let me guess, you're here to beg me not to go."

"Quite the opposite. I wondered if you knew how to defend yourself."

"Are you implying something?"

"Not at all. I'm asking about your background and whether you've undergone any training."

"And if I say no?"

"Then I'd ask if I could show you a few things. We have a couple of days before the rest of Avalon's warriors get here. I see no sense in wasting valuable time."

Zylah scoffed. "You think you can turn me into some kind of elite warrior in just two days?"

"No, but I can show you a few moves that might save your life in the event someone gets around that magic of yours." Saoirse hoped it was strong. It had certainly felt strong when the female had shoved her on her ass.

Zylah faced her. "I thought you were going to leave me alone."

Saoirse swallowed hard, "I said after all this is over, and clearly, it most certainly isn't. The least I can do is ensure your survival."

Zylah looked her up and down. "I don't want to be ridiculed."

"I won't ridicule you, nor will I make any sort of demeaning comments. I've trained plenty of novices and it gets a commander nowhere to bring down those who are trying to learn."

Zylah gazed out at the children again. "Fine. What do I do first?"

Saoirse faced her. "Widen your stance and bend your knees." Zylah hesitated then obeyed. "Good, now instead of coming straight at me, I want you to pivot to the side."

"Why?"

"Because your enemy will underestimate you and I plan to help you take full advantage of it."

Chapter Eighty-Four

TALON

alon wasn't sure which of the two sisters was more stubborn, the eldest or the youngest. It had taken all of them to convince Arianna to station herself in the town below and function as their healer rather than endanger herself by entering the royal city.

They were on a mission and if Niall intercepted them before they got the half-breeds out, there would be more than a few casualties. Their queen didn't need to be one of them.

None knew whether they were going to war or not, though most agreed that a fight was sure to break out. Talon just hoped a large portion of Ruadhán's warriors would follow their queen instead of the tyrant who sat on her throne. If they didn't, well, he supposed they'd cross that bridge when they got there.

Talon strolled through the woods, past the eyes of the watchful Fae guards and the tiny creatures he knew lingered somewhere among the trees.

Raevina was alone and seated on the lower thick branch of a tree, her back pressed against the trunk. One hand held a blade while the other ran a whetstone along its length.

The shrill sound pierced the otherwise peaceful woods, leaving everything deafeningly silent between the long strokes.

At least the rain had stopped.

Talon paused beside a tree and watched her methodic movement. She drew the stone across the blade again and again, staring at the edge as if she knew exactly how long it would take to reach perfection.

They were leaving in two days. If things went awry, they'd meet back here before fleeing to Levea. All were welcome, according to Avalon, and Saoirse claimed Brónach would send warriors to Levea's aid should Niall launch a full scale attack.

If Arianna didn't get her throne back, they'd make a new one for her in her home country.

Raevina hadn't said anything, leaving Talon to wonder if the female would continue serving her queen or return to Fiadh.

Their plans balanced precariously on too many what ifs and maybes. Talon wasn't accustomed to the uncertainties. Rion wasn't either; he could tell from the way the male's shoulders had tensed. But this was what Arianna wanted. She didn't want to risk their lives if they were outnumbered, nor did she want to leave Niall on the throne if he could be easily removed.

If removing a nine hundred-year-old male who could warp their reality could be called easy. Hopefully Gavin's training would pay off.

The young male had started early that morning and had recruited everyone else from Pádraigín. They had a simple goal: teach the warriors from the other three nations how to recognize a glamour. Even if they couldn't break it, the recognition would prevent unnecessary casualties. Talon couldn't help but remember the gruesome image of Rion's mouth covered in Arianna's blood. No, they definitely didn't need events to repeat themselves.

The whetstone continued and Talon studied Raevina.

They'd had a moment together, but every encounter since had been strained and uneasy. But maybe that was his fault. If so, he wanted to address it and set their future relationship straight, no matter what kind she wanted.

Raevina was beautiful beneath the dim light. Her long dark braids cascaded down her shoulders and her skin almost seemed to glimmer as if flecks of gold were woven into her flesh. He wondered what her animal shift might be. Certainly a predator. He knew no opponent would ever stand a chance if caught in her claws. She'd already captured him and he'd lost the fight before it had even begun.

Talon steeled himself, took a deep breath, and prowled forward on silent steps.

It was good timing, he reasoned. For once, Raevina wasn't surrounded by her warriors. All were lethal and graceful and trusted the others with their lives.

Talon envied them, if only because of the time they'd spent fighting at one another's sides. He'd get there eventually. He hoped. So long as the gods didn't see fit to tear him from the world early.

Talon stopped. Maybe he shouldn't be here at all. Raevina had already told him to come back with more experience. Perhaps she hadn't just meant it as an insult. Talon was incredibly young compared to her and her companions.

He faltered and stepped on a twig, then cursed to himself. Raevina didn't bother to look up.

"I don't like being disturbed before a battle," she said simply.

No hiding now. "I was hoping we could talk."

She examined her blade and ran her thumb across it. "I have nothing to say to you."

"But I do." He kept his temper in check. He wouldn't rise to the bait.

Raevina sighed and let the stone fall to her lap. "If this is about the kiss, save it. I didn't intend for it to make you follow me around like a puppy."

His heart thrummed in his ears. "It's about more than just the kiss and you know it."

She met his gaze. Her eyes simmered like molten spheres of amber. Talon swallowed hard. "You can't tell me you don't feel it." He had from the first moment they'd danced. A pull that drove him mad with need. A desire to be close to her and follow her everywhere she went.

But Raevina looked back at her blade as if she didn't have a care in the world. Several seconds passed and she sighed again as if annoyed. "A distraction."

"What?"

"The only thing you feel is a distraction. It will make you stupid and get you killed. You're better off forgetting about it. The rational mind makes better decisions."

Pain lanced through his chest as if she'd actually stabbed him. "You can't be serious."

"Oh, I'm quite serious."

Talon remained still for several seconds, but when Raevina lifted her stone to begin working on her blade again, he said, "We're going to Ruadhán in a few days to fight in a battle we're not guaranteed to win and you're content to leave things the way they are?"

She smirked at that. "And what would you like from me?" That cold gaze pinned him in place and her voice was mocking as she said, "You want a dainty little female who will cry over you? One who will run into your arms and beg you to live so that we can defy fate?" Raevina draped an arm over one knee. "I make my own fate. It steals nothing from me."

Talon just stared at her and after a long moment, Raevina's gaze softened slightly. "I don't know you, Talon of Móirín, but if you're going into this fight expecting to lose, then perhaps its best we keep it that way."

"I don't think we'll lose. I'm just weighing the odds."

Raevina shook her head. "You know nothing about odds."

"I've seen enough battles."

Her eyes flashed again. "You've barely begun. I've been in the field since before you were even a conceived thought in our universe. I've fought against enemies that would have you pissing yourself. If you have to question whether you'll win, then you've already lost."

Talon clenched his fists. "I almost killed The Demon." It felt as childish as it sounded.

Raevina made a show of clapping her hands together loudly and Talon cringed at her mockery. "And how many times did the two of you collide? Did you ever stop to think that he was pulling back to make you assume you were on equal footing? I've seen the way The Demon fights. If you're alive, it's because he wanted you that way. You were a knight among a group of pawns. An interesting toy he could play with and dispatch any time he wished." She smiled at him. "He was distracted and you got very lucky. Don't make the mistake of assuming you won anything."

Talon couldn't speak. Raevina continued her onslaught, spearing him through his chest with every word. "When you fight hundreds with nothing more than a few comrades to guard your back, when you swing your blade while stumbling over your own warrior's bloody corpses, when you find yourself promising vengeance upon your enemies no matter the costs, then maybe, *maybe* we'll talk about what you feel."

"You think I'm unworthy."

"I think you're a child. An arrogant male who allows little more than instinct to drive him. You're just like the fools who sacrifice their lives and have the audacity to call it glory." She smiled, a cruel, wicked thing. "The loudest ones are usually the first to run from a fight."

"I run from nothing."

Raevina smirked again and adjusted the stone in her hand. "I guess we'll see, won't we?"

CHAPTER EIGHTY-FIVE

ARIANNA

rianna didn't like the plan now any more than she had when they'd first agreed upon it. She was to remain hidden and safe while the rest of them risked their lives in order to subdue Niall.

Fae would die, she knew it and wished she could prevent it. She also knew that if Niall caught her, everyone would bow to him for her sake and they'd lose before they'd even begun.

Arianna clenched her fists. She wanted to do so much more. She had the power now. She could control the strange thing that roared in her veins, even if she didn't fully understand it. The group, her court, had brought that to her attention, too. Not knowing the extent of her power was just as dangerous as having it stripped away.

Two days passed swiftly. Arianna had healed any lingering injuries, including a rather nasty burn across Saoirse's upper back. She'd also tried to address Rion's achy joints, but her magic hadn't seemed to touch the pain.

Fine, that was the limit of it then.

Night descended too soon, blanketing the land in darkness. Fires dotted the landscape, courtesy of Raevina and her warriors. Gavin led those from Pádraigín to ensure they remained hidden from view, but most were spending time with their comrades, preparing for what could be the start of an intense battle. Perhaps even the start of another war.

She prayed it wouldn't come to that. Perhaps Niall would turn the throne over to her and fall to his knees begging his queen for forgiveness.

She seriously doubted it.

At dawn, they'd march the last few miles separating them from Ruadhán.

Their goals were simple. Find the half-breeds, get them out of the city, then attempt to recruit allies. Raevina claimed most would join her cause. Arianna prayed the female was right.

If they had the numbers, her father would lure Niall out, then his warriors would clap the male in irons before handing the city over to her. Not that she'd know what to do with it. The council members were dead and she had no direction. It would be a month of sorting through paperwork before she would even begin to understand how they'd run the place.

She sighed and watched Rion as her mate helped Talon drop off wood at the edges of already blazing fires. She was certain the two whispered amongst themselves, detailing plans to get her and Ellie to safety should things go wrong.

"You're looking better." Arianna almost jumped out of her skin at the sound of her father's deep voice. Rion's head whipped around, but upon spotting Avalon he relaxed again. He'd made a point to control his magic around her, for which she was silently grateful.

"I feel better." How could she not when she had Rion right in front of her? Sure, he was thinner than he used to be and she questioned whether he should be joining them at all. But Arianna knew wherever she went, he would follow.

"The bond is a gift." Arianna turned to find Avalon studying her mate. He and Talon were so close now, she knew they were planning something. Perhaps it was good they were working together, even if she was the likely topic of conversion. She hated to cause them so much worry.

Avalon cleared his throat. "I apologize for the part I played in trying to tear you two apart." Well, that certainly wasn't what she'd been expecting to hear.

"They said Ellie kept you informed about . . . things." Like her falling into a depressive state, though she was fairly certain that had all been Niall's doing.

"Your sister was worried." He looked her over and Arianna knew he was noting how thin she'd become as well. "I understand why."

Her anger rose despite his apology. Anger for everything he'd ever put her through. "You care so suddenly?"

Avalon lowered his head. "I deserved that." He looked away then, staring off into the distance until his gaze rose to the stars dotting the sky overhead. His voice was softer when he spoke again. "Sometimes I can still hear your mother's voice. She watches over us. Over you." Arianna swallowed the lump in her throat. "The way I acted toward you when you were a child wasn't fair. I treated you more like one of my subjects than my daughter." He was silent again. "I lost myself after your mother's passing and let grief consume me. I lost my way as Móirín's leader, and as your father."

Arianna had gone still. Her father was . . . apologizing to her.

"You carried a strength I couldn't see, something within that was far more powerful than any physical strength you possessed. Your mother had it, too. I think part of me saw the way you resembled her, and I just—" He shook his head. "I wanted to keep you from having to rely on it. I think I hoped I could protect you when I couldn't protect her."

Her father ambled toward a tree and placed his palm flat against the rough bark, almost as if he were feeling the life force within. He took a shaky breath. "I apologize for everything I put you through. I don't expect your forgiveness. Instead, I offer you the promise that I will do everything in my power to ensure you keep the throne beneath your rule. I will serve as your loyal subject, and I will never question your judgment."

Avalon turned to her and Arianna could have sworn his eyes shone. "I'm proud of everything you've overcome and all that you've accomplished. I offer you my full support and I hope one day I'm able to prove myself as a High Lord still worthy of his seat."

Her lips parted but words wouldn't form. She didn't know how to respond or react and when Arianna tried to clear her throat, she failed. Proud. That's all she'd ever wanted to hear from him and yet it didn't feel like enough. Not with the memory of his harsh voice still ringing in the back of her mind.

Time. It would take time. That's how healing was traditionally done.

Arianna nodded and turned her attention to her sister to break the tension. "What about Ellie?" Arianna wasn't sure what she'd do if her little sister had to return to Móirín anytime soon.

"I'll teach her everything she needs to know. No more tutors. She'll be learning directly from me." Avalon offered her a weak smile. "Unless the worst should happen tomorrow, of course. I just needed you to know that you have my blessing no matter what path you choose to walk."

The way he said it . . . Her father was usually so confident and his strength was something she needed right now. "You don't think we'll win?" Maybe they should retreat after all. Just focus on getting the half-breeds past Niall's guards and regroup in Levea. But if Whelan's vision came to pass and Niall raised an army, there was no telling what he might do.

Avalon watched those gathering by the fires. "I've seen many battles, yet I think this is the first time I've been so afraid." Arianna startled. Afraid? She'd never known her father to be afraid of anything.

"Why?"

He shrugged. "Maybe because it's my children's fate on the line instead of just my own" Avalon tilted his face to the stars again. "No matter what happens, be careful who you trust, and keep Talon and Ellie close."

Arianna swallowed her fear. "I will."

He looked her over again, then crossed the small space separating them and rested a comforting hand on her shoulder. "Be sure to get some rest tonight. You'll need it."

Her father tried to walk past with nothing more than a smile, but Arianna ducked beneath his arm and pulled him close, wrapping both arms tightly around his torso.

She thought she felt him tremble slightly as he held her.

They'd rebuild. After today, they'd rebuild more than just the continent. They'd rebuild their relationship and the relationships of those between every nation.

A home was built one brick at a time and this was where she would start.

"Be careful."

He patted her back. "You, too." Then he was gone, disappearing into the night to make preparations with his warriors as the High Lord of Móirín. She watched his retreating form and wondered who he'd turned to for comfort after her mother's passing. Maybe no one. Perhaps that was why he'd drowned for so many years.

Arianna found Rion waiting for her by a fire. She crossed the clearing but her mate didn't reach out. Her heart ached because of it. They were about to go to battle and he still felt so distant.

"What did your father say?"

She took her mate's hand and squeezed before leading him closer to the heat of the fire. The air wasn't cold, not by a long shot, but something about the warmth brought her comfort.

"He's afraid."

Rion studied the flames then bent to toss another log over them. Embers sprayed up like fireflies, then died.

"As am I."

Arianna tilted her head, trying to see his face. "You don't think we'll win either?"

"It's not about winning. It's about what direction everything will flow after tomorrow. Even if we win, the challenges won't stop there."

She sighed. "I know." And she'd likely have a target on her back for the rest of her life.

"I wish—" Rion stopped himself.

"What?"

He shook his head. "It's a selfish thought."

"Tell me anyway."

Rion ran a hand through his hair. "I just wish we had more time. I want to be alone with you and talk about everything that happened." He squeezed her hand. "I want to earn your trust back, but I guess an impending conflict doesn't really afford us that kind of time."

Arianna faced the flames again. "No, it doesn't." She felt the exact same way. She wanted to take him back to that little cabin in the woods and sit in the silence. She wanted to teach her body that Rion's touch wasn't something to be feared.

"Maybe after we win," she said.

"Yeah?"

Arianna nodded. "I'll set things in motion, then pass the reins to Ellie for a while."

"Should we worry about her setting everything on fire in our absence?"

Arianna smirked at that. "Maybe her and Saoirse can make the new council's lives interesting while we're away." If she got that far. Short of the ambassadors, Arianna didn't really know anyone from the other nations. She'd be hard pressed to replace Declan and the others.

"I spoke to Talon earlier." She inclined her head to listen. "He said they'll be able to handle things up top and that it's best if I stay with you."

"Good." They'd discussed a few possibilities but hadn't settled on a definitive yet. Both males probably thought the best way to keep her from joining the fray was to keep Rion out of it, too. They were right. She wasn't about to let Niall put him in iron again.

Silence stretched and an owl called from a nearby tree. Another answered, sentinels keeping watch. Hushed whispers floated through the air as others settled down for the night.

The fire crackled and Rion tossed another log into it. Arianna sighed, then leaned her head against Rion's shoulder. So much. There was so much about to happen.

"Well look who I found all huddled together as if we don't have a million things to do," Ellie said. Her sister carried a bowl in each hand with a chunk of bread sticking out from the top of each.

Arianna's heart jolted "Is there something you need help with?"

"No, I'm just teasing. Both of you do need to eat though." Ellie passed the bowls to them and Rion didn't even hesitate before digging in. Ellie just stared and it took Rion a moment to notice.

Her sister smiled. "Well, I guess that finally settles that." Rion offered Ellie the shadow of a smile. "Sorry, it's probably bland. We should have recruited Arianna to make it, but we didn't want to disturb you guys."

"Trust me," Rion said. "This is a feast compared to—" Rion stopped himself and glanced sidelong at his mate. "Well, it's a feast." Arianna wondered if he would ever feel comfortable enough to share his story. If he did, she'd be sure to listen to every detail.

"And before you go and try to offer him yours," Ellie said, pointing a spoon at her sister. "There's plenty to go around. I'll gladly go get you both a second bowl. Gods know you both need it."

Ellie wasn't wrong, but Arianna's face still flushed with embarrassment. Rion had lost weight being tortured, but she'd lost weight because she'd given up and refused to move. It was just another reminder of that weakness she was trying so desperately to purge from her body. Even if Niall had likely been the cause of it.

Arianna looked her mate over. She'd healed his wounds, but he had only rested for a short while. He'd been locked in captivity for months, then had fought for his life just a few short days ago. Maybe she'd made her decision too quickly.

"I think you should stay behind," Arianna finally said.

Rion didn't even look up from his food. "That's not an option."

"You need rest."

"I need you." The sudden intensity in his gaze had Ellie turning to face Kirian, who had just arrived with two more bowls in hand. Talon wasn't far off and she noticed he'd slowed his steps.

Rion lowered his voice, but it did little good with so many Fae around. "I can't be without you. Not again. Not after—" His voice caught and Arianna rested a hand on his forearm. She wouldn't put him through any more pain or stress.

"Fair enough." Because the truth was, she needed him, too. "We'll face Niall and everything he throws at us together."

"All right," Ellie said. "Don't get sappy. You all act as if we're not going to see tomorrow." Ellie laid back and folded her hands behind her head. "I personally plan to march in there and kick Niall's ass right off the edge of that city." They all chuckled.

"You two get some rest," Ellie said. "I'll keep an eye out."

"Are you sure?" Arianna asked.

Talon cut her sister off and said, "We have an early start and if we have to fight tomorrow, I'd rather do so knowing you two are well-rested."

Rion smirked. "Forced to fight alongside your enemy again."

Talon didn't rise to the challenge. Instead he said, "Enemy? I had rather thought we were past that." And Arianna swore something passed between the two that couldn't be put into words. Not quite friendship, but a step in the right direction. A brick to begin building.

Chapter Eighty-Six

Arianna

They moved with dawn, just as her father had promised. Arianna rode on horseback at the front of their line with Rion and The High Lord of Móirín at her side. Ellie, Saoirse, Raevina, Talon, Zylah, and Gavin rode behind them in two single file lines. Their small army followed on foot.

Kirian had been stationed at the rear to assist those who would carry supplies into the village below. He would also help prepare the villagers for evacuation should things take a heated turn. Eimear and the children had stayed back at the safe house along with a handful of guards.

Eimear wanted to fight, Arianna could see it in the female's eyes, but even she knew she was too weak to be anything more than a hindrance. They had promised to keep Niall alive if they could help it, if only so Eimear could look him in the eye and end him herself.

Four warriors from Pádraigín rode just outside their line keeping their advancing group hidden from the watchful eyes of Ruadhán's sentries. She was glad for their loyalty. Without them, sneaking in would have been nearly impossible.

Arianna had replayed the plan in her mind at least a hundred times since waking. She'd almost called the whole thing off at breakfast, but Zylah had caught her attention and the months they'd both spent shackled came rushing back as a reminder of why she couldn't afford to falter.

There were half-breeds who needed their help, and Arianna had promises to keep.

The sun continued to hide behind thick rolling clouds when they arrived at the edge of the village. A village the citizens of Ruadhán cared very little about.

It showed in the way some of the roofs sagged and in the cracks along the foundations. In the fields that weren't quite as lush as they could be and in the animals that were just a bit too thin.

Arianna tried to quiet her rage and focus on the task ahead. She'd reveal herself to the villagers as soon as her father and Raevina led their forces onto the platform. She didn't want to scare the citizens by having a small military force appear out of thin air in front of their ramshackle gates.

She tried to take a steadying breath. They would only be gone for a little while. Her father would signal her once they had the half-breeds out, then Arianna would rush to their aid.

It would take at least another thirty minutes for Raevina to sift through the warriors and either recruit them to her side or knock them out. She'd make a decision based upon numbers; after that Saoirse and Avalon would strike.

Then Arianna's real job began.

Arianna knew warriors from both sides would be brought to her and she'd be expected to heal them enough that they could rejoin the fray. If those who opposed her rule didn't change their minds by the time they got to her, Arianna was to put them in irons.

She bit the inside of her cheek. Not everyone would turn against Niall, whether from fear or loyalty. Five hundred years was a long time to rule. Many trusted him or feared him enough that they would never question his rule.

A light drizzle started again and Arianna sighed. More rain. Then the wind shifted and a horrid stench hit her delicate senses so hard she gagged and almost lost her meager breakfast.

She knew that smell. She'd never forget it. It conjured images of blistered hands and mangled bodies dumped into too shallow graves.

Arianna leapt from her horse and those who'd been riding alongside her followed along with four Móirín guards. Zylah and Ellie covered their noses, and Gavin had turned so pale Arianna wondered if the male might faint.

They moved east, their footsteps fast as the distance increased between her and the army at her back. No one dared speak, if only to avoid giving themselves away.

Her feet faltered as they rounded the corner of the homes and her eyes absorbed the carnage splayed across the ground.

Rion tried to turn her away, but Arianna pushed past him.

Bile rose in her throat as Arianna beheld the mounds of bodies just outside the village's perimeter. Scavengers were tearing through the carcasses and flies buzzed in the air, feasting on the long dead half-breeds. Their limbs were contorted at awkward angles and it didn't take long for Arianna to understand why.

They hadn't just died. No, they'd been thrown off the edge of the city while they were still alive. She could tell from the scorch marks on the earth and the greenery that lay broken and dead. Some had tried to stop their fall but their magic hadn't been strong enough.

No one spoke. Her father surveyed the scene as if he'd seen similar brutality before. Talon and Rion had gone unearthly still. Saoirse looked ready to rip someone in half. Zylah and Ellie were already crying and Raevina clenched her jaw in response, her gaze locked on the invisible city above. Gavin vomited.

Arianna's feet carried her forward. She wasn't sure why she tried to approach them. Maybe she hoped there was still something to be done, some way her magic might intervene and reverse the clock, but Rion's gentle hand took her upper arm and pulled her against his chest. She didn't resist this time.

Niall had done this. He'd murdered them, then let them rot as if half-breeds weren't worthy of a proper burial. They were garbage to him and he was using their deaths to send her a message. Niall wanted her afraid so she would return as his obedient puppet.

But fear was the last thing on her mind.

The scent of rot and decay filled Arianna's mouth with every breath and a rising wave built in her chest.

They'd made a plan, but she was done hiding.

"Arianna?" Rion's voice was gentle, yet she could sense the storm brewing beneath his skin. It was a fury that mirrored her own.

Her breath clouded in the air and frost gathered at her feet, forming tiny, jagged spears that crunched beneath her boots. She didn't even try to rein it in. Arianna was burning up from the inside as the ancient creature prowled its cage.

Free me, free me, free me, it seemed to say.

Arianna turned to Gavin. Her voice didn't sound like her own when she said, "Take us up."

Gavin retreated a step. He looked between Rion and Avalon as if waiting for their balks of protest. Both kept silent. "But—I thought the plan was to—"

Arianna stepped and Gavin retreated again. "Take. Us. Up."

Seconds later, Gavin was working the nearest platform, lifting them high into the air and toward the city. She'd burn it to the ground along with anyone who wished to stand with that monster.

The wind violently whipped at her tight braid, pulling tendrils of hair loose that stung every time they hit her face. Ellie had put it up for her that morning. She wore the same clothes she'd rescued Rion in and had just as many knives strapped across her chest alongside the twin blades Talon had gifted her. The rest of them were dressed in a similar fashion, ready to take on the world at her command.

She just wanted a glimpse. If Niall waited for her at the city's edge, then she'd send her father to gather their army and put an end to him once and for all.

No one questioned her shift in plans and part of her wondered if they could sense the mounting typhoon building in her core. She was going to kill Niall for this. Kill him, then leave his body out for the crows. She was done pretending everyone could change. Some people were just monsters and deserved to be put down.

Arianna didn't take her eyes off the city as they drew closer. Six guards peered over the edge, their weapons already drawn. She unsheathed the twin blades at her back, then heard steel sing through the air as the others prepared themselves.

Gavin's fear burned her nose, but she ignored it. So long as the male carried them into the city. He could flee afterward and she wouldn't brand him a coward.

Arianna growled and her magic erupted in a swirling storm of ice and snow. The guards stepped back and she leapt from the platform before Gavin had settled it into place.

Their gazes were . . . shocked, unsure as they beheld their queen and the raw magic circling her body. It begged her to tear them apart and make them pay for what they'd done. She reined it in. *Soon*, she promised. *Soon.*

Five flicked their gazes to a male at their front. The leader, then.

"You have three choices," Arianna said, her voice lethal. "Kneel, step aside, or fall where you stand." They looked between one another again, but the commander hadn't moved, as if transfixed.

"He told us you weren't coming back." Not a challenge or defiance. Still, her anger wouldn't abate.

"A mistake on your informant's part."

Arianna stepped and ice crackled across the stone path. The male quickly lowered to one knee and held his sword out as an offering. "My blade is yours, My Lady."

She scented the air, searching for a lie or a sign of any glamours. But this male wasn't from Pádraigín. His magic came from Brónach.

Another sank to the ground, followed by another. Only one remained upright.

"Traitors," he snarled. "Niall was right, you're all miserable traitors."

"Lower your weapon," the male's commander urged without turning. "Don't let the Regent confuse you."

"He is the rightful king, you coward." One flicker of magic was all it took for Rion to move. Her mate had crossed the space before she could blink. He twisted the male's weapon from his grasp with his bare hands and a sharp crack had the offender screaming as his shoulder dislocated.

Rion's magic crawled from beneath his clothes and wrapped around the male's throat to silence him. He fell still, but Arianna could still hear his heart beat.

"Spare him," the commander begged. "Please. He's my cousin. He's just young and confused. He hasn't even had his shift yet."

Rion watched her, waiting for the command.

"Bind him," Arianna ordered. Raevina obeyed.

The commander bowed his head. "Thank you, My Lady."

Arianna looked down the familiar streets. Familiar, yet different. The gems no longer sparkled and the gold she'd seen lining cracks and crevices no longer existed. The flowers weren't all in bloom and some of the homes carried rust along their metal railings.

The perfection had all been part of Niall's glamour. Her anger simmered and the beast beneath her skin rubbed against its cage. She wanted Niall and she wanted him now.

"There are others in the city who will fight for you," the male said.

There it was, the information they'd hoped for. Arianna glanced toward the city's edge. She couldn't get the image of the half-breeds out of her mind. How afraid had they been at the end?

"How many?" Rion asked. Her mate's magic circled him like a great serpent, wild and untamable. He also kept his distance, but something about the ancient magic strumming through her veins staved off her fear. Maybe it would eradicate it entirely.

"Enough to make a difference if you intend to stand against the Regent."

"Tell us everything you know," Talon demanded.

"He claims the new queen is young and idealistic, but that her ideas would lead to our ruination and eventual downfall. He's used the fear of the past to sway some, but many are reluctant."

"And where do you stand?" Avalon asked.

The male paled, seeming to realize who stood before him. He lowered his head again. "She is our queen. What are we fighting for if not her ideals?"

Arianna scented the air again. No lie. "Raevina." The female stepped forward, her shoulders squared as she awaited Arianna's command. "Accompany these five and gather those who will stand with us."

"We're fighting?" Talon asked. His eyes passed no judgement. He was simply a commander ready to function in whatever role she assigned him.

"We're fighting." Talon nodded his understanding, then Arianna turned to face Zylah. The female's face was stained with tears, but she looked more defiant than ever. "I want you in the village below. Get an infirmary set up. Warn the villagers and begin evacuating."

"I can fight." Everyone stopped to stare at the half-breed. Zylah had faced hardship and she'd seen the ugly side of war. Her scars were proof enough of the nightmares she'd endured. "Don't put me down there just because I'm not a pureblood."

"I wouldn't dream of it," Arianna said. "I'm placing you there because of your experience." Realization shone across Zylah's face. "I need someone with the ability to lead, to act in my stead. One who isn't prejudiced, to ensure everyone gets fair treatment no matter what kind of blood runs through their veins."

Zylah didn't respond at first, then she bowed. It was likely the first time the female had ever done so of her own free will. "I'll see that it's taken care of."

Arianna braced herself for what they were about to face. It had been inevitable from the start but after what she'd seen, she wouldn't stand on the sidelines. She wouldn't wait and let Niall hurt anyone else.

"Saoirse." The female inclined her head. Arianna saw the way she looked at Zylah with longing in her gaze. It would weaken them to split the pair. "I want you to join her. Niall will likely try to send warriors down to thwart our attempts at treating the wounded. Defend them."

Saoirse nodded. "On my honor."

Arianna turned to Talon, Rion, and her father next.

"If I may?" Her father asked and she nodded, grateful for someone with experience to guide what she prayed wasn't the biggest mistake of her life. "Our plans don't need to change much. Raevina will gather those she can. I can secure a perimeter and begin searching for the rest of the half-breeds." Arianna didn't let herself imagine what kind of conditions they might be living in.

Her mate closed the distance, keeping one eye on her as if waiting for her reaction. "If we get Niall in irons, his followers won't be so willing to fight."

"Go right for the king," Arianna said, thinking back to the board game they used to play in a library surrounded by books and thinking they had all the time in the world.

Rion looked at her and his chest seemed to swell with pride. "I think he's forgotten the queen gets to make any move she wants."

THEY SEPARATED and Arianna's heart pounded as they ran through the empty streets.

He knew. Niall knew they were coming for him and it only made sense that he would be in the manor, likely waiting in the great dining hall where he could make a spectacle of everything the way Gavin claimed he enjoyed.

Arianna would be the one making the spectacle today.

Zylah, Saoirse, Avalon, and Gavin all headed back to the village below where their small army awaited instruction. Avalon would find the rest of the half-breeds and send Raevina's warriors to chase her down. Apparently, the Fiadh female waited for no one.

Under normal circumstances, it might not have sat well with Arianna, but right now every second counted. She just prayed they would be able to evacuate the civilians before Niall threatened to use their safety against her.

The memory of him sickened her. He'd offered so many pretty words wrapped up with satin fabrics and ribbons only for those beautiful things to fall away and reveal the snake in hiding.

She'd been cautious of him, but never in a million lifetimes would she have thought Niall so ruthless and uncaring.

Tonight. Everything was changing tonight. The council was already dead. Niall was about to be imprisoned, then everything would be up to her. She'd serve the continent as a queen the way she should have done from the beginning.

Arianna tried not to let the thought overwhelm her. There were still battles to be fought, after all, and everything hinged on them coming out alive.

The gates to the manor were wide open and they slipped through without pausing. No guards stood on the threshold and, to her surprise, no one ambushed them from the shadows.

It was all just . . . empty.

The wind blew through the well-kept lawn and Arianna's hair stood on end. The front door was already open, as if inviting her inside.

"I don't like this," Talon said. Neither did she. It felt too much like a trap, an invitation that said, *come get me if you dare.*

But if they backed down now, they might never have another chance.

Arianna pushed forward with Rion to her front, Ellie behind her, and Talon bringing up the rear. The four guards had spaced themselves on either side, watching and waiting.

Their boots clicked on the marble floor, echoing through the dark space. The lights were off, casting everything in shadow. Someone had opened all the windows and the long drapes billowed out, obscuring their view of the halls.

Talon drew his weapon and surrounded them all with spears of ice. The Móirín guards followed his lead. Ellie pulled a long rapier from her belt and Rion clutched a sword in one hand while his magic mixed with Talon's, determined to defend them should anyone spring from the shadows.

Maybe Arianna should have had her father send a few more of his warriors her way. They'd still clung to the illusion of stealth. Foolish. Gavin had warned them Niall was always three steps ahead and she had ignored him.

The doors lining the hall were all closed and locked. Only one stood open and light spilled out from the doors like a beacon. A pair of servants stood on either side of the entry dressed in their finest attire as if waiting to escort her to dinner.

Arianna reached for Rion's free hand and squeezed tightly. He knew the feel of Niall's magic now, but she wasn't taking any chances. Arianna had a feeling Rion would be Niall's first target and she wouldn't allow the male to use her mate as his puppet.

The two servants bowed at the waist, seeming to ignore their weapons as they crossed the threshold into the dining hall.

Then Rion gripped her hand as if his life depended on it. "He's here."

CHAPTER EIGHTY-SEVEN

ARIANNA

Rion clenched his eyes shut and his entire body went rigid. Sand collected at his feet and swirled up around them, as if wanting to attack, yet not daring. His nostrils flared and Arianna stepped closer to her mate.

She squeezed his hand three times. It was the short code they'd discussed last night. Just something to let him know it was her still holding him instead of the images Niall would force him to see.

Rion squeezed back once, an acknowledgement. But he didn't squeeze again, which told her he was most certainly under some sort of glamour. Arianna prayed he could break it; if not, they were already a warrior short.

"So nice of the queen to finally join us, though I could have done without the riff raff." Niall eyed the four guards, Talon, Ellie, then Rion.

He sat in a navy blue plush armchair settled in the center of the vast space with one leg crossed over the other. Niall tipped a wine glass to his lips, staining them red. "You kept us waiting. Such an unqueenly thing to do."

A game. This was all a game to him. He wasn't even concerned with the weapons they'd drawn or the magic buzzing through the air.

Rion squeezed her hand again. She did the same. Three times to confirm they were all right. Rion's heart was racing. Faster, faster, faster. Sweat beaded his brow. Gods, what was Niall showing him? Arianna growled and bared her teeth.

Niall chuckled. "Now, now, behave. We wouldn't want things to turn hostile before the fun begins." He tilted his glass and warriors appeared around the room with arrows notched. They hadn't drawn, but she knew one movement from Niall would have them firing.

Arianna hadn't even scented the glamour that had concealed them.

Shit. They were surrounded and in such deep, unending shit.

"So," Niall swirled his glass. "Now that you know you're little," he paused to think, "mission has failed, I hope you might join me. I'm certain we can reach an agreeable compromise. It would make eternity a great deal easier for you if we did."

Niall set the glass down on the small round table to his left, then clapped his hands. Four servants entered. Two hauled another plush chair between them while the third clutched an extra glass and the last carried an unopened bottle of red wine.

Niall winked. "Just in case you thought I might try to poison you." They sat the chair, glass, and bottle down, then retreated back through a side door.

A power display, just for Niall to show off that those within Ruadhán were still willing to serve him. Curious that they'd avoided meeting her stare. Perhaps they weren't as loyal as Niall wanted to believe, which would only make things easier for her father and Raevina. She prayed they were safe, but Arianna couldn't worry about them right now. Not with a few dozen arrows pointed their way.

"She won't be discussing anything with you," Talon said.

Niall's eyes flashed, but it wasn't with amusement. "I wasn't aware the Queen needed her dog to speak for her." His gaze snapped back to her. "Since she's so willing to take on the role now."

He was angry. No, not angry, furious. Niall didn't want a conversation, he wanted a submission. For her to bend to his will because her friends' lives were on the line.

Arianna lifted her chin. She *was* here to play queen, just not the in way Niall wanted.

"I won't be joining you in anything."

"You don't wish to talk?"

"What I wish is for you to stand aside."

"That's her polite way of telling you to get on your knees," Ellie added.

If Arianna thought the look Niall had shot Talon was bad, it was nothing compared to the death glare he tossed at Ellie. Her sister didn't back down.

Niall picked up his glass again and sipped the wine as if he needed it to maintain his composure. "I'm afraid I've worked too hard for that." He pointed a long finger at Rion. "I've leashed that one. Quite easily I might add." Niall raised his free hand and waved. A pair of males entered the room and every muscle in Talon's body froze as they dragged a struggling Raevina between them.

Blood dripped from her nose and irons were clamped around her wrists, a short chain binding her hands together. She still managed to free one of her arms and slam an elbow into one of the guard's nose. He cursed and another two flew through the side door. The injured one drew a dagger and pressed it against the base of Raevina's throat.

She stilled, but it wasn't fear Arianna found in the female's gaze. It was cold, unrelenting hatred.

Niall smacked his lips. "Ah, do you hear that? I believe this is called checkmate."

A tang of fear floated around Talon that Arianna didn't quite understand. Her friend's throat bobbed, then she noted the way Talon seemed to tally every scrape and bruise along Raevina's skin. Almost as if he were tucking the information away for later.

Niall rose from his chair. "You're out of options," he said casually, then cast a sideward glance toward Ellie. "And if you so much as move, I'll make sure those arrows find your heart."

Ellie gritted her teeth but remained silent. Arianna hadn't realized her sister had palmed a dagger. She had likely planned to launch it at Niall's heart, cold as it was.

He drained the last of his wine and studied the bottom of the glass. "It's funny, isn't it? That the gods made us so powerful yet weakened us where our mates are concerned. It's no wonder my father loathes the idea of them."

Talon growled, but he didn't move. Arianna looked between him and Raevina again. Mates. She'd noticed Talon's attentions toward the female, but, gods. Niall had his mate.

Arianna's voice shook, but it wasn't for the reasons Niall assumed. "You already have the throne and the city. What do you want from me?"

"The people," he said simply. "They flock to you, their queen. You really should hear the way they speak of you with such reverence." Niall eyed Rion and she stepped closer to her mate as if she could shield him from the male's wrath. "The revered and the pariah." He chuckled. "Fate really is a cruel thing, isn't it?"

Arianna didn't respond. She didn't know how to.

"I tried doing things the noble way by attempting to win your heart, but it seems you won't allow that to happen with that one in the way." His gaze returned to her, but Arianna refused to back down, even as her body screamed at her to run, run, run.

"I could have made you happy, you know. You would have eventually forgotten about him and lived a life of comfort where the people adored you." Niall shook his head. "But we're beyond pleasantries now. I need you to declare me as the rightful king so my plans may continue."

"What makes you think I'd ever agree to that?" she seethed.

Niall raised a brow. "I'm certain you realize by now that you don't have any other choice. Unless of course you wish for this to end in bloodshed. I would, however, like to avoid ruining my tunic. The seamstress just finished it this morning."

Arianna chewed her lip and felt Rion's hand tighten. She squeezed it again. Three times. Niall seemed to notice.

He sighed. "I like order and I would very much like this night to go according to plan, but you get to ultimately decide how this ends." Niall lifted a hand and the archers surrounding them notched their arrows. "I can, for instance, command my warriors to fire and end the lives of everyone in this room." His hand lowered and the archers relaxed. "But that would leave you in a state of grief I'd rather avoid. Instead, those under my command could shackle your friends and place them in the dungeons where they'll be relatively cared for. So long as they behave, of course. And they'll remain alive so long as you comply with my demands."

Arianna studied the archers. "For someone claiming they need my assistance, you have an awful lot of Fae already willing to serve you."

Niall chuckled. "Yes, well, that's what centuries of work affords you. Loyalty. I've kept their lives comfortable and asked for very little in return. You, however, have come in here and threatened to tear down the very foundations our world was built upon."

Arianna eyed the guards again. She recognized a few faces, even if she couldn't place them. Arianna knew exactly what kind of comforts Niall referred to.

"Slavery isn't a comfort or a foundation."

"It's a very profitable business. And many rely on the income to maintain a certain lifestyle." Niall stepped closer, eyeing Rion for a moment. Arianna growled in warning and Niall's face contorted in anger. "I can promise you one thing: If you don't comply, the grief you suffered the last few months will feel like nothing compared to the agony you'll experience next. You had friends to care for you then. This time, you'll only have me."

Niall dropped his glass and it shattered on the floor, causing all of them to jump and tighten their hold on their weapons. Water and ice mixed together as the guards from Móirín readied themselves for a fight. The only one who didn't react was Rion.

Niall pointed to him. "Your mate can't hear us, in case you're wondering. I have him in a complete state of suspension. He's currently fighting his instincts to protect. Only in his case, your mate can't be sure of his enemies." Niall cocked his head. "I could keep him like that for eternity if I wished, though I think death would be more of a mercy, don't you?"

Arianna's throat went dry and Niall continued. "I still see hope in your eyes. Do you think your father will show up to rescue you?" He chuckled. "Let me tell you a little secret, Arianna of Móirín. I have manipulated and set things in motion that you can't even begin to imagine. I have eyes everywhere and I hear everything.

"There was once a male who thought he could challenge me. He was prodding in all the right places, unfortunately for him, and asking too many questions. My father demanded I deal with it, but the male was too powerful for me to simply kill. I needed him to continue in his role. Remember when I said I liked things easy? So, instead of removing him, I decided a distraction was in order."

Niall circled around the table and popped open the bottle of wine. "I tried little things at first, but it was never enough. Even his daughters couldn't distract the male from his pursuits. I increased the stakes to our game, but he was so damn stubborn." Niall shook his head. Arianna's heart was thundering now. "Unfortunately, I had to take drastic measures." He poured the blood red wine into his glass. "All this time, you've been hunting for the wrong culprit." Niall pointed to Talon. "Or rather, *you* have been hunting for the wrong one. It was such a brilliant plan."

"Bullshit," Talon snapped, but Arianna's heart felt as if Niall had shoved a javelin through it.

"Language," Niall tsked.

"What are you saying?" Arianna asked even as she already knew.

Niall smiled again, a cruel, vicious upturning of his lips. "Did you really think the High Lord of Fiadh came up with such an elaborate plan? That boorish male can't do much more than murder his own people. It's a shame, really. So much strength and potential wasted."

Grief settled over her heart. How many times was she going to hear a different story about her mother's death?

"I can't take all the credit, I suppose. My father was the one who gave the order."

"What does your father have to do with it?" Talon asked. What had Avalon been close to discovering, she wanted to add. But she couldn't move. Here she was, finally staring at the male who'd ordered her mother's murder. Or one of the males, at least. And she'd frozen in place.

Niall shrugged. "He has his own plans and doesn't feel the need to share them with his son." He tapped his nose. "Makes it easier to lie when you don't know the full story, but between us, I think he likes to play games a little too much."

"Says the male willing to imprison an innocent female for decades," Ellie said.

"Innocent?" Niall raised his brows. "Have you not been told the brutal histories of The Lady of Brónach?" He stopped himself. "No, I guess you wouldn't know them. I believe those stories were among the many things deleted from history." He pinched the bridge of his nose. "It's hard to keep track of everything these days. I can't fathom how my father manages it." He eyed Rion again. "Even The Demon doesn't understand the role he has played in shaping my father's idealistic future."

Arianna's face paled at that. He said "played" as if they were all nothing more than pawns on a chessboard waiting to be sacrificed.

Niall cleared his throat. "It seems we've gotten off track a bit. You'll know more soon enough. But it's time for you to make a decision."

He crossed the space and only paused once to glance at Raevina, who was struggling against her restraints despite the blade at her throat. Talon didn't move, but the guards charged. Niall flicked one hand and the four fell to their knees, clutching their throats as if trying to pry away invisible hands. They gasped for air and their magic died back.

Arianna didn't back away when Niall stopped directly in front of her. Ellie's eyes didn't leave the male.

"You are going to come upstairs with me." He leaned in and lowered his voice. "You're going to lie naked in my bed and I'm going to take what belongs to me." She shivered. "Afterward, we'll set a date for our official marriage ceremony and march across the continent. You will declare me as your mate, husband, and the King of Alastríona." She clenched her teeth. "And once you've produced a male heir, we will talk about the living conditions of your companions. Should they prove themselves compliant, then perhaps I'll even allow them to roam the manor in chains."

Bile rose in Arianna's throat at the mere thought of Niall's hands anywhere near her body. "And I'm just supposed to trust you to keep your word?"

He stepped over the ice at her feet and glided his hand beneath her chin. "Do you scent a lie?"

Arianna tried not to pull away. "And your father?"

He smirked. "Getting smart to our ways, aren't you? Yes, he'll let them live." Niall's gaze drifted toward Rion. "Though I can't make any promises on that one's condition. My father harbors a particularly nasty grudge toward his kind."

What did that mean? Niall leaned closer still and his windswept scent washed over and through her. "Well?"

Arianna met his gaze without flinching. She squeezed her mate's hand and studied his stiff shoulders and locked jaw. Then she looked at Talon who stared between Arianna and Raevina, his anger rising at how Niall had rendered him useless. Arianna met her little sister's gaze; she looked ready to leap in front of the arrows directed at Rion. Then her eyes locked with Raevina's. The female smiled.

"I want your word that no harm will come to any of them."

Niall's voice lowered and his eyes darkened with fantasies Arianna wanted no part of. "You have it." His lips were so close they brushed hers when he spoke. "All you have—"

Arianna plunged an iron blade into his gut, twisted, and shoved him so hard that they both toppled to the ground. Niall roared and Arianna heard the unmistakable twang of arrows as they loosened from their bows.

Talon's and Ellie's magic ripped from the air and the arrows bounced off their combined ice as it rose and domed to encase them in a protective shell.

Niall slammed his palm into the bottom of her chin, but Arianna buried another iron blade in his gut. She pushed it so deep she couldn't grasp the hilt anymore from all the blood coating it. Arianna grabbed his tunic and her magic broke free, covering his torso in a thick layer of ice to seal the wound and the iron inside his body.

Niall cursed and his long fingers wrapped around her throat. He slammed her head into the hard marble floor and stars shot through her vision. Arianna kneed him in the groin and the male gasped for air. She bucked her hips and rolled him so she sat on top, then Ellie clamped a shackle around one of his wrists.

Niall didn't stop fighting. He sank his fangs into Arianna' forearm, then the ground itself seemed to shake as Rion's magic billowed around them all. It clamped around Niall's arms, legs, and throat and squeezed until Niall released his hold. Arianna scrambled off him, her chest heaving.

Rion moved so fast she barely had time to watch him yank Niall to his feet only to slam the male to the ground again. Then Rion leapt on top of the male and punched Niall right in the face.

Again and again and again, Rion's fists came down. Blood sprayed and it felt as though everything around her had stopped. All eyes watched that rhythmic pounding and Arianna found that for once she didn't want to stop her mate. Let him kill Niall, let the world be rid of the filth.

Rion paused with a fist drawn back, his chest still heaving as he observed the bloody face pinned beneath his body. Niall coughed, spluttering blood, then he began laughing. A crazed sound that sent chills racing through Arianna's body.

Rion stood and turned toward her. He offered a single nod to indicate he was in control of himself.

Talon had already rushed toward Raevina, but the female kicked off the ground hard, using the distraction to flip over her captor's shoulders and drag her chains beneath his chin. She yanked once and the male's neck snapped. Talon threw a dagger into the other one and left the male to writhe on the ground as he clutched his throat and the blade protruding from it.

Her friend looked Raevina over, but he didn't reach for her. Raevina wiped the single line of blood from her neck and spit at the already dead male. Talon knelt to dig through the guard's pockets. For keys, she presumed.

Arianna loosed a shaky breath. They'd done it. They'd subdued Niall. Those with arrows stood in shocked silence, glancing between one another as if they didn't know what to do after firing upon their queen.

Judging from the anger rolling off her mate, running was likely their best option. She'd let them. They had too many other things to deal with as it was.

Niall choked on a mouthful of blood and gasped for air. "If I could clap for your efforts, I certainly would." His voice was strained and his teeth were coated in blood. She was pretty sure a few were missing. "I didn't think you had it in you." He chuckled again. "But you have no idea what you've just unleashed. Maybe my father really is the genius he claims to be."

Arianna exchanged an uneasy glance with Ellie, then opened her mouth to ask questions, but the very floor beneath her feet began quaking. Those in the room backed away and several outright fled. Arianna spread her arms wide for balance and the entire manor groaned as if threatening to fall in on itself.

Silence stretched for several long beats before the floor tilted. Everything went sailing to one end of the room and Arianna reached for Rion. His forearm gripped her own and his magic wrapped around their bodies to hold them steady.

The entire floor fell out from beneath them. Ellie shrieked, but their feet slammed against the hard marble a second later and Arianna's teeth painfully clacked together.

Talon growled at Niall. "What did you do?"

"Do?" Niall jeered. "Shouldn't you be asking what you've *undone*? I've kept this place maintained for centuries; did you think there wouldn't be consequences to unseating me?"

"There are people beneath the manor," Arianna said, remembering what Gavin had told them. Fae who were likely waking form whatever spell Niall had them under. And once their magic stopped working on the city . . .

Niall narrowed his eyes at her. "I'd love to know which council member was responsible for feeding you information." He tried to shrug but strained against the movement. "Not that it matters now." He smirked. "Many of those beneath us volunteered for their jobs; they just weren't privy to how long they'd be in servitude."

"You disgust me."

Niall's smile widened. "Be that as it may, you have pressing decisions to make. Those Fae are waking up and they're quite unaware that they're the only ones holding this place together."

Arianna's eyes widened. "Why resort to all this? What's the point?"

The ground shuddered beneath their feet again. "I'm not sure now is the best time to be asking such questions. Release me and I'll correct your mistake before the city plummets to the ground and kills everyone beneath it. Or do you no longer care for innocent lives?"

Arianna's heart beat wildly as she tried to formulate a plan. She needed to tell her father and evacuate the city. "Raevina," The female rubbed her wrists, but turned with determination in her gaze. "Take Ellie and clear out the city." Arianna looked at those who still stood on the outskirts of the room. Their eyes were wide. She raised her voice so everyone could hear. "Regardless of your loyalty, if you value your lives, you'll retreat and take your families with you."

Several scrambled from the room, but a few remained, casting wary glances at Niall as if they expected the male to have another plan of escape.

The floor tilted again in the opposite direction and Arianna slid a few feet, scrambling for purchase. The manor righted itself, but Arianna couldn't be sure for how long. Did they have seconds, minutes, or hours?

"Talon, bind him," she jerked her chin to Niall. "And get him to the nearest platform. Make sure a set of guards remains with him at all times, then come back to help the others evacuate the city. Rion, we need to—" Arianna stopped talking as the floor dropped from beneath them again. She gritted her teeth and dropped to her knees when it jerked to a sudden stop.

Her mate stared at the floor, then headed toward the door. She followed after him only to find everyone outside already running in a panicked frenzy. Arianna scented blood in the air, but those who'd been fighting had ceased and were scrambling toward the waiting platforms.

Warriors from Pádraigín stood at the city's edge, ready to carry the citizens to safety. Some didn't wait and leapt from the edge, taking their families with them. Arianna just prayed they were strong enough to stop their descent at the bottom.

Rion knelt and ran a hand along the ground. "I can slow it down."

"What?"

"It's rock, earth. I might not be able to stop it, but I can slow it down." He rose and turned to her. "The city is going to fall, and if it does, a lot of people will die. You and I both know they don't have enough time to evacuate. If I get under it, I can support the structure from below."

Her heart was beating in her throat. People were screaming and running as if their lives depended on it. "What if you can't get out?" she asked, taking in the enormity of the floating city. "What if—"

Rion pulled her flush against his body and crushed his lips into hers. His hands threaded through her hair and she let him tilt her head back, deepening their kiss. Her body ignited at his touch, remembering every sensation. She gripped his tunic tightly in her fists, desperate for this one moment to last forever.

Her mate pulled back, eyes full of a desperate emotion she didn't want to name. Rion's chest heaved and his hands traced her face. "If the city falls, you get on one of those platforms and get as far away as you can."

Rion tried to pull away, but Arianna yanked him back. She searched his unwavering gaze and her panic rose. "Promise me this isn't goodbye." His lips parted and the ground shook again. Tears filled her eyes. "Promise me."

Rion kissed her fiercely again, then pressed his forehead to hers. "I've never lied to you. I'm not going to start now."

Then he was gone, the cold breeze replacing the warmth of his body. She watched his back as he raced across the field, sprinting as fast as his legs could carry him. Then Rion disappeared off the city's edge.

CHAPTER EIGHTY-EIGHT

SAOIRSE

"What the hell is going on up there?" Zylah yelled as she draped a male's almost limp arm across her shoulders and began dragging him toward the two-story home she'd declared their infirmary.

The building had once been some sort of city hall. The residents hadn't been happy about Zylah's demands and they'd argued against it until Fae began falling from the sky. Literally.

No one questioned her again. Saoirse's warriors had jumped into action, assisting those who seemed as though they couldn't slow their descent fast enough. Many outright screamed for help and Saoirse wondered if the battle above was truly so frightening that Fae would leap from the city's edge without a guarantee of safety.

Zylah had called them idiots.

Saoirse sank her blade into another body and pivoted on her toes to thrust her magic through one who dared charge the half-breed at her side.

Saoirse was a whirlwind of movement as she kept their enemy at bay. Niall's warriors. She'd already broken through two glamours. Arianna had been right in assuming Niall would send a force down to deal with the village. It seemed as though he was willing to slaughter them all. A taunt to Arianna, she was sure.

Though most seemed to be fleeing the city, there were others chasing them down, screaming the word *traitor* as they tumbled through the sky. Saoirse didn't know whether the orders came from Niall or if they were simply acting on their own. She didn't care, either. If they came for Zylah, they were as good as dead.

Saoirse listened to the whispers of those who passed by, seeking shelter and assistance. They claimed the city would fall, but Saoirse didn't see any signs of it. The silhouette of the massive island was still hidden among the gray clouds. If they were right though, Saoirse wouldn't have long to grab Zylah and flee. Then the female would hate her even more than she already did.

"We need to move," Saoirse called over the fray.

Zylah rolled her eyes. "Do you see him?" She jerked her chin to the male in her gasp. "Does he look like he's moving any faster to you?"

"I mean we need to evacuate. The city is coming down."

Zylah tilted her head skyward. "What do you mean it's coming down?" Well, she certainly didn't appear to have Fae hearing. Or maybe she was simply too focused on her current task.

Saoirse slammed her blade into the gut of another male before kicking him away. "I mean, if you value your charges, you'll listen to me for once instead of arguing and start moving them away from the village." Saoirse's hair was standing on end now, every instinct telling her to run, run, run.

Zylah was frantic, her gaze searching the crowd. "If we can get one of those platforms over here, we could get them all out."

Saoirse yanked a dagger from her belt and launched it straight toward Zylah. It whizzed just past her left cheek and buried itself in another female's throat. The half-breed pulled at her magic and spun, yanking the male in her grasp. Her eyes widened at the sight of the female who'd been about to impale her, then she whipped back toward Saoirse with a scowl on her face.

"Are you out of your mind?"

Saoirse smirked. "Afraid I'd miss?"

"I felt the wind from that," Zylah screeched.

But Saoirse couldn't keep the laughter from her voice. "I have over a century of practice. I assure you, you were in no danger."

Something in the half-breed's gaze had Saoirse straightening. Zylah looked her over, as if appreciating her for the first time since their meeting in the tavern. It called to a primal instinct in Saoirse's blood, but she didn't have time to dwell on it. Instead, Saoirse plunged her blade into another warrior hell-bent on running her through.

Maybe all wasn't lost. Maybe, just maybe if they survived this, Saoirse would get the chance to court Zylah properly. She pivoted again, dancing around her opponents with feather-light steps.

Zylah was definitely watching and she'd make sure to give the female a show she wouldn't forget.

CHAPTER EIGHTY-NINE

ARIANNA

Raevina grabbed Arianna by her shoulders and shook her, drawing her away from the place where Rion had just leapt off the edge of the city.

Arianna turned to find Talon and her father's elite waiting for her command. She took a breath, trying to steady herself. Despite her aching heart, Arianna didn't have time to linger. She'd get these people to safety, then return to assist Rion in any way she could. Saoirse was already down there and if Rion could buy them time, it might save countless lives.

Arianna didn't ask Talon how he'd found the entrance to the underground cellar, she just followed and tried not to look too hard at the bodies of the fallen.

The battle had been brutal and even now she could hear the screams of the wounded. But they'd have to wait. There were others who needed her more.

The air chilled as they ran down the stairs and through a side door that led into what she could only call the hallway of a dungeon. Several cells were already open and they passed Fae who were carrying those unable to walk on their own.

Gods, how many had Niall kept in captivity? Were these males and females all dangerous, or innocents like Eimear, held against their will?

It was another matter she'd have to address later. They'd keep the prisoners in irons until then.

Another flight of stairs led them lower, and the carefully constructed stone dungeon shifted to a harsh, roughly carved rock hall. Torches lined the walls, but they were spaced so far apart Arianna had to rely on the light in Raevina's palm to see clearly.

Talon kicked open the cells as they went, and the line of warriors accompanying them grabbed the prisoners and carried them topside. Most were incapacitated in one way or another, barely able to speak, let alone move.

The city shuddered again. Arianna stumbled, struggling to find something to hold onto. She gripped the iron bars and Talon caged her with his body, as if he might block any falling debris. Thankfully, none came, but Arianna knew it wouldn't be long before the tunnels collapsed under the pressure of the rocking city.

They steadied themselves, then they were moving again, running as fast as their legs would carry them.

Her breath stalled when the area opened up into a room that would haunt Arianna's nightmares for the rest of her life.

Braziers were lit around the circular space, but they were barely more than embers casting eerie shadows across the Fae strewn about the area. Each individual sat in measured circles with strange glowing runes painted onto the floor. Their clothes hung from almost skeletal bodies and their hair had thinned so much that there were barely more than a few strands hanging from their scalps. Old, tattered clothes, the smell of their own filth, starved beyond reason. Just like Rion. Bile rose in Arianna's throat.

These weren't half-breeds. They were Fae. Pure Fae, and Niall still treated them as if they were tools to be used however he wished.

Arianna's head whipped toward the nearest one moaning in agony as he attempted to drag himself across the floor. She spotted another lying on her side, mouth open in a silent plea for help. Most were still locked in some sort of transfixed state, staring at nothing as their bodies glowed with whatever magic held them captive.

The warriors emerging from the long hall all seemed to move at once. Arianna's heart cracked when the Fae who'd awakened attempted to crawl away in terror. She didn't know how long they'd been here to end up in such a state. Each of them was barely alive, kept that way just so Niall could siphon their magic. What had he done with those who'd died? Did he honor their sacrifice or merely cast them aside and replace them with someone new?

The floor shifted again, falling, falling, falling. Her stomach plummeted with it, then fear tore through her when it didn't stop.

They were too late. She was going to die right here in this room with so many others.

The city slammed to a halt again and the warriors carrying the broken Fae barely kept to their feet. Talon's saddened gaze met her own and tears pricked her eyes as she understood.

The more they woke from their suspended state, the faster the city would fall. They couldn't save them, not unless Rion managed to stop the city from falling altogether. Even if he slowed them down, they couldn't get all the injured Fae to the surface. Not in time.

"Take those who are already awake," she commanded. Arianna approached a female who looked around the room as if seeing it for the first time. She wrapped an arm beneath her thin shoulders and lifted her frail body onto her back. The female didn't struggle. She likely didn't have the strength. Then Arianna headed back through the tunnel, turning once to gaze upon the dozens upon dozens of Fae still suspended by that strange magic.

A silent tear slid down her face as she turned away, knowing those trapped would never see daylight again.

CHAPTER NINETY

RION

The wind roared in Rion's ears as he fell and fell and fell. The ground raced toward him with quickening speed, but it still wasn't fast enough. *Promise me this isn't goodbye.*

Gods, he'd wanted to. He craved a long peaceful life with Arianna at his side. He wanted time to piece together everything that had been broken. But he wouldn't make promises he couldn't keep, and right now Rion had no idea what to expect.

He was still weak from Niall's torment. His body ached beyond reason and his stomach was twisted in knots from the food they'd eaten that morning.

But his magic wasn't weak. Ever since his shackles had broken, Rion had struggled to rein it in. The pulse beneath his skin was a roaring beast threatening to break loose, and he'd been saving it for a moment like this. He'd really been saving it for Niall, but Arianna had managed to subdue him herself. He would let his mother finish the job.

Rion threw his magic out to slow his fall, but when his feet hit the ground, his jaw still rattled from the impact. He ignored the stinging in his legs and turned toward those locked in combat.

Two warriors against Móirín's five on one side, and another three from Brónach locked in combat with a pair further down. They could handle those numbers without him.

Rion looked up toward the royal city still obscured by the clouds and thought of all the innocents who would die if it came crashing down.

He'd sworn to make a difference in the world, and Niall had stripped that opportunity from him before he'd barely begun. But maybe he could do this. Maybe if he successfully saved these people, they'd remember more than just the scars he'd carved into their history.

Maybe he'd be more than just a monster.

Smoke rose from some of the houses and Rion scented the air before sprinting west. He found Saoirse in less than a minute. She danced with her magic, leaves and trunks unfurling at her command. The siblings locked eyes and Rion tore her enemies away, launching their bodies through the air to give them a moment of reprieve.

"What's going on up there?" Saoirse asked, her blades covered in gore. Rion spotted Zylah behind her, assisting the injured onto a platform.

"The city is going to fall."

"I gathered as much. We're already evacuating."

"Good." He looked skyward again, then surveyed the village below. He'd never attempted something on such a massive scale, but his magic was roaring for release. He just prayed it would be enough.

"What are you planning?" Saoirse asked.

"I'm going to slow it down. Stop it, if I'm lucky."

Her lips parted as if to tell him such a thing wasn't possible, but she snapped her mouth shut. "You think you can do it?"

He loosed a breath. "Honestly. I don't know." Rion was about to say more when something in the air snapped. He couldn't quite explain the rush that flew over the area. Like an icy gust of wind that pricked one's skin, only there wasn't a breeze. Instead, everything … froze.

He counted the seconds, but Rion knew, deep in his bones, that whatever power had been holding the city high above their heads had just snapped.

Rion braced his feet. He didn't have time to think about those in the surrounding area. He couldn't watch to ensure no one was caught in the cross fire. He could only pray they moved fast enough as he sank his magic into the earth then jerked his hands upward.

Dozens of thick pillars rose from the ground at frightening speeds. They surrounded the area in a circle, but Rion knew they wouldn't be enough. He pulled more, another ring, then another further out. Rion pushed them up and up and up. Then he reached high, feeling for the city itself. It was massive and he strained against the distance. Rion imagined his magic forming into a massive pair of hands and gripping the enormous structure.

He gasped from the pressure.

Saoirse watched at his side, ready to run. For all he knew, the city could come crashing down and bury them all beneath his weight. It rushed down, faster and faster.

"Rion?" Saoirse's voice was questioning, uncertain, but she stood beside her sibling even as screams filled the air.

The massive city slammed into the first set of pillars and Rion grunted from the pressure threatening to break his spine. It felt as if he actually held the city above his head with his bare hands. Chunks of rock broke off from the pillars and several Fae stopped to shield civilians from the falling debris. Saoirse joined them, preventing one particularly large boulder from slamming into Rion's head.

The city crashed into the second row of pillars and they crumbled too, even as he pushed against it. More rocks fell, barreling to the earth with enough force to shake the ground beneath his feet.

It hit the third set of pillars and Rion crumpled to one knee from the weight bearing down on his body. But it was slowing. Not stopping, but slowing. Enough that the people just might be able to escape.

Saoirse looked him over once, then ran toward Zylah, likely commanding her to leave while she had the chance. The female didn't argue, though Rion thought he saw a longing look pass between the pair. He couldn't linger on it, not with the weight pushing against his body.

Tree trunks shot into the sky, reaching toward the underbelly of the city. They rose up and up and up, as high as the ones that guarded Nàdiar. But not high enough. They couldn't reach, not yet, but perhaps those who'd used the magic hoped it would help in the long run.

Giant pillars of ice formed, then lifted into the sky, higher and higher. Rion couldn't see when they collided with the base, but he could feel it. A slight lift of weight. He struggled for breath, braced himself, then rose back to his feet with a deafening roar.

Rion kept pulling at his magic, kept summoning the earth to climb up and repatch the pillars every time they crumbled.

Then the weight hit him again and Rion gasped against the pressure. Saoirse cursed and he followed her gaze to find Fae attacking those who were trying to assist him.

Saoirse moved, tearing their enemies apart with a precision she'd honed through the decades. Her warriors joined her, fighting, pushing, pivoting until their bodies were one with the magic they wielded.

Rion let them work and returned his attention to the city overhead. He pushed hard. Harder, fighting against the lightheadedness that threatened to pull him under. He wouldn't let it.

He would hold the city up until every last soul escaped from above and below, even if that meant he wouldn't follow.

CHAPTER NINETY-ONE

ARIANNA

The floor jolted and Arianna collapsed, grasping for anything to hold onto as the city shifted back and forth, tilting as if threatening to send them over the edge. When they'd fallen again, she thought it might be the end, but then she'd felt Rion's magic explode from his body. His very tired body. She chewed her lip, trying not to think about it as she carried the weak female toward one of the main platforms.

The tunnels below had collapsed, trapping any who hadn't escaped. Tears stung her eyes as she imagined all the Fae who would never taste freedom. She prayed they went peacefully and hoped their final moments hadn't been consumed by one of Niall's nightmares.

Arianna counted the platforms and grimaced. Some had come back, while others hadn't.

Bodies scrambled onto the edges before they'd even landed and Arianna searched through the faces for anyone familiar. Raevina pushed through the crowd, using her magic to stave off those who tried to run them over. Arianna hated every second of it. These were

Fae afraid for their lives and the lives of their families. Fae who simply wanted to flee the falling city however possible.

Arianna lowered the female onto the platform and several civilians lifted her up to prevent her from being trampled. Arianna nodded in thanks, then turned to leave.

Raevina grabbed her arm. "We need to get you out of here."

"I'll leave when everyone else is safe." She didn't mention that 'everyone' included Rion.

Raevina grimaced but stopped herself from stating the obvious. Not everyone was getting out of the city alive. There simply wasn't enough time.

"My Queen, please." Arianna wasn't sure Raevina had ever uttered the word. Arianna paused but didn't turn away. How could she just leave them all behind?

Arianna raised her voice. "How many of you are from Brónach?"

Several heads pivoted and one female stood. "How can we serve?"

"Can you make some sort of platform and lift more people to safety?"

The civilians exchanged determined glances. "We can try."

"That's all I ask."

Arianna tried to jump from the platform, but Raevina tightened her grip again. Her eyes were frantic now. "We have to go, there isn't time."

Arianna softened her gaze, knowing all Raevina wanted was to protect her queen and restore her people's honor.

Fae fell over the edges, shoved off by the crowd, but those from Brónach were already at work. They snatched falling bodies from the air while those from Móirín created even more platforms, trying to get as many civilians to safety as possible.

"I have to try." Arianna yanked from her grasp. She pushed through the crowd and ran toward the city's center. She needed to get to Rion, but pain shot through the back of her head and everything faded into nothing.

"WHAT THE hell are you doing?" Talon growled at Raevina as he jumped from the edge of the platform and ran to Arianna's side. He cradled her head and pulled Arianna into his arms.

"You know as well as I do that once these platforms leave, they won't be coming back. Would you rather see your queen as a statue to be honored or would you prefer to serve her while she's still breathing?"

Talon glared. "I'd rather you not strike her."

"And I'd like it if she listened, but it seems stubbornness runs rampant between the lot of you."

"She could try you for treason."

Raevina scoffed. "Then let me be tried knowing I saved her life."

Talon swore and looked over the edge to the ground racing toward them. His heart ached. Raevina was right. They were moving too fast and the city would fall with too many trapped on its surface. He looked out over the sea of desperate faces. There were so many left. So many innocents—

"Hey," a familiar voice called from the distance. Talon raised his head.

"By the gods."

Talon didn't know how Gavin had done it and he honestly didn't care. The male had reinforcements. Sort of. The flat structures weren't actual platforms, but they'd serve their purpose. When the citizens spotted them, their fearful screams turned to hopeful cheering.

No one was getting left behind after all.

CHAPTER NINETY-TWO

RION

He kept pushing.

Even after voices faded around him.

Even after he stopped scenting bodies and their movements.

Even when Arianna fell silent. Still breathing. Perfectly alive. But silent.

He wasn't worried. He knew they'd watch over their queen.

Rion cursed, gritting his teeth. The city wasn't slowing any more. His legs were weak and his body was nearly at its limit. He had pushed as hard as he could, but it hadn't been enough.

He'd told Saoirse to leave with her half-breed and help those who still needed it. She'd commanded him to make it out alive. He'd only nodded, knowing she'd scent the lie if he tried to speak.

The bond lengthened, telling him Arianna had escaped. She was safe, but he didn't know how many civilians were still above.

Rion's knee collided with the ground hard and the entire city tilted. He strained to keep it upright, but it wouldn't move. His mind teetered on the edge of darkness. Just a little more. He could hold it just a little more.

"I know you're not giving up already," a familiar voice said.

Panic laced through every cell in his body. Rion cracked his eyes open to find a pair of brown boots before him. He scented her magic and cursed again. "What the hell are you doing here?"

Ellie smirked as if they didn't have an entire city barreling toward them. "Saving your ass, what does it look like?"

"Dammit, get out of here." He pushed hard, willing strength to his body, but it wouldn't listen.

She looked around. "Yeah, I don't think that's an option for us at this point." Water formed along his skin and her magic flooded around his feet.

"Arianna can't lose you, too."

"Oh, I have no plans for her to lose either of us."

Rion wanted to yell at her, but he chuckled instead. "I don't think I've ever met a more stubborn Fae."

She tilted her head in amusement, but her face was determined, concentrated. "I'd like to think defiance is in my nature."

Her magic kept circling his body, but Rion couldn't figure out what she had planned. His vision was blurring. The sounds around him diming.

"Just a few more minutes," she promised, seeming to sense his fading magic. Would he feel it when the city crashed into his body? Would he hear Ellie's final scream? Rion swallowed hard. Would he feel the bond snap when his heart came to a sudden stop?

Rion's magic spluttered out and Ellie's arms circled his body before he hit the ground.

Rion wanted to tell Ellie so many things. He wanted to thank her for trusting him and treating him like a normal Fae when no one else ever had. He wanted to thank her for being his friend and for coming back for him. For not treating him like a monster.

He thought his lips hadn't formed words, but she whispered back, "You're welcome." Then they plunged into icy darkness.

CHAPTER NINETY-THREE

ELLIE

The sheer force of the impact above sent them shooting through the channel she'd dug a lot faster than Ellie had anticipated. She clutched Rion's limp hand, desperate to keep hold of him, but his fingers slipped from her grasp when the sideways underground current slammed into their bodies.

Ellie tugged at the water, willing it to obey, and reached for Rion again. She found his sleeve and clutched the material with every ounce of strength she possessed. She wouldn't lose him. If she did, she'd never be able to face her sister again.

Ellie propelled them through the water. She had intended to pull air down with them, but Rion's magic hadn't held out for as long as she'd hoped. Now she was left with a single mouthful of air and no idea when they'd reach the surface again.

Another current spun her in a circle then slammed her against a wall, knocking the little bit of breath she had from her lungs. She fought the urge to gasp and opened her eyes beneath the surging water. Black surrounded her on all sides.

Ellie summoned her magic and pushed them down, down, down, until they were propelled through the water again, riding a current so powerful she couldn't fight against it.

They tumbled through the freezing darkness and Ellie cradled her head with one hand. Her lungs burned, begging her to breathe. She hit another wall, then another.

Maybe this hadn't been her best idea, but it was better than getting crushed by a city. Or maybe she'd just sealed them in a watery grave where no one would find their bodies instead.

The burning increased and just as Ellie was about to open her mouth and accept her fate, the current spit them out into still water. It took several seconds for her to discern up from down, but Ellie followed the bubbles, pushing her body faster and faster, screaming at her magic to keep them alive.

She broke the surface and gasped for air, sucking down lungful after lungful. But Ellie didn't have time to stop. She grabbed Rion's body and propelled them toward the edge of the lake at breakneck speeds until they were on the bank.

She dropped to her knees and pressed an ear to his chest.

A heartbeat, but he wasn't breathing. She pressed her hands against his torso, grabbed the water in his lungs, then dragged it up and out of his mouth.

He didn't move.

"Do not make me give you mouth to mouth," she said and slammed her fists against his chest. No movement. Ellie did it again, then Rion gasped and rolled to one side, coughing as he sucked in breath. Ellie fell back onto the grass, resting one hand on her chest as she tried to steady her own breathing.

Water lapped against the shore and silence settled over the space. Her eyes burned and her lungs were on fire, but she laughed anyway. "See?" she said breathlessly. "Piece of cake."

Rion barely looked like he had the strength to lift himself onto his elbows. His arms were shaking, but he looked at her like she was the craziest being he'd ever met. "What did you do?"

Ellie waved one arm and realized she was trembling, too. "Oh, nothing special. I just found an underground current and threw us down it. Thank the gods for all the recent rain."

His eyes widened. "And you knew that would work?"

She shrugged. "It was an educated guess."

Rion collapsed again and started laughing, the sound deep and true. Ellie laughed with him, their breaths shaky and bodies spent, but just as she was about to comment further on their luck, a myriad of scents hit her all at once. Ellie leapt to her feet, yanking at the water in the lake behind them.

She clenched her teeth, staring down a dozen armed warriors standing atop the hill.

Chapter Ninety-Four

Talon

Talon stood at Arianna's side, watching his queen with his head half bowed. He knew the male had been changing for Arianna, but he never imagined Rion willing to sacrifice his life for the masses. Not after all the devastation Talon had seen him inflict on the battlefield.

Talon examined the amount of loose earth and sand surrounding the ruins of the once great city. He'd seen Rion's magic before, but never to this magnitude. It gave merit to Raevina's hurtful words before the battle. Talon shook his head. He was nothing compared to Rion's strength. Rion was, without a doubt, the strongest male on the continent. He was indeed Arianna's rightful mate and Alastríona's king.

King.

And the male had fallen before anyone had ever recognized him as such.

Talon wouldn't feel shame. He wouldn't grieve. He had to remain strong for Arianna. He would ensure the male received proper recognition for everything he'd done. He'd erect a monument in Rion's honor, even if he had to build it himself.

The world no longer made sense. The ancient texts. Their history. It was warped and filled with lies and false teachings.

The Fae weren't humans. They didn't forget their forefathers or their heroic deeds. They sang songs that stretched through the ages. They were a race that learned from their mistakes instead of repeating them.

Why then, had they believed Rion was a threat rather than royalty?

Even with Niall's dishonorable nature, the male was only nine hundred years old. He couldn't have been the one responsible. Not when the entire continent believed the same lie.

Talon couldn't wrap his mind around it. He'd speak to Avalon later, and Arianna—Once she felt up to it.

Talon studied his friend. His queen. She just sat there with tears running down her face. Talon prayed she wouldn't have another loss to mourn, not after Rion, but Ellie was missing, too.

He clenched his fists, feeling a lump rise in his throat. A warrior from Móirín had seen her running toward the falling city before they'd landed. The male had received a broken nose and a fractured wrist for attempting to restrain her.

Gods. He knew Ellie was fast and powerful in her own right. He'd trained her himself. But he also knew how deep her stubbornness ran. And Talon doubted she'd leave Rion to die alone.

Pain lanced through him again. Deep, unending pain. They might have saved Alastríona's queen, but they might have also just lost Móirín's future.

ARIANNA DIDN'T speak. She'd simply stood and Talon had followed.

His queen moved like a ghost and it reminded him of the months she'd spent without Rion. Would she sink into herself further? Could she pull herself together enough to lead at all?

Talon stepped around large boulders and chunks of the fractured city. He glimpsed a stone arm reaching toward the sky as if begging to be unearthed. Stained glass from the cathedral littered the area, catching the late afternoon sun and dotting the land in unfitting color.

A body lay covered in dust to their left, coiled in on itself, and Talon's heart clenched. He wanted to run to that body, examine it for signs of Ellie, but he kept himself still and nodded for one of the accompanying Móirín warriors to see to it.

Arianna wasn't paying attention to any of them. If she were, she might have sensed his racing heart and the fear that silently floated around him. They turned the figure over. Talon held his breath, but the warrior only shook their head.

Not Ellie.

They knew. All of them knew. He could sense his warriors' apprehension as they scanned the rubble, hoping, just as he was, that they wouldn't find a familiar face.

The place didn't even look like a city anymore, just a heaping pile of broken roads, shattered wood, and glass debris. The bases of a few homes—or what he assumed to be homes—stood out here and there, but the impact had broken everything and piled it all in on itself.

His eyes burned from the dust floating through the air. He knew they wouldn't find Ellie's or Rion's body out here. They'd be beneath the city's center, trapped under thousands of pounds of rock. But even so, Talon couldn't convince his eyes to stop searching.

His warriors drew their weapons suddenly and Talon followed suit, his heart jolting as he rushed to Arianna's side. Silhouettes of several moving bodies dotted the hazy horizon. Arianna just stared.

They waited for several tense moments and it was only when Talon spotted Avalon at their front that he relaxed and sheathed his weapon. Talon knew they'd escaped. Avalon had been working at the rear of the city during the evacuation.

But something in the way his High Lord smiled at them—no, at his daughter—had Talon's heart skipping for entirely different reasons.

He counted the warriors trailing Avalon, then spotted two figures limping at their center.

Ellie raised her arm in a weak wave, then Arianna was running. Talon followed, unable to keep his excitement at bay.

Alive. They were alive.

Both were soaked to the bone and covered from head to toe in mud. Ellie had one of Rion's arms slung across her shoulders and she fought to bear the male's weight. Rion had streaks of blood running down the left side of his face and something was clearly wrong with one of his legs.

But they were alive.

Ellie, gods, Ellie had to be the most beautiful sight he'd ever beheld.

Arianna slowed just enough to ensure she wouldn't knock her mate over, but she failed and they both crashed to the ground. Her hands were all over him, her mouth too as they kissed and whispered words no one else should have been privy to.

But Talon hardly cared as he grabbed Ellie and pulled her into a crushing embrace. She returned it and Talon felt her smile against his neck. He didn't know how long they stood like that, but when he pulled back, Ellie was smiling in the way only Ellie could.

"You," he said, ready to chastise her, yet finding himself unable to form the words. She was a heroine. She had run in when no one else was willing.

"I know, I know," she said a bit breathlessly and Talon wrapped her up again, grateful to whatever god had watched out for her. They certainly had their work cut out for them where she was concerned.

Talon didn't know how they'd managed it, but he would get the details later. Right now he turned his attention to the male still seated on the ground. Rion kept one hand around Arianna's waist as she healed the wounds across his body.

Rion's arms shook. He looked ready to collapse and Talon was certain Arianna was the only reason he hadn't. He would need several days to recover after . . . Talon glanced at the ruined city again. Gods, he'd actually managed to slow it down. Rion had bought them time. He'd saved so many lives.

Talon looked at the male who had once been his most brutal enemy.

A male who would one day rise as his future king.

He swallowed, his throat dry and stepped toward the pair. Talon didn't know where the lies began or how they would unravel their tainted history, but they would. One piece at a time.

Rion eyed him. Trust had to start somewhere and Rion had more than proven he was willing to go the distance to erase the scars of his past.

It was time to make some changes.

Talon extended his hand. "I could assist." Silence enveloped the pair. Arianna looked between them, tears staining her cheeks, but her smile could have lit up a room. To his surprise, Rion took his outstretched hand and Talon pulled his king to his feet.

CHAPTER NINETY-FIVE

ARIANNA

valon had planned further ahead than he'd previously let on. He'd found a neighboring village where the residents were more than willing to aid their queen.

Arianna's father had spoken with the elders and had put elaborate plans in place in case they needed to retreat. Instead, they simply needed somewhere to rest.

With Niall in irons and the royal city destroyed, the Fae in the large village welcomed those who sought sanctuary. In fact, they were so ecstatic to have their queen among them that a mated pair had even offered up their home for her to temporarily occupy.

Arianna had tried to refuse, but the pair wouldn't be persuaded. Talon said she deserved it, and when her friend's gaze lingered on Rion, she heard the words he didn't say.

He deserved it, too.

So she'd relented, just for one night, and walked into the small yet comfortable structure with her mate at her side.

Her father stationed guards at the doors and below the windows with a promise that no one would disturb them for the rest of the night. Thank the gods. She just needed one moment of reprieve after the near constant chaos of the last several days. Arianna pulled the curtains shut for good measure.

"We should clean up," Rion said from the foyer. He swayed on his feet and she wondered if he would collapse right there on the floor.

"Do you want to go first?"

He shook his head. "I think I need to sit. Just for a few minutes."

Arianna nodded and fell into awkward silence. At one time they would have bathed together, likely stayed beneath the steam for as long as the water remained hot. And she wanted to. She wanted Rion more than she craved breath, but that fear had started to return and he'd noticed it, too.

When his hands had grazed the scar on her arm, she'd jolted back as if she'd been burned. And when his lips had touched her throat, she'd stiffened and her breath had caught for all the wrong reasons.

"I'll make you some tea first," she offered. It was the least she could do, yet it didn't feel like nearly enough. Rion had just saved an entire city full of people and all she could offer him was tea. To say she felt pathetic was an understatement.

Arianna put an old kettle on the stove and turned the knob. Silence filled the small space again, but this time she took the time to study her surroundings.

There was an unlit fireplace along the back wall with a mantle full of pictures and trinkets that told the story of a family with two children. Toys leaned against one corner and two small pairs of slippers sat by the front door.

Everything about the home was kind and inviting. It was the type of place she longed for. Maybe she'd be blessed with a few children of her own one day. Arianna eyed Rion. Provided he wanted any. They'd never broached the subject and she'd been taking a preventative tonic since her return to Móirín. Just to be safe.

Rion sat in the wooden rocking chair and leaned his head back, exhaling as he closed his eyes. The sofa looked more comfortable, but he probably didn't want to dirty the furniture. Arianna examined herself and grimaced at the blood staining her shirt. She certainly looked like she'd been through hell.

The kettle screamed and both she and Rion jumped at the sound. Arianna scented his magic and her fear rose, coating the living space with its acrid tang. She tried to shove the feelings away to no avail.

Rion's face softened. "Sorry."

Her lips parted. She hated the way he looked at her. As if he were ashamed. She hated herself for causing those feelings. Nothing had been his fault. Nothing at all, and here he was having to keep himself in check so he wouldn't frighten her.

Arianna rummaged through the cabinets until she found a container of dry leaves. She popped the lid off then smelled the contents and sighed in contentment. Lavender and mint. Just what they both needed.

Maybe everything would go back to normal after a good night's sleep. They didn't have anything to worry about now, save for rebuilding. The hard part was convincing her mind it could rest.

Arianna filled a tea ball with leaves, then crossed the room and placed the steaming mug on the square end table.

"I won't be long," she promised. Rion only nodded, his eyes closing once again.

Arianna raced up the stairs, turned on the water, and scrubbed her body as fast as she could. She ripped the brush through her hair, threw on a pair of button up pajamas from the closet and promised herself that she'd clean everything she used first thing tomorrow morning. Afterward, she'd give the family their home back. There were enough people outside residing in makeshift tents. She wouldn't let those who normally lived here be among them.

CHAPTER NINETY-SIX

RION

Gods, she'd smelled absolutely divine. It was a perfume, no, a drug that appealed to his most primal instincts. Rion didn't care that he'd almost had a city crush him to dust nor that he'd almost drowned in a darkness he couldn't remember. He only cared about her.

And that was exactly the reason he'd kept his hands to himself and trudged up the stairs.

Dirt crumbled from his clothes with every step and littered the wooden staircase. He grimaced at the offending flakes, knowing the easiest way to clean them up would be to use his magic. Magic that scared his mate.

Rion sighed and silently shut the bathroom door. The tiny window on the far side of the space was cracked slightly. It let the steam roll out, yet did absolutely nothing to remove Arianna's scent.

The sweetness of it was intoxicating and his blood strummed through his veins, begging him to go to her and kiss her until he'd memorized every inch of her skin.

But he couldn't. She allowed him to hold her hand and she leaned into his warmth so long as he didn't lean too far back.

It was like dangling a bone just out of a starving dog's reach. He needed her. Was desperate for her. But Rion couldn't have her. Not yet. Maybe not ever.

He sighed, tugged his clothes off, and let them fall to the floor. The vanity was small and Rion couldn't glimpse himself in the already steamed mirror, but he knew well enough what he looked like. Years of honed muscles had faded from malnourishment. His skin was ashen and the black spots beneath his eyes were so prominent, he knew he looked as if he hadn't slept in weeks. Which wasn't entirely untrue.

He'd never considered himself a vain being, but his appearance made him feel inadequate somehow.

Rion turned the shower faucet to near scalding temperatures and stepped inside. He spun to let the heat hit his shoulders first and melt some of the tension from his body. Then Rion twisted so the hot water pelted against his face.

The feeling was magnificent.

This was only his second shower since his confinement. He hadn't felt clean after the first. Not even close. Even now, he wondered if he'd ever get the invisible dirt off his body.

Rion stretched his arms up and grimaced when his sore muscles protested the movement. He'd be lucky if he could move at all tomorrow.

He tilted his face up to the water again, then reached for the soap.

Everything in him coiled in on itself again. It smelled like her. It smelled like roses too, but Arianna's scent was everywhere all at once. It drove him wild, and Rion had to press his forehead against the cool tile to steady himself.

This was a new kind of hell.

After a brief reprieve, Rion grabbed the shampoo and ran his fingers through his filthy hair, scrubbing his scalp until it burned. He grabbed the damp rag, the same one Arianna had used, and washed himself from head to toe. It never felt like enough.

After a third pass, he gave up and let the water rinse the suds from his body. Bruises were forming and the scrapes across his skin burned from the soap, but Rion ignored it all as he finally let reality sink in.

They'd won.

He was free.

A knot finally began to unravel in his chest.

Free.

He wished he could summon his magic just to remind himself, but it was too weak. And he didn't want to frighten his mate, either.

Free, he kept repeating. Free, yet still caged by Niall's influence and actions.

It might as well have been iron keeping Arianna and him apart.

Rion clenched his aching fists trying to work the tension from his joints. He wouldn't push her. Not ever. If she needed time, he'd give her eternity. If she never wanted to share a bed with him again, then he'd take her hand every morning and relish the little bit of contact she allowed.

He'd bend and break himself to her will. Whatever she wanted.

Light footsteps echoed in the hall and stopped before the door. Rion froze, a dozen thoughts racing through his mind all at once.

Was Arianna injured? Had Niall somehow escaped and come to finish what he'd started? Was Pádraigín waiting outside to exact revenge?

The handle turned slowly and Rion exhaled. Arianna. He would know her anywhere. Her scent, the way she breathed, and that small tug on the bond that told him his mate was near.

"It's just me," she said. She'd probably sensed his sudden spike of fear. Rion waited for her to say more, but she just stood there, a silhouette behind the steamy pane of glass.

Then her shirt hit the floor. His heart began pounding when her pants followed, then she shed her undergarments.

Rion's mouth went dry and he was almost certain this had to be a glamour. A trick.

Arianna's bare feet padded across the short space separating her from the shower door, then she slid it open.

A low sound escaped his throat as he soaked in every beautiful detail. His mate stood before him. Bare, gorgeous, and utterly breathtaking.

His eyes roamed over her perfect curves and the way her damp hair hung over her shoulders. His gaze traveled lower, then lower again.

"Can I come in?"

Rion nodded, unsure if he remembered how to form words. He backed up a step to give her room.

Arianna swallowed hard and he sobered a bit at the sight of her clenched fists. Her fear stung his delicate senses and he wanted nothing more than to reach out and pull her close. But Rion remained still, as if he were nothing more than a statue within the manor's once beautiful garden.

Her body trembled. His did, too. "A-Arianna?" He stumbled across her name in a breathless whisper. Every instinct roared at him to claim her, claim her, claim her.

Arianna slid the glass door shut and stepped toward him.

He stepped back until his shoulders pressed against the cool tile wall.

Her brow furrowed. "Do you want me to leave?" Why in the unholiest of gods' names would he want her to—

"No."

She stepped toward him again. Her heart fluttered almost as fast as a humming bird's wings. He felt her desire down the bond and scented it from her as well. It almost broke his restraint.

"Can I touch you?" Why was she asking?

Rion cleared his throat, but his voice still came out unsteady. "I'm yours." She owned his body, his heart, his soul.

Arianna walked through the water and Rion watched it roll down her skin. Her body. Perfect. She was so utterly perfect. A shiver ran through him when her hands pressed against his chest, but shame accompanied it as he realized just how thin his body had become. He hated the way his ribs showed and loathed the strength he'd lost from being caged for so long.

But she didn't seem to notice those things as she traced his stomach, then tilted her head up to look at him. Those eyes. Those beautiful cerulean eyes. They captured his soul and set his body on fire. The way she gazed at him reminded Rion of the cabin, when he'd offered her his life and she'd captured his heart instead.

Arianna stepped closer and pressed her ear to his chest. Tentatively, Rion wrapped his arms around her shoulders. She shook so violently that he almost released her.

"I don't want to be afraid," she whispered.

Gods, he didn't want her to be afraid, either. "Tell me what to do."

Arianna tilted her head back to look at him. "Make it go away." Her gaze trailed to his lips and understanding swept through him. She wanted this. She wanted him.

Rion captured her mouth in a gentle kiss, but Arianna was greedy for him. She slid her tongue over his lip and a throaty moan escaped him before he could stop it. His laced his hands through her dripping hair, then Rion slid to the floor, pulling her down with him.

Arianna straddled his lap and he traced his hands over the thick scars along her back. "Summon your magic," he said. She eyed him for a moment, then did as he asked. "My wrists."

"Rion."

"Trust me." He knew it was asking a lot. She didn't trust him, that was the entire problem, but he was determined to change it. She wanted him to change it.

Water surrounded his wrists and Rion splayed his fingers over her waist. His breathing was ragged with want and unbridled desire threatened to burn him from the inside out.

"Tighter," he said and she obeyed. The rings of water circled his wrist as if they were alive. Firm, but not enough to hurt.

"You're in control," Rion said, his voice deep and husky. "Whatever you want or don't want is up to you."

Arianna nodded, studying her own magic as if confirming it to herself. She leaned forward and kissed him again, brushing her tongue against his lips. He devoured her then, kissing her deeply, basking in her scent and smell and taste. Rion kissed the side of her mouth, then trailed those kisses down to her neck. She froze and he silently cursed himself.

Instead of pulling away, he whispered in the shell of her ear. "Show me." She shifted slightly. "Show me you're in control." The water around his wrists tightened and she pulled his arm up, pinning them against the tile. Rion fought against the memory of the dungeon and his aching shoulders. He focused on the warm water instead the and beautiful female hovering over him. He didn't care what memories he had to suffer through. He'd suffer for her and give her whatever fractured piece of him she desired.

Rion studied her body and the way her chest rose and fell. "I'm yours," he said again. "Whatever you want."

Her heated gaze drank him in, then Arianna took everything.

CHAPTER NINETY-SEVEN

ARIANNA

The city was in absolute ruins. Most had survived the fall thanks to Gavin's return, but Arianna wouldn't forget the ones who hadn't, nor the strange magic that had held them in place. She'd never seen the markings before and wasn't even aware anyone could siphon magic to begin with.

There were other things at work. Things they'd forgotten and needed to uncover.

Arianna turned away from the bodies being pulled from the rubble. The Fae charged with digging were still finding them one at a time.

Arianna had been right about those jailed. Niall had imprisoned anyone who opposed him, including three council members Rion's mother knew by name. There were also a number of half-breeds and Fae who'd refused to bow to his rule. They'd attempted to overthrow him through the decades, but Niall had outsmarted every attempt.

Those who'd actually been criminals fled during the chaos. Maybe their time in the dungeons had changed them. Maybe not. She might send Talon to hunt them down in the future, but there were more pressing concerns to deal with before then.

Like how Niall had escaped, and the group of Fae that had helped him do it.

Rion had been livid, but whoever had freed Niall hadn't left any survivors to tell the story.

Rion and Eimear claimed Niall had likely fled back to Pádraigín. Which meant his father would soon get wind of everything that had transpired. Arianna wondered how much of the last few months had been orchestrated by The High Lord and what events Niall had planned himself.

She wouldn't forgive either male. Not after learning what had happened to her mother.

Avalon was sending word to Levea already, preparing his warriors should Pádraigín launch a full scale attack. Saoirse assured them Alec would join the fight too.

It was all too much too soon. Arianna didn't want to go to war. She was tired of the bloodshed already.

Arianna slipped on a loose stone, but Rion caught her arm and steadied her. She still jumped at his magic, which he tried not to use in her presence, but the drowning fear had all but dissipated after last night. She'd woken up in his arms, warm and protected and he constantly reminded her she was in control.

They followed his mother through the rubble, crawling toward the city's center. The further inward they ventured, the more intact things became. Buildings had still crumbled and nothing was unmarred, but it wasn't a complete scattered mess like the outskirts.

Eimear wore a green cloak with the hood up to cover her bare head, and she still hadn't removed the iron bracelet from around her wrist. Maybe that's how Rion had held up the city. His magic had been restrained for two months. Eimear claimed her magic had built up in the time she'd been held captive. Perhaps Rion's had done the same. Arianna didn't want to imagine what would happen when Eimear finally released hers.

The trio climbed higher and higher. Arianna crawled over fallen pillars and the remnants of shattered buildings. She carefully stepped around stained glass and crumbled stone gardens. Then found herself in the city's center. The manor. A place that now held nothing but a plethora of horrible memories.

Eimear paused to catch her breath. Rion had offered to carry her, but she'd declined, claiming she was tired of sitting still. Eimear needed to move and prove to herself that she was free.

Arianna understood.

His mother finally pointed down into an area that had collapsed into a small crater. Arianna didn't know what they would find inside, but her hands shook as she climbed the last few feet to stand at Eimear's side.

There, in the center of everything, with the temple roof collapsed around it, stood the statue of The Divine. The face had cracked and she was missing an arm, but she still stood, along with a part Arianna hadn't seen before.

"Long ago," Eimear began, "the Fae beneath Pádraigín's rule were ordered to destroy this piece of our history. But those still loyal to the true crown couldn't stomach having it erased." Eimear smiled faintly at the statue, as if she'd stood among those defiant Fae from centuries ago. "The High Lord burned books and altered our history. So, before their memories were taken away, they formed a secret pact and hid this one artifact. They hoped that someday, someone would find it and learn the truth."

Standing before them beside The Divine and previously hidden behind the walls of the temple was a male. A male with stones at his feet and grains of sand coursing down his arms. A male who stood beside The Divine as if he were ready to lay the world at her feet.

Not her enemy. Not a demon or an abomination. Her mate.

"I'd like to think they also hid a copy of the original ancient text, but I'm afraid I can't remember. You should order a trusted group of warriors to search the area, just in case."

"How do you know all this?" Arianna asked.

"As a seer, I've lived through countless lifetimes and the memories of others. I've witnessed things from our past, as well as events that have yet to unfold. The High Lord of Pádraigín did his best to alter my memories, but glamours don't work on a seer. At least not for long."

"That's why he imprisoned you."

"Niall imprisoned me. The High Lord ordered my death."

Right, Arianna kept forgetting they still had someone else to contend with. Someone who already sounded worse than Niall.

"I was tricked, and by the time I realized what was happening, there was iron around my wrists." Rion's fists clenched. "I guess I should be thankful Niall disobeyed his father. He made a mistake and now I'm free." The hollowness in her gaze made Arianna wonder if she really *was* free. How long would the nightmares last?

"Why change history at all?" Arianna asked. "What is his goal?"

Eimear shrugged. "That is one question I don't have an answer to. Many have done terrible things for power, but his is a plan that has stretched across the ages. There's more to it than simply obtaining the throne. I just don't know what."

"The current text is wrong then," Rion said. "About Arianna's mate coming from Pádraigín."

Eimear raised a brow. "I thought that would be obvious by now. It's wrong about a great deal of things. Namly, someone possessing your magic being a threat. You, my son, are the furthest thing from a threat. You're the protector of The Divine."

Rion's breath hitched. "So you're telling me . . ."

Eimear smiled as if Rion were a child again. "Yes. You are the rightful king of this continent, and the male carved in that stone was the best ruler this land has ever known."

CHAPTER NINETY-EIGHT

ARIANNA

Everyone told her to rest. They begged her not to help, but Arianna refused to listen. She wouldn't be coddled and most certainly wouldn't sit on a cushion while the rest of them were left to the elements.

There weren't enough homes to go around, and thus the village elders had agreed to build additional dwellings for those who wished to remain in the village. Everyone else was packing to accompany her father back to Levea.

Arianna healed those who'd been injured and carried bags to load wagons alongside everyone else.

Raevina and her warriors questioned the citizens of Ruadhán and wrote up detailed reports for Arianna to review at a later time. Thus far, Raevina had only locked up two individuals who she claimed were spies and still loyal to Niall. Arianna didn't question her.

Most, thankfully, seemed to have Alastríona's best interests at heart. Arianna had scolded a few who had sneered at the half-breeds and informed them that if their prejudices continued, they'd find themselves exiled. They'd quickly fallen silent and she hadn't heard a complaint since.

The villagers were surprisingly receptive to Rion's aid as he cleared debris and leveled the land. Rumor had spread that he'd been the one to slow the city down and had ultimately aided in their survival. Many were even offering him gifts while he worked, and Arianna smiled at the awkward exchanges. She never wandered far, just in case someone reached for a hidden blade. The factions were still out there, after all. Yet another thing they'd have to contend with.

Saoirse helped to plant and accelerate the growth of crops, though she mentioned something about a better harvest if the plants were left to grow on their own. Those from Fiadh kept the fires roaring, and warriors from Móirín watered the fields and replenished their wells.

When they weren't building, they were digging through the ruined city in search of bodies and salvageable supplies.

Even those from Pádraigín aided with the recovery effort as they moved heavy items and massive boulders from one location to another. Arianna wouldn't allow herself to be prejudiced against their magic. A citizen couldn't choose their leader.

Arianna studied the moving pieces. They were working together, and she was confident now more than ever that a unity between each nation is what would eventually bring them peace. Perhaps if they uncovered the original ancient texts, it would tell her what to do. It might also explain how Talon and Ellie had found their mates when the bond was said to be so rare.

Arianna finally spotted Talon in the crowd and ran to catch up with him. "Have you seen Ellie?"

Sweat rolled down the male's face but he shook his head. "I haven't seen her all morning." His brow furrowed. "Come to think of it, I haven't seen her since yesterday."

Arianna hadn't seen Kirian, either. She wondered if her sister was taking some time alone with the male after her recent brush with death. Still, Ellie should have told someone. With all the criminals that had escaped, Arianna couldn't help but worry for her little sister's safety.

Work continued well into late afternoon, then the villagers lit fires and the scent of roasted meat floated through the air, making her mouth water.

Just as they'd done the previous night, the villagers led Rion and Arianna toward the largest fire and the wooden tables that surrounded it. She didn't hesitate to dig into the immaculate food.

Arianna didn't sit at the head of a table here, and servants didn't rush to her every need, though a few villagers tried. She felt as if she were among the people, and they included her in their talk about their daily accomplishments. It was … normal. Like she was one of them.

Arianna looked past the crowd. Her father was set to leave in two days, and they planned to get at least two dozen more homes built before then. The weather was pleasant enough to sleep beneath the stars, but Arianna didn't want anyone stranded out in the rain.

Avalon agreed it would be an easy task.

Arianna studied the sea of faces again. She squinted between those nearest to her and those on the outskirts. She inclined her ears to listen, but couldn't hear the loud laugh that told her Ellie was near. Her sister wasn't one to miss dinner. Especially when the food tasted this good.

She stood and Rion stopped eating. "What's wrong?"

"Have you seen Ellie anywhere?"

His gaze scanned the area, then Rion was on his feet too, bowl forgotten. Her mate searched through the crowd, then furrowed his brow. Arianna tried not to panic as she walked the grounds, stopping at each fire to ask if anyone had seen her sister. They received the same answer every time.

Arianna spun on her heel, her heart hammering in her chest. The villagers were searching now too, scanning the outskirts, the empty houses, the fields. A small group even ran back toward the city ruins, curious if she had indeed snuck off with Kirian. Talon took to the sky.

An hour passed. No one had seen her, and they couldn't scent her either.

Arianna's mind whirled and she looked at no one in particular as her voice cracked with a new kind of fear. "Where is my sister?"

CHAPTER NINETY-NINE

ELLIE

Her head pounded and Ellie barely had the energy to lift it. Her blurry gaze took in a large fireplace with a gaping mouth the size of the entire wall. Embers burned within, casting an eerie glow on the stone lining the large structure. A pair of empty vintage chairs sat before the hearth with a table between them.

Her breath clouded and she shivered, moving to cover her bare arms with her hands. Chains rattled at her sides.

Chains.

Iron.

Ellie snapped awake and scanned her body. She was shackled at the wrists and ankles. The chains stretched between her limbs and away from her body where the other ends were clipped to bolts in the floor.

Props to her assailant for not underestimating her.

Ellie scanned the room. The last person she remembered with her was Kirian, but she didn't scent him now. She scented someone else. Someone ancient who smelled like old parchment and the winds that blew across the sea.

The hair along her arms rose and a small voice in the back of her mind begged Ellie to proceed with caution.

Ellie's gaze studied the room again. It didn't look like a dungeon. Dark like one. Cold like one. But the hearth and bookshelves and trinkets whispered of an old scholar's study. The tapestries didn't help. So many tapestries lined the walls. She couldn't see the pictures from where she knelt on the carpeted floor.

"I'm told you're quite the troublemaker for someone so young."

Her head whipped toward the voice in the corner. He'd been so still hidden among the shadows that she hadn't noticed him. Ellie tried to study his features, but they were lost to her in the darkness. He moved with an elegance she'd never seen, as if he walked on the air itself.

He was definitely from Pádraigín.

"Who are you?"

He didn't answer right away. Then, "A male who once fell in love and paid the price for it." Well, that certainly didn't give her any answers.

"What do you want?"

"A great many things, though fate has a way of denying me at every turn." Riddles. Why did older Fae always have to speak in riddles?

"Why am I here?" She tried again.

He took a long, deep breath and wandered toward the open fireplace. The male stared at it, then threw a log into the dying embers, scattering them like fireflies at his boots.

"Answering your question will only lead to more questions, so how about I tell you a story instead?"

Ellie wanted to bark at him. A story was the last thing she wanted to hear, but she also remembered her training with Talon. Any information while in the hands of an enemy was information she could use. It would give her time to search for an escape route, too.

She eyed her bound hands and the thick iron links that held them together, then grimaced. It would take a miracle to break them, but surely they'd move her to another location eventually. Or perhaps they'd allow her to relive herself in a proper toilet and she could try to escape then. Somehow Ellie doubted her current captor would fall for such a trick.

"Ten thousand years ago," he began, slowly walking toward one of the tapestries. "There were two younglings. A male and a female. The pair lived in a simple village and their families were very close friends. As neighbors, the two grew up side by side.

"When their teen years came about, the male and female found themselves in one another's arms most nights. They made promises in the dark. They swore to love and cherish one another no matter what life threw at them."

He moved to another tapestry, but Ellie still couldn't see it. "In those days, the King of Alastríona roamed the continent in search of his mate. It was a yearly event, and he stopped at village after village no matter how small. Everyone lined up to greet him and whisper praise and gratitude. He brought merchants and goods with him and the parties lasted for days."

The male turned toward her, but his face was hidden by shadow. "The land was a very different place back then. The Fae from the four nations weren't separated as they are now. They lived in harmony and protected one another from the dark creatures that roamed free."

He moved onto another tapestry, inching toward her. "The male and female refused to participate whenever the king arrived. They would hide away, preferring one another's company to the extravagant festival. They stole chocolates and souvenirs, of course, but they always avoided the male, especially after the female's unique gift made itself known."

"She was The Divine," Ellie breathed.

"She was, but she didn't want to be held captive by the mating bond. She thought that if she avoided the male, she'd never have to face it. Everything changed in her twenty fifth year. The female still hadn't had an animal shift, and her parents began to wonder if she might be their queen. Her parents sent word to the king against her wishes and he arrived without all the fanfare, just to see for himself."

The male before her loosed a breath, almost as if he were in pain. "When she stumbled into him, the bond took root."

"So she found her mate."

"She was shackled by a force she couldn't control." He growled. "She tried to resist, but in the end, she left with him."

"You were the young male." He didn't nod, but her skin crawled all the same. Holy gods. Ten thousand years. This male was ten thousand years old? Her father was barely over a thousand.

He ran his fingers over the fabric of the tapestry. "I vowed to save her from her fate. To free her from the bond. But as a simple farm boy, I couldn't even get close to her. So I climbed the ranks and dragged myself through the mud. Just for a chance to see her again. It took me a century." He fell silent again, but Ellie didn't interrupt. She just waited. "When I saw the swell of her stomach, I realized just how deep the king had her in his clutches."

Ellie blanched. "You didn't . . ."

"I'm not a barbarian, Evelyn. No one gets to choose who sires them. It didn't matter, she hid the child and I never found it."

The male moved on to the next bit of fabric, as if reading a story from the pictures. "It took a very long time, but I finally managed to kill the king. I thought she would be grateful, that once the bond broke, she'd be free from his grasp and we could go back to the way things were. But her rage—" He shook his head. "It was too late. The damage had been done. The queen who was prophesied to bring peace brought destruction instead. She burned everything in her conquest. Everything that I'd worked so hard to build."

"She was looking for you."

He chuckled. "Yes, and when we finally faced off against one another, I knew the only way to free her was to release her from this world."

Ellie's mouth went dry. "You . . . you killed The Divine?"

He paused at the final tapestry and Ellie could see the outlines of his jaw working. "The king took her from me in every sense of the word. He ensured I'd never have her, regardless of if he remained in this life or not." He laughed to himself. "Fate, or rather, the gods have a particular sense of humor. You see, the prophecy hadn't been fulfilled, so less than a century later, someone else with that vile magic was born. The people celebrated and revered the boy, claiming he would be another great king."

"You killed him."

"I killed several. The Fae began guarding the young king then, determined to protect him until he reached adulthood. It became apparent that I needed to do something else entirely." He looked directly at her. "But how does one change a prophecy written by the gods?"

"I didn't think we were supposed to."

He snickered. "Yes, perhaps that is where my problem lies. The fact that, despite being immortal, I do not possess celestial abilities." He stepped closer and she could see the color of his robes now illuminated by the firelight. Old robes, from ancient times. She'd only seen the runic designs in her history books.

He sighed. "I knew then that the only way to stop the endless cycle was to delete it from history. I raged wars. I swept over the continent. I burned everything in sight. And then I started writing my own histories, keeping the details as close to the original as I could while adding my own twists."

Ellie's stomach clenched. "But that would take—"

He turned to her, the faintest outline of his face visible. "Centuries? More? Yes, it would, and even then, those with old memories were hard to sway." He studied his hands as if he could see the blood of countless victims. "The young were easily swayed, especially those who neglected their studies. War killed the old, or I ensured it did. Why do you think there aren't many Fae over a thousand years old?"

She felt sick.

"I've successfully infiltrated every country and planted the ideals I wanted there. Afterward, I sat back and watched as elders fed it to generation after generation. Soon, no one questioned it. At least until Brónach's High Lady came along." He shook his head with disbelief.

"A seer. I almost couldn't believe it. It was like the gods were against me."

"So you had her imprisoned."

"No, I ordered her dead, but that son of mine wanted her as his play thing. I told him not to let her escape, but that is another unfortunate tale."

"But Rion. You didn't kill him."

The dim light illuminated his face enough that she caught his wicked smile. "You're right. I didn't, but I made his life hell. I'll admit, I was angry at first that he'd escaped. Brónach's High Lord was always a difficult one to influence. He asked too many questions and I'd bet all the gold in my coffers that he hesitated. His elder sister tried hiding him for a while, and he even survived several of my assassins. So I opted for a different route. I figured, why not bring him into my twisted game rather than eliminate him?"

The male chuckled. "It was too perfect. The male practically damned himself when he slaughtered his father's warriors and countless others. Then his brother, the new High Lord, sent him out on a mission. I paid him a personal visit. Not that he knew. I'll let you in on a little secret. Fear and anger are two of the most easily influenced emotions there are. And easily manipulated, as well. All it took was a little extra prodding and he pivoted from an angry teen to an outright murderous creature. Granted, there were rumors I spread, as well. Just to keep things interesting."

He pinned her with a deadly stare. "The King of Alastríona took everything from me. So I stripped everything from his successors and molded the one you call Rion into a tyrant to be feared."

"You—" Gods. Holy gods. He'd orchestrated Rion's entire life. He'd been the one from the very beginning. He'd—

Ellie's face paled and fear finally invaded her senses. If he could manipulate someone like Rion . . . "Why are you telling me all this?"

The male finally stepped close enough that she could see his face. He was young and fair, like all Fae. His light hair was pulled back, but half his head had been shaved. Thick scars ran along the left side of his face, with one slashing right through his left eye. It had left the pupil milky and useless.

"Because you aren't leaving," he whispered.

The male snapped his fingers and the door opened on the other side of the room. Ellie yanked against her bonds when she scented Kirian's blood, then tears pricked her eyes as two males hauled his broken body through the doorway. He didn't look up or move, but she could hear his heartbeat.

"Let him go," she yelled, and fought against her chains to no avail. They didn't budge and she could barely stand to her full height from how tightly they held her.

"No." He leaned closer. "It appears the boy wasn't fortunate in inheriting his father's genes. I'd say he has about a century or less to live." Ellie could hardly breath as she stared at Kirian's limp body, the blood pouring from his mouth, and his swollen eyes. "Don't fret. I won't kill him. He's going to stick around as a reminder. If you try to escape or do anything that displeases me, he'll pay the price." The male clicked his tongue. "Though right now, he doesn't look like he can take much more, so I'd be very, very careful. His life is in your hands."

"What do you want?" she seethed. "Arianna's secrets? Rion's?"

The male laughed out loud. "Heavens no, there's nothing you could tell me I don't already know." He stood. "What I want from you is far different." He crossed the room, then something about his words clicked into place.

"What did you mean when you said you could influence the mind? I thought those from Pádraigín controlled the air and cast illusions?"

"What is a false emotion but an illusion? What is a lie except an illusion? What is a false reality but an illusion? I've had a lot of time to hone my strength. More time than most."

"What's your goal, exactly? And no more riddles."

He knelt over Kirian and Ellie held her breath. "Destroy Alastríona and its prophecies. Once I'm certain they're gone, we'll move to a new continent and begin a new life. The Divine will cease to exist."

"That's genocide."

"Sometimes sacrifice is the only way to freedom." He returned to her and Ellie struggled against her bonds. "Now that you know why, perhaps you'll be a little more compliant." His gaze traveled to Kirian. "At least I hope you are, for your companion's sake."

He pressed his thumb to her head and a buzzing filled her ears before she was cast into shadow. Her stomach dropped and the world spun out of control. Ellie flailed, fighting for a foothold, but Kirian's bloody form flashed before her eyes and she stopped fighting, stopped moving as the darkness closed in and Ellie fell and fell and fell.

Author Bio

J.E. Reed is the #1 bestselling author of The Fae of Alastríona series, The Divine and the Cursed, The Revered and the Pariah. Reed loves writing magical stories full of love and adventure. She believes everyone deserves a happy ending.

Reed currently lives in Ohio with her husband, her son, and two cats. Her latest series has enabled her to pursue a full-time writing career and she plans to bring readers more heart-wrenching romance.

Visit Reed's website at www.jereedbooks.com
Follow her on Instagram: @jereedauthor
Follow her on Tiktok: @a_writers_quill
Follow her on Facebook: @J.E.Reed.author